THE LINDEN

AND

THE OAK

THE LINDEN
AND
THE OAK

A NOVEL

MARK WANSA

World Academy of Rusyn Culture

First published in Canada by
World Academy of Rusyn Culture
Toronto

This publication is made possible through the support of
    Steven Chepa
    President, Norstone Financial Corporation
    Toronto, Canada

For Mariya
and her boys.

Vichnaya pamyat!—Eternal memory!

Contents

THE LINDEN
AND
THE OAK

Prelude

HIGH ABOVE A RURAL PATH in an obscure corner of the Empire of Austria-Hungary, a lone falcon played the swirling highland air, gliding in graceful turns that concealed a craving purpose.

Across the northern horizon stretched the crest of the Carpathian Mountains—low hills in this particular section of the mountain range—dividing Central Europe into northern and southern halves. Below, in the Hungarian half of the empire, lay the valley of the Ondava Stream, in the heart of the region known locally as Makovytsya. Like other valleys in the area, it was cut through the landscape from north to south by water flowing from the great Carpathian watershed and descending southward in ever-broader rivers that eventually emptied into the wide Tisza near the vineyards at Tokay.

The falcon climbed higher into the blue September sky.

Nestled in the valleys were the thatch-roofed huts and rustic homesteads of a people desperately poor in all but spirit: a people forgotten and almost unknown; a people unified in language and faith but scattered in a thousand isolated villages; a folk lacking a precise notion of themselves as a *people*. When they were remembered at all by the outside world, they were often referred to as Ruthenians. To the native-born priests and poets among them they were known as Rusyns, a people speaking an eastern Slavic tongue rendered, like that of the Russians to the east, in Cyrillic script. But the common and often illiterate peasants who worked the land for absentee Hungarian landlords simply called themselves "our people" and spoke a language they called *po-nashomu*—"our way." In contrast, there were, in the surrounding lowlands to the north and south of the Carpathian Mountains, less ambiguous peoples, Poles, Ukrainians, Slovaks, Romanians, Czechs; peoples with well-articulated identities and visions of eventual autonomy within or independence from an empire whose hub was far away.

The falcon drifted in and out of the sun.

That imperial hub was the city of Vienna, where a stooped old man with generous side-whiskers was in the sixty-fifth year of his reign over his family's multiethnic domain. Old, venerable, and German, the Habsburg family over the centuries acquired and held together an empire that stretched from Poland to the Adriatic and from Bohemia to Transylvania—an empire in 1913 of fifty million as diverse as ancient Rome, its subjects speaking more than a dozen languages.

The falcon circled widely over the rural path.

The domains of the Rusyn families in the Ondava Valley, however, were measured not in geographical regions and millions of subjects but rather in arable plots and heads of livestock. The histories of these families were recorded in faded, inconstant script on water-damaged parish books. These families marked time by the harvests and the feast days of the saints; for them the world was immutable, affixed to a permanent cycle, and unaffected by the passage of time or kings. In these villages the people worked and slept in an ancient rhythm of day and night that admitted variation reluctantly. The men worked the land, watching the sky and dreading both drought and flood, while the women kept the house, raising the young and nursing the elderly. In times of celebration the musically inclined among the men would coax a dance from their battered fiddles, and the women would don richly embroidered blouses. When the occasion called for it, talented women of the village produced *pysankŷ,* multicolored eggs entirely designed and dyed with only beeswax and natural plant extracts. Infrequently, news from the outside world arrived late in the form of rumor or gossip, its meaning mysterious, its significance debated by the men and largely ignored by the women and children.

The falcon tightened its circle over the path.

The dominant structure of every village was its church. The walls and towers were constructed of massive hand-hewn logs, harvested from the local forests and intricately notched and fitted without the use of nails, unsuitable symbols of the Crucifixion. Atop each onion-domed tower was an ornate metal cross, each arm of which was fashioned as a smaller cross with arms branching into even tinier crosses; and from the ground they appeared like floating filigree dissolving in the firmament.

The falcon spotted movement below.

Like their Catholic brothers to the west, Rusyns gathered on Sundays in their wooden churches. However, unlike their Roman rite brothers, these Catholics celebrated the Resurrection according to the eastern Byzantine rite and chanted the Divine Liturgy of Saint John Chrysostom. In this tradition the people stood on the earthly side of the iconostasis, a wall with rows of icons of prophets, apostles, saints, and images of the Lord, both as infant, in the protective embrace of His Holy Mother, and as Christ Pantokrator, the risen Almighty One, under whose discriminating stare the faithful bowed. On the other side of the iconostasis, through the Royal Door, was the sanctuary, the eternal Heavenly realm of the Lord, whose mysterious presence in bread and wine was solemnly conveyed to the people by a priest.

The falcon's dispassionate eyes focused on a creature stirring below.

In any given village, a man might reappear after a long absence and tell of a fantastic land across the ocean where jobs were plentiful and where good money could be earned by those willing to work long hours in clamorous factories or dark coal mines. While some of his listeners shook their heads in disbelief, others lay awake at night staring into the darkness. Though these latter rose in the morning, troubled and distracted, the cycle continued: children came into the world, rivers flowed from the mountains, bees labored at the hive, and birds of prey circled and waited.

The falcon bore westward in one last sweeping turn and then veered abruptly eastward. The unsuspecting quarry was naked in the afternoon sunlight.

Tucking its wings, the falcon aimed its hooked bill and entered a killing dive.

PART ONE

Prophet Row

How lovely your dwelling,
  O Lord of hosts!
My soul yearns and pines
  for the courts of the Lord.
My heart and flesh cry out
  for the living God.
As the sparrow finds a home
  and the swallow a nest to settle
  her young.
My home is by your altars,
  Lord of hosts, my king and my God!

PSALM 84

CHAPTER ONE

Bird of Passage

VASYL RUSYNKO STOOD at the foot of a wayside crucifix under the tortured gaze of an almost life-sized wooden Christ. At the base of the cross were the words *"Khrest tvoye spaseniye!*—The Cross is your salvation!" Below this was inscribed the date, 1890—the year before Vasyl Rusynko was born. Vasyl crossed himself from right to left in the eastern fashion and whispered, *"Slava Ottsu y Sŷnu y Svyatomu Dukhu*—Glory be to the Father and to the Son and to the Holy Spirit."

Vasyl tossed his bundle to the ground and reclined in the tall grass at the foot of the Lord, resting his head against the black wrought iron fence that surrounded the shrine. Against the dark blue sky a lone sparrow flew northward up the valley. In the warm, heavy air buzzing insects courted madly about Vasyl's head, and he swatted them away to better view the little bird. The bird flapped, then glided, flapped, and glided, its course level and deliberate.

Vasyl shielded his eyes from the sun and cried to the bird, "Fly ahead and tell them I will be there soon!"

Then, in an instant, the sparrow disappeared in a small explosion of feathers. Vasyl twisted his neck to follow the flight of a falcon streaking eastward and vanishing beyond the trees. He looked back at the point of impact and muttered, *"Bozhe moi*—my God." Except for a few dark feathers floating to earth, the sky was empty.

Vasyl retrieved a tobacco pouch, pipe, and ten-penny nail from his pocket, sank back down on the grass, and set about the business of having a smoke. He tamped alternate layers with the head of the nail, struck a match against the bottom of his shoe, and ignited the pipe with a series of deep, quick puffs that momentarily shrouded him in white smoke. Bits of down swirled across the path.

Clouds that had gathered slowly all afternoon now towered ominously to the northwest. On the other side of the path stood a small copse of oaks and beyond was the *Potok* Ondava, a small stream bubbling faintly, an endless exhalation from the mountains. An anxious chipmunk raced up the path, stopped, rose on its haunches, and considered Vasyl and the intermittent billows of smoke. Satisfied or terrified, the creature dashed away into the thicket behind the wayside cross.

The topmost leaves of the oak trees fluttered in a light breeze. Vasyl slid down in the grass, rested his head on his bundle, and closed his eyes. The rippling river, the rustling leaves, the tobacco veil—all floated about his head and comforted his tired body. After some time, a faint ringing penetrated Vasyl's reverie—it was a sound he had not heard in years—the sound of a certain, distinct bell. It was an old bell that hung from the side of an old cart that was driven by an old man. Vasyl sat up and looked down the valley, where he saw that same ancient cart working its way slowly across a small meadow. Many years had passed since Vasyl, as a young passenger, had sat next to the old man—Old Mykhal he was called—and bounced along the rough roads to nearby villages. Old Mykhal had always enjoyed young Vasyl's company and often invited him to ring the bell to announce their arrival in a village.

Now, here was the old man himself approaching, older but essentially unchanged, swaying from side to side on the rocking cart and wearing the same old slouch hat—the only hat Vasyl had ever seen him wear. The bell clanged and Old Mykhal's horse, Sasha, nodded his head up and down while the old man waved and cried out, "*Slava Isusu Khrystu*—Glory to Jesus Christ— honored stranger!"

Vasyl stood, pulled his cap down tightly over his eyes, and dusted off his trousers as horse, cart, and driver came to a halt in the middle of the road. Old Mykhal belatedly pulled the reins, and the horse looked back at him as though annoyed at the unnecessary instruction. Vasyl removed the pipe from his mouth and touched the brim of his cap, being careful not to expose his face. "*Slava na viký*—Glory to Him forever! And God grant you a good day, Pan driver," said Vasyl, affecting an odd accent.

"Did you see her?" asked the old man. "Did you see her kill the sparrow? *Oi*, she is quick and deadly!" Old Mykhal unhooked the clapper from inside the bell and stored it under his seat. "The devil himself could not take your soul any quicker than the falcon takes the sparrow."

Vasyl laughed. "No, not without the Father's knowledge."

Old Mykhal brightened. "Ah, a scholar of the sacred Scriptures! Well," Mykhal winked, "you and I know that we are worth more than a whole flock of sparrows." Old Mykhal inspected Vasyl's foreign clothing and cap. "You are not from here, honored stranger."

Vasyl did not respond but merely puffed on his pipe.

Old Mykhal worked his nose, obviously enjoying the aroma of the tobacco.

Vasyl offered his pouch to the old man. "*Proshu*—please."

Old Mykhal reached down, taking the pouch and trying to observe the face beneath the cap bill. "Thank you, Pan . . ."

Vasyl ignored the probe. "I like your bell."

Old Mykhal smiled proudly and, using his little finger, tamped several pinches of Vasyl's tobacco into the bowl of his pipe. "I am known in these villages by the sound of this bell. I ring it whenever I enter one of them. Sometimes I ring it only to hear it ring. And sometimes I ring it in celebration."

"The falcon's kill," Vasyl suggested.

"Yes, she deserved a good ring." Puffing his pipe deeply, Old Mykhal studied Vasyl. "I wouldn't ask the honored stranger what he is doing here by the side of the road . . . but . . . finding a gentleman such as you deserves a ring. Do you not agree, Pan . . . ?"

Vasyl deflected the old man again. "I am looking for someone."

"Who is it you seek, friend?"

"Vasyl Rusynko. I am told he was born near here."

"Indeed he was—in Stara Polyanka. However, you will not find him there."

"How is that? He hasn't died, I hope."

"Only One can tell that for sure. But, God willing"—Mykhal bowed his head to the suffering Lord and crossed himself quickly from right to left—"God willing, he will come back to us someday."

"Then he is away?" Vasyl was enjoying himself.

"Away as a man can be, I suppose. He is in Ameryka. He left here four years ago, when he was eighteen years old. Now he would be . . . I would say . . ." Old Mykhal counted on his fingers, lost his place, started again, and then wiped his hand on his jacket. "He would be older now—a young man." Mykhal stroked his chin and squinted into the distance. "Vasyl was a good boy. He used to ride with me to some of the villages around here—Varadka, Yalynky, Niklova—and sometimes to Bekherov and Komlosha. He liked to feed my horse." Old Mykhal sighed deeply. "I miss him, honored stranger, and I often think of him over the sea in Ameryka so far from his people. He was such a good and handsome young man and everyone liked—"

Vasyl, reaching in his pocket, interrupted the old man. "Does Sasha still like apples?"

"Well, yes . . . but how did you know my horse's—"

Vasyl removed his cap and wiped his brow with his sleeve, the western sun fully illuminating an inverted grin. "It is good to see you again, Mykhal, old friend."

The old man removed his hat and stood slowly in the cart. "Vasyl," he whispered, "Vasyl Rusynko." His eyes moist, Old Mykhal sat down heavily and watched as Vasyl fed Sasha an apple.

"Mykhal, will you let me ride with you to Stara Polyanka?"

Old Mykhal sniffed loudly and motioned Vasyl aboard. Vasyl retrieved his bundle from the grass, tossed it into the back of the cart, and climbed up next to the old man. The old horse strained against the added load and the cart began to move. Mykhal snapped the reins redundantly and Sasha looked back in protest. The two men turned to the Lord and crossed themselves simultaneously and then rode in silence until the old man, somewhat recovered, coughed and wiped his nose with his thumb, flicking driblets into the air. He looked at Vasyl and shook his head. "Vasyl Rusynko . . . Vasyl Rusynko," he repeated, still accustoming himself to Vasyl's sudden reappearance. Vasyl raised his eyebrows and nodded at each reiteration as if somewhat surprised himself.

Eventually the two men spoke of many things: old friends, the history of recent crops, the malevolent forces of nature, the troubles brewing in the Balkans, and the odds of a military draft being called. But neither broached the subject of Vasyl's family. Old Mykhal respectfully steered the conversation toward innocuous topics; Vasyl would ask about his family when he was ready. Then there was silence and the men had nothing more to say.

Vasyl cleared his throat. "*Moya rodyna*—my family, Mykhal?"

The old man made a face and shook his head. "Your *nyanko*—your father—is not well, Vasyl. It's *sukhotý*—tuberculosis, you know. Ah! It is a curse to our people. It will take us all in the end." Mykhal coughed deeply—a forced hack as if to demonstrate his own imminent confinement.

Vasyl nodded soberly. "He was coughing up blood when I left. And my *mamka*?"

"Your mother manages the homestead by herself, the Lord bless her. She is a rare woman, Vasyl. She runs that household, milks the cow, makes butter—she even continues to keep your father's bees. She cares for your *nyanko* and her own *mamka,* too. The Lord has given her a great cross and a strong back to bear it."

"How are my *dido* and *baba*—my grandfather and grandmother?"

"Your *baba* misses you, Vasyl. She talks about you often. Your *dido* . . . well . . . he died. Two winters ago."

"Oh . . . I see. How?"

"You know how old people become confused. Bless me, even I get confused. Sometimes old people become confused and stay that way. That was how it was with your *dido*. Your *mamka* found him night after night in the barn sharpening the scythes and saying that the harvest must be brought in before it was ruined. Your *mamka* would remind him that the harvest had been brought in weeks ago, and she would take him inside and put him to bed. But the next night there he would be again out in the barn, sharpening. One evening your *dido* disappeared and half the village stomped about in the snow looking for him. At dark everyone went home except your *mamka* and your brother Petro. They searched most of the night by lantern without any luck. Your brother finally found him two days later in a thicket up the valley—frozen solid. Your brother had to chisel him off of the ground with an ax."

Vasyl shook his head, "God save him."

"Amen."

The two rode on in silence and Vasyl shuddered involuntarily before asking, "How is Petro?"

"Your brother is well. He married the spring after your *dido* died—one of the Senchak sisters."

"Oh? The Senchak sisters? You mean Paraska and Yevka? Which one did he marry?"

Mykhal looked up at the darkening sky. "The younger one."

"Not Yevka! She is only a child. He must have married Paraska."

"No. Paraska married Vasko Ivanchyn. And may the Lord have mercy on her and grant her a special seat in Heaven for such an act of charity in marrying such a fool. *On didko*—he's the devil! No, Petro married Yevka. I have cans for her in the back of the cart—cans for her egg dyes. She is no longer a child, Vasyl. And neither is your sister Anna. There is talk of an arrangement for her."

"To whom?"

"Petro Kotsur. The initial talks have gone well."

"Petro Kotsur? He is a boy!"

"You were a boy and now you are a man. You have been gone a long time, Vasyl."

"I suppose I have. And Andrii?"

Mykhal smiled and nodded knowingly. "You can guess, I imagine. The Lord blesses your young brother with a talent for the Scriptures and the written word. He is in school in Pryashev and when he comes home he continues his studies with Father Yaroslav. There is talk of Andrii studying to be a priest someday. Father Yaroslav and his wife are childless, and they treat Andrii as their own."

A rumbling from the black clouds over the mountains echoed down through the valley.

"It may rain," observed Vasyl.

The old man nodded. "Yes, the flies were biting earlier." He slapped his left forearm, a lingering gnat apparently troubling him still.

Vasyl shrugged, unconvinced. "Sometimes it rains whether they bite or not."

"It will rain."

The path detoured around a copse of oaks and then continued along the edge of a wide field. Two men with scythes balanced on their shoulders were walking across the field toward the path. The taller of the two walked with his shoulders hunched over, while the other man, considerably shorter than the first, swaggered with his head back as though shouting at the taller man.

Vasyl pulled his pipe from his mouth and cried delightedly to Mykhal, "Look! Vasko and Yurko!" And indeed they were. The shorter man was the very same Vasko Ivanchyn who had married Paraska Senchak the year before. The taller man was Yurko Kryak, a quiet giant of a man, slow of wit but quick with a spoon or cup of brandy.

"God save us!" hissed Mykhal between his teeth.

"Tell me, Mykhal, do Vasko and Yurko still fight and quarrel endlessly?"

The old man spat. "*Akh,* yes! They are inseparable."

The corners of Vasyl's mouth dropped sharply in an inverted grin. "Mykhal, should I ring the bell?"

"Feh!"

The two harvesters reached the path and were now walking along it toward Stara Polyanka. As the cart approached, Vasko waved them on without looking back. Vasyl pulled his cap down tightly, shading his face, and turned to Mykhal. "Don't tell them who I am. Let's stop and talk; we'll have some fun with them."

"You would have more fun speaking with my horse, Sasha."

"Stop the cart."

"Feh!"

Vasyl nudgedMykhal in the ribs. "Shh!" The old man pulled Sasha's reins; this time the old horse had not anticipated his master's wish. Vasko stopped and turned, yanking Yurko to a halt by his shirt.

Vasyl called out. "*Chestny Panove!*—Honored gentlemen! Is this the way to Stara Polyanka?"

Vasko contemplated the interrogator and flashed an impish grin across a begrimed face. "I will not say it is *the* way, honored visitor . . . I will only say that it is *one* way to the place you seek. But is Old Mykhal now so old that he cannot remember the way, or has he at last accepted what we always knew—that his horse has better sense than he and should be given a free rein?"

Mykhal leaned across Vasyl and jabbed his pipe at Vasko. "I am old enough to know that your mother could not remember the name of your father!"

Vasko laughed. "Thank you, dear papa, for reminding me! And how is my dear brother, Sasha?"

"I am not your papa! The devil himself is your papa! And I will thank you to leave Sasha out of this. Unlike you, he is one of God's innocent creatures!"

"No, dear Papa," Vasko said solemnly. "No one is innocent. Yurko here appears innocent but could just as easily be the dreaded Antichrist. We are all guilty: Yurko, my father, and your Sasha."

"Sasha is a horse!"

"*Oi!*" Vasko struck his forehead in mock astonishment. "A nonbeliever! Yes, old man, Brother Sasha is a horse. But among the five of us gathered here, he most resembles a horse and is therefore guilty of at least that!"

"FEH!"

Vasyl was delighted with the way things were going. "How long, then, to Stara Polyanka?" he asked, returning to the original question.

Vasko stroked his chin and grinned. "Only slightly longer than it takes the horse to get there. Once the horse arrives, you will not be far behind. Unless, of course, you find that on arriving you are no longer behind the horse's behind!"

Vasyl beamed at Mykhal. "Same old Vasko," he whispered. The old man stared ahead, chewing his pipe fiercely.

Vasko approached Sasha and stroked the horse's nose. "Tell me, Brother Sasha, where did you find Vasyl Rusynko, and why did you not tell me he was coming back to us from Ameryka?"

Vasyl removed his hat and threw it at Vasko. "When did you know it was I?"

"When you said, 'honored gentlemen.' No one ever calls me a *Pan*, not since you left. You are the only one who ever called me that. So they threw you out of Ameryka. I told him not to go, didn't I, Yurko?" His tall friend was staring at Sasha. During the preceding exchange, both Yurko and the horse had stood impassively, occasionally shifting their legs, indifferent to the conversation, but in no particular hurry to move on, and as content as such creatures can be when not eating or sleeping.

"Yurko likes your horse, old man," said Vasko.

Mykhal spat and studied the distant mountains. Vasko took an abrupt interest in the *Potok* Ondava—the Ondava Stream—gurgling nearby.

"Yurko! In the excitement, we nearly forgot! Yurko! A rock!" Vasko peered toward the stream and put out an open hand. Yurko fetched a stone from the path, placed it in his friend's outstretched hand, and watched as Vasko hurled the rock toward the flowing water. "Another, Yurko! *Skoro*—hurry!" The two men, working as a team, managed to rain a small volley of stones on a thicket, well short of the Ondava Stream. Many years before there had been a suicide in the Ondava near that spot.

Vasyl laughed. "Yes, my *baba*—my grandmother—used to have me do the same thing for her when we used to pass this way. We cannot have the dead haunting us, can we?" he teased.

Vasko put his hands on his hips. "Do you take me for an old woman? Even Yurko knows these things must be done. Isn't that true, Yurko? A man goes to Ameryka and forgets who he is. Now we must undo all the great damage that has been done to Vasyl so that he may once again join his people. I say that we all meet tonight at Yakov's tavern to begin the instruction."

"Ah, but I already know how to do this." Vasyl made the motion of lifting and drinking from a mug. "How is it with Yakov these days?"

Vasko waved his hand toward the south with a final gesture. "The *zhyd*—the Jew—is gone. He moved to Bardeyov two years ago. And good riddance."

Yakov had long ago suspended Vasko's credit at the tavern. "He sold the tavern to a man named Khudyk."

"Khudyk? I never heard of Khudyk." Vasyl looked to Mykhal, but the old man was still staring at the mountains, puffing his pipe, reflective and detached. He might have been alone with his cart and his horse enjoying a quiet late summer afternoon.

"After tonight, Vasyl, you shall place such ignorance behind you forever," said Vasko. "Andrii Khudyk is from Rostoky. His brother went to Ameryka and worked in mines in Penslovenya or Penslavyanskii or some such place. He came back with money and bought the tavern. Only, he died before he could work even one day there. His brother, Andrii Khudyk, then took it over."

"But why," asked Vasyl, "do you still call it 'Yakov's tavern' if it has been sold to this fellow Khudyk?"

"Because, honest Vasyl, that is its name." Vasko shook his head forlornly at Yurko to emphasize Vasyl's tragic decline.

For the horse the conversation was apparently finished. He stepped forward, the cart followed, and Mykhal gave a superfluous toss of the reins.

Vasyl waved to Yurko. "Yurko, my hat! Tonight, then—we meet at Yakov's!"

Yurko, still staring at Sasha, picked up Vasyl's hat and tossed it to him. The cart pulled past and Vasko and Yurko followed in its wake.

Vasko called out, "Vasyl!"

Vasyl turned in his seat.

"Take care that gelding delivers you safely!"

Vasyl waved.

"Vasyl!"

Vasyl turned again.

"I mean the one pulling the cart, not the one driving it!"

Vasyl grinned, the corners of his mouth dropping sharply. He looked at old Mykhal. The old man's neck was red and his jaw ground behind tight, thin lips. Vasyl tapped his pipe against the side of the cart, retrieved his tobacco from his pack and refilled the bowl for another smoke. He held the open pouch before Mykhal, but the old man was oblivious to the offer. Vasyl left the pouch on the seat between them and contented himself with watching for the first signs of the village.

Across the valley were the fields of Pan Kapishinskii, the wealthiest peasant in Stara Polyanka. His vast fields covered the western side of the valley, extending almost to the top of the ridge. Vasyl had earned money working in those fields before he left for Ameryka. Directly opposite those fields lay the village. Just around the final stand of oaks up ahead, the path would lead due north and straight into Stara Polyanka. Vasyl swallowed and fidgeted in his seat.

"Nervous?" Mykhal seemed to shout in his ear.

"No, why should I be?"

Old Mykhal shrugged, but smiled broadly. He nodded ahead. "Look."

There, towering above the crowns of surrounding linden trees, were the three onion-shaped wooden domes of the Church of the Protection of the Mother of God. Vasyl was baptized in this church as were his brothers and sisters, and nearly everyone else in the village. His parents were married there and his *dido*—his grandpa—would have been buried behind it two years ago.

"Stop the cart," said Vasyl.

Old Mykhal ignored him. Vasyl put his hand on Mykhal's arm. "Stop the cart, Mykhal."

Sasha came to a halt and Vasyl jumped down and grabbed his bundle from the back of the cart. He retrieved the clapper from under the seat and hooked it under the bell.

"You go on, Mykhal. I am going to walk around behind the church to my home. I want to see my family before I see anyone else. Go on, Mykhal. I will see you tonight at the tavern."

Old Mykhal touched his cap and watched Vasyl climb up the embankment and disappear into the trees. Sasha pulled forward, and Old Mykhal tossed the reins. With the bell clanging, the cart rumbled on into Stara Polyanka.

CHAPTER TWO

Stara Polyanka

SHE WAS THE FIRST TO SEE HIM—a lone figure circumventing the village, first visible near the expansive home of Pan Kapishinskii, then behind Pan Kapishinskii's barn, then behind the church. His distinctive gait—confident, but not proud—identified him. There was only one man from Stara Polyanka who walked this way. All the other village men either strutted, their chests undeservedly swollen, or shuffled, their backs prematurely bent. She squinted across the narrow valley. If it were truly him, he would emerge from behind the church on the upper path that could lead only to one home. She stepped out of the doorway of the hut for a better view of the entire village. There was Old Mykhal alighting from his cart. Several villagers were gathered around him—he would have her tin cans from Bardeyov. She looked again for the figure up the hill. He would be visible by now if he had taken the lower path; therefore, he must have taken the upper path and would come into view very soon. But Old Mykhal had told him about his grandfather and he would be at the graveside now. She waited and when the figure emerged on the upper trail heading toward an old hut above the tavern, she held her right hand across her chest and whispered, "Vasyl Rusynko."

"Yevka! Have you heard the news?" Startled, Yevka wheeled around. It was her sister, Paraska, who had married Vasko Ivanchyn. Paraska was annoyed and breathless as she brushed past Yevka and into the hut the two sisters shared with their husbands. Yevka looked back across the valley before following her sister inside. Vasyl was nearing the old Rusynko hut.

"What news, Paraska?"

"First, help me with these," said Paraska, holding her apron open and revealing half a dozen eggs. "Take these two, Yevka; they are the best—they are well-shaped and their shells are smooth. They will make good *pysanký*—

dyed eggs. Now, let me tell you: there is a *bosorka*—a witch—in the village, Yevka, and she is casting spells against us. First, that cow your husband, Petro, brought to this house has almost stopped giving milk. And now, the pig promised to us by Mariya Kavulya last spring has died! And here in my neck there is such a pain that I can barely breathe!"

Yevka closed her eyes, arched her eyebrows, and raised her hands in a gesture that acknowledged the string of bad luck but admitted clear evidence of neither dark magic nor witchcraft. Her sister had always been eager to attribute ill fortune to the scheming of a *bosorka* or even to the mischief of an *opyr*—a vampire. Paraska would chatter tirelessly about these latest omens and, in the end, the sisters would perform together one or more rites taught to them by their mother to ward off the effects of evil spirits.

"I tell you, the whole village is at risk. This rain that is coming will likely swell the Ondava and split the village in two. Yevka, bring that bucket of water to the hearth. We will find out who is casting spells against us. Put it there by the oven door." Paraska opened the little door and probed the coals with an iron poker. "Yes, there are three good little coals. Now, pay attention, Yevka—watch the bucket." Paraska reached into the oven with her bare hand and quickly chucked the three coals one after the other into the bucket of water calling out, "Man! Woman! Child!" Each coal hissed on impact and Paraska peered into the water. "Look, Yevka, 'woman' sank to the bottom! Just as I thought! Do you see? It is that witch—I won't say her name aloud—I knew it! *Tota bosorka*—that witch! *Tota huntsutka*—that troublemaker! Now sprinkle my neck with water from the bucket—it will ease my pain. Yes, Yevka, for now it is we who suffer, but soon, I tell you, soon . . ." Paraska continued to rant while Yevka dutifully sprinkled her sister's neck.

But Yevka was no longer listening to her sister. Yevka was looking out the door. Somewhere out there was the man with the inverted smile and the resolute walk—the man who was her husband's brother.

৩

Vasyl approached the hut of his childhood from the back. The building site was cut into the sloping grade, and here, the eaves of the high-pitched roof nearly reached the ground. The roof needed rethatching and the timbered walls rechinking with mud-and-straw plaster. On the north side of the home, the attached barn leaned precariously, its single door pushed closed as far as the structure's defects allowed. A rooster strutted to the threshold of the little barn, shook itself violently, and disappeared inside. Vasyl thrust his head in the doorway. Except for the rooster and three or four chickens, the barn was empty.

The hut had deteriorated during the four years Vasyl had been away. There was a time when necessary repairs never would have been postponed until late September. He walked around to the front of the hut, where he found the front door ajar. Vasyl stepped into a dark room illuminated by a lone candle burning before a small tin icon of the Mother of God in the corner. On the hearth a pot bubbled softly, rendering the air heavy with the earthy odor of potatoes. A cool breeze blew through the doorway, and distant thunder reverberated through the valley.

Far into the gloomy recesses of the room were the outlines of the bunks, framed with rough-hewn planks and raised high off the floor. As a child, Vasyl shared the upper platform with his older brother, Petro, and his younger brother, Palko. The two sisters, Anna and Helenka, slept in the lower bunk, while Andrii, the baby of the family, slept in a cradle suspended by ropes from the central beam.

In those days the boys played endless pranks on the girls, endured their father's resultant beatings, commiserated over their harsh treatment, and then vindictively plotted anew against the females. Once they managed to smuggle a cooperative pullet to the top bunk and from there drop it upon the unsuspecting sisters below. In the ensuing riot, the hen scratched Anna badly below her left eye, leaving a scar. Helenka jumped off the bunk and stood shrieking incoherently, pointing up to the silent top bunk lest there be any doubt concerning culpability. Their father yanked the poor bird off Anna and hurled it across the room, breaking its neck. The boys were next. Their father beat and kicked them, flailing furiously, while his wife pleaded for mercy on the boys' behalf in the name of the Holy Mother of God. Meanwhile, the girls, desperate to escape the indiscriminate blows of their father, hid themselves in the folds of their mother's skirt. Eventually exhausted, the father left for Yakov's tavern and returned home very late and very drunk.

One January day the fever came to Stara Polyanka. In the beginning the mothers dismissed it hopefully as nothing more than a bad winter cold. But the old women gossiped in small groups with their chins cupped in their hands and suppressed their murmurs at the approach of a young mother. By the end of January, two children, aged one year and two, were dead. February came and was merciless to a village of only forty households. In the first three weeks, eleven children between the ages of one year and six years succumbed. The old women comforted the wailing mothers; the men worked in the cemetery, carving little holes in the frozen ground. Then there was a week without a death and the villagers prayed that the worst was over.

The first day of March dawned cold and misty. During the early morning hours, Vasko Ivanchyn's two-year-old brother died. Just before midday Vasyl's brother Palko died, and during midafternoon a third child in the village died. It began to snow heavily at nightfall. The next morning, during a near blizzard, the seventeenth and eighteenth victims breathed their last. Number eighteen was Vasyl's sister Helenka. Vasyl's mother prepared her two children for burial and laid them tenderly in their tiny coffins. Vasyl and Anna, themselves very sick, missed the funerals. Their older brother, Petro, helped their father hack through snow and ice to dig the graves.

Before the funeral, Vasyl's mother went to the home of Mariya Senchak, the best *pysanka* artist in the village. Mariya had lost her own son, Hryhorii, in early February and her two young daughters, Paraska and Yevka, still lay ill in their bunk. Mariya Senchak alleviated her sorrow by creating a series of exquisite *pysankŷ* and presenting them to the other grieving mothers. The villagers long remembered these brightly dyed eggs as among the most beautiful ever made by an artist known for her incomparable work. Vasyl's mother was one of three mothers to receive two eggs. Mariya was waiting at her door when Vasyl's mother arrived, and wordlessly she handed Vasyl's mother the two carefully wrapped *pysankŷ*. Before his father affixed the wooden lids, Vasyl's mother placed an egg in each of her children's hands. She never spoke of them again.

The death of Palko created, or perhaps revealed, a breach between Vasyl and Petro. All interactions between the two older brothers had passed through the conduit, Palko. His antics and energy bound the three of them to a common allegiance. After Palko's death, Vasyl and Petro quickly polarized—two boys differing in all but name: Vasyl, smiling, likeable, and outgoing—the favorite of his *baba*—his grandmother; and Petro, unsmiling, preoccupied, and sullen—an enigma to all.

Now, standing in the dark room, Vasyl rubbed his growling stomach. He found a wooden spoon on the hearth and fished one of the potatoes out of the pot, setting it on the wooden table to cool. On a narrow shelf on the wall were the homemade tallow candles. Vasyl retrieved one, lit it from the hot coals, and ventured farther into the corners of the room, inspecting the bunks in the dim light. The beds were empty except for a heap of blankets on his parents' bunk. He moved along the windowed wall, examining the shelves and a pile of needles and yarn on a chair. On the dirt floor, next to a worn and stubby broom, was a small bundle of fresh reeds. Vasyl returned to his parents' bunk, this time scrutinizing the blankets more carefully.

There was movement in the covers. Coming closer with the candle, Vasyl noticed first the pallid hand feebly working the blanket's edge; and then, buried deeper in the blanket's folds, the sallow face and sunken, jaundiced eyes. Vasyl's father peered out vacantly, his breathing labored and uneven. Vasyl held the gaunt hand in his own and felt a faint squeeze. He sat with his father until the old man's eyes closed, and then, hearing voices outside, Vasyl went to the door.

Hurrying up the path from the center of the village were his mother and sister with his diminutive *baba* supported, or rather half carried, between them, her legs kicking out of step with her bearers, her feet occasionally slapping the earth. "*Skoro*—hurry!" she commanded. "I want to see my Vasyl!"

Vasyl stepped out of the doorway. His mother and sister halted, inadvertently releasing *Baba,* who stumbled forward, collapsing against her grandson and ejecting an abrupt "*Oi!*" Startled, she looked up and hollered, "MY VASYL!" in a voice incompatible with her size. She wrapped her arms around him and buried her head in his chest, moaning, "*Slava Hospodu!*—Glory to you, O Lord! You have brought home my Vasyl!" Vasyl's sister, Anna, hovered timidly to one side, while his mother stood back, both hands over her mouth, her eyes moist.

"Come over here," *Baba* beckoned to Anna. "You hold him and do not let him leave here, now and ever and forever." Anna put her head down and gave her brother a reserved hug. Vasyl kissed her forehead and she squirmed away shyly, but Vasyl grabbed her hand.

"Old Mykhal was right; you were a young girl when I left—now you are almost fit to be a bride."

Blushing, Anna pulled away from Vasyl and went to their mother's side. "Look, *Mamko*"—she wrapped an arm around her mother's shoulders and brought her closer—"it is Vasyl. Vasyl has come back to us."

Vasyl's mother waved her daughter inside. Anna followed *Baba,* who was shuffling to the door. The old woman pointed a crooked finger toward the barn. "Anna!" she shouted. "Go and chop the head off of the biggest chicken you can find, drain the blood, and then bring it to me. I'll pour hot water over it so you can pluck the feathers. Then help me cook a feast for my Vasyl!"

Vasyl stood alone with his mother in front of the hut. Her hair had grayed in four and a half years and her face was thin. He drew closer and stood quietly next to her. Then he pointed to the roof. "It needs rethatching. I will start tomorrow."

His mother nodded, and, sighing deeply, she wiped the streaks from her face. She took her son's hand and held it to her cheek, and when it began to rain softly, she led him inside the hut.

❧

Vasyl ate more than half the chicken because that is what the women placed before him. The three of them served him and fussed over him and watched him eat. *Baba* shuffled about the room maintaining a steady background chatter that everyone ignored, while, outside, the rain pounded against the thatched roof. Intermittently *Baba* sat, filled her mouth with food, and grinned at Vasyl. When Vasyl finished he fetched his pipe and tobacco pouch from his jacket hanging near the door. His mother smiled as she watched him fill the bowl.

"Petro smokes a pipe now, too," she said.

Vasyl inserted a stick into the fire and lit his pipe. "He had one before I went to Ameryka."

"Did he? I forgot," said his mother. She gazed at her son, who blew smoke toward the ceiling. Vasyl had become a man—the *gazda*—the head of the household. From now on, if there was village business to tend to, or the purchase of a goat or cow to be made, he would negotiate the transaction.

Vasyl puffed deeply. "When will I see Andriiko?"

Vasyl's mother took the empty potato pot off the hearth and placed it on the dirt floor near the window where the old roof leaked most noticeably. "When he returns from Pryashev."

Vasyl watched his mother, observing that she held her back as she straightened. "I will start the rethatching at that spot," he said.

"The whole roof is rotten!" cried *Baba*. "It will fall on us in our sleep and kill us all! The barn needs rebuilding, too!"

"It is not all that bad," said Vasyl's mother, wounded.

Vasyl stood and walked about the room with manly deliberation. The women marked his inspection: his mother anxiously wiping her hands on her apron, his *baba* sucking chicken grease from the ends of her fingers, and his sister standing in the corner by the hearth. He came to the bunks and looked into the dull, half-opened eyes. During dinner it had become increasingly obvious that Vasyl's father, though still breathing, ceased to live in the minds of the women, especially his mother's. They were accustomed to a nursing routine in which his father was like a sick barn animal, once prized, but now, hopelessly ill and deserving of a comfortable end commensurate with his former worth. To watch a man die takes strength; to watch a man die slowly over the years takes life out of those around him. Vasyl returned to the table and put his foot up on the stool. "You have done a fine job, *Mamko.*"

His mother reddened and waved indifferently, turning her back to her son and busying herself at the hearth. But she was pleased. Anna nodded and smiled at Vasyl, while *Baba* gave her fingers one last resounding smack. "All this fine work is for nothing if the roof falls tonight!" she said, inspecting her fingers.

Anna glowered at the old woman, but Vasyl laughed and, pulling his stool closer, wrapped his arms around his *baba*'s neck. "You are right, little stork. Who wants to nest on a rotted roof? Anna! Help me make up the barn for our guest, the stork, whose wings . . ." Vasyl sniffed her hands, ". . . feh . . . smell more like those of a chicken! She will be safe there—the barn's roof cannot fall any more than it has—" He grimaced at his thoughtless comment and stole a glance at his mother, who nevertheless remained occupied at the hearth.

"Ah, my Vasyl!" sighed *Baba*. "You must never leave us—never again."

Vasyl's mother stood behind her son and patted his shoulder. "Vasyl is a man. He will go where he will. I prayed for his return and God returned him to us. If he leaves again, I will pray again. And now, let Vasyl go. He has spent enough time with women. He thirsts for other company. Go, Vasyl."

Baba was agitated. "Go? Go where? In this weather he will drown before he gets to the garden gate!"

Anna took her grandmother's hand. "Come, *Babo*. Help me make a place for Vasyl to sleep. Is the top bunk all right, Vasyl?"

Vasyl nodded and stood. His mother appeared from a corner of the room with a coat over her arm. "Take this, Vasyl."

"But, *Mamko* . . ." said Vasyl glancing into the dark corner.

"Take it, Vasyl. He would want you to have it. Take it."

Vasyl put an arm into his father's old coat and rotated into the other sleeve held up by his mother. She straightened the collar and looked up at her son. "Go. You have been gone over four years. Your friends want to see you."

Vasyl took his hat off of a wall peg near the door and stepped out into a blowing deluge.

CHAPTER THREE

Yakov's Tavern

THE *KORCHMA*—the tavern—consisted of five small tables, several warped benches, an assortment of three- and four-legged stools, and a rough-hewn plank supported on each end by two empty beer barrels lashed together with rope. A stone fireplace heated the single room and, along with a kerosene lamp on the opposite wall, lighted it as well. A dozen men sat in little groups hunched over their drinks, smoking their pipes, their droning voices competing with mixed success with the torrent drumming on the roof. The most animated character in the place was the small, gray Andrii Khudyk, who was rolling a beer barrel into the room from a storage area in back.

Draped over a bench near the fire was an old coat. The owner of the coat—the new owner—took a swallow from his mug of beer and agreed to listen to Vasko Ivanchyn's argument one more time. "Tell me again, Vasko— but slowly, so that even I can understand."

Vasko stood and held his hands out in front of him with the palms up. "Vasyl, you know our custom concerning suicides, yes? The suicide must be buried where he committed his offense against God. Also, no suicide is to be buried in the church cemetery, on holy soil." Vasko smiled, placed his hands on his hips, and swayed unsteadily. "Do you not see?"

Vasyl feigned ignorance. "No."

Vasko explained again. "If one kills himself in the churchyard, where is he to be buried? Not in the churchyard; it is not allowed. But our way states he must be buried where he falls, which"—Vasko clapped his hands—"must be in the churchyard!"

Vasyl yawned. "Is that all?"

"Is that all!?" Vasko was incredulous. "Vasyl, where should the suicide be buried?"

Vasyl drained his mug. "In the road, just outside the churchyard gate."

"No, no, they cannot!" Vasko beamed. He had ensnared Vasyl. "He must be buried where he killed himself!"

Vasyl crossed the room and plunked his mug heavily on the plank bar. All the men in the tavern turned to hear his response. "All right, bury him just inside the churchyard gate." Andrii Khudyk filled Vasyl's mug.

Vasko massaged his temples—the conundrum apparently was causing a tremendous headache. "No, honest Vasyl, they cannot do that. Our ways do not permit such a thing. And Father Yaroslav would never allow it."

Vasyl returned to the bench. Old Mykhal was at the end of the table facing the fire, his eyes half shut. Vasyl put a hand on the old man's shoulder. "Mykhal, where should we bury Vasko's suicide?"

Old Mykhal turned from the fire, his head and upper body moving together stiffly. "Bury Vasko at the spot where he dies."

"No, old man, not me! Vasyl! Tell him!" Vasko tapped his mug on the table. "Khudyk! Whiskey!"

Ignoring Vasko, Andrii Khudyk threw two split pieces of *buk*—beech wood—on the fire. Vasyl prepared his pipe slowly and said, "We will make 'elekshyn' like they do in Ameryka. In Ameryka, when something this important must be decided—Vasyl puffed his pipe to life and eyed Vasko solemnly—"they make 'elekshyn.'"

Yurii Fedorochko raised his mug. "Tell us what to do, Vasyl!"

Vasyl stood and faced the men. "It is very simple. Everyone raises his hand once—and only once—for his choice of where to bury the suicide. I will count, and the choice with the most hands wins."

"No, no! This is not right!" Vasko had lost control. "Both choices are required by our custom, yet neither is acceptable!"

Vasyl ignored Vasko and asked for the vote. "Raise your hands if you favor a churchyard burial."

"No, no!"

"Quiet, Vasko! You had your say!" someone shouted.

"Raise your hands for the churchyard," repeated Vasyl. "One hand only, Ivan Dzyamba! One, two, three . . ." Vasko raised a hand. "Four. You are a fine man, Vasko. Now, raise your hands for burial in the road."

Vasko raised his hand again and Vasyl frowned. "You may choose only once, Vasko." Vasyl refused to count the vote until Vasko lowered his hand. The other men, weary of Vasko's poor humor, shouted at him.

"Lower your hand!"

"Someone tie his hands behind his back!"

"Yurko, throw Vasko out in the rain!"

"Throw him in the churchyard!"

"Throw him in the road *outside* the churchyard!"

After much laughter the vote was forgotten and the men returned to their drinks. Vasyl bought a whiskey, handed it to Yurko, and pointed him to the corner where his friend sulked. Vasko tossed back the drink in one swallow and pitched the empty cup back to Yurko. "Antichrist! Why did you not help me?" The crestfallen Yurko rejoined the small group sitting with Vasyl.

☙

The rain continued to fall outside and puddles of water collected on the dirt floor near the fireplace and by the door. Ivan Dzyamba had slid off his bench and now lay on the floor snoring, his mug still clutched in his hand, his body emitting an offensive odor. The members of Vasyl's circle, which was considerably smaller since he ran out of money, mumbled and smoked their pipes. Yurii Fedorochko, Vasko Ivanchyn, Yurko Kryak, and Old Mykhal—the latter, his eyes closed and his head nodding at intervals—listened as Vasyl told them about his travels.

"Vasyl, you tell a good story," scoffed Yurii Fedorochko when Vasyl described the immense size of a particular city across the ocean.

"It is no story, my friend."

Vasko leaned against Vasyl's shoulder. "Go on, Vasyl. Tell us more. Yurii is a nonbeliever and a friend of Yurko, the Antichrist."

Vasyl pushed Vasko away. "Don't call Yurko that. Can't you see he doesn't like it?"

Vasko snorted. "Tell us again, Vasyl. How big is this place you call Nu York?"

Vasyl placed a mug at each end of the table. "If this mug is Stara Polyanka and this one is Bardeyov, then all this area"—he indicated the surface of the table—"and even where Mykhal sits would be Nu York." Old Mykhal nodded and Yurii grunted. "But there is even more," said Vasyl. "There is Nu Dzyerzi over there across the river and my mug would be Yonkers—that is where I lived with my uncle Pavlo for four years. And there are many, many cities all around." He swept his hand well beyond the edge of the table.

Yurii grunted again and refilled his pipe. Vasyl retrieved a small box from his pocket, pulled out a match, struck it against the box, and ignited Yurii's pipe. Vasko inspected the box. "Is it from Ameryka, Vasyl?"

"Yes, I brought it from Nu York."

"What is this writing? Is it *po-amerykanský*—the American way?"

"Yes."

Vasko handed the box to Vasyl. "Can you read it?"

Vasyl studied the lettering on the box. "It says, 'Strayk ani ver.'"

"Well then, honest Vasyl," said Vasko, "what does that mean?"

"It means, my friend, that if I pull one of the matches against any rough, hard surface—let's say, your head—"

"Vasyl!"

"—then the match will flame up."

Yurii puffed on his pipe and frowned. "What the devil is that smell?"

Vasyl pointed to the floor. "It is Ivan."

"He smells like my pigs," snorted Yurii.

"Forget Ivan and your pigs," said Vasko. "Tell us about the ride on the boat, Vasyl. And tell us what you did in Ameryka."

"The ship to Ameryka was crowded with people from many places— our people and Slovaks and Germans and others—carrying everything they could fit into trunks and bundles. I slept down below in a big room with iron bunks near the engines. All the time we could hear and feel those big engines." Vasyl shook the table and groaned to demonstrate. "I lived here in Yonkers." He wrapped his hands around his mug. "On Pres-kot Street. I walked every day to faktri where they make carpet for the floor."

"They make what?" asked Yurii.

"Carpet. They are like thick blankets for the floor. It is what people in Ameryka want in their homes."

Yurii was incredulous. "In Ameryka people have money for such things?"

"In Ameryka, my friend, people have money for many such things."

Yurii stretched and yawned. "And so you left paradise where people have money for blankets on the floor—you left such a place to come back here. Why?"

"This is my home, my friend."

"A man can make his home anywhere. Most of our people go to Ameryka and stay. You came back."

Vasyl puffed on his pipe unsuccessfully, pulled it from his mouth, and turned the cold bowl in his hands. "I never wanted to stay in Ameryka. I went because my uncle Pavlo went the year before. I went because I wanted to earn money to buy land in Stara Polyanka. Only . . . I always wanted to come back here. This is my home."

"Honest Vasyl!" cried Vasko, slurring his words. "You sound like your brother Andrii! He always says every good Rusyn belongs in his homeland—at least, I think that is what he says. He always uses words I can't understand."

"Well then," said Vasyl raising his mug, "welcome me back, brothers! Here is where I will live"—he took a swallow—"and here is where I will die!"

Yurii shook his head. "So you came back here to live and die. Feh!"—he pointed to Ivan at his feet—"I'm dying now. We should throw him outside."

Vasko pounded his fist on the table. "Let the Antichrist drag him out!"

"Don't call Yurko that," said Vasyl. "I told you already, he doesn't like it."

Someone on the other side of the room called out, "What is that smell?"

"It is Ivan!" cried Vasko. "He passed out and now he has disgraced himself!"

The men gathered in a circle and contemplated the prostrate Ivan.

"He smells like the devil!"

"He got sick."

"He disgraced himself!"

"He disgusts me."

"He disgusts you? He lies there disgracing his family name! Do you think he cares if he disgusts you?"

"He smells awful."

"Is he dead?"

"No, he's not dead. Listen—he's breathing."

"He's not breathing, he's snoring"

"Idiot! How can he snore if he isn't breathing?"

"He smells like death."

"He disgraced himself."

"Let's drag him outside."

"He is a disciple of the Antichrist. Let the Antichrist drag him out!"

"Don't call him that."

"Help me drag him out."

"It's raining out."

"Throw him out!"

"It's raining like it did in Noah's time. We can't put him out in that."

"The rain will wash him off. He is disgusting."

"Listen to it! He will die out there."

"I am dying in here. Someone help me drag him."

"He will freeze!"

"Grab his legs!"

"You grab his legs! They are filthy!"

"For the Antichrist there is no such thing as filth! Let the Antichrist drag him out!"

"Don't call him that."

"Antichrist!"

"Yurko doesn't like to be called such a thing!"

"ANTICHRIST! ANTICHRIST!"

Yurko struck his friend sharply with the back of his hand, sending Vasko staggering backward over Ivan Dzyamba and through the circle of men who watched him land in a heap next to, and partly in, the fire. Vasyl vaulted the table, pulled Vasko's foot out of the fire and dragged his bleeding friend to safety in a corner. Shtefan Senchak leaped onto Yurko's back and rode him about the tavern, whooping like a madman until his mount fell back against the wall. The melee was, for the most part, a good-natured shoving match until Andrii Khudyk opened the tavern door and, with surprising strength and agility, began tossing men out into the mud. Vasko, revived now and holding his jaw, rose to his feet and charged the turned back of Andrii Khudyk, who stood in the doorway shaking his fist at the brawlers outside in the mud.

"Go home to your wives and mothers, if they will have you! You are— *phoooof!*" The airborne Vasko smashed into Andrii Khudyk and both men fell facedown in the mud.

Inside, near the crackling fire, Vasyl and Old Mykhal sat together with the snoring Ivan Dzyamba at their feet. Outside, the air rang with indictments; Vasko's tenor voice, distinct above the others, screamed recriminations with frequent references to the Antichrist.

"Tell me, Vasyl," said Old Mykhal, yawning. "Are there, in Ameryka, men who behave like this?"

Vasyl relit his pipe, puffed thoughtfully, and then said, "Yes—the Irish."

Presently Yurko came through the doorway carrying the groaning Vasko. "Put me down—I can walk!" cried Vasko. Yurko dropped his friend on the floor. "Help me up!" cried Vasko. "I cannot stand!" Yurko pulled him to his feet and Vasko promptly slid back down to the floor.

Andrii Khudyk staggered into the room, holding his head and pointing at Vasko. "Yurko! Get him out of my tavern—NOW! He is never to set foot in here again!"

Yurko turned his pathetic face to Vasyl, pleading for instruction. Vasyl rose and nodded at Vasko. "Let's take him home, Yurko."

Andrii Khudyk stood over Old Mykhal. On his overnight stops in Stara Polyanka Mykhal always slept in the tavern—but not tonight. "Everyone! *VON*—OUT!"

"Come, Mykhal," said Vasyl. "Tonight you stay with me."

Yurko picked up the muddy, whimpering Vasko, threw him over his shoulder, and followed Vasyl and Mykhal out the door, cracking his friend's head on the door frame.

CHAPTER FOUR

Awake

YEVKA LAY AWAKE IN BED, listening to the rain thumping the thatched roof above. Her husband, Petro Rusynko, snored next to her. Earlier that evening, after a full day's work in Pan Kapishinskii's fields, Vasko sat at the table, massaging his bare feet and chatting excitedly about meeting Vasyl Rusynko on the road south of the village. Paraska tapped her husband's shoulder, pointing to his muddy boots on the dirt floor near the hearth. Vasko picked up the boots, tossed them next to the doorway, and then walked around the table wiggling his toes.

"Vasyl will come to Yakov's tonight and it will be like old times," said Vasko, returning to his seat.

Paraska loomed over her husband with her fists into her hips. "Old times for him, perhaps, but not for you! You go to the tavern—you get drunk. You get drunk—you cause trouble. You cause trouble"—she struck her chest with her fist—"I have to make things right. Tonight you stay here. The ax handle is broken—you can fix it."

"Petro fixed it yesterday. Today he is in the hills cutting wood with it. Tomorrow I will help him bring the wood down, and tonight"—he slapped the table with an open hand—"tonight I will go to the tavern."

Paraska glared at her husband and then crossed the room to examine a shelf on the far wall. Finding nothing of interest on the shelf, Paraska sailed uncomfortably close past her husband on the return trip. Wincing, Vasko turned in his seat to better observe his wife. Neither husband nor wife spoke and a tense anticipation filled the room.

Yevka sat quietly against the wall, whittling a piece of brazilwood delivered that day by Old Mykhal along with tin cans from Bardeyov. The brazilwood was an unexpected surprise, the result of inquiries made by Mykhal on Yevka's behalf. The old man apologized to Yevka for the meager size of the piece, but Yevka squeezed his hand—Mykhal blushed—and told him she would make enough red dye from the precious shavings to last a year. She dropped the splinters in one of the tin cans, poured water over them, and placed the can on the hearth to boil. Yevka busied herself with the tools of her craft: a candle, a small cup of beeswax, and an old nail fitted with a wooden handle. Before her were the two eggs Paraska had selected earlier. Yevka carefully dabbed them clean and began to apply the first wax designs on the eggs.

Later, when Petro came up the path in the rain, Vasko bounded to the door to greet him, grateful for a release from the stony silence. Vasko told Petro of Vasyl's return, and, with hand gestures, grotesque faces, and nervous glances at Paraska's back, conveyed the recent domestic history. Petro tossed his hat but missed a peg on the wall and sat with a heavy thud on the bench. Yevka picked up the hat, hung it on the peg, and then fetched a dry shirt for her husband. She draped the wet shirt over the edge of their bunk and then helped Paraska with the meal.

At supper Petro and Vasko spoke briefly of the next day's work hauling down wood from the upland meadow's edge where Petro had worked all day. No one mentioned Vasyl Rusynko again. After the meal Petro smoked his pipe and Vasko dressed to go out, putting on his overcoat and hat while stealing glances at his wife. Petro climbed wearily into bed, and Vasko went out to the tavern.

Now, much later, Yevka stared into the darkness unable to sleep. She turned restlessly onto one side and then the other. She raised her head at the approaching sound of men laughing, arguing, and singing. The commotion escalated, rousing Paraska from her bed on the far side of the small partition at the other end of the room. "What the devil!" muttered Paraska, lighting a candle at the hearth. Fully awake now, she stomped across the room and threw open the door. "Who's there?" she demanded.

"Paraska! My dove! My angel-dove!" cried Vasko, his face bloody and his cap crooked on his head.

"Feh!" snarled Paraska, slamming the door in her husband's face.

Yevka rolled out of bed and went to her sister's side. "Paraska, what will you do?" she whispered.

"What his mother should have done—drown him!" There was a knock on the door. Paraska shook her head at Yevka. "He will sleep in the barn tonight."

A new voice called out, "Open the door, Paraska . . . please. This is Vasyl . . . Vasyl Rusynko."

Paraska lifted the latch while Yevka scurried behind her, out of view. Paraska peered out past Vasyl. "Who else is with you?"

Vasyl swayed to one side, sweeping his hand grandly. "Mykhal and Yurko!"

Paraska opened the door wider. "The three of you—Vasyl, Mykhal, Yurko—may enter." She moved aside, admitting all but Vasko. Yevka remained behind Paraska, her hands on her sister's shoulders, her eyes on the floor.

"My love! I am wet and cold!" cried Vasko as Paraska again closed the door in her husband's face.

"Please, Paraska, he is hurt. Let us bring him in," said Vasyl, peering over Paraska's shoulder. Yevka peeked at Vasyl, and then, quickly lowering her eyes, gripped Paraska's shoulders.

"Yes," Paraska said, scowling at Yurko. "I can guess how he was injured!" Yurko lowered his melancholy eyes and stared at his boots. "I also can guess that tomorrow—Yevka, you are hurting my shoulders—tomorrow I will have to make a visit to Andrii Khudyk and his wife." She noted the old man. "So, you were thrown out, too." Mykhal shrugged.

"Paraska, please," pleaded Vasyl. "You are an honorable woman. Let me bring him in. He is a good man and a good worker. He has always been like a . . ." Vasyl glanced toward the bunk where his brother Petro lay in the dark. "He has always been very close to me. If he is a sinful man, then I am a sinful man. There are men . . . women too . . . who are guilty of far worse offenses than long visits to the tavern." Yevka glanced up quickly, but Vasyl's eyes were fixed on Paraska's.

Paraska sighed and faced the door. On the other side, Vasko sang extemporaneously about burials in churchyards, banging his forehead against the door to mark the funereal rhythm of his tune. Paraska reached for the latch, but instead of opening the door, she handed the candle to Yevka and abruptly walked to the hearth, leaving her sister alone and wide-eyed next to Vasyl.

"Paraska, shall I let him in?" asked Vasyl.

While everyone awaited Paraska's decision, Yevka, biting her lower lip, stared at Vasyl. In the flickering light she studied his profile: a long, straight nose and strong jaw; an inverted smile; kind, luminous eyes . . . spirited eyes . . . eyes unlike . . . Suddenly, Vasyl turned those eyes upon Yevka and smiled, the corners of his mouth dropping sharply. Yevka looked down at the floor.

"Paraska, I am going to open the door now," said Vasyl. Paraska shrugged. When Vasyl lifted the latch, Vasko fell into his arms.

"*Ai!* My little dove!"

"I am not your 'little dove,'" said Vasyl, helping Vasko to the bench while Yevka closed the door behind them. Paraska brought water and strips of cloth to the table and mercilessly scrubbed her husband's face. Vasko held hands with both Paraska and Vasyl, flinching each time the cloth touched his open wounds.

"You are both so good, so honest," whimpered Vasko, kissing their hands. "Honest Vasyl! Honorable Paraska!"

"Shhh!" hissed Paraska. "You will wake the dead."

Vasko's eyes widened. "No, no, no! The dead must be left as they are. Promise, honest Vasyl, promise that the dead will not be disturbed and that— LORD HAVE MERCY, WOMAN! THAT HURTS!"

"Shhhhh!"

"Vasyl, the dead must not be disturbed until the Judgment. Promise me." Vasyl nodded. "Good, Vasyl, good. My brother died of the fever, do you re- member? You lost a brother and a sister. They must not awaken; not yet . . . *OI!* WIFE, NOT SO HARD! . . . They are buried well, our brothers and sis- ters. I want to be buried well, too. Ah, the Final Judgment! We must all be ready, no? You, and I, and Paraska—all of us! Even Old Mykhal—perhaps sooner than the rest of us." Vasko winked at Vasyl. "In the Bible do we not read the many warnings of the Final Judgment?"

"Fool!" snapped Paraska. "You do not even know how to read!"

Vasko raised his hands and looked to the ceiling. "Is Vasyl a sailor? Can he swim?"

Paraska pushed her husband's arms down on the table. "Sit still if you want me to clean you."

"But, honest wife, Vasyl is not a sailor and he cannot swim and yet when he says he sailed to Ameryka and back you do not correct him."

"You are drunk."

"Yes, gentle dove, but Vasyl is not a sailor. If he need not be a sailor to sail, then I need not be a reader to read."

"Vasyl did not swim to and from Ameryka. He went on a boat and other people—sailors—made the boat go. When you are in church, Father Yaroslav reads the Bible and you think you understand." Paraska rubbed her husband's wounds vigorously.

Vasko writhed in his seat. "They brought Vasyl back to us—he SAILED. Father Yaroslav proclaims the word of God to me—I READ!"

Paraska was very weary. "Will it make you quiet if I agree with you?"

"It will make me happy if you see why I am right."

"Very well. You can read . . . but you cannot write your own name."

Vasko opened his mouth, but Vasyl intervened. "Come, Mykhal. I have a roof to fix tomorrow and you have a cart to drive. We must sleep."

Vasko tightened his grip on Vasyl's hand. "Honest Vasyl! Like my own brother! Promise I will be buried well. Do not listen to the old man. Do not bury me where I fall. Bury me inside the churchyard with the holy ones, and not in the road with sinners. Promise, Vasyl."

"You have a long life ahead."

Vasko insisted. "Promise, Vasyl."

Paraska pleaded with Vasyl with tired eyes. Vasyl squeezed Vasko's hand. "I promise."

Vasko held his friend's hand. "One more thing . . . one more thing, Vasyl . . . before I go . . ."

Vasyl laughed. "Vasko, you are not dying, you are going to sleep."

"No, no. I've been dying since the day I was born. The Lord condemned us to death because Eve ate the forbidden fruit, and now we must make our way to death while we live. But before I go I must see that things are set right. Where is the old man, Vasyl?"

"Do you mean Mykhal? He is over there."

"Where? My sight fails me. Bring him here, Vasyl. Help me. Help me right the wrong that was done today."

Vasyl motioned to Yurko. "Bring him here," he instructed, pointing to Old Mykhal, who was leaning against the wall with his eyes closed. The old man suddenly found himself in Vasyl's place, holding Vasko's hand.

Vasko squeezed Mykhal's hand and whispered, "It is time for forgiveness, old friend. It is time to forget the wrongs of the past as we race to the Final Judgment." Mykhal looked imploringly at Vasyl, who yawned and shrugged with half-closed eyes. Vasko continued in a weak voice. "Forgiveness, old friend, is God's greatest gift besides life itself. When a man does a great wrong to another man, he should ask for forgiveness. Do you agree?"

Deeply moved, Old Mykhal nodded.

"I can't hear you," said Vasko in a surprisingly energetic voice.

"Yes," nodded Mykhal.

Vasko smiled piously. "Good. I forgive you. Now apologize to everyone else."

Old Mykhal jerked his hand back. "*Didku*—you devil!"

Vasko stood, clapping his hands and singing while the room was reduced to turmoil.

"*Didku!*"

"Father of the devil!" rejoined Vasko.

"*VON*—OUT!" roared Paraska. "You will all sleep with the pigs tonight!"

"ANTICHRIST!" accused Vasko, laughing hoarsely in Yurko's face.

Paraska grabbed a fistful of Vasko's hair, and, despite her husband's many pitiful "*ois*," propelled him out the door. Then, with her finger she beckoned to Yurko.

Vasyl gently conducted Yurko to the door. "Go, Yurko. Paraska is inviting you to spend the night in her barn." Vasyl then gathered up the trembling old man, helped him across the room, and, at the door, turned to address Paraska and Yevka.

"May God grant you"—he glanced toward the corner bunk—"and all in this house, good health. *Dobranich*—good night." Vasyl was smiling at Yevka as Paraska closed the door.

Paraska climbed into her bunk and flopped heavily onto her straw mattress. Vasko's tenor voice rang in the night air, cursing mud, pigs, wives, drivers, Antichrists, and tavern owners as he and Yurko made their beds in the barn. Yevka blew out the candle and climbed back into bed. The rain had stopped and she lay on her back, staring into the silent darkness. Next to her, Petro, who had propped himself up with his hands behind his head during Vasko's histrionics, turned silently onto his side, facing the wall.

Yevka rubbed her lower belly, where over the last two weeks a noticeable roundness had developed. That very morning, yielding to coercion from Paraska, Yevka had agreed very soon to inform Petro of his imminent fatherhood. But then, there was the unexpected reappearance of Vasyl after an absence of more than four years. Yevka did not tell Petro her news after all; she told Paraska that the news could wait until the next day, when Petro was not quite so tired. Yevka stopped rubbing her belly and turned on her side, away from Petro.

Vasyl Rusynko had returned to Stara Polyanka. After more than four years he had returned. Vasyl Rusynko . . . Vasyl . . .

☙

Vasyl and Old Mykhal stumbled through the dark village under a clearing sky that revealed a gibbous moon. "Yevka has become a woman," Vasyl said to the moon.

"Hmm?" grunted the old man.

"Yevka's not a child anymore. You were right, Mykhal. I was away from Stara Polyanka for a long time . . . she's a woman now . . . and I . . . I was gone a long time . . . too long, I think . . . too long . . ."

Vasyl held his arm tightly around the shoulders of the somnambulating old man, and the two men swayed up the narrow path to the Rusynko homestead.

CHAPTER FIVE

Andrii

THE NEWS OF VASYL'S RETURN from the mysterious land across the sea spread to nearby villages at the speed of a horse-drawn cart. From Vŷshnya Polyanka up the valley to Ondavka, then west across the ridge and down the steep and rugged trail to Bekherov, and, finally, south to Komlosha and Zborov, Old Mykhal shared the news and gossip with all those he encountered. At Zborov the old man entrusted the news of Vasyl's reappearance to a priest, Father Hodobai, who was returning to Pryashev from a visit to Yalynky. Father Hodobai knew the promising young student, Andrii Rusynko, from the "Alumneum," the eparchial boarding school in Pryashev. Father Hodobai promised Old Mykhal that he would inform Andrii of his brother's return from Ameryka. Turning his cart to the northeast, Old Mykhal tipped his hat to Father Hodobai and started the next, and loneliest, leg of his circuit: the open, windswept stretch to Smilno along which travelers journeyed in the shadows of the omnipresent soaring hawks.

After traveling by wagon to Bardeyov, Father Hodobai boarded the abysmally slow local train with its innumerable stops. At dinner that night in Pryashev, he sat next to Father Pavlo Goidych, the prefect of the Alumneum and one of Andrii's teachers. Father Hodobai related Vasyl's return to Father Goidych, who called young Andrii into his office the following day, gave him the news, and granted him permission to leave for Stara Polyanka the next afternoon.

And now Andrii sat in Old Mykhal's cart, ringing the bell as the horse, Sasha, slowed in front of Yakov's tavern. Andrii jumped from the moving cart and was halfway up the hill to the Rusynko place when he spotted Vasyl emerging from the hut. "Vasyl!" he shouted.

Vasyl's mouth arched downward in an inverted smile as he set his pipe on a bench near the door. The two brothers embraced in the little yard in front of the hut.

"Vasyl, you have come home to us!"

"*Bozhe moi*—my God—how long have I been gone?"

"Four years, Vasyl. You know that."

"Yes, of course. But I had a little brother when I left. Who are you?"

"Vasyl, it is I! It is Andrii!"

"No. Andriiko was a quiet little boy who followed after his *mamka* and his *baba* all day and read books with Father Yaroslav."

"Vasyl, I am sixteen years old now. I still read with Father Yaroslav when I am home. *Mamko,* Anna! Come out here! Look at Vasyl—look at him. He has come home to us! Our people leave the highlands by the hundreds for Ameryka never to be seen again. But here is a Rusyn who has come home where he belongs!"

"*Mamko,* Anna, do you two know this young man?" said Vasyl with mock concern.

Vasyl's mother shrugged. "Sometimes I'm not sure. Come inside, everyone."

Before they went inside, Andrii embraced first his mother and then Anna. Then, glancing around the property, Andrii asked, "Is Petro here?"

His mother motioned toward the hut. "He is inside." Then she smiled and winked at Andrii. "Petro and Vasyl were discussing the sale of one of our sheep." Anna reddened and whined, "*Mamko . . .*" And her mother added, "We think that Petro Kotsur will send shepherds to find her soon."

Andrii laughed, and, grabbing Anna's hand, spun her around in a circle until she pulled herself free and hurried into the hut, where she busied herself at the hearth with *Baba.*

The three Rusynko brothers sat at the table while their hovering *baba,* mother, and sister waited on them. After soup and bread, Petro stared at his empty bowl while Andrii chatted to Vasyl about his studies.

"After you went to Ameryka, Vasyl, I studied with Father Yaroslav here in the village. He taught me basic Magyar grammar and *prostopiniye*—our liturgical plainchant. He is sponsoring me at the Alumneum in Pryashev. Vasyl, it is wonderful there! I study with the priests, especially Father Goidych—oh, he is such a holy priest! He has such a reverence for the Holy Eucharist and such a tremendous devotion to the Mother of God—especially to the weeping icon of the Mother of God of Klokochovo. And we have liturgy every day in the cathedral and we sing it *po-staroslovyanský*—in Old Slavonic! Not in

Magyar, Vasyl, but in Old Slavonic! It is magnificent to hear. When we students sing, our voices carry the responses up and forward where our beautiful Slavic liturgy bounces off the iconostasis and rolls back over us like incense. You should hear 'Only Begotten Son' and the—you are smiling, Vasyl."

Vasyl tapped his pipe on the table and turned to the women at the hearth. *"Hospodi, pomilui*—Lord, have mercy! Does he talk like this all the time?"

Mamka stood behind Andrii and placed her hands on her youngest son's shoulders. "Yes, Vasyl. Your brother studies very hard. We are very proud of him. He shows me the books he reads and"—she shrugged—"I can't read their names and I still don't understand even after he reads them to me."

Petro looked up from his plate. "Hmph! Reading books doesn't bring the wood down from the hills."

"Petro, I will help," said Andrii frowning. "I always help when I am home. I may not be as strong as you, but I will help. When will we go?"

"Tomorrow," grunted Petro, pushing away from the table and standing.

"Good. Are you going, too, Vasyl? Yes? Well, then, wake me early."

Vasyl nodded but he was watching Petro, who now walked to the door and stared outside with his hands on his hips. Petro would cut wood even now if it weren't so late in the day; he lived for work.

"I always help when I'm home, don't I, *Mamko?*"

"Yes, Andrii, of course you do."

Vasyl continued to study his older brother. Petro would listen only to so much of Andrii's whining and then he would leave without saying a word.

"Then why does Petro criticize my reading and why does he always—"

And that was enough. Petro took his hat from a peg in the wall and walked out the door and down the path.

Andrii shook his head at Vasyl. "I wish he wouldn't act that way. He knows I'll help. Why is he always unhappy?"

Vasyl shrugged. "Forget it. He will be glad to see you in the morning. For now, he has new worries."

Andrii looked from Vasyl to his mother and back again. "What kind of worries? Why is Petro unhappy, *Mamko?*"

"Petro is not unhappy, Andrii. I don't know why Vasyl says that. Your brother is to be a father. He is worried, that is all."

Andrii opened his arms skyward. "Then I am to be an uncle! And you too, Vasyl!"

Vasyl did not respond but instead rose and went to the hearth. "Will you go to study at Father Yaroslav's tonight, Andrii?"

"Yes, but I won't stay too late."

"Will you take something to him?"

"Of course."

Vasyl retrieved a small bag from a shelf above the hearth and placed it on the table in front of Andrii. "It is a portion of what I earned in Ameryka— it is for the church."

"But Vasyl, you should take it to him."

"No, Andrii. You take it to him. Tell him it is from the Rusynko family. Tell him it is for whatever is most needed in the church."

Andrii peeked into the bag. "Vasyl, this is very generous. Father Yaroslav will be very pleased. For a while now he's wanted a new icon of *Mati Bozha*—the Mother of God."

"Good. Now come outside—I need your help in the barn before you go." The two brothers went outside to the barn, where Vasyl placed a hand on Andrii's shoulder. "I wanted to speak to you alone." Vasyl reached into his pocket and handed Andrii a pamphlet. "Here, Father Yaroslav might want to see this."

Andrii unfolded the pamphlet and read the Cyrillic title out loud. "*Fraternal Greetings to our Carpatho-Russian Brothers and Sisters Living in the Carpathian Mountains and in Ameryka,* by Mykhal Sharych, Saint Petersburg, 1893. Vasyl! Where did you get this? This is . . . this is forbidden! It is treason even to possess such a document!"

Vasyl smiled and stroked his chin. "Yes, this is true. Give it back and let me throw it in the fire."

"No, Vasyl, I will destroy it. But first . . ." Andrii opened the pamphlet and scanned the contents. "This is . . . this is unbelievable: '. . . from the capital of the Orthodox Russian tsar . . .' Vasyl, truly, where did you find this?"

"It is not difficult to find these in Ameryka. I got this in Yonkers. You have heard of the author?"

"Yes. Father Yaroslav has told me of Mykhal Sharych. He is a former Greek Catholic priest, and I think he is from Komlosha. Father Yaroslav says that Sharych's argument is that we Rusyns are really Russians—look, do you see, Vasyl? He calls us Carpatho-Russians and his pamphlet is in Russian. And because we are Rusyns—in his view, Russians—we should convert to Orthodoxy and 'return' to the Great Russian nation."

"Do you think our people want to be a part of Russia, Andriiko?"

"Some do. I think they resent having to learn Magyar in school and I know they dislike the liturgy sung in the Magyar language. In Pryashev I've heard people say that Magyar would never be allowed in a Russian Orthodox Church."

"Do you know what happened in Bekherov, Andriiko?"

Andrii nodded. "Yes, the conversions. We hear that quite a few have converted to Russian Orthodoxy."

"And you've heard about the trials, Andrii? The Magyar government is putting our people on trial for treason if they convert to Orthodoxy. There were articles in our people's newspapers in Ameryka."

"Yes, yes, I know all this, Vasyl. Why are you squeezing my shoulder so hard?"

Vasyl released his grip. "I'm sorry, Andriiko. I hear you talk of going to the seminary someday and of having to learn Magyar and I worry about you. I heard worrisome talk in Ameryka. I don't know what it all means. I only want you to be safe."

Andrii nodded solemnly. "Yes, there is much talk of this in certain circles in Pryashev—about our people being forced to become Magyars—about our people belonging in the Russian Orthodox Church because—God forgive me for saying this—our own Greek Catholic Church leaders seem eager to be more Magyar than the Magyars. And so our people suffer. Father Yaroslav says that a few years ago he was forbidden to call our people Rusyns. We were only to be called Magyars of the Greek Catholic faith. The government is sending more teachers to our village schools to teach Magyar. This is why our people are susceptible to pamphlets like this by Father Sharych. It encourages them to feel that there is still a way for them to be themselves—to be Rusyns—and not Magyars. Our language is similar to Russian and our church liturgy is the Old Slavonic version of the Greek liturgy of Saint John Chrysostom—the same liturgy used in the Russian Orthodox Church. Of course, we include prayers for the Pope and for our Emperor in Vienna instead of for the Tsar in Moscow."

Vasyl stroked his chin and studied his brother's young face. It was an eager face, a trusting face, the face of someone who could take up a cause and involve himself deeply in it. "Yes, Andriiko. I was only thinking of what you said earlier about Rusyns belonging here in the highlands. Do you think the

Magyar officials in Bardeyov and in Pryashev and in Budapest mind if you call yourself a Rusyn?"

"I say such things only to people I know and trust."

"Where will it lead, Andriiko? So you will become a priest and you will work among our people and you will tell them that they are good Rusyns and the Bishop will call you to Pryashev and correct you, saying that we are all good Magyars. Then our people, who can say only *'egy, kettő, három, négy, öt'*—'one, two, three, four, five'—and *'kérem'*—'please'—in Magyar, will hand you Sharych's pamphlet and they will say, 'Father Rusynko, would it not be easier for us to be Russians than Magyars? Don't make us what we are not.'"

Andrii smiled. "Vasyl, you never spoke like this before you went to Ameryka."

"I saw many things in Ameryka. I saw churches split in two when half the people became Orthodox and the other half remained Greek Catholic. Families split over this issue, and here in Makovytsya there are trials. So, I worry about you, Andrii. I don't know how Father Yaroslav feels about these things. I don't know how your teacher in Pryashev—"

"Father Goidych."

"Yes, Father Goidych. I don't know how he feels about these things. I don't know what ideas they are putting in your head in Pryashev."

"Vasyl, if I become a priest—or even if I do not—I could never turn my back on Rome. *Svyatýi Petro*—Saint Peter—went to Rome; he didn't go to Moscow. Father Goidych and Father Yaroslav feel the same way. But in Pryashev, Vasyl, there are so many ideas. Everyone talks about the church and about our people and how we should be called. Some say we should be allowed to call ourselves what we are: Rusyns. I agree and I think it's all very exciting."

"Yes, Andriiko, it is exciting to you. I know that in Pryashev there are many people who go to school and who read books and who talk about many things. But you are home now, home in the highlands, among farmers and woodcutters. Remember that. You are already more educated than they can ever hope to be. They don't understand this kind of talk. Be careful how you speak to them."

"You are treating me like a child, Vasyl."

"You are a child. You are full of big ideas. But you will get further if you speak with your people and not above them."

"Do you think I speak 'above' you?"

Vasyl chuckled. "Perhaps. I don't know. It will take me some time to get used to this new 'Andriiko'—so unlike the boy I knew when I left for Ameryka. But, if you are happy in school in Pryashev, then I am happy for you."

"I am very happy in school, Vasyl. Don't worry about me. It is only talk anyway. We are Rusyns and we are good at talking. It is probably what we do best."

CHAPTER SIX

The Ox

THE NEXT MORNING Vasyl and Andrii rose early to join Petro and Vasko in the *buk* forest—the beech forest—for a day of work hauling wood down to the village. The night before, their mother had made potato pirogi for them, and now the brothers stuffed these in their pockets and walked out into the chilly dawn.

Andrii rubbed his hands. "It is cold this morning."

Vasyl snorted. "There will be many cold mornings before there is another warm one. Put your hands in your pockets."

"It is still too cold."

"Perhaps you'd rather sit and read by the fire," teased Vasyl.

"That is not funny, Vasyl." Andrii pulled the pirogi from his pocket and inspected them. "I wish they were still warm."

Vasyl, who was heading into the barn, called back over his shoulder, "And I wish I lived in Pan Kapishinskii's wooden palace."

Momentarily, Vasyl emerged from the barn balancing an ax on his right shoulder. The two brothers, their efforts marked by surges of misty breath, followed the path behind the barn and began to ascend the valley.

Halfway up to the forest Vasyl stopped and lowered the ax to the ground. "I am awake now. Let's eat." The brothers retrieved pirogi and butter from their pockets and ate in silence as the beech forest on the opposite side of the valley turned golden brown with the first rays of light.

Between bites, Andrii swept his hand out over the valley, saying, "I think the *buk*—the beech tree—is my favorite tree—especially during the autumn. Look at the color, Vasyl. I wish we were walking into that beech forest. We would be walking in the warmth of the sun by now."

Vasyl swallowed and shook his head. "You wish for too many things you cannot have. The beech wood that was cut and stacked last year is in the forest on this side of the valley." He hoisted the ax to his shoulder and started up the path. "Hurry, Andrii. Petro will be angry if we are late."

Andrii wiped his hands on his pants and followed. "He will be angry with you, but he will say he is angry with me. It is no different than before you left. You remember how it was. He cannot speak comfortably with you."

"Yes, God only knows what troubles him."

"He is jealous of you, Vasyl."

"Jealous! Of me! Why?"

"Everyone likes you, Vasyl. The other men talk and joke with you. When you were gone they wondered about you—how you were, what you were doing. When Petro leaves a room, he is forgotten. He makes people uncomfortable." Andrii laughed. "But Vasyl makes no one uncomfortable—not the men and certainly not the girls. Among those who think it is their business to make matches, there is frantic activity. You made quite an impression when you returned, with your Amerykan pants and Amerykan shirt and Amerykan cap."

"And my Amerykan money," added Vasyl dryly. "Tell me, does Petro make you uncomfortable?"

"No. But I pity him, even though he is my older brother. That is not right. I shouldn't feel that way. Only, Vasyl, he is so unhappy."

"He has always been like that. Even with a beautiful bride he is still not happy. Soon he will be an unhappy father. With Yevka, Petro should—" Vasyl worked his jaw and marched forward, staring at the ground.

Andrii lowered his voice like their *baba* always did when she gossiped. "*Mamka* said that if you had come back last year, she would have matched you with Yevka."

Vasyl halted and spun around. "She told you this about Yevka?" Vasyl cried hoarsely.

Startled, Andrii stepped back. "Y-yes, Vasyl, because . . . because . . . well, everyone knows Yevka always had an eye for you."

"Everyone knows this?"

"Yes, Vasyl." Andrii avoided his brother's piercing stare and pointed to the ax. "Give it to me, Vasyl. I'll carry it now." Vasyl handed the ax to Andrii. Then, nodding slowly, he turned up the trail, his head down, his hands stuffed in his pockets.

The two walked awhile in silence and finally Vasyl said, "Is Petro angry that I came back?"

"He cannot understand why you would leave Ameryka."

Vasyl turned and squinted at Andrii. "I always said I would return."

"Petro says Uncle Pavlo stayed in Ameryka. He says you too should have stayed and that you should have sent money for the family to sail to Ameryka. He says that life could be better in Ameryka—"

"Petro says a great deal. He never cared about going to Ameryka before I went."

Andrii raised his palms to the sky. "Things have changed since then. We hear stories of a possible war to the south. Petro fears going into the army."

"Tell Petro not to worry. Those troubles are over." However, there was little conviction in Vasyl's voice. In Ameryka there had been much talk about Serbia and Bulgaria and Russia and Austria-Hungary and the possibility of war. It was all very confusing. One man, a Slovak co-worker at the carpet factory, had said to Vasyl, "Why you want to go back to the empire, eh? There will be war, you know? And you, a Russian, living in the Hungarian half of the Austrian Empire!" When Vasyl told the man he was not a Russian, the Slovak responded, "You talk like a Russian!" Vasyl did not know how to respond.

"Andrii, do you want to go to Ameryka?"

"Father Yaroslav says many of our people have gone to Ameryka and probably many more will go. When men like you come back and talk about Ameryka, it causes the men to think and to dream. Father Yaroslav hopes that most of our people will stay here in the homeland. He says Rusyns who go to Ameryka forget who they are."

Vasyl stopped. "I did not ask what Father Yaroslav thinks." The village lay below, shrouded under the flat haze of fifty newly stoked hearth fires. Bright rays from the rising sun now filtered through the trees, bathing the brothers in warm golden light.

"Father Yaroslav will sponsor my application to the seminary in Pryashev in a few years. My future is here, Vasyl."

"What about *Mamka* and *Baba*—what do they want?"

"*Mamka* says she is too old for changes."

Vasyl scowled. "She's not old; she's only forty-five!"

"*To pravda*—that's true. She is happy in Stara Polyanka. And she is happy that you are home. She feels the future will be good now."

Vasyl shrugged. "Maybe it will be. I gave some of the money to *Mamka*. She and *Nyanko*—papa—can buy land with it."

"*Nyanko* is too sick. *Mamka* says that now you are the *gazda*—the head of the family—and she is waiting for you to decide what to do with the money. The money is not enough to buy land and that is why Petro—" Andrii stopped.

"Go on," said Vasyl.

"I think I have said too much, Vasyl."

"Finish what you were going to say."

Andrii sighed and took a deep breath. "I know that you left some of your money in Ameryka—don't ask how I know this—and please don't look at me like that. When Petro learned of this he was very angry and told *Mamka* that you don't trust him. *Mamka* doesn't want to see you two quarreling, but she also doesn't know why you would leave some of your money in Ameryka. Why are you smiling, Vasyl?"

"I was wondering why my dear brother Petro would think that I don't trust him."

"*Ne znam*—I don't know. *Mamka* and Petro think that perhaps you will return to Ameryka someday."

"I've been to Ameryka—why would I go back?" Vasyl shook his head. "I don't understand. All this talk takes place behind my back. It seems that if I want to know anything I must ask my little brother."

"You have been gone a long time, Vasyl."

"I suppose I have . . ." Vasyl chuckled. "Honest Petro . . . honest brother Petro."

"Vasyl, please don't say that I told you any of this."

The brothers, Vasyl in the lead, continued up the trail toward the forest. Over his shoulder, Vasyl said, "It was four hundred Amerykan dolar, Andrii."

"What?"

"That is how much money I left in Ameryka with Uncle Pavlo. Now you know everything. I left the money in a box with Uncle Pavlo and told him I would send for it someday. He promised to keep it safe in Yonkers for me."

"Is it a lot of money—four hundred dolar?"

"Yes. I worked very hard for it. I suppose I did fear that there would be a war. It didn't seem like a good idea to bring that much money home with me. I felt that the money would be safer in Ameryka for now. I never thought of Petro. How strange that he thinks I don't trust him."

From farther up the trail came the echoing sound of an ax at work. The two brothers soon reached a small, level clearing in the center of which stood a high-sided cart with four enormous wooden wheels. Hitched to the great cart, an ox, bent and hapless under a large wooden yoke, watched their progress with vacant eyes. Nearby, Petro worked over a pile of wood, and from somewhere in the forest came the sound of Vasko's distinctive tenor voice improvising a song:

> *High in the mountains the great trees stand!*
> *They give their branches to only one man!*
> *He comes to them with ax in hand*
> *And says, "Tell me, tall ones, who I am."*
> *The trees raise their limbs and chant:*
> *"Vasko! Vasko! Vasko!"*

Vasyl and Andrii walked to the pile of wood and stood watching their older brother at work. Petro frowned at Andrii and said, "You are late."

"We will go help Vasko," volunteered Vasyl.

Petro pointed to the pile in front of them. "Andrii can help me load this first."

After Petro turned his back, Andrii made a face at Vasyl. Stifling a laugh, Vasyl shouldered his ax and followed the sound of Vasko's voice. The sun was streaming through the trees and a sparrow basked on a low branch, chirping and fluffing its feathers as Vasyl passed. When he came upon his friend struggling with a large log, Vasyl cried, "Hurry, Vasko! The evil one is near! I heard him singing in the forest—he sounded almost human. I have come to save you!"

Vasko straightened. "Very funny. You are late. Help me drag this log to the clearing. Someone left it here last winter instead of stacking it with the others."

"Is it dry?"

"Of course it is dry. I wouldn't be able to lift this end if it weren't. Loop this rope around it so we can pull it."

Vasyl tied the rope around the end of the log, leaving two loose ends. "Where is Yurko? I thought he was going to work with us."

"Feh! He'll arrive after the work is done."

"Where does Yurko live now?"

"He lives in his cousin's barn." Vasko laughed and shook his head. "He sleeps with the pigs!"

"Where does he sleep in the winter?"

"Always with the pigs! But I will guess that he stays warmer than many a man who sleeps with a wife. Now pull, Vasyl!"

The two men, snorting like draft horses, emerged from the trees, dragging the log behind them. Between huffs and puffs, Vasko's tenor voice once again pierced the highland air with song:

> *High in the mountains the great trees stand!*
> *They give their branches to only one man!*
> *He comes to them with ax in hand—*

And now Vasyl, the baritone, finished the tune:

> *But the trees scream out,*
> *"We'd rather burn than give ourselves*
> *To such an ugly, ugly little man!"*

Vasko released his end of the rope and took a wild swing at Vasyl who dropped his rope and ran across the little meadow, laughing and just managing to stay out of reach of his friend's flailing arms. Andrii whistled and clapped while Petro and the ox straightened and watched, both expressionless: the one insensitive and the other indifferent.

CHAPTER SEVEN

A True Rusyn

LATER THAT EVENING Yakov's tavern was filled with village men smoking pipes and drinking beer or other spirits. One among them was making his first visit to the tavern and was greeted by the regulars as an old friend. Earlier, after dinner, Vasyl had announced that an appropriate reward for a sunup to sundown day of hard work was a quick trip to the tavern, and Andrii certainly qualified for such a reward. Their mother ignored Andrii's beseeching eyes and *Baba's* prattle—"Let-the-boy-go-you-cannot-keep-him-from-there-forever-let-him-be-around-the-men-he-spends-too-much-time-with-us-women-Vasyl-will-take-good-care-of-him-he-will-not-be-your-baby-forever-can-you-not-see-that-he-is-a-man-now?"

"Do not worry, *Mamko,* your baby will be in good company," Vasyl said.

Their mother held up one finger, indicating her youngest son's limit at the tavern. Then, squeezing Vasyl's arm, she pleaded, "*Bozhe moi*—my God—Vasyl! Do not let Father Yaroslav learn where you have taken the boy!"

Now, sitting on a bench next to Vasyl, Andrii held aloft his third cup of brandy. Across the small table sat Old Mykhal, Yurko, and Vasko, the latter readmitted to Yakov's tavern by a small supply of kreuzer pieces—coins of the realm—and Vasyl's solemn promises to Andrii Khudyk of order and obedience.

"Listen, brothers!" slurred Andrii, raising his cup higher. "Brothers, will you not listen to me?"

Vasyl lowered his brother's arm. "Don't shout. We are sitting right next to you."

"But, Vasyl! I want to drink! I want to drink to your—to your return!"

"Very well, but do it quietly."

"I will, Vasyl! I will be quiet! I will be as quiet as a bird!"

"No louder than a *kukuchka*—a cuckoo bird," said Vasko.

"Yes, no louder than a *kukuchka*. To my brother, my brother, Vasyl, who saw Ameryka and who walked along Amerykan streets."

Vasko winked at Vasyl. "And who saw Amerykan women."

Vasyl snorted. "And what do you know about Amerykan women?"

"Only what you tell me, honest Vasyl."

"I have told you nothing."

"Your eyes speak of great adventures. There is fire in them."

"My eyes are red from drinking this kerosene that passes in this tavern for whiskey."

Vasko guffawed. "He is no *'pan'*—no gentleman."

Vasyl drained his cup and shook his head. "And this is no 'whiskey.'"

"Well," said Vasko, "what do you expect? Khudyk is not one of us. He is from farther east. I don't trust him, and neither should you. He doesn't even speak like us. Have you heard him, Vasyl? Instead of saying *'oblak*—window,' he says *'bolok.'"*

"And he says *'selo'* for 'village' instead of *'valal.'"* said Vasyl. "I've even heard him say—"

"*Oi*, Rusyn!" blurted Andrii, standing unsteadily. "May my tongue cleave to my palate if I remember you not!"

The tavern grew quiet as men turned and stared at Andrii. Vasyl made a drinking motion with his right hand, and the men returned to their drinks, smiling and winking knowingly at one another.

"Honest Vasyl, your brother is drunk," said Vasko.

"*Ne pravda*—not true, Vasyl! I am not drunk!"

"Then sit down, Andriiko. Sit down before you fall down."

"But, Vasyl, V-Vasko, I have been listening to the two of you. You should hear yourselves! 'They say this and we say that.' It doesn't matter! We are all Rusyns! Maybe one says *'hovoryu'*—'I speak'—and we say *'bisiduyu'* for the same thing. We are all Rusyns! Maybe in one place they say *selo*—village— and in Stara Polyanka we say *valal* for the same thing. It doesn't matter! We are all Rusyns! Andrii Khudyk sounds funny to Vasko and Vasko sounds funny to Andrii Khudyk. Probably in Pryashev there are Rusyns who laugh at how both of you sound!"

Vasko's jaw dropped and he blinked first at Vasyl and then at Andrii. "They laugh at us in Pryashev?"

"*Ne znam, ne znam*—I don't know, I don't know," said Andrii. "That was not my point. I am saying only what I am saying: that from valley to valley there are differences in how we say things, and from village to village we use some different words. But we are one people and we should see ourselves as one people: Rusyns all!"

Vasko, still genuinely shocked, looked at Vasyl. "Did you know that they laugh at us in Pryashev?"

Vasyl raised his eyebrows in mock astonishment. "Those dumb horses! What do they know?"

"No, no, no!" moaned Andrii. "Forget that. They don't laugh at us. I made that up." Andrii stood and slapped Yurko on the back. "Come, friend. Help me carry more drinks."

Vasyl reached into his pocket and called out, "Andriiko, you will need this!" Vasyl tossed his brother a coin. "And Yurko, see that he doesn't fall down."

Vasko leaned across the table. "Vasyl, why would your brother say that they laugh at us in Pryashev? Is he trying to make trouble?"

"No, Vasko. He is not trying to make trouble. He is trying to make a Rusyn out of you."

"But, Vasyl, what is the use of being a 'Rusyn' if no one knows what you are talking about?"

Vasyl laughed. "I don't know. I only know that he will be unhappy until you call yourself one."

Vasko shrugged. "I don't want trouble—but I won't have people laughing at us."

Andrii and Yurko returned to the table and distributed the drinks. "To Rusyns everywhere!" cried Andrii. "Who will join me in a drink to Rusyns everywhere?"

Vasko held up his cup. "Yes, to Rusyns everywhere—except those bastards in Pryashev! Who do they think they are? Who will go with me to Pryashev to thrash those idiots?"

Andrii choked on his drink and wiped his mouth on the back of his sleeve. "No, no! You would be fighting your own brother Rusyns!"

"Very well," said Vasko. "Who will go with me to Pryashev to break some Rusyn skulls?"

"No, no, Vasko!" groaned Andrii. "Why would you fight Rusyns when you yourself are also a Rusyn?"

Vasko shook his head at Vasyl. "Honest Vasyl, you are my friend and I have known you all my life. I honor Andrii because he is your brother. Only, you must tell him to stop calling me a Rusyn! I would rather be called a *tsygan*—a gypsy!"

Vasyl playfully shook Andrii by the shoulder. "You have made more work for yourself, dear brother! You are making more *tsygańy* than Rusyns!"

"It is not for me to make Rusyns!" cried Andrii. "God alone decides that! We have no choice in what we are. If you call a Pole a Pole and a Slovak a Slovak, they will nod and the conversation will move on to other matters. But when you call a Rusyn a Rusyn, he looks at you like a donkey and is annoyed that you are blocking his way to the tavern."

Vasyl cleared his throat and murmured, "Careful, Andriiko . . . careful."

Andrii propped his head in his hands. "We are Rusyns, all of us. *To ista pravda*—that's the honest truth."

Vasko reached across the table and patted Andrii's shoulder. "*Dobre, dobre*—very well, very well—because you are honest Vasyl's brother, you may call me a Rusyn if it pleases you. And if tomorrow is no worse than today, you may call me a Rusyn tomorrow also. As long as it costs me nothing, call my wife a Rusyn! Buy me a whiskey and you may call my papa, there at the end of the table, a Rusyn, too."

Old Mykhal opened his eyes and said, "I'm not your papa—the devil himself is your papa." Then the old man yawned and scratched his neck.

Andrii moaned, "*Oi*, Rusyn . . . *oi*, Rusyn!"

At that moment Ivan Dzyamba burst into the tavern and announced that a dead cow had been found on the trail to the gypsy camp. Vasko jabbed Yurko in the ribs and said, "There will be a fight among the *tsygańy*—the gypsies—for this! Maybe even a knifing! Vasyl, come with us!"

"It is too far."

"But, Vasyl, it will be worth the walk."

"It is too far."

"Feh! It is not that far, Vasyl."

"Why should I cross the river and walk over the hill halfway to Yalynky when I am warm and comfortable here? It will turn out to be nothing anyway."

Vasko shrugged and then left the tavern with Yurko, Old Mykhal, Ivan Dzyamba, and several other men.

Vasyl draped an arm over his brother's shoulder. "Andriiko, I will take you home now. Come, you are tired."

Andrii looked up, his eyes glassy. "Do you see, Vasyl? Do you see how it is with these farmers?"

"Yes, and I'm also one of these farmers."

"Yes, Vasyl, but you have been to Ameryka. You've seen things these farmers will never see. You know what I mean when I say that we are all Rusyns, don't you?"

"I know it is important to you, Andriiko."

"It should be important to you, Vasyl! Our own name identifies us! You are Vasyl Rusynko, not Vasyl What-you-will-ko! Ask a Rusyn in the highlands how he calls himself and he will say, 'I'm a farmer.' Ask him what language he speaks and he'll reply, 'Our way.' Ask him who lives in the surrounding villages and he'll say, 'Our people.' Why will he not see that he is part of a common people—the Rusyn people? What do people call themselves in Ameryka, Vasyl?"

"Amerykan."

"Of course. Do you see, Vasyl? They know who they are. They are all one people: they speak the same way, they worship the same way. Therefore, they call themselves Amerykan."

Vasyl stroked his chin. "I don't know . . . I don't know . . . Where I lived people spoke different languages and everyone had their own church. The only thing they did in common was call each other Amerykan."

Andrii shook his head. "And here we speak the same way and worship in the same church; but we allow someone else to decide how we should be called. Why is that?"

"Maybe you want too much from us, Andriiko. I'm a simple farmer, but I know it. If it makes you happy, call us Rusyns, but tomorrow we will have the same work to do whether you call us Rusyns or not."

Andrii massaged his temples. "So that is how it is, then. Ameryka is a very strange place where everyone is different and yet they call themselves the same thing: Amerykan. Here, we are all the same and yet we are happy to answer to any name. Well, Vasyl, at least in Ameryka a man knows who he is."

Vasyl laughed. "When I came home Vasko told me that in Ameryka a man forgets who he is. I think he is right. Maybe in the highlands we don't need a name. We know who we are."

"Then let me ask you this, Vasyl: why did you come home?"

"I always said I would—you know that."

"Life is very good in Ameryka, yes?"

Vasyl pulled his pipe and tobacco from his pocket and prepared for a smoke. "Yes, it can be, for some men. But for others . . ."

"For others, it can never be home. Is that why you came back?"

Vasyl laughed. "Yes, Andriiko. This is my home. I never thought of staying in Ameryka. I always missed this village—only God knows why. Something always called me home. You are smiling."

"You came home because you are a true Rusyn."

"Why do you say that?"

"Because it is true. You are as Rusyn as a Rusyn can be."

"Good! Let us drink to that! Take our cups and this coin to Andrii Khudyk while I light my pipe." Vasyl went to the fireplace and ignited his pipe with the glowing end of a stick. Andrii weaved back to the table with the drinks and Vasyl helped him into his seat. "Are you well?"

"I'm f-fine, Vasyl . . ." giggled Andrii. "I got dizzy when I stood."

"Maybe I should drink yours."

"Vasyl, I'm f-fine! Let us drink to you! To Vasyl Rusynko, the only true Rusyn I know! Now, true and honest Rusyn, you know that we must get you married."

"Oh?"

"Oh yes . . . yes, yes. Shall I tell you who she is?"

"No one has mentioned anyone to me yet. How is it you already know her name?"

"Oh, because, Vasyl, you are the main topic of the gossips in Stara Polyanka. And I know one of the main gossips."

"Who?"

"Mamka."

"Mamka! She has said nothing to me!"

"She will, Vasyl. The families are throwing their girls your way—one in particular."

"Who?"

"I shouldn't tell you."

"You've told me this much—tell me."

Andrii motioned Vasyl closer until their foreheads were touching. "If I tell you, you must promise never to say that I—"

"Yes, yes, I promise."

"Come closer."

"I can get no closer."

"Well, then . . . well, then . . . her name is Yevka—I mean"—Andrii snorted—"that was last year—what am I saying? I think I am drunk, Vasyl.

Her name is Mariya—Mariya Kavulya. What do you think, hmm? Why do stare at me that way? Here, take my whiskey. I don't think I should—"

"Drink it."

"But, Vasyl, I—"

"Drink it. Hurry up." Vasyl stood and, when his brother finished his whiskey, took the empty cup from his limp hand. "We will have another."

"*Mamka* said only one for me."

"You have had five," Vasyl snapped. "One more will not hurt." Vasyl went to the bar, fished a small coin out of his pocket, and slapped it, together with the two empty cups, on the plank before Andrii Khudyk. The few men remaining in the tavern mumbled over their drinks by the fire. Vasyl returned to the table and set one of the cups before his brother.

Andrii mumbled, "*Mamka* would be angry if she knew."

"Well, she won't know, will she? Drink up." Vasyl sipped his whiskey and glared at Andrii over the rim of the mug. Andrii's eyes were half-closed. The boy would be horribly ill in the morning, if not sooner.

"Vasyl, are you angry that I told you?"

"Told me what?"

"About Mariya Kavulya."

"I wasn't thinking about her. I was thinking about . . . something else. Drink."

"I can't. Here, you finish it. Mariya Kavulya is a fine girl, Vasyl."

"Is she?" Vasyl was peering into the fire at the frolicking lights and shadows.

"Yes. You two would make a fine match. You are good and honest and she—"

Vasyl banged his cup on the table, startling his brother. "Andriiko, do not think too well of me! I am only a simple *gazda*—a farmer—like any other, with faults and regrets and sins. Maybe Petro is right—maybe I should have stayed in Ameryka. Say no more to me about Mariya Kavulya. And no more nonsense about Rusyns!"

Andrii, confused, blinked to clear his moist eyes and then buried his head in his arms on the table, leaving his drink untouched.

Vasyl coaxed his pipe back to life with deep puffs, finished his whiskey, and then downed his brother's in one gulp. He stared into the gyrating flames and enveloped himself in a cloud of tobacco smoke.

After a long silence broken only by the occasional clunk of a cup or a small explosion of sparks in the fireplace, Petro Kotsur burst into the tavern and reported a fight near the gypsy camp.

Vasyl jumped up, and, pushing his way through the ring of men surrounding Petro Kotsur, shouted, "What happened? Move aside! Where are Vasko and Yurko? Where is Old Mykhal?"

"Old Mykhal is outside. Yurko—Yurko, we—we cannot find him," stammered Petro. "And—and Vasko . . . I think he is hurt . . . in the road . . . maybe stabbed!"

"WHAT!" cried the men in unison. Then, flexing their arms and hitching their trousers, they mumbled oaths and vowed revenge.

Vasyl silenced the men. "QUIET! Petro, why did you not bring him back here?"

"Well . . . Yurii told me to come here . . . to come for help."

From outside there came a voice in distress. Andrii Khudyk grabbed a kerosene lantern and led the men outside. Yurii Fedorochko and Old Mykhal, supporting a slumped figure between them, advanced into the yellow light. "Some help, brothers! Vasko is hurt!" cried Yurii. The men surrounded Vasko and his bearers, shouting angrily.

"Who did this?"

"Are you stabbed?"

"Tell us, Vasko! Tell us!"

"What happened?"

Old Mykhal's knees buckled and he grunted, "Help us get him inside."

"Yes! Let us carry him in!" cried the men. They hoisted Vasko to their shoulders eliciting a doubtful *"Oi?!"* from the patient.

Vasyl stepped forward to direct the human ambulance. "Turn him this way! No, the other way!" Half the men obeyed as they entered the doorway but the other half of the ambulance struck the side of the tavern, dropping Vasko on his head.

"Oi!"

The men dragged Vasko through the doorway and heaved him onto one of the tables. As Vasko moaned, the men coughed and gasped from their labors. Then, as one, they looked at Vasyl, who stood at the head of the patient. Other than a bloody face, Vasko's appearance was unremarkable.

Vasyl peered into his friend's inverted face. "Where are you hurt?"

Vasko sniveled. "Hmm?"

Vasyl leaned closer. "I said, where are you hurt?"

Vasko closed his eyes and made a sweeping gesture to indicate "everywhere."

"I see." Vasyl straightened. "Where is Petro Kotsur? There you are. Come and tell us what happened."

Petro Kotsur stepped forward. "We met three *tsyganŷ*—three gypsies—on our way to their camp. It turned out Ivan was wrong—there was no dead cow."

Vasyl looked around the room. "I see. Where is Ivan Dzyamba? Hmm, gone. Go on, Petro."

Petro Kotsur cleaned his ear with his little finger. "Well, he . . . Vasko, that is . . . well, you know how he is. He tried to . . . to . . . tell the *tsyganŷ*—the gypsies—that they were wrong . . . about the cow. He said . . . he told the *tsyganŷ* that they were all liars anyway and—and friends of the Antichrist. Then, well . . . they threatened us with rocks and we left."

Vasyl was skeptical. "Petro, why is Vasko's face bloody?"

"Well, you see, Vasko began to throw rocks at the *tsyganŷ* and Yurko . . . well, Yurko tried to stop him and then . . . then Vasko threw rocks at Yurko and shouted 'Antichrist!—Antichrist!' and . . . Yurko—"

Vasyl finished the narrative. ". . . and Yurko struck Vasko and ran away." Petro Kotsur nodded.

Vasko, his eyes still closed, raised his head, and whispered, "Antichrist."

The men shook their heads in disgust at Vasko's prostrate form and, grumbling among themselves, drifted back to their tables.

Vasyl went to the bar, placed a coin on the plank, and held up two fingers. Andrii Khudyk poured two whiskeys and Vasyl took the cups to his table, where Andrii now slept soundly, his head resting in his open hands. Vasyl sat down and draped his arm across his brother's shoulders. "Andriiko, what have I done to you?" Vasyl drank one whiskey in a single gulp and shoved the other one under Andrii's nose. The boy grunted and turned his head away. Vasyl sipped the whiskey and stared into the crackling fire. Vasyl yawned and mumbled, "My dear Andriiko. You love me as a brother and I make a *piyak*—a drunkard—out of you. That is something you should never be." Vasyl brushed back Andrii's hair and kissed him on the forehead. "Forgive me, Andriiko. Forgive me for what I have done to you . . ."

The boy was unresponsive.

Vasyl blinked his eyes and focused on the dancing flames. "Look, Andriiko.

There, in the flames—do you see? No? You don't see her, Andriiko, but I do. She belongs to someone else . . . to someone who didn't go to Ameryka . . . someone who should have gone to Ameryka. Now, it can never be . . . so . . . forgive me . . . whatever I do . . . forgive me . . ." Then he fell asleep with his head on Andrii's shoulder.

⁊⁊

A cold rush of air roused Vasyl from his sleep. Blinking his eyes, he looked up to see his brother, Petro, standing in the open doorway, scanning the patrons. The men glanced up, considering Petro briefly, and then returned to their drinks. Walking among the men, Petro came upon Vasko's snoring form curled up on one of the tables. Inspecting Vasko's bloody face, Petro grunted in disgust. He straightened and looked about the room, his gaze first passing and then returning to his two brothers in the corner. Petro crossed the room and frowned as he stood over Andrii. "Is he drunk?"

Vasyl slapped the table. "No more than I am, honored brother!"

Petro's eyes narrowed. "Are you drunk?"

"No more than you should be, Pan Rusynko!"

"Hmph! *Mamka* sent for me. She heard there was a fight and worried about Andrii."

Vasyl drew the unconscious Andrii closer. "Andriiko is safe with me!"

"Hmph, I can see that."

"Tell *Mamka* that her baby will be home as soon as he finishes his whiskey! Andriiko! Finish your whiskey! Your *mamka* and your big brother want to put you to bed!" Andrii raised his head and tried to focus his eyes. "You see," said Vasyl. "He is almost ready for a good night's sleep."

Petro reached under Andrii's arms to lift him to his feet. Vasyl pulled the boy away from his brother's grasp, and, rising unsteadily to his feet, shouted at Petro, "Do not touch Andriiko! Never touch him!"

Petro glanced around the room. The men had turned in their seats or stood to watch the drama unfolding in the corner. Petro's eyes came to rest on Vasko's prostrate form on the adjacent table. A crooked smile formed on his lips; he turned to Vasyl and said, "There is room on that table for another *piyak*—another drunk."

Vasyl lunged forward, but Petro swung his open hand, striking his brother with a resounding smack and sending him reeling against the wall. Vasyl slid to the floor and the other drinkers grumbled among themselves. Petro lifted Andrii to his feet. "Can you walk?" Andrii nodded, coughed, and then vomited on the floor. The men turned back to their drinks, while Andrii Khudyk stood nearby with his hands on his hips.

Petro held Andrii by the shoulders. "Are you finished?" Andrii nodded and then collapsed against his brother. Petro hoisted Andrii over his shoulder like a sack of grain and shook his head at Vasyl, stretched out on the tavern floor. "You never should have come back," he sneered. "You should have stayed in Ameryka." Then Petro stalked out into the night, carrying Andrii home.

Vasyl attempted to stand, but instead, slid to the floor and rolled onto his side. "I've been to Ameryka, honest brother," he mumbled. "I've been to Ameryka . . . and now . . . now I am home."

CHAPTER EIGHT

Shepherds

EIGHT WEEKS LATER, in early December, Paraska stood over her husband with her hands on her hips and said, "Hurry and get ready. Your uncle will be here soon."

Vasko was sitting at the table, a cup and a jug before him. He lifted the cup and swallowed the last of the brandy, licking the rim and smacking his lips. He wrinkled his nose and shook his head, greatly troubled. Paraska ignored him and wiped down the table. "Give me," she commanded, pointing to the jug.

Vasko placed a hand on the jug and frowned. "I am not sure it is the best quality *slyvovitsa*—plum brandy."

Paraska placed her hands on her hips. "Give me."

Vasko slid the jug closer to his wife but maintained a firm grip on the handle. "It is too harsh and it leaves a bad taste in the mouth." He shook his head. "It would be an insult to serve this."

Paraska slapped Vasko's hand and grabbed up the jug.

"I tell you, my beautiful swallow, it is an insult to God to serve *slyvovitsa* as bad as this to guests. Even to *tsyganŷ*—to gypsies—I would not serve it."

Paraska stored the jug on the shelf near the hearth. "No one is asking you to serve it to gypsies—and at two cups, your disapproval is not cheap! I would hate to hear your harsh judgment after three cups."

"I only wish to save the family from shame."

Paraska opened her mouth to speak but shook her head instead and stepped outside. She walked a few paces toward Yevka, who was coming up the path carrying a wooden pail of water, then abruptly turned and reentered the hut. Vasko, his shirt unfastened, and holding his pants up with one hand, was approaching the shelf near the hearth. "I am looking for my boots," he said, a feeble smile twitching on his lips.

Paraska crossed the room and, reaching around her husband, retrieved the jug from the shelf. She raised her right eyebrow at Vasko, sniffed loudly, and walked outside, setting the jug on a small bench outside the hut. Her sister had now reached the little Senchak yard. "How does your back feel?" asked Paraska.

Yevka set the pail on the bench next to the jug of *slyvovitsa*. "It is sore," she said, massaging her lower back.

"The baby is going to get much bigger over the next four months."

"Four and a half months," corrected Yevka.

"Yes, soon you will count the days." Paraska looked up the road. "Here come the men. Take the water inside—we'll make soup later. Tell Vasko that his uncle and the others are here."

Yevka went inside with the bucket while Paraska made her way to the road to welcome the approaching men. The leader, Ivan Ivanchyn, raised his shepherd's staff in greeting as he approached and called out, "*Slava Isusu Khrystu*—Glory to Jesus Christ!"

Paraska nodded. "*Slava na vikŷ*—Glory to Him forever. *Vitaite*—welcome."

Following Ivan Ivanchyn were two younger men: Ivan's son, Mikolai, and a nephew, Fedor. Ivan Ivanchyn stopped in front of Paraska and looked about the property. "Is he ready, Paraska?"

"Your nephew is trying to dress himself."

Ivan Ivanchyn laughed and pointed the staff toward the hut. "Well, he has had some success—here he comes now. I hope he has learned to wash himself by now."

Paraska pointed to the brandy by the door. "Vasko!" she bellowed. Her husband halted and took up the jug.

Ivan Ivanchyn handed the staff to Fedor. "Yes, we cannot forget the brandy. From here to Pryashev there is nothing better than Senchak brandy. Come, hand it over, Vasko!"

Vasko shambled down from the hut carrying the jug in one hand and scratching his neck with the other. Ivan Ivanchyn raised his eyebrows at Paraska and said, "He doesn't look much like a shepherd, does he?"

Paraska shrugged. "If you want a shepherd, get Shtefan Rozum. If you want someone to carry the brandy without spilling a drop of it, there is no one better for the task than my husband."

Ivan Ivanchyn held his hands out for the jug and, taking it from Vasko, raised it for the other two men to see. "Paraska, may I?" She nodded and Ivan Ivanchyn uncapped the jug and took a swallow. "*Ai,* Vasko, you are a lucky man to have married into the Senchak family." Vasko shrugged and gazed down the road.

Ivan Ivanchin replaced the cork and handed the jug back to Vasko. "Carry it with both hands like liquid gold. No one distills brandy finer than this. Mikolai, Fedor, my staff! Come, Vasko, let us make our visit."

The men walked down the road, turning onto the path that led to the Rusynko place, while Paraska went inside to help Yevka with the soup.

☙

In the Rusynko home Vasyl and Andrii sat on one side of the table and their mother sat on the other side, combing Anna's hair. "Petro should be here," their mother said. "He is the eldest."

At the hearth, *Baba* banged a wooden spoon on the edge of a pot she was tending and then she chuckled. "He is too full of shame."

Their mother glanced at Vasyl. "Petro should be here. Your father is . . . too ill."

The brothers glanced toward the bunk in the dark recesses of the room and Anna said, "Petro has his own household—he has agreed that Vasyl is now the *gazda*—the head of this house." Anna's eyes were closed and her head nodded with each stroke of her mother's comb. "And after that night at the tavern," continued Anna, "I don't think the two of them should be in the same room together. Did Petro ever apologize to you, Vasyl?"

"*To bŷlo nich*—it was nothing."

"It was awful of him to strike you."

"Anna, it was nothing."

Baba shook her spoon at Vasyl. "Nothing good ever comes from two brothers fighting!"

"Vasyl didn't fight," said Andrii. "Petro struck Vasyl. Vasyl never struck Petro."

Vasyl closed his eyes and sighed heavily. "Andrii, go to the door—I think I hear them coming."

Andrii looked outside. "I see no one."

"Only, I still think"—their mother stood as she spoke—"I still think Petro should be here." She smiled at Vasyl. "But you will talk for the family."

"Of course, *Mamko.*"

Baba shuffled to Vasyl's side and said gently, "You are a good *gazda.*" Vasyl shrugged and then *Baba* shook her finger in his face. "So, don't sit here idly! Hide your sister! They will be here soon, and they must not see her!"

At the door Andrii cried out, "I see them! They are at the bottom of the path!"

"Quickly, Vasyl! Andrii!" cried their mother, thrusting Anna into their midst. "Hide your sister in the barn. Here, cover her with this shawl. Move quickly!"

Baba shook her fist at the brothers. "Don't let her be seen! Any trouble will be on your heads if you do!"

The two brothers wrapped their sister in the shawl and the three ran outside, laughing and stumbling to the barn. Their sister safely concealed, the brothers returned to the front of the hut to meet the delegation.

Ivan Ivanchyn came up the path and, with great ceremony, addressed the two brothers as strangers, though he had known them since their births. "*Slava Isusu Khrystu*—Glory to Jesus Christ—honorable gentlemen!"

"*Slava na viky*—Glory to Him forever!" the brothers responded in unison.

Ivan Ivanchyn indicated his entourage. "My fellow shepherds and I have wandered these hills for days and we are in sore need of rest, kind strangers."

Vasyl opened his arms and swept his hands toward the door of the hut. "Enter, honorable shepherds, for this house never refuses those who come in the name of *Khrystos.*" The shepherds filed by the brothers and into the hut, Vasko passing last, winking and holding the jug of brandy aloft. Vasyl raised his eyebrows in mock astonishment and pushed Andrii and Vasko through the doorway.

Inside, the "shepherds" stood about awkwardly as Vasyl approached his mother and *Baba.* "These shepherds have stopped to rest in this house—they are very weary." Vasyl's mother smiled at the men and nodded quickly. Vasyl indicated the seating arrangements: Ivan Ivanchyn sat on one bench, his fellow shepherds standing behind him while Vasyl sat on the opposite bench with Andrii stationed behind him. Vasko placed the jug of brandy on the table, and the two Rusynko women maneuvered among the men, producing cups and plates of bread, cheese, and meat.

With everyone in their places, Ivan Ivanchyn leaned across the table and said quietly, "Vasyl, I understand I am to address you." Vasyl nodded and his mother affirmed her son's role with a pat on his shoulder. "Well, then," said the older man, indicating the jug.

Vasyl poured out two cups of *slyvovitsa*—plum brandy—and held his cup aloft. "*Dai vam Bozhe zdorovya*—May God grant you good health!"

Ivan Ivanchyn held up his cup and replied, "*Dai Bozhe i vam*—and may God grant it to you as well!" The two men tossed back their brandy and licked their lips. Vasyl's mother and *Baba* poured cups for the rest of the men—with a half-portion for Andrii—and two cups for themselves. With everyone invigorated, the convocation commenced.

"We shepherds have wandered all day in search of something," announced Ivan Ivanchyn.

"Oh?" said Vasyl, stroking his chin. "What is it you seek?"

"A lost sheep. In truth, a ewe. Our search has finally led us to this house."

"What makes you think the sheep has come here?"

"All our inquiries have led us here. We are told the sheep is on your property."

"Hmm . . . and if the sheep you seek is truly here, where will you take her?"

"To her true home."

"And which home is that?"

"The home of Petro Kotsur."

Vasyl nodded. "Yes, he is a good shepherd. And his is a good home."

"Then you have such a sheep?"

Vasyl drank from his cup. "Perhaps . . . perhaps we do. Only, if we have such an animal here, would you take her with you now?"

Ivan Ivanchyn smiled. "No, no. There are of course things to settle first. You have kept this sheep for some time on your property and Petro Kotsur is within his rights to ask for certain . . . certain payment for his trouble."

"Yes, yes, of course," said Vasyl. "We Rusynkos are an honorable family and we are prepared to offer what we can."

Ivan Ivanchyn opened his arms. "From generation to generation the Rusynko name has always been an honorable name. What the family lacks in property it more than makes up for in honesty. What can you offer, Vasyl Rusynko?"

"We offer two hens and a sow."

Ivan Ivanchyn stroked his chin. "I see . . . that is . . . honorable if not generous . . ."

Vasyl produced a small bag and dropped it on the table. "And silver."

Ivan Ivanchin opened the sack and then turned in his seat to display the contents to the shepherds, who, nodding their approval, held out their cups for Vasyl's mother and *Baba* to fill. Ivan Ivanchyn raised his cup. "To the Rusynko family! Long may the name live! And to you, Vasyl Rusynko—may your children inherit the virtue and honesty you possess!"

While everyone drank, Vasyl stood before his mother. "*Mamko,* I believe we have the very animal these shepherds seek in the barn."

His mother nodded and Vasyl turned to Ivan Ivanchyn. "We are happy her owner has sent for her."

Ivan Ivanchyn stood and shook Vasyl's hand. Vasyl nodded to his brother. "Now, Andrii." And Andrii went out the door and into the barn where Anna was pacing the straw-covered floor.

"Well?" she said, her eyes wide and dark.

Andrii beamed and placed a coin in her hand. "You are found. Go to the tavern. We will need more brandy."

Anna blushed and looked at the ground. Andrii led her out the barn door, pointed her down the hill, and gave her a playful push. Anna walked to the broken gate and then ran down the path, her hair bouncing loose and her scarf falling to the ground. She stopped and, after retrieving and retying the scarf, hurried on to the tavern.

❧

In the tavern, Andrii Khudyk, struggling with a beer keg, called to Yurii Fedorochko and Yurko Kryak for help. Together, Andrii and Yurii wrestled the keg into position on a table while Yurko watched.

When Anna, flushed and breathless, burst through the door, Andrii Khudyk smiled at her. "Ah, Anna Rusynko! I will guess why you have come. Is it for beer for Vasyl? No? Is it for whiskey for your *baba*? No no, of course not. Then it must be for brandy, eh? *Ai,* so it is. Who is it to be, then, Anna Rusynko? Who is the fortunate man?"

Anna looked at the floor. "Petro Kotsur," she said shyly.

"Petro Kotsur! A fine man. Here, take this, Anna Rusynko—no, keep your money—and tell your mother I want only the empty jug returned. Yurko, carry the brandy for Anna. I will guess there is a friend of yours at the Rusynko place."

Anna hurried out the door followed by the ungainly Yurko, who clasped the jug against his chest and struggled to keep pace.

Andrii Khudyk put on his coat and slapped Yurii Fedorochko on the back. "Yurii, watch the tavern while I go tell my wife that a marriage has been sealed between Petro Kotsur and Anna Rusynko!"

༄

Two weeks later the Christian villagers gathered in the Church of the Protection of the Mother of God for the Sunday liturgy. At the end of the service Petro and Anna came forward and stood before the iconostasis as Father Yaroslav Podhayetskii intoned the engagement blessings:

> O Eternal God, You have united those who were alone, and instituted an indissoluble bond of love in marriage for them. You blessed Isaac and Rebekah and made them heirs to your promise; now bless these your servants Petro and Anna, directing them in every good deed. For You are a merciful God who loves mankind; and we glorify You, Father, Son, and Holy Spirit, now and ever, and forever.

The congregation sang out, "AMEN!" Anna peeked at Petro Kotsur, who stood rigidly staring at an icon of the Risen Lord.

> O Lord our God, who espoused the Church, a pure virgin from among the gentile nations, bless this engagement and unite and keep these your servants in peace and oneness of mind. For to You, Father, Son, and Holy Spirit, is due all glory, honor, and worship, now and ever, and forever.

"AMEN!"

Father Yaroslav now blessed the couple, beginning with Petro Kotsur. "The servant of God, Petro, is engaged to the servant of God, Anna, in the name of the Father, and of the Son, and of the Holy Spirit. Amen." Then he blessed Anna, saying, "The servant of God, Anna, is engaged to the servant of God, Petro, in the name of the Father, and of the Son, and of the Holy Spirit. Amen. Glory be to You, O Christ, our God, our hope; glory be to you!"

The faithful sang in response: "Glory be to the Father, and to the Son, and to the Holy Spirit, now and ever, and forever. Amen. Lord, have mercy. Lord, have mercy. Lord, have mercy. Give the blessing!"

Father Yaroslav blessed the faithful:

May Christ, our true God, risen from the dead, have mercy on us and save us through the prayers of His most holy Mother, of the holy, glorious, and praiseworthy Apostles, and of all the Saints, for He is gracious and loves mankind.

"AMEN!"

"Grant, O Lord, to your servants Petro and Anna peace, health, and happiness for many years. *Mnohaya blahaya lita*—many happy years!"

And the congregation joyfully declared their good wishes singing:

God grant them many years;
God grant them many years;
God grant them many happy years.
In peace, health, and happiness,
God grant them many happy years!

CHAPTER NINE

Shabbes Goy

THE SNOW WAS ANKLE-DEEP on Stara Polyanka's fields and paths, and knee-deep against the windward side of the village's dark log huts and barns. The snow had begun the day before, on Friday, and now, on Saturday morning, Andrii Rusynko trudged through a light snowfall to the hut owned by Shlomo Lentz and his wife, Linka. The young Kavulya boy, Ivanko, was ill and Andrii had volunteered to assume the boy's role of *Shabbes goy*—the Sabbath gentile who fetched wood, built fires, drew water, and performed other daily chores for pious Jews in Stara Polyanka—chores that, as work, were forbidden to Jews on the Sabbath. Before he left the village to attend school in Pryashev, Andrii himself had been *Shabbes goy* to both Lentz families, those of Shlomo and his cousin, Yakov, who once owned the village tavern that still bore his name. For his work Andrii received cake or a coin or both, proportionate to his age and the amount of service rendered. Now that Yakov Lentz had sold the tavern and moved his family to Bardeyov, the only other Jewish household in Stara Polyanka, besides Shlomo's, was that of Vovk Edermann.

Upon reaching the Lentz hut, Andrii gathered two armfuls of firewood from the covered woodpile, and then went to the front of the building, tapping at the base of the door with his foot.

From inside, Shlomo's voice cried, "Enter! It is not latched!"

Andrii pushed the door open with his shoulder and entered the hut. Snow swirled in after him and, on the table, two candle flames strained in the draft.

"Welcome, old friend," said Shlomo. "Set the wood next to the hearth." Shlomo Lentz was dressed, like all male Jews in the villages of Makovytsya, in black from head to toe: black yarmulke, black caftan, black pants, and black boots. "*Chornŷ zhydŷ*—black Jews," the Rusyn villagers called them.

Streaked with sporadic gray lines, Shlomo's generous black beard tumbled over his chest. "That will be enough wood, Andrii," he said. "Make the fire a big one and it will last until after dark when the Sabbath ends. I can tend to it after that."

Shlomo Lentz's wife, Linka, emerged from behind a curtained corner of the room, greeting Andrii with a brief smile. Like her husband, she was dressed predominately in black, with the exception of her head covering—a white scarf drawn tightly around the periphery of her face. By her sad demeanor it was clear that their grandson was not doing well.

"He is no better?" asked Andrii.

Shlomo tossed his hands in the air. "With *sukhotŷ*—tuberculosis—who knows?"

"Shh!" scolded Linka. "You'll wake him. Besides, we don't know if it is *sukhotŷ*."

Shlomo rolled his eyes at his wife. "*Sukhotŷ* killed the boy's mother, didn't it?"

"No," said Linka, shaking her head vigorously. "Our daughter, Khava, died of a broken heart. She may have suffered from *sukhotŷ*, but she died of a broken heart when Yitzkhak went to Ameryka. Even Andrii knows this, yes?"

"Yes, I remember."

Shlomo and Linka's son-in-law, Yitzkhak Edermann, had left the village more than five years earlier and had not been heard from since. He left behind a wife, Khava, and a two-year-old son, David. Three years after Yitzkhak left, Khava died. And now, David was very ill. The hut had the faint smell of illness within it—the smell that one detects in another's home but not in one's own.

"Come join us at the table, Andrii," said Linka. "And tell us how your father is doing."

Andrii shoved a last piece of wood into the hearth and then sat at the table. "He is not well; but then, all winter he has gotten worse. *Mamka* didn't think he would last this long. He—" Andrii broke off. "I shouldn't say such things. It's not right . . . God will take us when He is ready."

"Well," Shlomo sighed, "your father has suffered long. He was always a good man—a hard worker like your brother Petro. Did you know, Andrii, I was in partnership with your father years ago? Yes, I was. We bought cows together. I bought them and your father raised them. 'Buy that one,' he would say; and I would say, 'But that one is small—it will amount to nothing.' Then your father would say, 'It is small and it is cheap. When I am done with it, it will be big and healthy and it will fetch a good price.'" Shlomo laughed. "And your father was always right. He always chose well, and we split a good profit between us."

"Yes," said Andrii. "I remember him telling that story." Andrii pulled up his coat collar, covering his neck.

"You are cold, Andrii," said Linka. "Warm yourself at the hearth."

"No, no. I'm fine. *Vonka zymno*—it's cold outside. I should have come earlier with the wood. I'm sorry you had to wait so long."

Shlomo dismissed Andrii's apology with a sweep of his hand. "You came when you could, and we are glad you are here. Now," said Shlomo, smiling, "it is soon, yes—the wedding of your sister Anna?"

"Three weeks."

"Ah. I will pray the weather clears and the periwinkle comes out. I wish her well with . . . Petro Kotsur, I think?"

"Yes, Petro Kotsur."

"And who is the *starosta*—the elder—arranging everything?"

"Ivan Ivanchyn. He is experienced in our ways. He is also uncle to both the groom and the best man."

"And who is the best man?"

"Vasko Ivanchyn."

Shlomo gasped and brought the fingers and thumb of his right hand together and pointed them to the ceiling. "Vasko Ivanchyn! Vasko Ivanchyn is a *meshuggener*—a crazy man! He is a-a . . . a *nudnik*—a pest! He is a-a-a—" and Shlomo struggled to find an appropriate non-Yiddish epithet for Vasko.

"Zhebrak?" said Andrii, trying to be helpful.

"Yes, he is a bum, but . . ."

"Piyak?"

"Yes, he is a drunk, however . . ."

"Huntsut?"

"Oh, yes—he is certainly a troublemaker . . ."

"Didko?"

Shlomo clapped his hands. "That's it! He's the devil! He nearly ruined my cousin's tavern with his bad credit and his tearful stories—the money was always just out of his grasp—'I will pay you tomorrow' or 'I will pay next week,' he always said."

"He is a good man," offered Andrii.

"Yes, yes, he is a good man when his business takes him to the household farthest from your own! I don't like the man. He—"

Shlomo's wife cleared her throat and her husband lowered his voice. "She doesn't like me speaking this way . . . not on the Sabbath." Shlomo always referred to his wife using the third-person pronouns, even when addressing her directly: "Is she happy with my work?" Yes, she would answer, she was happy with his work. Years before, when Andrii first began performing Sabbath chores at Shlomo's home, the conversations between the husband and wife baffled him.

The fire was burning well now and the room was filled with pleasant warmth radiating from the brick hearth. Andrii nevertheless forced another piece of split beech wood into the fire and snatched his hand back from the crackling flames.

"Careful, Andrii. Come, have cake. She made it sweet the way you like it, didn't she?"

"Yes," said Shlomo's wife. "It is there on the table by the hearth, Andrii. Pull a piece for yourself."

Andrii eagerly complied—he loved her cake—and sat at the table. Shlomo watched Andrii eat. "Your studies with Father Yaroslav take up much of your time when you are home from Pryashev, yes?"

Andrii nodded. "Father Yaroslav speaks only Magyar with me in his home now. He says it is necessary that I speak it well for the seminary. But we still sing the liturgy *po-staroslovyanský*—in Old Slavonic—at the church and—" Andrii stopped. "I really shouldn't speak about matters of language."

Shlomo smiled and said jokingly in Magyar, "*Nem értem*—I don't understand. Perhaps my business relationship with Pan Erdődy concerns you? That is all it is—a business venture. He is a Magyar who happens to hold a great deal of land up here in the highlands. I am a man who can add figures and that makes Pan Erdődy happy because he very much prefers hunting in the hills to peering over my shoulder. But you are right to hold your tongue about matters of the tongue. The Magyars rule us and they are sensitive about their language. They insist we speak it as well as they do if we are to do business with them. But I am glad your studies are going well." Shlomo leaned toward Linka. "Andrii will make a fine priest someday. Does she agree?"

Yes, she nodded, she thought so, too.

"You will be a good priest for your people," said Shlomo, "because you like to study and because you listen well. You understand things and people quickly see that in you." Shlomo and Linka watched Andrii finish his cake and then Shlomo said, "I have a nephew—her nephew, actually—who went to Bardeyov some years ago to study with the *rebbe*—the rabbi—there. There is a great synagogue in Bardeyov—have you ever seen it, Andrii? No? It is a beautiful synagogue with four great pillars supporting a great dome." Shlomo closed his eyes and waved his arms slowly over his head. "You look up and there is heaven above you."

"Is your nephew—her nephew—still there, in Bardeyov?" asked Andrii.

Shlomo opened his eyes and blinked at the wooden rafters and thatch above him. He nodded. "Yes, he is still at the yeshiva—the rabbinical school. He is a great scholar. And you, too, will be a great scholar in your own way, Andrii. You truly care for your people—that is obvious. You see a future for them, a future they cannot see—not yet. It is up to men like you and Father Yaroslav to help them see it and to make shorter the distance between the future and the present. There are those who say that my people have a future." Shlomo shrugged. "I have difficulty seeing what it might be. But our people, yours and mine, have much in common, don't you agree?" Shlomo was staring across the room.

Andrii nodded. "Yes, we share the same Old Testament; we are susceptible to the same dreaded *sukhotŷ*—tuberculosis; and we—"

But Shlomo's vision extended far beyond the huts and fields of Stara Polyanka. "Both our people are adrift among foreign nations and empires, Andrii. We have our own languages and we have our own faiths, and the men who rule over us do not speak our languages and do not worship in our synagogues or our churches. And we both seem destined for lives of great poverty. Of course, here in the hills, the highlands, away from the big marketplaces and railroads, what real hope do we have for anything more than we see around us now? If I were a younger man, I might think of going to the city to make my fortune. I might think like Yitzkhak who left us— left our daughter—years ago." Shlomo squinted into the dark corner of the room and twisted his beard. "I was angry with him when Khava died. Now little David is so sick. *Nu* . . . why be angry now? What is there for Yitzkhak here? I only wish that, before she died, he had written to her . . . given some account of himself." Shlomo looked at his wife, who closed her eyes and shrugged; they had discussed this many times. Shlomo threw up his hands. "He could be dead for all I know. What do I know of God's plans for any one of us . . . only God knows . . . yes, Andrii?"

Wiping the crumbs from his mouth, Andrii nodded. "The ways of the Lord are eternal and mysterious. The Lord sees us as clearly as we wish we could see Him. He reveals Himself to us in prayer, but we are capable of only a vague understanding of His extraordinary and merciful love. He not only loves us without reservations, but He forgives the truly penitent with the . . ." Shlomo and his wife were staring at Andrii and smiling.

"No, Andrii. Do not be embarrassed," said Shlomo. "If you were a Jew, you would be a good rabbi. We have watched you grow and now you blossom before us like the spring flowers in the meadows. Such wisdom from a . . . I was going to say 'a boy' but that is no longer the word to use. You have become a young man—a young man with a future. Tell me, Andrii, do you think you might someday go to Ameryka?"

The question seemed to surprise Andrii. "Well . . . no."

"Your brother, Vasyl, and your uncle went . . . only, your brother returned."

"Ameryka does not call me."

Shlomo was insistent. "Perhaps when you are a priest you will change your mind. There is a growing flock of your people to tend in Ameryka."

"I do not think that Ameryka will ever call me."

Shlomo beamed at Andrii. "No, I do not believe it will. But I hear Ameryka has called your oldest brother, Petro."

Andrii nodded and sighed. "Petro and Vasyl have argued about it all winter. Sometimes they shout at each other and curse one another with such fierce anger that I think . . . well, that maybe they enjoy it too much. Petro feels that Vasyl should have stayed in Ameryka and sent money for the rest of the family to come. Vasyl says he kept his word to our *nyanko*—our father— to come back with money to buy land. But Petro is angry because Vasyl left over half of the money he earned in Ameryka with Uncle Pavlo. Petro can't understand why Vasyl would do such a thing and when he asks, Vasyl says nothing."

Shlomo twisted his beard between thumb and index finger. "Perhaps Vasyl fears a military draft. It is possible, Andrii. There are still troubles in the south of the empire, you know."

Andrii shook his head. "He says he doesn't. Anyway, now Vasyl and Petro have reached an agreement. Vasyl gave Petro money—most of what would have been Vasyl's share in the land—and told Petro to do what he wants with it. Petro will leave for Ameryka after Anna's wedding and after Yevka's baby comes. Petro wanted to leave after the wedding, but Vasyl and *Mamka* said he should wait until his child is born—Vasyl even threatened to take his money back if Petro left before the child is born." Andrii shook his head. "Petro and Vasyl rarely speak to one another now."

Shlomo stretched his hands forward, running them over the surface of the table as though smoothing a wrinkled cloth. "Yes, Ameryka is a woman who has come between many men and who has broken up many families. Sometimes she pits brother against brother. Money is usually the cause. From what I've heard of Ameryka, there is no wisdom there—it is not a kosher land. Men find it easy to turn away from God in such a place. Ameryka is like 'Folly' in the Proverbs."

"Do you mean the verses about the banquets given by the woman Wisdom and the woman Folly?"

"Yes, Andrii. But in this case, it is Ameryka who is Folly and she is fickle. Do you know the lines about Folly—how she is inane and knows nothing?"

Andrii closed his eyes in concentration and, after a pause, recited:

> *. . . she is inane, and knows nothing.*
> *She sits at the door of her house*
> *upon a seat on the city heights,*
> *Calling to passers-by*
> *as they go on their straight way:*
> *"Let whoever is simple turn in here,*
> *or who lacks understanding; for to him I say,*
> *Stolen water is sweet,*
> *and bread gotten secretly is pleasing!"*
> *Little he knows that the shades are there,*
> *that in the depths of the nether world are her guests!*

Shlomo was pleased. "You remember the sacred words well. Remember this about Ameryka, Andrii: those who allow themselves to be seduced surely will be lost. I have seen it in my family and I have heard of it in others. Pray that your brother, Petro, resists the temptations of Ameryka. Your brother, Vasyl, seems to have come home the same man who left here. But, some men . . . some men change." Shlomo lifted his hands to the ceiling. "Well, well, Andrii. Enough of that—you will not go to Ameryka. That is good—that is good."

"Now, Andrii," said Linka. "Go to the shelf—there, do you see? On the wall. You will find a small bag. Yes, that one. Bring it here. No, please sit down and open it." Andrii untied the bag and found four silver pieces inside. "It is for you, Andrii," said Linka. "It is for your schooling."

"I cannot take this. It is—"

Shlomo raised his hand to silence Andrii.

"But, this is too much," protested Andrii. "I have done nothing today but bring wood. Ivanko Kavulya will be well before next Friday—in time for the Sabbath. You will need this for him."

"No, Andrii," said Shlomo hoarsely. "Take it. You have been good to us always. Take it. There is no more to be said."

"Thank you," said Andrii softly, pocketing the silver coins. "You will both come to the *hostyna*—the reception—after Anna's wedding? *Mamka* says she hopes you will come."

Shlomo nodded. "Of course. We will see you there. And come to see us whenever you are home from Pryashev. There will always be cake . . . sweet cake—the way you like it."

Andrii opened the hearth door and fed two more pieces of split beech wood to the flames. The fire crackled and hissed, and in the dark corner the boy, David, wheezed.

While Andrii and Shlomo shook hands, Linka returned to David's bedside in the corner. Andrii stepped outside, pulling the door closed after him. The snow now fell in large flake-clusters. Andrii pulled his hat down, stuffed his hands into his pockets, and trudged off, fading into the white silence.

CHAPTER TEN

The Procession

THE DAY OF ANNA'S WEDDING fell on an unusually mild and sunny day in late winter, two weeks before *Velykŷi Post*—Great Lent. Boiling atop the hearths of nearly every hut in Stara Polyanka were pots either of cabbage, soup, meats, or kasha. Men and women in these same huts spent the morning donning their finest flaxen clothes: colorfully embroidered shirts, vests, and skirts. In her own home, Yevka worked on a *pysanka* for Anna's *hostyna*— the wedding reception. She created the initial design rapidly, rotating the egg in her left hand and applying the hot beeswax with a series of quick strokes using a small nail she held in her right hand. When she finished, she carefully lowered the egg into a can filled with the first dye, a light yellow made from boiled onion skins.

Her husband, Petro, had left early, explaining neither his purpose nor his destination, and Yevka had not asked. But he had added wood to the fire before he left and now the room was warm.

Paraska was outside, and, in the corner bunk, Vasko snored loudly. Petro Kotsur had held his bachelor dance the night before around a great bonfire in the open area in front of the tavern. Pavlo Vantsa, a cousin of the Rusynko brothers, came from Varadka and played his locally famous fiddle, accompanied by fiddlers from Stara Polyanka. Vasko entertained everyone with his dancing and was well rewarded with brandy—"Fuel for my feet!" he declared with every drink he was offered. The women stood outside the yellow glow of the fire but pressed closer for a better view when Vasko cried, "Now, brothers, now! Join me!" The men raised a dust, stomping and turning with the music. "Faster, faster!" cried Vasko as the men jumped in the air, slapping their feet and thighs with open hands. One by one the men staggered out of the dance circle, panting and bending over with their hands on their knees. Then only

Vasko and Vasyl remained. "*Skoro*—faster, Vasyl!" cried Vasko. "Can you dance no faster?!" And finally, Vasyl spun out of the dance to the edge of the circle, where he gasped and held his sides. The girls standing nearby eyed him, giggling and whispering among themselves. Vasyl winked at them, eliciting squeals of delight. When he spotted Yevka in the shadows with the married women, Vasyl bowed his head and smiled.

Later, when the women left for the hills to gather periwinkle for the wedding crowns, Paraska lingered to watch her husband dance. When she turned to join the women in the hills, Ivan Dzyamba swayed into her path, shouting, "Vasko dances the way Pavlo Vantsa plays the fiddle! From the soul! From here!" he cried, striking his chest with his fist.

Paraska nodded, "*On didko*—he's the devil!"

Ivan Dzyamba laughed, "Yes, that's it! He's the devil!" And he staggered back to the dance.

Paraska repeated, "He's the devil, all right." But she smiled as she said it.

Now, the next morning, Yevka pulled the egg from the dye and set it on a small towel. The next dye would be a light red from Old Mykhal's slivers of brazilwood.

Paraska entered the hut and stood behind Yevka with her hands on her hips. "When the baby comes—and by the look of you, it could be any day—you will no longer have time for *pysankŷ*."

"I'm not due until after the start of *Velykŷi Post*—Great Lent."

"Hmph! Your baby will come when it comes. And then you can forget your eggs."

When Yevka mumbled a reply, Paraska said, "What?"

"I said, there must always be *pysankŷ*."

"*Tak*—yes, only, maybe not so many." Then Paraska went to her bed and examined the inert mound under the covers. "Look at him. Should I throw water on him or kick him?"

"Why don't you tap him on the shoulder and say, 'Get up'?" suggested Yevka, her eyes slightly crossed, concentrating on the egg in her hand.

Paraska opened her mouth to speak, changed her mind, and tapped her husband on the shoulder. "Get up!" she snapped.

Vasko turned onto his back and rubbed his eyes, struggling to focus on Paraska's looming face. "What is it . . . woman?" he mumbled. "Is it today . . . Petro Kotsur . . . is he . . . ?"

"Petro Kotsur is at his home. He's waiting for you."

"Are we . . . ?"

"*We* are at our home. Where *you* are, who knows?"

Vasko was awake now. "Woman, why did you not wake me earlier?" He slid out of the bunk and stumbled around in a small circle, stomping his feet. "The wedding is today and you stand there watching me sleep! Where are my clothes? HELP ME!"

"Stop shouting. Your clothes are behind you. Take them outside with you, wash yourself, and go to the barn to change. You are disturbing Yevka. She is making a *pysanka* for Anna."

Vasko gathered his things and, yawning and scratching himself, stood over his sister-in-law. "It is a beautiful *pysanka*, Yevka. Anna will be pleased."

Annoyed, Paraska cleared her throat and pointed to the door. When Vasko sneered at her, Paraska retaliated with an even more fearsome scowl. Vasko quickly scampered out into the sunlight.

Yevka slipped the egg into the red dye and then stood, grimacing and rubbing her lower back. Paraska, observing her sister, asked cautiously, "Nothing has happened, has it? Not now, not today!"

"No, nothing has happened. I told you, I'm not due yet."

"Well, I hope not. Today would be a fine time! Perhaps during the wedding. Maybe the *pysanka* should be for you!"

Yevka poked at the pot on the hearth. "Is all the cooking done?"

"All that we are providing, yes—don't touch that, you will burn yourself. Finish the *pysanka*. I will go give Vasko reasons to wish he were already at Petro Kotsur's."

❧

Ivan Ivanchyn stood in the doorway of the Kotsur hut, hands on hips, watching as the approaching Vasko sauntered down the road. "You are late, Vasko!"

Vasko shook his head and waved wearily in the direction of his home, suggesting perhaps that his tardiness was due to malevolent domestic forces.

"Well . . . ," said Ivan Ivanchyn, unconvinced of Vasko's innocence. "Whatever the reason, *skoro*—hurry. There is much to do."

Some of the groomsmen drifted out of the hut into the yard. Ivan Ivanchyn called them together. "Where is Mykhal Kavulya? As Petro Kotsur's godfather, he must lead the procession. Where is his flag?" The men were of dubious help.

"He is not here yet."

"Yes he is. He is inside."

"He is helping dress Petro."

"I did not see him."

"Mykhal Kavulya, are you there?"

"Yes!"

"Where is the *zastava*—the flag?"

"The women are almost finished with it. Here is the pole."

"That is a tree branch."

"It is a small trunk."

"What difference does it make?"

"Whittle it down."

"Any smaller and it will not support the flag."

"Make it smoother."

"Where is my ax?"

The men fussed over the wooden pole, and the women brought out the little flag and ribbons; everyone ignored Ivan Ivanchyn's instructions and appeals for order. When the musicians arrived and took their places outside the doorway, Pavlo Vantsa, the fiddler, glared at Vasko, who flashed an innocent smile and tapped his uncle, Ivan Ivanchyn, on the shoulder. "Why is that devil, Pavlo Vantsa, staring at me?"

The weary Ivan looked at Vasko with one eyebrow arched and said, "After last night I am surprised Pavlo does not fell you like a little beech tree."

Vasko reddened. "What happened last night?"

"How should I know? But knowing you, I am guessing Pavlo Vantsa has every right to cast the evil eye at you. Go inside and see if Petro Kotsur is ready—and stay out of trouble! Vasko! *Chekai*—wait—where is Yurko?"

"Asleep with his pigs!" cried Vasko.

Ivan Ivanchyn turned away from Vasko in disgust. "He calls you friend and yet you cannot trouble yourself to bring him with you? You there, Shtefan! Go find Yurko!"

Shtefan Guzii stepped out of the group assembling the *zastava*. "There is no need. Look, here he comes now!"

Everyone turned to see Yurko ambling down the road, attired only slightly more formally than he might dress for fieldwork.

"*Dobrŷi vechur*—good evening—Yurko!" someone yelled sarcastically. When the men laughed, Yurko stepped off the road and stood behind a small linden tree, his back turned, his hands in his pockets.

"If you men work any slower," cried Ivan Ivanchyn, "it *will* be evening soon! Shtefan and Hryhorii, stop staring at Yurko. He will join us when he is ready. Yurko, pay no attention to your friends! You are welcome to walk with me to protect the *zastava*." Ivan Ivanchyn went to the door of the hut and called out over the heads of the groomsmen, "Is Petro Kotsur ready?" Someone shushed him, pointing to the floor in the middle of the room where Petro knelt before his mother and father, asking for forgiveness and a blessing. Petro's parents blessed their son, made the sign of the cross over his bowed head, and then presented him with a small tin icon of the Lord. Petro crossed himself, rose to his feet, and walked outside.

Despite Ivan Ivanchyn's confusing instructions, the members of Petro's wedding party managed to take their proper places in the procession. Mykhal Kavulya took the lead position, raising the flag high in the air. Tucking their *husly*—their violins—under their chins, the musicians sawed their bows across their instruments, progressing gradually, and in several keys, toward a singular and recognizable tune. Ivan Ivanchyn took his place behind Mykhal Kavulya; Petro Kotsur and Vasko fell in next, with the groomsmen following; and the musicians, now harmonically reconciled, serenaded the procession from the rear.

Yurko, still standing by the road, watched as the pageant filed by. Ivan Ivanchyn beckoned to Yurko, who stumbled awkwardly in the young rye grass emerging along the road. Ivan Ivanchyn reached over, pulled Yurko into the column, and marched with his arm across the taller man's shoulders.

CHAPTER ELEVEN

Handmaiden Of God

AT THE RUSYNKO HOMESTEAD, *Baba* thrust a woman's scarf and shawl into Andrii's hands.

"I am too old for this," whined Andrii.

Baba pointed a crooked finger in her grandson's face. "And you are too old for a spanking! Do as you are told!"

Andrii pleaded with his eyes to Vasyl for help, but his brother ignored his pathetic expressions, saying, "Wait until after I present *Baba* and then be ready to go outside."

"But, Vasyl—"

"Remember, Andrii," explained Vasyl with mock seriousness. "You are doing a tremendous service for your family. I am certain that Father Yaroslav would agree that you will please the Lord. Now go outside and tell us when they arrive."

As he withdrew from the room, Andrii speculated aloud, "I doubt that the Lord has this sort of thing in mind when He awards merits."

In the corner, Paraska, Yevka, and the bridesmaids fussed over Anna, re-arranging her hair and pulling her dress this way and that, until the poor girl squirmed in protest under their clutches. "Hold still," commanded Paraska. "*Bozhe moi!*—My God!—I hope you don't give Petro Kotsur this much trouble tonight!" The bridesmaids, giggling and snorting, covered their mouths as Paraska threw her head back, roaring with laughter.

Vasyl watched the women clustered around his sister and noted the care-ful, gentle way in which Yevka combed Anna's hair. When Yevka glanced at Vasyl, they both looked away quickly. Vasyl joined his mother, who stood at the hearth pushing *holubkŷ*—stuffed cabbage—from side to side in a pot with a wooden spoon.

Vasyl held out his hand. "*Mamko,* give me the spoon and go sit. You look tired. I can chase *holubký* with a spoon as well as you can."

His mother looked up with moist eyes and whispered, "Go see *Nyanko*— your papa. Go see him and tell me what to do."

"What is it, *Mamko*? What is—"

His mother shook her head. "Shh! Do not speak—go."

Vasyl made his way past the giggling women to the bunk in the dark corner while Yevka, still brushing Anna's hair, followed his movements. Though Vasyl's back was turned, there was no misconstruing his sagging head and shoulders.

"Is that really true, Yevka?"

Distracted, Yevka ceased brushing Anna's hair. "What did you say, Anna?"

Anna now turned in her seat and was looking up. "Yevka, is it true?"

"Is what true?"

"What Paraska said about . . . you know . . . tonight . . . is it . . . is it true?"

"Well . . . I . . . I am not sure . . . I wasn't really—"

Paraska put her hands on her hips and squinted at Yevka. "What do you mean, you are not sure?"

"Well . . . well, then . . . yes, I suppose it is true."

Paraska threw her head back and laughed, while the bridesmaids giggled and whispered in Anna's ears.

Vasyl returned from his father's bedside and rejoined his mother. The two stood before the open hearth door, their faces auburn in the glare of the hot coals. "I am not sure what to do, Vasyl," said *Mamka* hoarsely. "God help us! Why today of all days? Tell me what to do."

Vasyl took his mother by the shoulders and turned her toward Anna and the bridesmaids. *Baba* was scolding the young women for dallying, and they in turn began to dance in a circle around her. "Look, *Mamko,*" whispered Vasyl. "Look at Anna—look how young and beautiful she is. You are to marry your daughter to a young man today—that is all. See your daughter married, and, before or after the ceremony, I will inform Father Yaroslav about . . . about *Nyanko*. Do not tell Anna—not until tomorrow. It is very simple, *Mamko.* Hang a blanket in front of Papa's bed so no one sees him. Now, I must get ready—I hear music."

Andrii burst into the room, proclaiming, "They are here!"

Vasyl pointed to the scarf and shawl. "Put them on now, Andrii—don't look at me like that. I wore them when our cousin Mariya married."

"But you were ten years old!"

"PUT THEM ON, ANDRII!" *Baba* thundered from across the room. "You are the closest thing we have to a ten-year-old boy. And you, young lady"—*Baba* inspected Anna from head to toe—"you are more beautiful than Petro Kotsur deserves."

From the back of the room *Mamka* dissented. "Petro deserves all the beauty Anna can give him," she said. "And she deserves all the beauty in him." *Mamka* finished hanging the blanket and stood over her daughter. "A life without beauty is no life. Be as beautiful as you can be for Petro, my dear Anna. Be beautiful for him and he will be beautiful for you. That will be something you will have with you always—no matter what happens in your lives." She kissed her daughter's hand and then held it against her cheek.

There was a tapping on the door, but only *Mamka* seemed to hear it. She nodded toward the door. "Open the door, Vasyl. They have come for Anna . . . and we will give her to them."

Blinking his moist eyes, Vasyl smiled at his mother. He pulled on his coat, and, straightening the collar, asked, "How do I look?"

"BEAUTIFUL!" bellowed *Baba*. "ANSWER THE DOOR!"

Vasyl kissed *Baba* loudly on the cheek and she pushed him away playfully. "Oh, my Vasyl!" she tittered.

Vasyl opened the door and stepped outside, where the entire colorful procession was arrayed before him: a sea of villagers dressed in sun-bleached flaxen garments decorated with red and black embroidery, all set against a background of green hills and whitewashed huts with brown thatched roofs. And in the blue sky above, the red ribbons tied to the *zastava* twisted and flapped in a light breeze. The fiddlers standing in the background finished their song with a wild flourish, thrusting their bows in the air like swordsmen brandishing sabers.

Vasyl bowed his head toward Ivan Ivanchyn, Petro Kotsur, and the groomsmen. "*Slava Isusu Khrystu!*—Glory to Jesus Christ, strangers!" he cried.

"*SLAVA NA VIKŶ!*—GLORY TO HIM FOREVER!" they shouted.

Vasyl crossed his arms and cupped his chin in his hand. "Brothers and sisters, why this warlike appearance? Do you mean to invade this peaceful home?"

Ivan Ivanchyn stepped forward and removed his hat with a grand sweeping motion. "Neither are we warlike, nor do we intend to invade your home. We are like you, peaceful. We are escorting a young man to church on the most important journey of his life."

Vasyl frowned. "I see no coffin in your midst."

Vasko snorted and jabbed his cousin, Petro Kotsur, in the ribs with his elbow. "That is good—did you hear him, Petro? 'No coffin.' Very good, Vasyl!'"

Ivan Ivanchyn smiled broadly. "No, not that journey, honest stranger. God has not yet asked him to make that journey. God has called him today to make a very different journey. Today is his wedding day, and we have come for his bride."

"Well, then," said Vasyl. "Go in peace on your journey. *Z Bohom!*—Go with God!" And with that, Vasyl turned to reenter the hut.

"No, wait," said Ivan Ivanchyn advancing to the door of the hut. "The bride we seek lives in this house."

"Here? In my house?"

"Yes."

Vasyl crossed his arms again, tapping his nose with his finger and gazing thoughtfully into the distance. "Yes, perhaps you are correct. She may in truth be here." Vasyl opened the door and reached inside for *Baba,* who whispered, "How do I look?"

"Beautiful. Take my hand," Vasyl murmured from the side of his mouth. "Yes, here she is!" He pulled *Baba* outside where she stood shyly next to Vasyl, blushing and adjusting the scarf on her head.

Ivan Ivanchyn raised his eyebrows at Petro Kotsur, who shook his head. "The groom tells me that this is not the agreed-upon bride."

Vasko shouted, "Vasyl! It is Petro Kotsur who is marrying today, not his widowed *dido*—his widowed grandfather!"

Baba made a horrible face at Vasko and he reciprocated.

"Ah," said Vasyl, his face brightening. He pushed *Baba* back inside and gestured to those assembled to be patient. Inside the hut, *Baba* and *Mamka* wrestled the reluctant Andrii into Vasyl's groping hands.

"Here is the one you seek!" cried Vasyl, presenting Andrii, his apron tied too high and his scarf crooked over his eyes.

Petro Kotsur shook his head vigorously and Vasko shouted again, "Look! It is a bride for Yurko!"

Everyone laughed. Yurko, standing next to Ivan Ivanchyn, watched the ribbons fluttering atop the pole held high in Mykhal Kavulya's hands.

Vasyl barred Andrii from reentering the hut as Vasko worked his way around the crowd. Andrii whined. "Vasyl, please." Vasko slipped behind Andrii, whisked the lightly tied apron from Andrii's waist and ran away brandishing the trophy high over his head. Andrii chased Vasko briefly in the yard and then stopped, examined his motives, and stomped back into the hut, pulling the scarf from his head and casting a vicious look at Vasyl.

Anna, standing just inside, presented her hand to Vasyl, but he reached around her and took Yevka's hand instead. *Baba* gasped, "She is married!" Vasyl thrust the startled Yevka into the sunlight, where she averted her face from the crowd.

Vasko called out again. "At last, Vasyl, the correct age and sex! But this hen already has a rooster and she lays many beautiful eggs. Show us another girl before you start a fight. Petro Kotsur may be a *kotsur*—a tomcat—but he is no match for Petro Rusynko!" And Vasko jabbed his cousin in the ribs.

Petro Kotsur, anxious and weary of Vasko's elbow, moved to the other side of Ivan Ivanchyn and whispered into his ear.

Ivan Ivanchin nodded. "Yes, yes, yes, Petro, of course. Now, Vasyl—or, rather, honorable stranger, we have come for the agreed-upon bride for Petro Kotsur. You have shown us many brides, each fine in her own way; only now, we ask you, give us the one and only true bride. That is all we ask."

Vasyl opened the door to allow Yevka to reenter the hut and then turned to face the crowd. "Honorable Ivan Ivanchyn—Pan Ivan Ivanchyn! I see now that you and your forces have merely come to see the fulfillment of a binding agreement between two peaceful families. You have behaved honestly and have presented Petro Kotsur, also an honorable man." Everyone looked at the groom, nodding and murmuring. "You have been patient," continued Vasyl. "So . . . now . . . I present to you . . . the bride!" Vasyl pulled Anna from the hut.

The assembly cheered and the fiddler, Pavlo Vantsa, began a fast tune that the other musicians mimicked with enthusiasm if not precision. Ivan Ivanchyn paraded Anna in a circle for all to admire. Vasko jabbed Petro Kotsur in the side again and pointed, lest there be any doubt whom Petro was to marry. *Baba, Mamka,* Paraska, Yevka, Andrii, and the bridesmaids emerged from the hut and arranged themselves in a row facing the crowd. Ivan Ivanchyn, holding Anna by the hand, now took Petro Kotsur's hand and led the couple to a spot in front of Vasyl and his mother.

Vasyl held up his hand, signaling an end to the music. "Thank you, honorable and most excellent musicians!" And then he turned to his mother. "Pani Rusynko, as mother of this young bride, you have raised a beautiful daughter, a handmaiden of God who trusts in the Lord, and who, as wife, will serve her husband and continue to obey the ways of the Lord. Petro Kotsur and all in this village thank you." He nodded to Anna. "Now."

Anna whispered, looking from her mother to Vasyl. "But what about *Nyanko*? Shouldn't I kneel also before *Nyanko*?"

Vasyl addressed Ivan Ivanchyn. "Her *nyanko* is very ill. We thought it would be better to remain outside."

Ivan Ivanchyn closed his eyes and nodded solemnly. "Of course, Vasyl. Anna, your brother is correct. Your *mamka*'s blessing is sufficient. You may kneel out here, Anna."

Anna knelt and asked for her mother's forgiveness and blessing. Her mother made the sign of the cross over her daughter and presented her with a small tin icon of the Mother of God. Anna stood and kissed her mother on both cheeks and then kissed her brothers. From her apron Anna produced a sprig of rosemary, which she held aloft for all to see. Then she affixed it to Petro Kotsur's hat.

Ivan Ivanchyn summoned Vasko, and the two men, each holding a hand ax, approached the doorway of the hut. Vasyl held the door while the two men incised a small cross on the door's rough surface. With evil now safely warded away from the wedding party, Ivan Ivanchyn directed Mykhal Kavulya to lead the procession on its way to the Church of the Protection of the Mother of God.

Vasyl whispered in Andrii's ear and then gripped the boy's shoulders when Andrii turned pale. Andrii blinked into Vasyl's eyes, slowly nodded, and then ran ahead of the procession and down the path to the center of the village. The wedding party wound out of the yard and only Vasyl remained behind. When the last musician disappeared from view, Vasyl reentered the hut and went to the back of the room.

He pulled down the hastily erected blanket and sat on the edge of the bunk, taking his father's cold hand into his own. His father's body was still flaccid and easy to manipulate. Vasyl went to the center of the room and dragged the two benches to the side of the bunk, where he placed them side by side, arranging the blanket over them. He lifted the wasted form and transferred it to the benches, securing it within the blanket but leaving the head, with slack jaw and half-closed eyes, exposed. From the cupboard next to the hearth, he retrieved a scarf and two copper coins that his mother had stored away for this long-anticipated day. With the kerchief he bound shut his father's jaw, tying a knot on the top of the head. He closed his father's eyes and weighted the lids with the two large coins. Then from a shelf on the back wall he brought down a bundle, which he unwrapped, revealing a folded shirt, vest, and trousers. These, his father's twenty-five-year-old wedding clothes, he arranged on the table. Later, his father would be dressed in them for burial.

The initial preparations completed, Vasyl stood in the open doorway. When a cool sigh of air brushed the back of his neck, he shuddered and stepped into the yard. Atop the woodpile a *straka*—a black bird—warily eyed Vasyl before hopping to the ground and strutting out of sight behind the barn. Somewhere a dog barked, and on the other side of the river a dozen or so of Pan Kapishinskii's cows dotted a green slope of pasture. The wedding procession had made its way to the center of the village, where the marchers passed by the front of Yakov's tavern.

Across the Ondava Stream, Petro Rusynko, finally finished with his day's work and dressed in his festive best, worked his way leisurely from his hut to the Rusynko place.

In the medium distance, the figures of Shlomo Lentz and his wife, Linka, appeared. Vasyl hurried forward to escort them to the hut. "Andrii has told us everything!" Shlomo called out. "We will watch. Go to the wedding. Your father will not be alone." Shlomo patted Vasyl on the back. "She and I will watch. Go, Vasyl. Don't miss your sister's wedding."

Vasyl strolled down the hill and met Petro coming up the path. "He is dead," said Vasyl, grinding his teeth.

"Who?"

"*Nyanko*—he is dead. Shlomo and Linka are sitting with him."

Petro gazed up at the Rusynko homestead and grunted. Then the two brothers turned and, with Petro in the lead, walked single file toward the Church of the Protection of the Mother of God.

CHAPTER TWELVE

Protection of the Mother of God

ANDRII RAN TO the Church of the Protection of the Mother of God, arriving at the entrance as the vested Father Yaroslav Podhayetskii emerged. "*Slava Isusu Khrystu*—Glory to Jesus Christ, Andrii!"

Andrii bowed his head. "*Slava na vikŷ, Otche*—Glory to Him forever, Father."

"What is wrong, Andrii? You are out of breath. Why are you not with the wedding party?"

"*Otche*—Father, would it be wrong . . . is it permitted . . ." The fiddles were audible now and Andrii glanced back down the hill.

"Tell me what is wrong, Andrii."

Andrii lowered his head. "My *nyanko* died . . . this morning. We are not sure when. Vasyl says we should go on with the wedding . . . only, I'm not sure . . ."

"Does Anna know?"

"No. Only *Mamka* and Vasyl know . . . and Shlomo Lentz and his wife. Vasyl told me to ask them to sit with the . . . to sit with *Nyanko*."

Father Yaroslav placed a hand on Andrii's shoulder. "You and Vasyl did well. Your father's death has been a long time coming. There is nothing more that can be done now except for you to assist in the marriage of your sister. We will tend to your father after the ceremony. We will ring the large bell tomorrow morning to announce your father's passing. Look, Andrii, they are approaching. Your brother is still at your home, yes? Good. He will come when he can. Now, Andrii, when the wedding party is ready to file into the church, I want you to begin the entrance psalm as you have practiced it. Do you feel well enough to do it? Good—here is the text. Now, stand here, outside the doors as I lead everyone inside."

When the colorful pageant formed in a semicircle in front of the church, the musicians bowed their last note and lowered their fiddles.

Father Yaroslav raised his hands in greeting to the people. *"Slava Isusu Khrystu!*—Glory to Jesus Christ!"

"SLAVA NA VIKŶ!—GLORY TO HIM FOREVER!"

Father Yaroslav gestured to Andrii, who cleared his throat and began to sing.

> *Happy are all who fear the Lord,*
> *who walk in the ways of God.*

The wedding party joined in singing the ancient chant as Father Yaroslav led them into the church.

> *What your hands provide you will enjoy;*
> *you will be happy and prosper.*

When Anna passed in front of Andrii, he took her hand and squeezed it. Their mother and *Baba* came next: the latter singing in a full voice; the former singing mechanically, her eyes red and moist.

> *Like a fruitful vine*
> *your wife within your home,*
> *Like olive plants*
> *your children around your table.*

Vasyl and Petro jogged up the path from the center of the village, entering the church with the last few villagers; among them, Paraska and Yevka.

> *Just so will they be blessed*
> *who fear the Lord.*

Passing through the congested vestibule, Yevka found herself entering the nave of the church with Vasyl rather than with her husband, Petro.

> *May the Lord bless you from Zion,*
> *all the days of your life*

That you may share Jerusalem's joy
and live to see your children's children.
Peace upon Israel!

At the conclusion of the psalm, Andrii stepped away from the front of the church, wiped his eyes, and gazed out over the village. There was the Rusynko homestead, where his father's lifeless body reposed; and there, on the hill behind the church and beneath the bare linden trees, was the Rusynko plot with its little cluster of listing wooden crosses. Andrii looked up at the great wooden tower that rose above the entrance to the church. High cirrus clouds moved eastward, and the tower resembled the mast of a ship straining and creaking westward. Atop the tower's iron cross a rusted sun radiated wriggling rays—*I am the light of the world . . .* How many of his people had passed through these doors to be baptized, to be married . . . and to be buried? And how many more would pass through before these wooden beams rotted away? Andrii started into the church, hesitated, and looked up to see a sparrow swooping around the tower from the east and flapping toward the Ondava Stream. Andrii smiled and entered the church.

ℭↄ

From the depths of Hell a fanged red beast disgorged the worm of sin. The serpent, ringed with bands of iniquities, slithered among the nations of the earth and past prophets and patriarchs, stopping at the figure of Adam kneeling at the foot of Christ the Judge, and there locked its jaws firmly on the original man's heel. Kneeling opposite Adam, was Eve, the first woman, her hands, like those of her husband, clasped in prayer.

Yevka, standing next to Paraska inside the church, closed her eyes and turned away from the small, window-sized icon of the Last Judgment that hung on the north wall of the church. When she opened them again she was facing the three Rusynko brothers—Andrii, Vasyl, and her husband, Petro—who all stood on the south side of the nave.

Father Yaroslav, having finished the Litany of Peace, now intoned:

O God most pure, Author of all creation, You in your love for mankind, transformed the rib of our forefather Adam into a woman, and blessed them, saying: "Be fruitful, multiply, fill the earth and subdue it."

Through marriage You made them two in one flesh; for this reason, a man shall leave his father and mother and be joined to his wife, and the two shall become one flesh. Those whom God has joined together, let no man put asunder.

Vasyl observed Yevka as she turned her attention once again to the icon with its crowds of saints and sinners and its promise of Heaven or Hell. In Paradise the Mother of God sat enthroned behind Jacob, Isaac, and Abraham into whose lap Saints Peter and Paul guided the saved.

In your loving kindness You blessed your servant Abraham; and, granting fruitfulness to Sarah, You made him the father of a multitude of nations.

Surrounding the Lord were his Holy Mother—appearing twice in the same icon—on the one side and the Baptist on the other; below were the apostles seated in a row, six behind Adam and six behind Eve.

You gave Isaac to Rebekah and blessed them with children. You joined Jacob and Rachel, raising from that union the twelve patriarchs. You united Joseph to Asenath and blessed them with children, Ephraim and Manasseh; and, accepting the prayer of Zachary and Elizabeth, You revealed in their child the Forerunner, John the Baptist.

Yevka glanced at Vasyl and turned away when their eyes met.

You caused the ever-virgin Mary to blossom forth in the order of nature from the root of Jesse, and You yourself became incarnate of her and were born of her for the salvation of the human race.

Yevka stared at the scene at the bottom of the icon where sinners suffered with an urgency that caused her to gasp.

In your indescribable graciousness and great goodness You came to Cana in Galilee, and blessed the marriage which took place there.

Racked, bound, and contorted, the souls of the condemned burned eternally in unquenchable and unconsuming flames.

Thus You made it clear that it is your will that there should be lawful marriage and from it the procreation of children. Now, most holy Master, hear the supplication of us, your servants. As You were there, so also be here with your invisible presence; and bless this marriage, granting to your servants Petro and Anna, a peaceful and long life, matrimonial chastity, mutual love in the bond of peace, a long-lived posterity, happiness in their children, and the unfading crown of glory.

Yevka's eyes widened at the plight of the figures in the lowest level of Hell, where an adulterous couple, locked in an eternal embrace, lay naked and helpless, derided by a hovering, red-winged fiend.

Keep their married life above reproach, and grant them to see their children's children; give them dew from heaven and the fruitfulness of the earth; provide them with an abundance of temporal good things, that they in turn may share their abundance with those in need; and grant to everyone here present with them all that is necessary for salvation.

Paraska squeezed her sister's arm and whispered, "What is wrong with you, Yevka? Are you ill? Is it the baby's time?"

Yevka shook her head. "No . . . n-no . . . I-I'm fine . . ."

"Well," whispered Paraska, "tell me if you are going to be sick and I will take you outside."

Yevka nodded and gazed across the church. Vasyl was staring at her with a look of concern. Yevka lowered her eyes and clasped her hands tightly over her belly.

Now, O Master, stretch forth your hand from your holy dwelling place and join these, your servants Petro and Anna; for You alone join the wife to her husband. Unite them in one mind and flesh, granting them fruitfulness and rewarding them with good children.

Astride the fanged beast sat the grinning devil, balancing the soul of Judas on his left knee, and holding out his right hand in a charming gesture of welcome.

Father Yaroslav now placed one of the periwinkle wedding crowns on Petro Kotsur's head, saying:

The servant of God, Petro, is crowned in marriage for the servant of
God, Anna, in the name of the Father, and of the Son, and of the Holy
Spirit. Amen.

Father Yaroslav placed the second crown on Anna's head saying:

The servant of God, Anna, is crowned in marriage for the servant of
God, Petro, in the name of the Father, and of the Son, and of the Holy
Spirit. Amen.

Then, making the sign of the cross over Petro and Anna, Father Yaroslav
chanted, "O Lord, our God, crown them with glory and honor!"

Paraska, wiping tears from her eyes, turned to Yevka and whispered, "*Oi,*
Yevka, what a happy day. It is like our own weddings, yes? Let me wipe your
eyes; you are even happier than I am!"

Now the lector was reading from the Epistle of Saint Paul the Apostle to
the Ephesians:

Be subordinate to one another out of reverence for Christ. Wives
should be subordinate to their husbands as to the Lord. For the husband is head of his wife just as Christ is head of the church . . .

Yevka gazed again at the icon of the Last Judgment and turned away shuddering, only to find Vasyl again staring quizzically at her. Then, to Yevka's
horror, Vasyl began scanning the same icon with obvious concern over the
source of her discomfort.

As the church is subordinate to Christ, so wives should be subordinate
to their husbands in everything.

Yevka bit her lower lip, whispering, "No, no, no . . ." as Vasyl studied the
icon.

Husbands, love your wives, even as Christ loved the church and handed
himself over for her to sanctify her, cleansing her by the bath of water
with the word . . .

Vasyl's scrutiny now progressed to the lower third of the icon.

So also husbands should love their wives as their own bodies. He who loves his wife loves himself . . .

Paraska grasped Yevka's arm and, peering into her face, whispered, "Are you sick, Yevka?"

For no one hates his own flesh but rather nourishes and cherishes it, even as Christ does the church, because we are members of his body . . .

Yevka swallowed and murmured, "I-I don't know . . ."

Paraska held out her arm. "Hold on to me—we will go outside. You there, move," she whispered to the women behind her. "Mariya, Anna Roman, move aside . . . move aside, Anastasiya Hryndyk . . . make room for a sick woman . . . yes, that is good . . . come, Yevka, we are almost there . . . move back, Mariya Korba—thank you. There now, Yevka, the air out here is cool—you will feel better now. This is my fault. I should have made you stay at home—it is too close to your time and you have been working too—"

"Paraska—"

"—hard and I—what is it, Yevka?"

"I'm better now."

"Do you want to go home?"

"No."

"You don't want to go back inside, do you?"

"No. I want to stay here until they come out. The air feels good."

"Do you want to go to the *hostyna*—the reception?"

"Yes . . . yes, I want to go. I have the egg for Anna. I want to present it to her."

"Very well. I will stay out here with you." Paraska and Yevka stood outside the church but close enough to the entrance for both to see and hear the remainder of the wedding service. "Anna looks beautiful on her wedding day. She reminds me of you, Yevka, on your wedding day."

"Me?"

"Yes. You were so lovely. I remember you were so nervous that I thought you would not make it to the ceremony. But then you and Petro walked into the church and you had such tears in your eyes! Then I knew how happy you were. Do you remember?"

"Yes . . . I—"

"Shh! Yevka, it is time for the *Otche nash*—the Our Father. We will join them."

And inside the church, the faithful raised their voices in prayer, singing:

Our Father, who art in heaven, hallowed be thy name, thy kingdom come, thy will be done, on earth as it is in heaven. Give us this day our daily bread, and forgive us our trespasses as we forgive those who trespass against us, and lead us not into temptation, but deliver us from evil.

Father Yaroslav then sang, "For thine is the kingdom and the power and the glory, Father, Son, and Holy Spirit, now and ever, and forever."

"AMEN!"

Paraska steered Yevka down the steps from the porch to the grassy area in front of the church. "Come, it is almost finished. We will sing when they come out. Do you feel like singing, Yevka?"

"Y-yes . . . only . . ."

"Only what?"

"It is nothing."

"If you are not well I will take you home."

"No, no . . . I'm . . . I'm much better now. Look, the service is finished—the musicians are coming out."

The musicians assembled outside the church entrance, where they serenaded the wedding party and guests as they filed out laughing and singing. As Petro and Anna Kotsur stepped out of the church, Paraska grasped Yevka by the arm and whispered gleefully, "Look, Yevka, look! Anna crossed the threshold first! Good for her! She will have the strong hand in that marriage! Do you remember my wedding, Yevka? Vasko and I almost knocked one another over racing for the threshold of the church. But I was faster. Do you remember? I crossed first!"

In a corner of the churchyard, the Rusynko brothers, Vasyl, Andrii, and Petro, deliberated solemnly with a number of the men, including Ivan Ivanchyn, Andrii Khudyk, and some of the Kotsur men. Pulling Anna away from her husband, the bridesmaids sang to Petro Kotsur: "*Yeshche nasha, zavtra vasha!*—She is still ours, tomorrow she will be yours!" And then the women congratulated Anna, teasing her and whispering in her ear.

Ivan Ivanchyn left the little conference in the corner of the churchyard and mounted the steps to the church entrance. "Quiet, please!" he shouted. "Quiet, please! My brothers and sisters! As you know, it is customary for the parents of the bride to hold a *hostyna*—a reception—in their home. Because of the large size of this wedding party and the . . . well . . . small size of the Rusynko home, the Rusynko family has come to an agreement with the Kotsur family. The two families will hold a joint *hostyna* at the tavern. The Kotsur family had planned theirs for the tavern anyway; and, I am told, the Rusynko family has already had their food and gifts for the couple delivered there. Let us then follow the musicians to Yakov's tavern!"

The musicians again tucked their fiddles under their chins and serenaded the procession down the hill to the tavern.

Yevka remained behind, entering the quiet church alone and bowing before the iconostasis. Her lips trembling, she avoided looking at the icon of the Last Judgment to her left, focusing, instead, on the icon of the Mother of God by the Royal Door. Sitting in the lap of his Holy Mother was the Savior of the world, his right hand raised in a blessing. The Virgin's lips formed a faint but benevolent smile and her right hand guided the faithful to her Son.

Yevka stared into the eyes of the Mother of God until her own eyes moistened. Then she began to weep softly: "*Panno Mariye*—Virgin Mary. *Panno Mariye,* pray for me." Then she wiped her eyes and prayed:

> Bohoroditse Divo—*Hail Mother of God,*
> *Virgin Mariya, full of grace,*
> *the Lord is with you.*
> *Blessed are you among women,*
> *and blessed is the fruit of your womb;*
> *For you gave birth to Christ, the Savior,*
> *and Redeemer of our souls.* Amin.

Yevka bowed before the iconostasis, crossed herself, and walked slowly out of the church. Making her way down the path toward the tavern, she met Paraska coming up the same path.

"Yevka! Where have you been? *Bozhe moi*—my God! I was worried when I lost you in the crowd. Are you well?"

"Yes, I'm fine."

"Where were you?"

"In the church."

"In the church? Did you lose something?"

"No, Paraska. I was praying."

"This is no time for prayer! *Skoro*—hurry! Father Yaroslav will bless the cup soon. And you have a *pysanka* for Anna. After that you can pray all you want to. Come." Paraska led the sisters down the path.

Yevka glanced back at the church. "*Panno Mariye*—Virgin Mariya," she whispered. "*Panno Mariye* . . . pray for me . . ."

CHAPTER THIRTEEN

Hostyna

AT THE ENTRANCE TO YAKOV'S TAVERN, Petro Kotsur's mother presented a plate of bread and salt to her new daughter-in-law, Anna—now Anna Kotsur. Bride and groom then entered the tavern, where they were immediately mobbed by women, who squeezed the resplendent Anna, and by men, who congratulated the bewildered Petro.

Father Yaroslav mounted a bench in the corner of the tavern and straightened, hitting his head on one of the wooden beams. Vasko laughed. "Careful, dear Father! You have either struck the ceiling of the tavern or the floor of Heaven above!"

Rubbing his head, Father Yaroslav frowned at Vasko. "Yes, Vasko. However, the way to Heaven is a long climb from the floor of a tavern!"

Ivan Barna and Hryhorii Hryndyk guffawed, elbowing Vasko, who smiled and bowed gallantly to Father Yaroslav.

"Brothers and sisters, your attention, please!" cried Father Yaroslav, ineffectually. "Brothers and sisters! Quiet, please. Quiet!"

"EVERYONE—QUIET!" boomed Paraska's voice from across the room. "That's better. Go on, dear Father."

"Yes . . . well . . . thank you, Paraska Ivanchyn. Petro and Anna, come forward, please. Yurko, will you and Mykolai and Fedor make room for Petro and Anna? There is no need to crowd and push—this is not the food line . . . not yet."

The guests laughed, while Mykolai and Fedor, embarrassed, made room for Anna and Petro. Yurko, however, remained rooted in place, staring at the lavish feast gracing the banquet table.

Father Yaroslav continued. "Mykolai, please bring the cup of wine. Anna, Petro, are you sure there is enough room for you?"

Vasko's tenor voice sang out, "This is good practice for Anna and Petro, dear Father! Tonight they will be this close . . . and EVEN CLOSER!"

Cheering, the men slapped Vasko's back. From across the room, Paraska roared, "QUIET, FOOL! Let Father continue!"

Father Yaroslav held up his hands. "Quiet, everyone, please. That's enough."

Mykolai squeezed through the crowd and set a cup of wine on the table.

"Very good, thank you, Mykolai. Everyone, it is time for the blessing of the Common Cup. Let us pray to the Lord!"

"LORD, HAVE MERCY!" the people sang.

Father Yaroslav then blessed the cup of wine:

O God, You have made all things by your power. You have established the world and have adorned man the crown of all your creatures. Now bless with your spiritual blessing this common cup which You give to those who are now united in the common life of marriage. For blessed is your Name and glorified is your kingdom, Father, Son, and Holy Spirit, now and ever, and forever.

"AMEN!"

Father Yaroslav handed the cup of wine to Petro Kotsur and continued. "Petro and Anna, when you were baptized in infancy, your lives were joined to Christ in a holy union built on the Lord's unending love for you. Now you have been joined together in a marriage that is also a holy union in Christ. As *Svyatýi Pavlo*—Saint Paul—reminds us, marriage is the divine will of God that a man and a woman should become one flesh and, therefore, one in Christ. So, just as you share a common cup of wine, so also will you share a common life in Christ. Love one another, Petro and Anna, and love the Church as Christ loves the Church." Then Petro and Anna each drank from the cup of wine.

Someone cried out, "*Tak dai Bozhe!*—May God grant it so!" And everyone cheered.

Now, Vasyl and Vasko busied themselves pouring brandy into a wide assortment of cups and mugs on loan by the guests for the occasion. The two men set aside the largest mugs for themselves, and, between filling the smaller vessels, splashed a bit more in their own mugs.

Vasko slurped the overflowing brandy from his mug and mounted one of the benches. "Brothers and sisters!" he cried. "As best man to Petro Kotsur,

I will make a toast to our honored couple. Vasyl will begin passing out the brandy. You men—you there, Yurko and Mykolai—help Vasyl. You too, Andrii. And Yurko, remember, each brandy needn't be sampled. It is good Senchak brandy!"

Paraska arched an eyebrow at her husband. "Hmph!"

Vasko continued. "Do not forget our good and wise priest, Vasyl! A mug for Father Yaroslav! Does everyone have a brandy?"

"YES!"

"Get on with it, Vasko!"

"We are hungry!

"Make it a quick toast!"

Vasko raised his mug. "To Petro Kotsur and Anna Rusynko—may you be like the couple who is father and mother to us all. When our father, Adam, first met our mother, Eve, he saw something in her that no man had ever seen before . . . mainly because there was no one else around to see . . . that is, there was no one before there was Adam and Eve . . . and Eve, coming from Adam's side—from his rib—was nothing to behold anyway, that is, not until—"

"Get on with it, Vasko!"

"Yes, enough! Good Father Yaroslav said a great deal in only a few words!"

"Say something quickly that we might drink and then eat!"

Vasko frowned and placed a fist on his hip. "I was merely trying to add to the wisdom expressed by our dear priest."

"Better then for you to be silent, Vasko!"

Amid much laughter, Vasko stepped down from the bench only to be pushed back onto his podium by Vasyl, who encouraged his friend with smiles and winks.

Vasko held up his cup. "Since you are all simple farmers, I will leave preaching to Father and say only this: to Petro and Anna; may you live long and well with each other! *NA ZDOROVYA!*—TO YOUR HEALTH!"

"*TAK DAI BOZHE*—MAY GOD GRANT IT SO!" cried the guests.

"Well said, Vasko!"

"A good speech, Vasko!"

"A good short speech, Vasko!"

"Let us now eat!"

The guests finished their brandy and crowded around the banquet table. Yurko emerged first with an impressive stack of *holubký*—stuffed cabbage—

and pirogi arranged over a thick bed of kasha. Vasko and Vasyl, watching their friend eat, shook their heads at one another in amazement. Vasyl patted Yurko on the back and said, "I wonder where you put all that food?"

Yurko looked up, kasha spilling from the corners of his mouth, and shrugged.

Vasyl patted him again. "Well, you work hard. You do the work of two men and you have a mighty appetite."

Vasko rolled his eyes and shook his head. "Come, Vasyl. Let us eat. Soon the dancing will begin. Let us get food while there is still some left. Yurko's stomach has a short memory."

In a corner, Andrii conferred with Father Yaroslav and then approached Vasyl. "Father and I are going to go see . . . we are going to the house."

Vasyl put his arm around Andrii's shoulders. "Does Father agree it is best not to tell Anna?"

"Yes. I told him that *Mamka* will tell her tomorrow. He agrees that is best. Only, Vasyl . . ."

"Yes?"

"Is it . . . it doesn't seem right to . . . to celebrate . . ."

"Andriiko, look at your sister. Do you see? Look how she laughs! Today is her day—let her have this day. There will always be time for funerals. Now, go. And send Shlomo and Linka here—they are honored guests! *Chekai*— wait, Andriiko!"

"What is it?"

"Smile. If you don't, Anna will know something is wrong."

In the corner, the women sang to Anna, removing her periwinkle marriage crown and replacing it with the *chepets*, the bonnet of a married woman. When the song ended, Yevka glanced over to the food line and saw Vasyl staring at her.

Vasko shot an elbow into Vasyl's ribs. "I think that in that group there is one with an eye for you."

"What?"

"Have you not noticed how Barbara Fedorochko looks at you? She has no shame. But Vasyl"—Vasko lowered his voice—"you can do better. Since that day when you returned from Ameryka last fall, there is another who has followed your every movement: Mariya Ivanchyn. Yes, Vasyl, yes. Don't roll your eyes and turn away. You are in demand, my friend. Name your price. Mariya Ivanchyn comes with cows and chickens and an ox and one of her father's plows. What more could a man want?"

Vasyl tilted his head, seeking Mariya Ivanchyn in the crowd of brides-maids. She was in the corner holding Anna's periwinkle crown. When she saw Vasyl looking her way she whispered into Anastasiya Korba's ear and both young ladies giggled.

"Yes," sighed Vasyl. "What more could a man want?"

"Certainly no more than she can offer." Vasko clasped his hands together. "Think of it, Vasyl! With your money to buy land and her dowry you would be second only to Pan Kapishinskii in Stara Polyanka. Think of the livestock, Vasyl!"

Vasyl looked at Mariya Ivanchyn again. "Yes, it is hard to think of any-thing else."

"Vasyl, just think! Someday I might even work for you!"

"Think of it!"

"Should I inform the proper parties that you might be interested?"

"Hmm . . . no—I think you should wait."

"Wait! Wait for what? Vasyl, there is no better match for you in any other village between here and Varadka."

"There is no other village between here and Varadka."

"Vasyl, you know what I mean. If you wait you may lose her to another."

Vasyl shrugged. "Misery is a daily risk in the highlands."

"I cannot imagine what more you could want."

"Well . . . I am not sure . . . perhaps love?"

"Love? Love? Love is for the rich. *Bozhe moi*—my God—Vasyl. You were too long in Ameryka. Love! Who can afford love?"

"Speaking of love . . ." Vasyl raised his eyebrows and tilted his head to-ward Paraska, who approached and pinched Vasko's arm.

"Hurry up and eat," she said. "The dance will begin soon."

"*Oi!* Not so hard, woman! Vasyl and I are speaking of important matters. We will dance when it suits us."

"You gossip like a *baba*," Paraska scolded. "And stop trying to talk Vasyl into a marriage he does not want."

"My dove, I have spoken with my uncle, Ivan Ivanchyn, and with Petro Korba and other men. I think we know what Vasyl wants."

"Truly? How would you know?"

"We know, honest dove, because we all have wives. We know what makes a good wife."

Paraska threw her head back and laughed. "Ha! Men get married and think they know something! All you husbands are the same. That is why God gives you all different faces so that we can tell you apart!" Paraska leaned into Vasko's face. "Mariya Ivanchyn? What are you thinking? Everyone who knows anything about these things knows that there is only one girl for Vasyl Rusynko." And with that Paraska turned and began to walk away.

Vasko and Vasyl blinked at one another and Vasko called after Paraska. "Who is it?"

Paraska sauntered back to Vasko's side, gazing distractedly about the room. "Hmm? Who is who?"

Vasko was irritated. "You know what I mean. Who is the one girl for Vasyl?"

"Oh that. Well, everyone knows that the best match for Vasyl is the girl who is young, quiet, and clever with her hands."

Vasko frowned. "And who is younger, quieter, and cleverer than Mariya Ivanchyn?"

"Fool! Mariya Kavulya is the only girl for Vasyl!"

"Mariya Kavulya!" sputtered Vasko. "Mariya Kavulya? My precious little dove, how much brandy did you drink during the toast?"

Paraska and Vasko continued to gossip, completely ignoring Vasyl, who quietly made his way to the circle of bridesmaids. Standing next to Mariya Ivanchyn, Yevka watched her brother-in-law approach. When Mariya Ivanchyn noticed Vasyl, she glided with quick little steps to his side.

"Vasyl Rusynko, what a blessed event is your sister's wedding—as are all weddings," she gushed, leaning lightly against Vasyl's shoulder and gazing up into his eyes. "I am disappointed that we did not return to your family's home from the church. I think I left my embroidery there."

Vasyl shifted his feet, separating himself from Mariya. "I will have Andriiko bring it to you."

"Oh, Vasyl, do not trouble yourself or your brother. I will come by tomorrow myself."

"Yes, I suppose you will." Vasyl motioned to his sister-in-law. "Yevka, come here, please."

Mariya Ivanchyn was not finished. "Vasyl, should I come by in the morning or in the afternoon?"

"Hmm? I don't know . . . whenever you think best."

"If tomorrow is not a good time . . ."

"Tomorrow is a fine time. Tomorrow morning would be fine."

"Tomorrow morning? Yes, well, perhaps that would be fine for you, however, now that I think about it, maybe the afternoon would be better. You see—"

"Yes, yes, fine—we will see you tomorrow afternoon."

"Well, if you would rather I did not come by at all . . ."

"Mariya Ivanchyn, I want you to come tomorrow! I want you to come to my house tomorrow afternoon!" The bridesmaids turned their heads and raised their eyebrows while Vasko flashed a triumphant grin at Paraska.

Mariya Ivanchyn smiled demurely and rested her chin on her shoulder. "Vasyl Rusynko, if you wish for me to come to your home tomorrow afternoon, I accept your invitation. I will go tell my mother and then"—Mariya's eyes widened significantly—"then, I will return." And Mariya faded into the crowd of women clustered around Anna.

Vasyl took a deep breath, ground his jaws together, and then turned to Yevka. "How are you feeling?"

"Better . . . I think."

"You looked ill during the ceremony. I thought that we would—that Petro would have to carry you out of the church."

"It was warm."

"Yes, it was." Vasyl jerked his head toward the group of women. "I don't know why I told Mariya to come tomorrow. Tomorrow will not be a good day."

"The family will be very busy."

"Yes, Yevka, we will be. You know about my father, don't you? Petro told you?"

"Yes."

"You won't tell Anna, will you?"

"Of course not," said Yevka softly. "I'm very sorry about your father."

"Thank you. He was a long time dying. But now he suffers no longer. Do you have the *pysanka* for Anna?"

Yevka retrieved a small box of her own making from her apron and opened the lid, revealing the egg nestled in a bed of straw.

"Yevka, it is beautiful. Anna will be pleased."

Mariya Ivanchyn returned and stood next to Vasyl. "I told my mother—she and I will see you tomorrow afternoon." She inspected the egg in Yevka's hand. "That is a pity," she said.

Vasyl frowned. "What is a pity?"

"The red is too dark. Do you see, Vasyl?" Mariya pressed herself against Vasyl. "It should be lighter. Don't you agree?"

Vasyl disengaged himself. "The red is fine as it is."

"Well, yes, it is close to the proper shade. Now I suppose if you—"

Vasyl whispered to Yevka, "Give the *pysanka* to Petro Kotsur's mother.

She may want it before the dance." As Yevka headed across the room, Vasyl turned his attention to Mariya Ivanchyn, who was still talking.

"—but, then, of course most would not know the difference. *Tsy tak*— isn't that so, Vasyl?"

"Mariya, excuse me. I must go help with the food and drinks."

"Well, then . . . *zavtra*—tomorrow, Vasyl Rusynko."

"What?"

"Oh, Vasyl! How you tease! I am coming tomorrow to fetch my embroidery."

"Oh, yes . . . well, tomorrow, then. Excuse me."

Vasyl returned to the food line, where the smug Vasko grinned at him knowingly. Vasyl pointed a finger in his friend's face. "Do not speak to me about Mariya or anyone else. Do not say a word—not one word."

In the middle of the room, Ivan Ivanchyn was trying unsuccessfully to call everyone's attention. "Brothers and sisters! Brothers and sisters! Quiet, please. Please be quiet!"

"EVERYONE—QUIET!" boomed a voice from the corner.

"Yes, thank you, Paraska—very nice. Brothers and sisters, it is time for the *ryadovi*—the bridal dance! Where is Petro Kotsur? He must be first. There he is! Some room, brothers! The rest of you line up and have your coins ready for the bride. Where is the bride?"

"A moment more, honorable *starosta*!" cried Paraska.

In the corner Petro Kotsur's mother inserted Yevka's *pysanka* down the front of Anna's dress, between her breasts, saying, "May you give birth as easily as this egg passes to the floor." Anna shimmied and the brides-maids giggled while Yevka and Paraska held a pillow at the foot of Anna's dress to cushion the *pysanka*'s fall. The bridesmaids clapped and Paraska whispered in Anna's ear. Anna gasped, covering her mouth, and convuls-ing in progressively louder giggles while Paraska threw back her head and howled. Yevka replaced the egg in the little box, tied the yarn, and gave it to Anna.

"Now, lovely Anna, your groom awaits you!" declared Ivan Ivanchyn. Come, Petro, dance with your bride. Musicians, play them a *chardash*!" Come, brothers! Bring your coins. Buy a dance with the bride. The line begins be-hind me!"

☙

Sitting in a corner of the tavern, Vasko, his eyes half-closed, swayed to the music of Pavlo Vantsa and his band of fiddlers. Vasyl slid onto the bench and tapped his friend on the shoulder. "Come, Vasko. It is time to go."

"I am in love, Vasyl. Do not bother me now."

"You are drunk."

"I am in love."

"*Dobre*—good, you are drunk and in love. Let's go."

"I am in love with the woman I married. LOOK AT HER, VASYL!" Across the room, Paraska turned her head and frowned at her husband. Vasko opened his eyes wide and worked his eyebrows up and down. Paraska turned away in disgust but suppressed a smile as she busied herself with Yevka at the banquet table.

"You are drunk and in love, Vasko. Come," insisted Vasyl.

"Yes, only so are you, but I do not go about bothering you. Why do you say nothing, honest Vasyl? You know I am right. But, Vasyl, you should either be drunk or in love but never both at the same time."

"Friend, you are drunk and in love at the same time."

"I am drunk with love . . . with love, Vasyl . . . with love. You are drunk with brandy and with love. You must decide between one or the other . . . it cannot be both."

"Then I must decide for love, my friend."

"Ha! You must first be sober to make a decision like that. Wait until tomorrow. Wait and then make your choice," said Vasko winking.

"My choice will still be for love, my friend."

"Yes, but Vasyl, who will it be?"

"What?"

"Who will it be? Mariya Ivanchyn"—Vasko nodded as he said the name—"or Mariya Kavulya?" Vasko shuddered and made a horrible face.

Vasyl watched Yevka and Paraska gather the remaining food. "Neither. I already told you. I choose love."

"But, Vasyl, to choose love one must have someone to love. You cannot be in love with no one. It would be like having a bag of salt but no meat to shake it on."

"Yes, I see."

"Then which 'Mariya' is it?"

"Neither."

"Then there is someone else! Who is it, Vasyl? Tell me."

"There is no one. Believe me, Vasko . . . I wish there were. Come, it is time to escort the bride and groom home."

Most of the guests spilled out of the tavern behind the musicians, while a few remained inside to finish their food and drink.

Vasko pointed at Yurko, who, spoon in hand, sat near the banquet table hunched over another plate of food. "Look, Vasyl. For Yurko there are no difficult choices. As long as there is food, he is happy!"

Across from Yurko sat Old Mykhal, who now bore Vasko's scrutiny. The old man eyed Vasko nervously, shifted in his seat, and took a sip of his drink. Vasko watched intently as the old man swallowed.

Old Mykhal put the mug down and squinted at Vasko. "What the devil are you looking at?" he asked Vasko.

"Blasphemer!" cried Vasko.

"W-what?" stammered the old man.

"Blasphemer! Where is Father Yaroslav! He should see this. Have you not read the Gospels, old man?"

"Well . . . I . . ."

"It is plainly written for those of us who have eyes to read. The Lord was very strict on this matter. Did He not warn against pouring new wine into old wineskins? Give me that." Vasko grabbed the old man's drink and tossed it back in one swallow. "Be warned, old man. Be warned! Come, Vasyl. This is no place for an honest man like you." And Vasko and Vasyl walked out of the tavern.

Old Mykhal sat silently working his lips, eventually shaking his fist and sputtering, "Feh!"

The remaining guests filed out of the tavern, leaving Yurko and the old man alone. Old Mykhal wiped his mouth with his sleeve and went to the door, beckoning to Yurko. "Come. They are escorting Petro and Anna. We will be late."

Yurko finished his food and rose to leave, running his tongue around the inside of his mouth and with loud sucking sounds dislodging pieces of meat wedged between his teeth.

❧

The night wore on. Outside Petro Kotsur's hut, Vasko led the men in singing ribald songs about wedding nights and related matters. Anna eventually lost patience for this time-honored convention and appeared at the front door, shaking her fist at Vasko and threatening him with one of her newly acquired cooking implements. Vasko sang louder:

> *On the wedding night, the couple never sleeps;*
> *On the wedding night, the village lies awake;*
> *On the wedding night, the forest is restless;*
> *Everyone stares in the darkness wondering:*
> *Will the bed hold out?*
> *Will the floor hold up?*
> *Will the walls cave in?*

Someone yelled from a neighboring hut that perhaps Anna was right— perhaps it was time to go home—time to go stoke the morning fire, because, as any fool could plainly see, the trees above the valley were already outlined by the light of dawn. Vasko yelled mighty oaths and invited his entourage to join him in a sound thrashing of the godless neighbor. Vasyl and Yurko restrained their friend, the other men gathered closer, and the inevitable scuffle ensued accompanied by many a shouted *"oi"* and *"Bozhe moi"* and one explosive "ANTICHRIST!" It ended quickly with the sound of a loud slap and Yurko's lanky shape running away into the darkness. The men dispersed, leaving Vasyl and Shtefan Rozum to bear home the bleeding, whimpering Vasko.

Not long after, the sun came up on the first day of Anna and Petro Kotsur's life together. Later in the morning, a few of the women, including Paraska and Yevka, returned to the tavern to finish cleaning. Finding Yurko asleep on a bench, they roused him, gave him a bowl of kasha, and sat him in a corner, out of the way, where he was content to eat and watch the women work.

Two days later the patriarch of the Rusynko family was buried in the family plot next to his children Palko and Helenka. Old Mykhal spent three nights sleeping in Yakov's tavern and remained in the village until the morning after the funeral. Before leaving, the old man removed his hat, wordlessly squeezed Vasyl's hand, and made his way to his old cart to begin the journey up the valley to Ondavka and Bekherov. There was much to share with the people of those villages. The old man packed his pipe with some of Vasyl's tobacco and rode out of Stara Polyanka, ringing his bell and rehearsing his narration of the last few days' events to the horse, Sasha.

The following week, the first week of *Velykŷi Post*—Great Lent, Yevka gave birth to a boy whom she named Daniyl—Danko. Ten days later Old Mykhal returned to Stara Polyanka and picked up a passenger bound for Ameryka. Petro Rusynko carried little with him for his journey and said nothing when Vasyl handed him a hand-drawn map showing routes into Galicia and Poland, where he would be least likely to encounter border guards. On the back of the map, Vasyl wrote their uncle Pavlo's address in Yonkers. When *Mamka* asked Petro how long it would be before he sent for Yevka and Danko, Petro merely shrugged. He said brief, perfunctory farewells to his wife and son and then climbed aboard Old Mykhal's cart. Sasha strained forward and the old man gave a belated toss of the reins. Petro, smoking his pipe, swayed in his seat next to Old Mykhal as the old man related the gossip of the surrounding villages.

The weeks passed, the days grew warmer, and the swallows, heralding spring's arrival, returned to Stara Polyanka. On *Velykden*—Easter Sunday— the people gathered in the Church of the Protection of the Mother of God, where they celebrated the Resurrection of the Lord and sang the triumphal, *"Khrystos voskrese!"*—"Christ is risen!" After the service Father Yaroslav blessed each family's Easter basket of bread, cheese, ham, sausage, salt, horseradish, and brightly dyed *pysankŷ*.

When the time came for the first cutting in the hills around the village, the men mowed the grass with their scythes and the women followed with pitchforks, turning the grass to dry in the sun. Later the hay was stacked against tall poles erected in the fields. As summer came the men coaxed life from the earth and tended their fields of wheat, rye, corn, and potatoes. In the huts, the women cared for the very young and the very old as they had for centuries.

Men and women, beasts and birds, and all other things filled with the breath of life basked in the warmth of holy creation. At night a million stars flickered feverishly, and, with the new dawn, popped and died like spent candles.

That change could come to such a world was unimaginable.

CHAPTER FOURTEEN

The Wagon

ANDRII, home from Pryashev for the summer, saw the wagon as he descended from one of the upper fields south of the village. Drawn by four horses and carrying three men, the wagon rolled slowly up the valley toward Stara Polyanka. Andrii stopped and shielded his eyes from the midday sun. The men were officials—Magyar officials; their dress, their hats, identified them. They were an unusual sight—something was wrong. Andrii quickened his step, then discarded his hoe and began to jog back to the village. When he reached the south end of the cemetery he began to run, leaping over tombstones and wooden crosses as he raced toward his home.

⁂

Paraska was in front of her hut, throwing seed to the chickens, when she saw the runner in the cemetery. "Yevka!" she cried. "Come outside!" Yevka emerged from the hut carrying Danko in her left arm. "Look up there," said Paraska pointing halfway up the side of the valley. "Your eyes are better than mine. Who is that fool jumping over the graves like a mad dog?"

Yevka squinted across the little valley. "It is Andrii—Andrii Rusynko."

"Are you sure?"

"Yes."

"What the devil is wrong with him? Is there a fire?"

Yevka glanced up the valley and shook her head. "I see no smoke. Look. He is going to the Rusynko place."

"Yevka, I don't like this."

Yevka pointed out a group of villagers gathering near the tavern, and, at that moment, a large wagon came into view. The little drama was attracting more actors. Now Father Yaroslav came hurrying down from his house, adjusting his overcoat.

Yevka saw another runner—this one broke out of the crowd near the tavern and raced up the path to the Rusynko homestead. "Look, Paraska. It is Yurko."

Paraska threw the rest of the feed to the chickens and brushed off her hands. "I'm going to see about this. I don't like it. I don't know where Vasko is—I don't like this sort of thing happening when I don't know where he is."

Yevka held her sister's arm. "Wait—look."

There was activity at the Rusynko place. The Rusynko women, *Mamka* and *Baba,* were stepping outside just as the two runners, Yurko and Andrii, converged simultaneously at the Rusynko hut. Andrii spoke with Yurko and then gesticulated first toward the wagon parked in front of the tavern and then toward the hills on the other side of the river. Yurko jogged off and then, prompted by Andrii's shouts, quickened his pace. Now Andrii himself ran along the path that led straight to Paraska and Yevka. The two women hurried down to meet him, Paraska in the lead with Yevka following close behind, holding Danko close to her chest.

"Andrii," cried Paraska. "Where is Vasko?"

Andrii, winded and red-faced, looked out over the valley. "I am not sure. I think he and Vasyl are working in Pan Kapishinskii's fields across the Ondava. I don't know . . . I think . . ."

Paraska grabbed Andrii's arm and squeezed. "What is it? What is happening?"

Andrii pointed to the wagon, now stopped in front of the tavern and surrounded by villagers. "Those are men from the army."

Paraska groaned. *"Bozhe moi!"*

Yevka rocked Danko tightly between her breasts. *"Oi Bozhe, moi Bozhe!"*

Andrii scanned the fields across the river. "I sent Yurko to find Vasyl and Vasko. It is a draft . . . a draft for the army."

❧

Vasyl and Vasko sat in the shade of a large oak tree. The leaves rustled overhead and Pan Kapishinskii's grain undulated in a light breeze.

"Honest Vasyl, tell me what you think. I want to know."

Vasyl waved aside Vasko's question. "You should ask Andrii these things. He is the scholar in the family."

"Andrii is a boy."

"Yes, but he knows better the things you ask. Ask him."

"I have asked him these things."

Vasyl reclined on the grass and yawned. "Well?"

"I don't understand his answers."

"Keep asking. He will explain if you persist."

"But Vasyl, what does it mean, to live even if one dies? At your father's funeral, Father Yaroslav told us that *Khrystos* said, 'I am the resurrection and the life; whoever believes in me, lives though he dies.'"

Vasyl finished the passage. "'And all who live and believe in me will never die.'"

"Yes, that is true. But Vasyl, what does it mean? How can one live even if he dies, *and* live and believe and never die?"

"Ask Andrii."

"Do you believe, Vasyl?"

"Believe what?"

"In eternal life?"

"Of course."

"But your father died and my father died, and they believed and yet they are dead."

"They are dead to this world."

"Are they in Heaven now?"

"If not now, then I suppose someday they will be. Only God knows."

"Vasyl, do you think Pan Kapishinskii will ever go to Heaven?"

"Only God knows. Why?"

"Father Yaroslav says it is easier for a camel to pass through the eye of a needle than it is for a rich man to enter Heaven. Pan Kapishinskii is a very rich man. But, Vasyl, what is a camel?"

"I have no idea. Ask Andrii."

"I did. He said he thinks it is an animal—like a horse."

"Well, then, there you are."

"But Vasyl, what if a camel is more like a flea?"

"What if it is?"

"Then Pan Kapishinskii has nothing to worry about."

Vasyl laughed. "I don't think the Lord had fleas in mind when he spoke of the rich. But when I see Pan Kapishinskii I will explain to him that you know he is assured of eternal life!"

"But, Vasyl, what is eternity?"

"It is forever, friend."

"Will it look like this?" Vasko swept his hands out over the valley.

"Ask Andrii."

"Will we look like we do now?"

"Ask Andrii."

Vasko paused. "Will there be women?"

Vasyl frowned. "Not the way you are thinking." Then Vasyl grinned. "But Paraska will be there."

Vasko paled. "Forever?"

"Yes, by your side . . ."

Vasko wrinkled his nose.

". . . forever . . ."

Vasko shifted on the grass.

". . . and ever . . ."

Vasko filled his cheeks with air.

". . . amen."

Vasko emptied his cheeks like a snorting horse. "But Vasyl, what will we do forever?"

"You won't do anything."

"Then what is the point?"

"Ask Andrii."

Still dissatisfied, Vasko reclined on his elbows and then, suddenly laughing, he pointed down the hill. "Look, where Yurko comes running. I thought he only moved that fast going to Yakov's tavern! Yurko! Yakov's is the other way!"

Vasyl chuckled but then stood and frowned. "Something is wrong."

Yurko stopped and beckoned to the two men, then turned and hurried back down the hill toward the village.

"Something is wrong," said Vasyl working his jaw. "Come, let us follow."

$$\text{\emph{e}}\text{\emph{\textasciitilde}}\text{\emph{o}}$$

Inside the Rusynko hut, Yevka sat at the table, rocking Danko and humming a nondescript tune. Her mother-in-law sat next to her, staring at the opposite wall. *Baba* stood by the hearth, her chin cupped in one hand. Paraska padded around the room and Andrii maintained a vigil at the doorway.

Andrii straightened. "I see them," he said and hurried down the path with

Paraska close behind him. *Mamka* went to her mother's side by the hearth and placed an arm around her shoulders.

"Where is my Vasyl?" asked *Baba*.

"He is coming," reassured *Mamka*.

"Where is Petro?" asked *Baba*.

Mamka frowned. "He left weeks ago. He went to Ameryka. You know that."

Baba shook her head slowly. "He should not have left." Then her face brightened. "My Vasyl!"

Vasyl entered the hut followed by Paraska, Vasko, and Andrii. *Baba* tottered to Vasyl's side and drew his right arm around her shoulders. Vasyl fixed his dark eyes on his mother and cleared his throat. "I was just speaking with Father Yaroslav. It seems that our Emperor's army is short several men." He attempted to laugh but coughed instead. "The gentlemen who have come to our village today are here to correct that shortage."

Baba pressed closer to her grandson. "*Bozhe moi!* My Vasyl, what will you do?"

Vasyl tightened his grip on *Baba*'s shoulders. "I will say good-bye . . . for now. Four names were called: Vasko, Yurko, Shtefan Guzii . . . and . . . me. When Shtefan heard that his name had been called, he went out the back of his barn and ran into the hills." Vasyl paused and looked at Yevka. "Petro was right. He knew this day would come."

The women looked at one another, blinking, trying to comprehend. Vasko leaned against the wall and stared at his boots. Yurko's form filled the doorway and he gestured to Vasyl, who, along with Andrii and Vasko, followed him outside.

Father Yaroslav came up the path, wheezing and wiping his forehead with a handkerchief. "Vasyl, they will eat in the tavern while you prepare to leave. That is all the time they will allow. They say that this is a general mobilization and that war is very likely. The latest news from Vienna is bad, Vasyl—very bad."

"Then I suppose . . . I suppose I should say good-bye," said an ashen Vasyl. He reentered the hut, passing Paraska, who stood in the doorway shaking her head and mumbling, "*Ni, ni*—no, no." After several moments, Vasyl, frowning and agitated, reemerged from the hut. "Where is *Baba*?" he asked of no one in particular. "She is not inside." He went around to the back of the hut and found his grandmother standing behind the barn, staring up the valley.

"*Babo* . . . I . . . I must go . . ." said Vasyl. Against the barn his *baba* looked small and insignificant. This was the woman who had long ago borne Vasyl and his brothers and sisters variously on her back on excursions to the woods to collect berries or mushrooms. It was she who made them aware of the beauty of the valley; it was she who taught them songs about the shepherds, the trees, and the healing waters of *Potok* Ondava—the Ondava Stream.

"*Babo* . . . I . . ."

"I will never see you again," murmured *Baba*.

Vasyl shuddered. He placed a hand on her shoulder and squeezed lightly. Her body was bony and frail. "*Babo* . . . I . . ."

"*Z Bohom*—go with God, Vasyl."

Vasyl left his *baba* next to the barn. When he took one last look at her, she was still gazing at the forest above the valley.

⌘

By the well in front of the tavern, the older men mingled and spoke in low voices, stealing glances at the wagon and the Magyar guard. Then the men nudged one another and pointed to the procession coming down the hill. First came Vasyl and Vasko, followed by Yurko, and finally, the Magyars and Father Yaroslav. Farther up the road, a pallid huddle—Paraska, Andrii, and Yevka clutching Danko—staggered after the men.

Yurko hoisted himself aboard the wagon. Vasko was poised to board next but blanched when Paraska shrieked, her unearthly scream piercing the silent vigil surrounding the wagon. Vasko, his face wild, turned around and shuffled toward his wife. Paraska broke free from Andrii, who had intended not to restrain her but rather to support her. Paraska enveloped Vasko in her arms and he buried his head on her chest.

As Father Yaroslav and Andrii Khudyk gently separated Vasko from Paraska, Vasyl embraced his brother. "Go back, Andriik—. . . go back, Andrii. Go back to *Mamka* . . . you are now the *gazda*—the head of the household. Help her all you can and tell her I will return." Vasko climbed aboard the wagon and held out a helping hand for Vasyl. "Go now, Andrii," said Vasyl, climbing aboard and taking a seat next to Vasko. "Tell *Mamka* I will see her again as soon as I can. Go to her now—she needs you."

Andrii, grateful for the instructions, nodded and ran back to the Rusynko hut. In his place now stood Yevka. Vasyl smiled at her—a modest smile, no more than the slight, downward turn of the corners of his mouth. Yevka returned the smile; and then, silently, her lips formed the benediction, "*Z Bohom*—go with God."

The wagon jerked forward and the men's heads bobbed in unison. Paraska's dreadful wail again split the valley and Vasko hid his face in his hands. Vasyl and Yevka maintained their mutual gaze until the wagon passed out of the village. Then Yevka, with determined strides and a tight hold around Danko, made her way to the trail above the road. From a clearing in the trees, she watched the wagon rock and bounce down the valley and out of sight.

☙

His bladder relieved, Old Mykhal buttoned his trousers and made his way back to the road. Watching his master emerge from the bushes, Sasha stood stoically harnessed to the ancient cart, his gray lower lip quivering as though mildly amused that one of them, after so many years, should exhibit any form of modesty.

"Sasha, tonight you shall sleep in a barn," said Old Mykhal, crossing himself and bowing to the wayside crucifix. "Bohdan, the smith, will look after your hoof, and I will sleep well at Yakov's tavern. Yes, and we may even see Vasyl tonight. He will know what to make of the news. He's a worldly man—he's been to Ameryka. He certainly knows more than the men in Yalynky and Niklova. They've never even been to Bardeyov!" In the villages of Yalynky and Niklova, the men had shared disturbing news with Old Mykhal: the Emperor's nephew and heir-apparent, Archduke Franz Ferdinand, had been shot, along with his wife, in the backseat of some sort of vehicle while they were touring some part of the empire where there were certain men who looked unfavorably upon the Emperor or his heir or both. Then the men in the villages had stroked their chins and told Old Mykhal that wagons bearing men from the army had been sighted on local roads.

Old Mykhal climbed into the seat of the cart and grasped the reins. He gave them a shake, and, when nothing happened, he shook them again, aiming an irritated wrinkle of the eyebrows at the back of Sasha's head. The horse, however, merely twitched his ears and stared intently at the path that led to Stara Polyanka. Then, from behind a stand of oak trees at a bend in the path, there appeared a large wagon drawn by four draft horses. The enormous horses considered the smaller Sasha briefly and then ambled down the road, nodding their massive heads. Only the passengers in the back of the wagon were familiar to Old Mykhal: Vasyl, Yurko, and Vasko, who, for once, seemed not to notice the old man. Among the passengers, only Vasyl acknowledged the old man, and then, only with a furrowed brow and a shake of the head. The wagon rolled slowly southward toward the lowlands.

So perplexed was Old Mykhal by this event that he sat mutely atop his cart, scratching his cheek. When he realized that his cart was moving he gave Sasha's reins a commanding toss. The cart rumbled up the trail toward Stara Polyanka and disappeared behind the oak trees.

The only remaining sign of life along this lonely little stretch of road was in the air above, where a falcon drifted slowly in the clear blue sky.

PART TWO

The Royal Door

Can you drink the cup that I am going to drink?

MATTHEW 20

CHAPTER FIFTEEN

The Pass

IN THE MIDDLE of a hot August afternoon on the Hungarian plain, a crush of peasants, black-garbed Jews, and local townspeople fanned themselves on a sparsely shaded train station platform. Working his way among the sweltering crowd, a lone peddler hawked sunflower seeds. For a small coin the peddler dipped a tin cup into a canvas bag he carried over his shoulder, scooped up the black seeds, and poured them into his customer's open hands or pockets. The peddler sold seeds from one end of the platform to the other and then back again; and when his bag was empty, he trotted behind the station to his wagon, where his son watered and fed their horse. From the back of the wagon the peddler filled his bag with more of the seeds from his vast supply and then hurried back to the platform to resume his lucrative business.

At the sound of a distant locomotive whistle, the people on the platform craned their necks for a view of a train approaching from the west. When they discerned uniformed figures leaning from the boxcars and carriages, the people shook their heads muttering, "Military," and spat the remains of their sunflower seeds onto the expanding piles of shells in the sun. The train rumbled through the station bound for Galicia, its cargo of men waving their caps at the sea of sullen, upturned faces. As the train, enveloped in dark gray smoke, receded from view, the civilians on the platform turned their heads to the west in anticipation of another train. The peddler continued hawking his seeds, and the coins jingled in his pocket as he walked.

Soon another train appeared and the crowd again craned their necks in anticipation. The peddler, at his wagon filling his bag with another load of seeds, smiled when he heard the exasperated groans of "Military" emanating from the platform. He returned to the platform in time to see the last carriage of waving soldiers pass through the station.

And so, the afternoon passed and the piles of sunflower shells grew as another military train, and another, and yet another passed through the station. The people began to drift away to their homes and businesses, despairing of making their journeys that day. A few resolute souls remained, squinting in the low western sun and blowing sunflower shells through their lips. The peddler, having made his last sale, folded his empty bag, climbed onto his cart next to his son, and drove home.

At last a train appeared from the west, slowing as it approached the station. There were no soldiers on this train, only grim-faced civilians filling every seat and standing in the aisles and open passageways between the carriages. The train stopped and the scattered few on the platform mounted its iron steps, pressing their way into the carriages. With the blast of a steam whistle, the long train chugged slowly out of the station.

Piles of sunflower shells littered the deserted station platform. As the sun set, a cooling breeze out of the distant Carpathian Mountains swirled softly across the platform, chasing scattered sunflower shells into the larger piles. Cumulous clouds, pink orange on the horizon, towered over the Carpathian Mountains.

Another train, this one shorter than previous trains but moving much faster, approached from the west. Flags bearing the insignia of the Austrian High Command fluttered wildly from the churning locomotive. The train roared through the empty station and, in its turbulent wake, swept the sunflower husks from the platform, scattering them onto the oily tracks and among the wheat stalks in the adjacent fields.

❧

A gray mist hovered over the Carpathian mountain pass. It had rained intermittently all morning, rendering the air heavy with the odor of saturated earth and dripping vegetation. The rail line from the lowlands branched into several sidings below the pass, and railroad workers moved among the smoking locomotives and wooden boxcars of idling trains. A switchman and a section manager for the railroad stood next to an immense locomotive, speaking Hungarian to one another in low voices.

"What time is it?" asked the switchman.

"Earlier than it looks—thirteen hundred. This train must be sided soon," said the section manager shaking his head. "We must tell them . . . soon."

"*You* must tell them. I am only a switchman. They are with the *Honvéd*—Royal Hungarian Army—and they are determined to have their way—especially the captain."

"Yes, he will want to pull the entire train across with one locomotive," said the section manager frowning. "Look at him there with his officers. They are speaking with János, the engineer. What does János know? They should be speaking with me."

The switchman shook his head. "Even János should know that this train must be split into two. A train this length must not be taken through the pass."

"You and I know this. But the army always wants things its own way, doesn't it? What does the army care about the proper use of locomotives, track, and rolling stock? The whole army is in a hurry to get to Galicia—that is all they care about. Did you hear what I told that pompous major this morning?"

"The cavalry major? The one with the trainload of horses?"

"Yes, that one."

"What did you tell him?"

"He said his train had to be in Galicia this afternoon and that if I continued to delay him it would be my fault if the Russians came pouring through the pass tonight. I told him that if he derailed his train in the pass he would not get into Galicia, and that the Russians then would be blocked from pouring through the mountains into Hungary, and that the war would be over before it could begin."

The switchman laughed. "What did he say?"

"What could he say? It was the truth. We split his train in two and sent him and his troopers and his horses on their way with a delay made twice as long as necessary by that obstinate major. By now he is in Galicia and, no doubt, on his way to Russia. May he find all the Russian enemies he desires."

The switchman spat on the tracks. "They care only for their precious cargo and their damn timetables. They care nothing about proper procedure."

A whistle blew and the two men looked down the track, where a dark ash cloud billowed just above the trees. "Another military train from Kassa," said the section manager. "Put it over there, on the second track. Soon we will run out of sidings."

The switchman trotted off and the section manager approached the captain and other *Honvéd* officers gathered around the engineer, János. "Captain, we must split this train," insisted the section manager.

The captain placed his left fist on his hip and hooked his right thumb over his leather holster. "Your engineer seems to think that one locomotive might be sufficient to make the crossing into Galicia." The other officers stared at the section manager, awaiting his reply, while, behind the captain's back, the wide-eyed János shook his head vigorously and raised his palms skyward. "I think we should consider his experience in these matters," continued the captain.

The section manager bowed slightly and smiled. "Yes, János is a great engineer who has mastered the smooth, level run from Budapest to Szeged. He is a peacetime engineer pressed into wartime service and he is in the high Beskyd Mountains now, not the Great *Alföld*—the Hungarian Plain. We can get half your train across now and the other half later; or, we can move the entire train to another siding and take it in two sections as soon as we find you another locomotive. There is no other way."

The switchman ran toward them across the tracks, calling out, "The colonel wants to know why there is a delay with this train!"

The captain sighed and motioned to the section manager, saying, "Will you please come with me? I may need your help explaining this." The two men, with the remaining officers in tow, made their way across the tracks to the waiting colonel while János scrambled up the ladder to the sanctuary of his locomotive cab.

The switchman chuckled as he sat on the bottom step of the locomotive's tender and filled his pipe with tobacco. Not far away, leaning against the tender, was a *Honvéd* infantryman from the train, holding in his hand a small kettle. The soldier's gray uniform was highlighted by distinctive Hungarian yellow lace winding on the upper thighs and running down the outside of the pant legs, and by a red First Class marksman's lanyard suspended from his left shoulder strap. His black-billed gray cap was adorned with a small metal cockade bearing the royal monogram, "1FJ"—Franz Josef I. The starless collar identified the infantryman as a private.

The switchman nodded a greeting at the soldier and then, noting the kettle, jerked his head toward the locomotive. "You want hot water? They will get you hot water."

The infantryman touched his cap and approached one of the firemen, whom he addressed in Magyar with a heavy Slavic accent. "*Van meleg víz?*—Is there hot water?"

The firemen pulled a rag from his back pocket, directed the soldier to hold the kettle just so, and opened a valve, filling the container with steaming water.

The infantryman covered the kettle with a wooden plug and, touching the brim of his cap, said, "*Köszönöm*—thanks." He walked back to the long line of boxcars, nodding at the switchman as he passed.

☙

"Vasyl! Did you get hot water?" cried Vasko.

Nodding, Vasyl held the little kettle aloft.

Vasko stuck his head back in the railcar, exulting, "I told you that he would get us hot water!" Vasko jumped from the boxcar and jogged to Vasyl's side. "Let me carry the water, Vasyl. *Oi!* It is hot! Why did you not tell me it was so hot?"

Vasyl slapped away Vasko's hand. "No. You will spill it. Since when is it necessary to tell you that hot water is hot? Stop. I told you I would carry it."

"Yes, Vasyl—yes, of course. Now, what did you learn? You were there at the front of the train for a long time. What did they say? Will we be here all day?"

"Hop up there and take this . . . BY THE HANDLE . . . now set it down before you spill it." Vasyl pulled himself up into the boxcar and then he and Vasko set about to make coffee.

"Rusynko! Did you bring enough water for everyone else?" The voice was deep and came from beneath a cap covering the face of a large soldier lying on the boxcar floor near the sliding door.

Vasyl did not look up, but continued to prepare his coffee. "No, Varkhol. I filled this little kettle with only enough water for two men. If you would like hot water for yourself, I will tell you of a place where there is always enough hot water, even for you."

Vasko snickered and slapped Vasyl on the shoulder. "That is good, Vasyl. Tell him where to go to get all the hot water he could ever want."

Varkhol pushed his cap back on his head and stood looming over Vasyl. "Yes, tell me where to go."

At that moment, the company's first sergeant, Sergeant Haletskii, walked up to the open door and shouted, "Everyone off the train! We may be here until nightfall! Varkhol! You and Kravets, come back to the kitchen car and help unload the stew wagons. The rest of you—" He eyed Vasyl and Vasko and their kettle. "Where did you get the hot water, Rusynko?"

"The locomotive boiler."

Sergeant Haletskii raised his eyebrows. "Good thinking. Varkhol, Kravets, follow me."

Varkhol glared at Vasyl, who lifted his mug as in a toast. Vasko snickered again. "Varkhol is the devil. Do not turn your back on him, Vasyl. Only, tell me, what did you learn? The sergeant says we may be here till nightfall."

"Yes," said Vasyl. "I think we may stay here well after dark."

"*Bozhe moi*—my God—Vasyl! More waiting! We could have walked to Galicia by now!"

Vasyl grinned. "Don't be so impatient. The army knows what is good for you. Come, let us get off the train." The two men jumped down onto the ballast and then retrieved their tin cups from the floor of the boxcar. Vasyl pointed across the tracks. "Look there—do you see the colonel and the captain? I think that they want to take this train to the north across the mountains and into Galicia with only one locomotive. Only, I'm not sure. My Magyar is not very good. There are many trains passing north and south—maybe that causes delays. I don't know."

Several men from the same boxcar gathered around, and one of them, Petro Matsko from Tsigla, spoke up. "Is it possible, Vasyl? Can one locomotive pull such a train?"

Vasyl shrugged. "Last year I rode a freight train across the mountains from Krosno and it had to be broken in two for the pass."

Vasko stepped in front of Vasyl, puffed out his chest, and threw a thumb over his shoulder. "Ask him why he was coming down from Krosno." The men looked mutely from Vasko to Vasyl and back again. "Tell them, Vasyl," said Vasko. "Tell them why you were in Krosno."

"I was passing through on my way from Hamburg."

Vasko addressed the men while indicating Vasyl with a sweeping gesture. "He was coming back from Ameryka. He lived and worked in Ameryka for four years, and when he returned he brought Amerykan money with him and bought brandy and whiskey for everyone at Yakov's, our tavern in Stara Polyanka."

The men squinted at Vasyl, who shrugged and explained. "I brought home money for my family. My father was going to buy land in our village."

Mykhal Slyvka from Výshnii Verlykh shook his head in disgust. "A fellow in our village went to Ameryka, came back, and bought land and built a big house. Then another went and did the same thing and soon the price of land became too high for honest farmers. These men changed. They became too important for their friends. I wish they had stayed in Ameryka."

"I can tell you I would have stayed in Ameryka," said Petro Roman from

Komlosha. "Men who come back from Ameryka have money. I would never leave a place where there was that much money."

The men stared at Vasyl in silence until Petro Matsko jerked his head toward the locomotive and addressed Mykhal Slyvka and Petro Roman. "Come, let's get hot water."

Vasyl and Vasko followed the men and stood back studying the massive locomotive. Wisps of steam emanated from a dozen valves and the faces of the two men in the cab glowed in the red light of the open firebox. Somewhere deep inside the locomotive a valve opened and closed, paused, and opened and closed repeatedly, its snapping rhythm punctuated by little bursts of steam from the dark, dripping underbelly.

Vasko sipped his coffee and then flourished his free hand impatiently. "How do men build such a thing as this? How do they know what to do?"

Vasyl drank his coffee and wiped his mouth with his sleeve. "There are men who know what is to be built and they direct other men to build it."

"Why don't they build it themselves if they know what to do?"

"Because there are bosses and there are workers. Pan Kapishinskii doesn't work his own fields—we do. He is the boss and we are the workers."

"But, Vasyl, Pan Kapishinskii could work the fields if he wanted to or had to."

"Yes, but he has money and can afford to pay men like us to do his work."

"If I had money I would still want to do some of the work. That would leave more money for me."

"If you had money, you would spend it all at Yakov's tavern."

"No, honest Vasyl. If I had money I would buy one of those great stone statues like the ones we saw in the cemeteries in Kassa."

"They are for the wealthy, my friend."

"Yes, and I would have my name carved in the stone in big letters: Ivanchyn."

"You wouldn't be able to read it."

"I could. I can read my own name, Vasyl. Besides, I would be dead. What need would I have for reading then?"

Vasyl finished his coffee and shook the remaining drops out on the ground. "Well that is true. You certainly haven't needed it so far."

"No, I haven't. You read, Vasyl. What has reading gained for you?"

Vasyl scratched the whiskers on his left cheek. "Well, I got on the right boat going to Ameryka and I got on the right boat coming back. That is something, I suppose."

"Ha, Vasyl, ha! Better that you never learned to read, then, and better that you never went to Ameryka. What did Ameryka do for you? Look, another train."

A train approached from the north—from Galicia—and the section manager directed it to a siding in front of Vasyl and Vasko. This was a passenger train, not a military train, and through the windows weary civilians gazed blankly at the two infantrymen standing outside the car. At the bottom of one window a small boy pressed his hands and face to the glass. Vasko removed his hat, swept it to his chest, and bowed his head. The boy's mouth opened slightly and he turned to speak to a woman sitting nearby.

Vasko grinned at Vasyl, who muttered, "Refugees."

"Where are they going, Vasyl?"

"God only knows—Budapest—Vienna—Pozsony."

"Why would they leave their homes?"

"I don't know. Perhaps their homes were destroyed. Maybe the war has started."

"I would stay and protect my home—wouldn't you, Vasyl?"

"Yes, I suppose I would. Let's go eat."

As the two men walked back toward their own train, Vasko glanced back to see the boy, whose features were now blurred by condensation on the window.

❧

"I think your friend Yurko is looking for you," said a smiling Sergeant Haletskii, who was leaning against one of the boxcars and munching on bread. "Tell me, Rusynko, was it wise to put him with the stew wagons? I never saw anyone eat like he does."

"He has always been a big eater, Sergeant," explained Vasyl.

"I've never seen anyone eat like that. At least he waits until everyone else has eaten. Go on, he hasn't seen you two all day."

Vasyl and Vasko made their way to the back of the train, where they found Yurko serving the men clustered around the steaming pots.

Vasko called out. "Yurko! Don't pour any stew down your gullet yet. There are still two very important mouths to feed."

Vasyl and Vasko produced their tins and handed them to Yurko. "Don't serve to me from the top," said Vasko. "Stir that good meat up from the bottom. Yes, that's it. Now see if you can do the same for Vasyl here."

Vasyl held out his tin for Yurko to fill. "Thank you, Yurko. You are a good man." Vasyl followed Vasko to the end of the wagon, where they set their plates on an inverted crate. Raising his voice above the murmurs from the small groups of men, Vasyl continued, "Yes, Vasko, as I was saying, Yurko is a good man! He takes good care of us! This stew, for instance, is going to be especially good. Do you know why?" Vasko shrugged and the assembled men waited for the explanation, their spoons poised in midair. "Because, Vasko, when Yurko stirred this stew, he USED BOTH HANDS!"

The men laughed and Petro Matsko slapped Vasyl on the back. Even Varkhol stood and stomped his foot, snorting and raising his cup in a toast to Vasyl. Vasko reddened and chuckled self-consciously as he, too, recalled a warm day near Kassa many weeks earlier.

On that day a drill corporal was introducing the men to riflery and was dismayed to learn that many of the men could not tell him if they were right-handed or left-handed. Before the corporal, there towered a placid, vacant-eyed soldier.

The corporal shouted up into the tall man's nostrils. "Can you write?"

No answer.

After a pause, a soldier with a tenor voice sang out from the group of men. "He can't write, Corporal!"

The corporal continued to stare at the tall soldier. "Can't you talk?"

No answer.

The tenor again: "He doesn't say much, Corporal!"

The corporal stared into the soldier's nostrils and then smiled. He backed away and searched the ground for an appropriate stone. Finding one, he picked it up and held it aloft for the tall man to see; then he tossed it to him with an underhand motion. The stone struck the soldier in the chest and dropped to the ground.

The tenor sang out again: "He can't catch either, Corporal!"

The men snickered and the corporal, his face reddening, stepped closer, bellowing into the taller man's chest, "What is your name?"

No answer.

Again it was the tenor in the crowd of onlookers who responded. "His name is Yurko! Yurko Kryak from the village of Stara Polyanka on the Ondava!"

The corporal stared up into the nostrils, thought for a moment, and then smiled. "Tell me, Kryak, when you urinate, which hand do you hold it in?"

No answer.

The tenor again: "HE USES BOTH HANDS, CORPORAL!"

Now, these weeks later, Vasko's helpful shouts to the corporal were still fondly remembered in the company, and Vasyl was often called upon to relate the incident to the curious who were not present that day.

ᏒᎧ

Later that evening it rained heavily. Vasyl lay awake, staring out the half-opened boxcar door and listening to the riotous downpour. When the fury slackened, he rose and stood at the open door, where he lit a cigarette. Only a light drizzle fell now and he jumped down to the ballast, shuddering at the cold water that dripped inside his collar from the roof of the boxcar. From the north, a train materialized out of the mist and came to a slow and clamorous halt in front of Vasyl. The fireman climbed down from the train, buttoned up his coat, and yelled in Magyar to the engineer, who appeared at the open cab window, laughing and tapping the bowl of his pipe against the side of the locomotive. The train was made up of passenger cars, the first of which bore a large emblem featuring a cross and the Habsburg coat of arms ringed with the inscription, *Österreichische Gesellschaft vom Roten Kreuze*—Austrian Society of the Red Cross.

Vasyl walked past both the locomotive and the first car. At the second car he glanced in both directions, took a last draw on his cigarette, flicked the butt aside, and climbed aboard. Inside he winced at the contending odors of antiseptics and decaying flesh that greeted him.

All the seats had been removed and replaced with stacks of bunks, each occupied by a bandaged man. From the closest bunk there dangled a pale arm, stark against the dark blanket. Vasyl moved closer and inspected an equally pale face with chapped, parted lips and half-shut eyes, framed by an utter stillness.

In the bunk above, the blankets were tucked around a bandaged head that revealed only a mouth, a nose, and an opened left eye, which followed Vasyl's movements. Vasyl nodded at the head and noticed the lips forming a word. He leaned closer and heard the wrapped head whisper in German, *"Cigaretten?"*

Vasyl reached in his jacket pocket and pulled out a box of matches and a cigarette. He placed the cigarette in his mouth, lit it, and then held it in front of the bandaged head. The exposed mouth pulled deeply and the eye closed as the smoke streamed out of the nose. Vasyl retrieved another cigarette for himself and ignited it from the wounded man's cigarette. The two men smoked in silence, Vasyl alternately drawing from his own cigarette and holding the other one to the exposed mouth. When he finished his cigarette, the wounded man held out his left hand, took Vasyl's hand in his own, and squeezed weakly.

From the other end of the car, a nurse suddenly shouted in German, startling both men. Vasyl shrugged apologetically to the bandaged head and bolted from the car, jumping to the ballast. He jogged back to his own train, where the firemen were busy stoking the engine's firebox for the long mountain run into Galicia.

CHAPTER SIXTEEN

Happy To Try

FOR SERGEANT HALETSKII the army had been a way of life for almost ten years. Twice he took part in maneuvers in the Balkans when it appeared that Austria-Hungary would be drawn into conflicts in the south. Those expeditions were fairly small and certainly more easily managed than this massive invasion force of over a million men marching through Galicia toward Russia. Now, after three days of marching, Sergeant Haletskii stood with his hands on his hips, watching troops on a distant road move forward across the low, rolling hills. He mumbled something and Vasyl, who was standing nearby, approached him and asked, "What did you say, Sergeant?"

Sergeant Haletskii swept his arms out toward the horizon. "Look, Rusynko. Look at the dust raised by so many boots. Remember this sight and tell your children about it someday. Tell your grandchildren when you are old. You may not see something like this again in your lifetime. We are endless columns marching on endless roads. It makes you wonder—how long it would take us to march to where the head of this column is right now—a day— two days?"

Vasyl looked out over the terrain that receded down and away into a distant afternoon haze. "And if it took two days, what of it, Sergeant?"

Sergeant Haletskii smiled and shook his head. "It is nothing, Vasyl. I worry about things that should be of no concern to me. Only . . ." He pointed again toward the northeast. "Only, I wonder what would become of our forward force if they engaged the Russians and had to wait two days for us to come up? But, it is nothing for us, is it? Come, we are moving forward again."

Sergeant Haletskii headed to the company's rear, yelling, "Everyone up— we are moving forward again! Everyone up!" Vasyl returned to the tree where he had left Vasko reclining on the ground. He found his friend lying on his side, one hand supporting his head, and the thumb and index of the other hand working at his nose.

"Up, Vasko," said Vasyl. "We are moving forward again."

Vasko stood among the other lounging men and wiped his hand on his trousers. "Vasyl, all day we march in the heat and for the first time we find shade. But you spend your time talking in the sun. There are those who would say that makes you mad."

Vasyl entered the shade ring of the tree and removed his hat. "And you, Vasko? What would you say I am?" he asked, wiping his brow with his sleeve.

"A man whose mind is his own, in or out of the sun."

Varkhol stood and stretched. "Feh! Vasyl, he called you mad the moment you walked out of the shade."

Vasko's eyes widened and he smirked. "He's a *huntsut*—a troublemaker! Don't listen to Varkhol, Vasyl. Trust him as you would the devil."

Varkhol loomed over Vasko. "You called your friend 'mad' and now you deny it. You yourself are the devil!"

Vasko hastily repositioned himself with Vasyl in the middle of the three men. "Vasyl, who has always been your best friend?"

Vasyl bent down for his pack and hoisted it on his back. "My brother Andrii, of course."

"No, no, outside your family—who do you trust more than all others?"

"Sergeant Haletskii. Put your pack on."

"No, no. Who is your greatest friend, not of your own family, and who has no higher rank than ours?"

Vasyl stroked the stubble on his chin and then smoothed his mustache. "I see. There is only one, then, who answers to that: Yurko."

"Yurko! Vasyl . . . please."

"He feeds me well. What more could a man want?"

Varkhol slapped Vasko on the back. "You see? Your friend is not mad at all. Perhaps you should go to Ameryka so that you can come back with as much sense as your friend."

One of the men, adjusting his pack and shouldering his rifle, asked, "Who has been to Ameryka?"

Vasko raised his arm and pointed to Vasyl. "He has. He lived and worked in Ameryka for four years and when he returned he brought Amerykan money with him and he bought brandy and whiskey for—"

"How is it with Ret Soks?" asked the man, brushing past Vasko.

Vasyl grinned. "Good—very good—much better than with Yan-kis. Did you live in Bo-ston?"

"Yes, nearby. I saw Ret Soks play once before I came home. They won."

Vasyl nodded solemnly. "Ret Soks are very good," he said. "I heard that last year they won sir-is."

"COMPANY FORWARD!" shouted Sergeant Haletskii from the rear, and the men re-formed their column and resumed their eastward march.

"What is 'Res tak' and 'Yaki'?" asked Vasko.

"Ret Soks and Yan-kis," corrected Vasyl. "It is bes-bol. It is a game in Ameryka between two gangs of men who take turns to hit a ball with a big wooden club. People watch them play the game."

"People watch the game?"

"Yes. They pay money and sit outside and watch."

"Who pays?"

"The people who watch. The men who play are paid to play."

"Who pays them?"

"I don't know—the men who own the team, I suppose."

"Where do they get the money?"

"From the people who pay to watch them."

"People *pay* to watch them?"

"Yes, I just told you that."

"Do they get to try to hit the ball?"

"Who?"

"The people who pay the money to sit outside."

"No. They watch men who are paid to try to hit the ball."

"The men who try to hit the ball don't have to pay, but the people who can only watch must pay—*pravda*—true?" asked Vasko incredulously.

Vasyl nodded. "*To ista pravda*—that's the honest truth."

Vasko shook his head in disbelief at the men marching around him, emphasizing the extraordinary folly of such a game. "Honest Vasyl . . . who but a madman would *pay* to *watch* others play a game? I'd as soon pay to watch Yurko eat."

Vasyl shrugged. "That is the way in Ameryka, my friend."

Vasko wrinkled his nose. "Vasyl, you were right to return to the highlands where an honest man can breathe honest air, and there is no charge for it."

At the sound of shouting, Vasyl looked over the tops of the men's heads. "Look, here comes Sergeant Haletskii. He is in a hurry."

The red-faced sergeant was motioning the men to the side of the road as he approached, calling out, "Make way for cavalry! Move back! Make way for cavalry!" He stopped near Vasyl and said, "I would tell everyone not to look at them, but what is the use? Everyone will look anyway. Damned cavalry— always making a show. Look out— here they come."

A small contingent of Hungarian Hussars approached from the east, escorting a dozen captive Russian cavalrymen toward the rear. The victorious Hussars studiously ignored the infantrymen while their proud horses condescended to nod briefly at the dusty, gawking foot soldiers. Bloodied and bandaged, the mounted prisoners sang *Bozhe Tsarya khrani*—God Save the Tsar, and when they finished the Russian Imperial anthem, their captain looked over his shoulder and cried, "Well done, men!" The Russians responded, "HAPPY TO TRY, SIR!"

As horses and riders continued westward, Vasko appeared at Vasyl's side. "Vasyl! Did you hear?"

"Hear what?"

"The Russians said, 'Happy to try.'"

"Did they?"

"Yes. They have been beaten. But even in defeat the Russians are 'Happy to try!' I like that. And at least they are still on their horses. They are better off than we are with this endless marching."

"Well," said Vasyl. "For now, try to be happy on your feet. Come, we are moving forward again. And don't carry your rifle like that."

"But, Vasyl, it is too heavy and it is too hot. It is easier to carry it in one hand at my side."

"Shoulder your rifle before Sergeant Haletskii has to correct you."

"I don't see why the train could not take us farther," Vasko mumbled, shouldering his rifle. "They made us get off the train only to march. Why did they not bring us at least this far? We have passed several rail lines."

Vasyl laughed. "You are never happy! Three or four days ago you said you could walk faster than our train—and now you are! Stop complaining—the army knows what is best for you."

"But, Vasyl, how much longer do you think?"

"Until what?"

"Until we get there—how much longer until we get to wherever we are going?"

"I don't know."

"Where are we going?"

"I don't know."

"How long do you think the war will last, Vasyl?"

"I don't know."

"I heard until autumn," said a voice from the ranks.

"I heard, at least until the rains," said another.

"*Bozhe moi*—my God!" cried Vasko. "Another month of this? Is that possible, Vasyl?"

"Anything is possible," said Vasyl. "Be quiet and march." Vasko mumbled a reply and Vasyl said, "What did you say?"

"I said, 'Happy to try, sir!'"

The men marched, choking on the chalky dust raised by thousands of pairs of boots, and, at the end of the day, they encamped along the edge of a wood. After dinner, in the lingering summer twilight, the men lounged in the grass, smoking pipes or cigarettes. A low, distant rumble to the east was evidence enough to some that a storm was gathering beyond the horizon. Vasyl and a few other men observed that Sergeant Haletskii chewed on his pipe and tensed with each flash on the eastern horizon.

That night Vasyl slept poorly. The next morning, well before dawn, the men were roused, told to eat quickly, and prepare to move on.

☙

The men marched all morning and stopped at noon just long enough to drink water and swallow dark bread. They pressed forward, too tired to complain, and stared down at the monotonous cycle of advancing hob-nailed heels before them—left . . . right . . . left . . . right . . . As the afternoon progressed, couriers raced up and down the length of the column on frenzied horses whose dark necks were streaked with white foam. While the first of these mounted messengers aroused the infantrymen's interest, the men eventually grew weary of the spectacle and the tiresome shower of earth and dust raised by each galloping horse.

When, by midafternoon, it became clear that some change was occurring at the head of the column, tense excitement replaced the men's fatigue. The sergeants trotted up and down the column, shouting at the men and directing them, by company, into positions on either side of the road. From the rear, an uninterrupted flow of men advanced and fanned out along this growing line of force.

Vasyl and Vasko lay in a slight depression not far from the road. Extending to their left and right were rows of their gray-clad comrades, packs forming mounds on their backs, rifles at their sides, a vast field of yellow wheat before them. On the other side of this field stood a row of trees, and beyond their shimmering leaves came the sounds of booming artillery and popping rifle fire. Vasyl glanced over at Vasko to say something but his friend was resting his forehead on the barrel of his rifle. The sound of rifle fire increased, especially to the right, where it was joined now by an insistent knocking, like the perpetual rhythm of the thundering factories across the ocean.

This is where the war would begin for these men—here in the rolling fields of Galicia, where narrow-winged swifts streaked across the clear blue sky and a westerly breeze brushed the men's backs.

A shadow fell across Vasyl and he looked up to see Sergeant Haletskii standing behind him and staring out across the field. The sergeant was biting his lower lip and his eyes were dark. Then Sergeant Haletskii shouted, "LOAD!" All along the line, other sergeants barked the same order and, breech mechanisms snapping open by the hundreds, the infantrymen loaded five rounds of ammunition in their rifle magazines. The sergeants ordered an advance, and the men stood, adjusting their packs and clutching their rifles to their chests. Vasyl looked at Vasko, but his friend was staring across the field. The westerly breeze picked up slightly, and, as if this were the anticipated signal, Sergeant Haletskii shouted in unison with the other sergeants and the long line of men stepped forward into the wheat field.

CHAPTER SEVENTEEN

The Harvest

AS THE MEN MARCHED across the field, the wheat crumpled under their boots, scattering the ripe grain. Vasyl looked back at the ruined crop and then at Vasko, who nodded and closed his eyes as if to say, "I know—it's a shame." They came to a section of the field ruined by the prior passage of infantry. Several little gray mounds dotted the trampled yellow wheat, and as the men approached they stopped to gawk, despite Sergeant Haletskii's orders to continue. The mound at Vasyl and Vasko's feet was a young Austro-Hungarian soldier lying on his back, his right leg drawn awkwardly beneath him. His eyes were half-opened and flies walked over his face and into his mouth. Vasyl and Vasko stared at the man until Sergeant Haletskii's shouts prodded them forward.

Vasyl looked down at his own uniform and boots as he walked. The dead man wore the same boots—his gray trousers bore the same yellow lace trim. He would have fastened his tunic and eaten breakfast that morning and felt the same wheat rustle against his legs. Vasyl glanced over at Vasko, but his friend's rigid face was fixed on the earth.

They reached the trees on the other side of the field without incident and came to a halt. To the right and left officers and sergeants conferred in little groups and then returned to their men, shouting and directing them forward. The men continued through the row of trees, emerging onto another field almost wholly flattened by the earlier passage of troops. On the opposite side of this field, smoke rose above another row of trees and drifted eastward. As the men marched toward the sound of gunfire, a horse-drawn ambulance passed them, bouncing slowly rearward, its heavily bandaged wounded staring vacantly from beneath a torn canvas cover.

To the right was a dressing station where more of the wounded waited in the sun, calling hoarsely to the orderlies for water. To the left, the right flank of another regiment swept into position. Well behind this new group of men, an Austrian battery now went into action. Each volley from these guns was preceded by the same pantomime: a flurry of activity from the gunners, then the dusty recoil of the guns, followed by the delayed report as the gunners threw open the breeches to load the next artillery shells.

Sergeant Haletskii walked backward in front of the men, his hands cupped around his mouth, his shouts competing unsuccessfully with the Austrian battery. A lieutenant hurried to the sergeant's side and as the two men conferred, the lieutenant gesticulated toward the east and the sergeant nodded slowly. The lieutenant hurried down the line of men while Sergeant Haletskii, with a wave of his arm, directed the men along a slightly altered course.

The company followed Sergeant Haletskii across a wheat field toward a distant line of trees shrouded in smoky haze. Behind the men, another Austrian battery fired a volley. In the distance the earth rose and tree branches twisted violently and fell to the ground. Suddenly, a different sound, a metallic rattle, filled the air and the sergeants screamed, "DOWN! DOWN! EVERYONE DOWN!"

Russian shells exploded in the rear behind the Austrian batteries, jarring the earth and lifting great columns of Galician soil into the air. Ensuing volleys roared overhead, probing closer and closer to the Austrian guns. The artillerymen loaded and fired with desperation, but the Russian shells were finding their targets among the Austrian guns and their horse-drawn caissons.

During a lull in the shelling, the infantrymen turned on their sides and looked toward the rear where the once orderly batteries were now reduced to ruins. The piercing screams of wounded horses rose from the smoke and chaos as frantic artillerymen attempted to right their guns.

Vasko tapped Vasyl's shoulder and pointed to one of the upended caissons, where a horse, stabbing and pawing at the ground with its forelegs, struggled to pull itself out of a shell hole. The horse strained, paused, and then, with a violent shudder, collapsed on its side. There was no shell hole; the horse's hindquarters had been shot away and the wretched animal was simply trying to stand. Vasyl shook his head at Vasko and the two men turned toward the east and waited.

Sergeant Haletskii walked up and down the company, counseling his men, "Everyone stay low—keep your rifle actions clean. Stay low, my children—the time is near."

The Russian guns began firing again and after a metallic rattle in the air, two explosions erupted not far behind the line of infantry, knocking Sergeant Haletskii to the ground. Holding his hands over his ears, the sergeant rolled onto his stomach near Vasyl. Russian shells rattled out of the sky, bursting near the men, who clung to the bouncing earth.

Sergeant Haletskii yelled, "We can't stay here! Where is the lieutenant?" The sergeant raised his head and looked up and down the line. "Someone should give the order! Where the devil is the lieutenant?" Another shell landed nearby and the wounded screamed as soil rained down on them. Sergeant Haletskii ground his fists into the earth and cried, "*Oi*, my children! My children! Where is the damn lieutenant?" The sergeant rose to his feet and ran along the line of men.

The earth exploded nearby and a stone struck Vasyl's neck and rolled down his shoulder. He pressed his face into the soil, clasping his hands over his neck and drawing his forearms over his ears. The moist earth filled his nostrils and he groaned out of the side of his mouth, "*Bozhe moi*—my God!"

The barrage suddenly stopped and the hellish racket was replaced by the cries of the wounded and the shouts of the sergeants. Vasyl wiped the soil from his nose and surveyed the scene around him. Most of the men were gazing about them in stunned silence. To the right, orderlies tended to moaning men while ignoring lifeless forms. Vasko stirred next to Vasyl, blinking and coughing as though waking from a sound sleep.

"Vasyl, are you all right?"

"Y-yes . . . I think so."

Sergeants to the left and right blew their whistles and shouted, "PREPARE TO ATTACK! PREPARE TO ATTACK!"

One of the infantrymen, a man with a sonorous voice began to pray: "*Hospody Isuse Khryste!*—Lord Jesus Christ!"

"PREPARE TO ATTACK!"

Now others joined in the prayer: "*Syne Bozhii!*—Son of God!"

"PREPARE TO ATTACK!"

"*Pomilui mya, hreshnoho!*—Have mercy on me, a sinner!"

Sergeant Haletskii, standing almost directly in front of Vasyl, shouted, "COMPANY, UP! PREPARE TO ATTACK!"

"*Hospody Isuse Khryste!*"

Vasyl rose to his feet and called out, "Vasko! It is time!"

"COMPANY, UP!"

"Syne Bozhii!"

Vasko brushed frantically at his rifle's action while to the left and right men began to stand. Vasyl called again, "Vasko! Come! It is time!"

The sergeants blew their whistles. "COMPANY, FORWARD!"

"Pomilui mya, hreshnoho!"

Vasko stood and held out his rifle. "Vasyl! Look!" he cried, showing Vasyl the open action filled with dirt.

"Bozhe moi, Vasko! You can't fire it like that!" Vasyl ejected all five rounds from Vasko's rifle. "Here, put them in your pouch! Hurry! It is time!"

"EVERYONE, FORWARD! DO NOT STOP FOR WOUNDED!"

"Hospody Isuse Khryste!"

The earth exploded, showering Vasyl and Vasko with dirt, and then a second explosion knocked them to the ground. Vasyl rose to his knees, wiping his eyes and coughing from the harsh explosive fumes. Picking up his rifle, he struggled to his feet and looked for Vasko. To his left, his comrades advanced in an orderly line, while to his right the men seemed to hesitate as though unsure of their course. Everyone seemed to be moving far too slowly—without urgency. Vasyl recognized Vasko in the group to his right and sprinted after him.

From the shadows of the trees on the other side of the field came the persistent knocking of machine guns—the Russian Maxims—firing into the advancing men. A man on Vasyl's right dropped to his knees, throwing out his arms, and crying, *"Syne Bozhii!*—Son of God!" as he fell on his face. On the left, the Maxims clattered and six men, one after the other, fell to the ground, the last one struggling to his knees before finally sinking into the yellow wheat.

The Russian guns clattered from the left, right, and center. Men in front of Vasyl began to fall—some dropping without a sound, others screaming, and still others falling forward with a groan as if greatly and sorrowfully disappointed. The remaining men hesitated but continued toward the distant trees.

A wounded man waved desperately to Vasyl, who dropped to his knees at the man's side. "Look!" panted the soldier, his face pale and his lips colorless. "Do you see? What am I to do?" He tore feebly at his dark-stained abdomen. *"Bozhe moi,* what am I to do? Everything is coming out!" Vasyl grimaced at the awful wound and its foul odor. The wounded man's head fell back on the wheat and he turned his face away from Vasyl, mumbling, *"Bozhe moi . . .* everything . . . everything is coming out . . ."

"You there!" shouted a passing lieutenant. "Do not stop for wounded!"

Vasyl grabbed his rifle and rose to his feet.

"Move forward—do not stop! The wounded will be tended to!"

Vasyl ran to catch up with the other infantrymen, who, in their dwindling numbers, were scattered far and wide in the ruined wheat field. Sprinting toward a wagon path, Vasyl dropped his rifle and dove to the ground when the Maxims fired short bursts from the trees. He landed safely in a shallow ditch, finding himself in the company of three other men who lay on their backs gasping.

"*Bozhe moi!* I'm thirsty!" cried a familiar voice and Vasyl looked over to see Vasko's filthy face near his own. The other men he recognized as Petro Matsko and a man named Shtefan. The men helped one another with their bulky packs, found their water, and drank, keeping their heads low.

Vasyl peeked at the field the men had just crossed. Except for a lone, gray figure limping toward the rear, no one was visible. "Where is everyone?" muttered Vasyl.

The Russian Maxims were silent and all sounds of war were remote and muffled. The four men lay on their backs, staring up at the sky. The sun was very low now and the long dusk would soon begin.

℘

When Vasyl opened his eyes the sun had set and the guns of both armies rumbled like distant thunder. Vasyl drank from his water flask and shook Vasko by the shoulder.

"I'm awake, Vasyl. We were waiting for you to wake up."

"How long was I asleep?"

"Not long. I think I slept too."

"I never felt so tired."

"Vasyl?" It was Vasko's voice again.

"Yes?"

"What do we do now?"

"I don't know."

"Do you think we will ever have to do that again?"

"Do what?"

"Run across a field at the Russians. Vasyl . . . all those men . . . so many fell."

"I know . . . I know."

"I never thought it would be like that. I hope we never have to do that again—never . . . forever and ever . . ."

Petro Matsko slid closer and whispered, "Keep your voices low. The Russians are inside the trees in front of us. What should we do? Where is our company?"

"How close are the Russians?" asked Vasyl.

"No more than a stone's throw. I can hear them talking."

Vasyl tilted his head to the left and right. "My head still pounds—I can't hear them."

"What should we do?" repeated Petro Matsko.

Their dirty faces indistinguishable in the late evening, the three men stared at Vasyl, entrusting all decision making to him. Vasyl surveyed the dim landscape. The tree line from which they had begun the attack was a black shape rising to the faded sky; to the left, the evening star hung low. "Since the Russians didn't counterattack, our regiment must have held its ground," whispered Vasyl. "We should go in the direction of the evening star—maybe just to the right of it. We should run into our regiment once we reach the trees. We won't be seen in the dark. I don't think we should stay here, unless we wish to become prisoners of our Russian brothers."

The other three men nodded and sighed deeply—Vasyl's decision was sound and they were happy with it. They shouldered their packs, picked up their rifles, and, crouching low, made their way across the field, stepping over the dead and dying as they went.

And during the night, along the broad Galician front, men of both armies died, calling out in their dark solitude to a thousand mothers and one God in half a dozen languages.

CHAPTER EIGHTEEN

Sneg

IN SEPTEMBER 1914, Vasyl and Vasko marched with their dwindling company and dispirited army into the town of Rava Ruska. As they marched through the *rynek*—the marketplace—Jews in black hats and long, dusty black coats stood in doorways under indecipherable Hebrew signs while their womenfolk peeked out from behind small, rippled-glass windows. For the Jews, the sight of an army passing through was no longer the novel event of a few weeks earlier. For the infantrymen, the sight of entire villages and neighborhoods of somber-costumed Jews was of interest to only a very few.

Vasko spat the dust from his mouth and wiped the dribble from his chin. "Dymitrii Roman says that the *zhydŷ*—the Jews—don't read their letters like we do. They read theirs from the end to the beginning."

Vasyl smiled and continued to stare down at the tramping boots in front of him. "You can't read. What difference does it make to you?"

"Is that how our *zhydŷ* read in Stara Polyanka, Vasyl?"

"I don't know—maybe."

Vasko chuckled. "If I ever learn to read, I think I would rather read forwards than backwards."

At the head of the marching column, the men spread out in a large square and lined up in front of the stew wagons. Vasko jabbed Vasyl in the ribs. "Look! It is Yurko! He will feed us well."

Vasyl and Vasko stood in line at the wagon manned by their friend and watched a filthy, matted dog slouch past them to a spot under the wagon where it collapsed in a panting heap. "Yurko!" cried Vasko. "Look where your brother lies at your feet!"

Corporal Brynda, in charge of the stew wagon, nudged Yurko with an elbow and pointed to Vasko. "Don't overfill his bowl, Yurko. We must leave some for the dog!"

"Fill one bowl and let them share. You'll feed two dogs!" offered someone in line.

The men laughed and Vasko made a vicious face at Corporal Brynda.

Sergeant Haletskii sat next to Vasyl and ate in silence, staring into his bowl.

Vasyl wiped his mouth with his sleeve and said quietly, "Sergeant, I hear we lost the lieutenant yesterday."

Sergeant Haletskii nodded. "He was still alive when they took him from the field . . . but . . ." The sergeant flourished his spoon. "It is a bad business, all of this. It will get much worse before it gets better. The Russians fight well against us."

"There are some who say the war may not end until the rains come," said Vasyl.

"Yes, yes, we will all be very wet before this is through. And, I think, very cold . . . yes, very cold."

☙

After lunch some of the men strolled around the *rynek,* where Jewish merchants hawked a variety of wares from their covered stalls. One enterprising merchant sold tin cap badges depicting patriotic slogans, patron saints, and Austro-Hungarian military unit insignia. Vasko made a purchase at this stand and then went in search of Vasyl, finding him sitting in the shade with Mykhal Varkhol and Petro Matsko.

Wrinkling his nose, Vasko joined the men. "Feh! These *zhydŷ* eat raw onions. They sit at their tables with a knife in one hand and an onion in the other. This whole town smells like onions."

Vasyl laughed. "How would you know? How can you smell anything with all that raw garlic you eat?"

Vasko ignored his friend and displayed a new badge now pinned to his cap. "Look—do you see? They have many like this, but I picked this one because it has the prettiest girl on it. What does the writing mean, Vasyl?" Vasko handed his cap to his friend.

Vasyl squinted at the badge and then tossed the cap back to Vasko. "It says, 'Beware! Badge-wearer carries syphilis.'"

Petro Matsko laughed and Mykhal Varkhol slapped Vasyl on the back.

"Vasyl!" cried Vasko. "Truly, what does it say?"

"I don't know—it is in German. But she is *Svyata Barbara*—Saint Barbara. I can read that much of it. She is, I think, the patroness of miners."

"Miners?" Vasko stroked his chin. "Very well. She will protect me—we spend much time close to the earth. She will do very well for me."

That evening the men were ordered back out of town to new positions near the ones they had occupied in the morning. They marched past the same Jewish homes and shops they had passed earlier in the day, now dark and lit from within by yellow candlelight, which silhouetted the dark, silent forms watching from the doorways.

Outside of town Sergeant Haletskii appeared next to Vasyl and walked beside him in silence. Eventually he said to Vasyl, "Do you hear?"

Vasyl turned an ear forward. "No . . . I don't think so."

"There! Do you hear now?"

Vasyl concentrated and Vasko, moving up closer from behind, said, "I hear it, Sergeant."

There was a distant rumble like thunder. "Yes, now I hear it," nodded Vasyl.

"Now we are in for it, children." Sergeant Haletskii paused. "Yes, we are likely to meet our Russian brothers in force now. They will want that rat trap, filthy hole of a town behind us and we are going to stand in their way."

"What do they want with that town?" asked Vasyl.

"The railroad. Did you not see the yards and the tracks coming and going from the town? Our Russian brothers will want them. Oh, yes, they will want them badly."

The men marched most of the night, and in the predawn chill they came to a little ridge somewhere south of Rava Ruska. The guns were silent now, but there were other sounds in the air: coughing men shuffling on unfamiliar ground; snorting horses shaking their harnesses; cursing drivers bouncing off the inadequate paths. The men stacked their rifles and settled on the cold ground, pulling up the collars of their summer tunics and thrusting their hands into their pockets.

And somewhere in front of them, in the direction of the approaching dawn, another army was shivering in the dark and waiting.

乄

Vasyl gazed eastward as the morning mist began to dissipate. There were no signs of the Russians, but the clearing skies seemed to serve as a signal to artillerymen of both armies. The first shells arched overhead, passing each other at their apexes before falling on their opposite targets. The clatter of machine guns—both Russian Maxims and Austrian Schwarzloses—and the crackle of rifle fire combined with exploding artillery shells in a crescendo along a broad front.

On the company's left flank, Sergeant Haletskii conferred with a lieutenant. When the two men parted the sergeant hurried down the line, stopping every so often to address the prone infantrymen. When he flopped down near Vasyl, the sergeant removed his cap and wiped his forehead with his sleeve.

"We can't stay here," Sergeant Haletskii explained. "The Russians have broken through on either side of us. The lieutenant says we are too exposed. We may get help on our left, but we must fall back to that little ridge where the artillery units are already falling back." The sergeant waved to another sergeant on the company's right flank and then stood. "Listen, men! We will WALK toward that ridge and form a firing line! Company . . . UP!"

The men struggled to their feet, adjusted their packs, and followed the sergeant. Russian shells rattled overhead and exploded among the retreating artillery units. To the left, infantrymen of the collapsing right flank began to run. To the right, other units now ran toward the rear, shedding their equipment and looking anxiously over their shoulders. Vasyl and the men around him, caught up in the contagious panic, also began to run.

Vasko stumbled into Vasyl and the two men fell to the ground. "Vasko! Take off your pack!" The two men struggled out of their packs and Vasyl stood, holding both their rifles. "Here, Vasko! Take your rifle!"

The two men ran to the ridge, where they were met by two mounted officers, brandishing sabers and screaming in Magyar at the retreating mob. Sergeant Haletskii placed himself between his men and the officers and translated the officers' orders into Rusyn: "Form a firing line here! A firing line here! Stop or you will be shot!" Vasyl and Vasko threw themselves to the ground gasping.

"*Bozhe moi!* I am thirsty!" cried Vasko, fumbling for his water flask.

One of the mounted officers shook his head in disgust and growled something in Magyar at Vasko before prodding his horse into a turn and disappearing behind the low ridge.

Vasko called to Sergeant Haletskii, "What did he say, Sergeant?"

"He said that the rains will come soon, and because you threw away your pack you will sleep in the water and suffer no longer from thirst." Now the sergeant cupped his hands over his mouth and addressed the men. "Listen to me! Everyone, check your rifles! Clean them if you must! Load them and await the order to fire!"

Someone to the left shouted, "There they are!"

Vasyl looked out over the field toward the low rise that the men had lately occupied and that now bore a sparkling crown along its entire length.

Sergeant Haletskii shouted, "Yes, I see the sun on their bayonets! Prepare yourselves, my children! Prepare yourselves!"

From the right came the sound of Austrian rifle fire, at first sporadic, then incessant and intense.

"Here they come! Load! Prepare to fire!"

Vasyl pulled back his rifle's bolt, inserted five rounds, thrust the bolt forward to the receiver, loading the first round, and aimed the rifle across the field.

"FIRE!"

☙

For a week the armies of Russia and Austria battled near the town of Rava Ruska. For both armies, trained almost exclusively in concepts of advance and attack, losses were enormous. In many units, the apparatus of command simply dissolved with the slaughter of junior officers. On both sides, isolated groups of enlisted men, often leaderless, but placing faith in resourceful peers, improvised and fought their way back to their units. Other men, out of fear or exhaustion or both, simply surrendered. Eventually the Austrian army abandoned its positions around Rava Ruska and retreated to the west, burning villages and crops and anything else of use to the pursuing Russians.

☙

"Vasyl, come quickly!" cried Vasko, trotting from the direction of a burning village. Vasyl was writing slowly on a piece of paper; when he finished he pinned the note to the tunic of the dead officer at his feet.

"Vasyl, what is that? What did you write?"

Vasyl stood and shouldered his rifle. "It reads, 'Russian brothers—bury our lieutenant—his name is Strumer—he fought well.' I don't want to leave him out here in the open . . . but . . ."

"Only, Vasyl, he wasn't really our lieutenant, was he? We never saw him before today."

"Yes, he was our lieutenant—if only for a day. I don't want to leave him like this. We don't have time to bury him . . . the Russians will tend to him, I think."

"Was that his name—Strumer? I never knew his name."

"I think so—someone called him that. I think that is what I heard. His identity disk is missing from around his neck and I can't find it. His neck is open—I think the disk was shot away. Anyway, 'Strumer' is what I wrote. Where are the others?"

"Follow me," said Vasko.

To their right a village with familiar-looking huts burned brightly in the gray dusk. The huts were almost identical to those in Stara Polyanka. The intense heat stung Vasyl's cheek, and he turned and lowered his head as if struggling against a strong wind. "We are too close, Vasko—we are heading for the Russian lines."

"There is no danger. The Russians are on the other side of the village. We saw them and Petro Matsko even spoke with them. They want no trouble from us, Vasyl, and we want no trouble from them—not now. Look at the village burn."

"Yes, it is hot."

"Vasyl, the farmers around here look and talk just like us. Why must we burn their homes? Where will they go?"

"I don't know. They have nowhere to go. You have seen the roads—there are almost as many refugees as soldiers on the roads."

"But, Vasyl, it makes no sense. Why must we burn their homes? These people have done nothing wrong—how is it that they are our enemy?"

"We do what we are told to do because that is what the army wishes. Who are these men in front of us? Is that Petro Matsko?"

Indeed, it was Petro Matsko who stood over a figure lying in the wheat field. Vasyl peered at the body and turned to Petro. "Who is he?"

"He is a Russian—a private," said Petro Matsko. "Where is the lieutenant?"

"Dead. Is this man alive?"

"Yes," said Petro Matsko. "Do you hear that rattle? That's him trying to breathe."

Vasyl knelt by the man and motioned to Vasko to move aside and not to block the light from the burning village. "His eyes are open," said Vasyl, running his hands over the Russian's arms, down his chest, and over his hips. "*Bozhe moi . . . Bozhe moi . . .*" said Vasyl, standing and wiping his hands on his pants.

"What is it, Vasyl?" said Vasko, leaning over the wounded man. "Is it bad?"

"Yes. I think his belly is open all the way down . . . it is . . . it is very bloody."

"Is it over for him, Vasyl?"

"Yes—soon. Where are the rest of our men?"

Petro Matsko pointed toward the village. "There are Ivan and Shtefan and the new man—I don't know his name." Petro whistled and the three silhouettes near the village paused, looked about, and then changed course and approached.

Shtefan called out, "Where is the lieutenant?"

"Dead," answered Vasko and Petro simultaneously.

Ivan looked at the form on the ground. "Is that him?"

"That is a Russian," said Vasko. "The lieutenant is over there. Vasyl put a note on him asking the Russians to bury him."

"He did what?"

Other members of the company appeared from out of the darkness and the group formed a circle around the dying Russian.

"He put a note on him," explained Vasko. "So the Russians will bury him."

"Who is to be buried?"

"The lieutenant."

"The lieutenant is dead?"

"Yes! If you had listened, you would have heard!"

"I just got here! How the devil would I know the lieutenant is dead?"

"Is this the lieutenant?"

"*Bozhe moi!* No! This is a Russian!"

"Respect the dead—keep your voice quiet."

"He's not dead—not yet."

"I thought you just said he was dead."

"The lieutenant is dead—this is a Russian. Vasyl, you tell them."

Vasyl held up his hand and knelt next to the Russian. "Quiet! All of you, quiet. He is trying to say something."

A man squeezed in next to Vasko for a closer look and whispered, "I thought the lieutenant was dead."

"*Oi!*"

Vasyl held up his hand again. "Tsh! Now, what is it, brother?" Vasyl bent down with his ear near the man's mouth.

The Russian pointed a trembling finger toward the village and whispered, "*Sneg.*"

Vasyl followed the Russian's gaze toward the burning village where swirling ash blew across the fields. He shook his head at the soldier. "*Ne sneg*—not snow—ash."

The Russian twitched his finger again. "*Sneg.*"

Vasyl opened his mouth to speak, but paused instead and looked back at the village. The ashes shimmered in the flaming light and fell softly among the men. Vasyl nodded at the soldier. "*Da . . . sneg*—yes . . . *sneg*—snow."

Vasko tapped Vasyl on the shoulder. "Vasyl . . . Vasyl . . . come, Vasyl. We must go. Petro Matsko says the Russians are moving again on the other side of the village and will be here soon. They will look after their brother."

"Give me his blanket, Vasko," said Vasyl. "It is there, by his feet. Good—no, don't unroll it—now hand it to me." Vasyl lifted the Russian's head and rested it on the blanket. He stood and took his rifle from Vasko. "Where are the others," he asked, looking around.

"There, on the road. Come, Vasyl. Hurry!"

Vasyl slung his rifle over his shoulder and waved his hand, indicating that Vasko should lead the way to the road. The two men struck out toward their comrades, and Vasyl looked back at the Russian lying on the trampled grain and staring into the swirling sky.

"Vasyl, what are you thinking?" asked Vasko without turning around.

"What makes you think I'm thinking?"

"Because, honest Vasyl, you always push me ahead when you want to think without me following you and bothering you."

Vasyl snorted. "If that is true, what good is it to me? You are bothering me now, yes?"

"What are you thinking, Vasyl?"

"Nothing."

"Then I will tell you what I am thinking . . . do you want to hear, Vasyl?"

"No."

"I'll tell you anyway. I think it is horrible to die alone in a field. That Russian is just like you and me—an infantryman. He looks like us except for his uniform. He is young and I wonder—"

"Vasko."

"What?"

"Think about something else. Thoughts like those will keep you from sleeping."

Vasko stopped and turned to face the village. The flames flickered in his eyes and his grimy cheeks shone a dull orange. "Do you think he is still alive, or . . . ?"

Vasyl brushed by without looking back and took the lead. "I'm not thinking anything right now. Don't talk about him again. Come."

Vasko studied the sky. "Do you want to know what I'm thinking now? In a few weeks it could snow. Vasyl, I said, in a few weeks it could snow . . . Vasyl? Now you won't answer me. I hope the war ends before the snows come. But before the snow comes, the rains will begin and maybe the war will be over—who can fight in the rain? That is all I was thinking about. That and the Russian—I know you said not to talk about him. The war will have to end before the snows come, don't you agree, Vasyl? Who can fight in the snow? That is all I was thinking about . . . rain and snow . . . and the Russian. I hope the Russians find their brother soon . . ."

☙

Along the entire front the Austrian armies collapsed in the face of relentless Russian pressure and retreated to regroup on the western side of the San River. And as the miserable Austrian armies marched in long, shuffling columns, the autumn rains descended upon them.

CHAPTER NINETEEN

To the San

THE FIRST LARGE RAIN DROPS struck the road with such force that dust erupted from the perimeter of each impact. The rain quickly muddied the road, soaking everyone and everything on it. The downpour muffled the hubbub of a weary army in flight—the grumbling infantry; the cursing teamsters, whipping their exhausted horses; the creaking wagon wheels; the groaning wounded. The men in the column knew the meaning of this downpour. It was the beginning of the autumn rains; life that previously had been merely miserable would now be miserable and wet.

Vasko appeared at Vasyl's side and shouted, "We should go under the trees!"

Vasyl nodded but kept walking—too weary to change course.

"Vasyl, let's go to the trees!"

Vasyl nodded again and felt Vasko's hand pull him off the road. They stumbled through the brush and into the forest, where men already sat, preparing their pipes, or leaned against trees, studying the sky. The two men moved farther back into the woods where it was dark and fairly dry, and began collecting wood for a fire. Vasko cleared the forest floor with his foot, creating a large circle, and Vasyl used small twigs and brush to build a small fire into which the two men fed progressively larger pieces of wood. When the fire was well established and crackling, Vasko sat on his heels and stared into the yellow flames.

"Vasko, hand me your rifle," said Vasyl. He secured the two rifles by their stacking hooks and propped them upright. "We need a third leg—hand me something to hold them up."

At that moment Petro Matsko, along with two men, both named Shtefan, appeared, each carrying an armful of wood. "More firewood for you, brothers!" announced Petro.

Vasyl nodded to a pile of wood. "Dump it there and give me your rifles—we'll stack them together. Who has a canvas for a cover? Good, Petro—that will do. Cover the muzzles."

The men retrieved various items of food from their packs and discussed the prospects of a meal. Petro Matsko produced a half cabbage, while the others provided one potato apiece. The men pooled their water into a tin pan, added sectioned potatoes, and placed the pan on a pile of hot coals they sequestered on the edge of the fire. Vasyl, to the delight of all, passed around his pouch of tobacco and paper, and the men busied themselves with rolling cigarettes.

"It is the last of the tobacco I brought from Ameryka," Vasyl sighed. "Enjoy it, brothers." He inserted the end of a stick into the fire, ignited his cigarette, and passed the glowing twig to Vasko.

High above them the rain continued to fall on the trees and to drip down on the men. But the rain, like the war, receded in the men's minds as they basked in the little warm circle and succumbed to the spell induced by their tobacco.

Vasko poked at the potatoes in the pan and sprinkled salt from a pouch into the bubbling water. Satisfied that the potatoes were nearly done, he added the cabbage and stirred the pot. The men ate in silence. After the meal they repeated the ritual with paper and tobacco. Then Vasko gave voice to a thought that was on all their minds: "Do you think the war is over?"

Vasyl blew smoke into the fire. "If it is, who would tell us?"

The men considered this for a moment. "We've been at this war almost two months," said Vasko hopefully. "When does a war end?"

The men pondered again and then each voiced his thoughts.

"It ends when one side loses."

"Then it's over—we've lost. Soon we could go home."

"We haven't lost simply because you say we've lost."

"We're running away."

"We're retreating."

"I think we're retreating to fight again."

"I agree. I've been through this too many times over the last few weeks."

"It is true. We run and then we stand again."

"I hope it ends soon."

"We all do."

"I miss my family."

"Don't talk of it."

"Well, I do. I can't help it."

"Don't speak of them. I miss mine too. Speaking about them doesn't bring you any closer to home."

"No, but I miss them all the same—especially on a day like today."

Petro Matsko nodded. "Yes, I agree. On days like this we would sit indoors and build a big fire in the hearth. My wife and *baba* would make soup and my father would play his fiddle. We'd have my wife's *slyvovitsa*—plum brandy—before soup and then afterward my wife and *baba* would dance."

"My wife makes the best *slyvovitsa* in our village," offered Vasko.

Petro Macko nodded. "*Slyvovitsa* would be good now. After two gulps of *slyvovitsa* at home, I would sing songs as my father played his fiddle."

"Vasyl's cousin from Varadka plays the fiddle. Everyone knows Pavlo Vantsa. He plays at all the weddings around Varadka and Stara Polyanka. He played at mine."

One of the Shtefans took a last, deep drag on his cigarette and flicked the butt into the fire. "I married a month before I was called to active duty. A month! Now I'm here in Galicia. I wonder how much longer she must wait for me?"

"It is good to have a wife waiting for you," said Petro Matsko. "And you, Vasyl, is someone waiting for you?"

"No."

Vasko chuckled. "They are all waiting for Vasyl! He will have his choice of any young girl in Stara Polyanka. When we go home he only has to point to the one of his choosing. *Tsy tak*—isn't that so, Vasyl?"

"Maybe. Only, I cannot remember her name—is it Mariya Kavulya or Mariya Ivanchyn?"

"Hmph!" snorted Vasko. "I know which I would choose. You men don't know Vasyl as well as I do. He can make a good match if he wants to. Only, that is not important to him. What is important to Vasyl is love. *Tsy tak*, Vasyl?"

"If you say so."

"If I say so? You told me that yourself—at your sister's wedding."

"Did I?"

"You know you did. You said that love is more important to you than a good dowry."

"I married three years ago," said the other Shtefan. "I married for the dowry,

but now . . . now, I think maybe she and I have love, too. We have two children—a boy and a girl—and I miss them. I think we must have love because
I miss my wife like in the old songs. Do you know the songs I mean?"

Petro Matsko nodded. "Yes, I think I do. We sang songs like that in our
village. I remember one:

> *It rained the evening*
> *They took me for the army.*
> *A last embrace with Mariya,*
> *Final kisses on her rosy cheeks!*
>
> *No more will I see Mariya!*
> *No more her green eyes!*
> *No more her silken hair!*
> *No more—"*

"No more singing!" cried Vasko, shaking his head in disgust. "*Bozhe moi!*
Can you sing anything sadder than that?"

One of the Shtefans cleared his throat and sang:

> *Do not weep when you receive the news.*
> *Know that I am buried beneath a linden tree*
> *In a distant foreign land.*
> *But do not weep for me;*
> *No, do not weep.*

"Enough!" cried Vasko. "Any more of this and these trees will weep! Who
knows '*Ne budu dobrŷi*—I Won't Be Good'? Sing it with me, Vasyl!"

Vasyl nodded. "Maybe our brother also knows it. Welcome, brother. Join
us by the fire." The men followed Vasyl's gaze to a lone figure standing outside their orange circle in the dim flutter of firelight and shadows. Vasyl invited him again. "Come to the fire and warm yourself."

A young peasant approached, wringing his hands. When Vasko moved
aside, making room, the peasant squatted and thrust his hands nearly into
the fire.

Frowning, Vasko studied the newcomer. "Are you mad? Be careful! You'll
burn yourself."

The peasant pulled his hands back slightly. "It is good—" His voice broke and he coughed fitfully. Vasyl poured a tin of water and passed it from man to man around the fire to Vasko who offered it to the peasant. The man drank and handed the cup back to Vasko, nodding his thanks. "Blessings on you all, brothers. It is good to sit with one's own people. I think, by your speech, you are from these mountains."

Vasyl nodded. "Yes, we are all from the other side of these mountains— from the highlands."

The peasant nodded and held his hands closer to the fire. "Yes, *verkhovyna*— the highlands. It is good to speak *po-nashomu*—our way—with friends, and to hear songs sung our way. They are like songs from my village . . . good songs about our beautiful land and our trees . . . and . . . better times . . ." He closed his eyes.

Vasko watched with concern as the peasant's hands neared the flames. "Doesn't that hurt your hands?"

The peasant pulled his hands back. "Yes . . . yes, it does."

"Then why the devil do you do it?"

"I don't know. Maybe some chills are best warmed directly in fire. My brother, have you never been that cold?"

Vasko snorted and looked at Vasyl. "I've never been so cold that I wanted to burn instead."

"I envy you," mumbled the peasant, staring into the fire.

Vasyl indicated the little pot of cabbage and potatoes. "Are you hungry, brother?"

"No . . . I don't think so . . . I haven't eaten . . . I think for two days."

Vasko was irritated. "Then you would like to eat?"

"No."

Vasko frowned at the peasant and, pointing to his own forehead, shook his head at Vasyl. Vasyl, however, was intrigued and tossed his pouch to Vasko. "Then you will want a smoke. Give it to him, Vasko."

The peasant took the pouch, rolled himself a cigarette, and then leaned close to the fire to ignite it.

"*Bozhe moi!*" cried Vasko. "Use a stick! The devil himself doesn't put his face in fire! Vasyl, look at him! Do you see how he burns himself?"

The peasant pulled back, puffing and smiled broadly at Vasko. "Yes, this fire is too hot . . . even for the devil." He blew smoke into the fire and nod-ded to Vasyl. "I thank you greatly for the tobacco. We see little of it around here and when we do, we consider ourselves blessed. Yes . . . we consider ourselves blessed." He inhaled deeply and then blew the smoke into the fire. "Blessings are rare these days—these are terrible times for all. Clearly the devil walks among us and works his mischief in the souls of the unwary." The peasant stared at Vasko and leaned closer to the fire. "Only, brothers, I can tell you that some men do not wait for the devil to knock on the door of their souls, but they go out to greet him with deeds already done. Yes . . . yes, with deeds already done. God will judge us all, but some will have a short hearing and then . . . *fft!* . . . the flames of judgment . . . yes, brothers, the flames of judgment."

Vasko edged away. "Vasyl . . ."

Vasyl held up a hand to silence his friend and then nodded at the peasant. "Go on, brother, tell us about yourself. There are no flames of judgment here."

The peasant nodded and exhaled slowly into the fire. The flames flickered in his eyes and when he leaned back, drawing deeply on his cigarette, the shadow of his nose divided his shiny forehead. "There is no end to soldiers such as you," he said. First the Russian army, then the Austrian army, and then the Russians again. I said it would never end, but she said it would all pass and that God would save us. She was carrying low—her time was near—but she said over and over that God never abandons those who need him. Yes . . . God would save us . . . He never abandons, she said. It was our first child. Her brother went to Ameryka last year and was to send for us—perhaps next year . . . yes, perhaps next year."

Vasko pointed at Vasyl and opened his mouth to speak but was silenced by Vasyl, who, with a shake of his head and two quick gestures, indicated that Vasko should not interrupt and that the peasant should go on.

The peasant smiled at Vasko, took a long puff on his cigarette, and continued. "Then the Russians began to burn the village before retreating, and all the people packed their things, and, out of fear, followed them. Fear, my brothers, is like the devil—once you say 'yes' to it, it is almost impossible to say 'no.' Men threw everything in their carts, and loaded wives and children and old people on top of it all. My neighbor's mother sat on their cart and stared back at her burning home—her eyes were wide like a frightened cow's and her hair was white as salt—yes, my brothers . . . white as salt. We followed the Russians and there was fighting around us every night. We kept to the thickest parts of the forest out of fear." The peasant blew smoke from his nostrils and nodded. "Yes, white . . . white as salt."

The peasant rocked on his haunches, smoking and humming. Vasko pointed to his own forehead again and Vasyl said softly, "Continue, brother. You are among friends."

The peasant looked up and squinted at Vasyl. "Hmm?"

"You were telling us that you had to hide in the forest with your wife."

"Yes . . . that is true. We had to hide and then . . . then her time came. The others went on and we stayed behind—alone in the forest. All day and long into the night she called out in pain and she cried . . . *oi,* how she cried! The fighting came close to us in the middle of the night and I beat the ground with my fists. The baby finally came before sunup and I placed it on her stomach and held it there—she was too weak to hold it. In the morning she was dead and that baby was crying . . . yes, that baby was crying." The peasant took a last drag on the cigarette and flicked it into the fire. The men sat motionless while water dripped from the leaves overhead, plopping on the ground and sizzling on the glowing coals.

"You see . . . a child must have its mother," continued the peasant, speaking very softly now and leaning closer to the fire. "It cannot live without its mother. I dug her grave as deep as I could—I used a plank from the cart. I lowered her into the hole and put that crying baby on her chest. I filled the hole as fast as I could and then I ran. I left the cart and ran deeper into the woods and kept running until morning. I have been wandering in these woods for days . . . days and nights . . . nights without sleep, brothers . . . yes, maybe forty days and forty nights . . ."

Vasko gathered his pack and moved to a spot on the other side of the fire between Vasyl and Petro Matsko. "Give me room, Vasyl. I'll not sleep near him tonight. Move your feet, Petro—you too, Shtefan." Vasko untied his pack, pulled out his blanket, and made a bed among the leaves. He shook out his empty pack and draped it over a branch to dry. The other men followed suit and then they all reclined, closing their eyes. The peasant, however, remained squatting by the fire, staring into the flames.

"Yes, yes," the peasant mumbled. "A child must have its mother . . . yes, yes . . . a child must have its mother . . . it cannot live without her . . . do you see? It cannot live . . ."

Vasyl, lying on his side, felt a jab in his back.

"Make him stop, Vasyl," whispered Vasko. "Who can sleep hearing that? It's like having the very devil himself among us."

"Yes . . . yes . . . he walks among us . . . guard your soul . . . guard your soul . . ."

Vasyl pushed Vasko's hand away. "Go to sleep—everyone, go to sleep"

"Yes . . . yes, yes . . . *oi,* as white as salt . . . yes . . ."

"QUIET!"

"Yes . . . hmm, hmm . . . hmm . . ."

⁂

Early in the morning, Vasyl made his way back to the campsite, where he shook his friend from a sound sleep. "Get up, Vasko. Our Russian brothers are not far away. All of you, up! I just spoke with Sergeant Haletskii. He says our company has been ordered to form a rear guard. Hurry up."

Coughing and stretching, the men rose and began packing their gear. Vasko pointed to the vacant spot on the other side of the smoldering coals. "Look—he's gone. The devil is gone. Where do you think he went?"

Vasyl and the other men shrugged and busied themselves tying up their packs and stepping back into the trees to relieve their bladders.

Vasko shouldered his pack and uncovered the stacked rifles. "Look. Vasyl, come here. Look—my strap is missing from my rifle."

Vasyl and the two Shtefans gathered around the rifles and one of the Shtefans said, "My strap is missing also."

Vasyl shrugged. "We'll worry about them later. Come—we must hurry."

"But, Vasyl, who would steal rifle slings?"

Petro Matsko emerged from the trees buttoning his pants. "No one stole your sling, Vasko. Your friend borrowed it."

"My friend?"

"Your devil-friend by the fire. He is back in the trees over there. You will have to cut him down—but then, there won't be much left of your rifle sling, unless you take it from around his neck."

Vasko frowned. "Vasyl . . . why did that devil have to use mine?"

"Hmph! He used mine too," said one of the Shtefans.

Vasyl shouldered his rifle. "Come. We must go. Hurry."

The men gathered their rifles and made their way through the trees to the road, where Sergeant Haletskii deployed them in defensive positions to await the advancing Russians. In the brief skirmish that ensued, one of the Shtefans—the one who had married a month before his call to active duty—was badly wounded and had to be left behind to the care of the Russians. The remaining men scurried westward on the muddy road to rejoin their comrades in the long retreat to the San River.

∾

The Russian armies followed the fleeing Austro-Hungarian forces across the San River westward toward Kraków and southward into the Carpathian Mountains. Through the winter of 1914 to 1915, the Austro-Hungarian and Russian armies battled to a stalemate in the Carpathians. The wounded overwhelmed the medical staffs of both armies; prisoners of war clogged the roads of rear areas, where their captors scrambled to feed and shelter the multitudes. By the spring of 1915, casualties among the armies of Austria-Hungary totaled almost two million. Losses among the Russians, who, to the north, faced German as well as Austro-Hungarian armies, also approached two million.

And the war was only nine months old.

CHAPTER TWENTY

Our People

IN THE SPRING OF 1915, Vasyl, Vasko, and the remnants of their company were encamped, along with other reserve infantry units, behind the front lines in the Carpathian Mountains. Sergeant Haletskii and Vasyl were finishing their lunch and enjoying their army rum ration when Vasko joined them. The sergeant wiped his spoon on his shirt and said, "I can't go with you, Rusynko. The lieutenant wants to speak with me. I'll go later. I've already sent Varkhol and Matsko. The men coming back say the lines are long, so you'd better hurry—it looks like it might rain later." The sergeant chuckled. "It is funny, Rusynko. Have you noticed how the men have a new attitude about the Germans?"

"I think so."

Sergeant Haletskii stood and stretched. "It is true; they have a new attitude. At first our men complained about the Germans being here in our sector. They hated the Germans—they resented them for their better uniforms and their better equipment. They hated the way the Germans looked at us— the way they smiled and shook their heads at each other as if to say, 'Look at the poor Austrian Slavs trying to be soldiers!' But now, our men like the Germans. Or, they like the women the Germans brought with them. Are you going, Ivanchyn?"

Vasko lowered his flask of rum and wiped his mouth with the back of his sleeve. "Yes, Sergeant."

Vasyl grinned and then tapped Vasko's leg with his boot. "What would Paraska say?" he asked.

"I want to see the German women," Vasko said, shrugging, his mouth full.

"Very well," said Sergeant Haletskii. "Take this with you, Rusynko." He handed Vasyl a full flask of rum and then called over his shoulder as he walked away, "I'm going to see the lieutenant. I will see both of you this evening, either here or at the camp."

"How many German women do you think there will be, Vasyl?" asked Vasko.

"I don't know. Hurry up."

"I've never seen German women, Vasyl. You were in Germany last year when you came home from Ameryka, yes?"

"Yes. Finish eating."

What did the German women look like?"

"What do you mean, what do they look like? They look like women everywhere. Hurry up."

Vasko licked his spoon, inserted it into his tunic pocket, and rose to his feet. "I'm ready, Vasyl. Let's go before it rains."

Vasyl stood, brushing his trousers and looking at the sky. "I wonder, how far is it? I don't want to get wet."

"Don't you want to go?"

Vasyl shrugged and the corners of his mouth arched downward. *"Chom nit*—why not?" Vasyl took a swallow of rum and handed the flask to Vasko.

The two friends struck out toward the rearward area on a crowded road they shared with oncoming German and Austrian supply wagons. Teamsters whistled and bellowed to their enormous draft horses, lumbering on the heels of the little Austrian mountain carts driven by harried Slovaks, Hungarians, and Rusyns.

Vasyl and Vasko stepped off the road and waited as a large horse-drawn artillery piece rumbled past. "I wish I were in the German army, don't you, Vasyl?" shouted Vasko.

"No. Why would I want to be in their army?" The two stepped back onto the road.

"Because, Vasyl, when they do something, they do it in a big way—in the right way. If I have to be in an army, I wish I were in their army. I hear they defeat the Russians whenever they want to. The Germans always come to our aid because our army cannot defeat Russians. Do you know what the Russians call our army?"

"How would I know?"

"They call us the 'gypsy bazaar.' What do you think of that? 'Gypsy bazaar!' I heard it from Petro Burda, who was escorting Russian prisoners to the rear last week. They think we are a bunch of *tsyganŷ*—gypsies!"

Vasyl laughed. "I suppose we are an odd-looking army. I think I can see why they would call us that."

"Yes, Vasyl, only, *tsyganŷ*! I think I would have them call us anything but that! At least the Germans don't call us *tsyganŷ*."

"No, probably not. God only knows what they call us."

"But, Vasyl, they must not think too badly of us. They brought their women for us."

Vasyl laughed. "Well, that is something, I guess!"

"Have you heard the rumors, Vasyl?"

"Yes."

"What have you heard?"

"The same things you've heard."

"What have you heard?"

Vasyl stopped and searched his pockets. "Wait, Vasko. I want a cigarette. Do you have tobacco?"

"No. What did you hear?"

"Never mind, I have some. I heard that the Germans might make an attack against the Russians with our army in support. Do you have papers?"

"No. I heard the same thing. Where did you hear this, Vasyl?"

"From you. Never mind, I have papers, too."

Vasyl rolled a cigarette, handed it to Vasko, and then rolled another for himself. Producing a box of matches from his tunic, Vasyl ignited both cigarettes and the two men walked in silence, smoking and sipping from the flask of rum.

Along a particularly quiet stretch of road they approached a large roadside crucifix with both cross and corpus rendered in stone and set upon a concrete base. Vasko slipped the flask inside his tunic, shielding it from the gaze of the Lord. The two men paused, crossed themselves, and continued on their way.

Vasyl pulled Vasko off the road. "Look."

Approaching from the south was a German army vehicle, its driver sporting goggles and struggling with the steering wheel. In the backseat was a German officer. Vasko straightened and saluted while Vasyl stepped back from the road. Neither the driver nor the officer paid the slightest attention to the two haggard infantrymen of their Austrian allies' army standing beside the road. Vasyl and Vasko, coughing and waving the dust from their faces, continued along the road.

Vasyl laughed. "There is your beloved German army. He didn't even return your salute. Do you still wish you were in his army?"

"*To nich*—it is nothing, Vasyl. Look, Germans. They will show us where to go."

On the side of the road stood five German soldiers, smoking cigarettes and sharing a large bottle of wine. Upon noticing Vasyl and Vasko, one of the Germans brandished the wine bottle and shouted. The other Germans laughed and nodded to each other.

Vasko reddened. "What did he say?"

"I don't know," said Vasyl.

The two friends approached the soldiers and stopped. The Germans inspected the two Austro-Hungarian infantrymen with amused interest, pointing and making comments among themselves. One of the Germans directed his comrades' attention to the faded yellow lace pattern on Vasyl's and Vasko's trousers. "*Ungarin*—Hungarians?" asked the German.

Vasyl hesitated and then nodded. "*Ungarin.*"

Out of the corner of his mouth, Vasko whispered, "Vasyl, we're not Hungarians."

Vasyl, also whispering out of the corner of his mouth, replied, "What does it matter?"

The German with the wine bottle offered Vasko a drink. "*Ungarisch Wein! Prost!*—Hungarian wine! Cheers!"

Vasko took a swallow and handed the bottle to Vasyl. "Ask about the German women."

"I don't speak enough German to ask that."

One of the other Germans addressed Vasyl, who shrugged, indicating he did not understand. The German made a vulgar gesture and his friends laughed. Vasyl nodded—now he understood. The Germans pointed to a wooded area across a nearby field. Vasyl and Vasko nodded their thanks for the wine and went on their way.

Out of the dark western skies came the distant rumble of thunder, and the two friends quickened their pace to the trees where soldiers of the Austro-Hungarian Army lounged.

One of these soldiers stood and called out in Slovak, "Come, brothers! You are almost there! Heaven awaits you!"

Vasyl and Vasko reached the trees as a light rain began to fall. The Slovak who had welcomed them offered Vasyl a bottle. "Drink, brother!" he shouted.

Vasyl took a swallow and grimaced.

The Slovak laughed. "Homemade *borovichka,* my brother!"

Vasyl took another long drink, made a face, and passed the pine-flavored whiskey to Vasko. "*Dobra*—good," said Vasyl. "Bitter, but good."

Vasko swallowed and wiped his chin. "*Oi!*" He took another long drink. "*Oi!*"

Vasyl took the bottle from Vasko, had one more swallow, and handed it back to the Slovak. "Where do we go?" asked Vasyl.

The Slovak pointed through the trees. "You are almost there. Hurry before there is nothing left." He took a sip of *borovichka* and, looking at Vasko, tapped the bottle. "*Dobra, áno*—good, yes?"

"*Oi!*"

With the Slovak roaring with delight behind them, Vasyl and Vasko followed the trail into the woods, where they soon reached a large clearing. German and Austro-Hungarian soldiers stood in long lines facing a row of canvas tents pitched in a semicircle at the clearing's edge.

Vasko tapped Vasyl's shoulder. "Look! Varkhol and Petro Matsko!"

With a jug in his hand, Varkhol swayed to their side. "Welcome, brothers!" he cried, slapping Vasyl on the back and draping an arm around Vasko's shoulders. "Dear brothers! Honest comrades! Vasko, drink! Yes, that is the way—big swallows for the little man!"

"*Oi!*"

Varkhol took the jug from Vasko and pushed it into Vasyl's hands. "Drink, brother! It's not bad wine. Petro! Hold my place! You two must go to the end of the line. These crazy soldiers will tear you and me apart if you try to join me in line. In the trenches they are your comrades, but here, it is every man for himself! Do you see that old man by the big beech tree? You must go to him first. He will take your money—then you get in this line. He will sell you wine and vodka, if you can afford it. He has two daughters in the tents and, I hear, a wife!"

Vasko sputtered, "A wife! *Bozhe moi*—my God! How old is she?"

Varkhol slapped Vasko on the back. "What difference does it make? She's a woman, not a horse!"

A soldier in line turned around and said, "I've seen her. By the time you finish this jug she'll be as young as you can dream—so long as you can dream with your eyes shut!"

Vasyl put out his hand. "Give me your money, Vasko. Hold a place in line for us. I'll go pay for both of us."

"I don't have any money," said Vasko.

"No money! Then what are you doing here?"

"I'll pay you back later."

"*Bozhe moi!* Stay here!" Greatly annoyed, Vasyl staggered to the line under the beech tree. When he reached the head of this line he displayed a handful of coins to the old man, saying, "*Zwei, bitte*—two, please."

The old man picked out a number of coins from Vasyl's hand and responded in Rusyn, "You don't have to speak German to me. I speak *po-nashomu*—our way. You want whiskey, wine, vodka?"

Vasyl was surprised. "You are not German?"

"No. You want whiskey, wine, vodka?"

Vasyl examined the meager supply of coins remaining in his hand. "How much for vodka?"

"Twenty."

"Twenty? The women cost only fifteen!"

"Vodka is hard to find. You want vodka, it's twenty. You want wine, it's ten."

Vasyl slapped the coins in the old man's hand. "*Bozhe moi!* Give me the vodka."

The old man reached behind his seat and held up a small bottle. "When you finish the vodka, return the bottle. I'll pay you for it."

Grumbling, Vasyl snatched the bottle and stalked away.

The old man called after him. "You want your change? You have change coming for the vodka." The old man held up a coin.

Vasyl turned around and squinted at the tiny coin. "How much is it worth?"

"Not much."

"Keep it." Vasyl rejoined his friend in the line, opened the vodka, took a swig, and handed it to Vasko.

"*Dyakuyu*—thanks, Vasyl. I'll pay you back. You know that I will."

"Yes, yes! What the hell!" snapped Vasyl. Then he smiled and jabbed Vasko in the ribs playfully. "Yes, I know you will pay me back—just as you always re-paid Yakov in the old days."

What had been a light rain suddenly became a furious downpour. The men pulled up their collars and tilted their bottles to their mouths, shut-ting their eyes tightly against the deluge. Laughing and shoving one another good-naturedly, they shouted oaths above the rain's racket.

Vasyl pulled his cap down tightly over his eyes and took a swallow of vodka before handing the bottle to Vasko. "Do you remember Yakov's she-cat?" he shouted to Vasko.

"His what?"

"Yakov's she-cat—do you remember her?"

"The gray? The one he had when we were children?"

"Yes!"

"I remember—what about her, Vasyl?"

"Do you remember when it was her time—how the tomcats circled her and took their turn with her?"

Vasko took a swallow of vodka. "Honest Vasyl, you are drunk!"

"Yes, but mostly I am wet. I remember that the tomcats had the sense to stop while it rained."

"But, Vasyl, we can't leave now. We've waited so long to see the German women. Look, the line is much shorter."

"Yes, and I am much wetter. Give me the vodka."

Eventually the rain abated, transforming into a cold mist. The line moved forward and Vasyl and Vasko found themselves at the front of the line, where an old woman, missing her lower front teeth and wielding a crooked cane, directed Vasyl to one of the tents.

Shaking the water out of his cap, Vasyl walked around the tent to the entrance, turned the flap aside, and entered. Inside, he found a wooden cot like those used by officers, an inverted wooden supply crate, and on the floor, a muddy canvas mat—but no woman. Vasyl picked up a small icon sitting on the crate and was examining it when a feminine voice startled him.

"*Panna Mariya*—the Virgin Mary," said the voice in the same Lemko dialect spoken by the old man under the beech tree. She was young—younger than Vasyl—and wearing only wooden shoes and a long, white open blouse. Slightly plump, but by no means fat, she was a stark contrast to the gaunt peasant refugees who roamed the countryside and begged from passing armies. She entered the tent, closed the flap behind her, and stepped out of her wooden shoes, pushing them under the cot with her toes. She stretched and, scratching her white belly, reclined on the cot. The bottoms of her feet were black with caked mud. She yawned and said, "Well?"

Vasyl, still holding the icon, stared at her until she took the icon from him and replaced it on the inverted crate. "There is not much time, soldier," she said. "They only allow you a little time—the lines are long." She was one of Vasyl's people; she looked like almost any girl in Stara Polyanka. "Do you want to look at icons, soldier, or do you want to look at me?"

Vasyl closed his eyes and murmured, *"Nem értem*—I don't understand."

"Ah, you are Magyar, soldier. I don't speak Magyar—only '*kérem*—please,' '*köszönöm*—thank you,' and maybe a few other words. You can't understand me at all, can you? Maybe you speak a little German, hmm? *Verstehen Sie*—do you understand?"

"Nem értem," said Vasyl, opening his eyes and struggling to focus on the girl.

"To shkoda—that's too bad. You look like a good boy—I like you. When I came inside the tent I thought, 'He looks like our people.'" She pointed to her feet. "Shoes off, hmm? No muddy boots on the cot." Then she gestured with her hands. "Pants stay on—open them, but keep them on. *Igen*—yes, that is good." She held her arms open. "Now come to me." She reached for Vasyl's arms, but he held up a hand, stopping her.

"What is it, soldier? Hmm?"

Vasyl reached over to the crate and turned the icon of the Mother of God facedown. The woman chuckled and then covered her mouth and wheezed with laughter, her face contorting and her breasts and well-fed belly trembling.

☙

Vasyl tied the laces of his boots and then stood and pulled the tent flap aside. He paused and, without looking back, said, *"Köszönöm*—thank you."

From the cot came a reply in midyawn, *"Szívesen*—you're welcome."

Vasyl stepped outside into the damp chilly air and, cocking his ear, listened to the commotion issuing from one of the tents. He grinned and snorted at the sound of an unmistakable tenor voice: *"Oi-ioi! Oi-ioi! Oi-ioi! Oi-ioi!"*

Varkhol and Petro Matsko, standing under the trees with other recent veterans of the tents, beckoned to Vasyl, who joined the laughing men.

"Vasyl, do you hear him?" cried a gleeful Varkhol.

"Yes, I hear him."

Varkhol turned to the other men. "Remember what I said—wait until he comes out of the tent and then everyone together! You too, Vasyl. Wait for my command."

The tent of interest was silent now. The men snickered and awaited Varkhol's signal. When Vasko emerged, Varkhol shouted, "Now!" The men chanted in unison, *"Oi-ioi! Oi-ioi! Oi-ioi! Oi-ioi!"*

Startled, the red-faced Vasko made a quick bow and trotted to Vasyl's side. "Let's go, Vasyl," he said. "I'm hungry."

Vasyl slapped Vasko on the back. "I'm sure you are. You worked hard! *Oi-ioi!*"

The men still waiting in line laughed coarsely at Vasko and jostled him back and forth until he escaped their clutches and trotted after Vasyl, who had started back toward the company's camp with Varkhol and Petro Matsko. The road was a muddy mess, and though the rain had ceased, the clouds lingered, clinging close to the earth and rolling slowly over the fields. Waving Varkhol and Petro Matsko ahead, Vasyl waited for his friend. Vasko's hands were stuffed in his pockets and he walked with his head down.

"Not too much farther," said Vasyl. "Soon you can eat."

Vasko nodded and the two walked in silence. Then Vasko mumbled something and Vasyl said, "What?"

"They were *nash narod*—our people," Vasko repeated.

"Who?"

"The girls in the tents."

"Yes . . . yes, I know. All of them: the old man who took our money—my money, the *baba* with the cane, the girls."

"I thought they would be German, Vasyl. I remember this morning, in our camp, someone said that the Germans brought their women with them."

"Well, they were wrong. The Germans brought our women with them."

"It doesn't seem right . . . it just doesn't seem right . . ."

"What doesn't seem right?"

"If I had known the women were *nash narod*. I would not have come here. It isn't right."

Vasyl snorted. "It seemed right to you when you thought they were German. You didn't run out of the tent and ask for a return of your money—my money."

"I was drunk—what did I know? It wasn't right, Vasyl . . . it wasn't right. It would have been better if she had been German. Then . . . I wouldn't feel this way. We should have left."

"We'd already spent my money."

"I know . . . I know. I'll pay you back. It just wasn't right—not with our people. I didn't know what to say when she spoke to me *po-nashomu*—our way. What did you say to yours?"

"Not much. She thought I was Magyar."

"Why would she think that?"

"Because when she spoke, I answered, '*Nem értem*—I don't understand.'"

Vasko chuckled. "You pretended to be a Magyar. I wish I'd thought of that. Do you see, honest Vasyl? You didn't think it was right either."

Again, they walked in silence until they came to the same lonely wayside crucifix they had passed earlier. They stopped, crossed themselves, and Vasyl said, "Let's rest here. I want a cigarette."

Vasyl retrieved tobacco and papers from one of his tunic pockets, and the two men rolled cigarettes for themselves. They lit their cigarettes, inhaled deeply, and stared at the Lord.

"Look at him, Vasyl. Look how He suffers. Do you think He knows where we've been?"

"Of course."

Vasko groaned. After a pause, he said, "Vasyl . . ."

"Yes?"

"Are you . . . are you afraid of hell?"

"Yes . . . yes, I am."

"So am I, Vasyl. So am I." Vasko shook his head. "And it is *Velykŷi Post*— Great Lent."

"*To pravda*—that's true."

"*Bozhe moi*," moaned Vasko.

"Yes, *Bozhe moi*."

"I want to tell you something, Vasyl. I don't want you to laugh at me."

"I never laugh at you."

"Only you do, Vasyl. Maybe you don't laugh aloud—but with your eyes, you laugh."

"I won't laugh, my friend."

"*Dobre*—very well. I . . . I miss Paraska."

"I know you do."

Vasko smiled. "How do you know?"

"Because I can see it in your face—ever since we've been in the mountains."

"Yes, I think of her always. I try not to, only . . . only I can't help it. I hope she is safe in Stara Polyanka. I hope they are all safe. They say there was fighting in the mountains west of here. Look how the Lord faces that way— maybe He knows something . . ."

Vasyl nodded. "Yes, I heard that Makovytsya is in Russian hands and—*Bozhe moi,* Vasko! What the devil is wrong with you?"

Vasko's eyes were wide and his cigarette twitched in his mouth. He removed the cigarette from his lips and pointed to the base of the cross. "Vasyl, look! Lilacs! Someone put lilacs at the Lord's feet. They were not there when we passed by here earlier!"

"No, perhaps not. They are only lilacs, Vasko. What is wrong with you?"

"Do you see lilacs in bloom anywhere around here, Vasyl? It is too early for lilacs. Where did they come from?"

"I don't know—perhaps from the lowlands, where it is warmer already. Calm yourself, Vasko."

Vasko inhaled a last time from his cigarette and then flicked it onto the road, shaking his head. "Do you remember?" he murmured. "In the spring in Stara Polyanka, we used to cut lilacs and place them on the graves. Something is wrong, Vasyl. Someone is dead."

Vasyl put a hand on Vasko's shoulder. "There is nothing wrong. No one is dead. Come, you are hungry, remember? Let's go back to the camp and eat. Come."

The two men returned to their company in silence, Vasko scowling as he walked.

 C/3

Back at the camp, the smoke from the regimental stew wagons hung low in the chilly evening air, and the men reporting for supper were greeted by the smell of fresh-baked bread from the field ovens. Vasyl and Vasko retrieved their tins and stood in line, where Yurko served goulash from a steaming pot. Without a word, Vasko disappeared with his tin while Vasyl ate with other men from the company.

Later, at sundown, Vasyl found Vasko sitting alone against a tree. Vasyl sat against a neighboring tree while the western sky dissolved from yellow to orange . . . then to red . . . then purple . . . and, finally, gray. When Vasko stood to leave, Vasyl joined him and the two walked together back toward camp.

After a few steps in the twilight, Vasko grasped Vasyl by the shoulder, bringing his friend to a halt. "You miss someone too, Vasyl."

"Oh?"

"Yes. There is love in your eyes."

Vasyl smiled. "Oh, yes. Only, I cannot remember her name. Is it Mariya Ivanchyn or Mariya Kavulya?"

Vasko shrugged and snorted. "I don't remember anymore. I have forgotten. But I know that you miss someone, honest Vasyl. Only, I don't think her name is Mariya."

"I miss my family."

"Of course. And you are in love. I can see it."

"I told you once before, there is no one."

"Yes, I remember. But, Vasyl, if I tell you something, do you promise you will not laugh at me?"

Vasyl laughed. "Why do you always think that I am laughing at you?"

"You are laughing now."

"I'm laughing because you never believe me."

"Well, you can laugh if you want. I don't know if I should tell you this, only I remembered something while I sat under that tree. I remembered when you were in Ameryka and your brother Petro married Yevka. I thought it wasn't right. I remember thinking, Vasyl should marry Yevka. Now you may laugh, Vasyl."

Vasyl sighed and murmured, "There is no reason for me to laugh, my friend."

"You miss her, don't you, Vasyl? I know you do. Don't say anything. I will never mention it again. Only, I thought about these things under that tree and I wanted to tell you. I don't know why. I will never mention it again—forever and ever. But it wasn't right . . . it just wasn't right . . ."

❧

Holy Week began two weeks later and there were outdoor celebrations of the Divine Liturgy for Rusyn units. Greek Catholic priests sat in the woods and heard individual confessions. Great numbers of infantryman, Vasyl and Vasko among them, stood in long lines in the cool spring air and then knelt on the forest floor to confess their sins.

The following Sunday was *Velykden*—Easter. The Greek Catholics among the Austro-Hungarian troops sang the triumphal hymn of the Lord's

Resurrection in Old Slavonic. Across no man's land, beyond the rows of trenches and barbed wire, the Orthodox Russian army sang the same triumphal hymn in the same Old Slavonic:

Khrystos voskrese iz mertvykh!
Smertiyu smert poprav,
I sushchim vo hrobikh zhivot darovav.

Christ is risen from the dead!
By death he conquered death,
And to those in the graves He granted life.

CHAPTER TWENTY-ONE

Lime

IN THE SPRING OF 1915 GERMAN FORCES, with Austro-Hungarian armies in support, attacked Russian defenses on a broad front between Gorlice and Tarnów in western Galicia. After hours of constant shelling, German and Austrian units advanced across a churned landscape strewn with Russian dead and dying. Stunned and wounded Russian survivors, greeting the advancing troops with vacant stares, sat placidly while awaiting medical attention from German and Austrian orderlies. The Russian lines destroyed, German and Austrian troops streamed into the open country east of Gorlice and Tarnów. To avoid being outflanked, Russian units in the Carpathian Mountains withdrew from their defenses and fled to the north and east. Ferocious Russian resistance delayed the German and Austrian pursuers, but could not stem the disaster. The Great Russian Retreat of 1915 had begun.

❧

Vasyl returned from the stew wagon with another plate of goulash, rejoining his weary comrades reclining in the shade of three oak trees bordering a broad wheat field. When a light easterly breeze rustled the wheat, Vasko grimaced and wrinkled his nose. "Feh! It never leaves us," he grumbled.

Vasyl shrugged. "As long as the war lasts . . . it will stay with us."

Petro Matsko swallowed and wiped his chin. "The heat doesn't help. Another day like yesterday and the smell will be unbearable."

"And it is only early June," said another man. "We have a long summer ahead of us."

Vasko wiped his plate clean with a piece of bread. "The winter was cold, but at least there was no smell. They should bury them faster in the summer."

Vasyl shook his head. "There's not enough time or men for the job. The Russians may be retreating, but they are making our pursuit costly."

Varkhol snorted. "Have you all not heard? Do you think they pulled us from the front to get fat and sleep in the grass? Eat all your goulash, brothers. After this meal you will trade your rifle for a shovel."

Vasko frowned. "Varkhol knows nothing. Rumors pass through him like dung."

Varkhol smiled. "When you get your shovel, remember who told you."

Vasko tapped Vasyl's shoulder. "We will see to it that Varkhol gets a large shovel so he can dig all the way down to his future eternal home! What do you think, Vasyl?"

Vasyl ignored Vasko and pointed his spoon toward a young soldier sitting nearby.

"You are new."

The men glanced up from their goulash, regarded the new man briefly, and returned to their food.

"What is your name and where are you from?" asked Vasyl.

"Fedor Prybula—of Marhan."

"Marhan . . . Marhan . . ." Vasyl pondered the name. "On which river is it located?"

"The Topla."

"Above or below Bardeyov?"

"Below."

"Do you know Stara Polyanka on the Ondava?" asked Vasko.

Fedor squinted and then said, "Is it near Tsigla?"

"Yes," said Vasyl. "To the north. Is there any news of Stara Polyanka?"

"I think it is gone."

Both Vasyl and Vasko leaned forward, crying, "Gone?"

"There was fighting for a long time around Zborov and the roads to the north," said Fedor. "Some of the villages were burned."

Vasko turned to Vasyl. "*Bozhe moi,* do you think—"

Vasyl hushed his friend with a raised hand. "What did you hear of Stara Polyanka, friend?"

"It is hard to say. There was much fighting there, I think."

"You said before that you thought it was gone," said Vasyl.

"There were refugees everywhere. There was much talk about this village or that village. Many people went to the hills to hide from the fighting."

Vasyl grasped Fedor's arm. "What about Stara Polyanka?"

Fedor shrugged. "I don't know. Some people came to Reshov. But I think they were from Nŷzhnya Polyanka. The army brought them south because their homes were destroyed or their village was occupied by the Russians."

Vasyl looked at Vasko and said, "I know Reshov. It's not far from Bardeyov."

Vasyl tightened his grip on Fedor's arm. "Were there any people in Reshov from Stara Polyanka?"

"Maybe. I don't really remember."

"Do you remember the name Rusynko?"

"Or Ivanchyn?" asked Vasko. "Squeeze it from him, Vasyl."

Fedor pulled away from Vasyl. "Let go of me." He rubbed his arm and said, "Did you say Rusynko?"

"Yes. Do you remember the name Rusynko?"

Fedor nodded. "I was in Reshov one day and I think there was a couple with that name. His name was Vasyl and hers was . . . Mariya, I think. Do you know them?"

"Yes," said Vasyl. "He might be my father's cousin. They are from Niklova. Were there any others by that name?"

"I don't know—maybe. It was a bad time. I don't know. They took me for the army very soon after the Russians crossed the mountains."

Vasyl and Vasko looked at one another, and then Vasko kicked his heel into the earth. "How much longer, Vasyl?"

"What?"

"How much longer will this war last?"

"I don't know."

"Well, I know," said Varkhol. "With the Germans in charge of this offensive, it can't last much longer. The Russians can't beat the Germans. They have lost—we'll be home at summer's end."

"Do you think that's possible, Vasyl?" asked Vasko.

"Anything is possible."

At that moment Sergeant Haletskii rode up in a heavy cart pulled by two draft horses. An identical rig was not far behind. "Rusynko and Matsko! Come with me."

Vasko jumped up. "Do you need a third, Sergeant?"

"No, Ivanchyn. Rusynko and Matsko will do."

Vasyl handed his tin plate to Vasko and climbed onto the cart, sitting next to Sergeant Haletskii, while Petro Matsko climbed up onto the second cart. Vasko trotted behind. "Where are you going? One more won't be in the way!"

Sergeant Haletskii waved Vasko back. "No, Ivanchyn. You will have your work to do."

"But Sergeant, I don't want to dig graves!"

Sergeant Haletskii turned to Vasyl. "How did he know?"

Vasyl sniffed the air and winced. "There is nothing wrong with his nose, Sergeant." Then Vasyl looked down at his friend. "Go back, Vasko, before Varkhol worries that his little dog is lost!"

Vasko shouted, "Happy to try, sir!" Then he grunted and shuffled back to the shade of the oak trees.

Sergeant Haletskii smiled at Vasyl. "Your friend doesn't like to work hard."

Vasyl shook his head. "It's not the digging he minds—it's the tossing of fifty or a hundred men into one grave that gives him restless nights. Where are we going, Sergeant?"

"For lime. Our supply ran out yesterday." When Vasyl frowned, Sergeant Haletskii laughed. "You didn't think we were going to get wine for the Colonel did you? Our German friends have offered us some of their supply of lime. The Germans never run out of it. They plan ahead. They always have plenty of what an army needs. They know before any offensive that they will need many men and many guns and many shovels and many bags of lime. Our army never plans as well as the German army."

The two carts bounced far to the rear under increasingly dark, threatening skies. At the sound of a distant and rolling rumble, Sergeant Haletskii brought his cart to a halt and turned in his seat. "Artillery," he said, closing his eyes and turning an ear eastward. "Theirs." The other cart came to a halt and all four men listened to the intensifying barrage.

Sergeant Haletskii turned both ways in his seat. "I don't think it is against us. It sounds like it is on our left." He turned his head again. "Yes . . . I'm sure it is on our left. Perhaps the retreating Russians have found something worth defending." The sergeant motioned to the men behind, and the two carts continued on their way.

Later, Sergeant Haletskii stopped again and the men in both carts turned in their seats and listened. "I don't like it," said the sergeant. "No . . . I don't like it. Do you hear that? Those are our guns. That other, that low *boom* . . . *boom* . . . *boom* . . . those are our Russian brothers. I don't think that is on our left. And I don't think it is on our right either."

"Do you think we should turn around?" asked Vasyl.

"No. We're almost there. We can't go back without the lime."

Eventually the men reached the German supply post, where Sergeant Haletskii presented his written request to a German sergeant, who pointed down the road, said something in German, and laughed. Sergeant Haletskii climbed back onto the cart and indicated that Vasyl should now take the reins.

Vasyl asked the sergeant, "What was he laughing about?"

"How would I know? I don't speak German."

The two carts pulled into the assigned area and, donning gloves, the men loaded the carts with sacks of lime. As they worked, the four men glanced nervously toward the frontlines and the constant, low roll of artillery. The cargo stowed, Sergeant Haletskii once again took the reins and steered the lead cart back toward the front.

ↂ

The return journey was slow for the anxious men, who could merely listen to the growing magnitude of the struggle in front of them. At a crossroads they were forced to wait as long gray lines of German infantry, stabbing the air with the points of their *Pickelhauben*—their spiked leather helmets—marched up from the south and turned onto the same road. Sitting on the reins, Sergeant Haletskii pulled his pipe and pouch from a pocket, prepared a smoke, and handed the pouch to Vasyl. "I don't have any papers. *Tsy mash faiku?*"

"Yes, I have a pipe," replied Vasyl, reaching inside his field jacket. "A few days ago it belonged to someone else—he will never need it again." The sergeant produced a wooden match, struck it against the side of the cart, and shielded it with a hand as the two, in turn, ignited their pipes.

Sergeant Haletskii flicked the match to the road. "This is bad. These men are reinforcing us." He sighed heavily. "The Germans must always reinforce us." He looked behind him at the low western sunlight streaming through the gathering clouds. "It will be dark soon—and wet."

The men smoked idly until the end of the German column marched past them. Sergeant Haletskii tossed the reins and the two carts rolled forward in the dust raised by German boots. At sundown, when they reached the same wheat field and oak trees, they were waved off the road by a lieutenant.

"Park your carts over there, Sergeant. Your company was sent forward earlier. Get your rifles and follow this road. You will run into them directly." The lieutenant turned and disappeared into a sea of Austrian uniforms.

Sergeant Haletskii shrugged. "Let's go find our rifles." After a lengthy search in the dark, the four men found their rifles and headed toward the sound of the guns. Flashes from the horizon silhouetted trees, stumps, and men with their equipment frozen in various attitudes. When they came upon a group of men from another company, Sergeant Haletskii went off to search for someone in charge.

The ground beneath Vasyl's feet vibrated as he looked toward the north, where, in the medium distance, the explosive flashes were most intense. The light breeze that had come up at sundown now gusted and whipped the branches of the trees.

Sergeant Haletskii gathered the men around him. "No one knows the location of our company. Apparently they were called forward just after we left this afternoon. The Russians counterattacked along our front and broke through before dark and moved in behind our lines. Now the officers here are trying to decide which position to take—the Germans have already moved up ahead of us. They think the Russian counterattack has been stopped, but no one is sure. There are rumors that the Russians who broke through are surrendering."

Vasyl studied Sergeant Haletskii's face, which, illuminated intermittently by the distant flashes, resembled the hand-cranked images from the penny arcades on the other side of the ocean. Along with the wind now came raindrops, and the artillery flashes on the horizon were joined by lightning above.

From the direction of the front came the sound of shouting and the men craned their necks for a better look. The men parted as a Red Cross orderly shouted, "Make way for wounded! Make way there! Step back!" The rain fell heavily now on the shuffling wounded and the unscathed onlookers. A caisson pulled by three men harnessed to the broken wooden tongue rumbled by carrying four roughly bandaged men. In the lightning flashes, Vasyl made out a familiar form among the men pulling the cart and he fell in step with them.

"Yurko, is that you? You are not hurt?" Yurko shook his head. Vasyl fell back to scrutinize the men in the caisson and then again came abreast of his friend. "Yurko, where is Vasko?" Yurko glanced back toward the glowing front. "Yurko, is that where our company was sent today?" Yurko nodded.

"Rusynko!" Sergeant Haletskii gestured to Vasyl to rejoin the group. "No one here seems to know what to do. I think it is best that we head toward the front and help our wounded. Stack and cover your rifles—then follow me."

Vasyl, Petro Matsko, and a few others stored their rifles and followed the sergeant in the rain against the endless flow of wounded. For most of the night they helped carry and escort the injured into the yellow lantern light of a hastily erected Red Cross dressing station. Vasyl, studying muddy faces in his search for Vasko, was heartened when Yurko staggered into the tent carrying a man from one of the caissons. But Yurko shook his head at Vasyl, deposited the man on a cot, and hurried back out into the rain.

After midnight the rain finally stopped, but the torrent of wounded and dying men continued all night and throughout the following day.

CHAPTER TWENTY-TWO

The Grave

TWO SLOVAK STRETCHER BEARERS, wearing the arm patch of the *Roten Kreuze*—the Red Cross—and carrying between them a rolled canvas stretcher, slogged across a muddy shell-pitted landscape. The other two members of their team, both Magyars, had gone forward in the search for wounded. One of the Slovaks, Anton, had been at the front since the previous September and was taking a new stretcher bearer, Jozef, a young student from Pryashev, into the field for the first time. The new man struggled in the mud and listened to the older man's discourse on his experiences at the front.

"You will see, Jozef, my friend, how it will take us all morning for only four or five cases. In this mud we might not even bring in that many. Arm and leg cases are the best ones to find and head wounds if they aren't too bad. They'll all want water—they'll want all the water you have, so use a cup—never hand them the whole flask—they'll empty it. Stomachs are the last priority, especially after all the cases we brought in last night. There are plenty of other cases to keep the doctors busy without bringing in hopeless stomach cases. They always want water and you can't give it to them because their bellies are open. All the way to the dressing station they cry for water. See there—do you see those two in the shell hole? Look there, do you not see them waving to us? I can see from here that they are both leg cases. After a few days out here you will learn quickly to spot the living—even in such a valley of death as this. Feh! Pray it is not warm again—we shall not be able to stand the smell or the black clouds of flies. We'll let the others take those two in and we'll go on." He turned around and, whistling to two teams toward the rear, pointed to the shell hole. "Tomas!" he cried. "Two leg cases!" One of the men raised his hand and then beckoned his comrades to follow him to the shell hole.

Anton continued. "Did you see how those wounded waved to us? Those were men with the strong spark of life within them. You will see others who are much weaker and who don't realize their hopeless state." They resumed their search and soon spotted a wounded infantryman in the shadow of a broken cart. His left arm reduced to a dark-stained stump just below the shoulder, the wounded man guzzled water from the tin cup proffered by Jozef. Anton whistled to the two Magyars, who halted their search and came to help bear the soldier from the field.

By midmorning the team had transported three men, a Russian and two Slovaks, to the carts bound for the dressing station. In their progress through the mud the men had passed many a corpse and many a man passing from this world with labored breath and parched, trembling lips. Far into the field the four men stopped and took turns from a flask of water.

Anton pointed across the field. "We haven't searched over there yet. Come." The four men made their way to a part of the field where the ground had been churned violently, and where men and pieces of men lay imbedded in mud or partially submerged in flooded shell holes. In the middle of the dreadful scene lay two dead horses, one torn in two and the other on its back with its legs pointed skyward. The violence of the scene evoked a gasp from Jozef and the two men halted. The dead and their equipment were strewn widely and the area was completely silent. Yet somewhere amid the flutter of torn bits of uniforms and flapping soiled bandages there was life. Hearing a human voice, the men scanned the landscape for the source.

Anton tapped Jozef on the shoulder and pointed. The men picked their way through the carnage and advanced toward the wounded man whose raspy voice demanded, "*Voda . . . voda*—water . . . water."

Anton handed Jozef a flask and said, "Here, pour it in your cup. Where is your cup? Never mind. Take mine—and don't lose it. Give him what he wants—he's a leg case."

While Jozef tended to the thirsty soldier, Anton whistled to the two Magyar stretcher bearers. Then he knelt next to the wounded man and asked in Slovak, "*Ako sa voláte*—what is your name?"

The wounded man, between gulps of water, wheezed, "Varkhol."

"Very well, Varkhol. We are going to carry you to the dressing station." He examined the wound; the right leg was open and black from the midthigh to the knee and the foot was turned back at an unnatural angle. "Amputation," he murmured to Jozef. The other leg, while lacerated and muddy, appeared relatively intact. Anton stood and placed his hands on his hips. "What the devil is keeping them?" And he whistled again to the Magyars.

While they awaited the other two stretcher bearers, Jozef pointed. "Look—over there." Nearby, a wounded man lay in the mud, staring in their direction and beckoning with a feeble twitch of his wrist.

"Yes, Jozef, I see him. He is hopeless. Help me get this one on the stretcher. Wrap the bad leg to the good one." The wounded man, Varkhol, groaned as the men bound the legs together. "Now, slide the good leg on from this side and the other leg will follow." Varkhol arched his back, crying, *"Ayyy!"* before collapsing unconscious on the stretcher.

Jozef stole a glance at the other wounded man—the hopeless case—who now beckoned again. Jozef looked away quickly. "He wants me to go to him."

Anton shook his head. "He is hopeless. There is nothing we can do for a man with no legs, an open belly, and a mangled arm. He would not survive the move to a stretcher."

"Perhaps he wants water."

Anton snorted. "Water would kill—" He stopped and considered the feeble gesturing of the broken man. "Very well. Here, take him water. But hurry. This leg case can be saved—he needs us. And don't give away all your water!"

Jozef hurried away with the flask as Anton straightened the stretcher handles and secured Varkhol's arms tightly to his sides. "There," he said. "We don't want you thrashing when you wake up—you'll spill into the mud and take us with you." When the Magyars finally arrived, Anton raised his head to call Jozef, but was surprised to see him on his hands and knees with his ear turned to the legless soldier's mouth. Jozef then nodded slowly to the hopeless case, gave him water, and then returned to his comrades.

The Magyars took the front stretcher handles while the two Slovaks grabbed the rear handles; together the four men lifted the groaning man. Jozef looked back over his shoulder, but the broken infantryman was very still now.

"What did that man say to you?" asked Anton. Jozef merely shook his head and struggled forward in the mud.

Panting and groaning, the four made their way out of the churned terrain, their boots encrusted with mud. "We'll stop here," Anton announced to Jozef. "My arms are giving out and I can't lift my boots any longer." Anton addressed the other stretcher bearers in Magyar: *"Álljon meg itt*—stop here!" They carefully lowered their still-unconscious man on the trampled grain and reclined on either side of him. "Sit so your shadows shade his face," said Anton.

Jozef rubbed his tired arms and, after a pause, mumbled, "He asked me to promise him something."

"Who?"

"The hopeless case back there—the one with no legs. You asked me what he said."

"What did he say?"

"He said, 'Don't leave me here—bury me in the churchyard with the holy ones and not in the road with sinners.'"

"He said that? What did you say?"

Jozef lowered his head. "I promised him."

"You cannot promise such a thing as that."

"I know . . . I know."

The four sat awhile longer. From the east came the distant rumble of artillery. Anton stood. "Come. Let's get this one back and then we'll eat." They lifted the stretcher and continued on to the dressing station, their legs rustling through the young wheat.

ॐ

"Corporal Rusynko! Corporal Rusynko!"

Vasyl, working with a group of soldiers over a pile of battlefield-scavenged rifles, straightened and raised a hand. "Yes, over here."

A corporal from a nearby company hurried toward Vasyl. "You're Corporal Rusynko?" The corporal examined Vasyl's plain collar.

"Yes—since yesterday. I don't have my collar stars yet."

"Sergeant Lukacs wants to see you," said the corporal. "Your friend has gone mad. Come."

Vasyl grabbed the corporal's shoulder. "Vasko? You found Vasko?"

"If he is the tall, quiet one, then, yes."

"That would be Yurko." Vasyl addressed the men working with the rifles. "When you men finish with this pile, take the salvageable rifles to Sergeant Buryk's squad for repair. Then come back here and wait for more broken rifles. Very well, Corporal, let's go. Take me to your sergeant and tell me what happened."

The corporal threw his hands in the air as if imitating an explosion. "He's gone mad!"

"Yes, you said that. What's wrong? Where is Yurko?"

"He's with a burial party."

"Is he not well?"

"Your friend refuses to bury any more men."

Vasyl shrugged. "No one likes burial duty."

The corporal shook his head. "He's gone mad."

The two walked along the same road Vasyl had traveled two days earlier with Sergeant Haletskii in the quest for lime. Carts laden with corpses rumbled by slowly and the men stepped off the road into the ruined wheat to let them pass. Vasyl and the corporal followed the carts to the tree-lined edge of a field where teams of men worked at digging and filling great holes in the earth. Next to one freshly dug pit, a crew unloaded a cart and lined the bottom of the pit with corpses in Russian, German, and Austrian uniforms, shoulder to shoulder. Along the edges of another pit, men with rags tied around their faces spread lime on the bodies below.

The corporal tapped Vasyl's arm and said, "Over there. That's Sergeant Lukacs."

The corporal led Vasyl to the edge of a pit where the sergeant stood shaking his head slowly. He acknowledged the two corporals with a nod and then swept his arms out over the grave. "An awful business, my friends—an awful, evil business. So many men . . . so many . . . We can only dig so fast, but not as fast as shrapnel kills, eh? Are you Rusynko? Yes? Very well, Rusynko, your friend is over there at the end of this pit. Take him with you. There is no point in keeping him here. I can only yell at a man so much. Tell him he can take his dog and bury it anywhere he likes."

Vasyl frowned. "His dog?"

"Yes, that awful thing that always sat under the stew wagon. Your friend found his dog's carcass somewhere, and he won't let any of us near it. I've known men like him before. He's slow, isn't he? A thousand men can die before his eyes and he can snore all night; but let a dog die and he'll cry for hours. He's not right in the head—but never mind—he's a good man. He's done the work of two men all day. He's earned a rest. Take him with you, Rusynko."

Vasyl walked around the edge of the corpse-lined pit and stood over his friend. Yurko was sitting on the ground with his legs crossed, his head in his hands. "Come, Yurko. Let's go," said Vasyl gently.

Yurko shook his head without looking up.

Behind Yurko was a small mound covered with one of the discarded lime sacks. "What do you have there, Yurko? What did you find? Is it that old dog? Every dog must die someday. You know that." Vasyl squatted next to his friend. "Come, Yurko. The sergeant says you can take it with you and bury it wherever you like."

Yurko pulled back the sack, revealing a human form. Vasyl stared at what first appeared to be a child in uniform. When he noticed the legs were missing, the form began to look familiar. "Yurko . . . it's . . . it's . . ." Vasyl stood and Yurko, covering the form, gazed up at Vasyl with moist, red eyes. Vasyl took a deep breath and turned away, looking across the field at the crews unloading yet another cart next to an unfinished pit. Pairs of men, one at the head of each corpse, the other at the feet, bore the sagging, mud-caked forms to the lifeless row extending along the edge of the grave. Leaning on their shovels, the workers in the pit watched the procession with listless eyes, and then spat, leaned down, and lifted another shower of dirt over their shoulders.

Sergeant Lukacs appeared next to Vasyl. "Well?" asked the sergeant.

"It's not a dog, Sergeant." Vasyl closed his eyes and massaged his temples with his left hand.

"What?"

"It's not a dog. Yurko found someone he knows on the carts . . . it's someone we both know . . . we are all from the same village . . . and . . . they were close friends . . . they were cousins . . . distant cousins, I think . . . but, really, they were friends . . . *we* were friends. The three of us were good friends . . . very, very . . . good friends . . ."

"*Ay,*" said the sergeant, looking over Vasyl's shoulder at Yurko. "It's an awful business . . . awful. So he found a friend. His friend must be buried. Will Yurko let us bury him?"

Vasyl kicked at the dirt. "Well . . . no. I think Yurko would like to bury him somewhere else."

"These soldiers must be buried here."

"I know, Sergeant. But I think I know where Yurko would like to bury this one man. They were very close friends."

"Friends or not . . . I don't think . . . I can't allow him to remove his friend from this field." There was little conviction in Sergeant Lukacs's voice.

"Sergeant, if I stay here and help Yurko fill in this pit, will you let him . . . will you let us bury our friend?"

The sergeant shrugged. "It's an awful business. Give me the identity disk before you leave."

Vasyl nodded. "Thank you, Sergeant." And then he went to Yurko's side to explain the compromise.

Sergeant Lukacs stared into the pit at the soldiers of three armies, barely distinguishable under mud and dust and dark, fatal stains. Some, no doubt, were from the sergeant's own company; but who could recognize men such as these—broken, incomplete, bloated, and whose faces were stretched and twisted from sun and violent death? What a blessing for a man to be recognized among so many by a friend!

"I hope a friend buries me someday," murmured the sergeant.

The workers walked over the dead, spreading lime, as Yurko and Vasyl joined the men toiling with shovels around the rim of the pit. The dead men's uniforms took on the same dusty appearance, colored one and all by the same chalky, Galician soil into which they slowly submerged and disappeared—another one hundred men returned to dust.

"It's an awful, awful business . . ."

࿋

The graves filled and covered, the weary remnants of the regiment were again on the march, shambling eastward in pursuit of the Russian armies. The men, still shaken from the ferocity of the Russian counterattack, chatted nervously and scanned the horizon at every distant noise.

"How many are we now?"

"I heard we lost forty."

"*Bozhe!* We were only a hundred and fifty or so to begin with."

"Then how many are we now?"

"Well, if I had a hundred and fifty sheep and I lost forty . . . I would have . . . well . . . it would be . . . very bad."

"Forget your sheep—answer the man! And if you can't, I will. We are now only one hundred."

"One hundred and *ten*."

"Yes, one hundred and ten. It's a bad business. It's like tracking a bear. The Magyars who owned our hills once came to our village to hunt in the mountains. They had guns and servants and wagons and horses. They came upon a bear and shot it, wounding it only, and then tracked it for days. When they cornered the animal it charged one of the Magyars. Even though he managed to get off two shots into the bear's chest, the bear mauled the

Magyar and killed him. Yes, we, too, are tracking a wounded bear and now we are mauled. It is a bad business."

"Was the bear killed?"

"The bear ran into the woods and lived."

"Bozhe moi!"

The sky was dark now and ominous flashes on the horizon silhouetted distant hills and trees.

"I wish we had rum. I could drink a lot of rum now."

"So could I. They should give us another rum ration after all we've been through."

"Does anyone know what happened to the lieutenant?"

"He was killed—I saw his body yesterday afternoon."

"What was his name—I don't remember."

"It was Kubek."

"No it wasn't—that was the name of the last lieutenant. This one was a German from Budapest."

"Koppel?"

"That's it!"

"What happened to Kubek?"

"He became ill."

"I heard he died."

"Of what?"

"Who knows? He's dead, isn't he? What does it matter?"

"I would hate to be a lieutenant. We've had so many."

"You've only been with us a few months. I've seen five."

"I remember six. Who remembers more than six?"

"Sergeant Haletskii would remember more than six. He's been at the front since last summer. His company has seen many lieutenants—some killed, some wounded, others transferred."

"Our Sergeant Lukacs has seen as many lieutenants as Sergeant Haletskii."

"I heard that Sergeant Lukacs let that idiot from Sergeant Haletskii's company bury a dog yesterday."

"A what!"

"A dog."

"Which idiot?"

"The tall one at the stew wagons—the one who never speaks."

"Yurko?"

"I think that's his name. He and Corporal Rusynko buried a dog."

"Yes, that's his name—Yurko. Only, I heard it wasn't a dog they buried."

"What did they bury?"

"I heard it was a man they buried."

"I was there. It was a dog."

"Did you see it?"

"No, but I heard someone from the burial detail talking about it."

"It wasn't a dog—it was a man. Sergeant Lukacs showed the identity disk to someone in my cousin's platoon and then my cousin told me about it. It was that little rooster Varkhol always picked on."

"Ivanchyn?"

"Yes. Corporal Rusynko and Yurko were his friends, so the sergeant let them bury him in a churchyard."

"A churchyard? Why?"

"I don't know. All I know is that they carried him to a village near here and buried him in the churchyard at night."

"How does one infantryman, this Ivanchyn, deserve his own grave?"

"I don't know."

"Well, I wouldn't want to be buried in a pit."

"Neither would I."

"Nor I."

"What does it matter once you are dead?"

"It matters to me!"

"And to me!"

"Well, it doesn't matter to me."

"No, I suppose it doesn't. No . . . it doesn't matter—not at all. Only somehow it does. It matters very much if you think about it."

It began to rain and the men, groaning in unison, staggered numbly toward the rumble of the Russian guns.

CHAPTER TWENTY-THREE

Reunion

THE GREAT RUSSIAN RETREAT across the Galician landscape continued through the summer of 1915, finally ending in the fall when the cursed autumn rains blessed the wretched armies of both sides with impassable roads. With the exception of a small corner of eastern Galicia, the Russians had been driven from Austrian territory. The exhausted German and Austrian pursuers and the tormented Russian millions entrenched for the winter along a seven-hundred-mile front. In a little over a year, over four million men from both sides had been killed, wounded, or captured in the Carpathian Mountains, in the hills of Galicia, and on the plains of Russian Poland.

In the spring of 1916 the armies paused as winter's monotonous mantle melted, saturating and cleansing the soil. Along the Eastern Front wildflowers rose from the dead earth and fragrant life budded from skeleton trees as the world was born anew.

ↀ

Vasyl walked alone along a quiet dirt road, his hands in his pockets, a pipe dangling from his lips. He had eaten a hearty lunch at the stew wagon and was returning to his platoon when, from a good distance behind him, a familiar voice called his name. His mouth forming an inverted grin, Vasyl turned around with a name on his lips, a name he hadn't pronounced in almost two years: "Andrii." There, along a stretch of the road where the sun broke through the leafing trees, stood his brother in the uniform of an Austrian infantryman. Andrii waved his cap until he was satisfied he had been seen and then he raced to his brother's side.

"Vasyl!"

"Andrii!"

The brothers embraced, laughing and squeezing one another.

"Vasyl, I have found you!"

Vasyl fumbled for words. "Andrii, what is . . . why . . . how is it you are here?"

Andrii, breathless and exuberant, placed his hands on his brother's shoulders and danced him in a circle laughing. "Last year's draft. They sent me into the army last fall. *Bozhe moi,* Vasyl! You are alive! I have been at the front for more than a month and every time my sergeant has permitted it, I have searched for you. And now, look at you!" Andrii rubbed the three little stars on Vasyl's collar. "You are a sergeant! What do I call you? 'Sergeant Rusynko?' 'Sergeant Brother?'"

"'Brother' is good," chuckled Vasyl. "But 'Sergeant' if anyone is listening. I'm afraid the Emperor insists." Andrii laughed. He was a man now, tall— Vasyl was able to look him in the eye—with a long, angular face and dark, pessimistic eyes that betrayed an unhappy maturity. The two brothers joked about the army and the food the army fed them, and Andrii complained that all he had done since arriving at the front was dig trenches and latrines.

Vasyl shook his head. "Be glad you are not digging—" but he checked himself and then continued. "Be glad you are with me now and not digging. But tell me, Andrii, how are *Mamka* and *Baba*? How is everyone in the village?"

Andrii shook his head. "*Baba* died, Vasyl—in the fall after you left. The war made her so much older so quickly. She got sick during the Russian occupation of Stara Polyanka. When Father Yaroslav heard that she had stopped eating, he went to the Russians and they sent a doctor to tend to her. But there was nothing they could do for *Baba*. She asked about you at the end and I told her you were well even though we had no idea if you were alive or dead."

Vasyl looked away and then asked hoarsely, "And *Mamka*?"

Andrii lowered his head. "She is . . . she is . . . well. After *Baba* died she went to Niklova in the fall of 1914 to stay with Aunt Mariya. Later, Anna and Petro joined her in Niklova."

Vasyl placed a hand on his brother's shoulder. "Look at me, Andrii. *Mamka* is not well, is she?"

Andrii shook his head. "No . . . no. First you were taken for the army, then there was fighting in the village, and finally, *Baba*'s death—it was all too much for her, Vasyl. She seems well . . . but, in here"—Andrii pointed to his heart—"in here, she is not well. *Slabe serdtse*—a weak heart, I think."

"And the rest of the village, Andrii?"

"There was fighting in the fall and again in the spring. The village was almost destroyed in the fighting. Our beautiful church"—Andrii's voice broke—"our beautiful church . . . the Protection of the Mother of God burned to the ground. Embers from a burning hut landed on the roof. Everyone ran to her and we saved the icons and everything we could carry." Andrii wiped his eyes.

"Go on, Andrii," said Vasyl gently.

"Andrii Khudyk was killed right outside his tavern and Ivan Ivanchyn's sister, Mariya, died on the Dzyamba family's footbridge over *Potok* Ondava. Many were injured, Vasyl, including Paraska. But her sister, Yevka, saved her life. You would have been proud of your sister-in-law. *Bozhe moi,* it was a terrible time. I don't think—"

Vasyl raised a hand to stop his brother. "What happened to Paraska?"

Andrii rubbed the outer portion of his right thigh. "She was hurt here. Yevka saved her and even the Russians who witnessed it said she was a hero. The village was shelled by both the Russian and Austrian armies, and there was great confusion. Some of the huts caught fire and many of the people ran for the hills. Yevka, Danko, and Paraska headed toward the trees above the village. A shell landed nearby and they were thrown to the ground. When they got up they found that Paraska was bleeding from her leg and could not walk. Yevka took Paraska upon her back and held Danko close to her chest and carried them both up to the trees. She carried them both, Vasyl. Can you believe it? And Paraska was pregnant at the time. Yevka carried them up into the forest." Andrii stopped to catch his breath.

"Paraska was pregnant?"

"Yes. She had a boy. She named him Mykhal—Myko she calls him."

"Myko will be fatherless, Andrii," said Vasyl.

"Vasko? He is dead? *Ai!* Poor Paraska . . . poor Paraska. When?"

"Last summer."

"I see . . . and Paraska doesn't know . . . *Bozhe moi,* poor Paraska."

"Where is everyone now, Andrii?"

"The last time I saw them they were on their way to Niklova in Old Mykhal's cart. Everyone left, Vasyl . . . they are all gone."

"They must have come back to the village by now. The Russians are nowhere near the area any longer. When were you called for the draft? Where were you living when they called you?"

Andrii ignored Vasyl and pointed to a spot beneath a tall pine. "Vasyl, let's sit." The brothers reclined under a tree and Andrii deflected Vasyl's inquiries about Stara Polyanka and instead told anecdotes about his life in the army thus far, episodes that he related with droll sophistication and insightful sarcasm. Andrii mimicked junior officers and then, with lavish apologies to Vasyl, he parodied sergeants with devastating effect. Vasyl shook with laughter—they were all familiar types and it was a humorous portrayal of an army Vasyl knew well, told by a brother he scarcely recognized.

When Andrii finished he sighed and shook his head. "The only redeeming thing about this army, Vasyl, is that they allow us to have our icons at the front. I was happy to find icons of the Mother of God and *Svyatŷi Nikolai*—Saint Nicholas—in our trenches."

"Yes," said Vasyl. "Each company is allowed to display the icons." After a pause, Vasyl again pressed his brother. "Where were you when you were called for the army? They would have come for you in the village, but you don't seem to have been in the village for some time."

Andrii fiddled with his tunic buttons and then said, "You are right, Vasyl. I left the village soon after the German and Austro-Hungarian armies pushed the Russians across the Carpathians. I left when Magyar officials entered the village and arrested me."

"What!"

"They actually came to arrest Father Yaroslav. They were arresting priests from the entire region. They accused him of collaborating with the Russians. The charge was nonsense, of course. I went to Father Yaroslav's side to protest his arrest and they took me with him. They took us by wagon and then by train to a camp of little wooden buildings surrounded by wire. There were many priests from our region—from around Vŷshnii Svidnyk and Medzilabortse and Humenne. All of us were accused of being sympathetic to the Russian cause in the war, some merely for identifying themselves as Rusyn, which the Magyars took to mean 'Russian,' and others, like Father Yaroslav, for serving as priests in Russian-occupied territory. The Magyars simply assumed that we had all welcomed the Russians as brothers and liberators."

"What happened to Father Yaroslav, Andrii?"

"I don't know. They took me from the camp after a month and put me in the Austrian army. Since then I've heard that Rusyn Orthodox priests and

Rusyn peasants were arrested north of the mountains and shot or hanged. The Emperor's hangmen strung up Rusyn Orthodox priests like common criminals, Vasyl. Can you believe it? Like common criminals . . ."

Andrii reclined on the ground, locking his fingers together over his belly and closing his eyes. The two remained silent for a time. In the trees, unseen birds chattered and somewhere men laughed.

At last Andrii broke the silence. "I don't intend to stay very long at the front, Vasyl."

"Oh?" There was little surprise in Vasyl's voice.

"At the first chance I shall walk to the Russian lines and give myself up. I will not remain in the army that arrests our people and our priests and hangs and shoots us. It is a case of right versus wrong. For me it is a clear choice."

Vasyl nodded. "I see."

"You are shocked, Vasyl?"

"No."

"You are disappointed in me?"

"No."

"Will you join me?"

"No, Andrii, I will not join you."

"So instead, you will remain in the army of our persecutors."

Vasyl stared into his brother's eyes and Andrii turned away, uncomfortable and ashamed. A group of young soldiers walked by, laughing and jostling one another in their spotless uniforms. "It's been almost two years since that day in 1914 when I was taken from Stara Polyanka and placed in the army," said Vasyl. "In two years I've seen things I could never dream. I've lost friends and buried friends. I've marched in heat and snow until I thought I could not take another step. Then, when I am most tired, I have been ordered to fire my rifle until the barrel is too hot to touch and then to get up and run forward or backward as the luck of the day would have it. I've stood by helplessly as men have died before my eyes and I've watched ravens feed on the dead between the forward lines. I've felt—no, Andrii, do not interrupt me— I've felt hunger and thirst such as I've never felt in my life—the thirst after battle is the most painful of all. Every night I dread doing any of it again; all I dream of is going home." Vasyl closed his eyes tightly as if he were seeing the dream before him now.

Vasyl opened his eyes. "I dream of seeing you, Andrii, and *Mamka* and Anna and . . . others. But when I awake I see young men like you and older men like myself—those of us unbelievably still alive—and I can't think of doing what you ask me to do. These men look to me for advice and help in everything. Some are so poorly trained they are unsure how to load their rifles. They are almost like you—brothers all to me. I know nothing about empires and emperors, and I see little difference between myself and the men in the opposite trenches. I don't think I remember much about what is right and what is wrong or what is true and what is false. I would guess that there are still things that are right and things that are wrong, and if you tell me that is the case I will believe you. But here at the front none of that seems to matter anymore. I understand nothing of this war except what I see around me, and usually I can see no farther than the man next to me. I suppose the longer this war lasts the more sense it makes to surrender. I've heard men talk of it and I've known some who gave themselves over in the night. Something inside me keeps me from doing it and I have no idea what it is. You are wiser than I, Andrii—you are well schooled and well read. Your choice is probably best. Whatever you do, you have my blessing." Vasyl placed his arm across Andrii's shoulders. "Your eyes are wet."

Andrii sniffed and looked away. "*To nich*—it is nothing."

Vasyl smiled. "They are tears of love. If I could still shed them I would join you."

Andrii wiped his eyes. "I've never heard you speak this way. But I see now why you are a sergeant, Vasyl."

"Not by choice."

"No, but you have become one. The men of the village always listened to you. Here at the front men look to other men they can trust—men who are natural leaders—men like you. I have seen this in my own company, and even though I feel no part of it I understand it. Most men long to be led well and look for leaders they trust. The men are loyal to you and you to them. That is why you could never leave here, Vasyl."

Vasyl shrugged. "We had a sergeant once—a good one—Sergeant Haletskii was his name. He was, as you say, a natural leader. I learned everything I know about being a leader from him. He was with us from the beginning, in the summer of 1914, until this last winter, when he became ill. He stayed at the front until he could no longer stand on his own. The army sent him home and made me a sergeant. I hope I am half the sergeant that Sergeant Haletskii was."

Andrii nodded. "Your men are fortunate to be led by you."

"They are good men, Andrii. Maybe they are loyal—maybe not. They all know how to use their rifles. They listen to me and they say, 'Yes, Sergeant!' when I ask them to do something. But when the time comes for them to stand against the Russians . . . I don't know . . . I don't know . . . The army is changing. I see it in the replacements. The lieutenants ask me about the men and I tell them that they are ready—that they will stand up well against the Russians. But I only say this to satisfy the officers. In truth, I don't know what the men will do." Vasyl threw up his hands. "We will see . . . we will see. And you, Andrii, when will you leave?"

Andrii shook his head. "I don't know yet. There are several in the company who say it is best to wait until there is an attack—either by us or the Russians. Then, perhaps we will go to the forest and wait for the Russians to pass. We have spoken of several plans and discuss our ideas quietly."

"Make sure you speak very quietly, Andrii. If you are discovered you will be shot. The army has big ears. Be careful of what you say."

Andrii wrinkled his nose and gazed down the road. "I need to report back."

Vasyl forced a laugh. "Yes, go back before someone like me comes looking for you. Only, I must tell you, Andrii, there are rumors, mostly from prisoners, that the Russians are concentrating opposite us. They are led well by a general named Brusilov. Many of us think he means to attack with strength in this sector."

Andrii nodded solemnly but said nothing. The brothers stood and dusted themselves off excessively and when they had finally stared at each other's boots long enough Vasyl said, "*Z Bohom*—go with God. Or should I say, '*Do svidaniya*—good-bye'—like the Russians?"

Andrii grasped his brother's right hand. "'*Z Bohom*' is best. Go in health with God, Vasyl. *Z Bohom.*"

The brothers embraced, looked briefly into each other's eyes, and then walked down the road, each in his own direction.

CHAPTER TWENTY-FOUR

Brusilov

A WEEK AFTER HIS REUNION WITH ANDRII, Vasyl sat in a front-line communication trench, listening as a lieutenant questioned two scouts who had just returned from a predawn reconnoitering of the Russian forward line. One of the scouts watched the brightening eastern skyline intently while his comrade, still out of breath, related events.

"The Russians have dug up close to our first line, sir. They are so close that our men in forward posts can speak to them without shouting."

The lieutenant frowned. "Did you speak to any Russians?"

The scout hesitated. "Well . . ."

The lieutenant rapped the man on the knee. "Come, then. Tell me. Did you speak to any Russians?"

The scout pulled a pouch from his shirt pocket and handed it to the lieutenant. "Yes, sir. Last night."

"You traded with them?"

"Yes, sir."

"It is forbidden to trade with the enemy. You know that."

Vasyl cleared his throat and intervened. "May I see the traded item, sir?"

The lieutenant handed the pouch to Vasyl, who opened it and pulled out a pinch of tobacco. "What do you think, Sergeant?"

Vasyl sniffed the tobacco. "Russian *makhorka*." Then he took a paper from his vest pocket and rolled himself a cigarette.

The lieutenant watched Vasyl's fingers twist the paper and tobacco into shape and then squinted as Vasyl placed the cigarette in his mouth, lit it, and inhaled deeply. "Sergeant, what do you think it means?" asked the lieutenant.

Vasyl exhaled and considered his answer carefully before speaking. "It means . . . there are Russians just outside our lines, sir."

The lieutenant nodded and returned the pouch to the scout. "Why do you suppose, Sergeant, that the Russians would dig up to our lines in this sector when, as we can hear even now, the main thrust of their attention appears to be north of us—well north of us—where they have obviously concentrated a great deal of artillery fire for days now?"

Pondering the lieutenant's long-winded question, Vasyl inhaled the pungent Russian tobacco and then swept his free hand toward the Russian lines. "They will attack on a broad front, sir. They will attack here."

The lieutenant was skeptical. "Because of a little traded tobacco you think this?"

Vasyl shook his head. "No, sir, not only because of the tobacco, but also because of the two Russian deserters the other day. They both had new underwear."

The lieutenant raised his eyebrows. "Why was I not told?"

Vasyl inhaled deeply and shrugged. "You weren't here, sir."

"Sergeant, do you believe the issuance of new underwear among Russian recruits is significant?"

"Perhaps not, sir. But to the two Russians it meant they could expect to attack soon."

"And you think they will?"

"I think the Russian deserters think they will."

The lieutenant clasped his fingers, cracking the knuckles one by one, and then studied the backs of his hands in the waxing dawn. After a period of silence he motioned the two scouts toward the rear. "You two get some sleep. Sergeant, come with me. I would like the captain to hear your theories."

The scouts disappeared down the trench and Vasyl tossed his cigarette to the ground, stepping on it as he fell in behind the lieutenant.

☙

Vasyl and the lieutenant were well behind the forward line when the first Russian shells rattled in the air behind them. The lieutenant began to run and Vasyl threw himself to the floor of the trench. The shells exploded to the right and to the left of the trench, knocking the lieutenant backward, his neck snapping as he hit the ground. Another cluster of shells exploded, collapsing a section of the trench. Partially buried, Vasyl struggled out from under the dirt and, crouching low, scrambled over the dead lieutenant on his way to the second line of trenches. He dashed through smoke and falling earth to the main trench, where he nearly ran into a frightened young soldier's bayonet before collapsing, exhausted, against the earthworks.

The Austrian machine gunners in the first line were firing sporadically into the dust and smoke raised by the Russian shells; in the confused, asphyxiating conditions they soon abandoned the few functioning guns, climbed out of their trench, and ran back to the next line of defense. Vasyl peeked over the parapet of his trench and watched the desperate men dodging the exploding towers of earth. Some threw themselves to the ground under the raining earth and then scrambled to their feet to continue the race. Others remained still, rising again only as limp forms in the exploding earth. Some simply vanished in the dust. Those who survived dove into the trenches and lay on their backs gasping, holding their wounds and crying for water.

When the Russian barrage lifted, Vasyl grabbed a rifle and stood on the fire step—the top step of the trench. Through the smoke he could discern two or three Russian caps and Russian bayonets bobbing up and down in the forward trenches—the former Austrian front lines. Vasyl stepped down and called to two young recruits cowering on the floor of the trench, "You there! Go find rifles and get up on the fire step. Now!" The two nodded and obeyed. Vasyl worked his way down the trench instructing and encouraging the men. "Listen, my children! Check your rifle actions! Make sure they are clean before you load! You there! You are new. What is your name?"

"Kravets, Sergeant."

"Welcome to the front, Kravets. Get up on the fire step."

"Yes, Sergeant."

"Is someone looking after the injured?"

"Yes, Sergeant! But we need more water!"

"We have plenty of water, Sergeant! They can have some of ours!"

"Very well, then! Share the water. Only don't give it all away—you'll need it yourselves. Everyone else, get up on the fire step!"

"YES, SERGEANT!"

"Our Russian brothers will attack soon. Plevka, where is your rifle?"

"I can't find it, Sergeant. I just came back from the field bakery with bread."

"Very well. Here, take mine. It's not loaded. Do you need ammunition?"

"No, Sergeant. I have ammunition pouches with me."

"Good. You there, Brynda and Markovich! You are responsible for the icons. Protect them and carry them if we fall back."

"Yes, Sergeant!"

"Very well, my children! Stand ready!"

Suddenly, the Russian guns rumbled along the eastern horizon and out of the sky came a shrieking wind. Russian shells landed in front of the trench system and advanced toward the Austrian lines where they exploded among the earthworks, raining earth and timber among the riflemen. Vasyl pressed against the trench walls with his arms over his head and neck. Wounded men screamed in agony, and from the right came the shout, "Russians!" Wild-eyed Austrian infantrymen dropped their rifles and stumbled down the trench past Vasyl and then down a collapsed communication trench toward the third and final defensive line. Vasyl, raising his arms, ordered the men to halt. The terrified men threw Vasyl to the trench floor, trampling him in their panic.

Vasyl struggled to his feet, calling to Brynda and Markovich, "The icons! Get the icons!"

"Yes, Sergeant!"

A deafening blast knocked Vasyl on his back and obliterated Brynda, Markovich, and the icons. A mangled soldier torn open by the explosion landed on top of Vasyl and both were buried by the collapsing trench wall. Vasyl clawed at the dark earth, his hands finding the warm intestines of the dying man. Pulling himself toward the light of day, he squirmed to the surface and emerged from the earth, choking and coughing. Spitting mud and wiping his eyes, Vasyl scrambled over the dead and dying, climbed out of the trench, and ran westward, joining his fleeing comrades.

ᕙᕗ

The road was a congested mass of soldiers and refugees. Driven by fear, their faces caked with the soil of Russia, they fled westward, gasping in the suffocating mix of heat and dust. A humming noise, like the drone of countless bees, hung over the shuffling column. But unlike the sound of rushing life surging from the hive, this was the collective lament of fading hope and ebbing life. While few squandered their energy on speech, persistent rumors of pursuing Cossacks swept the length of the column like a hot wind, eliciting waves of collective groans.

Discarded equipment, broken wagons, and dead horses lined the ditches alongside the road. At the edges of the adjacent fields, beseeching peasants—hungry, thirsty, and dying—extended their wasted arms in limp supplication.

Exhausted, Vasyl shouldered his way out of the column, stepping off the road and into a field of wheat, where he bent over, his hands on his knees, gasping and coughing. From the north and east came the roll of Russian guns harrying the rear of the retreating Austrian Army. From the south came the sporadic reply of Austrian guns.

Vasyl cut through the stalks of wheat on a course parallel with the retreating column. Not far ahead, two groups of men wrestled with a pair of field guns outside the smoldering remains of a village. The men aimed the guns to the north while, to the rear, another group chocked the wheels of a caisson. Noting that the battery was undermanned, Vasyl veered toward the road to melt once again into the retreating mob. He made only two strides back to safe anonymity when he heard a voice call out: "Sergeant!"

Vasyl ignored the voice.

"SERGEANT!"

Vasyl sighed and made his way to the gesturing lieutenant in charge of the battery. The distraught young officer addressed Vasyl in a mix of Slovak and Rusyn. "We fire guns. Help with shells. You understand?" He pointed toward the caissons on the edge of the village. "Help with shells. *Skoro*—hurry!"

Vasyl nodded and ran toward the village, mumbling, "What a bad idea." When he reached the village, he ducked inside the doorway of a charred building with a collapsed roof and Hebrew lettering over the entrance. Crossing the cluttered floor, he went out a back door and headed toward the retreating column. As he passed the skeleton of another building, Vasyl noticed a form in the blackened doorway. It was a young Austrian infantryman, no more than a boy, his eyes moist, his lips trembling. Vasyl beckoned but the boy was unresponsive. When a gun from the Austrian battery roared, the boy nearly fell over.

Vasyl went to the boy's side, steadying him and saying, "You shouldn't stay here. Do you speak *po-nashomu*—our way? That battery will draw Russian fire. Do you understand me?"

The gun fired again and the startled boy shook violently and fell against Vasyl's chest. Vasyl put his arm around the boy and pulled him out of the doorway. "Come with me," said Vasyl. The boy shuffled his feet and Vasyl, tightening his grip on the boy's shoulders, shouted, "Pick up your feet! I can't carry you!" The boy obeyed and the two walked out of the village, rejoining the long column.

Now aware of the Austrian battery, Russian gunners to the north began returning fire. Shells exploding in and around the village rained charred timbers and clods of earth dangerously close to the column. Vasyl gripped the boy's shoulders tightly and shouted, "Hurry!"

West of the village the column split briefly, passing on either side of a stalled cart. Vasyl steered the boy past the right side of the cart and came face-to-face with two Jews, an older and a younger man, standing over their collapsed horse. Both men were garbed and capped entirely in black; only the white tassels of their prayer shawls dangling from under their coats, and the older man's gray beard, provided variation from their somber appearance. The melancholy patriarch of the stranded family bowed his head slightly at Vasyl. In the back of the cart the Jewish womenfolk trembled and an unseen infant cried. Explosions rocked the village and a young girl in the cart screamed, clutching frantically at an old woman, who tried to calm her.

Vasyl sighed and leaned the young soldier against the cart, saying, "Don't move." Then he approached the patriarch and the younger man. "You can't stay here." The two Jews stared at Vasyl and, at the sound of more explosions, glanced toward the village. Vasyl raised his voice. "This road is under fire— you must get off this road! *Verstehen Sie*—do you understand?"

The old man nodded and the younger man spoke. "We speak Polish and a little of your way."

Vasyl shrugged. "Well, that will have to do. You must take these women off this cart and get them away from here."

The young man nodded but did not move. The ground shook from the exploding shells and the horse, its tongue rolling out onto the dirt, closed its eyes.

Vasyl beckoned to the two men. "Come here. Take them away." Vasyl motioned to the three passengers to alight from the cart, but they remained frozen. In the middle of the little group, a young mother, her clothing streaked with dark stains, held a newborn infant in her arms. Next to her, still comforting the young girl, lay the old woman, wearing a filthy bandage wrapped around her right leg.

Vasyl closed his eyes and shook his head. Passing soldiers, panicked by more rumors of Cossacks, jostled the cart. Vasyl retrieved the young soldier from the side of the cart, placed his arm across his shoulders, and, without looking at the patriarch, shouted, "The road is under fire! You can't stay here!" Vasyl and the boy rejoined the crush of fleeing men.

At the crest of a low hill, Vasyl pulled the boy to the side of the road and, shading his eyes, studied the road below. A voice behind Vasyl called out, "Come take a rest from the war!" Sitting in the shade of a small tree was an infantry sergeant, his head and left hand wrapped with dirty rags. Vasyl and the boy joined the sergeant, who swept his uninjured hand to the west. "If you want to keep fighting, you will have to run to catch up with the senior officers."

"Have you seen any officers?" asked Vasyl.

"No, brother Sergeant—not since yesterday. I've seen a few of those little rabbits with a silver star or two on their collars. One came by here earlier with two field pieces."

Vasyl jerked his head toward the east. "I saw him with two Škodas—two field artillery pieces—in the village."

The sergeant made a face. "Feh! That lieutenant is an insane rabbit! All who joined him are worse than madmen—they should have known better. They passed here earlier, the lieutenant threatening to shoot all who got in his way. Madmen!" The sergeant peered at the boy. "What is wrong with your friend?"

Vasyl shook his head. "He can't talk right now."

"Well, that's honest—there are no words for what is happening here, brother Sergeant." The man spat and then said, "Your stupid *zhydŷ* are still there."

"What?"

"The *zhydŷ*—the Jews you spoke to—see there? They still sit and watch the soldiers pass. I watched you speak to them. You weren't the first to stop and tell them to move on. But you can't tell *zhydŷ* anything. They'll speak your language when it's convenient for them, but when you need something from them, ha!—suddenly they speak only their own language. But don't be confused, friend, they understand everything."

Vasyl squinted at the distant family and nodded. "Yes, they understood. In the back of the cart was a woman who had trouble in childbirth. There was also an old woman with a bad leg. And now their horse is dead."

The sergeant dismissed the Jews with a toss of his bandaged hand. "It's no matter. The war is over. I've surrendered already. The enemy doesn't know it yet, but as soon as the first Russian comes by, I will be happy to be his prisoner and a guest of the Tsar for the remainder of the war. Sit, friends, and we'll wait together."

Russian shells exploded on either side of the road near the village, sending columns of earth into the air. The boy shuddered violently and Vasyl looked again toward the west. "I think we will go on."

The sergeant snorted. "Why, friend? So that you can rejoin your unit? What is the use? After a hot meal, you will be rewarded with another chance to face our Russian brothers. And they are our brothers—do not doubt it. I understand their language and they understand mine. That is more than I can say about officers in my own army. You don't want to kill your brother, do you? I know I don't want to. I'll not be Cain to the next Russian Abel I see. Sit with me, brother, and wait for them."

Another shell landed nearby, this one blasting a bloody hole in the retreating column. Vasyl led the boy back to the road, calling over his shoulder, "We will go, on at least until dark."

The sergeant raised his bandaged hand as the two men melted once again into the column. "Well then, brothers, *z Bohom*—go with God!" he shouted. Then he shook his head and muttered, "Madmen."

☙

Streaking out of the sky, the Russian shell plunged lethally toward the road. Every distinct sound—the panting of a terrified boy, the scraping of hundreds of boots on the gravel road, the neighing of a nervous horse—all seemed to hush in anticipation. Vasyl dug his fingers into the boy's shoulder and yanked him to the left in order to throw him to the ground.

The shell burst like hot stinging sand, obliterating the boy and tossing Vasyl across the road where he landed on his back atop discarded officers' luggage. Vasyl closed his eyes, shielding them from the falling dirt and debris with his left arm. His right shoulder throbbed and the right arm was useless.

Opening his eyes, Vasyl propped himself up on his left arm. Heaped around a smoking hole in the ground were the ragged remains of men. Outside the fatal circumference of the blast, the wounded struggled to their feet. One man, on his knees, held his abdomen while another, missing his lower left leg, dragged himself to the side of the road. The retreating column pressed on, the men stepping over the dead and ignoring the cries of the wounded. The ground shook beneath Vasyl's bed of luggage and he closed his eyes, briefly losing consciousness.

When Vasyl awoke, he blinked his eyes at movement in the sky above. A flock of black birds circled overhead, flapping their wings in slow, methodical strokes. Vasyl tried to raise himself on his right side, but cried out in pain.

"*Hospody, pomilui*—Lord have mercy!" cried Vasyl weakly. Breathing quickly, he stared at the black birds. *"Hospody, pomilui!"*

He turned his head and vomited, coughing and spitting the bitter bile from his mouth. The ground no longer jumped, and overhead the birds had disappeared. *"Hospody, pomilui,"* he whimpered.

Vasyl's eyes gradually closed and he lay very still, his uneven respirations almost imperceptible.

CHAPTER TWENTY-FIVE

Sister Frances

AT THE RUSSIAN FIELD HOSPITAL behind General Brusilov's advancing armies, Sister Frances, a Red Cross nurse from London via Moscow, stood in the rain squinting into the darkness at the wounded. "There are so many . . . too many," she whispered to herself in her native English. For two days the surgery tents had been full of the most serious cases. Though army surgeons from Moscow and Petrograd worked quickly day and night, there seemed to be no end to the stream of Russian and Austrian wounded. Most came by cart, delivered by Russian orderlies who distinguished not between friend and foe but between living and dead, between salvageable and unsalvageable. Many arrived on foot, directly from the front, hastily bandaged by their comrades, and now sitting or lying stoically in the mud, wiping the rain from their eyes and holding their service caps over the faces of those too weak to shelter themselves.

Sister Frances spotted the orderly, Semyon, and shouted to him in Russian, "Over here! *Bystro*—hurry! Did you find the torch?"

Semyon held a little metal box aloft. "I don't know how to operate it, Sister."

"Well then, hand it to me," said Sister Frances. Turning on the device she aimed a jittering yellow oval on the ground. "Here, Semyon, now you take the torch and hold it like this. Direct the light so I can find the men that Sister Anastasiya and I tagged earlier. Help me look for men with ribbon on their tunics. The ones who need attention first will be in this area closest to the tents. The ones out near the road came later and will have to wait."

Sister Frances identified three men and sent Semyon for help. Seeing a familiar figure outside the surgery tent, she called out, "Sister Anastasiya! They are over here—the three with our ribbons."

Sister Anastasiya stepped cautiously through the mud to Sister Frances's side and looked down in the oval of light at the drenched wounded. "Yes, I see. Where are the canvas tents? Why do we still have no cover for these men?"

"The tents are up on the other side of the road. There are no more tents for these men. There are so many, Sister Anastasiya. There are more wounded than we can treat."

Sister Anastasiya took the lantern from Sister Frances. "Have the orderlies taken out the dead?"

"Semyon and the others moved them under the tree behind the surgery."

Sister Anastasiya frowned. "The dead have no use for the shelter of a tree."

"It wasn't raining when they moved them."

"Hmph. Have the orderlies bring these three inside." Sister Anastasiya carefully headed back to the surgery.

When Semyon returned with three orderlies and two canvas stretchers, Sister Frances indicated one of the figures on the ground. "The Austrian is an arm case. He has been here since last night while we tended the stomach and head cases. Be careful—his right arm is fragile—there isn't much left of it."

Semyon directed two of the orderlies to transfer the arm case into the surgery.

"Now then," continued Sister Frances. "This man over here is a leg case. Give him to Doctor Grigorii Konstantinovich. Lift him at the hips—one on either side—both legs are gone at the knees. This last man, this lieutenant, is a head case that just came in and he is—" Sister Frances paused and pressed her index and middle fingers under the jaw, searching for a pulse. "Well, he is dead. You know where to take him, Semyon."

Semyon, squatting next to the lieutenant's body, grinned in the yellow torch light. "I think that on a night like this, the good sister wishes she were home in *Angliya*."

"No, Semyon, I do not wish I were home in England. Russia's cause is Britain's cause. My sisters in England are doing their part for our British boys. I have a sister in France, serving as a nurse near Amiens. We have a brother in the trenches, probably not far from there. But, Semyon, my place is here with the Russian Army. I lived in Russia before the war, and it seemed a natural thing for me to stay and volunteer once war was declared. I am where I belong. Take the leg case inside, Semyon. When you are finished, deposit the lieutenant under the tree. Make sure his identity disk is clearly visible for the burial party."

"Yes, Sister," said Semyon, wiping the rain from his eyes. He motioned to the other orderly. "You there! Vanya! Help me."

❧

The surgery tent contained six wooden tables illuminated by kerosene lamps suspended from the central support posts. Doctor Grigorii Konstantinovich, assisting Doctor Aleksei Vasilevich with a bowel case at the next-to-last table, looked up when Sister Anastasiya passed by. "What do you have for us, Sister?" he asked.

"An arm case, Doctor." Sister Anastasiya directed the orderlies, Semyon and Ivan, to bring their wounded man to the last table. "Place him here," she said. The two orderlies transferred the wounded man to the operating table.

Sister Anastasiya stood next to Grigorii Konstantinovich. "His right arm is shattered, Doctor, and . . . and he's an Austrian."

"Yes, I can see that," said Grigorii Konstantinovich, smiling at Sister Anastasiya. "He is a wounded man, Sister. We don't treat men based on their uniform or language."

"Yes, Doctor."

"We hope for the sake of our own gallant young men that the Austrian and German medical staffs do the same. It is our job to relieve suffering, Sister, not to make war on the wounded."

"Yes, Doctor."

"Semyon!" cried Doctor Grigorii Konstantinovich.

"Here, Your Honor!"

"Am I to assume that we are finally down to arm and leg cases?"

"I don't know, Your Honor. The wounded continue to arrive. For every one we bring in, another takes his place. Sister Frances says that the Austrian has been here almost two days and that he should be looked at."

"Well, she is right. That's too long for any wounded man to—" the doctor broke off abruptly and frowned at Semyon. "Why are you grinning like a madman?"

Semyon pointed to the surgery entrance where a Russian soldier—a private— stood in the rain holding his crudely bandaged left hand.

Grigorii Konstantinovich addressed the soldier brusquely. "Yes, what is it?"

Bowing his head the young soldier displayed his bandaged hand. "*Vashe blagorodie*—Your Honor, please, it hurts," he said softly.

"Go see one of the sisters—they will clean your wound and decide if one of us needs to look at it. We are all very busy. You must wait like all the others."

"Please, Your Honor, please." The soldier stepped closer and unwound the dark bandage, thrusting his hand, one end of the filthy cloth still fixed to the clotted wound, into the yellow lantern light. "Please. It hurts."

Greatly annoyed, Grigorii Konstantinovich stepped away from the table and inspected the wound, roughly turning the hand in the light.

"*Oi!*" cried the soldier piteously. "Have mercy, Your Honor!"

"Tell me, *golubchik*—little dove," said Doctor Grigorii Konstantinovich, using the Russian gentry's patronizing term for peasant soldiers. "Who shot you?"

The soldier considered the question carefully. "The . . . enemy, Your Honor."

"You mean the Austrians?"

"Y-yes . . . yes, Your Honor." The soldier grew apprehensive under the doctor's cross-examination.

"Did you see them?"

The soldier paused. "No . . ."

"They were too far away? Come, come! Answer the question. Where was the enemy?"

"F-far . . . Your Honor. Far away—across a great field."

"A sad effort and a poor lie, *golubchik!*" The doctor shook his head and his tone became sardonic. "Yours is a close-range wound inflicted not by an enemy of the Tsar but rather by yourself or an equally misguided and cowardly comrade for whom you undoubtedly returned the favor. While you may be in a hurry to leave the front, we are in no hurry to tend to you. You will wait like the others." The doctor turned to the orderly. "Semyon, take him out by the road where he may sit in the rain and contemplate his treasonous doings. Bring in all but close-range hand and foot wounds. Let them wait."

"Yes, Your Honor! Come, you." Semyon opened the tent flap for the dejected soldier.

Indignant, Grigorii Konstantinovich muttered to himself, "The *golubchik* is a young fool. I would think by now that all *samostreltsy*—self-wounded men—in the army would know that muzzle burns betray a close-range wound. This fool doesn't know enough to shoot himself through a loaf of bread like every other coward!"

Overhearing the doctor, the young Russian soldier paused on his way out of the tent. "But . . . but, *vashe blagorodie*—Your Honor, bread is precious."

Startled, Grigorii Konstantinovich contemplated this pathetic young soldier who was soaking wet and covered with mud. "How long have you been at the front, *golubchik*?"

"Since last year, Your Honor. Just after *Rozhdestvo*—Christmas."

The doctor was incredulous. "You have been at the front for a year and a half?"

"Yes, Your Honor."

The doctor raised his eyebrows and then, nodding slowly, said, "I see . . . a year and a half. Yes . . . I see. Semyon!"

"Here, Your Honor!"

"Semyon, take this . . . take this soldier to Sister Frances. Ask her to clean and dress his hand immediately. If she feels the wound needs further care, bring him back."

"Yes, Your Honor. Come, you. Follow me."

Doctor Grigorii Konstantinovich watched as Semyon and the young Russian vanished in the rain. "A year and a half . . . ," he murmured. Then he turned to Sister Anastasiya. "Now, Sister, the Austrian. Give him the anesthetic and prepare the site and give him the injection. Hold up the bandage . . . yes . . . good. The wound is not badly infected; however, the hand is nearly shot away and the ulna and the radius are shattered beyond repair—this shouldn't take too long. When I am finished you may help suture the flap, Sister. Now, these lateral lacerations from the arm pit to the iliac crest—"

"Shrapnel, doctor."

"Yes. Has it all been removed?"

"Sister Frances tended to it before the rain. She said there were bone fragments with the shrapnel."

"Sister Frances does good work. Ivan! Ah, there you are. I will need another bone saw for this tray."

"Yes, Your Honor."

"I want the saw with the heavier wooden handle. Do you know which one I mean, Ivan?"

"Yes, Your Honor!"

"Good. That one is easier on my hand. I'll be of no use to anyone if I develop blisters on my hand."

Grigorii Konstantinovich scrubbed his hands in one basin and then held them over a second basin as Sister Anastasiya rinsed them with a pitcher of water. The doctor looked over the shoulder of Aleksei Vasilevich, who was finishing the bowel case. "I am going to remove this arm quickly," he said. "And then I will step outside for a cigarette. I don't think I've been out of this room since this morning." Aleksei Vasilevich nodded without looking up and Grigorii Konstantinovich went to Sister Anastasiya's side. "Has the anesthesia taken effect, sister?"

"Yes, Doctor."

"Very well . . . a scalpel, please."

☙

When the rain stopped the orderlies took advantage of the change in weather to move the wounded from the postoperative tents. Sister Frances was directing the transfer of patients into the wagons that would carry the wounded to the train and then on to the base hospital. "Ivan!" she called, when she saw the passing orderly. "Will you help here? What have you there?"

"An arm, Sister—for the shed. I will help on my way back."

"I will take it to the shed if you will help load these men on the wagons. I can't lift them anyway."

"Yes, Sister."

Sister Frances took the wrapped arm from Ivan and walked past the rows of canvas-covered dead lying under the broad canopy of the tree near the surgery. Near the little shed where amputated limbs were stored for burial, four men were digging by the yellow light of a kerosene lantern. One of the laborers called out, "Is it a limb, Sister?"

"Yes, an arm. Shall I take it to the shed?"

"No, bring it here, Sister," answered the same laborer. "The good doctor, Grigorii Konstantinovich, says we should bury the limbs first. The flies were fearsome at the shed yesterday. Set it on the pile there, Sister."

Sister Frances peered into the dark at an enormous mound of arms and legs. "Are all of these from the shed?"

"Yes, Sister," answered the second laborer. "The good doctors have been busy. They say the Austrians are beginning to stand and fight again and the offensive might slow down. We'll be digging many a pit such as this."

The third laborer said, "Maybe the war will end with this offensive."

"Feh!" cried the last man, leaning on his shovel. "You are a child! It will take more bloodshed than this to end the war. But whose blood, eh? Whose blood will end the war? Enough red blood has been spilt—it will take the spilling of blue blood to end this war!"

"Hush, you! Enough of your treasonous talk," said the first laborer. "Pay no attention to him, Sister—he has spent too much time listening to trouble-makers."

Sister Frances smiled good-naturedly as the men continued arguing.

"They are not troublemakers!" cried the man leaning on his shovel. "They are university students. You should listen to them sometime. They make sense!"

"They are godless revolutionaries and you are a traitor to the Tsar!" shouted the third laborer. "Who will sing, *'Bozhe Tsarya khrani'*—'God Save the Tsar' with me?"

"Hush—both of you—and dig!" said the first laborer. "I am tired and I want to sleep, so hurry and dig. Tomorrow we will be digging bigger pits. Leave the arm on the pile, Sister. We will take care of it. Dig faster, all of you. *Bystro*—hurry! And no more talking! You spend more time talking than digging. If you dug with your mouths we'd be finished by now!"

Sister Frances headed back to the postoperative tent past the lifeless forms concealed under broad lengths of canvas. "The sheeted dead . . . ," she murmured in English. "There was something in *Hamlet* about the sheeted dead . . . how does it go? 'The sheeted dead . . .' Ah, yes, 'The graves stood tenantless and the sheeted dead / Did squeak and gibber in the Roman streets.' The sheeted dead . . ."

The shadow of one of the other sisters glided across the side of the post-operative tent as Sister Frances pulled back the flap and entered.

☙

"You are awake. Sister Anastasiya told me that you spoke a little English while under anesthesia. Can you understand my Russian? Don't try to speak—nod if you understand, or shake your—ah, good—you do understand. I heard we were facing Rusyn troops in this sector. I have spoken with some of your people who were taken prisoner—your language is very similar to Russian. I am Sister Frances and I'm from London. I am going to look at your sutures and your dressing. Have you ever been to London? No? I haven't been home since . . . two . . . almost three years before the war. I have a brother your age serving in France. It is difficult here at the front to get much news from an-other front so far away. I am curious how you know any English words. Have you been to America? Ah, you nod 'yes,' I see—that explains it. I'm going to lift this cover so that I can change your dressing. No more hemorrhage—that is good. I know you may not appreciate this now, but you are very fortunate, for when you were first brought in you were considered a near hopeless case. Very few suffering as much blood loss as you survive surgery. Did you leave family in America? No? Then you have loved ones near here . . . yes, I see. I'm sorry if this hurts. A wife? No—maybe a girl waiting for you? Ah, yes, you opened your eyes. A girl in your village is awaiting your return, yes? Yes, I see— there is love in your eyes—you think about her often. Have you been home since the war began? No? Well, God willing, the war will be over soon and you will be released and allowed to return. I'm going to move this lantern closer so I can inspect the wound. It is funny—the phrase, 'God willing'—I never said such a thing in England. But here, in Russia, and ever since I came to the front in the fall of 1914, I say it all the time. Perhaps it is because I hear it all the time, but I doubt it. That would be mere mimicry, whereas, in truth, I believe now that anything and everything that happens is due to God's will. In London, such a thought never occurred to me. Perhaps in London it was possible to ignore God's will. This may hurt—I will try to be gentle. In Saint Petersburg—I should call it Petrograd now, but I always forget—in Petrograd I was governess to three young ladies whose parents felt their children would benefit immeasurably from instruction in the French and English languages. On Sundays I attended church services with the family. Of course, I did not take communion—it is not permitted to the non-Orthodox—so I observed, and while I did not understand all that took place I was entranced by the majesty of the Orthodox service. Somehow, as a result, 'God willing' has seemed a natural expression since. Did that hurt? I'm sorry—I'll try to be gentler. Please lie quietly; you cannot afford to expend energy. There, look to the fellow beside you while I apply the new dressing. He is a Russian—from the south, I think. If you two are ever awake at the same time, you will find him easy to talk to. My Russian has improved remarkably in two years and, although he speaks a dialect that two years ago would have been incomprehensible to me, I find I can understand him reasonably well. I believe he can understand me. If he cannot, he certainly makes a good show of it. Anyway, you two should have no trouble at all—two former enemies side by side in hospital. He was a farmer and I will venture a guess that you were also. I know what you are thinking: how will he farm without legs? Well, he may have a son at home or a brother or—there, the worst is over. Now for the new dressing. Please be still. No, it is best that you don't look. Please, you mustn't exert . . . please . . . lay your head back down. Please . . . please, you may burst the sutures . . . oh . . . oh, my poor boy! I see—yes, I understand now. Dear God! Dear God! My poor boy! You didn't know. No one has told you. My poor boy. Then yes, you must look. They took the arm off here, above the elbow. It could not be saved. Take my hand in yours. Now squeeze. Do you understand? Squeeze my hand, hold it tightly. Yes, that's it. Do you feel that? You have one good strong hand. God willing, you will come to see how fortunate you are. One arm is gone but the other will become stronger. You will see. I have seen hundreds . . . no . . . thousands of young men just like you who have lost arms and legs. And I have seen just as many who have lain before me and lost so much more . . . everything . . . Squeeze again . . . harder! Be strong . . . be strong and, God willing, return to your village and your family and the girl you love! Now, squeeze my hand. Yes! That is good! Squeeze it! Again . . . good!"

CHAPTER TWENTY-SIX

The Camp

ON A CRISP NOVEMBER AFTERNOON IN 1916, three hundred Austrian prisoners of war shuffled into a Russian military camp. Exhaling misty puffs from their mouths and nostrils, the prisoners slowly gathered in an open area that was surrounded by shabby wooden barracks. Dark clouds clung closely to the earth and threatened an imminent snowfall. When the three hundred were fully assembled, the mounted Russian escorts turned their horses back toward the rail station.

A captain of the Imperial Russian Army, an immaculate great coat draped over his shoulders, emerged from a small wooden building and surveyed the new group of prisoners from the edge of a little covered porch. Two guards with bayonet-tipped rifles at their sides stood in front of the building.

"Welcome, Slav brothers!" the captain cried. "I call you 'Slavs' because that is what you are and I call you 'brothers' because every Slav is my brother, whether he is from Belgrade or Prague, Warsaw or Kraków, Lvov or Moscow. We are one people brought into conflict against each other by unfortunate circumstances. It is not the natural desire of a Slav to take up arms against his brother Slav. This great fratricidal war is a crime against Slavic unity and brotherhood. It is a tragic war initiated by non-Slavic politicians who seek to mold Europe into a base for world domination. This course of action ignores the natural and peaceful desires of all Slavs, who, by virtue of their language and culture, are destined to coexist in a unified Slavic state. For now, you are prisoners of war; however, when this war ends there will be created under the benevolent patronage of the Tsar of All the Russias, His Imperial Majesty, a great Slavic empire for Slavs and governed by Slavs. We will all be a part of one great Slavic state. It is the destiny of His Imperial Majesty—"

The captain's monologue was suddenly interrupted by a loud, lengthy yawn, by no means sarcastic or bitter, but rather reflective of a desperate soul's need for rest. One of the guards hobbled through the crowd of men and came to a prisoner with bloodshot eyes who was surprised to find himself an object of attention. As the captain made his way through the crowd, the ragged prisoners stepped aside, peering at the officer's uniform and carefully trimmed beard.

The captain stood behind the guard. "Corporal, is this the man?"

The corporal nodded, "Yes, Your Honor," and stepped aside.

The startled prisoner looked up into the captain's eyes. The captain smiled and said, "You are tired, Private." The captain's light stress on the adjective made it unclear whether this was a question or an observation. Confused, the prisoner merely blinked. "What is your name?" asked the captain.

"Mykulyak, Your Honor. Mykulyak, Mykolai."

The captain smiled at the prisoner. "Perhaps, Private Mykulyak, you do not agree that all Slavs belong in one great state."

A voice from the crowd of prisoners broke the silence. "He meant no offense, Your Honor. We are all tired."

The captain faced this new speaker. "Your Russian is very good. I surmise from the three faded stars on your collar that you are a sergeant."

"Yes, Your Honor."

"Although your Russian is good, your pronunciation betrays you. While you give the *geh* a good effort, your natural inclination to pronounce the letter as *heh* is perceptible. What is your name, Sergeant?"

"Rusynko, Your Honor. Rusynko, Vasyl."

"Sergeant Rusynko, I once knew a man from Galicia. You sound like him. You also are from Galicia." Again the captain blurred the distinction between question and statement.

"No, Your Honor. I am from Stara Polyanka, a small village."

"This village, then, is not in Galicia." The captain smiled. "Perhaps I should say, 'Halicia.'"

"No, Your Honor. It is near Pryashev—Eperjes as the Magyars call it."

"Ah, Eperjes! The Hungarian Kingdom! You are one of our lost Slavic cousins from across the mountains. We have many of your Rusyn brothers in this camp." The captain turned to the Russian guard at his side. "Corporal, take these men to their barracks so they may rest and warm themselves." The corporal hobbled through the crowd of prisoners, bidding them to follow. The captain again addressed Vasyl. "There was terrible fighting in your mountains during the first year of the war. Were you there?"

"No, Your Honor. I was in Galicia and Russia."

The captain inspected Vasyl's jacket. "Your right sleeve is empty, Sergeant."

"Yes, Your Honor."

"Where did you lose your arm?"

"Near Brody—last summer. It was two or three days after our lines collapsed."

The captain nodded. "Yes, last summer during the Austrian retreat. That was a tremendous defeat for the Austrians. This camp is full of men taken last summer in that sector. We had so many prisoners that we were forced to let them sleep in the open fields. It took the entire autumn to build enough compounds for all the men. We built no fences—no need to—where would you go?" The captain paused and patted his right shoulder. "My right sleeve is also empty, Sergeant. I lost my arm the year before you did—in the summer of 1915, during our retreat before your army and the German army. It was just outside some filthy little hamlet between Lublin and Chelm. I don't know who was more miserable, the Jews in the village or the peasants on the farms. Typhus was rampant and the people were so sick they could scarcely bury their dead. One morning the Germans appeared in front of us. Their artillery rendered my men senseless. As chaotic as it was, and as stunned as my men were, they stood heroically and did not break and run." The captain sighed and gazed up at the clouds. "My men died in great numbers—it was a tremendous sight that I shall never forget. At some point I found myself on a stretcher being carried from the field, eventually to the dressing station, then to the surgery, then to the base hospital, then to home in Moscow, and then . . . then, here." The captain paused. "It will snow soon. Tell me, Sergeant Rusynko, do you sometimes feel the cold on your missing arm?"

Vasyl thought for a moment and then nodded. "Yes, it often is sore where the hand should be."

The captain nodded solemnly. "It has been a year and a half and still I have pain below my shoulder. I also have sensation where my missing hand should be. The doctors told me it would happen, but they never told me if or when it would stop. I often wonder at the odd power of the mind that it would stubbornly insist that, despite all powers of human reason, a limb, long removed, still exists in empty space—in an empty sleeve—a ghost of an arm haunting its former owner." The captain held out his gloved left hand in the fading light. "There, do you see? It is snowing. Good night, Sergeant Rusynko. Keep yourself warm. It is going to be a long winter." The captain went into the building and closed the door.

The same limping Russian corporal who had identified the yawning Mykolai to the captain appeared and joined Vasyl in the walk to the barracks. They walked in silence until they stood outside a long wooden building, where the Russian guard finally spoke. "Your barracks, Sergeant. They are serving supper. What do you think of my captain?"

Vasyl studied the corporal in the yellow glow issuing from the open barracks door. The man was about Vasyl's age and wore a bushy mustache that accentuated a smirking mouth. "I don't know, Corporal," said Vasyl. "I suppose he seems like a sad man."

The corporal's smirk broadened. "Yes, he is sad. He is sad because he lives in the past." The corporal abruptly turned and limped away in the dark.

Vasyl stepped inside the building into the light of a kerosene lamp. Down the length of the room were several long rows of three- and four-tiered bunks. Mykolai, the yawner, spotted Vasyl.

"Sergeant!" cried Mykolai. "I saved you a bunk—the middle one because I thought it would be easier for you—with only one arm. Look, no climbing, no bending or crawling. I'll take the lower one. There's a kettle in the middle of the room. It's not much—only water and onions. But there's a fair supply of black bread. Some of the men here think that you might recognize the cook. He's been here since last summer."

Vasyl and Mykolai made their way to the center of the barrack, where the men were crowded around a large steaming pot. The corners of Vasyl's mouth dropped in an inverted smile. There, stirring the soup with both hands was Yurko Kryak.

❦

A few days later, Vasyl and Mykolai, standing outside their barrack, noted a small but animated discussion taking place among some of the prisoners in front of the captain's quarters. Mykolai went to investigate and then beckoned urgently to Vasyl. As Vasyl approached, Mykolai handed him a typed page. "Look, Vasyl. It is from the captain. It is about the Emperor—he is dead."

Vasyl took the paper from Mikolai and read:

To all Austrian prisoners of war—Your sovereign, Emperor Franz Josef, Emperor of Austria and King of Hungary, has died. His obstinate insistence on a one-sided remedy to the intricate series of events that unfolded in the summer of 1914 brought war to all of Europe and loosed an unnatural and fratricidal conflict between the Slavs within his Empire on the one hand and the Tsar's Imperial forces on the other. In the south, Serbs were also forced to defend themselves against the Emperor's captive Slav brothers. Now the old monarch is dead. Pray that wisdom prevails in the Viennese court and that the end of the war may come soon.

Captain Zernov

Vasyl returned the paper to Mikolai who asked, "Do you think it means the end of the war, Vasyl?"

Vasyl shrugged. "I don't know what it means."

The men gathered nearby were also unsure of the significance of the announcement.

"Who will be the new Emperor?"

"The war will surely end now."

"Why should it end? The Kaiser and the Tsar are still alive."

"When do we go home?"

"They should let us go soon—before the snows are too deep."

"The war will continue, friends. Believe me. This will not end it."

"He is right! If the last emperor would not end the war, why should the next one?"

The men continued to debate the prospects of war or peace while Vasyl edged away from the group and made his way back to his barracks. On the way he came across the Russian corporal who had escorted him to his barracks on the first day in the camp.

The corporal nodded a greeting and asked Vasyl, "Have you read the captain's notice?"

"Yes, I have." Vasyl noted the smirk on the corporal's lips. "The death of the Emperor is amusing to you, Corporal?"

"That his death causes concern to the captain amuses me."

"You do not like your captain?"

"I dislike those who dislike change."

"Your captain said, 'Pray the end is near.' The end of the war would be a change."

"Yes, it would."

"Do you feel the end is near?"

The corporal's smile flattened into a scornful grimace. "One way or the other—the war . . . other things."

The corporal's manner was unsettling and Vasyl pressed him further. "Tell me, Corporal, how do you come to limp so badly?"

"Artillery during the retreat in 1915. I lost half my foot and my knee was shattered. I'll never be able to bend it again. I still have shrapnel in my calf." The man's limp increased in the telling.

Vasyl redirected the conversation. "I have a brother—a younger brother—he was in a company not too far from mine. I often wonder how he is . . . where he might be at this moment. Do you have any brothers, Corporal?"

"My oldest brother was killed in Poland during the first summer of the war. A second brother was killed during the advance in Galicia last year. I have a younger brother who is trained in war industry production and therefore exempt. He is with the workers in Petrograd. Here is your barracks."

The Russian corporal's behavior and cryptic comments intrigued Vasyl, who began to notice frequent encounters among the Russian guards in the camp, usually with the enigmatic corporal at their center. These small groups of four or five men stood in circles in their long winter coats, stamping their feet, their faces veiled by puffs of cloudy breath. These men, including the corporal, murmured secretly among themselves and seemed to share a dislike for the captain.

One of the guards, however, did not join in the corporal's clandestine groups. Nikolai Petrovich was a simple peasant with a gray beard and matching gray mustache, stained tobacco-brown beneath the nostrils. When the weather was clear he often visited with Vasyl in the compound, where the two men smoked cigarettes made with Russian *makhorka* as they spoke of farming and shared their dreams of life after the war. One day Vasyl told Nikolai Petrovich that he had spent four years overseas.

"Four years on the other side of the earth!" cried Nikolai, his mouth open in disbelief. "Away from your family for four years! I am away only two years from mine and I am sad every day. Tell me, Vasyl, what does a farmer do in a place like Ameryka where he has no land?"

"I did what all farmers from my people's villages do when they go to Ameryka—I worked in a factory."

Nikolai Petrovich leaned over, blew smoke to the ground, and tried to spit. When he straightened, a stream of foamy spittle trailed into his beard. "Feh! Factory! Men who work in factories become old and sad early and they drink too much and become mean. They dream up fantastic ideas and speak badly of the Little Father—the Blessed Tsar. They talk about revolution and things I cannot pronounce. But farmers like you and me stay young even when we are old, and we don't forget how to laugh, and when we drink we sing rather than blaspheme the Tsar. Factory! Feh! What did you make in the factory?"

"Long rolls of carpet. *Verst* after *verst* of carpet for Amerykan homes."

Nikolai Petrovich slapped his knee and again leaned forward blowing smoke to the ground. "Yes! Even in Russia there are people who put blankets on the floor—blankets to keep the floor warm! But you came back to your farm."

"Yes. I wanted to buy land."

Nikolai Petovich's eyes widened and he nodded solemnly. "That is good. A man with land needs no blankets on his floors." The Russian eyed Vasyl's empty sleeve. "You will farm as well with one arm as some men with two. I see that in you. You have a wife—children? No? I have a wife and three sons—daughters also—but three sons, Vasyl Rusynko. You have brothers, yes? Good, then—they will help. You will all work together. I have three brothers—had three brothers—one is dead in this war—and three sons. We who come home, God willing, will work together and soon things will be as they were before the war."

℘

The long, dark Russian winter fell over the camp. There were rumors of food shortages and unrest in Petrograd and Moscow, and the feeling that all was not well in Russia prevailed among the Austrian prisoners.

CHAPTER TWENTY-SEVEN

The Time of Troubles

IN EARLY MARCH OF 1917, Vasyl and Mykolai were walking across the camp compound when they noticed a group of Russian guards standing outside the captain's quarters. Among the guards was Nikolai Petrovich, who, upon seeing the two men, broke away from the group and hurried across the compound. "Vasyl, Mykolai, something has happened to the Tsar. We are awaiting word from the captain. Come wait with us if you want."

"What has happened?" asked Mykolai.

"I don't know—something serious. Wait for the captain. You too, Vasyl."

The men stood in the sun outside the captain's quarters as a small crowd of curious fellow prisoners gathered. The men murmured among themselves and turned their collars up against a sporadic but brisk evening breeze.

When the captain emerged from his quarters, he was hatless and he held in his left hand a folded document. With his one hand the captain opened the document, stared at it, and then slipped it into his great coat. He coughed and then addressed the assembled men in a weak voice:

"I think it is right that I share . . . that I tell all of you . . . sad but important news. There will be many changes in the coming months . . . perhaps sooner. The Tsar has abdicated for himself and for the Tsarevich—his son—in favor of his brother, the Grand Duke Mikhail. The Grand Duke has also abdicated . . . and, so . . . so, it is finished. Three hundred years of history have come to an end with just a few words written on a piece of paper . . . just a few dozen words. The old ways are passing from our sight and a new age is upon us." The captain paused and looked about him, his sad eyes moist and red. "Three hundred years ago a Russian dynasty ended and a time of unrest, confusion, and pretenders prevailed—a Time of Troubles. I wonder, now who will play the role of Boris Godunov, hmm?" The captain sighed deeply and ran his hand over his bare head. "Well . . . what do you think of that? I've left my cap inside. So . . . so . . . I . . . I know there is a shortage of bread and other food in the camp. Perhaps the political changes will result in a better system of supply. I hope so. Good night . . . good night to you all." The captain returned to his quarters, leaving the prisoners and guards to murmur among themselves.

"*Bozhe moi!*" blurted Nikolai Petrovich. "What does it mean? No Tsar? How can that be?"

"The people's will, old friend," said the limping corporal, whose smirk now expanded into a grin.

Nikolai Petrovich snorted. "Feh! It isn't my will! It is the will of troublemakers! Troublemakers like you!" Nikolai Petrovich stalked away grumbling.

"Tell me, Corporal," asked Vasyl, "why does the fall of emperors always bring you such happiness?"

"It is change that brings me happiness."

"And why will this change bring you happiness?"

"Because the age of privilege is over. Now comes the age of collective rule."

"Collective rule?"

"Yes. All men, not a privileged few, will hold equal power and 'Bread and Peace' will become reality and not merely words shouted in the streets and written on banners."

Vasyl jerked his head toward the captain's quarters. "Will everyone have bread and peace?"

"The captain, like all men, will have what he deserves and what he has earned. Those who protest are the enemy."

"The enemy?"

"Big changes are coming, Vasyl Rusynko. Those who live in the past are the enemy. Good night. Sleep well."

ℭℭ

A month later Vasyl was picking his way across the muddy compound when he heard the sound of motorized vehicles. Bouncing through the compound gate were three automobiles bearing flags of the Russian Provisional Government on the front fenders. The vehicles came to a halt in front of the captain's residence. The passengers, in military uniforms, stepped out of their vehicles and filed into the building.

Vasyl made his way to one of the barracks and leaned against the wall in the shade. A few curious men emerged from the barracks and slowly made their way to the captain's quarters.

After a short while the men emerged from the quarters and began addressing the small crowd of prisoners gathered outside the building. Vasyl remained in the shade of the barracks, observing the Russian speakers and the growing crowd of prisoners. A Slovak prisoner named Stanislav emerged from the crowd and hurried past Vasyl.

"Vasyl, come listen!"

Vasyl remained leaning against the barracks. "What is it, Stanislav?"

"Those men are from the Russian government and they have an offer for us—" Stanislav glanced at Vasyl's empty right sleeve. "For some of us. Come listen, Vasyl."

Vasyl shrugged and made his way to the crowd as Stanislav went into the barracks to spread the word. Vasyl stood at the back of the crowd and listened to the young speaker, a member of a Russian Army recruitment committee.

"Slovak and Rusyn brothers! I come to you today as your comrade. I am, like many of you, a Rusyn, born in the Carpathian Mountains under the foreign rule of a distant king. I, like all of you, was unjustly called to fight against my brother Slavs. Men whose language and culture are foreign to me forced me to take arms against men whose language and culture are similar to mine. The Russians are brothers to the Slovaks and the Rusyns! Russians are our natural allies in all matters, and it is under their protection and tutelage that we can hope one day to rule ourselves. Imagine living in your own Slovak or Rusyn state!"

Vasyl moved closer.

"The old order—the order that called you to leave your loved ones and to kill your Slav brothers—that order is dead. A new age in history is upon us! Through the power of democracy, the Russian people will never again be subject to the whim of privileged leaders. But, brothers, the price for peace is strength in arms. There are those who prefer a weak Russia to a strong Russia. The eyes of the world are upon Russia! And now Russia needs her Slavic brothers. Now is the time to join the ranks of those you were formerly and unnaturally asked to oppose!"

Someone near Vasyl shouted, "As guests of the Russian Army, we are starving. How will it be as members of your army?"

The speaker took a step forward and pushed his cap back on his head and spoke as though imparting a confidence to this one prisoner. "You will eat as a soldier should expect to eat, brother. Any concerns you have will not be for your belly."

Another voice called, "I want to go home!"

"So do I! I don't want to fight!"

"WE ALL WANT TO GO HOME!"

The young speaker held up his hands. "Yes, brothers, we all do! The quickest way to your homes is in the wake of a strong and speedy peace. Once there is peace, we will all go home. There are Slavic units of former soldiers of the Austro-Hungarian Army in formation now for the Russian Army. The men come from camps such as this one. They all want to go home as much as you do. But they recognize that there can be no peace until Austria-Hungary and Germany are defeated."

The men murmured among themselves and shouted questions to the recruiters. Vasyl returned to the rear of the crowd, but continued to pay particular attention to the Rusyn recruiter, who, presenting himself with poise and confidence, stepped down from the porch and mingled with the prisoners, fielding individual questions, and earnestly addressing each soldier's concerns. Vasyl returned to his spot in the shade of one of the barracks.

Stanislav drew near Vasyl and excitedly summarized the young speaker's offers. "Go speak with him, Vasyl. He is very sincere."

"I'm sure he is."

"Talk to him yourself, Vasyl."

"No, Stanislav. I don't think I will. His way is not my way."

"Joining the Russian Army could be no worse than staying here and starving to death. Go join that group and get to know him. You will see." Stanislav dashed off to his barracks.

"I already know him," whispered Vasyl. "He is my brother . . . my brother Andrii."

☙

The recruiters worked well after sundown, signing up prisoners for Slavic units in the Russian Army. Eventually, Vasyl turned his back on the little crowd and gazed up at the evening star hanging just above the western horizon. "How far is it?" he murmured. "How far is it to Stara Polyanka?" Vasyl started back to his barracks but stopped when he heard a familiar voice.

"A moment, please, brother." It was Andrii, approaching in the dark. "I see you have lost an arm. There is a need for more than just fighting men. You may have skills that can serve you and Russia and, hence, all Slavs well."

"And for this you would give me bread?" asked Vasyl without turning around.

"Yes. Bread and more. What is your name, brother?"

"What about peace?"

"Peace will come in time."

"For now, you offer bread alone."

Andrii moved a few steps closer. "The world is hungry for more than just bread and peace, brother. The world craves a lasting peace. Do I know you? Have we met?"

Vasyl turned around. In the dark both brothers' faces were indistinct. When Vasyl spoke again, his voice shook slightly and his words were slurred. "Do they feed you well?"

Andrii seemed surprised. "The Russian Army? Yes . . . yes, they do."

"Would you continue recruiting your own people for the Russian Army if they didn't feed you?"

"I act out of a desire to help my people. I believe that the best hope for the future of my people—our people, brother—is through the patronage of the Russian government. Your voice sounds familiar. Do I know—"

"Will you feed me?"

"What?" Andrii was startled.

"I am hungry. Will you feed me?"

"Well . . . I . . ."

"Must I join your army before you will feed me?"

"You misunderstand. I don't feed people. I recruit them for the army, where they will be fed and taken care of and—"

"And killed."

"Well, not necessarily . . . but, yes, they could be killed, but not the way you say. Men die in this camp. They die without hope and they live without hope. We are offering a chance for them to be part of something greater—something that will change history and lead to—"

"How many men have joined your army?" Vasyl interrupted.

"I don't know—hundreds, thousands, I suppose. Do . . . do I know you? Your voice . . . something about you—"

Vasyl was insistent. "How many have joined your Russian Army to change the world and how many have joined to eat?"

"I don't think your question is—"

"I will tell you that not one man from this camp will join your army for the reasons you would like. They will join in order to eat and for no other reason. They will do anything to eat . . . anything. Go offer your promises elsewhere. Don't offer them here—don't offer them to me."

The two men faced one another in the dark until Andrii, sighing, said, "It is late—I will return to my comrades now. I hope you will reconsider joining us. Good night."

"*Z Bohom*—go with God, brother," Vasyl said softly.

Andrii nodded in the dark. "Yes, *Z Bohom*." He turned away and then paused. "I am sure I know your voice. What is your name?"

Breathing quickly through his mouth, Vasyl turned away and walked silently toward his barracks. Andrii followed and placed a hand on Vasyl's left shoulder. "Wait. Who are you, brother?"

Vasyl nodded.

"You will tell me your name?" asked Andrii.

Vasyl nodded again and then whispered, "You have said it . . . brother."

"I have said it?"

"Yes . . . brother."

"I . . . *B-Bozhe* . . . *Bozhe moi* . . . is it you . . . is it you, Vasyl?" Andrii's voice was scarcely audible.

Vasyl nodded.

Andrii's voice cracked. "Vasyl! I . . ." Andrii shuddered and then fell to his knees and wept. Vasyl laid his hand on Andrii's head, whispering over and over, "Brother, brother, brother . . ."

Finally composing himself, Andrii sniffed and sighed heavily. "I had almost given up hope. For months I have passed endless graves and mass graves. I dared not look at them—I dared not think of it. Every camp we visited I looked at each man hoping one would be you, Vasyl. Tonight I thought of you when I spoke with the men here. I thought, any one of these could be you. They are all so thin . . . you are so thin, Vasyl. What . . . what happened to your arm?"

"Russian artillery."

Andrii groaned. "And here I am trying to get you to join their army."

Vasyl snorted and began to laugh.

Andrii was horrified. "Vasyl, please . . . stop. It is wrong to laugh. Stop laughing. It is really not funny."

But Vasyl's laughter was contagious. Andrii, sputtering and covering his mouth, finally succumbed and the two brothers locked arms and shook together.

"No, you are right," said Vasyl taking a deep breath. "It is not funny. But it feels good to laugh—for any reason. When do you and your Russian friends leave?"

"Tomorrow . . ."

"Will you go with them?"

"Of course, Vasyl . . . I must."

"I see," said Vasyl. "Yurko is here in the camp."

"Yurko!" cried Andrii. "And how is he?"

"Thinner but just as tall and quiet as you remember him."

The two men stood in silence until Andrii cleared his throat. "I must report back."

Vasyl chuckled. "We have done this before."

"Yes . . . we have. Vasyl . . . *Z Bohom*—go with God."

"*Z Bohom,* Andrii."

"Vasyl?"

"Yes?"

"Will I see you in the morning?"

"I don't think so . . . no."

"When will I see you, Vasyl? When do you think we—"

"Only God knows. *Z Bohom,* Andrii."

و∙د

Many left the camp to join the Slavic units of the Russian Army. The Slovak, Stanislav, marched out of the camp, waving to Vasyl and shouting, "I will see you again, Sergeant—maybe in the streets of Pryashev!" Vasyl waved and smiled. Just as many prisoners, however, declined the Russian offer and remained in the camp. Mykolai, the prisoner in the bunk below Vasyl's, had listened with interest to the offers but, in the end, decided that he had seen enough of the war.

By midsummer of 1917, rumors of a new Russian offensive were confirmed by the sudden transfer to front-line duty of all able-bodied guards, including Nikolai Petrovich.

Nikolai came to see Vasyl on the way out of the camp. "Not much longer,

God willing, before you and I shoulder scythes instead of rifles, eh, Sergeant Rusynko?"

"Yes," said Vasyl. "Trust in God, but keep your head low."

Nikolai Petrovich laughed and then somberly patted his chest. "I have my protection here, sewn into my shirt. It is an icon of the Mother of God holding and protecting the Lord. She also protects me. But, just in case she is too busy for the likes of me"—Nikolai pulled a short piece of rope from his pocket—"I have this. It was used to hang a murderer. Such talismans are hard to find now, Vasyl Rusynko." He replaced the rope and patted the pocket. "With charms such as these, I have little to fear."

And so the old guards and other Russians formerly deemed fit only for rear area duty marched out of the compound and to the trains headed for the front.

Two months later, news arrived announcing that the Russian offensive was a failure, that casualties were enormous, and that in Petrograd there were bread riots and strikes.

❦

By the end of October, the captain had disappeared from his quarters and a new flag—blood red—flew above the camp. Vasyl and the other prisoners debated its meaning.

"What is that?"

"It is the flag of revolution."

"Who raised it?"

"I don't know."

"Has there been another revolution?"

"Who knows?"

"I'm tired of revolutions."

"Do you think the war is over, Sergeant?"

"No, the Russians would have told us by now."

"I want to go home."

"Go then. They won't stop you. There are hardly any guards left. And there are no fences."

"No fences . . . yes, it is tempting . . ."

"You'll be frozen before morning."

"I didn't say I would go now—not in winter. I just meant I want to go home sometime."

"I would go in the spring."

"Yes, the spring—the spring is the time to go."

"When would you go, Vasyl?"

"I don't know—the spring, I suppose."

"It is a long walk, no matter when you go."

"It is too long—you'd starve."

"Does anyone know where we are?"

"Now you're thinking! It would be good to know where you are first, before you wander off into the forests!"

"It's too cold now to think about it anyway. I'm going back inside."

"I'm coming with you."

"Wait for me. I'll not stay out here alone. I hope it will be an early spring—an early and warm spring."

❧

During the winter of 1917–1918, typhoid fever swept through the camp and the dead were stacked outside on the frozen ground to await burial in the spring. The interminable snows submerged the camp in a sea of white and the sky remained gray for weeks at a time. In their icy wooden barracks, the prisoners despaired of ever going home again.

CHAPTER TWENTY-EIGHT

The Last Winter

A HOWLING BLIZZARD BUFFETED THE BARRACKS, whistling through myriad cracks and driving snow under the doorways. Yurko dragged a corpse down the center aisle of the barracks past lice-infested bunks where sick and dying men lay helplessly in their own filth. Yurko dropped the dead man's feet halfway to the barracks door and leaned against the bunks to catch his breath. He had made the trip over a dozen times in the past few days, usually with help, but now, as the only ambulatory prisoner in the barracks, he worked alone. Across the aisle from Yurko, in the top bunk, lay a man from Uzhhorod, his face contorted in pain. In the middle bunk, Vasyl breathed irregularly through his mouth and observed Yurko's movements with blood-shot eyes.

Yurko swayed across the aisle, pulled back Vasyl's blanket, scraped the fat squirming lice from around his friend's neck, and flicked them to the floor.

Vasyl closed his eyes and whispered hoarsely, "You are a good man."

Yurko ran his finger nails along the inside of Vasyl's tunic collar, scooping the yellow vermin into his hand and throwing them onto the floor. Then Yurko dropped to his knees and leaned into the lower bunk occupied by the lifeless Mykolai. His cold jaw agape, frozen in an eternal yawn, Mykolai was as fatigued in death as he had been on that first day in camp during the captain's speech. Yurko pulled the blanket over Mykolai's dull half-closed eyes.

Yurko swung out from the lower bunk, grabbed the ankles of the dead man on the floor and resumed the journey to the barracks door. Lifting the door latch with his elbow, Yurko leaned against the door, pushing it open against the gusting wind. Snow swirled inside the barracks and the door banged against the corpse and slammed shut as Yurko pulled the body through the doorway. Yurko deposited the body against the base of a great white mound, and trudged back to the barracks.

Back inside, shivering men near the door cursed Yurko and rebuked him, shouting, "Don't open that damn door again!" Yurko staggered to Vasyl's bunk, where he found his friend semiconscious. He scooped another handful of lice from inside Vasyl's tunic and threw them to the floor.

When Vasyl closed his eyes, Yurko, weak and exhausted, leaned into the bottom bunk, rolled Mykolai's body onto the floor, and with his feet pushed the body across the floor next to the adjacent lower bunk. Yurko then collapsed onto the vacant bunk and closed his eyes.

Outside the barracks, the corpse, now veiled in white, froze to the ground next to the stack of its icebound comrades.

❧

The night wind continued its assault on the barracks. Inside, the wood stove in the center of the long room cast a dull amber glow. From the long rows of bunks came the labored breathing, coughing, and murmuring of the prisoners. Yurko, awakened by Vasyl's humming in the upper bunk, slowly rolled out of his bed, struggled to his feet, and supporting himself against the bunk, examined his friend. Vasyl's eyes were closed and his forehead was hot.

Vasyl, delirious, asked in a raspy voice, "How are the children? Are they eating well? Hmm? Yes? Good . . . good. I heard that you didn't finish your work . . . but all is well now. There was no harm done. Father would be angry . . . if he knew. But he won't know . . . he won't know . . . will he? No . . . no, of course not. Look at the sun on the hills." Vasyl, his eyes still closed, tapped the frost-covered wooden barracks wall. "Out there . . . do you see? Do you see them? I see every one of them. There are so many . . . so many. Who knew there would be so many? Hmm? Are the children eating well? Yes? Good. They must eat well . . . they must eat well. The little ones . . . they are so very, very hungry. There are so many . . . so . . . many . . ." Vasyl drifted off to sleep.

Yurko lowered himself to his bunk and lay on his side. Mykolai's body was, as before, on the floor, only now there were two large rats hunched atop his chest. Yurko swung a leg out from his bunk, kicking one of the rats down the floor between the rows of bunks. When the spinning rodent came to a stop it slowly crawled into a dark corner, dragging its useless hind legs. The other rat returned to Mykolai's chest and continued feeding, oblivious to Yurko's choking sobs.

ℰℐ

Vasyl awoke in the dark, his fever momentarily broken, and called feebly to his friend. "Yurko . . . Yurko. I think . . . I think maybe you can hear me. I know you are sick, Yurko. I think I have been sick a long time . . . I don't know how long. I don't remember much, but . . . but I . . . I do remember some things. The fever will come back to me—this I know. I remember things I said during my fever . . . I remember things I saw. Some of it was true—some of it was not. Maybe all of it was true—I don't know. But I must tell you, Yurko—you must hear this—Yurko, do you hear me? When I die, drag me outside to freeze. Don't leave me in here on the floor. Do you hear me, Yurko? You must promise me this. And if you die, I will take your body outside—I promise. I will take you outside if it is the last thing I ever do . . . now and ever . . . and forever . . ."

ℰℐ

In early 1918 the frozen earth dissolved into a sea of mud, as the living emerged from their barracks to bury the thawing dead. Yurko worked with a party of Rusyns and Slovaks to dig a pit on the edge of the compound while Vasyl, still not fully recovered from his illness, organized a group of six men to pry apart the dead and drag them to the pit. The men struggled with the frozen corpses, complaining as they labored.

"This morning I was cold—now I am hot."

"You will be cold again. Believe me—winter is not yet over."

"I never want to be as cold and sick as I was this winter—never again."

"Our comrade on the ground has found a way to avoid misery. Look at him—he will never be cold or sick again. He is past feeling anything."

"There is little comfort in that!"

"Pick up your end! I'm doing all the work."

"I'm doing what I can. I don't have the strength for this work."

"If you have strength to complain, you have strength to work."

"Quit arguing, you two. Respect the dead. You are carrying a man. He may not look like one now—but once he was a man."

"Yes, Sergeant."

"Very well, Sergeant."

"You there, Anton, help me pull this one to the pit."

"Yes, Sergeant."

"There, do you see? The sergeant has only one arm and yet he works as though he had two. And he is still ill—he shouldn't be out here. Do you hear him complaining?"

"No."

"Well, then."

"Has anyone heard news of the war?"

"Not I."

"Nor I."

"Since they raised the red flag, they say it will be over soon."

"Feh! They said that in the autumn. And still the war goes on."

"Maybe there has been another revolution."

"No. Look, the red flag still waves."

"We suffer because of that flag."

"How do you mean?"

"Look around you, my friend. We are sick, we are hungry, we are dead."

"He is right. It wasn't this bad last winter."

"No, and last winter the red flag did not hang from that post."

"Fool! It is not the red flag that makes us suffer."

"That was not his meaning. It is those who raised the flag who make us suffer."

"This is true. I hear the Russians are starving. Don't pull so hard on that arm—you'll break it off."

"What, then, will become of us?"

"We are starving now—what do you think will become of us?"

"Some say we should go home."

"Go home! How?"

"Walk."

"Walk! Are you mad? Do you know how far it is?"

"Yes, I know. But here . . . here there is nothing for me but death."

"And death will follow you, friend. It will follow you out of this camp."

"He is right. You would not survive a night—you would freeze."

"I would wait until it no longer freezes at night. This one is loose. Help me pull him."

"Yes. We could walk at night and sleep during the day."

"Yes, you are right. And the guards—the few left—they will not miss us."

"This is true. Fewer of us means more food for them."

"And what of the war? Somewhere between here and home, the war goes on. Someone will stop you—either their army or ours."

"I'll go if someone goes with me. These two are frozen at the shoulder."

"We can drag them together."

"Not through this mud."

"Use your spade—put the blade between their shoulders and strike the handle."

"Yes, I see. It is a clean break."

"I wonder what the sergeant will do? Will he walk home?"

"He will stay. He has only one arm. He was near death this winter. He would be a fool to go."

"If I had any money, I would bet it on the sergeant. I say he will go."

"I agree."

"So do I."

"Well, if I were fool enough to want to go, he would be the one I would want to go with. I think we can all agree on that. Pick up your end—I can't carry this man by myself."

༒

It was late afternoon when the men finished burying their comrades. Vasyl and Yurko were walking slowly back to their barracks when Vasyl placed his hand on his friend's shoulder. "Stop, Yurko. I want to tell you something. Many of the men are talking about going home. Some have asked me what I will do. I have thought about it for some time now and I have made a decision. We are going home. I am not certain how. It is a long way. But, we are going home. Do you understand?"

Yurko nodded.

Vasyl continued. "We have spent our last winter in Russia. We have buried many friends today. Somehow we are still alive. Next winter we may not be so fortunate. Soon we will go." Vasyl studied the sky. "Very soon. Maybe in a few weeks. We will need to repair our boots—they will need good soles. We will live off the land—we will take what we need from farms we pass. We will walk—perhaps hide on trains if we can—but mostly . . . mostly, I think, we will walk. We will follow the sun, to the west, and then to our mountains, and, then . . . then, home—home to Stara Polyanka. We have spent our last winter in Russia."

Yurko nodded.

Vasyl patted Yurko's shoulder. "*Dobre*—good, Yurko. *Dobre.* I'm glad you feel the same way. Now, let's get something to eat."

☙

Over the course of the next few weeks, Vasyl and Yurko made preparations for their journey. Like-minded prisoners also gathered supplies and began leaving the camp in small groups of three or four at night or in the early-morning hours.

Vasyl and Yurko found adequate boots among those salvaged from their dead comrades. Working in their bunks with nails pulled from discarded boots, they reinforced four pairs of boots—two pairs for each man. One evening, a man named Anton, from a village on the Uzh River, watched the two at work. Vasyl, holding a boot between his knees, pressed a small nail into the sole and then hammered it home with a rock.

"For a man with one arm you are a good cobbler, Sergeant," said Anton, propped up in his bunk.

Vasyl chuckled. "My new trade—by necessity." He pressed another nail in place and struck it with the rock. "Anton, have you thought about what I told you?" Vasyl pressed another nail in place.

"Yes," said Anton. "I have. But . . . but, I think I will stay."

"You are welcome to come with us."

"I know. Thank you, Sergeant. If I could, I would go. Only . . ."

"Only what?"

"Only, I've been coughing up blood for some time now. I would only slow you down. I will stay. The war can't last forever."

Vasyl slipped his right foot into the boot and stood to test the fit. He hobbled between the bunks and then nodded to Yurko. "This one is good. And you are right, Anton. The war will not last forever. Don't worry—when it ends, the Russians will send you home in a train. You will look out your window and you will see two tired infantrymen of the old Austrian Army stumbling along the tracks in worn-out boots. Wave to us as you pass, Anton. We will envy you."

Anton laughed weakly until he began to wheeze. Then he collapsed onto his bunk, coughing and moaning.

Yurko and Vasyl laced up their reconditioned boots and went outside for their long daily march around the compound.

〇〇

On a clear, cold evening three weeks later, Vasyl, carrying two pairs of boots, walked across the compound, past the limp, scarlet flag of revolution, to the edge of the fields that bordered the camp. He waited in the growing dark for Yurko, who soon appeared with a canvas bag over his shoulder.

"Open it, Yurko. Let me see."

Yurko opened the bag, revealing two dozen potatoes.

"Our dinner for the next few nights, Yurko. And this "—Vasyl retrieved a pouch from inside his jacket—"this is tobacco. It is from Anton. He said it hurts too much to smoke now. He said to remember him when we enjoy his tobacco. And we will—tonight when we stop. Anton will never leave Russia and he knows it."

The two men stood at the edge of the field and gazed one last time at the squalid prisoner-of-war camp with its decrepit little buildings and its mass graves.

"So many men, Yurko . . . so many good men."

Yurko nodded.

"We have a long way to go, Yurko. Perhaps we are leaving too early in the year—it might snow again. In fact, I'm certain of it. But I think we must leave now. Russia is a dangerous place—who knows what could happen here."

Vasyl turned away from the camp and pointed to the sky. "Do you see that star, Yurko? It is the evening star. It follows the sun and so will we. If I die on the way home, you follow the sun. Do you hear me? You follow the sun in the day and you follow that star in the evening until you reach our mountains. Come, Yurko. Let's go home."

They walked along the edge of the field and then onto a cart path to a road that led toward the fading western light.

CHAPTER TWENTY-NINE

Enemies of the Revolution

FOR MORE THAN TWO WEEKS the two men followed a main east–west railway line, scurrying off the tracks into hiding at the approach of trains and spending nights in the forests or in trackside maintenance sheds. After almost a week of good weather, this day began with a light snow. By evening the countryside was frozen white and the temperature was falling. At a point where the track branched to the right, Vasyl called over his shoulder, "Yurko, there appears to be a town up ahead. Let's follow this siding and look for shelter. I don't want to sleep in the snow tonight."

They walked past the black hulks of two locomotives that were stripped of every salvageable part while the bellies of their broken boilers rested on the rails. Their Imperial Russian insignia were canceled, but not obliterated, by contemptuously deep scratches hacked into their rusting skin. Farther down the siding they encountered several ax-wielding peasants and Jews dismantling the carcasses of four wooden boxcars. Vasyl approached the nearest peasants and offered help in exchange for a night's shelter.

"Be gone," muttered one man stacking splintered planks in a pile. The other peasants eyed Vasyl and Yurko with suspicion and continued their scavenging.

At another boxcar, Vasyl saw a group of bearded Jews in long black coats laboring with their axes. "We will work for a bed of straw in your barn!" he cried out to them. When they ignored him, Vasyl shrugged and said to Yurko, "Come, we will seek shelter in town."

As the two men passed the last boxcar, a lone young Jew called to Vasyl. "You may sleep in my storage room if you will help me carry this wood."

Vasyl and Yurko joined the Jew at the end of the boxcar, where Vasyl extended his arm, saying, "Fill the wood to my shoulder, Yurko." Noticing the quizzical look on the Jew's face, Vasyl nodded reassuringly. "I know it's only one armful—we'll come back for more."

The Jew tore at the railcar with an ax. "There isn't enough time. Soon it will be dark. After dark it is too dangerous to be outside—especially alone. There are many ruffians roaming the countryside."

Yurko finished loading Vasyl's arm and then hefted a prodigious stack of wood in his own arms. The Jew slipped his ax inside his black coat and loaded himself with splintered planks. "Follow me," he said over his shoulder.

The three men walked along the rail siding into town and then, leaving the railway, they made their way among blackened stone pillars. "The railway station," said the Jew pointing to the pillars. "It burned down last fall." In the waning light the men stepped over the building's foundation stones and onto a broad street lined with Jewish shops. Little windows cut into the sagging brick and wooden facades cast a dismal yellow light onto the snow-covered street. As they walked past a block of charred ruins, the Jew explained, "Some locals rioted against us two weeks ago—a pogrom."

Shortly they arrived at a modest wooden storefront and the Jew tapped the door with his boot. The young woman who opened the door greeted the Jew but immediately withdrew into the room at the sight of Vasyl and Yurko. The Jew addressed the woman in Yiddish and then turned to Vasyl. "She is my wife. She is afraid of . . . strangers." He spoke to his wife sharply, and she scurried out of sight into a back room where she was greeted by children's voices.

"Where shall we put the wood?" asked Vasyl.

"Hmm? Oh, yes," said the Jew distractedly. "Here on the floor. Put it anywhere. I still must chop it up for the fire."

Vasyl and Yurko piled the wood on the floor and then Vasyl said, "We will go now."

The Jew nodded and sighed heavily. "Yes . . . yes . . . I . . . I suppose it would be better if you left. There have been . . . troubles . . . troubles with locals, troubles with outsiders, troubles with everyone. The war was bad enough, now the peace is . . . well, the peace is no peace at all. It is a terrible peace."

Vasyl pushed Yurko gently toward the door. "We will go."

"Wait," said the Jew. "I must pay you for the work. I have no money. What will you take for helping me with the wood?"

Vasyl looked about the empty room and then back to the Jew. "Do you have any potatoes?"

"Yes . . . a few."

"We'll take four if you can spare them."

"Wait here." The Jew went to the back room and then paused in the doorway. "Do you have salt?"

Vasyl shook his head. "Not much."

"I will also bring salt." And he disappeared through the doorway. Again there was the hushed but animated discussion between the Jew and his wife accompanied now by the insistent cries of a baby. After a moment the Jew returned to the front room and handed Vasyl a small bag. "Salt," he said, and then he drew potatoes from his pockets and gave them to Yurko. "They are small, so I am giving you six."

Vasyl put the salt inside his coat and, nodding at the Jew, stepped outside with Yurko. It was still snowing lightly and the town was very dark. From the doorway the Jew said, "Do you see that street over there? Try down there. There are Christians living on that street."

Vasyl and Yurko trudged down the street to an intersection and turned the corner. At the first small dark building, Vasyl knocked on the door. Receiving no answer, he motioned to Yurko to follow him. "All these buildings are dark in front. Let's go around back."

At the rear of one building a sickly yellow light shone from a small window set deep in the rough-hewn wall. When Vasyl rapped on the door, shadows flickered across the window.

"Who is there?" called a woman's muffled voice from inside.

"We are seeking shelter," said Vasyl. "There are two of us."

"Go away!"

Vasyl shook his head in disgust at Yurko. Then he rapped lightly on the door again.

The same voice called out, "Go away!"

"We offer work in exchange for shelter!" offered Vasyl.

"Are you mad? Go away!"

"Bozhe!" muttered Vasyl. "What kind of town is this? Come, Yurko. We will freeze to death before anyone takes us in here."

As the men walked away, the back door of the store opened a crack. "Come back here." It was the woman's voice. "Do you swear there are only two of you?"

The men returned to the door and Vasyl held out his hand, indicating Yurko. "There are only two of us, as you yourself can see."

The woman opened the door and popped her uncovered head out into the alley, looking quickly in both directions. "Collect as much firewood as you both can carry. Bring it to the door on the street." She shut the door abruptly in the men's faces.

"Come, Yurko," said Vasyl. The two men returned to the main street lined with Jewish shops and then made their way to the ruins of the railway station and finally to the spur and the splintered remains of old Russian rolling stock. They loaded themselves with wood and returned to the front of the house, where Vasyl tapped the door with his boot. Receiving no response, Vasyl kicked the door, rattling the adjacent window. A yellow light faintly illuminated the window from within and there was the sound of a heavy door latch.

"Who do you think you are, kicking my door in?" grumbled the old woman as she admitted the men. Her hair was mostly gray and her right eye was swollen shut. "Stack the wood in that corner." She pointed to Vasyl's smaller load. "That's all you brought?" Vasyl lifted his empty right sleeve and dropped it. "Hmph!" shrugged the woman.

"Where do we sleep?" asked Vasyl.

"In here, on the floor. At sunrise you will leave." The woman narrowed her left eye menacingly. "My husband has a pistol." Then she inspected the men's greatcoats. "Are you deserters?"

"No," said Vasyl, shaking his head wearily. "We are only walking home." He pointed westward. "That way."

"Hmph! You are either deserters or prisoners of war. You will leave at sunrise." The woman grabbed several pieces of wood and took them with her into the back room, bolting the door from the other side.

Vasyl and Yurko settled in for the night on the wood plank floor. Vasyl stared at the dim glow under the back room door. "I'm glad we ate before we came to this town, Yurko. I don't know how we would cook in this place without going outside. Anyway, I'm too tired to do anything but lie down. At sunrise we will leave this town and make a fire in the woods where we will cook our potatoes. We will eat them with our salt and then we will continue to the west as we have done now for . . . two weeks . . . three weeks . . . I don't remember. But I think just a few more weeks—maybe four or five at the most—and we will be home . . . home with our own fire." Vasyl turned onto his side away from the back room door.

Curled under his woolen greatcoat, Yurko was already snoring lightly.

∾

Vasyl was roused from his sleep by a piercing whistle. "What the devil!"

Yurko was already at the window, wiping at it with his coat sleeve and peering outside when Vasyl came to his side. "What is it, Yurko? Do you see anything?"

Yurko shook his head. At the sound of another whistle Vasyl said, "It's a train—but that's too long a blast. It's not regulation—an engineer would never blow it that long." Vasyl unbolted the door and gazed down the street. "The snow has stopped, but I can't see anything. It's too dark. I hear loud voices, though."

The door to the back room suddenly flew open and the old woman hurried to the window, her husband hobbling behind her. "Close that door!" she shouted to Vasyl. "Bolt it! Dymitro, stay in the back room! You, I told you to close that door!"

Vasyl ignored the woman and stepped out into the snow-covered street. "Watch for me, Yurko. I'll be right back." Yurko nodded and barred the woman from bolting the door.

Vasyl trudged through the snow to the middle of the main street, where he could look down the length of the Jewish shops to the ruins of the railway station. Somewhere near the main tracks there was the sound of uproarious singing accompanied by accordions. A Jew, his long black coat waving wildly behind him, ran up the street toward Vasyl. Vasyl stepped in front of the man and cried, "Who are they? What is happening?"

"Russians!" shouted the Jew, weaving around Vasyl. "Pogrom!"

At that moment Russian soldiers singing and carrying torches staggered up the street, gathering bricks from the ruins of deserted shops. In front of a large synagogue, the Russians stopped and threw their bricks through the building's narrow arched windows. The door of the synagogue opened and an elderly Jew stepped outside, waving his arms at the soldiers. One soldier raised his rifle butt and struck the Jew in the head. With a wild cry the soldiers charged into the synagogue, trampling the Jew under their boots.

As other gangs fanned out from the railway, the dreaded shout, "Pogrom!" spread up and down the streets until it was rendered superfluous by the crash of breaking glass and the crack of rifle fire.

Vasyl returned down the side street and found Yurko standing in the doorway fending off the gray-haired woman's flailing arms. When she saw Vasyl, the woman screamed, "Tell this idiot to let me pass! We must hang the cross! Let us hang the cross!"

Vasyl pulled Yurko out of the doorway. "Come, Yurko. Let her out."

The woman secured a small wooden cross to the door and then yelled to her husband, "Dymitro, the icon!" Her husband handed her a small icon, which she placed in the window. The woman stood back looking at her home with satisfaction. "There, very well. They are here to rob the Jews—we will be spared."

Russian soldiers reeled around a corner and, spotting the little group assembled in front of the old woman's house, cried, "Jews!"

The woman screamed, "No! No! This is my house! There are no Jews here! They are all down that street! *Na pravo! Na pravo!*—To the right! To the right! This is not a Jewish street!"

One of the Russians waved his torch in Vasyl and Yurko's faces. "Who are you?" he slurred.

"They are escaped prisoners," declared the woman. "They broke into our home."

Vasyl shook his head. "She's lying. She gave us a room for the night in exchange for firewood."

"Liar!" shouted the woman. "I would never allow enemies of the Russian Army into my house!" She jabbed a gnarled finger in Vasyl's face. "We had to let them in—they threatened us."

Vasyl glared at the old woman. "We did no such thing."

The woman snorted. "Of course you deny it!" Then, addressing the Russians, she lowered her voice confidentially. "The tall one is an idiot—he never speaks. But this one"—she jerked her head toward Vasyl—"this one is trouble!"

One of the Russian infantrymen leveled his rifle and lightly jabbed the bayonet in Vasyl's midsection. Yurko quickly intervened, deflecting the rifle barrel with one hand and backhanding the Russian in the face with the other. The startled Russian fell backward onto the snow, his rifle firing harmlessly into the sky. The terrified old woman covered her ears and screamed.

"No, Yurko!" cried Vasyl, grabbing Yurko's collar. But as two other Russians removed their rifles from their shoulders Vasyl pushed his friend away. "Run, Yurko! RUN!" One of the Russians thrust his rifle butt into Vasyl's ribs, knocking him to the ground. Propping himself up on his one arm, Vasyl gasped, "Follow the star and the sun, Yurko! Run!"

His feet kicking up snow, Yurko ran awkwardly toward a side street. The two Russians raised their rifles, aimed, and fired.

"I hit him!" cried one of the Russians.

"The hell you did," said the second Russian. "He's gone around the corner there."

"I tell you, I hit him! I'll go have a look."

"Don't waste your time—he's halfway to Zhitomir by now."

"I know I hit him," said the first Russian over his shoulder as he cautiously approached the corner. He looked down the dark street, and then, slinging his rifle, rejoined the group shaking his head. "He's gone. I'm sure I hit him. I know I hit him."

Vasyl closed his eyes and sighed heavily. "Good man, Yurko," he murmured softly. "Follow the star and the sun . . . follow them home to Stara Polyanka."

A soldier brandishing a pistol approached from the direction of the station. "What is happening here?" he cried. "Why are these men on their backs in the snow?"

The Russian whom Yurko had knocked to the ground now stood, rubbing his face and brushing snow from his coat. "This bastard's friend hit me and ran away," he said.

The Russian pointed his pistol at Vasyl's head. "Get up. Who are you—what are you doing here?"

Vasyl struggled to his feet and nodded in the direction of the old woman. "My friend and I stayed in her home. We gave her firewood in exchange for shelter for the night."

"They threatened my husband and me," croaked the old woman. "He and his friend are escaped prisoners."

"We did not escape. We were walking home. That is all."

The Russian lowered his pistol. "Show your collar."

Vasyl unfastened the top of his coat.

"The old woman is right," said the Russian. "He's an Austrian—a sergeant." The Russian turned to the old woman. "You are very helpful."

The old woman grinned. "I always try to be—especially with the army."

"What are you doing in the street?" Now it was the Russian who grinned.

The old woman's countenance fell. "I am—I was giving the army directions to the Jewish street. I—"

The Russian shoved three of his comrades toward the old woman's house. "Have a look," he said. The three men trudged through the snow with the protesting old woman on their heels.

"Now," said the Russian, returning his attention to Vasyl. "You are a spy sent behind our lines by your army."

"I am not a spy. Would my army send a one-armed man to spy?" Vasyl waved his empty right coat sleeve.

The Russian smirked. "How the devil would I know what your army might do? Where did you get the firewood?"

Vasyl hesitated. "At . . . near the railway."

"I see," said the Russian. "So, you are a thief."

"No. I am not a thief."

The Russian chuckled. "You are not many things. You are not a thief, you are not a spy, you are not an escaped prisoner of war. And yet, here you are."

From the doorway of the old woman's home a Russian called out, "You should see this place! The *starukha*—the crone—has a cellar full of *samogon*—homebrew!"

The Russian stuffed his pistol under his belt and laughed. "I knew she was up to something. Bring her out here!"

The three Russians, each brandishing a jug of homemade liquor, escorted the indignant old woman back out into the street.

The Russian shook his head at the woman. "So, while the people in the cities starve, you horde grain and brew *samogon*."

Defiant, the old woman thrust out her chin. "Talk to my husband. Who knows what he has been up to?"

One of the riflemen shook his head. "The back door is open and there is no one else in the place."

"How could I know such things were in my cellar?" cried the old woman. "Look at my legs! Do I look like someone who could walk up and down cellar steps?"

"Nevertheless," said the Russian. "Your cellar is full of *samogon*."

Flustered, the old woman blurted, "I put a cross on my door! And an icon in my window! You are here for the Jews! Why bother honest Christians?"

"Honest!" cried the Russian. "Honest! And with a cellar full of *samogon* under your feet! You are an enemy of the revolution who grows fat like the Jew on the misery and labor of others! While your comrades in the cities starve, you turn precious grain into *samogon!*"

"I'm an honest Christian, I tell you!"

"You are as honest as the Jew in your calculation of profit for yourself! We are here to strike at the Jews and the bourgeoisie. You are all the same to me!" The Russian snapped his fingers at two of the soldiers swilling from upturned jugs. "Take her with this Austrian sergeant. Put them in the synagogue on the Jewish street with the others. They are enemies of the revolution."

The soldiers surrendered their jugs to their comrades and leveled their rifles at Vasyl and the old woman. "Go on, prisoners," slurred one of the Russians, stirring the air menacingly with his bayonet. "To the synagogue with you."

The icy street crunched beneath the prisoners' boots and the old woman, clutching Vasyl's arm for support, grumbled, "I put a cross on my door . . ."

At the entrance to the synagogue, a Russian was brandishing a pistol in the face of an old Jew bent with age, his hands raised in supplication. "Now, be gone!" the Russian barked at the old Jew. "Your synagogue is closed to any more of you—only prisoners may enter. Be gone!" Seeing Vasyl and the old woman, the Russian queried the escorts, "What do you have there?"

"Enemies of the revolution," answered one of the guards, slinging his rifle over his shoulder.

"Hmph! You've told me nothing. They're all enemies of the revolution!" He opened the door and waved Vasyl and the old woman into the synagogue with his pistol. As he closed the door behind them, the Russian turned to the old Jew. "Now, what have I told you? Be gone!"

The interior of the synagogue was dimly lit by candles and smelled of old wood and musty books. Scattered about the floor were bits of manuscript and torn lengths of curled parchment. Six Jewish men worked patiently and methodically on their knees, reassembling the sacred remnants of their ancient tradition.

"Look at me!" wailed the old woman. "An honest Christian in a roomful of Jews! I had a cross on my door and yet the soldiers ransacked my house! Have they no fear of God?" She stood in front of Vasyl and glowered at him. "Do you hear me? A cross on my door!"

"Perhaps," said Vasyl dryly, "your cross is too small. Now, shut up and sit down somewhere."

Startled, the old woman blinked her eyes and backed away from Vasyl, mumbling, "A cross on my door . . ."

વ્ઝ

Vasyl, his eyes closed, sat on the synagogue floor against a stone pillar, listening to the sounds of breaking glass, screaming women, and the occasional crack of a rifle. Near the door, the old woman sat on a bench and mumbled to herself. Vasyl was falling asleep when the door of the synagogue opened, admitting another prisoner.

"I see they also brought you here," said a familiar voice. Vasyl opened his eyes and looked up to see the same young Jew with whom he and Yurko had collected wood when they first arrived in the town.

"Yes," said Vasyl, standing and nodding a greeting. "Apparently I am a spy." Vasyl unfastened his top coat button and exposed the stars on his collar.

"And your friend—the tall one?"

"He ran away. He is heading home to our village. And you? Why are you here?"

"I hid my family in the forest . . . as I always do during times like this. I came back to get my in-laws but was picked up in the street by Russian soldiers."

"How long will the Russians stay in this town?"

The Jew shook his head. "They will rob my people until there is nothing left to take. They will rob and kill until they are tired of it. Their stay may depend on how much liquor they find."

Vasyl glared at the old woman by the door. "They found plenty of that. And what will become of those of us locked up in here?"

"I don't know," said the Jew. "The Russians are unpredictable. Some people they shoot in the street—some they lock up. There may be good news, though. I overheard Russians at the railway discussing the German advance."

Vasyl was surprised. "The Germans are advancing?"

As the two men spoke, an old Jew, a tattered prayer shawl drawn tightly over his unkempt gray hair, shuffled up to Vasyl and stood quietly next to him.

Vasyl nodded politely at the old man and then looked intently at the younger Jew. "Why are the Germans advancing? I heard there was an armistice and the Bolsheviks and the Germans were discussing peace."

"They were. However, it seems that the Bolsheviks are slow to accept German terms. Now the Germans are negotiating with bullets and shells. In fact, according to the Russians I overheard, there is a rumor that an armored train full of Germans may be on its way here from the next town. If this is true, the Russians will flee from here soon. They are in no position to fight the Germans right now."

"No, they are not," said Vasyl, shaking his head. "They are no longer an army—they are a mob. And yet, the war continues."

"Yes, the war continues," said the Jew. "And for my people, the best hope is that the Germans arrive soon. They will restore order."

The old Jew standing next to Vasyl began to chant softly and then looked up at Vasyl as if awaiting an answer.

Vasyl raised his eyebrows at the younger man. "What did he say?"

The Jew smiled and shook his head. "He said, 'You must always try to water trees.' Pay no attention to him—he is an old, old man."

When the old man repeated his chant, Vasyl said, "He is mad then?"

"Perhaps. The quotation is from the writings of a *tzaddik*—a holy man. It refers to finding wisdom and deliverance in time of terror." The younger Jew stroked his beard. "Perhaps he is not mad at all."

The old Jew tugged at Vasyl's empty sleeve and spoke.

"What now?" Vasyl asked the younger Jew.

"He asks who you are."

"Tell him I am nothing, only a soldier going home."

As the young Jew translated, the old man's eyes widened. He grasped Vasyl's empty sleeve with both hands and spoke at length and with such animation that his prayer shawl slipped from his head.

Vasyl looked at the younger Jew. "What is this all about?"

"He is excited because you were in the army. He is asking about a story that has circulated widely since the war began. The story deals with the large number of my people serving in both the Russian and Austrian armies. In this story, a Jew from one army finds himself on the battlefield in single combat with a soldier from the other army. The Jewish soldier thrusts his bayonet into the other soldier and is horrified when his enemy falls, crying out, '*Shma Yisroel*—Hear, O Israel!' This is the opening of the last prayer every Jew utters before he dies. The thought of Jews killing one another troubles many of my people—especially the elderly."

"I see," said Vasyl. "Tell him that I never witnessed any such thing. No, wait. Tell him no such thing ever happened."

"Yes . . . yes, of course," said the young Jew, and he began to translate.

The old man listened intently and then looked into Vasyl's eyes. He released Vasyl's empty sleeve and, groping for the other sleeve, found Vasyl's hand and pressed it in his own.

From outside came the sounds of gunfire and men shouting. The rattle of a machine gun echoed in the distance. Vasyl smiled at the young Jew. "The rumors are true. That is a German machine gun you hear." Vasyl gazed upward where yellow light played on the broken arched windows above the door and cast flickering shadows throughout the synagogue. "I think the Russians are torching the town."

"They will burn us alive!" cried the old woman, rising from her seat. "Who will help an honest Christian?"

Vasyl squeezed the woman's arm and forced her back in her seat. "Sit down and shut up!" he ordered. Then he turned to the young Jew. "Is there another way out of here?"

"Yes, but it is secured from the outside. I could see the barricade before I came in."

"It is all your fault!" cried the old woman, aiming a crooked finger at Vasyl. "You and your tall friend, the idiot! If it weren't for you two, I'd be home in a warm bed right now!"

There was a loud pounding on the synagogue door and then a clanking of keys.

The old woman cowered behind Vasyl. "Lord, have mercy! They are coming to shoot us all!"

The door suddenly swung open, revealing Yurko.

"*Slava Bohu*—Glory to God!" cried the old woman, throwing her arms in the air. "It's the idiot!"

"Yurko!" shouted Vasyl, brushing past the old woman and slapping his friend on the back. "You came back!" Squeezing past Yurko into the synagogue was the old Jew who had pleaded outside the door with the now-vanished Russian guard. The Jew pocketed the synagogue keys and then joined his people in collecting parchment scraps from the floor. "Come, Yurko," said Vasyl, his arm across his friend's shoulders. "Let's leave this place."

When they stepped outside into the gloomy dawn, they shielded their faces from the intense heat of a building burning furiously across the street. Snow had begun to fall again during the night and dark smoke rose from several points around the town.

The young Jew followed them outside and grasped Yurko's arm. "Have the Russians left?"

Yurko nodded.

"And the Germans are here?"

Yurko pointed down the street toward the railway station ruins where a long train, its locomotive billowing black smoke, was poised to lurch eastward. Artillery pieces, their barrels covered with canvas, were mounted on flat cars, and helmeted Germans manned machine guns on the rooftops of boxcars.

Halfway down the street, a squad of German riflemen marched three Russian stragglers out of a building. Suddenly, one of the Russians bolted from the group and raced up the street in the direction of the synagogue. The German captain in command shouted and pulled a pistol from his holster.

Vasyl threw himself onto the snow. "Down!" he yelled.

Yurko and the Jew flopped down next to him as the German captain fired a single shot. The Russian stumbled forward and fell with a grunt in the middle of the street. Vasyl raised his head cautiously. The Russian struggled to stand but was hit by a second shot. Now lying on his stomach gasping, the Russian glanced back at the German looming over him. The captain aimed his pistol at the back of the Russian's head and fired a single shot.

Seeing the young Jew next to Vasyl, the German called out, *"Jude, kommen Sie hier!"* The Jew rose to his feet and approached the German.

Vasyl whispered to Yurko, "Be very still. Do whatever the German tells you to do." Yurko nodded solemnly.

The Jew returned to Vasyl's side. "The captain wants us to carry this dead Russian and follow him. I told him you two are locals. I think it is best if he does not see the stars on your tunic collar. The Germans are going to execute these Russians."

The German squad had now marched their remaining two prisoners to the middle of the street next to the body of their fallen comrade. The captain barked a series of orders which the Jew translated. "You two," he pointed to the Russians, "and you two," he pointed to Vasyl and Yurko, "are to carry this man down this street and halt behind the synagogue."

While the German captain continued to shout, Yurko and one of the Russians each grabbed one of the dead man's arms while Vasyl and the other Russian each took a leg. The four men slogged through the snow swinging the dead man face down between them.

The Russian staggering next to Vasyl was very drunk. "I knew I hit your friend," the Russian slurred.

Vasyl frowned. "You what?"

"Your friend—the tall silent one—last night when he ran around the corner. We fired at him. Look at his coat—under the left arm. Do you see the two holes? In and out—there's no blood. But, it's all the same—I hit him."

Vasyl studied the young Russian's face. "So that was you? You were one of the riflemen?"

"In and out."

"And now you will be shot."

"It's all the same . . ."

"'Rape and murder,' that's what the German captain said."

"You speak German?" The Russian stumbled along with half-closed eyes.

"Enough to understand *Vergewaltigung* and *Mord*."

"It's all the same." The Russian shrugged. "Anyway, your friend didn't run far. Ivan was wrong—'Halfway to Zhitomir,' he said. You were wrong, Ivan. Do you hear me?"

When the Russian struggling in the snow next to Yurko did not answer, Vasyl said, "Ivan didn't hear you."

"Ivan is facedown between us. You carry him by his right leg. He's facing hell and he will hear me soon enough. 'Halfway to Zhitomir,' he said. Your friend stayed behind—to help you. He is a good friend."

"Yes, he is."

When the group reached the back of the synagogue, the captain barked orders that the Jew translated. "Drop the body here. Prisoners to the wall!"

The bearers lowered Ivan's body onto the snow. The Russian next to Yurko began to shake and sob. The Russian at Vasyl's side removed his greatcoat and handed it to Yurko. "There are no holes in this one. Take it. I won't need it where I'm going." Then he put his arm out to the other Russian. "Come, Nikolai. It is too late for tears. Look at our two friends." The two Russians walked backward through the snow to the brick wall of the synagogue. "Look at them, Nikolai. Theirs are the last kind faces we'll see before the Devil's own."

The German captain ordered the squad into formation.

"It's all the same," said the Russian, his gaze fixed on Vasyl.

At the command, "FIRE!" Vasyl closed his eyes.

The concussion of the rifle volley shattered the quiet courtyard, loosening a clinging band of snow from the synagogue eaves onto the two crumpled men below. The Russian who had given his coat to Yurko lay on his side, his eyelids fluttering and a bright red discharge flowing from his mouth onto the white snow. Pulling his pistol from his holster, the captain walked across the courtyard and fired a single shot into the back of each Russian's head.

Holstering his firearm, the captain shouted orders to his squad. All but two of the German riflemen marched out of the courtyard. The captain then spoke to the Jew, who, in turn, translated for the benefit of Vasyl and Yurko as the captain left the courtyard.

"There is a shed on the other side of this courtyard wall. The captain wants us to drag these men through the gate and place them in the shed for burial later. These two soldiers will supervise and then rejoin their squad."

Vasyl, Yurko, and the Jew carried the three corpses to the shed outside the synagogue courtyard while the two Germans smoked and chatted with each other. When the three men completed their task, the Jew whispered to Vasyl, "You two stay here." He reentered the courtyard, spoke briefly with the Germans, and then reemerged. "We may go now. Are you ready to resume your journey?"

"More than ready." Vasyl nodded.

"Then come with me," said the Jew. "I must go to the forest on the west side of town to collect my family."

The three men made their way past smoldering buildings and grim little groups of Jewish men conferring in the middle of the street. These somber men nodded salutations to the young Jew and cast wary looks at Vasyl and Yurko. In front of one building, Jewish women wailed over three dark-clad forms prostrate on the frozen street.

When they reached the edge of town, the Jew pointed to a well-trod path. "This is the path to the woods. We will follow it and I will show you how to get to the railway before we reach the trees."

Walking along the path, the men could see on their left a second German train squealing gradually to a halt, its cargo of soldiers already leaping from boxcars and forming ranks in the snow. The locomotive of the first train, billowing great gray black clouds of ash, now lurched eastward in pursuit of the Russian Army. As German occupation troops marched into town and past the brick synagogue, a rifle volley reverberated through the side streets.

The Jew stopped in the middle of a field. "Here is where I leave you. You will go in that direction to the railway." He turned and started toward the woods.

"Wait," said Vasyl.

"Yes?"

Vasyl extended his hand. "Thank you."

The young Jew hesitated, and then grasped Vasyl's left hand briefly with his own left hand. He abruptly turned and hurried off toward the woods.

Vasyl and Yurko headed across the field toward the railway. Though it continued to snow lightly, the air was warmer than the previous day. As they reached the tracks, Vasyl said, "I think, Yurko, that I will not mind sleeping outside tonight. I think I have had enough of towns for a while. Perhaps we will find a small railway trestle for cover. That way we can have a fire at night that won't be seen by passing trains. We might even—" He stopped when Yurko tugged sharply on his empty sleeve. "What is it, Yurko? What do you see?"

Yurko pointed across the field to the edge of the forest where a column of men, women, and children emerged from the trees and tramped across the snowy field toward the town.

"Yes, Yurko. The Jews are returning home."

But Yurko pointed insistently to one little family in the procession: a young woman holding hands with two small children, and behind her, a man clutching a bundle tightly to his chest with one arm while waving with his other arm. Yurko held up his arm in acknowledgment.

"Yes, Yurko, now I see them," said Vasyl holding up his arm. "It will be safe for them to go home now that the Germans are restoring order." Vasyl patted his friend gently on the back. "Come, Yurko. Let us walk as far as we can today. I, too, want to go home."

The two men turned westward and followed the parallel rails that seemed to converge at the white horizon.

CHAPTER THIRTY

A World Gone Mad

ON A WARM SPRING DAY Vasyl and Yurko emerged from the edge of a thicket and stepped onto a deserted road. Austrian and Russian armies had clashed in the area during the first year of the war and the land still bore the wounds and debris: collapsed trenches, rusted wheels, sun-bleached horse rib cages, and overgrown mass graves. Vasyl looked up at the sun and studied the shadows in an effort to secure his bearings. Two days earlier, he and Yurko had crossed the Bug River north of Lvov, and now it was only a matter of days until they would be able to see the low outline of the Carpathian Mountains on the southern horizon.

Vasyl pointed to the south. "Yurko, look. There is a village. We will make our camp outside the village and, after nightfall, we will look for food." Vasyl pointed northward. "I think this road leads to Rava Ruska. Do you remember that place?" Yurko nodded but he was looking in the other direction, toward the village. Vasyl continued, "If we circle around the north and west sides of Lvov and then head south, we will come to the road to Przemyśl. At Przemyśl we will come to the San River. At that point we will head south and cross the San River near Sanok. We buried Vasko in a village near the San River—do you remember? What is it, Yurko? Do you see someone on the road?"

Yurko pointed south toward the village, where there was commotion in the road.

Vasyl nodded. "Yes, Yurko, I see. They are mounted—two dozen at least. They have rifles, Yurko—I see rifles. Come, let's hurry. To the trees, Yurko!" The two men ran across the road, then through the knee-high grass and into the shady refuge of the trees, where they knelt out of view. The rhythmic clopping of numerous horses' hooves swelled until thirty riders passed on the road, all of them dressed in mixed and matched uniforms of several armies, and all of them heavily armed with an assortment of rifles: Russian Mosin-Nagants, German Mausers, and Austrian Mannlichers.

Vasyl and Yurko waited until the noise from the mounted irregulars faded and the dust raised by their horses settled. When they ventured back out onto the road, they were startled by a voice, calling out in Russian, "Vasyl Rusynko, is that you?" The two men froze in place.

"Vasyl Rusynko!"

Vasyl turned toward the sound of the voice. "What the devil, Yurko! Do you see anyone?"

"Vasyl Rusynko! Over here!"

Yurko tapped Vasyl on the shoulder and pointed to a figure waving from the tree line along the road leading toward the village. The corners of Vasyl's mouth dropped slowly, forming a smile. "Come, Yurko. It is old Nikolai Petrovich from the camp in Russia!" Vasyl and Yurko jogged up the road and cut through the grass to the edge of the forest. Their old Russian guard stood in the sunlight smiling, his beard perhaps somewhat grayer and his mustache still stained tobacco-brown beneath the nostrils.

Nikolai locked arms with Vasyl and patted Yurko on the shoulder. "Brothers! It is good to see you again. You are on your way home. Come, have soup with us. It is thin. Expect more nourishment from our conversation than from our kettle!"

Vasyl laughed. "It is good to see an old friend—an old friend preserved by the Mother of God and a piece of rope!"

"Yes, Vasyl, did I not tell you I would be safe? So, you and Yurko decided to leave my beloved Russia—well, it is a troubled land now—an angry, troubled land. We live in a world gone mad! But, enough of that! Come, brothers, and meet new friends." Nikolai led the two men into the woods to a campsite where two other men sat on either side of a small fire. Near them a pale figure with black, sunken eyes lay wrapped in blankets. Nikolai pointed to the men by the fire. "This is Ivan Andreevich and this is Mikhail Sergeevich. Brothers, welcome our brothers from the mountains. This is Vasyl Rusynko and this is Yurko. They are honest farmers from the same village. Vasyl Rusynko lost his arm through no fault of his own or ours, but, rather, through the mischief of one of our artillery shells. Yurko is his friend and they are walking back to their farms just as we are, but in the other direction. We are all former prisoners of each other's army and no longer foes. Yurko doesn't like to talk much, so ask him nothing. He'll speak if the Spirit wills it."

The men nodded greetings to each other, and Yurko studied the sickly man lying on the ground.

Nikolai introduced him also. "That is Pyotr Andreevich." Nikolai lowered his voice. "He is very ill. We've been here two days because Pyotr cannot travel any farther. I'm afraid he'll never travel beyond here. Tonight—tomorrow, perhaps . . . he's not long for this world."

Ivan Andreevich and Mikhail Sergeevich removed the little army kettle from the fire with a stick and the men produced an assortment of mugs, bowls, and spoons. Nikolai served Vasyl and Yurko first, and then the five men sat around the fire slurping their hot soup.

Nikolai scraped at his bowl. "I wish we had fresh bread with this. We have *sukharki*—dried black bread. Help yourselves, Vasyl and Yurko. Soak it in your soup so you can eat it. We had fresh bread two days ago when we passed through the village. But then that band of gunmen came through and we haven't been back."

"Who were they?" asked Vasyl.

"From what I've heard, they are deserters: Germans, Poles, Slovaks, Czechs, your people and mine. Some probably were like us once—fellows trying to get home from war, fellows who got caught up with these bands for safety in a dangerous world. Now these gangs are everywhere! They hide in the forests and prey on villagers and travelers and the unwary. Not one of them wants to return to his own army. They are their own comrades—they answer to no one. But, stay clear of them—they rape, steal, and murder. It's a world gone mad, I tell you! Whatever the two of you decide to do tomorrow, Vasyl, don't go near that village. It will do you no good. We've been in villages these gangs have visited. It's a horrible sight you would not soon forget."

"Yes," Vasyl said, nodding. "We've seen what mobs and gangs can do. Yurko and I stay away from villages and towns when we can. In fact, we avoid people as much as possible."

"Yes," said Ivan Andreevich. "Stay too close to the towns and risk being picked up by your government's police. But, wander too far into the country and risk an encounter with the roving bands."

Nikolai set his empty bowl on the ground. "Vasyl, these murderers have little use for broken-down old infantrymen like us; it is best to leave the road to them. You two were wise to hide in the forest this afternoon."

When Mikhail Sergeevich produced a pouch of tobacco, the men pulled their pipes from their pockets and passed the welcome treat around the circle.

They sat in silence, blowing smoke up toward the fading patch of blue sky above the trees. The sickly Pyotr shivered under his blankets and began to cough—a shallow, morbid rattle. The men stirred uncomfortably and cast sidelong glances at their comrade. Pyotr turned on his side, gasping for air until, utterly exhausted, he fell into a fitful sleep.

Nikolai leaned toward Vasyl and Yurko and whispered, "Perhaps in the morning I will be digging a hole. There is a nice spot back in the woods, in a little opening. There are wildflowers and at noon a little sunlight shines down through the trees."

Yurko peered into the forest and then rose and disappeared into the trees.

Nikolai puffed on his pipe and raised his eyebrows at Vasyl. "Your friend passes food quickly."

Vasyl shook his head. "He's gone to earn our supper."

"We have plenty of wood. There is no charge for food among friends."

Vasyl glanced at Pyotr. "Yurko didn't go to collect wood . . ."

"Oh . . . yes, I see."

"He's dug many graves, Nikolai Petrovich. Despite the war, he is still strong and he digs quickly."

"Your friend is a good man, Vasyl Rusynko."

"He is that. I can't remember the last time he ever spoke. I don't think he has said a word to me since the war started—perhaps not even before the war. And yet, he always seems to know what to do and when to do it. I'm glad he's with me."

Vasyl finished his pipe and reclined with his head on his rolled greatcoat—comfortable, sleepy, and content with this little circle of men. He turned on his side and observed the three men as they cleaned their kettles and bowls and wiped their spoons on their shirts. It was twilight now—that time after the sun has set when everything is illuminated by a diffuse light that reveals details which, during the day, are often lost in sunny brilliance: Nikolai's eyes crossing slightly as he inspected his spoon, Ivan's dark cheeks collapsing with each puff of his pipe, a dying man's blanket laboriously rising and falling. Closing his eyes, Vasyl fell asleep before Yurko returned from the forest clearing.

᷈

In the morning all the men awoke but one. Nikolai, Ivan, and Mikhail wrapped Pyotr Andreevich in his own blanket and carried him to the grave in the clearing prepared by Yurko the night before. The three men lowered the body into the ground and then stood over the open grave. Nikolai announced, "Let us send Pyotr on his journey with *Vichnaya pamyat.*" Following Nikolai's lead, the men began to sing:

> *Vichnaya pamyat.*
> *Vichnaya pamyat.*
> *Blazhennii pokoi;*
> *Vichnaya pamyat.*
>
> Eternal memory.
> Eternal memory.
> Blessed repose;
> Eternal memory.

The men crossed themselves and filled the hole with dirt, stamping it firmly with their boots. Ivan and Yurko gathered large stones and formed the image of the three-armed eastern cross on top of the grave.

The men then packed up their few belongings and hiked through the woods to the road. Nikolai grasped Vasyl's arm. "God be with you, Vasya," he said. "I will remember you fondly as Vasya—and God be with you, Yurko."

Vasyl embraced Nikolai. "*Z Bohom*—go with God, Kolya."

Nikolai sniffed and brushed tears from his eyes. "Yes, remember me as Kolya. We all have a long journey before us. We are only three now, and we pray that we will be three when we reach home. And we pray that the two of you will find your homes and families as you left them. To our farms, brothers! And to our new lives in a world gone mad!"

☙

Vasyl and Yurko gave the village a wide berth but passed closely enough to observe village men digging in the churchyard. The workers leaned on their shovels, warily eyeing the two men as they crossed the distant fields. Once around the village, Vasyl and Yurko rejoined the road and followed it for the remainder of the day, hiding in ditches and forests at the approach of other travelers. They slept again that night in the woods, and two days later they reached the outer ruins of the old Austrian fortress system surrounding the city of Przemyśl. Before dawn they crossed the treeless landscape where, in the summer of 1914, the Austrian garrison had cut down an entire forest to create a clear field of fire against the armies of Russia. By day they slept among the shell-damaged walls of the once-imposing Fortress I. That night, under a full moon, they entered Przemyśl, where the taverns were doing boisterous business with crowds of drunken German and Austrian troops spilling out into the streets. Vasyl and Yurko avoided the soldiers by slipping down narrow streets and alleys, pausing to rest in the shadows of great stone churches and synagogues. A small barking dog, its tail wagging, followed them along one stone street.

Vasyl picked up a rock. "What kind of dog wags his tail as he barks? Yurko, throw this at him. This dog will draw attention to us. I don't want to be held for questioning—not now. We've come so far and we are so close to home."

Yurko, however, was down on his haunches, holding his hand out with the palm up. The dog ceased barking and approached cautiously, allowing Yurko to pet him.

When the dog crawled into Yurko's lap, Vasyl said, "That's enough of that. We can't take him home with us. Put him down, Yurko."

Yurko set the dog on the street and gave it a gentle push. The dog trotted down the street, turned, and resumed wagging its tail and barking at the two men. Yurko shook his head at the dog and held a finger to his lips. The dog ceased barking and sat, content to watch the men as they disappeared around a corner.

Vasyl and Yurko emerged on the southwest side of Przemyśl on the road to Sanok. In the approaching dawn they set up their camp in another of the ruined Austrian fortresses ringing Przemyśl. They built a fire under the brick arched entrance to one of the old barracks and cut up three potatoes into a little pot of water. Vasyl climbed up a flight of stone steps to the ramparts and gazed to the south. "They should be there," he whispered. "They should be there, along the horizon." Then he saw them. Out of the uncertain haze of early dawn was the growing outline of the Carpathians, still distant, but reassuringly immutable—a fixed goal for weary travelers.

Vasyl called down to Yurko by the fire and beckoned to him. Yurko made his way up the steps to Vasyl's side and followed his gaze.

"Look, Yurko. Do you see? Look there—our mountains." Yurko stretched his neck forward a little like an anxious horse. "Only a few more days, Yurko, and we will be home." Vasyl pointed to two darting birds. "Look, Yurko!

Swallows! They are this far north already. By now they are building their nests in Stara Polyanka."

The two men watched as the mountains grew brighter in the waxing dawn. When the first rays popped over the eastern hills, Vasyl and Yurko closed their eyes and warmed their faces in the morning sun.

PART THREE

Christ Pantokrator

Today, You arose from the grave, O Merciful Lord;
You rescued us from the gates of death.
Today, Adam sings in exultation and Eve rejoices.
With them, the Prophets and Patriarchs ever praise
the might of Your divine power.

THE DIVINE LITURGY OF
SAINT JOHN CHRYSOSTOM

CHAPTER THIRTY-ONE

Trespassers

BY THE SPRING OF 1918 more than three years had passed since the Russian occupation of Stara Polyanka. The battles in the village and the surrounding countryside between the Russians and the combined forces of Germany and Austria-Hungary had scarred the land with shell holes, trenches, and graves. No building in Stara Polyanka escaped the effects of war. Some huts had burned to the ground; some were damaged beyond repair. The remaining huts, though wounded and sagging, produced smoky evidence of occupancy curling from their broken chimneys.

The Church of the Protection of the Mother of God was gone. Its former site was a mere outline of crumbling and blackened foundation stones. But deeply rooted on either side of the stone steps leading up to the former church site were two venerable linden trees. The two towering sentinels, green and unblemished, bore, beneath their canopy of heart-shaped leaves, the promise of abundant blossoms in July.

And amid the ruins, Stara Polyanka's Rusyn peasants, the remnant of a population reduced by death and panicked flight, bore their wounds stoically. Hampered by a shortage of labor and a dearth of livestock, the young, the old, and the infirm eked out a living working the soil by hand.

Often, in the evening or late at night, small groups of Rusyn and Slovak men—veterans of four years of warfare in Galicia and Russia—wandered homeward through the hills, begging for food or stealing from near-empty barns. The villagers endured these incursions and prayed that the men would resume their travels in the morning.

༄

In the fading evening light, Paraska limped to the side of the hut, the ends of her apron gathered in her hands. She squinted across the valley at the old Rusynko hut, where two figures carried wood into the old hut. Paraska shook her head and mumbled, "Trespassers."

When Yevka emerged from the hut, Paraska pointed toward the Rusynko place. "Yevka, do you see? More trespassers at the old Rusynko hut. Someday that place will burn down or fall down. It is little more than a lean-to now— a lean-to with half a roof." Paraska massaged her right thigh.

"They must have just arrived," said Yevka. "There was no one there earlier today. Does your leg hurt?"

"It always hurts. Look—do you see what I found?" Paraska opened her apron. "Potatoes and turnips."

"Where did you find so many?"

"At the Kavulya place."

"Paraska! That is stealing. They may come back. They only went to Zborov because of the war. What if they come back?"

"If they come back, they will understand that we had to feed the boys. I don't know—maybe it is wrong. But maybe God doesn't mind if sometimes you take a thing from its owner. Maybe God will understand. Anyway, at least the boys will eat."

Yevka smiled at her sister. Paraska's fingers were dirty from digging up the hoard of potatoes and turnips, and the muscles of her lean forearms flexed beneath the skin. "Yes, you are right," said Yevka. "God might be angry if the food were wasted." Yevka peered at the Rusynko place. "How many are there this time?"

"I don't know. I saw two—there may be more. I hope there won't be trouble like there was with the last group. Maybe these men will keep to themselves and move on quietly. To be safe, we should hide the potatoes and turnips. Only, let's feed the boys—they are hungry."

The sisters entered their hut and secured the door. Up the hill, at the old Rusynko hut, the smoke of a cooking fire climbed from the open roof toward the stars emerging in the dusk.

☙

Early the next morning Yevka called to her sister in the hut, "Paraska! Come outside!"

"What is it?"

"Come outside."

Paraska appeared at the doorway. "What is it, Yevka? Give me your arm—my leg is stiff this morning. What is wrong?"

Yevka pointed. "Look at the Rusynko place."

"Is there trouble? Your eyes are better than mine, Yevka. There is not enough daylight yet. I do see two men. They are on the roof. What are they doing on the roof?"

"It is strange . . ."

"What is strange, Yevka? What are they doing?"

"They are fixing the roof."

Paraska put her hands on her hips. "It is not theirs to fix! It is not their home! They have no right to take what is not theirs. Why would they do that?"

Yevka shook her head slowly. "*Ne znam*—I don't know . . ." She squinted in the brightening dawn. "*Ne znam* . . . it is strange . . . only . . ." Yevka placed a hand over her mouth and swallowed.

"Only what, Yevka? *Bozhe moi!* You look ill. What is wrong with you?"

Yevka sat down on the little bench outside the entrance to the hut and buried her face in her hands.

"Yevka, what is wrong? Are you ill?"

Yevka shook her head and wiped her eyes with her apron.

"What is it, Yevka?"

Yevka straightened her apron in her lap and sighed deeply. "They have returned, Paraska. They have come home to Stara Polyanka."

Paraska's eyes widened and she whispered, *"Bozhe moi!"*

❧

Standing outside the old Rusynko hut, Vasyl tossed a branch to Yurko, who was balanced precariously at the edge of a hole in the roof. "Yurko, lash this branch to the end of that broken limb. Do you see? Will it extend out over the side? Good. I'll hold the end. Make it strong. It must hold the thatch and the weight of snow in winter. Now, take this piece and place it over the widest part of the hole—with the thick end up on the roof ridge. Take it, Yurko. Yurko, do you hear me?"

Though Yurko nodded, he was preoccupied by something on the far side of the hut.

"What is it, Yurko? What do you see?"

With a hand gesture, Yurko indicated that Vasyl should go to the front of the hut.

Curious, Vasyl walked to the end of the hut and nearly ran into Paraska coming around the corner. "Paraska!" Vasyl cried.

Paraska, her eyes darting about the Rusynko grounds, nodded at Vasyl. "Vasyl, it is . . . it is you." Her gaze fixed on Vasyl's empty right sleeve.

"Yes, most of me." Vasyl smiled weakly, his mouth turning down at the corners. "And Yevka!"

Yevka appeared behind Paraska and, with one hand on her sister's shoulder, peered shyly at Vasyl. A small boy peeked out from behind Yevka's dress.

Vasyl crouched down and looked up at Yevka. "This is Danko, yes? Danko, I'm your uncle—your uncle Vasyl. You must be . . ." Vasyl thought for a moment. "You must be four years old now." The boy grinned and disappeared behind Yevka's dress. Now, from among the folds of Paraska's dress, there appeared a second boy, this one younger than Danko. Vasyl raised his eyes to Paraska.

Paraska placed her hand on the boy's head. "Myko, come. Come see Vasyl."

"Yours, Paraska?" asked Vasyl.

Paraska nodded. "Yes, he is Vasko's son. He was born the winter after you men were taken by the army. Myko is three years old." Paraska gazed around the empty yard, then up to Yurko on the roof, and finally back to Vasyl, who stared at the ground avoiding her eyes. Vasyl shifted his feet, cleared his throat, and finally looked at Paraska and shook his head.

Paraska closed her eyes and nodded. "Yes . . . well . . . well . . . well then . . . I see . . . I see . . . yes . . . I understand." She turned and stared at the beech trees high atop the east side of the valley. "Well . . . well, Yurko, Vasyl . . . welcome . . . welcome home." She sighed and walked away slowly, hand in hand with Myko.

Yevka watched her sister pass out of sight around the corner of the hut. When Yevka turned around, Vasyl stood before her.

"Yevka."

Yevka stared at the empty sleeve and Vasyl extended his one hand. "Give me your hand, Yevka. Let me squeeze it. Do you feel that? I am grateful for that—it is the strength of one good hand. Someone once told me that there are greater losses than the loss of an arm." He released Yevka's hand and glanced around the corner of the hut and murmured, "And it is true . . . very true."

"I am glad to see you . . . Vasyl," said Yevka. Vasyl grasped Yevka's hand again and she squeezed his calloused fingers, and then pulled back her hand and looked away. "I must go to Paraska now," she said, and then she disappeared around the corner of the hut with Danko running after her.

Vasyl beckoned Yurko, and the two men went to the front of the hut, where they stood at a respectful distance from the two sisters.

Paraska gazed across the valley, Yevka at her side. "Give me your hand, Yevka," whispered Paraska. "Yes, that is good . . . thank you . . . that is good. I think . . . I knew I would never see him again . . . I knew it the day he left. Sometimes I thought that there was a chance . . . but, now . . . well, now I know for certain . . . and, so, that is the end of that." Paraska sighed and blinked her eyes. "Where is Vasyl? There you are. Vasyl, sometime you will tell me about Vasko—where he is buried . . . how you remember him. Only now, Vasyl, you and Yurko are welcome to our table for dinner tonight. Yevka and I don't have much, but you are welcome to what we have."

"Yurko and I will be there," said Vasyl softly.

Danko tugged at Yevka's dress and pointed to an animal at the entrance to the Rusynko hut. "Look, *Mamko!* What is that?"

Yevka stroked her son's hair. "*Koza*—a goat, Danko."

Paraska cried, "*Bozhe moi,* Vasyl! Where did you get it? I haven't seen a goat in two years."

"Yurko and I . . . we brought it . . . that is . . . we found it in the mountains a few days ago and—"

"Yes," nodded Paraska. "If one is willing to look in the right places there are many things to be found: potatoes, turnips, goats. Yevka, come. Come, boys."

The sisters, their sons in tow, wound down the path while Vasyl and Yurko resumed their repairs on the roof of the old Rusynko hut.

❧

The dinner was meager—potatoes and cabbage and a thin kasha. Yurko swiftly ate everything the women placed before him; when he was finished, he sat with his hands clasped in his lap until someone thought to dish more food onto his plate. Then, with a flurry of hands and elbows, Yurko dispatched the second helping. Yevka's Danko and Paraska's Myko were spellbound by the exhibition and watched Yurko with open mouths. Then the boys looked at each other with wide eyes and tittered as they ate their food.

Yevka placed another potato on Yurko's plate and scolded Danko with her eyes. She glanced toward Vasyl while he was engaged in conversation with Paraska; when he gazed up at her, Yevka reddened and sat on the other side of Yurko.

Paraska was talking about life in Stara Polyanka. "The armies that passed through the village during the first year of the war took almost everything we had. First one army and then another. They took the cows and the chickens. They left very little. Last winter was dreadful, Vasyl. There was never enough food. It was good of you and Yurko to give us the goat. Now the boys will have milk and cheese. These are such bad times, Vasyl . . . such bad times. I often wonder what will become of us. I wonder how we will survive another winter. Many of the old became very ill last winter. Almost every household lost someone. I don't know how we will—"

Vasyl interrupted Paraska with a raised hand. "And my family, Paraska? Are they still in Niklova?"

"Yes. How did you know they were in Niklova?"

"Andrii told me. I saw him at the front in the spring of 1916. I know that my *baba* died."

"I see. Your mama is with her sister, Mariya Hryndyk in Niklova. Anna and her husband, Petro Kotsur, are also in Niklova. Anna is very well—she has a girl the age of my Myko and she will soon have another child. Petro Kotsur returned from the army last winter and he is well—only, I think he was hurt in the war. I don't remember—he seems fine."

"How is my mother?"

Paraska shrugged. "I haven't seen your mother since she left the village. I hear that she is well. Father Yaroslav is in the village. He is well, but his wife died two years ago—she was ill even before the war. Father Yaroslav celebrates liturgy in the Parish House now. He also serves at churches in other villages." Pointing to Vasyl's boots, Paraska remarked, "Those won't last much longer."

Vasyl laughed. "No, they weren't much good to begin with. Yurko and I started home from Russia with two pairs of boots each. We threw away the first worn-out boots after we crossed the Bug River. We walked the rest of the way in our second boots, and now . . ." He shook his head forlornly at the ragged boots. "Well, maybe Yurko and I can fit our last pairs with new soles."

After a lengthy exchange of meaningful glances between the two sisters, Yevka went to the back of the hut and disappeared into the storage room. Puzzled, Vasyl asked, "What was that about, Paraska?"

Paraska held up a hand. "Be patient. We may have something for you and Yurko."

Yevka emerged from the storage room carrying three pairs of boots. She set them on the floor between Vasyl and Yurko. "Try these on."

Vasyl picked up one of the boots. *"Bozhe!"* he cried in amazement. "German boots! Almost new! Where did you two get these?"

Paraska cleared her throat. "One . . . only has to know where to look."

Vasyl inspected the other boots. "And Russian boots! And they are big—they will fit Yurko! Try them, Yurko—you've always liked Russian boots. This German pair will fit me nicely. Where the devil did you two find boots like these?"

Again Paraska cleared her throat. "It doesn't matter. Take them as a gift. You gave us a gift. We appreciate the goat. And the boys . . . the boys also appreciate the goat. *Tsy tak*—isn't that so, Myko and Danko?"

The boys nodded. Then Danko said softly, "We want to see the goat again."

"Maybe later," said Paraska.

Vasyl stood in his new German boots and stomped around the room. "I don't understand. These boots can't be more than six months old. Is there a black market? In Russia, even an old pair of boots can cost several boxes of cigarettes. What did you have to pay for these?"

The two sisters were silent and uneasy. Flustered, Yevka called the boys. "Come, Danko, come Myko, let's go see the goat."

Danko tugged at Yevka's skirt again. "We want Yurko to come with us."

Yevka put her hand on Danko's head and pushed him toward Yurko. "Ask him." Danko twisted out from under his mother's hand and buried his face in the folds of her dress.

Yurko got up from the table, retrieved his hat from a peg in the wall, and stepped outside, happy in his new boots. Yevka and the boys followed Yurko outside, leaving Paraska and Vasyl alone in the hut.

"Is Yevka angry with me, Paraska?" asked Vasyl.

"No. She's not angry. She's ashamed."

"Ashamed? She didn't steal the boots, did she?"

"No, Vasyl—not really. She's ashamed—but she shouldn't be. She took the boots from the feet of dead men. What good are boots to the dead?"

Vasyl sat on the bench and closed his eyes.

"It was early in the war," continued Paraska. "The soldiers' boots and clothes were still almost new. After our church burned down, there was fighting almost every day up and down the valley—in the hills and in the villages. One evening Mariya Guzii came to the door and told us that north of Stara Polyanka, along Petro Dzyamba's rye field, there was a ditch full of dead soldiers. No one had stripped them yet, she said—maybe we could help her. I was still in bed with my bad leg, so, after the moon rose, Yevka and Mariya went to Petro Dzyamba's field. Yevka carried home boots and jackets. We still have one of the jackets in the back room—it has two holes in it. But it should fit you or Yurko. You are welcome to it."

"*Bozhe,*" murmured Vasyl, rubbing his forehead.

The hut was silent except for the muffled crackling of coals behind the hearth door. After a reflective pause, Paraska spoke. "I don't think it was really stealing . . . not the way we used to think of stealing. It is like potatoes and turnips. Why should they rot just because the owners are not around to eat them? God understands, I think, if you take something that is no longer being used by the owner."

From outside came the sound of the boys' laughter. Paraska rose from the table with a groan and hobbled to the door. "I'm going to put an end to this," she grumbled. "If I know those boys, they will let that goat out of the barn. I don't want to spend all night chasing a goat." Paraska went out the door, calling, "Yurko! Don't let that goat out of the barn! Hmph! He didn't hear me."

Vasyl rummaged through his pocket for a cigarette, went to the hearth for a light, and then stepped outside. Behind the barn, Yurko ran in and out of the bushes chasing the goat, while the boys, close on Yurko's heels, giggled wildly. Paraska, limping in slow pursuit, shouted at Yurko and the boys, but to no avail. Vasyl joined Yevka, who was standing alone outside the hut, watching the commotion.

"Yevka . . ." Vasyl said the name softly and with a tenderness that startled them both. Yevka, her lips trembling and tears streaming from her eyes, looked at Vasyl briefly, and then turned away. "Yevka, I . . . I'm . . ." Vasyl took a puff on his cigarette. "Thank you, Yevka . . . thank you . . . for the boots."

Yevka shook her head. "*To nich*—it's nothing," she sniffled. Then wiping her eyes and composing herself, she said, "Here comes Paraska. You should talk to her. She will want to know about Vasko."

Paraska went to Yevka's side. "They can chase that goat all night! I'm tired of yelling at them."

Vasyl chuckled. "They are having fun, Paraska."

"Are they? Well, I don't know . . . perhaps they are. What about Yurko?"

"Yurko doesn't mind. I think he is having fun also. He enjoys the boys, Paraska. He is very much like them."

Paraska smiled. "Well then, I suppose there is no harm."

Vasyl cleared his throat. "Earlier, Paraska, you . . . you asked me about Vasko."

Paraska clasped her hands over her apron and looked down at the ground. "Yes, I . . . I wanted to ask you . . . well, I don't know . . . nothing too important really . . . and maybe you don't even know. I want to know when was . . . when did . . . when did Vasko . . . die?"

Vasyl took a puff of his cigarette and exhaled slowly. "It was in the spring," he said. "The spring of 1915 . . . the spring after we left Stara Polyanka."

Paraska's eyes glistened. "Yes, in the spring. His son, Myko, was born late in the winter. I don't know why, but it is good to know that Vasko was alive when Myko was born. Did you . . . did you see Vasko at the end? You are not comfortable with my questions—I see that. Only, Vasyl, I knew . . . on the day he left for the army . . . I knew . . . when they came for him and for you and the others . . . I knew I would never see him again. When I saw you earlier at your hut, I knew he would not be there with you. Only, I had to see for myself. I knew he would not come back because I see him in my dreams, and always he is walking away, and I can never catch up to him to see his face once again. So, Vasyl, please tell me—did you see him at the end?"

Vasyl placed the cigarette to his lips and inhaled deeply. "Yes."

"How did he look?"

Vasyl shrugged and exhaled smoke toward the sunset. "He looked just as you remember him, but asleep."

"Where is he buried?"

"In a churchyard north of the mountains." Puffs of smoke accompanied each syllable.

"Ah! In a churchyard—he would like that. Was a priest present for the funeral?"

Unprepared for this question, Vasyl paused. "Yes, a priest was present," he lied. "There was always a priest for funerals."

"I am sorry to ask so many questions, Vasyl. It was sad for us when the war came here and so many soldiers were killed. There was no time to bury them properly, so the soldiers dug long pits and put all the young soldiers in those holes and covered them—so many young boys! I cried for them—I cried for them because I always thought of Vasko. But I am glad Vasko is in a churchyard. He would be glad if he knew . . . I would like to think that somehow he does know . . . Look, Vasyl! Yurko caught the goat."

Danko and Myko were jumping up and down in circles around Yurko, who was dragging the stubborn goat home by her horns. When Yevka called for the boys to come inside, they ignored her. Paraska bellowed, "DANKO—MYKO—NOW!" The boys grumbled to one another as they marched past Paraska and Vasyl and then followed Yevka into the hut.

Paraska bowed her head toward Vasyl. "I thank you again, Vasyl. Why are you smiling?"

Vasyl pulled his cigarette from his mouth. "I was thinking that you would have made a good sergeant in the army—or, even a good foreman in a factory in Ameryka. You have the voice for it."

"Hmph! Goodnight, Vasyl. GOODNIGHT, YURKO!"

Yurko hurried up from the barn and joined Vasyl for the dark walk back to the old Rusynko hut.

CHAPTER THIRTY-TWO

Hunger

A FEW DAYS LATER, Paraska entered the hut holding the corners of her apron together in one hand. Yevka, feeding wood into the hearth, nodded a greeting to her sister, closed the hearth door, and placed a pot of water over the flames. Paraska opened her apron, revealing six potatoes.

"These are all I could find, Yevka. I don't know what we will do after this. Where are the boys?"

"They went with Yurko to pick plums at the Kavulya place."

"Hmph! It will take more than plums to keep us alive!"

Yevka, busy with the potatoes, did not respond.

Paraska moved closer to her sister. "Don't you agree, Yevka? We will need more than plums and a few potatoes now and then to survive, yes?"

Yevka nodded and continued to cut the potatoes.

"Yevka?"

No answer.

"Yevka?"

Yevka sighed heavily. "Yes?"

"Yevka, did you think about what I asked you?"

Yevka dropped the potato slices into the water. "Yes."

"He is your brother-in-law."

"*Znam*—I know."

"I would ask, but I don't think it is right. Will you do it?"

Yevka paused. "I'd rather not."

"But, Yevka, the boys are always hungry. I'm hungry. Are you not hungry?"

Yevka closed her eyes. It was warm near the hearth and her forehead was beaded with sweat.

"Yevka, tell me, are you not hungry?"

"Yes . . . yes, I am always hungry."

"I know it is a difficult thing to ask him, but he returned from Ameryka with money. He must still have it somewhere. We could pay him back when Petro comes home to Stara Polyanka. Or, when Petro sends money for you to come to Ameryka, you could pay Vasyl what we owe. They say that soon it will be possible to write to Ameryka again. You could ask Petro for the money, and we could pay Vasyl back then. I would ask, only he is your brother-in-law and—did you say something, Yevka?"

Yevka had stepped away from the hearth and now stood in the corner of the room, before a small icon of the Mother of God. "I said, I will think about it," she said.

☙

Vasyl was holding his pipe between his knees and scraping out the bowl with a knife when he saw Yevka climbing the path toward him. He set the knife on the log next to him and struck the pipe against the log to dislodge the loosened tobacco residue. Yevka looked up toward the knocking sound and, seeing Vasyl, hesitated before continuing the climb.

"Yevka, I am happy to see you."

Yevka entered the little Rusynko yard. Vasyl stood, holding his pipe aloft and turning it in the early afternoon light. "I always liked this pipe. I missed it during the war. Having a smoke from this pipe is one of the few pleasures I can provide myself. I know Yurko doesn't mind rolling cigarettes for me, but it is good for a man to be able to do some things for himself."

Yevka nodded and cleared her throat. "Yurko is a good man."

Vasyl smiled. "Yes, he is. He is not here—he should be back soon."

Yevka lowered her eyes and stared at the ground.

Vasyl twisted the pipe in his hand and studied Yevka. "How is Paraska?"

Yevka nodded at the ground indicating that her sister was well.

"Her leg doesn't trouble her, I hope."

Yevka turned slightly and ran her hand up and down her right thigh. "It always hurts, here . . . almost four years. She doesn't complain much—only, little pieces of metal sometimes come out and I think—" Yevka stopped abruptly— Vasyl was watching the motion of her hand on her thigh.

Vasyl looked away quickly, pocketing his pipe and fumbling with his jacket. "And the boys, Yevka . . . the boys . . . how are they?"

"They are well."

"*Dobre*—good. Yurko enjoys them. He is like a child himself. I think he would be happy to spend all day and night with them. He is—Yevka, what is wrong?"

Yevka frowned. "They are not well."

"Oh? The boys are not well?"

"The boys are both sick. They are with Paraska . . . and they . . ."

"What is it, Yevka? What is wrong?"

Yevka worked her apron with her hands and her eyes moistened. "The boys . . ."

Vasyl placed his hand on Yevka's shoulder and felt the bone beneath a scant veneer of cloth and skin. Though she turned her face away from Vasyl, she pressed her shoulder against his hand. "Yevka, the boys are hungry, yes? Yes, of course they are—I see. Come inside." Yevka followed Vasyl into the hut and held out her apron to receive two eggs and two potatoes. "Tell Paraska that Yurko and I will bring more food when we can."

Yevka stared into the apron. "What will you eat?"

Vasyl trivialized Yevka's question with an impatient toss of his hand. "We have all we need."

Yevka wiped her face and looked briefly into Vasyl's eyes. She walked to the doorway, then stopped and turned. "God bless you, Vasyl." She then hurried down the hill.

Vasyl retrieved his pipe and tobacco from his pocket, prepared a smoke, and ignited it with a stick he thrust into the hearth. Later he would tell Yurko that they would have no supper that night.

❧

Paraska pulled a blanket over the legs of Myko and Danko and straightened, massaging her lower back with her hands. She looked down at the boys, shook her head, and sat at the table across from her sister. "*Oi*, Yevka," she said, slumping to the bench. When Yevka failed to respond, Paraska sighed loudly and shook her head slowly from side to side. Still failing to evoke a response, Paraska clasped her hands on the table and stared at her sister. "Yevka, did you ask him?"

Yevka evaded her sister's stare. "The boys ate tonight, yes?"

"Yes, they did. You didn't ask him, did you?"

"He gave us food—I couldn't. It would not have been right."

"Yevka, we will starve . . . the boys will starve. You must ask."

Yevka bit her lower lip and said, "We have the goat . . ."

"Yes, yes," said Paraska impatiently. "You always say that. And what if the goat dies, hmm? What if the goat dies—or what if it is stolen? Men from the war come through the village at night. Do you remember the ones who came through Stara Polyanka a year ago? What if men like that come here and steal the goat?"

Yevka merely shrugged.

Paraska leaned toward her sister. "Yevka, let me remind you: Vasyl came back from Ameryka with money. He may still have it. Yes, I know, he may have given it to his mother. But he may have kept some. We need to know, Yevka. You must speak to him."

"I can't," said Yevka.

"We can pay him back, Yevka. I don't know when or how—but we will pay him back. People say that the war is over. Soon, maybe your Petro will come back to Stara Polyanka with money. We can pay back what we owe to Vasyl then. But, of course, Petro may not come back from Ameryka and—wait, Yevka. I'm not finished. Where are you going?"

Yevka went to the hearth and stared down at the glowing coals. Paraska was leading into a topic that, for almost a year now, she had broached often with Yevka—the talk of leaving Stara Polyanka. "I'm listening," mumbled Yevka.

"You know, Yevka, if your Petro is doing well in Ameryka, he might want to stay. They say that in Ameryka there is food for all who can work."

Yevka nodded. "The boys need more food."

Emboldened, Paraska went to the hearth and leaned against her sister. "Yevka, Petro said he would send for you one day, yes?"

"Well . . . he didn't really say it . . . I'm not sure if—"

"Of course he did, Yevka. Of course he wants his wife and son with him. Do you think he would send enough money to bring Myko and me over also? They say that women work in Ameryka. They say that in Ameryka there is no shame in women working for money. I would pay Petro back. I would give everything back, to the last kreuzer."

"Well . . . I . . ."

"If he sends for you, you won't leave me here, will you?"

"I don't know—I . . . it is not for me—"

"*Bozhe moi,* Yevka! There is nothing for me here! In Ameryka there is work. In Ameryka there is money! In Ameryka there is food! They say that people are safe in Ameryka—that there is no war. What about the boys, Yevka? Don't you want them to be safe and to have enough to eat?"

Yevka grimaced. "Of course I do. Only . . ."

"Only what?"

"Petro never really promised he would send for Danko and me. Maybe he meant to—I don't know. Only, Paraska, that was four years ago. What if he . . . what if he has made a new life for himself?"

"Tsh, Yevka! You are his life—you and Danko. He will send for you when the war ends. None of our people has heard from their people in Ameryka since the war began. He will write—or have someone write—when the war is over. But never mind. Tomorrow we will have Vasyl and Yurko here and we will try to feed them well. It is the least we can do for them."

❧

Vasyl and Yurko sat on one side of the table, and Paraska and Yevka sat on the other side with Myko and Danko between them on the bench. Yurko once again delighted the boys with his aggressive work with his spoon. Paraska filled Yurko's bowl with more thin soup and sat down on the bench, trying to catch Yevka's eye.

Vasyl finished his food, arched his back, and stretched his arm. "Yevka, you and your sister are making a happy man out of Yurko. He doesn't enjoy his own cooking this much."

Yevka acknowledged Vasyl with a brief nod and then quickly looked away. Paraska frowned at her sister and turned to Vasyl. "We are grateful for the food, Vasyl. Since the war started, it seems that all we think about is food. For all the thinking we do about it, we see very little of it." Paraska widened her eyes at Yevka, who abruptly stood and busied herself at the hearth. Irritated, Paraska stared at Yevka's back and then continued, "Vasyl, do the people in Ameryka go hungry during wars?"

Vasyl raised his eyebrows and smiled. "I don't know, Paraska. When I was in Ameryka there was no war. Why do you ask?"

"Well . . . I . . . I think about food often and I wonder . . . I wonder how Petro is doing now . . . and I wonder if he has enough to eat."

Vasyl shrugged. "If he is working, he is eating. In Ameryka, there is plenty of everything if you are willing to work for it." Vasyl looked at Yevka. "And you know Petro is a good worker."

Paraska began clearing the table. "How much can a good worker earn in Ameryka, Vasyl?"

Vasyl pressed his tongue down on his lower lip and looked from Paraska to Yevka, who quickly busied herself helping her sister. "Hmm, let me think. What does one of our people earn in Ameryka? Petro has been in Ameryka four years—about as long as I was there. I suppose he could have saved several hundred dolar by now—if he has lived simply—not spent anything— worked steadily the whole time. Have you two heard from Petro?"

"No, Vasyl," said Paraska. "Did you save several hundred dolar when you worked in Ameryka?"

Yevka bit her lower lip and stole a glance at Vasyl, whose mouth arched downward in a sharp smile. He said nothing but rather stared at the sisters until they both turned red, first Yevka and then Paraska. In the awkward silence, Paraska retreated to the hearth and stood with her back to the rest of the room. Yevka went to a corner of the hut, where she prepared the boys' bunk for the night.

Vasyl finally stood and stretched his arm over and behind his head. "We thank you for the meal, Paraska, Yevka. Good night, boys. Come, Yurko."

Paraska followed the men to the doorway and watched them disappear down the trail and into the gray dusk. "Hmph," she grumbled. "Hmph!" And she closed the door.

✧

Late the next morning Anna Rusynko hurried up the path to the Rusynko homestead with her husband, Petro Kotsur, in tow. When she was close enough to be heard, Anna cried out, "Vasyl! Vasyl!"

Vasyl came to the doorway of the hut and waited for his sister. When Anna saw her brother she ran to him. "Vasyl! We heard you came home! Anastasiya Burii came to Niklova yesterday and said you were—" and then Anna saw her brother's empty sleeve. "Vasyl . . ."

"Anna."

"Vasyl . . . it is true, then . . . about your arm . . . it is true."

Vasyl placed his left arm across his sister's shoulders. "It is good to see you, Anna. Yes, it is true." Vasyl acknowledged Petro Kotsur with a nod. "So, Anna, I hear you have a daughter and, now, another on the way!"

Anna blushed. "Yes. Little Marya is with her *baba*—our *mamka*."

"How is *Mamka*?"

Anna shook her head slowly. "She's tired, Vasyl. She's very, very tired. She cannot travel because she is so tired. Also, she is sad. But she made me promise to bring you to Niklova to see her. Will you come, Vasyl?"

"Of course. This afternoon we will go. How are you, Petro? I see you walk with a limp."

Petro opened his mouth, but it was Anna who spoke. "Petro was hurt in the war. He was taken by the army the year after you left us. They took many of the men for the army, Vasyl. They even took Father Yaroslav and Andrii."

Vasyl pointed at Petro Kotsur's foot. "How were you hurt?"

Again, it was Anna who spoke. "They shot him, Vasyl. The Russians shot him through the foot. He is lucky to be alive."

Vasyl looked at Petro's foot and then smiled at his brother-in-law. "Through the foot, hmm? Yes . . . well . . . it was good of the Russians to aim low."

Petro Kotsur looked down at his foot and then gazed across the valley. Anna looked into her brother's eyes. "So many are dead, Vasyl. So many . . . these are sad, sad times. When the first soldiers came to Stara Polyanka, we left for Niklova. We took *Baba,* but she . . . she didn't live through the first winter of the war."

"Yes, I know."

"You know this? How do you know?"

"Andrii told me."

Anna brightened. "Andrii is alive?"

"He was two years ago."

"You must tell *Mamka,* Vasyl."

"I will." Vasyl looked at Petro Kotsur. "Do you have a cart?"

Again, Anna: "We walked. No one has a horse anymore. No one except Old Mykhal. He and Sasha hid in the forest when the soldiers came. He kept his horse and his cart through the whole war. He will come through Stara Polyanka soon. He will be glad to see you, Vasyl."

"And I will be glad to see him. Come, come inside, both of you. We will eat a little something before our walk to Niklova. Come, Petro, go inside and sit. Rest your wounded foot."

Petro Kotsur, his limp now more pronounced, made his way to the hut with Anna, while Vasyl followed, suppressing a grin.

❧

After soup and bread, Vasyl walked to Niklova with Anna and Petro Kotsur. They reached the home of Aunt Mariya, the sister of Vasyl's mother, before midafternoon. Vasyl's mother covered her mouth when her son entered the little room where she lay on a cot, her head and shoulders propped up on pillows. She closed her eyes and wept quietly when she saw the empty sleeve. Vasyl sat on the edge of the little cot holding hands with his mother, who finally wiped her eyes and nose.

"I cried when Anastasiya Burii told us that they took your arm," his mother sighed. "But then I praised God you were alive. I said I wouldn't cry when I saw you, but . . ." She shook silently, her face contorted and her eyes closed. Her hair was almost totally gray now and the backs of her thin hands were spotted. She stopped trembling and shook her head slowly. "Vasyl . . . Vasyl . . ."

Anna spoke. "Vasyl, tell *Mamka* about Andrii."

Vasyl's mother clutched her son's arm. "What? You have news? He is alive?"

"Well, I don't know that—it's been two years since I saw him . . . at the front. He was well at that time. He told me about *Baba* and the fighting in Stara Polyanka."

Mamka closed her eyes again. "Yes, *Baba* . . . and others . . . all dead. Before *Baba* died, the soldiers came to arrest Father Yaroslav. Andrii tried to protect Father, so they took him, too. Later, they released Father Yaroslav and he returned to Stara Polyanka. But, about Andrii we've heard nothing."

Vasyl told his mother and Anna about his time spent as a prisoner of the Russians, and of his long walk home with Yurko. He related everything he could remember of his conversation with Andrii—the one at the front in 1916—but mentioned nothing about their meeting in the Russian prisoner-of-war camp in 1917.

Later, after Anna and Petro had left the room, Vasyl stood and stretched. "*Mamko,* do you . . . do you have enough . . . enough to eat?"

"Vasyl, there is never enough to eat. We never have more than two or three days' supply of food in the house. Mariya and her family work hard, but there is so little. Mariya is good to me, Vasyl. I wish I could help her . . . only I cannot. I cannot leave here, Vasyl. I cannot leave this room."

"Why can't you leave?"

His mother closed her eyes and rubbed her temples with the index finger and thumb of her right hand. "No . . . no . . . no . . . I can't leave here . . . no . . . no, not now . . . not yet. I remember too much, Vasyl. I remember too many . . . too many . . ."

Vasyl took his mother's hand in his again. "The war is over for our people, *Mamko*. It is over. Now we rebuild and go on as before."

"Go on as before? I don't remember what life was like before the war. Do you believe it, Vasyl? I remember almost nothing . . . nothing. I can't remember what your father looked like. I don't remember my own mother and father. I do remember the church—but they say it is gone now. I think our hut in Stara Polyanka was up the path from Yakov's tavern. Is it still there?"

"Yakov's or our hut?"

"Our hut . . . and, I suppose, the tavern."

"The hut is there—most of it. Yurko helps me. We are putting on a new roof. The tavern is nothing more than four walls—four walls and no roof. There is nothing else for us to do but to rebuild and carry on, *Mamko*." Vasyl held his mother's hand lightly in his own, and when she fell asleep he rose and left the room.

❧

Vasyl left Niklova late that afternoon to walk home alone to Stara Polyanka. At the midpoint of his journey, he stopped and sat in the shade of an old oak tree and pulled out his pipe and tobacco. After filling, tamping, and lighting the pipe, he leaned against the tree and blew smoke into the overhanging branches. He could lie here all day. Here there was nothing but sunlight and trees and singing birds. Behind him was Niklova, where his mother lay asleep in a dark room. In front of him was Stara Polyanka, where his own dark room awaited him. Tonight he would endure what had become, since his safe arrival in Stara Polyanka, a nightly ordeal of terrifying dreams and eternal darkness.

But now in the pleasant afternoon breeze, Vasyl pulled the pipe from his mouth and began to doze. When he opened his eyes again his surroundings appeared exactly the same, yet something had changed. He sat up, pocketed his pipe, and then heard the bell. Coming down the path from Stara Polyanka was Old Mykhal, rocking from side to side on his cart and waving his hat in the air.

Vasyl laughed and returned the old man's wave. "Yes, *Mamko*," he whispered. "We will go on as before—just as in the old days. Nothing changes nor needs to change. Everything will be just as it was before the war. We will go on and on just like Old Mykhal. That is all we can do." Vasyl stood and waited for the old man. "It is all we can do . . ."

CHAPTER THIRTY-THREE

A Ghost

YURKO WAS AWAKENED in the middle of the night by muffled cries and hollow shouts from Vasyl's bunk across the room. Yawning, Yurko sat up in bed and then swung his legs over the edge of his bunk. At the sound of a growling call, Yurko crossed the room and shook Vasyl by the shoulder until his friend grunted, "Yes, Yurko, yes . . . yes . . . I'm . . . I'm awake."

Yurko shuffled to the hearth, where he lit a candle and retrieved a pouch of tobacco and a package of cigarette papers from the little shelf to the right of the cooking area. His eyes half closed, Yurko mechanically rolled two cigarettes, picked up the candle, and went to Vasyl's bunk.

Vasyl was now sitting on the edge of his bunk, rubbing his face with his hand. He looked up at Yurko and shook his head. "I'm sorry, old friend. The dreams are . . . bad . . . very bad. I wake you every night now, don't I? I shouldn't try to sleep at night. I try, but the dreams always come . . . Then I always end up walking around the village, from one end to the other, over and over until dawn."

Vasyl slipped on his boots and then took both cigarettes from Yurko's open hand, placing one behind his left ear and the other between his lips. Yurko held out the candle, and Vasyl, his hand shaking, pulled the candle close to the cigarette, splattering hot wax on Yurko's hand. His role in this nightly routine complete, Yurko blew out the candle and returned to his bunk at the other end of the room, where he quickly resumed his night's sleep.

Vasyl now rose and retrieved his jacket hanging near the door. He slipped his left arm into the jacket and draped the other sleeve over his right shoulder before stepping outside into the moonless night. The bright canopy of stars silhouetting the surrounding tree-covered hills confirmed that the wet chill and welcome birdsong of impending dawn were still far, far away. As Vasyl drew hot tobacco smoke deeply into his lungs, the end of the cigarette radiated a hot, orange glow. His eyes adjusted now to the dim starlight, Vasyl headed down the path for his nightly roam through Stara Polyanka.

❧

Yevka returned to the front of her hut, balancing firewood in one hand and steadying herself against the wooden walls with the other. A light, predawn breeze rustled the leaves of the linden trees growing along the banks of *Potok Ondava*—the Ondava Stream. Yevka squinted toward the lower half of the village, but in the dark she could see no sign of other early risers preparing their morning fires. She turned to enter the hut and then abruptly looked back toward the village, peering intently into the darkness. Something had caught her eye—a flash of light perhaps. She stared into the darkness and waited. Then she saw it again: a faint light that glowed bright orange and then quickly waned. After a pause, it appeared again. Yevka moved from side to side and, with her keen eyesight, attempted to determine the location of the glowing light. It faded, and then suddenly reappeared to her right. Yevka took a step forward—the orange light originated from the footpath that passed near her own hut. The glow faded. Yevka waited and watched until she was satisfied that the mysterious light had vanished. She shuddered and went inside to stoke the hearth fire.

❧

Two nights later Yevka awoke from a fitful sleep. She tossed in her bunk until her son, Danko, asleep next to her, groaned in protest at her restlessness. Finally, unable to fall back asleep, Yevka rolled slowly off the straw mattress and wrapped her shawl around her shoulders. Nearby, Paraska snored lightly in the bunk that she shared with her son, Myko. Yevka walked outside and secured the door behind her.

In the cool and silent night, Yevka stood in front of the hut, looking up at the stars. The little points flickered, each one faint and insignificant by itself, but, in massed groups, they glowed and fused into bright patches that illuminated the heavens. Yevka moved away from the hut to a spot near the road. Though the earth was a mere shadow beneath the starlight, Yevka knew the valley well. Somewhere in the darkness to her left was the Parish House, where Father Yaroslav would celebrate the Divine Liturgy next Sunday. Before her was the *Potok* Ondava, gurgling and flowing endlessly on its little course through Stara Polyanka, and then along the road south of town where the crucified Lord gazed at passersby: "*Khrest tvoye spaseniye*—the Cross is your salvation!" To Yevka's right was the Kavula house and beyond it was the Fedorochko house—both indistinguishable in the blackness. Across the *Potok* Ondava was the former site of the Church of the Protection of the Mother of God. Before the war, from this spot near the road, Yevka was always able to see the church. Even on moonless nights such as this, she could see the western tower of the church silhouetted by the canopy of stars. But now, there was nothing—the church was long gone, burned to the ground during the war. She rested her chin on her fist and then closed her eyes. It was peaceful outside under the infinite sky.

There was a sound—perhaps a stone shifted and tumbled under the Ondava's flowing water. Yevka opened her eyes, blinked, and then gasped. A little orange light glowed from the main path—from almost the same spot where the glow had appeared two nights earlier. Yevka moved to the right and then to the left as the light maintained its suspended position in the path, glowing brighter than any star in the heavens above. Yevka eased backward toward her hut and stopped. The ground beneath her feet felt uneven—she had veered off the path and now peered frantically into the darkness, searching for her hut. The orange glow remained fixed in the middle of the main path directly before her. It was mesmerizing—alternately glowing, fading, and dancing in the air.

Somewhere across the Ondava was the former site of the Church of the Protection of the Mother of God. "*Panno Mariye*—Virgin Mary," whispered Yevka. "*Panno Mariye,* pray for me . . . pray for me."

Yevka sighed and her shoulders sagged. She stepped forward, stopped, and advanced again, until she stood close enough to touch the enticing light. The orange glow fell to the earth and exploded in a small shower of sparks. Yevka nodded and whispered, "Yes . . . yes." She thrust out her hand and was drawn into the darkness.

❧

"Yevka, you know I am right," said Paraska, stirring a pot of water with a long wooden spoon. When Yevka did not respond, Paraska turned from her work at the hearth. "Did you hear me? I said, you know I am right."

Yevka stood and placed the potatoes from her apron on the shelf next to the hearth.

"You have nothing to say, Yevka?"

Yevka shrugged. "Yes, you are right."

Paraska set the spoon down and placed her hands on her hips. "You agree with me so that I will stop talking, but you don't believe me. Ask anyone and they will tell you the same thing: there is a ghost who walks our village every night. Don't shake your head."

"I didn't shake my head."

Paraska returned to the pot. "You were going to shake your head. Everyone is talking about it. It is not one of the soldiers passing through on his way home—everyone agrees on that. This one doesn't move on, but, rather, returns each night. Anna Kavula says she saw it two nights ago by the old tavern and Mariya Guzii says it tried to get into her home a few nights ago—she heard it knocking at the walls like a branch in the wind."

"Maybe it was a branch in the wind."

"Don't mock me, Yevka. You are young and there is much you do not know about the spirits of the dead who walk among us, troubling us with their mischief. A ghost is walking about Stara Polyanka at night and you are not worried. I think you should be more concerned." Paraska pointed to the pot on the fire. "Put the potatoes in the pot. Where are Danko and Myko?"

Yevka placed the last potato in the pot and tilted her head toward the open door. "They are outside. They are supposed to help with the garden, but you know they—"

Paraska suddenly grabbed Yevka by the shoulders and yanked her away from the doorway.

"*Oi!* Paraska, you are hurting me!"

Paraska, her eyes large and dark, pulled Yevka close to her. "You know who it is, don't you?"

"What?" cried Yevka trying to pry Paraska's grip from her shoulder. "You are hurting me!"

Paraska released her hold on Yevka and sat at the table with her head in her hands. "You know who it is."

Yevka rubbed her shoulder and did not answer.

"Yevka, by your silence, I know you know who it is."

"I know nothing."

"Yes, you do, and you care for me and you do not wish to see me hurt."

Paraska, with wet eyes and quivering lips, faced Yevka and whispered, "I know who it is."

Yevka swallowed and looked away.

Paraska stood and cried, "It is Vasko!"

"What!"

"Yes, Yevka! He has come back to me! I dream of him always—always he is leaving me, walking away from me. His death in the war was unnatural—and now he has come back to haunt our village. His spirit is looking for me! *Oi,* Yevka, what shall I do? Because of me, the village is now cursed and troubled!" Paraska slumped back onto the bench and sobbed into her hands.

Yevka closed the door to the hut, and then sat on the bench with her arm over her sister's shoulders. "Vasko is not haunting our village, Paraska. I am sure of it. Please, don't ask me how I know. He is gone—he is never coming back. It is not the ghost of Vasko who walks throughout the village at night . . . no." Yevka stroked her sister's hair and stared into the glow of the hearth coals. "No, it is not Vasko's ghost. It is the ghost of . . . of someone else . . ."

⌘

That night Paraska turned in her sleep and called out sleepily, "Hmm?" A noise awoke her and she sat up rubbing her eyes. It was Danko, crying in the bunk he shared with his mother. Paraska leaned toward the neighboring bunk, being careful not to awaken Myko next to her. "Yevka . . . Yevka," she whispered. Receiving no response, Paraska reached over to shake her sister but found only the whimpering Danko. Paraska slid next to the boy and placed her arm around him. "Shh . . . shh." The boy fell back to sleep and Paraska herself drifted in and out of sleep until Yevka shook her by the shoulder.

Paraska slid from the bunk and returned to her own bed, drowsily chiding her sister. "Yevka . . . you should . . . empty your bladder . . . before you go to bed."

Later, when Paraska awoke, Yevka was building a fire in the hearth.

⌘

Several nights later, Paraska awoke to a whistling wind and realized the door to the hut was wide open. She got up, closed it, and returned to her bunk. Fully awake now, she reached over to feel for Yevka's form but found only the sleeping Danko. Paraska turned over in her own bunk mumbling, "Better to take care of that before bedtime," and then fell asleep.

In the morning, Paraska frowned at Yevka. "Are you well?"

Yevka was surprised. "Yes . . . why do you ask?"

"You didn't latch the door last night when you went out and I had to get up to close it. You should take care of that before you go to bed."

"I am sorry, Paraska. You are right."

❧

The weeks passed, and during that time the villagers brought in the first small harvest of hay, working late into the evenings and returning to their huts exhausted. One night, under a full moon, they bundled and stacked hay until very late. When they retired to their huts, they were, though weary, inspired by the hope of a good summer and the gradual return to a life of peace and good harvests.

On that particular night, Paraska went to bed early and was too tired to respond when Yevka whispered, "Paraska, are you awake?" Paraska was about to fall asleep when Yevka again asked her, "Paraska, are you awake?" Paraska was very much awake now, but she did not respond to her sister. Instead, she breathed rhythmically and remained still, listening for any sounds in the dark. After a long pause, she heard the bunk next to her creak, followed by the sound of slow steps across the room and then the click of the door latch. The room was briefly bathed in moonlight, and then Yevka's shadow passed outside, followed by the sound of the door closing.

Paraska swung out of bed and tiptoed across the room, stopping at the door to listen. When the sound of Yevka's footsteps faded, Paraska opened the door and glanced about in the moonlight. Yevka was walking down the path. Paraska stepped outside, closed the door softly behind her, and followed her sister, staying in the shadows and out of the bright moonlight. There, in the middle of the road that led to the center of the village, stood Yevka. In the dark shadows under the trees across the road, Paraska could just make out a small orange glow. "The ghost," Paraska gasped and held her hand over her mouth. Out of the trees a figure emerged and approached Yevka—the two became one form in the moonlight. They then glided down the road and Paraska followed.

Yevka and the ghost reached the center of the village, while Paraska remained well hidden within the shadows of the trees near the road. Outside

Yakov's roofless old tavern, the pair stopped, and the ghost tossed the orange glowing object to the ground, where it bounced and sparked. The ghost spoke in low tones and his empty right sleeve flapped in a light breeze. Paraska's jaw fell and she groaned, "Vasyl . . . Vasyl . . . no . . . no." Yevka rested her head on Vasyl's left shoulder and he placed his arm around her waist. Then Vasyl opened the door to the ruined tavern, admitted Yevka, and then closed the door behind him.

Paraska's shoulders sagged, and she stood in the shadows until her wounded right thigh throbbed. Finally, she turned and slowly limped back up the path to the hut where the boys still slept soundly. As she lowered herself onto the bunk next to Myko, Paraska murmured, "Yevka, Yevka . . . *akh!* Yevka! *Hospodi, pomilui*—Lord, have mercy!"

CHAPTER THIRTY-FOUR

The Oak

ON A COOL AUTUMN MORNING IN 1918, the vanguard migrants from impending winter flapped southward, their raucous calls descending through the crisp highland air: "KYU-YU! KYU-YU! KYU-YU!" Confined to the footpaths below, another migrant walked southward across the mountains toward the village of his birth. He stopped, and, shading his eyes from the sun, looked up to watch the V-shaped flight of geese. He cupped his hands on the sides of his mouth.

"Kyu-yu!" he called to the birds. "Kyu-yu!"

And the birds responded, "KYU-YU! KYU-YU!"

"Yes, Kyu-yu, my angels! Fly to the Lord! For He is your Master and mine! Tell Him I want to go home to Stara Polyanka. If He will have me back, I will be His."

"KYU-YU! KYU-YU!"

"Beg Him to forgive me!"

"KYU-YU! KYU-YU!"

"Beg Him to teach me humility in all things."

"KYU-YU! KYU-YU!"

"Yes, 'Kyu-yu!' Is that all you can say to me? Only, do not rebuke me, my angels! Unlike you, I am flesh, a breeze that passes by, never to return. But you angels soar above the sinful mud that weights the boots of mortals. How I envy your heavenly progress and how I detest my earthly stagnation! Fly, my angels! Fly!"

"KYU-YU! KYU-YU!"

"Yes, yes! Kyu-yu! Kyu-yu!" He laughed and continued southward in the shadow of the geese.

☙

Vasyl and Yurko had been stacking firewood all morning in front of the Rusynko home and were almost finished when Yurko tapped Vasyl on the shoulder and pointed toward the upper valley.

Vasyl squinted at a distant figure walking along a high trail. "Yes, I see him, Yurko. He is alone." The two men watched the figure approach. Vasyl smiled. "I think I know who that is." Yurko nodded and stretched his neck forward. Vasyl laughed and slapped Yurko on the back. "Yes, I know now who it is! It is my brother! It is Andrii! He has come home to us!"

Andrii drew nearer and, when he saw he was being observed, slowed, recognized his observers, and quickened his step. When he closed within a few steps, he lowered his head and stopped. "Vasyl . . . Yurko . . . *Slava Isusu Khrystu*—Glory to Jesus Christ."

Vasyl took his brother by the arm. "*Slava na vikŷ*—Glory to Him forever! *Vitai domu, brate*—welcome home, brother."

Andrii smiled shyly. "I don't suppose there is a fatted calf to feed the prodigal son . . ."

"No, Andrii, but there is plenty of thin cabbage soup." Andrii nodded and Vasyl studied his brother's face. It was still youthful, but under the eyes were dark circles of fatigue and hunger. These, time would erase; but outside their dark confines were minuscule cracks in the veneer of Andrii's youthful skin. These were the thin lines of enduring sadness that Vasyl had seen on so many young faces. "So, Andrii, you are tired of Russian winters?"

"Yes, Vasyl. That land is cold, and the wind that I thought would bring a warm spring of hope has become instead a bitter chill that will, I fear, bring only longer and colder winters. The hope for our people will come from within, not from without. I was foolish to think it could be any other way."

"You are not foolish, Andrii. But I am glad you have come home."

"It is good of you, Vasyl, not to hate me."

"Hate you! How could I ever hate you?"

"I turned my back on you. I went east when I should have come home. I turned my back on you—on our people—on God Himself."

Vasyl placed his arm across his brother's shoulders. "You are home. Think no more about it. God forgives all."

"Yes, but I need to go to confession. Is there a priest in the village?"

"Of course. Father Yaroslav is here."

"He is alive?"

"Well, he was last Sunday during *Sluzhba Bozha*—the liturgical service."

Andrii covered his mouth and gazed skyward. He sniffed and wiped his eyes, murmuring, "God is truly merciful and gracious." Andrii crossed himself and sighed deeply.

"He keeps bees now," said Vasyl.

Andrii blinked in confusion. "Bees? Who keeps bees?"

"Father Yaroslav. He has two hives in the little field below the cemetery—next to the site of the old church—not far from the linden trees."

Andrii smiled. "He always wanted to keep bees."

"He's making a third hive in his barn. He will want to see you."

"Yes, first thing tomorrow morning I will go to him." Andrii paused. "Have you seen *Mamka,* Vasyl?"

"Yes. She is living in Niklova with Aunt Mariya, just as you remember. Anna and Petro live there also. But *Mamka* is not well—neither here nor here." Vasyl pointed to his heart and then to his head. "Prepare yourself before you go to see her, Andrii."

Andrii nodded solemnly. Then the two brothers went inside, where they chatted about their routes home. Vasyl asked about the places he remembered from his journey home from Russia. Andrii, too, had passed through Przemyśl and had his first look at his mountain homeland just south of that city. They talked late into the night, while Yurko fed them and made up his own bunk for Andrii. Finally, when Vasyl and Andrii retired to their beds, they discovered that Yurko had gone to the barn to sleep in the little stall that once housed the Rusynko pigs.

✂

The following day the news of Andrii's return to Stara Polyanka spread through the village. In the late morning, Paraska walked up the hill to the Rusynko hut and announced that Andrii's return called for a celebration.

"Andrii, *vitai domu*—welcome home. You are to come to our hut this afternoon for dinner. I haven't seen you since the beginning of the war. I would not have recognized you. Yurko, you are also invited, of course. We will have buckwheat bread and mushroom soup and *slyvovitsa*—plum brandy. Yes, Yurko, *slyvovitsa*—I think this is the first time I've seen you smile since . . . well, before the war anyway. *Bozhe moi!* Perhaps the miracle of speech will overcome you tonight! Come this afternoon. We will have a gathering like the old days." Paraska started out the doorway, and then stopped, turning to Vasyl and saying,

"And, of course, Vasyl! How could I forget Vasyl! You are always invited. But, then, you already know that, don't you, Vasyl? I will see you all later."

That afternoon the men arrived with cabbage and a length of vine with four tomatoes. Paraska and Yevka seated the men at the table and served them bread and soup.

After supper, Vasyl sipped from his mug holding the *slyvovitsa* against his palate with his tongue and letting it run down the back of his throat. He closed his eyes and clucked his tongue. Next to him, Andrii also closed his eyes and savored the liquor, while across the table, Yurko licked his lips as well as the inside rim of his mug.

Paraska poured herself a little brandy and pushed the jug toward the men. "There is more."

"Yes," said Vasyl, placing his hand over the proffered jug. "But not yet. Let us enjoy this first taste. Let us remember the work that went into creating this fine drink. It is not to be lapped like water, Yurko, but tasted." Vasyl took another sip, demonstrating the proper technique to enjoy the liquor.

Andrii finished his drink and slid the mug next to the jug. "Fill it, Vasyl. I wish to make a toast." Vasyl poured all around, including the mug offered by Yevka. Andrii raised his mug. "To all that we lost, and to all that will take the place of our losses—for it is to the future that we look now."

❧

Vasyl stepped out of the hut after supper, puffing his pipe. He found Andrii, preoccupied with a pencil and small notebook, sitting on the chopping block. Vasyl stood behind his brother, peering over his shoulder until Andrii smelled the tobacco and snapped his book shut. "Vasyl, how long have you been standing there?"

"Since three puffs on this pipe. What are you writing?"

Andrii reddened and pocketed both book and pencil. "Oh . . . nothing . . . words . . . Words that come to me when it is quiet—especially in the evening—sometimes in the morning—but, usually in the evening."

"Words, Andrii?"

"Yes. Words I hear in the light wind that moves up and down the valley. Do you see how the birds float in the air and let the breeze take them where it will? It is like that with the poems I write. I don't search them out—they come to me. I have heard that there are musicians who compose songs like that."

The corners of Vasyl's mouth fell sharply in a smile. *"Bozhe moi,* Andrii! When did you become a poet?"

Andrii shrugged. "I don't really know. During the war—in Russia. Or, perhaps earlier . . . maybe in prison with Father Yaroslav. I don't know. I didn't start writing poems until I was in Russia. They weren't very good. They were poems about the things that happened during the war. There were many poems that I thought up—they are still in my head. Every day I pick through them and write a few notes."

"You should write them all down."

Andrii smiled. "No, not until I stop trying to write the words. I must write only what I hear."

"What do you hear, Andrii?"

"I hear sounds—the rustle of the leaves in the trees, the Ondava flowing out of the hills, the birds calling, and also . . . well . . . you will laugh when I tell you what else I hear."

"I won't laugh."

Andrii lowered his head. "I hear voices."

Vasyl pulled his pipe from his mouth. "Voices?"

"Yes. You don't think I'm mad, do you?"

Vasyl shook his head. "Whose voices do you hear?"

"Everyone I know or have ever known: you, Father Yaroslav, *Mamka,* our father, Petro, Anna, and Old Mykhal. I've even heard—and now you will laugh—I've even heard Yurko's voice, even though I cannot remember what his voice sounds like. I only know that when I hear it, it is his."

Vasyl laughed. "The priesthood is losing a good man."

Andrii opened his hands to the sky and then clasped them in his lap. "The priesthood probably still calls me—I don't know. This is not the time for me to think about it. Too much has happened. I want to have time to think and pray about the priesthood, but every time I try, I am distracted by poetry."

Vasyl was both amused and intrigued. "There are priests who write poetry."

"I don't know, Vasyl . . . I don't know. I do know that there are men who should be priests, and there are men who want to be priests who should be poets. And there are men who want to be poets who should be shot. Feh! You should read some of the foul-smelling waste that gets printed."

Vasyl laughed. "And so you are a poet. Read me one of your poems, Andrii."

Andrii shook his head. "I told you, I have only sketches of poems. I threw away the ones I wrote in Russia. They were about people and places—they weren't really poems. I wrote them when I tried to grab the voices from the air, and before I let the words come floating to me in their own time. Those times filled me with despair, and I longed to be here in Stara Polyanka. I remembered the psalm, 'I lie awake and moan, like a lone sparrow on the roof.' And so I lay awake at night, unable to sleep—a lonely sparrow—a coward really."

Vasyl was surprised. "A coward?"

"Yes, Vasyl, a coward. When I was in prison, I saw that Father Yaroslav was willing to die at the end of a rope for the faith. I was too angry to die for the faith. I lost all desire to become a priest—at the very moment when I should have desired more than ever to be a priest. Angry men should not become priests. You lost your arm in loyalty and service to our emperor. I ran to the first Russians I could find. Father Yaroslav was willing to give his life. You gave your arm. I offered nothing and I lost nothing. Now, I find refuge in poetry, because in poetry no one asks anything of me. I am as brave as I care to be, with words no one will ever see—thus, a coward."

The waning autumn sun cast shadows in the thin lines around Andrii's eyes. He looked twice his twenty-two years. Vasyl prodded his brother again. "Read me a poem, Andrii."

"I told you, I'm a coward."

"Stop it—you are not a coward. Read me a poem."

"They are mostly in my head. I haven't really written too many down on paper . . ."

"Tell me one, then."

Andrii bit his lower lip. "I'll tell you the story of a poem. It is one of the poems I started in my head. It is one I started after seeing you in the Russian camp last year. Would you like to hear about that one?"

Vasyl nodded.

"It is about loss, Vasyl. It is about the memory of something that can never be replaced. It is about an idea that comes from loss. I told you I no longer write about important people and events and historical processes. Now my poems are about the mountains and this valley. They are about trees and the light and rain that feed them and about birds that nest in the trees. The birds are angels, Vasyl. God sends them to us, to fly overhead and to sing and to draw our faces up to see the pure blue sky—up towards God. But my poems are more than songs about birds and trees. They are about the *gazda*—the farmer—who tills the field and about his wife—the *gazdynya*—who bears the next generation. They are about us."

"Us?"

"Yes, Vasyl, they are poems about *nash narod*—our people. I found a book while I was in Russia called *The Way of a Pilgrim*. In it a pilgrim recites the Jesus Prayer over and over in response to the Apostle Paul's instruction to 'pray without ceasing.' And so the pilgrim wanders throughout Russia praying, '*Hospodi Isuse Khryste, syne Bozhii, pomilui mya, hreshnoho*—Lord Jesus Christ, Son of God, have mercy on me, a sinner!' You know that prayer."

"Yes . . . yes, I know it."

"I said that prayer, Vasyl, as I walked. I said it as I fell asleep at night, and I said it when I awoke. At first, I concentrated on the words, but the song of the birds in the trees drew my gaze upwards, and I began to see images of our people in the branches of the trees and in the patterns of the clouds. I came to realize that the lives of our people are like prayers. So, I prayed and began to hear the voices of our people. The voices sounded like they were in prayer. It was then I realized that everything we do is a prayer: Petro going to Ameryka, Father Yaroslav going to prison, you going to war—they are all prayers to God. Everything we do is a prayer to God—our thoughts, our actions, our virtues and our sins. In my poem—"

Vasyl pulled his pipe from his mouth. "Our sins?"

"Yes, Vasyl, everything. Even our sins. Now, in my poem—"

"How is sin a prayer?"

"Because we feel guilt. And the act of guilt is our last prayer before we actually sin. Our guilt is our prayer for forgiveness. But, Vasyl, my poem—"

"What if we feel no guilt?"

"We all feel guilt over our sins—everyone but a madman. The Lord sees and hears our sin, Vasyl. When Adam eats fruit from the forbidden tree, God asks, 'Where are you?' Do you think God did not know where Adam and Eva were? Of course He knew. By asking them, God forces them to acknowledge Him. Of course, Adam blames Eva for his sin. But, it is truly Adam's sin. But, Vasyl, my poem—"

"If a man fails to repent—what then?"

Andrii shook his head. "Then he has failed to respond to God. God desires us to be with Him, not estranged from Him. We know when we sin, and by failing to respond to God's call to us to put away sin, we offend God and sin further. In his Epistle to the Romans, *Svyatÿi* Pavlo—Saint Paul—reminds us that, just as one son of God—Adam—brought sin into the world, so another son—*Khrystos*—Christ—took our sins upon His back for our salvation. Do not carry sin with you knowingly, Vasyl."

"What if the thing that causes one to sin is . . . is always nearby?"

"Then you must remove it or remove yourself. You must remove the temptation."

Vasyl rubbed his arm above the stump. "What if the sin . . . is not . . . what if the sin harms no one—"

Andrii frowned and shook his head. "Every sin, large or small, is an affront to God. Father Yaroslav says that whether a bird is tethered with a thread or a chain, the result is the same: the bird cannot fly. Only by cutting the string or chain can the bird fly again. Both can be cut—one much easier than the other. We can never rise to heaven if we are tied to sin." Andrii stood and stretched. "But, Vasyl, I was telling you about my poem, the one that came to me in your voice after I saw you in Russia."

"Hmm? Yes . . . yes, you were. What is it called?"

"I call it '*Dub*—The Oak.' It is about the oak that loses a limb but continues to grow—something else replaces the loss. We long for things we lose and long even more passionately for things we never had. A man loses an arm and misses it because he remembers having one. A man born without an arm can miss what he never had only by seeing others using both arms. It is a poem about a tree, but really it is about our people."

"And what does this have to do with our people?"

"Our people long for their own homeland."

"We do?"

"Yes, Vasyl, I think we do. We have our own unique language and faith. Our bishops answer to Rome, but our liturgy is almost identical to the Russian Orthodox. We have our own traditions. I've heard that there are leaders in Ameryka and Western Europe who say that all unique peoples should have their own homeland and that the creation of these homelands will be at the expense of the losers in the current war. You remember how it was at the front, Vasyl—the ranks were full of our people from both sides of the mountains. I met men from Uzhhorod and Mukachevo and Sanok and villages near those cities who felt the same way—that we are all one people spread across unfortunate political boundaries—boundaries imposed upon us by powerful people far from here who know nothing about our ways and our desires. There are others, however, who feel we are latecomers to the nationalism debate and—you are smiling, Vasyl. You are laughing at me."

"I'm not laughing at you. I was only thinking how good it is to have you home again." Vasyl yawned and stretched his arm. "You should go to the town of Výshnii Svidnyk, Andrii. I hear that men there talk of these things, and that they meet with men from Prague and Bratislava. I am only a simple one-armed *gazda*—farmer. I don't even know many of the words you use."

Andrii lowered his head and murmured, "Did you still want to hear about my poems?"

"Yes, but tell me about the trees and the birds—those I can understand. All this talk about nations and peace conferences makes me sleepy."

"I have a poem for Yevka, too."

Vasyl was startled. "You what?" Andrii, however, was looking over Vasyl's shoulder at Yevka, who was emerging from the hut hand in hand with her son, Danko.

Andrii called to her. "Yevka, I was telling Vasyl that I have a poem about you. It is about the *pysankŷ*—the dyed eggs—you make. I haven't written it yet, but I've heard some of it in my head. When will you make *pysankŷ* again, that I may watch you and learn for my poem?"

"In the late winter or early spring. Maybe sooner."

"Good. May I come watch you?"

"Yes, of course."

Paraska emerged from the hut, followed by Yurko, who carried a giggling Myko on his shoulders. Paraska stood next to Yevka with her fists on her hips. "What of the spring? What will happen? What is Andrii talking about?"

Andrii stroked Danko's hair. "I want to learn to make *pysankŷ* for a poem that stirs in my head. And a poem for you, Danko—I will make up one for you. Your face is soft and pink—you shall be a peach tree."

Paraska looked at Vasyl. "What is this all about? Why is Danko a peach tree?"

Vasyl shrugged. "Andrii is a poet now. He writes about trees and birds."

Paraska frowned. "Trees and birds? What about trees and birds?"

Andrii indicated the sky with a sweeping gesture. "The birds are God's angels. They draw our eyes upward to God, who sees us and who knows our thoughts and hears our prayers. The birds also—"

Paraska interrupted with a deep chuckle. "Good thing we have roofs over our heads."

Andrii scratched his cheek. "I don't understand."

"Well," said Paraska, looking not at Andrii, but, rather, at Yevka. "We don't want God seeing everything, do we?"

Andrii shrugged. "Well, I don't think it really matters if there is a roof because, after all—"

"Think of it, Yevka," laughed Paraska. "Aren't you happy we have a roof over our heads? I know I wouldn't want birds flying over my head all day and all night describing my actions to God. What about you, Yevka?"

"Well . . ."

"No! Of course you wouldn't! Thank God for roofs! And what about you, Vasyl? Aren't you grateful for roofs on houses . . . and on barns . . . and even on old taverns? Of course, here in Stara Polyanka the tavern has no roof. What a pity! What do you think, honest Vasyl? Hmm? What do you think?"

Vasyl stared at Paraska while Yevka quickly retreated into the hut with Danko in tow. Finally, Vasyl removed his pipe from his mouth and, in a measured tone, said, "I think I am grateful for one thing: my brother Andrii writes about birds that soar and not about hens that cluck. Come, Andrii; come, Yurko."

Yurko lowered Myko to the ground and gently pushed the boy toward the entrance to the hut. Yurko then hurried after the two Rusynko brothers.

Paraska stood alone in the little yard grinding her fists into her hips and watching the men make their way to the Rusynko homestead. "Well, well," she murmured. "Well, well, Vasyl Rusynko . . . who do you think you are, hmm? Who do you think you are?"

CHAPTER THIRTY-FIVE

Miraculous Tears

MIDAUTUMN OF 1918 was particularly cold in Stara Polyanka. Frigid air pouring over the Carpathian Mountains assailed the village's wretched little huts and whistled through myriad defects in walls and roof thatch. After sunset one evening, the temperature plunged and the villagers huddled by their fires.

In the Senchak hut, Paraska fed pieces of *buk*—beech wood—into the fire box, closed the little iron door, and then held her hands over the hot surface of the hearth. In the corner, Yevka finished putting Myko and Danko to bed and then, blowing into her hands, crossed the room to the hearth. The sole source of light was a single burning candle on the table in the middle of the room.

Silently, Paraska made room and cast extended, sidelong glances at her sister.

Growing uncomfortable, Yevka shifted her feet. "Paraska, why do you stare at me?" she asked apprehensively.

Paraska chuckled and shook her head. "I'm not staring at you, honest sister."

"No?"

"No."

"Then why do you look at me that way?"

"How am I looking at you, honest Yevka? Hmm? Maybe I'm proud of you. Would it be wrong for me to be proud of you?"

"I don't know, Paraska . . . I don't know. You haven't said much to me for days. Now you are staring at me. I am only asking why you are staring at me."

Paraska tossed her hands up in the air. "Well then, honest Yevka, I will tell you. I am not staring at you—I'm staring at your belly, and I am thinking what a lucky wife you are."

"Oh . . . ?"

"Yes, Yevka. I see many things in our village. I see many things, especially when it is cold and the days are shorter and shorter. It seems that the less sunlight there is, the better I am able to see. I see how little food there is since the war. I see how much less food there is when the cold weather comes. I see these things and I think how happy Petro would be if he could see you now."

"I see . . ."

"Do you, Yevka? Do you see? Then I am happy for you . . . while the rest of us starve, you get bigger, and all right here!" Paraska slapped her own waistline for emphasis. "All in one place! Do you still see, Yevka? Do you see how happy I am for you?"

"Paraska . . . please . . . I—"

"No, Yevka, do not interrupt me. I am too full of happiness for you! I have spent every waking moment trying to get food for my Myko and for Danko—your son by your husband—your husband, Petro. Sometimes I have worried about you getting enough to eat, and I have cried myself to sleep. But now I am happy because I see that you have managed to get a little something inside you!"

"*Oi*, Paraska!" Yevka buried her face in her hands.

"*Oi*, Yevka! Do not cry in front of me! I have cried too many tears while you run to the arm of your lover! *Rozumim vshŷtko*—I understand everything! These tears, Yevka! They are too much! Look at yourself—trying to outweep the Mother of God! At Klokochovo, her icon wept real tears—miraculous tears. Do not insult the Mother of God with your false tears of guilt and pleasure! The Mother of God and I cry tears of sorrow!"

"*Oi*, Paraska . . . *oi* . . ." Yevka retreated to a dark corner and hid her face in her hands.

Paraska remained at the hearth, her lips twitching, listening to Yevka's sobs. Finally, Paraska went to the corner of the room and placed her arm around her sister's shoulders and stroked her hair. "You know, Yevka"—Paraska purred in her sister's ear—"since last summer I have worried how we could ever repay Vasyl for all the food and help he has given us. I am so happy you found a way."

Yevka squirmed out from under Paraska's arm and rushed to the darkest corner of the hut, where she collapsed on the floor and sobbed.

Myko and Danko, huddled in their bunks, turned their wide eyes on Paraska, who limped to the table and slumped onto a bench. "Hmph!" she snorted. "I work all day trying to feed Myko and Danko while you run around at night making babies with men named Rusynko! What will your Petro say about this? Hmm? What will the people in every village along the Ondava say? Now we'll never get to Ameryka . . . *nygda*—never!"

ℭℴ

Early the next morning, before the boys awoke, the sisters rose and began preparations for a meager breakfast. Yevka, her eyes still swollen from crying the night before, avoided Paraska's cold stares and tended to the hearth fire. Paraska stomped about the hut, muttering, until finally she stood behind her sister, glaring at the back of Yevka's head. Paraska breathed deeply and her nostrils flared as she spoke.

"You know, Yevka, there will be talk in the village."

"I know that."

"It will be difficult for you."

"Yes, I know."

"I, of course, will help you."

"Oh?"

"Yes, Yevka. I will do everything I can to protect you from the loose tongues in the village. But there will be talk . . . much talk . . . especially when the father's name becomes known."

"I know, Paraska . . . I know."

"Yes, yes—I know you think you know. When will you tell Vasyl?"

"I have already told him."

"You told him? What did he say?"

"*Nich*—nothing."

"You told Vasyl that he will be a father by his brother's wife and he said nothing?"

"Paraska . . . please . . ."

"When did you tell him?"

"Three weeks ago."

"Three weeks ago! You told him three weeks ago? Your own sister has to find out by asking, but the one who says nothing has known for three weeks!" Paraska, her fury growing, clasped her hands in a ball against her forehead. Grinding her jaws together, she composed herself. Then she comforted her sister. "Of course, Yevka, you know that I only wish to protect you from shame."

"*Dyakuyu*—thank you."

"Yes, it is my duty to protect you." Paraska paused and stared up at the thatched roof. When she continued, she arched an eyebrow and leaned toward her sister. "Yevka, do you remember the girl everyone talked about when we were young—the one who went to Ondavka to marry the beekeeper's boy?"

"Maybe . . . what about her?"

"Do you remember how the people talked about her?"

"I think so . . . I don't think I remember what they said."

"Well, Yevka, I will tell you so that you do remember. People said all sorts of horrible things about her. You were very young at the time—you were probably too young to understand. So it does not surprise me that you don't remember. There were rumors about her—that she had slept with another boy—"

"Paraska—"

"—that she had—"

"Paraska, why are we talking about this?"

"*Chekai*—wait, Yevka. I'm only trying to help you. There was a rumor that this other boy—not the one she was to marry—this other boy had made her with child. Everyone talked about it and the beekeeper heard about it and demanded that the rumor be proved true or false before he would allow the girl to marry his son. And do you know what happened? The rumor became just that—a rumor! The girl married the beekeeper's boy and the old rumor was forgotten. You see, Yevka, it is possible to make a rumor go away. Do you understand what I am saying?"

"No . . . I don't think so . . ."

Paraska leaned closer to Yevka and spoke in a low, confidential voice. "There is, in a village near here, a woman—she's not a witch or a sorcerer—who can make a rumor disappear. The girl went to that woman for help. There are herbs and there are other ways to—"

"Paraska!"

"Tsh! You'll wake the boys, Yevka."

"Paraska! Say no more of this! How can you say such a thing?"

"Yevka, please! Lower your voice. I am trying to . . . to . . . to help you. I want to save you from shame and from—"

"I won't murder my child to save myself from shame!"

"*Bozhe moi,* Yevka! What will everyone think? What about my shame? Yes, Yevka, what about my shame? Stop thinking only of yourself! Think of me! People will point at me, too! They will say, 'She is her sister! She is like Yevka!'"

"Say no more about this!"

"Please, Yevka—the shame, the shame! And what about Ameryka? How can we go to Ameryka now? What will Petro say?"

"Enough, Paraska!"

"It would be so much easier to go to Ameryka if you only had Danko with you. Think about it, Yevka—think about it."

"*Nygda*—never," murmured Yevka, her hands clasped over her abdomen. "*Nygda . . . nygda.*"

"Yevka, I only want to help you."

"Get away from me."

"Yevka, please . . . I only . . . where are you going?" Paraska placed a hand on Yevka's shoulder. "It is too cold outside. You mustn't go out. Please don't go."

Yevka's face was rigid and her eyes were black. "Let me go—now!" Yevka wrapped her shawl over her head and around her shoulders, opened the door, and stepped outside, slamming the door behind her.

Paraska leaned against the wall and found herself facing the little tin icon of the Mother of God, presenting in her left arm the infant Savior of the world. Paraska cringed against the wall and held her hand over her eyes. "*Mati Bozha*—Mother of God!" she whimpered. "Oh, don't look at me that way! *Mati Bozha!*" Paraska lowered her hand and stared at the icon. "What have I done? *Mati Bozha!*"

❧

During the night the wind abated and by morning a light snow fell from the gray sky, blanching the quiet earth. Yevka retrieved a bundle of wood from the pile beside the little barn and stepped carefully on the thin white layer as she worked her way slowly to the door of the hut. The boys were still asleep and Paraska was beginning to stir. Yevka stoked the hearth, placed a little kettle of water over the old coals, and stood back clasping her arms under her shawl for warmth and turning her back on the rising Paraska.

"Yevka," came her sister's sleep-heavy voice from the corner. "Yevka . . . is it . . . is it still snowing?"

Silence.

"Yevka, did you get wood?"

Silence.

Paraska rose to a sitting position on the edge of the bunk that she shared with Myko. Shuddering, she pulled her shawl over her shoulders and rubbed her right thigh. She stood with a groan and shuffled across the dirt floor to her sister's side, where she warmed her hands over the fire.

"Yevka . . . I think Danko cried out last night. I thought I heard him . . . last night . . . or maybe . . . Well, I thought it was Danko . . . perhaps it was Myko . . . I don't know." Paraska bit her lower lip and rubbed her hands together. "*Bozhe,* it's cold this morning. I can't get warm. Look, I am shaking." Then she leaned toward her sister, hopefully. "Yes? Did you say something, Yevka?"

"I said nothing," said Yevka.

Paraska captured her upper lip between her teeth, held it there, and nodded. "Yes," she said, relaxing her jaw. "Yes . . . well . . . well . . . I . . ."

"Paraska, you don't have to speak. You have said much these last two days."

Paraska nodded quickly. "Yes, yes, I . . . I said too much . . . I was worried about you, Yevka."

"You were worried about me?"

"Yes. I am worried . . . worried about your health . . ."

"You don't need to worry about me."

"But, Yevka, you are going to have a baby, and I am worried that there will not be enough food for you. When there is a baby, you must eat more. I want to take care of you and help you to—"

"You don't have to do anything for me, Paraska."

"Of course I do, Yevka—you are my sister. What must you think of me— that I won't help you? The baby will come in the spring, yes? Well then, we must prepare. We must begin today. I will do everything, Yevka . . . everything . . . anything you need . . ."

Yevka walked to the door and reached for the latch, but Paraska stepped in front of her. "No, Yevka, you must not go out into the snow—I will get what you need—I will not permit you to work—I will not—"

"Paraska—"

"What is it, Yevka? Tell me what to do."

"Move away from the door."

"Yevka, please let me help you. Yesterday . . . yesterday . . . I was . . . I said things . . . I never . . . oh, *Mati Bozha*—Mother of God! I let the devil take me by the tongue! I never should have said those things to you . . . and I—"

ai, Yevka, I would cut out my tongue before I ever hurt you again! Yevka, help me to help you!"

"Very well."

"Good, Yevka! What can I do?"

"Move away from the door."

"But, Yevka, I told you—I want to help—"

"Unless you can move the latrine indoors, you cannot help me."

"Yes, yes, Yevka, of course. What else can I do?"

"Close the door after me."

∾

When Yevka came back inside, Paraska was on the floor near the hearth. Myko was on his knees at her side, sobbing.

Danko ran to Yevka's side. *"Mamko! Teta* Paraska fell! She was walking and suddenly she fell!"

Yevka rushed to her sister. "Paraska! *Bozhe!* What happened?"

Paraska's eyes were closed, and she breathed with difficulty. "My head!" she gasped.

"Did you hit your head, Paraska? Is it bleeding?"

"No, Yevka. Help me up. Get me to the bed."

Yevka directed the boys toward the hearth. "Danko, Myko, go stand by the hearth and get warm. Stop crying, Myko. Your mother will be all right. Now, Paraska, rise to your knees."

"Oi, Yevka! My head! There is such a pounding inside! I'll stay on my knees. I won't be able to stand. I know I will fall again if I try to stand. I can make it to the bed like this."

Yevka moved the bench and table to make room for Paraska, who crawled to her bunk on all fours, pausing frequently to rest and moan. When she reached the side of the bed, she hung her head and struggled for air.

Yevka knelt at Paraska's side, cradling her sister's head in her arms. *"Bozhe,* Paraska, *Bozhe!* You are hot—your skin is on fire! You must get into bed—get up now!" Yevka, grasping her sister from behind, under her arms, pulled her up to her feet and pushed her forward onto the bed. Then Yevka swung Paraska's legs onto the bed, and covered her sister with a down-filled blanket.

Paraska shivered violently under the covers. "My legs, Yevka . . . they . . .

they became weak . . . I . . . I couldn't stand. I . . . I fell . . . *Bozhe moi,* I'm so cold!"

Yevka, her eyes moist, stroked her sister's hair. "Paraska . . . Paraska . . ."

"Yevka, listen to me," choked Paraska. "It is my fault . . . I brought this on myself. It is my sin. Go to Father Yaroslav. Tell him I'm sick. Bring him quickly—I may not have long!"

"*Oi,* Paraska!"

"It's my own fault, Yevka! My sin is so great! Honest Yevka! You are so good to cry for me—to cry such good tears of sorrow. Bring Father. *Skoro—*quickly!"

Yevka wrapped herself in warm clothing and ran outside.

Myko and Danko huddled next to the hearth while Paraska shivered in bed, working the edges of the blanket with her fingers, and lamenting, "My fault—it is my fault . . . *Mati Bozha*—Mother of God—pray for me!"

❧

While Yevka fed the boys, Father Yaroslav heard Paraska's confession and then anointed her. When he was finished, he sat wearily at the table, where Yevka poured him a cup of hot *rumyankovŷi chai*—chamomile tea.

"Thank you, Yevka. *Ai,* that is good."

"Father, what . . . what do you think? Is she . . . how bad is it?"

Father Yaroslav shrugged and took another sip of tea. "She is very ill, Yevka—very ill. It is *Yspanska khvoroba*—Spanish influenza. I've heard that there are many fatal cases in Pryashev and Bardeyov. Four people became ill in Nŷzhnya Polyanka yesterday. Paraska's case is the second one in Stara Polyanka. Ivan Burii became ill last night. The sickness is moving up the Ondava Valley. It is very serious, Yevka."

Yevka nodded. "I understand. You look very tired. Are you well?"

Father Yaroslav smiled. "*Ya ne khvorŷi*—I'm not sick. I was at the Burii home late last night—very late. How are the boys?"

"They are well. Myko was very frightened when his mother fell to the floor."

"Yes, I can understand that. I've been told that when one is stricken with this illness, it is like being hit on the head with a board."

Yevka rose at the sound of urgent knocking at the door. She opened the door, admitting Mykhal Roman. "*Slava Isusu Khrystu*—Glory to Jesus Christ," he said, removing his hat.

"*Slava na viký*—Glory to Him forever," said Yevka and Father Yaroslav, returning the greeting simultaneously.

"*Proshu*—please, Father," said Mykhal Roman rotating his hat in his hands. "It is *moya zhena*—my wife," he said, his voice breaking.

Father Yaroslav took a last sip of tea and rose from the table. "Thank you, Yevka. Let me know if there is anything else I can do for Paraska. It seems we have another case of *Yspanska khvoroba.*" He went to the door and patted Mykhal Roman's back as the two men went outside. "Come, Mykhal. Let us go to your Anna."

Yevka closed the door behind the two men, and went to her sister's bedside. "Are you awake, Paraska?"

"I don't know . . . I don't know. I'm so cold—the devil is in me, Yevka."

"Shh," soothed Yevka. "Don't say such things. You must be quiet. You are very sick."

Paraska closed her eyes. "I'm going to die—I know I'm going to die. Oh, Yevka! I prayed you would not have your baby—I wanted you to see that woman with the herbs. The devil heard my evil prayer! I brought the devil to Stara Polyanka. I am being punished for my evil thoughts! If you get sick, Yevka, you will lose the child. Don't get sick, Yevka! *Bozhe,* don't get sick!"

"Oh, Paraska! Please don't talk! Rest, Paraska, rest."

"Everything is my fault—my fault . . . *Mati Bozha*—Mother of God! Yevka! Yevka! The tears of the Mother of God! Oh, don't weep! *Proshu*—please, don't weep."

"I'm not weeping, Paraska."

"No . . . no, Yevka . . . not you . . . *Mati Bozha*—the Mother of God. Do not weep!"

"*Mati Bozha* is not here," said Yevka, feeling Paraska's forehead. "You are on fire with fever. Please lie still, Paraska."

"Don't you hear her, Yevka? Listen!"

"No . . . no, I don't hear—"

"Hush, Yevka! She is weeping . . . *tykho*—quietly . . . *tykho* . . . *tykho* . . . listen to her. She weeps for us, Yevka, because she knows how her Son suffered for us. She weeps because we are unworthy of His suffering. She weeps because I invited the devil to Stara Polyanka . . . the evil one roams the village, striking down the innocent because of me."

"No, no, Paraska! Father says this illness is influenza—not the work of the evil—"

"*Mati Bozha*—Mother of God!" cried Paraska. "*Mati Bozha,* go to your

Son! Tell Him I am sorry!" Paraska's eyes widened. "Yevka, our icons! There in the corner!" Paraska propped herself up on her elbows. "Go look at the Mother of God and tell me what you see. *Skoro*—hurry! Yevka, the Mother of God is weeping—look!"

Yevka went to the corner and peered at the small tin icon of the Mother of God hanging on the wall. "She is not weeping, Paraska."

Paraska crossed herself. "Oh, Yevka, do you see how she looks at us? Do you see?"

"No, Paraska. I see nothing but the little icon."

"Yevka, are you blind? She is weeping next to you. Look behind you, by the wall. Offer her something to wipe her face."

Yevka looked behind her and then returned to Paraska's side. "Paraska, calm yourself—there is no one there."

"Yevka, are there tears on the floor? Look closely."

"There are no tears, Paraska. The floor is dry. Please lie down."

"Yes, of course—they are miraculous tears, Yevka. She is here to help us . . . she weeps for me . . . she weeps for you . . . she weeps for all of us . . . all of us . . ." Paraska's voice broke. "All will be well, Yevka . . . all will be well. She heard my prayer . . . she will go to her Son . . . all will be well . . ." Paraska sank back onto her pillow.

Yevka sat on the edge of Paraska's sick bed, stroking her sister's hair. "Yes, Paraska . . . all will be well. Now, sleep . . . *tykho*—quietly . . . sleep . . . sleep . . . *tykho* . . ."

ↄ

The influenza epidemic lingered in Stara Polyanka and the other villages of Makovytsya, striking its victims without warning or partiality. Mykhal Roman's wife, Anna, died after a two-day illness, and was followed in death by Ivan Burii and Mariya Korba. Father Yaroslav fell ill one Sunday at the close of *Sluzhba Bozha*—the Sunday service—and had to be carried to bed. The only dwelling untouched by the pandemic was the Rusynko hut. During the course of the epidemic, Vasyl and Yurko—Andrii was in Pryashev at the time—subsisted almost entirely on a prophylactic regimen of garlic and *slyvovitsa*—plum brandy. The fact that neither Vasyl nor Yurko fell ill, but, on the contrary, spent more than two weeks tending the fields and barns of sick villagers, digging graves, and nursing the stricken Father Yaroslav back to health was, to many villagers, compelling evidence, indeed, of the merits of their chosen therapy.

Then the contagion visited the Senchak hut again, striking down Yevka and both Myko and Danko. Paraska, improving but still very weak, cared for the household, weeping and rebuking herself, saying over and over, "It is my fault! It is all my fault!"

☙

One morning, Yevka felt better—or, rather, not as ill as before. She rose from her bed, and shuffled to the table, where she sat on one of the benches, exhausted and out of breath.

The door opened, and Paraska entered the hut, pushing the boys in front of her. "*Bozhe moi,* you two! Behave yourselves! Yevka! What are you doing out of bed? Are you mad? *Bozhe!* You didn't lose the baby, did you?"

"No."

"*Dobre*—good. Get back in bed and stop being selfish—you have someone else to think about besides yourself."

"I suppose I should get back in bed. I thought I was stronger."

Paraska frowned at Yevka. "What are you smiling about?"

Yevka shook her head. "Nothing. Only, I'm happy that you are well again, Paraska. I thought we were going to lose you."

"Hmph! It was nothing."

"It is good to know that you will help me in the coming months."

"Of course I will. I said I would, didn't I? Now get back in bed before I become angry with you. Stand up and hold my arm. *Bozhe,* you are weak! Now, walk slowly to the bed. What were you thinking, by getting up before you are ready?"

"I wanted to see the icon—I wanted to see if she wept."

"You wanted to see if who wept?"

"*Mati Bozha*—the Mother of God."

"Yevka, what are you talking about?"

"Don't you remember? You said you heard the Mother of God weeping when you were sick."

"Yevka, I heard and saw many things when I was sick."

"But, Paraska, don't you remember? You heard her weeping, and you said there were tears on the floor."

"Yes, yes, yes—of course, Yevka, if you say so. Look, you made it across the room. Now climb back into bed. There you are—now pull up the covers and get warm."

"You said she weeps for us because we are not worthy of her Son's sacrifice."

"Yes, yes, Yevka, of course she weeps for us. We all know that. Our mother taught us this when we were young."

"She did? *Mamka* told us about the Mother of God weeping?"

"Yes."

"What did *Mamka* say?"

Paraska shrugged. "*Ne znam*—I don't know. It was something about *Mati Bozha* weeping for us because we are sinners."

"Yes, yes—what else, Paraska? What else did she say about *Mati Bozha*?"

Paraska glowered at the boys, who were playing noisily in the corner. "She is probably weeping for us now—only who can hear her with all this noise? Myko, Danko! Shush!"

"What else did *Mamka* say?" said Yevka insistently.

Paraska sighed. "If I tell you, will you go to sleep?"

"Yes."

"The only other thing I remember *Mamka* saying was that one had to be very quiet to hear the Mother of God weeping. She weeps very quietly. '*Tykho*—quietly,' *Mamka* would say. '*Tykho . . . tykho.*'"

"Yes," nodded Yevka. "*Tykho . . . tykho . . .*"

"Now will you go to sleep?"

"Yes, Paraska, yes. Thank you."

"Very well. Now I'm going to put the boys to work before they drive me mad. Danko! Hush! Your *mamka* is trying to sleep. Myko! Hush! Your *teta*—your aunt—is trying to sleep. Go outside, both of you! You will help me outside. Myko, close the door after me."

The room was quiet now as Yevka, drifting to sleep in her bed, murmured, "*Tykho*—quietly . . . *tykho . . . tykho . . .*"

CHAPTER THIRTY-SIX

A Small Circle

IN EARLY NOVEMBER *Yspanska khvoroba*—the Spanish influenza—was still ravaging the villages of Makovytsya. In Stara Polyanka there were funerals, each with a *Panakhida*—a memorial service—and presided over by a very pale and weak Father Yaroslav. When Father Emyliyan of Varadka became ill, Father Yaroslav served, with Andrii Rusynko's assistance, at a funeral in that village. After the funeral, they returned to Stara Polyanka, where Andrii helped put the exhausted priest to bed. Then he ran to the Rusynko hut, bursting through the door with an armful of newspapers.

"Vasyl! Vasyl, there you are! And Yurko! You must both hear the most won-drous news!" Andrii unfolded the papers and spread them on the table. "After the funeral in Varadka, I walked to Nŷzhnya Polyanka and bought all these newspapers. Old Mykhal had just delivered them today. Look, it is all the lat-est news! The war is finally over! The Germans have agreed to an armistice. Everything is happening so quickly. Look at these headlines!" Andrii flipped through the newspapers. "There is anarchy in Vienna! The Poles have declared a republic in Warsaw! The Kaiser abdicated in Germany! Emperor Karl abdi-cated the thrones of Austria and Hungary! A single Republic of Czechs and Slovaks has been declared! And look at this—Rusyns met in Stara Lyubovna and rejected any Rusyn union with Hungary! No more union with Hungary! Can you believe it, Vasyl? Wait, there is more! There will be a conference of nations to decide upon peace terms. Prezident Vylson of Ameryka is coming to Europe! He says all people will have a voice in how they are governed. Even Rusyns! Can you imagine that? What do you both think?"

Vasyl and Yurko merely stared at Andrii.

"Well, I thought it was good news," said Andrii. "You two don't look very happy about it."

"It is good news," said Vasyl quietly. "It is very good news, and I am very happy for you."

Andrii beamed. "Yes, Vasyl, but be happy *with* me! It is good news for all of us! It is the best news our people have ever had. The future looks very good for Rusyns. Do you want to read the news yourself, Vasyl?"

"No, Andrii. You tell us the news."

"Well, I think you should read it yourself—there is so much to tell. This is what I've been talking about since I returned from the war. Do you see? People will listen to us now! There are those in the world—especially among our people in Ameryka—who remember us and wish to see our dreams fulfilled. Prezident Vylson of Ameryka says that all people have the right to self-determination. I once read that he gave a speech that outlined fourteen ways the war could end and how peace could come again to the world. Prezident Vylson of Ameryka is a great man, Vasyl. Was he prezident when you were in Ameryka?"

"Not when I arrived. I think he was when I left Ameryka—I never really paid much attention to—"

Andrii, however, was not listening, but was pacing about the room, waving one of the documents. "I tell you, Vasyl, this letter inspires me! It was issued recently—after a meeting in Stara Lyubovna—a meeting of the Russka Narodna Rada—the Rusyn National Council. I wish I could have been in Stara Lyubovna when they wrote words like these: '. . . we are imbued with the democratic spirit of the times . . .' It was an historic moment, Vasyl. It happened because Prezident Vylson has made it possible for people to talk this way. Tell me, when was Prezident Vylson of Ameryka elected? How much longer will he be prezident? Ameryka is the model of democracy, yes, Vasyl?"

"Well, I don't really know much about—"

Andrii interrupted again. "I want to read to you the words of the council leaders from Stara Lyubovna. Listen to this, Vasyl:

We are Rusyns! Because we live in the Carpathians, we are called Carpathian Rusyns. But we know that Rusyns similar to us live beyond the Carpathians. Their speech, customs, and faith are the same as ours, as they are our brothers. With them we ethnographically form one great multi-million people.

The Rusyns in Stara Lyubovna are reaching out to Rusyns north of the mountains. Can you imagine it, Vasyl? We here in Stara Polyanka could find ourselves in the middle of a Rusyn nation—a newborn Rusyn nation! 'Rusyns beyond the Carpathians . . . they are our brothers.' Those are inspiring words, Vasyl, yes?"

"They mean something to you, Andrii. To me they are nothing more than long words. I only—"

"But, Vasyl, do you not see? Foreigners have ruled over our people for hundreds of years. Here, south of the mountains, the Magyars have owned our lands and taken our taxes and belittled our language far too long. Prezident Vylson says that Poles, Romanians, Slovaks, Slovenes, and Czechs and every other 'multi-million people'—even Rusyns—will decide for themselves how to exist on the world political stage. Tell me that does not inspire you, Vasyl. Tell me!"

"You are young, Andrii, and to you the world is a big and wonderful place."

Andrii frowned and looked at Yurko. "Vasyl is laughing at me again."

Yurko's eyes were closed and he was scraping his teeth with a dirty fingernail.

"Look, do you see, Vasyl? Yurko does not laugh at me. He understands the bright promise we now enjoy."

Vasyl scolded his brother with his eyes. "No, he doesn't, Andrii, and you know that. You are young and you have big dreams about the future. After the last four years of war, it is good that anyone can have hope in anything. You want a Rusyn nation? Here in the highlands there is too much work to do—we don't have time to worry about building a Rusyn nation. Let those in the cities talk of such ideas. I wish you well, but I think it is hopeless. Now, enough of this talk. Yurko and I need to finish the plowing, and we need your help to plant *zhŷto*—rye—for the spring. You can begin building a Rusyn nation once the *zhŷto* is in the ground."

☙

Two days later, a Jewish peddler passed through Stara Polyanka on foot selling buttons, brass hooks, needles, and other sundries. He also had with him a three-day-old newspaper from Pryashev, containing a news item announcing an upcoming meeting of the Russka Narodna Rada—the Rusyn National Council—in Bardeyov. Ecstatic, Andrii gave the peddler a small coin for the newspaper, and, as an afterthought, another small coin for three brass buttons. Andrii slapped the three buttons on the table, opened the paper to the story about the meeting in Bardeyov, and announced, "There! Look, Vasyl! What do you think of that?"

"*Dobre, dobre*—very good," nodded Vasyl.

"I knew you would become interested once you saw this, Vasyl!"

"Yes . . . yes I am. Only . . ."

"Only what, Vasyl?"

"Only, my Sunday vest needs five buttons, not three."

"Vasyl!" Andrii whined.

Throughout the day Andrii pestered Vasyl so persistently to attend the meeting in Bardeyov that Vasyl finally proposed a compromise.

"Andrii, I will go with you as far as Niklova. I will stay there with *Mamka*. You go on to Bardeyov, attend all the meetings you desire, and then return to Niklova, where *Mamka* and I will listen to everything you have learned."

"But, Vasyl, you should come with me to the meeting. Let me tell you the reasons why you should—"

"No."

"But, Vasyl, you haven't heard the reasons."

"I don't wish to hear the reasons."

"Well . . . I think you should think about going to the meeting, Vasyl."

"Thank you—I have. I will be very happy to stay in Niklova with *Mamka*. Now, when is the meeting?"

"In four days."

"That is *sereda*—Wednesday. Today is *sobota*—Saturday. Tomorrow is *nedilya*—Sunday. If we leave after *Sluzhba Bozha*—the church service—for Niklova, we will arrive there in the evening. The next day is *ponedilok*—Monday. Old Mykhal should arrive from Nýzhnya Polyanka on that day, and you can travel with him as far as Zborov."

Andrii beamed. "Yes, Sergeant Rusynko!"

Vasyl's mouth formed a flat, grim smile. "Why do you call me that?"

"Because you sound like my sergeant at the front during the war. When shall we advance, Sergeant?"

"As soon as you stop calling me 'Sergeant.'"

❧

On their way to Niklova, Vasyl and Andrii stopped at the *korchma*—the tavern—in Nýzhnya Polyanka. Andrii went straight to the day-old newspapers on the counter, and perused the headlines while Vasyl went to the other end of the counter. The Jewish tavern owner, Moshko Edermann, was twisting the long strands of his graying beard as he studied a large crack in the wall behind the counter. He was dressed in a black kaftan and wore a round black yarmulke over his long graying hair. Moshko turned around when Vasyl cleared his throat.

"Vasyl Rusynko! *Dai Bozhe shchastya*—God grant you happiness!"

"*Dai Bozhe i vam*—God grant it to you as well," nodded Vasyl.

"And Andrii! *Dobrŷi den*—good day!" cried Moshko.

"*Dobrŷi,*" murmured Andrii, not looking up from the newspapers.

"You boys are on your way to Niklova to see your *maty*—your mother—yes?"

"*Hei*—yes," nodded Vasyl.

Moshko jerked his head toward Andrii and, smiling, said to Vasyl, "Your brother, the scholar—always reading, always studying. I like to see that in a young man."

"He's going to make a nation."

"A nation?"

"Yes, a Rusyn nation."

"Ah," said Moshko stroking his beard. "Are you on your way to the meeting in Bardeyov, Andrii?"

Again, Andrii nodded without looking up from the newspapers.

"Well, that is good," said Moshko. "So, Vasyl, what will you have?"

"Vodka—two." Vasyl pulled a coin from his pocket and placed it on the counter.

Moshko pulled two glasses out from under the counter, inspecting each at arm's length with a farsighted squint before pouring the vodka.

Vasyl called to Andrii, "Come, you can read later. Come, drink."

Andrii reluctantly interrupted his studies and joined Vasyl and Moshko at the end of the counter. The brothers clicked their glasses.

"*Na zdorovya*—to your health!"

"*Na zdorovya!*"

The brothers downed their drinks, Vasyl with one swallow, Andrii with two, and set their glasses upside down on the counter. Andrii returned to the newspapers, and Vasyl pointed to the large crack in the wall behind the counter. "What happened?"

Moshko waved a hand in disgust. "Feh! I don't want to talk about it. Poor workmanship! What else can anyone expect from prisoners of war? Especially Russian prisoners! It's not their town—why should they care? You should hear what the people say about me, Vasyl. 'That Edermann—that *zhyd*—that Jew! He got more! We got little! He got much!'"

"More what?" asked Vasyl.

Moshko shook his head. "I don't want to talk about it." He held out his left hand with the palm up like an open book, and then with his right index finger he tallied his grievances. "In the fall of 1914 the retreating Austrians burned Nýzhnya Polyanka. I lost everything! The Russians came and took what was left of the village. Such a big victory for them! Only Mitro Hmotrykh's house was still standing! The next year the Austrian and Hungarian armies came back. They brought Russian prisoners of war with them and made them rebuild the village. Everyone said, 'Look at the damned Jew, Edermann! He gets a big house and a *korchma*—a tavern!'" Moshko jabbed his finger into the palm of his left hand. "I got more because I lost more! Feh! I don't want to talk about it."

Vasyl smiled. "Some people are never happy."

Moshko shrugged. "They are unhappy with the little brick buildings they received. Have you seen them, Vasyl? I, too, would be unhappy. They are so small that if, God forbid, you should want to turn around in your house, you have to back your way outside through the front door, turn around and back yourself inside."

Vasyl laughed. "I'd hate to see the latrines!"

Moshko tapped the bottle of vodka. "*Kapurkova*—one for the road? My treat."

The corners of Vasyl's mouth dropped sharply. "*Hei, chom nit*—sure, why not?" Vasyl rapped his knuckles on the counter. "Andrii, *kapurkova*—one for the road."

Andrii laid aside the newspapers for good and once again joined his brother and Moshko Edermann. "Not too much," he said to Moshko, holding his thumb and index finger slightly apart. "*Lem kus*—only a bit."

Moshko poured vodka into both glasses, these portions being the same size as the original servings.

"*Velykýi kus*—a big bit," Andrii grunted.

Moshko laughed heartily. "'*Velykýi kus*—a big bit!' That is good!"

The brothers downed their drinks as they had before, with Andrii requiring three swallows this time. Vasyl turned his glass over and set it on the counter. "So, Moshko, how much longer must I walk all the way to your *korchma* just to have someone pour me a glass of vodka?"

"Not much longer, friend. My cousin, Shlomo Lentz, in Stara Polyanka, will open a *korchma* soon—probably in the spring. He says he doesn't want to open one, but I've been talking to him. I'll even handle ordering supplies for him! It couldn't be easier! And still he hesitates! Feh! I don't want to talk about it." Moshko reached under the counter and presented a pipe to Vasyl. "Do you want it? It's a nice one—new. One of my suppliers gave it to me last week. I don't smoke anymore, but I know you like a good pipe."

Vasyl turned the pipe in his hand. "Very nice. I like my old pipe, but . . ." he winked at Moshko, and jerked his head toward Andrii.

Moshko nodded. *"Chom nit—*why not?"

Vasyl handed the pipe to Andrii. "It's yours. We'll have a smoke after dinner tonight."

Andrii, his eyes half-closed, shrugged. *"Chom nit?"*

Vasyl and Andrii said good-bye to Moshko Edermann and resumed their walk, heading west on the main road. To their left, over halfway up a steep hill in the beech forest, three gypsies worked with shovels and picks amid the ruins of the old Austrian bunkers.

"It's been four years since those trenches were manned with soldiers," said Andrii, pointing unsteadily at the workers. "But still the *tsyganŷ*—the gypsies—find bits of metal scrap and discarded equipment. Only God knows what they do with it all."

The brothers continued on the road toward the crossroads, where the path to Niklova branched to the left, and, a few paces farther to the west, the path to Yalynkŷ branched to the right. Vasyl stopped, retrieved a cigarette from his shirt pocket, and lit it with a wooden match, which he ignited with a stroke along the bottom of his shoe.

Andrii pointed to a man working in an adjacent field. "Look, Vasyl! A *gazda*—a farmer. We will speak with him. It will be good to hear the natural wisdom of the people before I go to Bardeyov." Andrii, his words indistinct, called out, *"Slava Isusu Khrystu—*Glory to Jesus Christ!"

The *gazda* looked up from his work. *"Slava na vikŷ—*Glory to Him forever!" he cried, waving his hat. *"De idete, panove—*where are you going, gentlemen?"

Andrii cupped his hands to his mouth. "As far as the Lord will allow. I am going to a place where I will watch the birth of a Rusyn state. Then, after that, who knows how far I will go? Maybe Prague, maybe Paris!"

The *gazda* gazed blankly at Andrii. Vasyl shouted, "We're going to Niklova!"

The *gazda* brightened. "Ah, that is a place I've heard of—in fact, it is the place where I live. You are Mariya Hryndyk's nephews, yes? *Dobre*—very well. You know the way to Niklova. I don't know if there is a road anywhere in Makovytsya that will take you to those other places. Are they a long way from here?"

Andrii cupped his hands to his mouth again. "A long way indeed! But distance is of no consequence to those who trust in God. The time spent traveling to such places, in such a new world as this that we now enjoy, is directly proportional to the love God has for his too-long overlooked Rusyn servants. God's love transcends time and distance!"

Again, the blank stare.

"Can't you just speak *po-nashomu*—our way—plainly to him?" said Vasyl, rolling his eyes at his brother. Vasyl cupped his hand to the side of his mouth. "I think my brother is saying: the journey will depend on how well God loves Rusyns!"

The *gazda* nodded grimly. "Ah, then you will have a long journey indeed, friends . . . a long journey indeed."

Vasyl snorted. "Do you want to move on now, Andrii? Or do you want to hear more wisdom of the people?"

"I don't want to talk about it," scowled Andrii.

They turned left and walked south to Niklova, along a path that passed through vast fields of freshly plowed earth.

"Do you smell that, Vasyl?" asked Andrii, walking with his eyes closed and his whiffing nose pointed skyward.

"Yes."

"Do you know what that is?" asked Andrii.

"Yes. It is freshly plowed earth."

"No, Vasyl, it is more than that. It is the soil of our little region, Makovytsya. It is fertile soil, where, by spring, a new nation will be born—a Rusyn nation." Andrii jumped up and down, turning and landing four times in all four directions of the compass. "*Sevŷr! Vŷkhod! Yuh! Zapad!*—North! East! South! West!" he shouted. "There are Rusyns in every direction from here, Vasyl! Here in Makovytsya we are in the middle of everything that is Rusyn on earth! Tell me what you think of that."

Vasyl took a long drag on his cigarette, exhaled, and yawned. "I still think it smells like freshly plowed earth."

Andrii dismissed Vasyl with a toss of his hands. "There is no point in discussing this with you, Vasyl."

Then Andrii pointed out a stone wayside cross to their right, just off the road. "Look, the Lord watches over Makovytsya." The two brothers crossed themselves from right to left as they passed the stone crucifix. When Vasyl finished his cigarette and ground the butt under his boot, the two brothers skidded and laughed their way down the steep little hill into Niklova.

☙

That evening after supper, Vasyl and Andrii smoked their pipes while their mother and their *teta*—their aunt Mariya Hryndyk—cleaned up the plates and utensils. The brothers sat on opposite benches, and between them, on the table, stood a kerosene lamp, its yellow flame casting a sickly glow about the room.

"*Mamko,* Vasyl won't go to the meeting in Bardeyov with me," tattled Andrii.

"No? Why not?" asked *Mamka,* mildly amused. Vasyl watched his mother shuffling around the room. She was bent and aged, and her gray hair was unkempt. "Vasyl, why won't you go to the meeting with your brother?"

Vasyl shrugged. "Andrii refuses to tell me anything about it. I ask him over and over, 'Andrii, what is a Rusyn?' 'Andrii, what would a Rusyn nation be like?' He won't answer me—not one word."

Andrii gasped. "*Ne pravda*—not true! I've told you everything!"

Vasyl laughed. "Really? I must not have been listening. When did you tell me everything?"

"I'm ignoring you, Vasyl. But, I tell you, if you come with me to Bardeyov, you will be as excited as I am about our people's future."

"No one can be as excited as you are."

"Vasyl, the world is changing before our eyes. All those who died in the last four years will not have died in vain. The war was fought for a purpose. The original reasons for the war have been replaced by higher ideals. Vylson has made this possible."

"I never saw Vylson at the front," snorted Vasyl.

"Vylson redefined the war in such a way as to make it possible to end it," explained Andrii.

Teta Mariya asked, "Who is Vylson? Will he be at the meeting?"

"Vylson is prezident of Ameryka," said Andrii.

The brothers' *mamka* was startled. "And he's coming to Bardeyov?"

"No, no, *Mamko.*" Andrii smiled. "He will be in Paris with other world leaders. In Bardeyov, there will be local Rusyn intellectuals and other leaders who are planning our people's future in accordance with the principles of self-determination set forth by Prezident Vylson."

Mamka and *Teta* Mariya stared at Andrii, and then looked at Vasyl with raised eyebrows. Vasyl merely shrugged. "Andrii talks like this now . . . *furt—* all the time."

ℰℐ

Late the next morning, Old Mykhal arrived. Andrii bade his mother and *Teta* Mariya farewell and walked with Vasyl to the *korchma*—the tavern in the middle of Niklova, where the old man and his horse, Sasha, awaited. Vasyl shook hands with Andrii, who then climbed aboard the old cart.

"I wish you would come with me, Vasyl," said Andrii.

Vasyl shook his head and laughed. "You nag like an old woman. Go, Andrii. Speak well for *nash narod*—our people." Then Vasyl addressed Old Mykhal. "You are taking Andrii as far as Zborov, yes?"

Old Mykhal nodded. "We will stop at Yalynkŷ and Smilno first. We will be in Zborov tomorrow, and Andrii will ride on to Bardeyov from there."

Vasyl stroked Old Sasha's neck. "Sasha is getting old. Can he still make it up the little hill on the way out of Niklova?"

Old Mykhal shrugged. "He is slow . . . slower than he used to be. He can still do it. We will have to stop at the top to rest him."

Old Sasha pulled the cart forward and the old man, startled by the sudden movement, tossed the reins.

On the slow ride up the hill out of Niklova, Andrii chatted excitedly about Rusyns, self-determination, and nation building, while Old Mykhal smoked his pipe and nodded good-naturedly at all the incomprehensible words and ideas. Eventually, after Andrii had exhausted his own knowledge of Prezident Vylson's Fourteen Points—he really only knew about the tenth point, which dealt with the inhabitants of the former Austro-Hungarian Empire—the two men rode in silence.

The old man pointed to the clouds on the horizon, casually mumbling something about the possibility of rain, or even snow, later that night.

"Yes, clouds!" cried Andrii. "Let me tell you about clouds!" And Andrii began a monologue on his latest poem—it was all in his head, he would write it down when he had time. It was a long poem about many things. But chiefly it was about the clouds high overhead that obscure heaven from men's eyes. And it was about the fact that, even though men may feel that God is hidden from them, God actually prefers to view his favorite creatures through a gray mist that dulls the thorny edges of mankind's sinful nature.

თ

After Andrii left Niklova, Vasyl returned to the Hryndyk hut and had lunch with his mother and *Teta* Mariya. After lunch *Teta* Mariya left to call on a sick friend. Vasyl sat in his mother's room and told her about Yevka.

"*Bozhe*—oh, God," murmured his mother, shaking her head, her eyes closed. "*Bozhe.*"

"*Mamko,* I wanted you to hear this from me. No one else knows—not even Andrii. There will be gossip at some point. I did not want you to have to ask me about rumors."

"*Bozhe.*"

"*Mamko,* listen to me. No one must hurt you over this. If anyone gossips about this and you are hurt by it, I will . . . I don't know . . . I will . . . put a stop to it."

Vasyl's mother smiled at her son. "I'm not bothered by what people think or say. Maybe you should be."

"No one's opinion has ever bothered me."

"No one's? Don't you think you should worry about God's opinion?"

Vasyl looked at the floor and sighed. "I don't want to talk about it."

His mother closed her eyes and rubbed her temples. "*Bozhe.* I will be a *baba*—a grandmother—again. When?"

"*Zyma*—winter. Maybe *yar*—spring."

"I see . . . I see. You and Yevka! I always wondered about the two of you—not because of anything you ever said, but because of the way Yevka always looked at you. This was before you went to Ameryka. Of course, you never noticed Yevka—all the girls looked at you! But, Yevka . . . she . . . well, I suppose I never should have arranged a match between Petro and Yevka. You and Yevka! *Bozhe!*"

"It is my fault and mine alone, *Mamko.*"

"A baby out of wedlock isn't made through one person's sin. It's the work of the devil. Nothing like this happens unless two people turn their backs on God, Vasyl."

"Yes . . . I know."

"Have you gone to confession?"

Vasyl lowered his head and drummed his fingers on his thigh.

"I can't hear you, son."

"I didn't say anything."

"No, you didn't say a word. See a priest soon, Vasyl. Don't carry this sin on your back too long."

"No . . . I suppose I shouldn't."

"Death is never far from any of us, Vasyl."

"*Znam*—I know . . ."

"*Dobre*—very well. I've said what a mother should say. Now, how is Yevka?"

"*Dobre.*"

"What will you do when the baby comes?"

"What will I do?"

"Yes. What will you do? Will you attend the baptism? Will you write a letter to Petro? What will you do?"

"*Ne znam*—I don't know."

Vasyl's mother sighed. "*Bozhe . . . Bozhe.* Keep your soul close to God, son. I'm sure Yevka is keeping her soul close to God. Do that, and you will be fine. *Bozhe!* Yevka . . . *Bozhe!*"

⁓

Andrii returned to Niklova four days later. At dinner, he began discussing the growing tensions between the emerging government in Prague and Bela Kun's Hungarian Bolsheviks in Eastern Slovakia. Both Vasyl and *Teta* Mariya tried to discourage Andrii's discourse with subtle expressions and shifting glances at *Mamka,* whose eyes were closed and whose face was contorted as if in pain. When these reproachful looks failed, and Andrii began discussing the possibility of fighting in the lowlands, Vasyl glowered at his brother and said, "We'll talk of this later. Tomorrow we will bring firewood inside for *Teta* and *Mamka* and then we will leave in the afternoon for Stara Polyanka."

Andrii, confused, nodded and ate in silence. After dinner, and after *Teta*

Mariya had helped their tired mother to bed in her back room, Andrii whispered to Vasyl, "What is wrong? What did I say?"

"*Mamka* is very tired. All your talk of Bolsheviks and Czech armies doesn't help. She is not well . . . here"—Vasyl held his hand over his heart—"or here." Vasyl pointed to his head.

Teta Mariya reentered the room and shook her finger in Andrii's face. "Your poor mother! The war was very hard on her, and you talk of more war. I won't have that talk in this house. Are you blind? Can you not see that she is ill?"

Crestfallen, Andrii held his head in his hands and chided himself under his breath. "I should have realized . . . how selfish . . . how uncaring . . . I should be beaten . . . I should—"

Vasyl patted Andrii on the back. "*Dobre*—very well. That's enough. If it will make you feel better, I'll slap you in the morning. Now it is time for sleep. We will have a long day tomorrow."

Teta Mariya helped the brothers prepare their beds in the main room of the house, and then she padded back to the little room next to her sister's. The brothers extinguished the kerosene lamp on the table and climbed into their beds. From the glowing hearth in the corner came the intermittent hissing of expiring coals.

"Vasyl?" whispered Andrii, lying on his back and staring into the dark.

"Yes."

"Do you remember when we were young and *Nyanko*—Papa—was still alive?"

"Of course."

"Do you remember how it was—how safe we felt?"

"Safe?"

"Yes. He took care of us, and he took care of *Mamka*. He was in charge of everything, and we followed him and did what we were told."

"We were children then, Andrii."

"Yes, I know. We felt safe because we trusted him; he provided for us. I remember those days and I wish I could feel that way again, except with God in the place of *Nyanko*. Why can't I trust God the way I trusted *Nyanko*? Is it lack of faith on my part? Am I not the Christian I should be? Do I—"

"Andrii, try to sleep. It will be a long day tomorrow."

"Yes, Sergeant. We will talk tomorrow."

"Yes, tomorrow."

Pause. "Vasyl?"

"Yes?"

"May I tell you one more thing?"

"Only if it is short and requires no comments from me."

"*Dobre*—very well. I'm glad I went to the meeting in Bardeyov. I realize more than ever that we need to put our trust in God, not in people. That is what I wanted to tell you. I want to trust in God with the same childish trust I had in *Nyanko* when we were young. That is all I wanted to say. Although I should tell you that I am thinking of the seminary in Pryashev again. I never really stopped thinking of the seminary. I don't think I have a talent for politics. I'm too impatient. It seems that in politics one must always settle for far less than one originally desired. I suppose God feels the same way about us. What do you think, Vasyl?"

Silence.

"*Dobre* . . . you are asleep." Andrii yawned. "I will pray that I be given the grace to trust God like a child . . . and not to worry about things . . . to be as I was when I was a child . . . when I was a child . . . I spoke like a child . . . I thought like a child . . . and . . . and these three . . . hope . . . faith . . . and . . . love . . . love never . . . fails . . . forever and ever . . ." Andrii's voice trailed off and his breathing became deep and rhythmic.

Vasyl rose, put on his boots, and donned his coat. He retrieved a cigarette from his large supply in the coat pocket, lit it using a splinter of wood thrust into the hearth coals, and then slipped out the door.

He walked through the village of Niklova, from one end to the other and back again all night long, chain-smoking his supply of cigarettes, and listening to *Potok* Ondava babbling, unseen in the dark . . . *tykho*—quietly.

～

It was late afternoon when Vasyl and Andrii finished stacking firewood outside the Hryndyk hut. When the brothers walked out of Niklova, Andrii spoke at length about the meeting he had attended in Bardeyov.

"Things are chaotic, Vasyl. I don't know what to think. I know less about the future of our people now than I did before I attended the meeting. I am discouraged. These people in Bardeyov will turn over our future to the politicians at the peace conference in Paris. We will fall under the rule of anyone who happens to make a good case for including us within their borders."

"Are you sorry you went to Bardeyov?"

"No, Vasyl. I'm not sorry. I feel older, though." Andrii smiled sheepishly.

Vasyl stopped and lit a cigarette. "Tell me what you learned," he said, inhaling deeply.

Andrii threw his hands in the air. "From what I could understand, we have several choices. 'Choices!' There's a word—'choices.' Whatever happens will happen despite our final 'choice,' I can tell you that! Rusyns to the east may want some sort of self-government within Hungary. There was talk of Rusyns joining Russia. What a notion! Even some Russians don't want to join Russia! That country is too far away and in too much turmoil. Some think we should join the Ukrainians, but they are across the mountains, and Russia hovers over them like a big mass of snow ready to avalanche without warning."

Vasyl pulled his cigarette from his mouth. "Russia will do what without warning?"

"'Avalanche.' You know, slide down from the mountains and sweep away everything in its path."

"I never saw mountains in Russia."

"What?"

"I never saw mountains. You said Russia would slide down a mountain."

"No, no, I meant it figuratively. Russia will always be some sort of threat to Ukrainians."

"*Dobre*—very well," nodded Vasyl. "That I can understand. Go on."

"Realistically, the best I think we can hope for is some sort of union with the new Czech-Slovak state. The Slovaks have declared themselves bound to the Czechs. I think that whatever the Slovaks do, western-dwelling Rusyns will inevitably have to follow. Maybe we can argue for self-rule."

"I thought you went to Bardeyov to watch the birth of a Rusyn state," said Vasyl, the corners of his mouth dropping.

Andrii nodded enthusiastically. "Yes, of course. But there are problems. A truly separate Rusyn nation would look something like an elongated oval from Stara Lyubovna in the west, to the headwaters of the Tisa River in the east. I suppose here in the western part of such a nation, the border would have to include Sanok to the north and everything south of Gorlice. Here, on the southern slopes of the Carpathians, we would have to include everything down to Bardeyov. Bardeyov itself would be good to have and then, of course, there is Pryashev. What do you think the chances are that the Slovaks will allow a Rusyn state to include Bardeyov and Pryashev?"

Vasyl thought for a moment and then said, "I suppose it depends on how much God loves Rusyns."

Andrii was annoyed. "Are you making fun of me?"

Vasyl laughed. "No, Andrii. I would never make fun of you."

Andrii brushed away his brother's comments with a flip of his hand. "You are making fun of me, but I don't mind. There are Rusyns to the north, across the mountains in Poland, who are prepared to join us Rusyns here to the south. Perhaps they could be part of the Czech-Slovak state. There will be a meeting next week in Poland, in the village of Florynka. I plan to attend and give them my support."

"I am happy for you, Andrii."

"You are?" asked Andrii guardedly.

"Yes. The men at these meetings need people like you—people with your talents."

"Would you like to come with me to Florynka, Vasyl? No, of course you wouldn't. Why do I bother to ask?"

"You go, Andrii. *Nash narod*—our people—need more men like you. I wish I could be like you. But I only wish to live quietly in the highlands." Vasyl lit another cigarette from the fading remains of his old cigarette. "I have been on this earth for twenty-seven years, and tonight I feel more peace here in my heart than I have known in a long time. I don't know why, Andrii . . . I don't know why." Vasyl looked up at the scintillating stars. "Maybe it's the sky. It looked just like this at the front, during the war."

Andrii laughed. "Of course—the sky is the same here as it is across the mountains."

"Is it? Well, yes . . . I suppose it is. Only . . . at the front there was something else . . . something very different. Maybe it was something on the ground. Everything was smaller."

"'Smaller?'"

"Yes, Andrii. Everything was smaller. We lived in the ground and never saw anything but the sky above." Vasyl snorted. "I was at the front too long. You will laugh, Andrii, but I think . . . I think there are times when I miss the front. I don't miss the death and fear. I miss the life I had in a small circle of men—men who are almost all dead now. I want only to live within a small circle with Stara Polyanka at the center. I don't want to think about anything outside that circle."

The sun set before the brothers reached Nŷzhnya Polyanka, and it was completely dark when they turned left on the road to Stara Polyanka. Vasyl stopped.

"Listen, Andrii."

Andrii cocked his head to the side. "What is it? What do you hear?"

"Wild pigs. They are near the Ondava."

"Yes, Vasyl, now I hear them. They are in front of us, yes? Let's avoid them and their sharp tusks."

Vasyl picked up two stones from the path and handed one to Andrii. "If they charge us, throw this."

Andrii turned the stone in his hand and gazed up at the stars. "On such a night as this, King David must have seen a similar sky." And Andrii quoted from the Book of Psalms:

> *When I see your heavens, the work of your fingers,*
>   *the moon and the stars that you set in place—*
> *What are humans that you are mindful of them,*
>   *mere mortals that you care for them?*

The brothers resumed their walk, while, near the banks of *Potok* Ondava, wild pigs snorted in the fallow potato fields.

CHAPTER THIRTY-SEVEN

The Linden Tree

IN FEBRUARY 1919, all households in Stara Polyanka eagerly awaited the warmer temperatures of approaching spring. In the Senchak household, eagerness was tempered with apprehension.

"How do you feel this morning, Yevka?" asked Paraska.

"*Dobre*—well. My back is sore, though."

"That's no surprise. There are only a few more weeks until the baby comes. How much longer do you think, hmm? Five weeks? Six weeks?"

Yevka ran her hands over her belly. "I think no more than six weeks."

"No more than six weeks," repeated Paraska, tapping her fingers on the table six times for emphasis. "Six weeks will pass quickly."

"Yes," said Yevka. "I suppose they will."

"And what will you tell people after six weeks?"

Yevka sat at the table with a weary sigh. "I don't know, Paraska . . . I don't know."

Paraska sat on the opposite side of the table. "Perhaps we should talk about it, Yevka."

"Today? You want to talk about it again?"

"Yes, Yevka—I want to talk about it again—today. Do you think you will be able to hide the baby when it comes? Of course not! People will talk soon, if they haven't started already. Your layers of clothing have hidden your belly all winter, but now . . . now it doesn't matter. Your belly is big, and you waddle when you walk. You haven't been to church in three weeks. I tell people you have *hryp*—the influenza—again. Others in the village are sick again, so I think people believe you might be ill. But, Yevka, I think some of the gossips in the village know something is different about you. And in six weeks they will know everything."

Yevka closed her eyes. "I know, Paraska . . . I know."

Paraska inspected her fingernails. "Andrii is coming today to watch you make *pysanký*. You could tell him while he is here," she suggested casually.

"No."

"Yevka, you have to start with someone. Vasyl probably already told him."

"Vasyl will not tell anyone."

"No . . . I suppose he won't." Paraska drummed her fingers lightly on the table. "Yevka?"

"Yes?"

"Yevka, I think you should announce your pregnancy to the village—let me tell you why. *Chekai*—wait—don't interrupt. Let me finish, and then I will say no more about this. I think it will make things easier for you when the baby comes. Let people talk all they want to about it. Then, after the birth, they will have nothing to say, except 'it is a boy' or 'it is a girl.' They will still say things about you behind your back, but they will appreciate your honesty. If they don't find out until the baby is born, they will resent you. Look at me, Yevka. Do you understand me? They will feel foolish for not knowing. I think some of the women already know—I'm almost certain. Women have a sense about these things. Already, there may be evil gossip among some women. You can blunt their mischief, Yevka."

Yevka laid her hands across her belly and said nothing.

Paraska reached across the table and touched her sister's shoulder. "These are only thoughts, Yevka. I will do or say whatever you wish."

"Thank you."

Paraska sighed heavily. "I am afraid, Yevka, that no matter what happens, you will be hurt."

"I know, Paraska . . . I know."

Paraska rose and went to the shelf by the hearth, where she gathered Yevka's *pysanký* tools and jars of dye, and brought them back to the table. She pulled an egg from her pocket and set it on the table. Then she went to the door. "I think I hear the boys. Yes, here they come with Andrii. You should move closer to the table, Yevka, if you don't want Andrii to know anything yet."

Myko and Danko entered the hut laughing and followed by Andrii, who doffed his hat and announced, "*Slava Isusu Khrystu*—Glory to Jesus Christ!"

"*Slava na viký*—Glory to Him forever," responded the sisters.

Andrii closed the door and hung his hat on a wall peg. "I hope I am not too late," he said. "Myko and Danko think I am a horse. They like to ride on my shoulders, over and over again, first one and then the other."

"We want to do it again!" shouted Danko.

"M-m-me f-f-first!" cried Paraska's Myko.

"Shush, both of you!" scolded Paraska.

Danko was insistent. "But, *Teto*—Aunt, it was FUN!"

"Y-y-yes, *M-Mamko!* F-fun!"

"Shush, both of you!" shouted Paraska. "I won't listen to this. Sit quietly at the end of the table—both of you. Now you will have kasha. Do you want kasha, Andrii?"

"Yes, that would be good. Yevka, how are you? I hear you have been ill."

"I'm better . . . much better now, thank you. We hear you have been away for a while."

"Yes, I was over the mountains in Poland. I was in Florynka and Sanok, to meet with our Lemko Rusyn brothers who wish to join with us who live south of the mountains." Andrii sat down when Paraska placed a bowl of kasha on the table. "It looks good, Paraska, thank you." Andrii described his experiences in Poland, and when he finished eating he turned to Yevka. "I want to get started, if you are ready, Yevka."

"Yes." Yevka indicated the egg and tools on the table. "How do you want to begin?"

Andrii tossed his hands in the air. "I want to know everything about *pysankŷ*. On the way home from Russia at the end of the war, I thought about writing poems about our people. I remembered your *pysankŷ*, and in the back of my head I stored the idea for a poem about them. Do everything you would normally do to produce one *pysanka*, Yevka. But as you work, tell me what you are doing and what you are thinking."

"What I'm thinking?"

"Yes. Tell me what you are thinking as you make your designs. I brought a notebook and pencil—I will observe you and make a few notes. You talk and I will listen and learn."

Yevka nodded and picked up the egg. "I'm not sure what I can say about an egg—I suppose we use the egg because it is round and light in color and because—"

Andrii had begun writing but stopped and interrupted Yevka. "Yes, Yevka, the egg is round and oblong. There is something in an egg's shape—in its perfect form—it is the womb from which we all emerged. It is—"

Paraska cleared her throat. "*To pravda*—that is true!" She picked up the empty bowls in front of the boys. "'The womb' is true. Is that what you were thinking, Yevka?"

"Well . . ."

Andrii scribbled notes and continued. "It is more than just an egg or an image of a womb. The egg is our people's quiet world in miniature—a world we can hold in our hand—a decorated shell of earthly color surrounding life within. While the iconostasis in the church is a physical representation of everything holy and invisible in our faith, each egg is an image of everything earthly and visible in our daily lives. It is the—" Andrii stopped when Yevka held the egg over a dish of water. "I'm sorry, Yevka. I'm talking too much. I will only listen from now on. You will not hear another word from me until I leave. *Proshu*—please, go on."

"This is rainwater," Yevka explained, lowering the egg into the dish. "Rainwater is pure—like the tears of the Mother of God."

Andrii's eyes widened as he scribbled in his notebook and mumbled, "'The tears of the Mother of God!' That is good! Very good!"

"Her tears produce pure water," continued Yevka. "Not salty tears like ours. Her tears clean the egg."

"Yes, salty tears," grunted Paraska. "Salty tears from sinful eyes." Paraska sat at the spinning wheel in the corner, arranging unspun flax on the distaff.

Yevka pulled the egg from the water and dried it with the kerchief. "We do not use cooked eggs for *pysankŷ*—that would kill the life inside. Nor do we empty the egg after we dye it. It is best to keep the life in the egg."

"Yes," professed Paraska. "There is life in that womb." Paraska began turning the spinning wheel and drawing flaxen thread from the distaff.

While holding the egg in her left hand, Yevka heated a small tin of blackened beeswax over the lone candle in the middle of the table. "The beeswax must come from the church," she said. "That is the best wax for this kind of work."

Andrii looked up from his notebook. "Yevka, this is beeswax from the candles made by Father Yaroslav, yes?"

"Yes."

"*Dobre*—good," nodded Andrii scribbling in his notebook.

When the wax melted, Yevka moved it to the side of the candle, close enough to the heat to remain fluid but not close enough to burn. She held the egg between the tips of the fingers of her left hand, and with her right hand, dipped the nail into the melted wax, and then touched the nail to the egg, making a small, round dot, and then drew the nail toward her, creating the pointed tail of an inverted teardrop. She moved the nail in and out of the beeswax and onto the surface of the egg quickly, turning the egg deftly and creating a wax line from pole to pole and up the other side of the egg. Then, she turned the egg a quarter turn and made three long strokes: a single stroke with a wing stroke on each side. "The swallow—he comes to us each spring, and the warm weather follows."

Yevka lowered the egg into the yellow dye and explained to Andrii, "Where there is wax, no dye will stain. When I remove the wax, those parts will be white—the swallow will be white—it will be pure like the rainwater."

Yevka retrieved the egg from the dye with a wooden spoon and patted it dry. She dipped the nail into the wax and drew on each face of the egg, centered below the swallows, a ring of wax strokes with the tails pointing outward. "The sun—light for the world."

"Yes," nodded Andrii. "The sun, like *Khrystos*—light for the world."

Yevka lowered the egg into the green dye and set the wooden spoon aside. "When this last wax is removed, the yellow color will be revealed."

Andrii picked up the nail, holding it like a pen. Yevka pushed the little tin of wax closer to Andrii. "Try it yourself," she said. "Dip the nail in the wax and then draw the wax across your thumbnail."

"My thumbnail?"

"Yes. It is like the shell of an egg."

Andrii dipped the nail into the wax and touched it to his thumbnail. But instead of creating a smooth stroke, he smeared his thumbnail with black wax. When he attempted to scrape the wax into the desired shape, Yevka shook her head.

"There is no fixing it once the wax has touched the surface," she explained, taking back the *pysaltse*—the writing tool. "If you made a mistake like that on an egg, the design would be ruined."

"Oh, yes," said a flustered Andrii. "I see . . . yes, I see . . ."

Yevka pulled the egg from the green dye, patted it dry and then made a series of strokes along the lines running pole to pole. "Green—eternal life."

Yevka lowered the egg into the red dye. "The final color—red—the color of blood . . . the blood of *Khrystos,* who died that we may live."

"*Slava Isusu Khrystu!*" cried Paraska, working the flaxen threads through her fingers.

Yevka extracted the egg from the red dye, patted it dry, and handed it to Andrii. "Hold it close to the flame, and when the wax melts, wipe it away. Hold it closer."

"*Oi!*"

"Not that close—you will burn yourself—yes, that's it . . . like that."

Andrii turned the egg, wiping away the black wax and gradually the colors and design emerged. "Yevka!" he gasped. "It is a miracle! Look at the sun! It is just as you said, the 'Light for the World.' And the swallow! Look how it sweeps its wings in flight above the green leaves. You are a poet, Yevka!"

Yevka smiled. "I am?"

Andrii nodded vigorously. "Yes! Yes, Yevka—you are writing poetry on eggs, just as I am writing poetry on paper. My poems are about the birds and the trees and our people and our ways. Your poems are identical to mine— only on eggshells. You write about the natural world that surrounds us, and so do I. Today I listen to your thoughts as you create a *pysanka,* and then I write what you say. The best poetry is sometimes nothing more than writing dictation." Andrii wrote in his notebook. "Your poem will be about the new life God brings to the earth in the spring."

"*Tak dai Bozhe*—may God grant it!" cried Paraska.

Yevka reddened. "I thought the poem was about *pysankŷ.*"

"It is. But it is about more than just *pysankŷ,* Yevka. Every poem is about something and everything. Your egg shows pictures of birds and the sun and green plants, but it tells the story of new life in spring and of salvation and eternal life—something and everything. What shall I call your poem?" Andrii stroked his chin and studied the egg. Suddenly he gasped, *"Bozhe!"* Then he covered his mouth. "I shouldn't call on God like that. But I just realized something. The wax is from the candles in the church! *To pravda,* Yevka?"

"*To pravda*—that is true."

"And the wax is from the beehive!"

"Of course it is," said Paraska, her foot rhythmically slapping the pedal of the spinning wheel. "What of it?"

"Father Yaroslav harvests honey from his hives. The bees make honey from the nectar of the linden tree flowers. *Lypŷ*—the linden trees—stand next to the church—well, they stand where the church once stood and where it will stand again someday. Father Yaroslav will bless the *pysankŷ* on *Velykden*— Easter. He will bless them outside, under the linden trees—the same trees that produce the flowers that attract the bees who make the wax that is used for the church candles that burn down to small wax smudges that are used to make the *pysankŷ* that are blessed under the linden tree!" Andrii took a deep breath. "It is a circle—uninterrupted and eternal." Andrii's eyes widened. "*Ioi!* That is good! *Dobre*—good . . . *dobre* . . ." he muttered as he scribbled in his notebook. "Eternal life . . . each spring . . . God's creation . . . new life . . ."

Yevka glanced at Paraska, but her sister merely smiled and continued to pull the thread from the distaff.

Andrii stood and paced the room, organizing his thoughts. "I will call the poem, '*Lypa*'—The Linden Tree. It will be about a woman's skill with the *pysaltse,* that is, how she 'writes' on the surface of an egg. But it will also be about the yearning of our people to write our own history and destiny on the face of the earth—oh, that is good! I like that!" Andrii sat down and scribbled in his notebook. "The poem will draw together some of the other ideas from other poems I have on paper and in my head—like Vasyl's, and the one I haven't finished about Father Yaroslav—and it will form a picture . . . a painting made up of words in our language for us and . . ."

Yevka turned the egg in her hand. The endless tangled branches of green leaves encircled this little creation, and the light seemed to originate from within. And there, in the cloudless sky, the unrestrained swallow soared above the living earth.

"And in each poem I will re-create a part of our way. It will be a book of poems—yes, a book—and I will start with simple verses of common events in our lives and in the green life around us—the green life God gives us every spring—the living creation that, despite war and misery and death, continues to move about us. Yes, it is God at work around us, creating for us and through us in endless, timeless circles while we, in our brief lives—"

Yevka closed her hand around the egg while Paraska turned the spinning wheel and collected the flaxen threads on the spindle.

CHAPTER THIRTY-EIGHT

Fruit

ON AN AFTERNOON IN LATE WINTER, Paraska and Yevka, both heavily bundled against the cold, walked together toward the lower half of Stara Polyanka. Large dark clouds moved slowly across the sky, and an icy breeze blew intermittently from the north. The boys, Myko and Danko, walked in front of their mothers, laughing and jostling one another.

"Myko, let's run!" cried Danko.

"*Ch-ch-chekai*—w-w-wait! N-n-not so f-f-fast!"

Danko ran ahead anyway, with the slower Myko trailing behind and pumping his arms wildly.

"Look, Yevka," said Paraska, shaking her head. "Look at my Myko. What am I going to do?"

Yevka looked at Myko and then at Paraska. "What are you going to do about what?"

"Have you heard him speak? Have you not heard?"

"Do you mean his stammer?"

"Yes, Yevka. You know that is what I meant. Women in the village are starting to talk about it."

"Well . . . I don't think it is that noticeable."

"Of course you don't, Yevka! Your Danko doesn't stammer. He speaks well."

"He is eight or nine months older than your Myko."

"No, Yevka. Age has nothing to do with it. My Myko is a stammerer." Paraska sighed heavily. "It is either Vasko's fault or mine. I'll never know for certain. One of us sinned—that is all that is certain. Now, Myko carries the price for our sin in his voice."

Yevka took her sister's hand and squeezed. "You don't know that. Myko is a good, sweet boy."

"Of course he is! He is my son! But . . . when he tries to speak . . . I know that one of us . . . one of us . . . Vasko or I . . . one of us sinned." Paraska stopped and massaged her thigh.

"Does it hurt?" asked Yevka.

"Yes, it always hurts—now more than most times—probably because the air is so cold when it blows. Listen to your Danko. Do you hear how well he speaks? I would think that with a father like Vasko, my Myko would be a great talker. Vasko was no stammerer. Do you remember how Vasko could talk, Yevka? *Bozhe!* He could go on and on!"

"I remember, Paraska."

Paraska gave her thigh one last squeeze. "*Dobre*—very well—let's go." The sisters followed their boys toward the old Dzyamba house. "Do you think I sinned, Yevka? Do you think I am to blame for Myko's speech?"

"Of course not."

"Then you must think it is Vasko's fault."

"I don't think it is anyone's fault."

"But, Yevka, it is due to someone's sin or to some evil action. How else can it be explained?"

Yevka shrugged. "*Ne znam*—I don't know. Myko was born during the fighting here in Stara Polyanka. Maybe, while you still carried Myko within you, his voice was touched by the war." Yevka shrugged again. "*Mozhe . . . ne znam*—maybe . . . I don't know."

Paraska's eyes widened and she gripped Yevka's arm as they walked. "Yes, Yevka! I never thought of that! *Mash pravdu*—you are right! It was the war—the war made my Myko a stammerer—not I and not Vasko. It was the war. Think of it! Do you remember the guns, Yevka? Do you remember their sound?"

"Yes, they were loud."

"Yes, yes, they were loud. But do you remember how they sounded? 'Du-du-du-du-du-du!' Do you remember?"

"Yes. I don't think I will ever forget . . ."

"And now my Myko's voice gets stuck like those guns when he tries to speak: du-du-du-du-du-du! You are right, Yevka, *mash pravdu*—you are right! It was the war." Paraska smiled and nodded. "It was the war," she murmured. "Only the war and nothing else. *Lem voina bŷla*—it was only the war."

The boys waited by the entrance to the old Dzyamba place, and then followed their mothers through the yard and past the charred ruins of the old log house to a little orchard in the back of the property.

Paraska pointed to the only two trees remaining in the orchard. "Soon, Yevka, this apple tree and this plum tree will leaf and blossom. You can help them—you are pregnant and so are they. Walk around the trees while I speak to them."

Yevka was doubtful and raised an eyebrow at her sister. "These are not our trees."

"No, Yevka, they are not. But it would be a sin to let the fruit go to waste."

"I don't know . . . it seems to me that it is stealing. If we steal while I am pregnant, my child might grow up to be a thief."

Paraska placed her hands on her waist and chided her sister. "No, Yevka. It is stealing only if the owners still lived here. They are gone, and we are tending the trees until they return. You must help. I have pruned them so that this season they will bear great fruit. Last year these damn trees produced little and"—Paraska covered her mouth and then whispered to Yevka—"I shouldn't have cursed the trees—what must they think of me? They will produce nothing this year if I speak poorly of them. I hope they didn't hear me. You must help, Yevka. Walk around the trees."

Yevka rubbed her belly. "Well . . ."

"Go on, Yevka. Begin with the plum tree and I will do the talking. You will see—this year we will have fruit." Yevka began walking around the plum tree while Paraska nodded her approval. "Yes, Yevka, that is good." Then Paraska addressed the plum tree. "Now, plum tree, you listen to me. May you be full of life like the woman who walks around you: may you bear much fruit! Yes, Yevka, *dobre*—good. Go around again. Go three times! Are you paying attention, plum tree? Be like this woman—bear fruit! Now, Yevka, walk around the apple tree. Yes, *dobre*. Do you see this woman, apple tree? Do you see how easily she bears fruit? May you be like this woman and bear good fruit. Yevka, *ishi raz*—again!"

After the third time around the apple tree, Yevka stood at her sister's side. "Do you really think this will work, Paraska?"

"Of course." Then Paraska whispered out of the corner of her mouth, "Ask me about the ax."

"What?"

"The ax, Yevka, the ax," hissed Paraska. "Don't you remember? We talked about it this morning."

"Oh, yes—the ax." Yevka faced the trees and carefully enunciated, "Paraska-do-we-have-an-AX-at-our-house?"

"Why, yes, indeed we do, Yevka. It is a very sharp ax! Later this year we will use it to cut down dead, unproductive trees—trees that, for selfish reasons known only to themselves, refuse to bear fruit. Yes, Yevka, it is a VERY SHARP AX." Paraska leaned closer to Yevka's ear and chuckled softly. "That should do it. If these trees have any sense at all, they'll know what they need to do. *Dobre*—good! We can go home now."

The sisters herded the boys in front of them, and headed back through the yard to the road. There they encountered Yurko on his way to the upper half of the village. Paraska stopped and held up her shawl to cover Yevka's face.

"Paraska, I can't see."

"Hush, Yevka—I know what is best. *Slava Isusu Khrystu*—Glory to Jesus Christ, Yurko! No, don't stop, Yurko—continue on your way. *Dobrÿi den*—good day."

Yevka attempted to wave aside her sister's shawl. "Paraska, I can't see."

"*Chekai*—wait, Yevka. He's passing."

"Paraska, something is wrong. I—"

"Shh, Yevka!"

"But, Paraska, I—"

Paraska lowered the shawl and shuddered. "He is gone, Yevka. It is good I covered your eyes in time. You mustn't look at anyone like Yurko—not until after the birth. You don't want your child to grow up to be an idiot, do you?"

Yevka shook her head. "No, I suppose not. But—"

"No, I didn't think so."

"Only . . . I . . ."

"No, Yevka, do not feel badly for Yurko. He can't help what he is. What is it, Yevka? You don't look well. What is wrong?"

"I think it is time."

"Time for what?"

"The baby."

"The baby! What makes you think it is time?"

"It is wet down my legs."

"*Oi*, Yevka! Why didn't you tell me sooner? Hurry! It is not far! Go home and I will go find Mariya—come boys, hurry!"

The sisters struggled to their destinations, one limping to fetch the midwife, Mariya Vantsa, and the other waddling back to the Senchak house.

ᏗᎣ

Later that evening, long after Myko and Danko had fallen asleep on the bed in a dark corner of the room, Paraska worked under Mariya Vantsa's supervision, untying knots in clothing and linens around the hut. "Untie all of them," ordered Mariya. "The baby will come much easier if there are no knots in the home. Look, Paraska, your own scarf has a knot." Paraska pulled the scarf off her head and was loosening the offending knot when both she and Mariya were summoned to Yevka's side by another in a series of ever more frequent wails.

"*Oiii!*"

Paraska wiped Yevka's sweating temples and looked at Mariya Vantsa positioned at Yevka's open knees. "It is now, yes?"

"No, no, no. It won't come for a while. We have a long wait ahead of us." Mariya glanced about the room.

"What is it?" asked Paraska. "Are there more knots? Did I miss some?"

"No . . . no," said Mariya slowly. "I was thinking . . . it is a cold evening . . . perhaps it will snow . . . do you have any of that good *slyvovitsa*— plum brandy—that you make."

Paraska studied Yevka's face and then sat next to Mariya. "Do you really think she should have *slyvovitsa*?"

Mariya laughed. "Not for Yevka—for us! It is going to be a long, cold night."

Paraska blinked at Mariya and then went to a shelf near the table, where she retrieved a bottle and a small cup.

"Two cups," ordered Mariya. "Don't make me drink alone."

Paraska fetched a second cup from the shelf and returned to Mariya's side, where she poured the *slyvovitsa* into the cups. "How long, do you think, until the baby comes?"

Mariya shook her head. "*Ne znam*—I don't know. It could be all night . . . or . . . this is her second child . . . so . . . maybe not so long. The baby will come when it is ready. *Na zdorovya*—to your health!" Mariya clicked her cup against Paraska's cup and the two women downed their drinks in one swallow. "Ah, that is good, Paraska!" Mariya squinted at Yevka. "Where is her garlic? I don't see it."

Paraska searched the bed and then found it on the floor. "Here it is."

Mariya shook her head in disgust. "*Bozhe moi,* Paraska! Place it by her neck. If you have any concern for the future of your sister's child, don't let her lose it again. Only it can protect against the work of the evil one." Mariya tapped the side of her cup with a finger and cleared her throat. "Maybe one more . . . hmm, Paraska?"

"Yes . . . yes, of course. Here is the bottle."

Mariya poured two cups of *slyvovitsa* and handed one to Paraska. "Here, let us drink to the health of the child."

Paraska took her cup and the two women drank, smacking their lips in unison afterward. "No one makes *slyvovitsa* like this! Paraska, you are an artist!" Mariya banged her cup on the table and leaned her head toward Paraska. "So! *Khto nyanko*—who is the papa? It can't be Yevka's husband, Petro—he hasn't been in Stara Polyanka for years. I think I should at least know who the father is. Don't you agree, Paraska?"

"Well . . . yes . . . I suppose you should."

"After all, you asked me to deliver the child."

"Yes . . . yes, I did."

"I won't tell a soul, Paraska."

Paraska looked into her empty cup and sighed. "No . . . you must not tell anyone."

"God knows there are plenty of rumors about the father."

Paraska closed her eyes. "Everyone discusses this?"

Mariya raised her cup to her lips and tapped the bottom to dislodge any lingering drop of alcohol. "What else do gossipy women have to discuss? The war is over—the influenza seems to have run its course. So, they talk about your sister."

Paraska swallowed hard, looked at her sister, and then leaned closer to Mariya. "You must not tell anyone."

Mariya closed her eyes and shook her head. "Not a soul."

Paraska opened her mouth, paused, and then whispered, "Vasyl . . . Vasyl Rusynko."

Mariya gleefully slapped her knee. "I knew it! *Ya mala pravdu*—I was right! I knew it!" Then she quickly composed herself and held a finger to her lips. "Not a soul, Paraska—not a soul."

Paraska groaned and poured two generous servings of *slyvovitsa*. Raising her cup, Paraska toasted Mariya. "*Na zdorovya*—to your health."

"*Na zdorovya,* Paraska. To the health of the mother! *Ioi,* that's good *slyvovitsa.* You know, Paraska, if you didn't want every loose tongue between here and Zborov wagging about your sister, you should have announced her pregnancy long ago, along with the name of the father. Nothing keeps hens from clucking like a few scraps of food. Believe me, Paraska, there are wicked gossips in this valley. You were right to trust me, though. What is that awful noise? Who is yelling at this hour of the night?"

Paraska stood, a little unsteadily, and shuffled to her sister's side. "I think it was Yevka. Yevka, was that you? Do you need something?"

Yevka's moist face was red and her eyes were shut tightly. "No . . . no," she panted. "It hurts . . . *Bozhe moi,* it hurts!"

Paraska shouted to Mariya Vantsa, "Yevka says it hurts!"

"OF COURSE IT HURTS!" roared Mariya. "She's having a baby!"

Yevka cried out again. Paraska, her lower lip trembling, whimpered, "Mariya, shouldn't we do something? Can't we ease her pain?" Paraska felt Yevka's forehead and cheeks. "*Bozhe!* She's so hot!"

Mariya gestured toward the little window near the door. "Paraska, place your hands against the cold glass, and then hold her face in your hands."

Paraska obeyed, and, as she held her hands to Yevka's hot cheeks, Mariya staggered to the bedside with the bottle of *slyvovitsa.* "Get another cup, Paraska," said Mariya.

"Another cup?"

"Yes," nodded Mariya. "Get a cup for Yevka."

Paraska retrieved another cup from the shelf on the wall and handed it to Mariya. "Do you think she should have this? Is it a good idea?"

Mariya filled the little cup with *slyvovitsa.* "Of course she should have some. It will help. It will relax her. Here, take it to her." Mariya handed the cup to Paraska and then returned to her seat at the table.

Paraska pushed the cup against her sister's lips. "Here, Yevka, take this. Mariya said it will make things easier for you." Paraska tipped the drink into Yevka's mouth.

Yevka coughed and gasped. "Take that away! *Bozhe,* I'll be sick!"

Paraska shuffled to her seat next to Mariya. "Well?" said Mariya. "Did she drink it?"

Paraska tilted the cup to her lips. "Yes—I think so—the cup was almost empty."

"Good!" shouted Mariya. "That is good! Here, Paraska, I poured two more cups of your famous *slyvovitsa*. Let us drink to the health of the father!" Mariya jabbed her elbow into Paraska's side and winked. "Whoever he may be!"

"Yes . . . well . . ."

The two women drank and then banged their cups on the table. Mariya began to giggle and Paraska happily joined her. "What . . . *he-he-he* . . . are we laughing about, Mariya?"

"I was thinking, Paraska, that I wish I had some of your *slyvovitsa* when I delivered my three children." Mariya snorted and then roared, "*Bozhe moi!* I wish I had some of your *slyvovitsa* when I *conceived* my three children! You laugh, Paraska, but you don't know my husband, Mykolai. The clumsy ox! We're lucky we had any children at all!"

Paraska and Mariya leaned forward and wheezed uncontrollably with laughter.

Another series of cries from the bed brought both women upright in their seats. "What the devil was that!" cried Mariya.

Paraska staggered to Yevka's side. "It was Yevka! Mariya, come look at her! I think I see the child's head appearing!"

Mariya appeared at the foot of the bed. "Pull the blanket off of her legs, Paraska. How can you see anything with that blanket in the way?"

Paraska giggled. "Oh . . . of course . . . you are right."

"Yes," said Mariya swaying unsteadily. "It won't be long now. Look, do you see how open she is? There is the child's head. Very soon now . . . very soon."

Paraska nodded and arranged several garlic cloves around Yevka's neck. "Yevka, did you hear? Mariya says it will not be much longer."

Yevka arched her back and hissed through her teeth, the saliva bubbling at the white-caked corners of her mouth.

Moist-eyed, Paraska looked from the pain on her sister's contorted face to the clinical concern on Mariya Vantsa's face and opened her mouth to speak. The sound that emanated came not from her own lips but, rather, from her sister's: "*OI!*" It came from deep within an exhausted soul with a passion and urgency that startled Myko and Danko from their drowsy state in their bunk and brought their hands to their ears. The cries filled the hut, and outside a dog barked.

Paraska blinked her eyes dry, and then noticed that Mariya was speaking to her above the din. "Take it, Paraska!" Mariya was shouting. "Take it!"

Paraska picked up a sheepskin blanket and opened it to receive the slimy infant whose piercing cries now replaced Yevka's. Paraska wrapped the child tightly inside the warm wool and placed the bundle on Yevka's chest.

After a light tapping from outside the hut, the door opened to admit merely the scarfed heads of Anna Barna and Mariya Guzii. "Well?" queried Anna. "We've stood in the snow half the night, and now we hear the cry of a baby. What did she have?"

"Hmm?" mumbled Paraska and Mariya Vantsa simultaneously.

"Is it a boy or a girl?" snapped Mariya Guzii. "Haven't you looked?"

Paraska and Mariya Vantsa blinked at one another. "We forgot to look," slurred Paraska as she peeled back layers of sheepskin. "Mariya, come here. Mariya, did you hear me?"

"Hmm?" mumbled Mariya Vantsa, her eyes half shut.

"Look at the child, Mariya. I can't see. Is it a boy or is it a girl?"

Mariya opened her eyes, swooped her head almost into the sheepskin, and straightened. "Tell Vasyl Rusynko he has a daughter!" she announced. Anna Barna and Mariya Guzii giggled and their heads disappeared behind the closing door.

Paraska's jaw dropped and she sputtered at Mariya, "You—you clucking hen! *Huntsutko*—you troublemaker! You—"

"Paraska," pleaded an exhausted Yevka. "Not so loud."

"Take your hands off Yevka's child, *bosorko*—you witch!" screamed Paraska. "Get out of our house, *suko*—you bitch!" Paraska grabbed Mariya Vantsa by the neck and hustled her to the door. "*Idy von*—get out! Never return!"

Mariya Vantsa stumbled outside into the darkness shrieking, "How dare you throw me out!"

"*Idy do didka, sobako*—go to the devil, you dog!" barked Paraska, slamming the door. "*Tota sobaka*—that dog! *Tota suka*—that bitch!" Mumbling incoherently, Paraska returned to Yevka's side and leaned over Yevka. "How is my niece?" she slurred.

"It's not your niece," sighed Yevka wearily. "He's your nephew."

Paraska closed her eyes. "She's my what?"

"Paraska, listen to me. Try to understand. It's a boy, not a girl."

Paraska opened her eyes. "*To ye khlopets*—this is a boy?"

"*Hei, khlopets*—yes, a boy." Yevka opened the sheepskin. "Look, Paraska, can you see?"

Paraska peeked at the naked child and then massaged her temples. "Mariya Vantsa is blinder than I am. How much did she have to drink? *Tota piyachka*—that drunk! I'll send her a bill for all the *slyvovitsa* she drank! I'll go to Shlomo Lentz in the morning. The *zhyd*—the Jew—will write a bill for me. As payment I will milk that cow of his for a month! And I will pay Mariya exactly nothing for the delivery—*nich*! You did almost all the work yourself, Yevka! *Tota bosorka*—that witch—Mariya told everyone you had a daughter! And that Vasyl is the father! Feh, Mariya Vantsa! *Tota piyachka*—that drunk! *Tota suka*—that bitch!"

"Paraska, please, not so loud."

"Of course, Yevka. I will be quiet. Don't worry. Everything is fine now. Everything will be even better when Mariya—that bitch!—when Mariya gets my bill. Now, Yevka, there is one more thing to do."

"What is it, Paraska?"

"We need to tie the cord."

Yevka bit her lip nervously. "Do you think you can do it, Paraska?"

"Of course I can! Has the afterbirth come out yet?"

"Yes . . . I think so . . . but . . ."

"I'll get the knife."

"Yes, but . . . oh, Paraska . . . I don't know—"

"Yes, this knife is good—it is a good sharp knife."

"Paraska?"

"Yes?"

"Are you sure you can do this? You had a great amount of *slyvovitsa*."

Paraska nodded solemnly. "Yes, but I don't get drunk on my own *slyvovitsa*. Besides, I'm too angry at Mariya Vantsa to be drunk. I'm fine now. Don't worry—I can tie and cut. I won't hurt the boy." Paraska picked up the placenta. "It's big. I'll bury it in the garden in the morning—we'll plant a plum tree over it this year. Now, Yevka, hold two fingers around your son's cord so I can measure for the knot. *Dobre*—good. Now, hold the cord tightly while I tie it. *Dobre*. Now one last cut. *Tak*—like so! Look, Yevka. What do you think?"

"*Dyakuyu*—thank you, Paraska. He looks good, yes?"

"Yes. Yes, he does. But be careful, Yevka. Too many compliments can bring bad luck." Paraska smiled at the boy and made puckering sounds with her lips. "Look, Yevka—he has curly black hair—that means that he will be wealthy. He doesn't clench his fists, so he will share his wealth with his family and others. His wealth probably won't be measured in bags of gold or silver but he will be known someday as a generous man." Paraska kissed the boy's hand and then became serious. "Yevka, we must prevent an exchange by a *bosorka*—a witch." Paraska reached into her pocket and held up a length of red thread. "Do you see? I am prepared. We'll tie it around his wrist— loosely, but not too loosely. If one morning we find the boy without the thread around his wrist, we will know he was stolen during the night by a *bosorka*—no doubt Mariya Vantsa herself!—and replaced with an evil child. The evil spirits are always at work around us, Yevka. The next few days are the most dangerous. It is best that we take turns keeping an eye on the boy." Yawning, Paraska sat on one of the benches. "You close your eyes and rest, Yevka. I'll watch now." Paraska put her head down on the table. "You rest . . . and I'll watch the boy . . . such a good boy . . . a shame to lose him to a *bosorka* . . . let Mariya Vantsa come for him, *tota bosorka*—that witch . . . I'll throw her in the Ondava . . . *suka*—bitch . . . *suka* . . ." Paraska closed her eyes and began to snore softly.

Yevka cradled her son in one arm, stroking his cheek with her free hand. His eyes were shut tight, and he pressed his face against his mother's probing finger. Yevka cupped the boy's head in her hand and whispered, "*Sŷne moi*— my son, what will they say to you? What names will they call you behind your back?" She kissed his forehead. "They will never hurt you—*nygda*— never . . . *nygda, sŷne moi . . . nygda . . .*"

CHAPTER THIRTY-NINE

The Inheritance

IN THE MORNING Paraska prepared the boy's first bath. On the table in the middle of the Senchak hut, she placed a small pot of hot water and two small towels. Propped up in bed against a small stack of pillows, Yevka breast-fed her baby.

Rummaging about the room, Paraska gathered a variety of objects which she placed on a small piece of sheepskin next to the pot of hot water. Then, after scolding Myko and Danko for dawdling over breakfast, Paraska ordered the boys to sweep the snow from the entrance to the hut. "And don't take too long about it—it is cold outside. Yevka, is he done feeding yet?"

"Almost. He's on the other nipple now."

"*Dobre*—good," said Paraska. "I'll give him his first bath. As midwife, Mariya Vantsa should be here to do it, but, as long as I breathe she will never enter this house again. *Nygda*—never! *Tota huntsutka*—that troublemaker! *Tota sobaka*—that dog! *Tota*—"

"Paraska, please!" interrupted Yevka. "The boys . . ."

Paraska ushered the boys outside, handing them reed brooms. "Go. Sweep. Now." She closed the door behind the boys. "Mariya Vantsa—feh! *Tota sobaka*—"

Again, Yevka interrupted. "Is the bath ready, Paraska?"

"No—I haven't put anything in the water yet. Is he done feeding?"

"I think so . . . he's asleep."

"Well then, he's done. I'm going to add everything to the water now. Let's see . . . what do we have? I'm putting in garlic to keep evil away from him. And here are two old links of iron chain so he will be strong. I borrowed a silver coin—a nice big one from Father Yaroslav: it goes in the water so the boy will be wealthy someday. So that he will work well in the forest, I'm adding the head of an ax. Is there anything else you want me to add, Yevka?"

"Yes—sugar and salt."

"Ah, yes, of course!" said Paraska, going to the shelf near the hearth. "Sugar and . . . yes, there it is . . . salt . . . *dobre*—good." Paraska returned to the hot water pot and added a pinch of each additional item. "Sugar, so he will have a sweet manner about him, and salt, so he will be agreeable."

Myko and Danko came inside and ran across the room to warm themselves at the hearth. "Did you bathe him yet?" asked Danko.

"Soon," said Paraska. "You boys may watch if you don't get in the way. Yevka, I'll take the boy now."

"I'll bring him."

"Yevka, don't be foolish. You are too weak. Hand me the baby before you drop him. And take care that his feet don't point to the doorway like a corpse to be taken for burial."

"*Dobre*—good, take him," said Yevka. "I'll sit at the table and watch." She shuffled to the table and lowered herself gingerly onto one of the benches.

Paraska positioned the boy on the sheepskin with his feet pointing away from the doorway and lowered one of the cloths into the warm water, wringing it out and folding it in half before gently wiping clean the boy's arms and legs.

"Why don't you just pick him up and dunk him in the pot?" suggested Danko.

"Because, he is not a chicken to be boiled," explained Paraska, wiping the boy's face and neck. "This is the first good look you boys have had of him. Danko, this is *tvoi brat*—your brother; Myko, he is *tvoi bratanets*—your cousin."

"He l-l-looks f-f-funny, *Mamko*," observed Myko.

"That," explained Paraska, "is because he was born just last night. His head will look misshapen for a few days. It doesn't look too bad, does it, Yevka?"

"No . . . I don't think so . . ." Yevka smiled proudly. "He is very hand—"

Paraska placed a finger over her sister's lips. "Shh, Yevka. Keep your voice low if you are going to say things that might tempt the evil spirits. Be careful . . . very careful. Don't say what you really feel. Don't bring bad luck on the boy. The evil spirits are always listening."

Yevka nodded. "Yes, I understand. He's . . . he's . . . *brydkŷi*—ugly, isn't he?"

Paraska nodded vigorously. "He's the ugliest child I ever saw!" And she spat generously on the dirt floor.

Myko and Danko giggled.

"W-w-we w-want to—"

"We want to spit, too!"

Paraska showed them the boy. "What do you think of him?"

"H-h-he's *br-br*—"

"HE'S *BRYDKÝI!*"

"*Tak*—it is so," nodded Paraska. "He's very ugly indeed."

The boys laughed and spat on the floor.

"*Bozhe,*" sighed Paraska. "Yevka, listen to my Myko. His speech gets worse each day."

"He sounds the same to me."

"I'm his mother, Yevka. Believe me, he gets worse every day." Paraska shook her head. "Well, never mind. What do you think, Yevka," said Paraska studying the baby's face carefully. "Should we make any improvements?"

"Hmm . . . I don't think he could look uglier, do you?"

Paraska stroked her chin. "Well . . . maybe we could make him a dimple on the chin . . . *tak*—like so." Paraska pressed her little finger lightly into the boy's chin. "Yes, he's much uglier now." She winked at Yevka and whispered, "A dimple for the girls someday, yes?"

Yevka nodded and whispered, "Yes, he will have a good face . . . a good face."

Myko and Danko spat on the floor and danced in a circle around the table.

"B-b-b—"

"*BRYDKÝI!*"

◆

On the morning after he returned to Stara Polyanka from a meeting in Pryashev, Andrii sat at the dining table in the Parish House with Father Yaroslav. "I didn't even know she was pregnant," complained Andrii. "I can understand others not knowing, but . . . how could I not know? And my own brother . . . I can't believe it . . . I just can't believe it. My own brother—the father! Three nights ago I became an uncle and I didn't even know Yevka was pregnant! I was in Pryashev worrying myself over the birth of a new Rusyn state while here in Stara Polyanka there was the birth of a new Rusyn in my own family!"

Father Yaroslav held his plate next to a large bowl and spooned a generous serving onto his plate. He pushed the bowl across the table. "Here, Andrii, take it. Be careful—it is very hot. Mariya Guzii makes wonderful *halushkŷ*— noodles. Once a week she brings me enough for three meals."

But Andrii had not finished his rant. "Who could have predicted this? It seems that the odds were better that I become an uncle to an illegitimate child than a witness to the birth of a legitimate state!"

Father Yaroslav pushed the *halushkŷ* a little closer to Andrii. "Go on, take it. You must eat."

Andrii served himself a small portion. "Why did I not see what was happening? How long has this been going on?" Andrii thrust his fork in to the air. "Well, obviously for at least nine months! How long have you known about this?"

Father Yaroslav smiled. "I can't answer a question like that."

"No, no, of course not. I'm sorry, Father."

"These are difficult times, Andrii. Our village has suffered; our people have suffered. The Mother of God weeps for her poor children of Makovytsya. And yet, Andrii, our people will survive and continue to live here as they have for centuries. Children will be born and—"

"Yes, Father, my brother will see to that!"

Father Yaroslav smiled. "You are young, Andrii, and your opinions are harsh. Are you angry with your brother because he sinned, or are you angry because your family is the subject of gossip?"

"Father, Yevka is married to our brother! How could Vasyl do such a thing?"

"Can you not forgive him?"

"I don't know . . . I don't know why I should."

"I see. The Lord can forgive your brother, but you cannot."

"Father, my brother has betrayed Petro."

"And so you will cast him out like Cain, a marked and despised man."

Andrii glared at Father Yaroslav. "You know I could never do that. I'm angry, yes. But I suppose it will pass."

"Temper your anger, Andrii. It is unattractive before the Lord."

"Father, I'm angry because I am hurt. I am hurt because I love Vasyl." Andrii sniffed loudly and looked away.

Father Yaroslav ate in silence until Andrii composed himself and began eating. "You will come to the baptism of your nephew tomorrow?" asked Father.

"Of course. It will be a joyous sacrament to celebrate. I hear that . . . that the boy has a name. Yevka says he will be called Tomas—Tomashko affectionately—and that you know about it."

"Yes, she and I have spoken. 'Tomas' was the name of her uncle—an uncle she loved very much."

"So you will not insist on an odd name for the boy, Father?"

"No, that old custom of branding an illegitimate child with an untypical name does not sit well with me. 'Tomas' is a fine name, and I will be happy to baptize him tomorrow."

"*Dobre*—good," said Andrii smiling. "Have you seen the boy?"

"No, not yet."

Andrii beamed. "He is handsome! *Oi,* I should watch what I say!" Andrii covered his mouth, but then laughed. "I've been around Paraska too much. Those old pagan superstitions have no place in our lives today. But, truly, my nephew is handsome with his dark hair and large dark eyes." Then Andrii frowned. "Of course, he will have nothing but his good looks to offer a young girl someday. His fate is sealed."

"Why is that?"

"Father, you know better than I the hard life an illegitimate child faces. Tomashko will forever bear the stain of his parents' sin."

"Andrii, you know that is not true. God does not visit the sins of a parent upon the child. The only stain Tomashko bears originated with Adam, and that stain will be erased in his baptism tomorrow."

"But, Father, he will always be judged by people for what he is—illegitimate."

"God will not judge him by his parents. Do not forget the story of the man born blind. *Hospod Isus Khrystos*—the Lord Jesus Christ—made it very clear that neither parent sinned. The affliction suffered by the blind man is for the manifestation of God's love. What is the Greek text held in the Lord's hands in our icon by the Royal Doors?"

"*Ego eimi to phos tou kosmou*—I am the light of the world."

"Very good, Andrii. Never forget that the man's blindness—his darkness—was cured by the Light of the World. God's love became manifest through the cure of the blind man."

"I know this here." Andrii pointed to his head. Then he placed his hand over his heart. "But here, I feel pain for Tomashko and his future."

Father Yaroslav nodded. "God guarantees us nothing in this corrupt and worldly life, except death. He sent His Son to guarantee us the next life, a life purchased for us in the sufferings of the Son. *Svyatŷi Pavlo*—Saint Paul—tells us in his First Letter to the Corinthians that 'flesh and blood cannot inherit the kingdom of God.'"

Andrii completed the quotation: "No, 'nor does corruption inherit incorruption.'"

Father Yaroslav smiled. "*To ista pravda*—this is the honest truth. There is great change in store for all of us if we believe and love. The sufferings of this world, while painful, are fleeting. The glory and peace of the next world are eternal. Our glorification will render us unrecognizable—we will have been delivered from the filth of a dark, corrupt world into the eternal presence of the True Light—the same True Light that will be poured into the soul of little Tomashko tomorrow."

Andrii wiped his wet eyes and dried his cheeks with his sleeves. "But, meanwhile, in this dark world, Tomashko is so innocent and helpless."

"Innocent, yes. Helpless . . . maybe not."

"How can a newborn be anything other than helpless, Father? He cannot speak, he cannot feed himself, he cannot walk, and he can never be legitimate. In the eyes of the civil authorities, he will always be illegitimate—he will never be able to claim an inheritance. He will have to rely on the mercy and kindness of those around him."

"Yes, Andrii, 'so that the works of God might be made visible through him.'"

Andrii closed his eyes. "For now, Tomashko can only cry and hope to be heard."

"Well, Andrii, perhaps Tomashko's cry will be heard. Perhaps it has already been heard. And perhaps"—Father Yaroslav pushed his chair away from the table, stood, and winked at Andrii—"Perhaps tomorrow there will be a miracle, and the works of God will be made visible."

გ

On the day of the baptism, when it came time to go to the Parish House, Paraska passed Tomashko through the window of the hut and into the waiting arms of his godmother. To further confound the constantly lurking evil spirits, Paraska then placed a loaf of bread in Tomashko's wooden cradle, which hung from the hut's truss beam. "They will never know he is out of the house," whispered Paraska to Yevka.

During the ceremony in the Parish House, Tomashko woke briefly, wrinkling his nose in annoyance at the water dripping onto his forehead. Afterward, while the baptism party returned to the Senchak hut for the reception, Father Yaroslav entered Tomashko's name in the *Matryka*—the parish registry book. When he finished, he called over Andrii, who was waiting to walk with him to the reception.

"Andrii, I want you to see what I have written. It may not be quite the miracle I promised, but it will serve its purpose."

Andrii read the entry and, at the column listing the father's name, he read aloud, "'Petro Rusynko.' 'Petro Rusynko?' You've made a mistake, Father."

"Read the last column, Andrii."

And Andrii read: "'The child's father has been in Ameryka for five years.'" Confused, Andrii blinked at Father Yaroslav. "I don't understand."

"Tomashko and his descendants cannot be deprived of their inheritance by any civil authority."

"But, Father, Vasyl is the father, not Petro."

"Yes, I know. I prayed to God last night, asking what I should do for Tomashko. Two things became clear to me as the result of prayer: Tomashko will suffer the stigma of illegitimacy throughout his life; and, God knew Tomashko before the boy was even formed in the womb. The first is temporal, the second is eternal. Therefore, since a child is never to blame for its own birth, Tomashko is and always will be legitimate in God's eyes."

"What will Petro say if he ever sees what you wrote in the *Matryka*?"

"I hope he will understand. Andrii, I am not playing a cruel joke on Petro Rusynko in Ameryka. The earth and all that it contains are passing. All of us are passing: the Tsar and the beggar, the humble and the proud, the peasant and the priest. The world has changed in the last five years, and so have all of us who still live. The world can never be as it was, nor can we be who we once were. Tomashko is now baptized into a new world. Regardless of anyone's opinion on the subject, he and his heirs cannot be deprived of any inheritance that is due them."

Andrii lowered his voice. "But, Father, is it . . . is it proper to record a birth in this way?"

"I hope so. Anyway, what I have written, I have written." Father Yaroslav chuckled. "I never thought I would quote Pontius Pilate for anyone's benefit. Come, let us go to the reception."

☙

At the entrance to the Senchak hut, Paraska and Yevka greeted Ivan Guzii and Paraska Dzyamba with great ceremony and with the respect due to the godparents of Tomashko. The neighbors, Mykhal and Mariya Burii, and Fedor and Mariya Fedorochko, also came to the reception. In their excitement, Myko and Danko ran in and out of the hut and among the guests. When Yurko arrived the boys hopped on his back in turns, demanding to be borne at high speed around the hut and to the Ondava and back.

After all the guests had arrived, Yevka whispered to Paraska, "Did you . . . did you . . . ask Andrii?"

"Did I ask Andrii about what?"

"You know . . . about . . . about Vasyl."

Paraska snorted. "Yes—and Andrii said the same thing I told you. Vasyl didn't come to Tomashko's baptism and he won't come to the reception."

"Well . . . I thought . . . maybe . . . maybe he would come."

"Feh, Yevka! Feh! If he didn't come to see his son when he was born, he certainly won't come to see him on his baptism day. God knows he was at the conception—he certainly showed up for that! Stop worrying about Vasyl. He's probably hiding in Niklova behind his *mamka* and his *teta*. If she weren't so ill, his *mamka* would crawl to Stara Polyanka to be at her grandson's baptism. But not Vasyl! You'll find him drinking at the *korchma* of the *zhyd*—the Jew, Moshko, in Nýzhnya Polyanka before you ever find him at the baptism of his son. Soon, Vasyl won't have to go that far to avoid you or his son; Shlomo Lentz soon will open a *korchma* here in Stara Polyanka and Vasyl will have a new home! Yevka, forget about Vasyl. Now, come—we have guests." Paraska called everyone's attention. "Listen, everyone! Normally, the midwife would now make a wish for the future of the newly baptized child; however, Mariya Vantsa is . . . well, she is not here . . . she is . . . ill. Therefore the godmother, Paraska Dzyamba, has graciously agreed to welcome Tomashko into this house. Pani Dzyamba, please."

Paraska Dzyamba made her way to the middle of the room. "Thank you, Paraska. Yevka, thank you for asking Ivan Guzii and me to be godparents to

Tomashko. We are very honored and happy to be called to God's service."
Paraska Dzyamba cleared her throat and recited:

> *We took him to church a pagan*
> *We have brought him home a Christian.*
> *May he grow up to be good and strong*
> *For God and for his parents and for his godparents.*
> *May he not forget God and always go to church,*
> *But may he always have friends in the tavern.*
> *May he always have health*
> *And never lack money.*
> *And may he be strong enough to handle plow and scythe,*
> *But also bright enough to wield a pen.*

"Well spoken, Pani Dzyamba," said Paraska, picking up the sleeping
Tomashko. "Now, everyone, please help set up the food on the table. I hope
Father Yaroslav will be here soon to give the blessing. Yevka, where are Myko
and Danko?"

"I think they are outside with Yurko."

Paraska went to the doorway with Tomashko cradled in her arm and
shouted, "MYKO—DANKO! COME IN TO EAT! YOU TOO, YURKO!"
Startled, Tomashko opened his eyes and began to cry. Paraska thrust the boy
into her sister's arms. "I thought he was asleep. Here, Yevka, he wants you.
MYKO—DANKO! NOW! Ah, and here come Father Yaroslav and Andrii.
Now we are all here."

❧

In the spring of 1919, Andrii, with guarded optimism, traveled east to Uzhhorod
to observe the proceedings of the Tsentralna Russka Narodna Rada—the
Central Rusyn National Council. At the conclusion of the weeklong conference, he returned to Stara Polyanka. It was a warm day in May when he
found Father Yaroslav outside the Parish House putting the finishing touches
on a new beehive.

"*Slava Isusu Khrystu*—Glory to Jesus Christ, Father!"

Father Yaroslav looked up from his work. "*Slava na vikŷ*—Glory to Him forever! Andrii, it is good to see you. So, you are back from Uzhhorod. By the look on your face, I will guess that developments were not favorable."

Andrii shrugged. "I am disappointed but not surprised."

"Tell me, then, Andrii, what you learned."

"I learned that, for Rusyns, compromise means conceding everything in the hope of receiving something in return. Rusyns to the east will enjoy some measure of autonomy within the new state of Czechoslovakia. So, that is something to celebrate, I suppose. We here in the area north of Pryashev will fall under Slovak rule. Our Lemko Rusyn brothers in Galicia, north of the mountains, will live under Polish rule."

Father Yaroslav pointed to a small shelf. "Hand me that can of paint and a small brush, will you? My beehives are not complete without a verse from scripture." When Andrii brought the requested items, Father Yaroslav began painting yellow letters on the side of his new beehive. "So, Andrii, there will be no Rusyn state after all. What will you do now?"

"*Ne znam*—I don't know. I think I would like to go into the seminary; but then, I also wish to continue writing—or trying to write—poetry. Perhaps now that our people's destiny is fixed, I will have no more excuses to wander around from Pryashev to Uzhhorod to Sanok to Florynka. Since the war, it has been difficult for me to stay in one place for very long. Too many exciting things have happened. Maybe I should stay in Stara Polyanka and be a farmer for a while."

"Perhaps you should keep bees," suggested Father Yaroslav, still painting.

"I don't think I have the patience to tend to bees. My father kept bees, and my mother tended them after he died—at least, until the war. I was always afraid of being stung."

Father Yaroslav nodded. "I, too, was once afraid of the bee's sting. But, I decided it was a fear worth conquering. I went to Varadka and learned everything about beekeeping from Mykhal Matsko. He told me one day how to achieve happiness in life. If you want to be happy for a day, he said, go to the *korchma* and drink. If you want to be happy for a month, get married. But, if you want to be happy all your life, keep bees."

Andrii laughed, and then frowned. "I'm not sure I understand. I thought Mykhal Matsko was happy in his marriage."

Father Yaroslav smiled. "He is, Andrii. He is very happy. His is one of the happiest marriages I know. The point of his parable is that earthly things are fleeting. A man who keeps bees understands that if he disturbs a bee, he may be stung. Therefore, he must be calm. His calm must originate in an inner peace that can come only from God."

Father Yaroslav set aside the paint brush and turned the beehive around. "Read the verse, Andrii."

And Andrii read: "'Learn to savor how good the Lord is; happy are those who take refuge in him.'"

"Our refuge is the Lord, Andrii. Once we sample his goodness, we can never be satisfied with anything less. Likewise, once we taste honey from the bee, nothing else is half so sweet."

Andrii read the inscription again to himself and smiled. "I think I'm still afraid of being stung."

"Then beekeeping is not for you," said Father Yaroslav, laughing.

Andrii ran his hand over the hive. "I may not be able to take care of bees; but, as a priest, I could perhaps help our people 'Learn to savor how good the Lord is.'"

"Yes, you could," said Father Yaroslav encouragingly. "The church is our great institution, Andrii. Our liturgy, our *prostopiniye*—our plainchant— these are what we Rusyns have when we have nothing else."

"The church is our refuge, Father. Like your hives for bees."

"Yes, Andrii. *To ista pravda*—that is the honest truth." Then Father Yaroslav tapped the top of the beehive with a finger. "Do you know how bees spend the winter, Andrii? They huddle inside the hive. The colder the winter, the more tightly they cling to one another, and the bigger the colony that survives. It is the same for us Rusyns. Tsars and empires will come and go, but our church, the Greek Catholic church endures—in it we find refuge in the Lord. While worldly leaders may treat us as bastard children with no rights or legacy, we are as legitimate as your nephew Tomashko in the eyes of the Lord. We will huddle in our church, while, outside, any manner of disasters or wars may rage. The church is our hive in our wintry exile from the family of nations. It is our inheritance and a gift to our descendants."

CHAPTER FORTY

Svyatŷi Vechur

AND SO THE YEAR 1919 PASSED—a year of blossoming trees, potato planting, harvests, wood cutting, and autumn plowing. Then came December.

Vasyl and Andrii spent the feast of *Svyatŷi Nikolai*—Saint Nicholas—in Niklova with their mother and their *teta* Mariya Hryndyk. The brothers were surprised when their mother announced that she would leave her sister's home to attend the service in the Church of the Protection of the Mother of God in Niklova. The brothers were further astounded after the liturgy when, at the dinner table in *Teta* Mariya's home, their mother expressed a desire to celebrate Christmas in Stara Polyanka.

Overjoyed, Andrii reached across the table and took his mother's hand. "*Mamko moya*—my mother! You are coming home to Stara Polyanka!"

"No, Andrii," said *Mamka*. "I only want to spend Christmas there. My home is here in Niklova with my sister, Mariya. I want to celebrate *Svyatŷi Vechur*—the Holy Supper on Christmas Eve—as we did in the old days . . . before the war . . ."

Vasyl studied his mother's haggard face and said, "Are you strong enough for the journey to Stara Polyanka?"

Mamka nodded. "I walked to church and home again today, yes? I will ride to Stara Polyanka with Old Mykhal—he, of course, is invited to the dinner. We will all be together like the old days . . . *ishi raz*—one more time . . ."

Vasyl frowned at his mother. "Why do you say it that way? You make it sound as if it would be for the last time."

"It will be the last time," said *Mamka*. "Tell him, Andrii."

Vasyl turned to face his brother. "Tell me what?"

Andrii shook his head. "I only just heard the news myself. Anna and Petro Kotsur are planning to go to Ameryka. It seems that next year, after the war-imposed interruption, Ameryka again will start receiving people re-settling from Europe. Petro Kotsur has a brother in Ameryka—in a place called Bai-something—"

"Bayonne?" offered Vasyl.

"Yes, I think that is it. This brother wrote that he will send money for Petro and Anna to come to Ameryka. He says there is good work there."

"Do you see, Vasyl?" said *Mamka*. "It will be our last time all together—one last *Svyatŷi Vechur*—as it was in the old days. We will all be there: Mariya and I; you, Andrii, Anna and Petro Kotsur and their girls, Marya and Terka; Old Mykhal and Yurko; Paraska and Yevka and their three boys . . ."

Vasyl stared at the table in silence. *Teta* Mariya rose from the table, and, with her eyes, motioned to Andrii to follow her to the other end of the room, leaving Vasyl alone with his mother.

"I want you to lead the prayers, Vasyl," said *Mamka*. "I want you to take us to the river for the washing and make the toasts at the table. Vasyl . . . Vasyl . . ."

Vasyl looked up into his mother's pleading eyes.

Mamka glanced at Andrii and Mariya and lowered her voice. "Vasyl, I want to see all my family—all my grandchildren—I want to see them all to-gether one last time."

Vasyl peered into *Mamka*'s eyes until she conceded a significant and sin-gular nod.

"No . . . *Mamko* . . ." Vasyl groaned.

"Don't weep for me, Vasyl. When God calls, we must go." *Mamka* smiled and whispered, "Will you do this for me?"

Vasyl sighed and took his mother's hand in his own. "Of course, *Mamko* . . . of course. It will be just as in the old days. I will see to it." He leaned toward her and whispered, "Does Andrii . . . does he know?"

Mamka shook her head. "He would be too upset."

"What about *Teta* Mariya?"

"Yes," said *Mamka*. "She knows and she is caring for me." She squeezed Vasyl's hand. "I'm very happy, *sŷne moi*—my son . . . very happy. One last time . . . just as in the old days . . ."

∽

Eighteen days later *Mamka* and *Teta* Mariya arrived in Stara Polyanka, rid-ing on Old Mykhal's cart and bundled heavily against the cold. For the first time in almost five years, the Rusynko hut benefited from a discriminating feminine eye. *Mamka* was shocked at the condition of her old home. "When was the last time any cleaning was done?" she asked in disgust.

"Yesterday," said Andrii.

Mamka sighed deeply and began pointing about the hut, indicating the areas in most desperate need of cleaning. "Well, don't stand there, Andrii. Help me—we haven't much time. Everything must be done before this evening."

Teta Mariya took charge of the cooking chores, putting Yurko and Old Mykhal to work peeling potatoes and garlic.

When Vasyl entered the hut, *Mamka* noticed the pail he set near the door. "Is that the same *diinŷk*—milking pail—your father used on this holy day?" she asked.

"The same," said Vasyl, nodding. "I have another surprise." He stepped outside briefly and returned with a small evergreen tree, no more than waist-high to *Mamka*. "*Smerek*—a spruce tree—to hang from the main beam."

Mamka was pleased. "Your father always brought home a small *smerek*."

The corners of Vasyl's mouth dropped in a smile. "As in the old days, *Mamko*."

"*Tak dai Bozhe*—God grant it so!" said *Mamka*.

Vasyl borrowed Yurko, assuring Old Mykhal that his co-worker would soon return. Yurko climbed onto a bench, took the *smerek* tree from the outstretched hand of Vasyl, and secured it by its base to the main roof beam with a length of cord.

"*Dobre*—good," said Andrii, inspecting the inverted tree. "It looks very good. You should also—"

Mamka thrust a small broom into Andrii's idle hands. "You should also sweep. There isn't much time." She pulled a bench away from the wall. "*Ioi!* Sweep here also. This hasn't been swept since the war! How do you live in such a place?"

Paraska and Yevka arrived with the three boys. Paraska carried a container of *slyvova pidlyvka*—plum sauce—and a plate of *pyrohŷ z kapustov*—cabbage pirogi. Yevka carried a sleeping Tomashko cradled in her left arm.

A little later, Anna and Petro Kotsur arrived with their daughters, Marya and Terka. Petro carried *pyrohŷ z bandurkov*—potato pirogi—and a plate of dried fish.

In the late afternoon, Andrii announced that the time had come to go to the Ondava for the ritual washing. Everyone filed outside, where Vasyl stood with the *diinŷk*—the milking bucket. Vasyl scanned the little group and said, "*Dobre,* follow me to the Ondava!"

The group followed Vasyl down the little path to the frozen stream. Upstream and downstream, other families could be seen and heard carrying out this ancient tradition. Vasyl pointed to Yurko, who nodded and, armed with an ax, stepped out onto the frozen surface of the stream. Yurko scored a circle on the surface of the ice with the ax, and then tapped the ice until it fissured and broke, exposing a small watery hole. Yurko took the *diinŷk* from Vasyl and dipped it into the hole. He set the filled bucket on the banks of the stream and rejoined the group.

Vasyl began chanting and the others joined in:

> *Bŷstra vodichka,*
> *Tŷ nasha matichka.*
> *Umyvash tŷ pisok kaminya*
> *I yshŷtko stvorenya*
>
> *Umŷi moï kostŷ*
> *Od ushytkoi nedohlivostŷ*
> *Od panskoi karnostŷ*
> *A ludskei nenavistŷ.*
>
> Running water,
> You are our mother;
> You wash the sand from the stones
> And all creation.
>
> Wash from my bones
> Every weakness,
> Landlord's oppression,
> And people's hatred.

After they finished the ancient chant, the family took turns washing their hands and faces in the frigid water.

The sun set as they returned to the hut. Inside, Vasyl directed Yurko to place the bucket on the floor next to the table where all nine dishes of food were displayed. Vasyl nodded to his brother. "Now, Andrii—a little from each dish into the bucket."

Andrii tore a piece of bread from the loaf in the center of the table and then worked his way around the table as Yurko followed him with the bucket in hand. Once the bucket contained a small portion from each of the nine dishes, Vasyl, Andrii, Yurko, Old Mykhal, Petro Kotsur, and Paraska's boy, Myko, and Yevka's son, Danko, all left for the barn.

"The barn isn't what it once was," said a wistful Vasyl. He handed the bucket to Old Mykhal. "Here, old friend. Feed Sasha first. He is an honored guest in our barn tonight. Andrii, feed the goat next. Where we once had a cow and pigs, pour a little of the water on the straw. Maybe that will bring us good fortune in the coming year. Yurko, fetch some clean straw for the supper table. Boys, do you want to feed the chickens?"

Myko nodded and Danko said, "*Hei, strỹiku*—yes, Uncle!" Andrii passed the bucket to the boys, who then poured the remaining mix of food and water into a shallow pan for the chickens.

In his one arm Vasyl clutched the straw Yurko handed him and then jerked his head toward the barn door. "Let's go back now." As he walked out of the barn, Vasyl called over his shoulder, "Andrii, Yurko, don't forget the chain." Yurko removed a length of chain from a hook in the barn wall and slung it over his shoulder.

It was twilight now and the light was fading quickly. Andrii explained to Myko and Danko, "We don't eat until the first star appears. Do you see a *zvizda*—a star?" The boys scanned the sky, and then simultaneously pointed to the same faint spot of light.

"*Zv-v-v—*" stammered Myko.

"*Zvizda!*" shouted Danko. "*Persha zvizda*—the first star!"

"Yes," said Andrii. "*Persha zvizda*. Well done, boys. Vasyl! The boys have seen the first star. Do you see?"

"Yes, I see it," said Vasyl without looking up. "Run inside boys. Tell them you saw the first star."

The boys ran into the hut, calling to their mothers:

"*M-M-Mamko!*"

"*Mamko!*"

"*P-p-p—*"

"*Persha zvizda!*"

"N-n-now w-we—"

"NOW WE EAT!"

"Shh! Both of you!" scolded Paraska. "You eat when I tell you. First we pray and sing. Now, wait for the men to come inside. Listen and don't talk."

Vasyl entered the room first and announced, "*Khrystos razhdayetsya*—Christ is born!"

"*SLAVYTE YOHO*—GLORIFY HIM!" cried the family standing around the table.

Gracing the table was a white linen cloth, a symbol of the first swaddling clothes worn by the Son of God. In strict observance of the fast of *Svyatŷi Vechur,* nine dishes containing no meat or milk products were placed on the table. In the center of the table was a round loaf of bread with, in its middle, a burning candle—the Light of the World.

Vasyl spread the clean straw on the floor around the table, and, motioning to Yurko and Andrii, said, "Now the chain." Everyone stepped back as the men wrapped the chain around the legs of the table, letting it rest on the straw.

Danko tugged at his mother's dress. "*Mamko,* when do we eat?" he whispered.

"Not yet," said Yevka. "Be patient."

"Andrii," said Vasyl, "you have the best voice. Lead us in '*Rozhdestvo Tvoye*—Your Birth.'"

Andrii cleared his throat and began to sing '*Rozhdestvo Tvoye Khryste Bozhe nash*—Your birth, O Christ our God . . .' Everyone joined him in the singing of the old liturgical hymn:

> *Your birth, O Christ our God,*
> *Has shed upon the world the light of knowledge;*
> *For through it, those who worshipped the stars,*
> *Have learned from a star to worship You, the Sun of Justice,*
> *And to recognize You as the Orient from On High.*
> *Glory be to You, O Lord.*

"Now do we eat?" whispered Danko.

"Shh," hushed Yevka gently.

"*Slava tebi Hospodi*—Glory be to You, O Lord," repeated Vasyl. "Now, let us sit."

Everyone took a seat, avoiding a conspicuously empty chair at the end of the table. "Who s-s-sits in th-th-that ch-ch-chair?" stammered Paraska's son, Myko.

Andrii lifted Myko and set him on the bench next to his mother. "We don't sit in that chair, Myko. That is a special chair. *Prorok Iliya*—the Prophet

Elijah—sits there. He is the one who announces the coming of the Messiah. But it is also for the souls of our dead loved ones who rejoin us on this night."

The boys' eyes widened and Danko exclaimed, "Are they all here now?"

"Yes," nodded *Mamka*. "Vasyl's and Andrii's brother Palko and their sister Helenka; their father, their father's parents, my parents . . ."

"My husband," added Aunt Mariya.

"*Moya mamka ta moi nyanko*—my mama and my papa," added Old Mykhal his eyes growing misty.

Paraska put her arm around Myko and held him tightly. "*Tvoi nyanko*—your papa . . ." she whispered.

Myko looked up at Paraska. "M-m-my p-p-papa is there?"

Paraska closed her eyes and nodded.

"They all fit in that one chair?" asked Danko incredulously.

Everyone nodded.

"Yes."

"Yes, Danko."

"Yes, they are all there."

Danko whispered to his mother, "Now do we eat?"

Vasyl's mother laughed. "Almost, Danko." Then she picked up a small plate from the table. "*Chesnok z medom*—garlic with honey," said *Mamka*. "I will make the sign of the cross on each of your foreheads with this garlic and honey. Usually I start with the oldest and end with the youngest. But tonight I will start with the youngest. Though there may be bitterness in our lives there is also sweetness. Though we all die, there is always new life."

"*Tak dai Bozhe*—may God grant it!" responded Paraska.

"Yes," everyone agreed. "*Tak dai Bozhe!*"

"Begin serving the food, Vasyl," said *Mamka*. "I will start the blessings." While everyone chatted excitedly and passed the dishes around the table, *Mamka* went to Yevka's side and sat next to her. Admiring her grandson, *Mamka* said, "He is a handsome baby. He looks sleepy."

"Yes," said Yevka. "It has been a long day. He will—"

"Yevka," interrupted *Mamka* in a whisper. The room was noisy with the sounds of clinking plates, conversation, and Paraska's hearty laughter. "Yevka," whispered *Mamka* again. "Forgive me . . ."

"Forgive? Forgive what?"

Mamka closed her eyes. "It is my fault. I should have made the match between you and Vasyl, not Petro. It never should have been Petro. *Nygda*—never . . ."

Yevka grasped *Mamka*'s hand and the two women pressed their foreheads together briefly. Sniffing and clearing her throat, *Mamka* dipped the garlic into the honey, saying, "We remember the new life promised to us by the Lord. From the bitterness of the cross came the sweetness of eternal life with God." With the garlic, she made the sign of the cross on Tomashko's forehead. "*Slava Ottsu y Sŷnu y Svyatomu Dukhu*—Glory be to the Father and to the Son and to the Holy Spirit."

"*Amin*," said Yevka.

Mamka stood with a groan and began working her way around the room, blessing family and friends. When she reached Paraska, she said, "I hear you have a treat for us."

Paraska reached into a basket at her feet. "*Slyvovitsa*," she announced, setting the bottle of plum brandy on the table. Yurko rose from the table and quickly moved about the hut, collecting an assortment of cups and mugs from shelves, cupboards, and drawers, depositing one in front of each adult.

"Yurko, you should move so fast at harvest time," snickered Paraska.

The bottle made its way around the table until all adults had a portion— some more generous than others—in front of them. *Mamka* finished the blessings on the foreheads and took her place as Vasyl stood. "*Khrystos razhdayetsya!*—Christ is born!"

Everyone stood and responded, "*SLAVYTE YOHO!*—GLORIFY HIM!"

"*Dai Bozhe shchastya!*—God grant happiness!" said Vasyl raising his glass.

"*DAI BOZHE!*—GOD GRANT IT!*"

Vasyl continued: "May He grant us all good health and good fortune as we prepare to celebrate the Nativity of His Son. We pray that we will all live to see another *Svyatŷi Vechur*." As *Mamka* and Vasyl exchanged brief glances, the adults raised their glasses and nodded, "*Dai Bozhe*—God grant it . . . Dai Bozhe." Vasyl continued. "And we ask God's blessing on us all—even on those who would harm us. And we ask God's blessing on this food." Vasyl raised his cup. "*Khrystos razhdayetsya*—Christ is born!"

"*SLAVYTE YOHO!*—GLORIFY HIM!" cried everyone, and they swallowed their drinks and sat down.

Vasyl leaned toward the boys. "Do you know what we do now, Danko?"

Everyone looked at Danko, who shyly lowered his head and shifted closer to Yevka.

Vasyl slapped the edge of the table with his hand. "WE EAT!"

The cabbage pirogi now depleted, the plate of potato pirogi began its journey around the table. As he had with the cabbage pirogi, Vasyl removed a potato pirogi and placed it on a plate at the chair for the Prophet Elijah and the souls of the dead.

As the potato pirogi were passed from place to place, Aunt Mariya began ladling mushroom soup into wooden bowls. When she served Myko his soup, she noticed that the boy was kicking at the chain that ringed the table. "Do you boys know why we put a chain on the floor on this night?" The boys shook their heads. "The chain," explained Aunt Mariya, "is strong and binds us all together as it binds together the legs of the table. If we rest our feet on the iron links we will also become as strong as the iron itself in the coming year." Aunt Mariya looked at Vasyl's and Andrii's mother. "Isn't that right, *sestro*—sister?"

"*To ista pravda*—it's the honest truth," said *Mamka*. "Yurko, pass the bottle of *slyvovitsa*. We will have another toast." Yurko handed her the empty bottle across the table. *Mamka* turned the bottle in her hand and shrugged. "Well . . . another toast would have been nice . . ."

"*Chekai*—wait," said Paraska, reaching again into her basket on the floor. "Knowing that Yurko would be here tonight, I brought another bottle. No, Yurko—sit down. You are too kind and, perhaps, too eager to help. We will pass the bottle the other way this time."

Old Mykhal took the bottle from Paraska, poured himself a cup of the plum brandy, and passed the bottle to Anna and Petro Kotsur.

Mamka rose to her feet and proposed a toast. "You must all know by now that this is the last *Svyatŷi Vechur* we will all celebrate together. My daughter Anna and her husband, Petro, and my granddaughters, Marya and Terka, all will be leaving us soon. They are . . . they are going . . . to Ameryka." *Mamka* faltered as her eyes began to moisten. "Petro will have good work in Ameryka . . . with his brother, Pavlo. So . . . let us . . ."

Vasyl stood. "Thank you, *Mamko*. Now, to Anna and Petro Kotsur! *Dai Bozhe shchastya*—God grant you happiness!"

"*DAI BOZHE!*—GOD GRANT IT!" Everyone threw back their drinks, laughing and hugging Anna, and slapping Petro on the back.

Mamka sat wearily and smiled gratefully at Vasyl.

Everyone reclaimed their seats and continued eating. At the sound of singing from without, Vasyl held up his hand to silence everyone in the room. "*Kolyadnykŷ*—carolers," he said.

Danko tugged at his mother's arm. "Who is it? Is it *Isus*—Jesus?"

"You will see when the door opens," said Yevka.

Andrii took both Myko and Danko by the hands and led them to the door. "On this night," he explained to the boys, "young people in the village go from door to door singing *kolyadŷ*—Christmas carols. We will invite them inside to warm themselves and to sing for us."

Accompanying a knock at the door was the muffled shout of a small chorus of voices: "*Hei, gazdove*—O, you farmers!" When Andrii opened the door, five boys and girls ranging from ages five to fourteen or so, pressed into the doorway, shouting, "*KHRYSTOS RAZHDAYETSYA!*—CHRIST IS BORN!"

"*SLAVYTE YOHO!*—GLORIFY HIM!" came the joyful response from around the Rusynko table.

Andrii motioned the carolers inside and closed the door behind them. "Are you Petro?" he asked the oldest boy.

"Yes—Petro Burii."

"You've grown tall quickly. *Kilko tobi rokiv*—how old are you?"

"*Mam shtyrnadtsat rokiv*—I'm fourteen years old."

"What will you sing for us, Petro?" asked Vasyl.

Petro Burii conferred with his young friends and then announced, "*Divnaya Novyna*—Wondrous News."

Murmurs of approval came from the dinner table as the children sang:

> *Divnaya novyna,*
> *Nŷni Diva Sŷna,*
> *Porodyla v Vifleyemi*
> *Mariya yedyna.*
>
> *Ne v tsarskoi palati.*
> *No mezhdu bŷdlyati,*
> *Vo pustŷni, vo yaskŷni,*
> *Treba to vsim znati.*
>
> Wondrous news
> A son today of the Virgin
> Bore in Bethlehem
> Mary, the chosen one.
>
> Not in a king's palace
> By the ox and donkey
> In the desert, in a stable
> But all should know of this.

Moved by the children's singing, *Mamka* clasped her hands together over her mouth and swayed in her seat to the rhythm of the familiar old carol. Vasyl sat on the bench next to his mother as the children began to sing *Rozhdestvo tvoye Khryste Bozhe nash*—Your birth, O Christ our God. "It is a good evening," said Vasyl. "It is a good *Svyatŷi Vechur,* yes, *Mamko?*"

Mamka took Vasyl's hand and squeezed it between her own. "It is like the old days . . . just like the old days . . . Look, do you see the two little ones? They are like your sister and brother, Helenka and Palko—both gone now so many years. And, yet, look at those two! So much like them! Whose children are they?"

"They are from the Barna household," said Vasyl. "She is Marya and he is Ivanko."

"Call them over when they finish singing, Vasyl."

When the children finished, everyone applauded and gave the children small sweets. Vasyl brought Marya and Ivanko to *Mamka* as Andrii was leading everyone in *Z namy Boh*—God Is with Us:

> *Z namy Boh, z namy Boh!*
> *Rozumiyti yazŷtsi*
> *I pokaryaitysya, i pokaryaitysya*
> *Yako z namy Boh,*
> *Yako z namy Boh!*

> God is with us, God is with us!
> Understand, all you nations,
> And humble yourselves, and humble yourselves
> For God is with us,
> For God is with us!

Mamka said to Vasyl, "Go to the cupboard next to the hearth. Look on the top shelf, under the scarf. Bring both coins." When Vasyl hesitated, *Mamka* smiled reassuringly. "I need the coins now. When the time comes, you will have to find two more. Go, Vasyl—bring me the coins." Vasyl went to fetch the coins and *Mamka* took the children by their hands. "Look at you two! So little, but with such big voices that you can sing with the older children! I have something for you both. My son will bring it soon. Are you two enjoying *Svyatŷi Vechur?*"

Marya nodded and Ivanko said, "This is our first house. Petro says we must visit at least three houses."

"Do you know why you must sing at three houses?" asked *Mamka*.

Marya and Ivanko shook their heads.

"*Svyata Troitsa*—the Holy Trinity—*Otets, Sŷn, i Svyatŷi Dukh*—Father, Son, and Holy Spirit. Never forget that. Ah, *dobre*—good, Vasyl, you found the coins. Here is one for you, Marya, and one for you, Ivanko. Show them to your parents when you get home, after the third house. Now, again, why three houses?"

Marya and Ivanko looked at one another and then shook their heads.

"*Svyata* . . ." hinted *Mamka*.

"*Svyata* . . ." repeated Marya and Ivanko.

"*Troitsa*."

"*Svyata Troitsa*—Holy Trinity!" the brother and sister pronounced triumphantly.

"*Dobre*," nodded *Mamka*. "*Svyata Troitsa . . . dobre . . .*"

Andrii herded Mariya and Ivanko together with Myko and Danko out the door. "Come!" Andrii shouted. "We will all go together to the next house to sing! Come, children! Come, Yurko, Anna, and Petro! Come, everyone who wants to sing!"

Vasyl sat at his mother's side. "Three houses, *Svyata Troitsa*—Holy Trinity? I never heard that before," he said, the corners of his mouth dropping sharply.

Mamka laughed. "It was all I could think of! Maybe they will remember!"

❧

After caroling, most villagers attended the midnight liturgy at the Parish House. Afterward, there were more carols while up and down the Ondava Valley came cries of:

"*KHRYSTOS RAZHDAYETSYA!*—CHRIST IS BORN!"

"*SLAVYTE YOHO!*—GLORIFY HIM!"

Andrii and Vasyl helped their exhausted *Mamka* back to the old Rusynko place. She and her sister would spend one more night in Stara Polyanka. The brothers hung a sheet from the truss beam to afford their *Mamka* and *Teta* Mariya privacy. After their *teta* and *Mamka* were in bed, the brothers heard their mother's voice.

"Andrii . . . Vasyl . . ."

"Yes, *Mamko,*" said the brothers.

"Thank you for a wondrous *Svyatŷi Vechur.* It was just as in the old days . . . Tonight I saw . . . Helenka and Palko . . . *Prorok Iliya*—the Prophet Elijah . . . and Helenka . . . and Palko . . . they were all here . . . tonight . . . Helenka and Palko . . . as in the old days . . . one last time . . ."

Andrii opened his mouth to speak, but Vasyl shook his head and the two brothers made their own beds on the floor near the hearth.

Somewhere outside in the crisp, black night, a lone male voice sang:

> *Z namy Boh, z namy Boh!*
> *Rozumiyti yazŷtsi*
> *I pokaryaitysya, i pokaryaitysya*
> *Yako z namy Boh,*
> *Yako z namy Boh!*

> God is with us, God is with us!
> Understand, all you nations,
> And humble yourselves, and humble yourselves
> For God is with us,
> For God is with us!

❧

In February of 1920, *Mamka* died in her sleep at her sister's home in Niklova.

Her funeral took place in Stara Polyanka in the Parish House where family and villagers sang the ancient *Panakhida*—the memorial service for the dead.

Father Yaroslav concluded the service with the words:

May Christ, our true God, risen from the dead, Who rules over the
Living and the dead, place the soul of His departed servant, Anna
Rusynko, in the abode of the Saints, grant her rest in the bosom of
Abraham, and number her among the Just through the prayers of
His most pure Mother, of the holy, glorious, and illustrious Apostles,
Of our venerable and God-bearing Fathers, and of all the Saints; may
He have mercy on us and save us, for He is gracious and loves mankind.

"Amin," intoned the congregation.

Again, Father Yaroslav: "In blessed repose, grant, O Lord, eternal rest to the soul of your servant, Anna Rusynko, and remember her forever." Father Yaroslav nodded to Andrii, who, with tears streaming down his cheeks, led the last, slow chant:

> *Vichnaya pamyat,*
> *Vichnaya pamyat.*
> *Blazhennii pokoi;*
> *Vichnaya pamyat.*
>
> Eternal memory,
> Eternal memory.
> Blessed repose;
> Eternal memory.

After the ceremony, *Mamka* was buried in the Rusynko section of the cemetery. At her feet were her children Palko and Helenka, and at her side was her husband.

Just as in the old days.

CHAPTER FORTY-ONE

Z Bohom

TWO MONTHS AFTER THE DEATH OF *MAMKA,* Anna and Petro Kotsur received a letter from Petro Kotsur's brother, Pavlo, and together they went to
see Vasyl on a cold and windy April afternoon.

"Vasyl, look," said Anna. "It is from Petro's brother in Ameryka. The letter arrived quickly—only four weeks! Do you see?"

Vasyl inspected the letter and the envelope.

Anna continued. "Pavlo wrote on 19 March 1920. He wrote from a village
called . . . Bai-on."

"Bayonne," corrected Vasyl. "Bayonne, Nu Dzyerzi. And it took six weeks
to get here—not four weeks."

"But, Vasyl, the date," insisted Anna.

"It is a different calendar. Our calendar is two weeks behind. It doesn't
matter—it is not important. What news does he have?"

"Pavlo says he can get Petro a job at faktri and that we can live with him.
He has a house and a wife he met in Nu Dzyerzi who comes from a village near Bardeyov. They have three children. He says there are many of our
people there and a church with our priests. He says it's almost like being in
one of our villages except it is much bigger."

Vasyl handed the letter back to Anna. "I see. So, when do you leave?"

"We leave as soon as we can," replied Anna. "Andrii says we must have
papers. He will help us learn to get the right papers. We will stay in Varadka
with Petro's cousin until it is time to leave."

"When you go, Anna, will you take a letter to our uncle Pavlo in Yonkers?"

"Of course, Vasyl."

"I wrote to him last year asking him to send me the money I left with him
before I came home to Stara Polyanka. I never heard back from Uncle Pavlo."

"We will find him, Vasyl. Don't worry."

"Good, Anna." Vasyl looked at Petro's leg. "Can you walk without limping?"

Anna replied on behalf of her husband. "His leg is fine."

Vasyl was amused and continued to address Petro. "I ask because, when you land at the island, the guards will send you back if you are not well."

Anna said, "His leg is fine," and then she glanced at Vasyl's empty sleeve. "Do you think you will come to Ameryka someday, Vasyl?"

"I've been to Ameryka, Anna."

ՇԴ

With Andrii's help, Anna and Petro Kotsur were soon ready to be on their way. In early May they packed their belongings and bundled their children against the wind and rain of a particularly unpleasant day.

Vasyl and Andrii walked to Varadka to see them off. Old Mykhal and his horse, Sasha, were waiting outside an old wooden hut. Andrii would ride with them to Nýzhnya Polyanka to pick up the latest newspapers and then walk home later in the day.

Anna looked up at the dark gray sky. "*To shkoda*—too bad," she said. "I didn't want to leave in such weather. I hate to remember my brothers standing in the rain."

"This is good weather for farmers," said Vasyl smiling. "As we always say:

> *Mokrýi mai,*
> *V stodoli rai!*

> Wet May,
> Paradise in the barn!

The three stood in silence. Finally, Anna spoke. "Vasyl . . ."

"Yes?"

"Will you . . .will you give us your blessing?"

"Of course."

"Vasyl . . . I . . . don't know if . . . I don't think we will come back to Stara Polyanka. I don't know if I'll see you—"

Vasyl took his sister's hand and smiled. "Of course we will see each other again! You and your Petro, Andrii and I—we will all be together again someday. Pay no attention to Andrii—he is crying because he is looking forward to that happy day. Anna, Petro, I give you both my blessing and I wish you safe travel. *Z Bohom*—go with God, Anna." He kissed his sister's forehead and extended his hand to his brother-in-law. "Take care of her, Petro— *Z Bohom*." Vasyl held out his arm. "Anna, hand me Terka." Anna placed her youngest daughter in Vasyl's arm. "Now, let me kiss Marya." Anna picked up her oldest daughter, who grabbed both ends of Vasyl's mustache and giggled. *"Ioi!"* cried Vasyl playfully. "The mustache is a part of me—you can't take that with you, Marya!" Anna handed Marya to her husband, who placed her on the seat next to Old Mykhal.

Anna, her eyes moist, turned again to her brother. "Vasyl . . . I . . ."

"Go, Anna . . . go," said Vasyl softly. *"Z Bohom*—go with God."

Anna's lips quivered. *"Z Bohom . . ."*

Petro and Andrii helped Anna onto the seat next to Old Mykhal, and then the two men climbed into the back of the cart.

Vasyl kissed Terka on her forehead, handed the sleeping child to Anna, and then quickly walked to the back of the cart.

"I will see you tonight, Andrii," said Vasyl.

Andrii nodded.

Old Mykhal removed his pipe from his mouth and smiled sadly at Vasyl. "It seems anymore that Sasha and I serve only to take our people on the first leg of their journey to Ameryka. They are all tired from years of war and food shortages. So many are leaving Makovytsya, Vasyl. From Ondavka, Výshnya Polyanka, Varadka, Nýzhnya Polyanka, Yalynký, Niklova, Bekherov, Komlosha . . . Stara Polyanka . . ." The old man sniffed loudly.

Vasyl patted the old horse's flank. "How is my old friend Sasha?"

"Old Sasha can't work as he once did. We will go as far as Smilno today and then we will come back. I think from now on our route will be only *Ondavska Dolyna*—the Ondava Valley. We will only ride from Nýzhnya Polyanka to Ondavka and back. A short route—and it's not too steep to Ondavka."

Anna blinked her eyes dry and looked back at Vasyl, who raised his left hand and waved, his empty right sleeve flapping in the cold breeze. When the cart reached the bend in the road between the Roman place on one side of the road and the Vantsa place on the other, Anna looked back again, but Vasyl was already gone from view.

At Nýzhnya Polyanka, Andrii disembarked after a handshake with Petro, an emotional farewell to Anna, and innumerable kisses for Marya and Terka. From the steps of Moshko's tavern, Andrii watched the cart trundle slowly down the road toward Smilno.

Along many such cart paths and roads, there came a slow but constant exodus of Rusyns, descending from the Carpathian hills in countless carts like Old Mykhal's. In cities and towns, families alighted from old carts and boarded small trains that rumbled off to the larger cities, where they boarded larger trains to Prague. From Prague, they went to the Dutch port city of Rotterdam, where they embarked on ships to the vast country in the New World that once again had opened her doors to the masses from foreign shores.

೧

Summer came and the villagers busied themselves during the long days, working in the fields, harvesting grain for themselves and fodder for their animals. In their potato fields, the people erected stick and branch figures adorned with bits of dangling metal to frighten away the aggressive wild pigs.

Children were born in the Guzii, Korba, and Barna households. But the two most talked-about newcomers to the village arrived at the Burii and Fedorochko households. Because of their family connections in villages to the south, the Burii and Fedorochko families were able to bring the first new cows to Stara Polyanka since the war. The Burii family named their cow Yahoda—Strawberry, and the Fedorochko family named their cow Malyna—Raspberry.

At the Senchak place, while there was nothing on the property so impressive as a milk cow, there was still the white goat, Bila, brought across the mountains by Vasyl and Yurko after the war. After *Velykden*—Easter, Father Yaroslav presented Paraska and Yevka with a rooster and two chickens in appreciation for meals the sisters had provided for the priest. The sisters diligently worked their rows of vegetables and cared for their boys with patience and resolution. Now, with a munching goat chained to the front of the house and chickens roaming the yard, the Senchak hut was beginning to resemble its prewar appearance. When the cabbage ripened, the sisters and their boys harvested the vegetables and carried them inside to the cold storage room. Paraska and Yevka set up a cutting board between them, while Myko and Danko carried in the last load of cabbage.

Paraska pointed to a large open barrel in the corner of the room. "Now, boys," she said. "Do what I told you earlier."

Barefoot, Myko and Danko jumped into the barrel, which came up to their chests, rolled up their pants, and waited for instructions.

Paraska shook her head forlornly. "Look, Yevka, look how skinny the boys are. They fit so easily in the barrel!"

Yevka wrapped Tomashko in a linen sling, tied the ends around her neck, and suspended the boy across her chest. Her hands free for work, she began chopping and slicing cabbage with Paraska. The sisters worked quickly until there was a mound of sliced cabbage on the cutting board. Paraska set the edge of the board on the lip of the barrel. "You boys, stand against the other side of the barrel," she commanded. Then she dumped the cabbage into the barrel.

Myko asked, "*M-M-Mamko,* n-now do we j-j-jump?"

"You boys wait until we cut up the apples and onions and then you can mix them with your feet. Do *not* jump up and down—you'll tip the barrel over."

Yevka began cutting up onions while Paraska rummaged about in the dark room for apples. From the other room came a knock.

"*Bozhe,*" said Paraska, annoyed. "Go see who is bothering us, will you, Yevka?"

Yevka rose and entered the main room of the hut where she found Andrii standing in the doorway. "Yevka," he said. "*Slava Isusu Khrystu*—Glory to Jesus Christ!"

Yevka nodded, "*Slava na viký*—Glory to Him forever."

Andrii held a small bag in his hands, which jingled when he nervously exchanged it from one hand to the other.

"*Proshu*—please—come in," invited Yevka.

"No, *dyakuyu*—thank you. I . . . I . . . I am here to . . . to give you a gift from someone. I wish he had done this himself . . . but . . . well, here I am." Andrii handed Yevka the bag. "It is from Vasyl. It is some of the money he earned working in Ameryka before the war. Our *mamka* had it among her possessions in Niklova when she died. Vasyl . . . he . . . Vasyl wants you and Paraska to have it."

Yevka looked inside the bag. "It looks like a lot of money—we can't take this. Please thank him, but tell him it is too much."

Andrii refused the bag. "No, Yevka. It is yours. I cannot go back with it. It is yours—take it."

"Andrii, it is too much. We could never repay this."

"Take it, Yevka. Use it for the boys. Or . . . maybe . . . maybe for Ameryka. Vasyl knows Paraska wants to go to Ameryka. He . . . he doesn't know how you feel about going to Ameryka. It is not to be repaid—that is all I know." Andrii abruptly turned and walked down the path.

Yevka looked inside the bag again and went back to the cold storage room. As she entered the room, Paraska was scolding the boys. "I told you NOT to jump! Stop it, both of you!" Paraska slipped off her wooden shoes and hitched up her long skirt. "Like this!" she said marching around the room. "Move your feet up and down—like you are marching through snow. *Vydite*—do you see?" The boys imitated Paraska, marching in a circle inside the barrel, giggling and poking each other in the ribs. Paraska looked up at Yevka and shook her head. "I'm too tired to yell at these boys anymore." Noticing the bag in Yevka's hand Paraska asked, "Who came visiting?"

"Andrii."

"What is in the bag?"

"*Pinyazi*—money."

"*Pinyazi?*"

"Yes." Yevka handed the bag to her sister.

Paraska looked in the bag and then, dropping her jaw, she looked at Yevka. "*BOZHE!* Where did he get all this?"

"From Vasyl. He earned it in Ameryka before the war. His mother had it with her in Niklova," explained Yevka, picking up a cabbage and resuming her work at the cutting board.

Paraska looked in the bag again and then handed it to Yevka. "Why did he give it to you?"

Yevka set the bag on the floor at her feet and shook her head. "He didn't give it to me—he gave it to both of us."

"Why? We can never pay it back."

"It is a gift. It is not to be paid back."

The boys were kicking the cabbage at each other and screaming with delight. Paraska raised an open hand over the barrel. "*Bozhe!* Be quiet, boys!" She raised her hand higher. "Or you'll get this!" Paraska sat at the cutting board and resumed slicing cabbage. "It is not to be paid back?"

"No."

Paraska lifted the cutting board, dumping another pile of sliced cabbage at the boys' feet. "Did Vasyl mention to Andrii a purpose for the money?" she asked, reaching for another cabbage.

Yevka nodded. "He said it is for the boys . . ."

"Oh . . ."

"Or . . . or, to go to Ameryka . . ."

Paraska's eyes widened. "Vasyl told Andrii this?"

"Yes. He knows you want to go to Ameryka."

"Vasyl said this? He said he knows I want to go to Ameryka? What did you say to Andrii?"

"*Nich*—nothing. I took the bag." Tomashko began to stir at that moment. Yevka laid her knife on the chopping board and lifted her blouse, exposing a breast for Tomashko to suckle.

With slow knife strokes, Paraska cut a cabbage in half, and then into quarters, and finally into thin wedges. Absentmindedly, she tossed the pieces in the general direction of the barrel, striking both Myko and Danko on their heads, eliciting gleeful surprise from both boys. "What," asked Paraska deliberately, "do you think you should—I mean, *we*—what do you think we should do with the money?"

Yevka sighed. "*Ne znam*—I don't know . . . *ne znam* . . ."

Paraska snorted. "*Tÿ ne znash*—you don't know? You've told me we can't go to Ameryka because we don't have money. Now we have the money, but you don't know what we should do with it?!"

Yevka stroked Tomashko's head through the linen sling. "Maybe . . . maybe I'm not sure about Ameryka."

"Not sure!" cried Paraska, her knife slicing sharply through a head of cabbage and nearly tipping over the cutting board. Paraska caught a whole head of cabbage before it rolled to the floor. "You are not sure! Before the war, your Petro went to Ameryka and said he would send for you one day. Then after the—"

"Well . . . he never really said he would send for us," suggested Yevka. "I don't know if he—"

"Of course he planned to send for you! Either that or he changed his mind and planned to return to Stara Polyanka. But you know how he felt about this village. He never wanted to come back. After the war—once we heard about Vasko—you agreed with me that we should think about going to Ameryka. When Vasyl came home, we asked to borrow money so we could go to Ameryka. He had no money at that time. Then you and Vasyl—well, we know what happened next—there's no need to go over all that again. You told me that the only thing keeping us from going to Ameryka was money! Now we have it, and you are not sure you want to go! *BOZHE!*"

"Please, Paraska, you are upsetting the boys."

"MYKO!" bellowed Paraska without taking her dark eyes off of her sister. "Are you upset?"

"N-n-no, *M-M-Mamko*."

"DANKO! Are you upset?"

"No, *Teto!* And I'm not jumping either! See?"

"*Dobre*—good, boys, *dobre*. You are mixing the cabbage well. So, you see, Yevka, the boys are not upset. And I'm not upset either, dear sister—I'm not upset at all! Why should I be? Before we had the money, I was upset that we could not afford to go to Ameryka. Now we have the money, only you have changed your mind! Why the devil should I be upset?!" Paraska chopped her knife viciously on the cutting board and threw the diced cabbage into the barrel. She selected another whole cabbage from the pile on the floor and rolled it back and forth on the cutting board. Once she had calmed herself, Paraska tried a different approach. "Yevka," she said affecting concern. "I know it doesn't bother you when you hear what women in the village say about you. Only . . . what about Tomashko? Don't you worry about the things these cruel gossips say about him?"

"I don't know. Yes . . . I suppose I do worry . . ."

"Yes, I'm sure you do. How will Tomashko feel someday, hmm? Just think what other children will call him."

Yevka closed her eyes. "Yes . . . I can imagine . . ."

Encouraged, Paraska tossed more cabbage at the boys' feet. "Why don't you want to go to Ameryka? Is it because of Vasyl? He wants you to go! Why do you think he gave you—gave *us*—the money? Are you afraid to go to Ameryka because your husband is there? Aha! You bit your lip! So that's it! You are worried about Petro, yes?"

Yevka shrugged. "Yes . . . perhaps. I have nightmares with him finding out about Tomashko."

"Well!" exulted Paraska. "That's nothing to worry about! No one knows where your Petro is. Ameryka is a big place, yes? Vasyl has told us how big it is—and he has been there. Don't you think Petro would have written to you by now if he had really wanted to see you again? Petro went to Ameryka to stay. He will not come back here. He has made a new life for himself in Ameryka, Yevka. You have nothing to worry about from Petro. Imagine yourself in Ameryka, Yevka. Just imagine seeing Petro one day in Ameryka—what would he say to you? 'I'm sorry I never sent for you'? 'I'm sorry I never wrote to you'? Why, Yevka, if we went to Ameryka—I know you don't want to go, I'm only saying *if* we went—you could just walk right by Petro as if you didn't see him. What right would he have even to look at the wife he abandoned? I tell you, he would have no right! No right at all! *To ista pravda*—that's the honest truth!"

Yevka bit her lower lip and stared at the cabbage barrel, oblivious to Tomashko's restlessness in her arms.

"That breast is empty," said Paraska. "He's ready for the other one."

"Oh, yes . . ." said Yevka, shifting Tomashko to her other side.

All the heads of cabbage cut up, Paraska ordered Myko and Danko out of the barrel, raising an open hand at an intimidating height when the boys protested. Then, with the boys' help, she covered the barrel with a wooden lid, pointing out the marks on both barrel and lid that, when aligned properly, provided the best fit inside the vat. She weighted the lid with two old grindstones to compress the cabbage mix and press the air out of the barrel.

"Yes," said Paraska, shaking her head. "You have nothing to worry about, Yevka. You will never see Petro again . . . not for the rest of your life."

☙

Summer came to an end and the days grew noticeably shorter. On a clear day in late November, Vasyl heard Old Mykhal's bell and headed down the path to the ruins of Yakov's tavern. The old man chatted with the villagers gathered around his cart, but upon seeing Vasyl, he flourished a letter over his head. "For you, Vasyl—from Ameryka! From Anna!"

Vasyl took the letter and said, "Come join us for dinner, Mykhal." Vasyl helped Old Mykhal down from the cart and together they walked—slowly for the old man's benefit—up the hill to the Rusynko place.

Old Mykhal retrieved a pouch from his coat pocket and handed it to Vasyl. "Tobacco. For you."

"*Bozhe moi,* old friend! How did you come by it?"

Old Mykhal winked. "I have friends, Vasyl—many friends."

Vasyl laughed. "Yes, I know you do. Tonight, you and I will have a smoke after dinner."

Inside the hut, Mykhal visited with Andrii and Yurko, while Vasyl sat near the hearth and read the letter by candlelight.

October 5, 1920   *Bayonne, New Jersey*

Vasyl—We are in Ameryka. Our ship arrived in August. Petro's brother Pavlo got job for my Petro at faktri. I help Pavlo's Mariya at their house. We cook and clean all day. Men from our homeland stay here and pay for a bed and meals. One man sleeps until he goes to work and then another man comes home from work, he eats and then sleeps in the same bed until the other man comes home from his work. It is very crowded here. Petro and I sleep in a small room by the kitchen with Marya and Terka. It is noisy from trains nearby. The girls cry at night from the noise. I am going to have a baby in the spring. Tell Andrii yes the men on the island make you read. I read about how the poor are blessed. My Petro went to Yonkers to look for our brother Petro. He found out that our Uncle Pavlo died in Yonkers in 1916. Our brother lived with Uncle Pavlo on Preskat street in a boarding house. The same boarding house you lived in with Uncle Pavlo. My Petro said he asked priest at Saint Nicholas Church if he knows where our brother is. The priest hasn't seen Petro since Uncle Pavlo's funeral four years ago. We asked at the church of Saint John the Baptist here in Bayonne but no one knows him or where he is. My Petro says our brother maybe went to Pennsylvania. No one knows if our brother is still alive.

Anna

Vasyl handed the letter to Andrii and tossed more wood into the hearth. "Oh, he's alive," Vasyl murmured to himself. "He is alive and now he has my money. He's alive . . . and well . . . alive and well . . . somewhere in Ameryka."

⌘

Once Paraska heard that Vasyl had received news from Anna in Ameryka and that Andrii had also read the letter, she hunted down Andrii and wrung the contents of the letter from him. Armed with the news, Paraska left Andrii and marched home.

"Yevka!" she shouted as she opened the door to their hut. "Are you here? YEVKA!"

"Yes, I'm here," answered Yevka, just putting a sleepy Tomashko in his hanging cradle. "What is the trouble?"

"Your Petro may be dead."

"What!" gasped Yevka. "What has happened?"

"Vasyl received a letter from his sister Anna. She doesn't know if Petro is alive or dead! Anna's Petro went to many places in Ameryka looking for your Petro. No one has seen him in years." Paraska allowed Yevka to absorb the news and then said, "He either died or started a new life somewhere in Ameryka. Either way . . . he's in God's hands now."

Yevka pushed Tomashko's cradle, sending it into a gentle sway above the floor of the hut.

"Yes," Paraska continued. "He's in God's hands now. *To ista pravda*— that's the honest truth."

CHAPTER FORTY-TWO

Abram's Lie

ON A COOL SPRING DAY IN 1921, Old Mykhal drove his old cart into Stara Polyanka and came to a halt in front of the ruins of Yakov's tavern. He remained sitting on the cart, scanning the hills above the village, while Sasha, his ears twitching, chewed his bit and shifted his feet nervously.

Andrii was walking up the path from the river, carrying his books in one hand and his pencils in the other, when he saw the old man descending slowly from the cart. "Mykhal!" he shouted, startling the old man. "Why did you not ring your bell? How is one to know you are in the village?"

Mykhal waited until Andrii was near and then looked from side to side before saying quietly, "Where is Vasyl?"

Andrii laughed. "What is it, Mykhal? Why the secrecy?"

"Where is Vasyl?"

"Probably at home," said Andrii, now concerned. "What is it, Mykhal? Is it bad news?"

"Yes . . . I think so. It could be very bad. I must see Vasyl."

"Very well, Mykhal—let us go find him. We will look first at the hut; if he is not there, I will look for him at Shlomo's tavern at the north end of the village. Will you not tell me what is wrong?"

"I will tell you, Andrii, but only while we look for Vasyl."

"Very well."

☙

At the Rusynko hut Yurko was chopping wood. Under Vasyl's watchful gaze he split several pieces from the woodpile. When Yurko finished, Vasyl pointed to the smaller cut pieces and extended his arm in front of him. "Yurko, put those in my arm. I will take them inside while you split the bigger ones." Vasyl turned the corner of the hut and, hearing his name called, looked toward the village to see Andrii hurrying toward him.

Vasyl frowned and cried, "Where have you been? Write your poems at night or when the snows come—now we need your help with wood. Go help Yurko."

Andrii shook his head and took the wood from his brother. "I'll carry that. Come inside, Vasyl. Mykhal is behind me—he has something to tell you. I'm going to find Paraska and Yevka and the boys. Meet us at their hut." Inside, Andrii dropped the wood near the hearth and headed for the door.

"What is this, Andrii? Stop! Tell me."

"There is no time, Vasyl. Here he is—Mykhal, tell Vasyl what you told me."

Andrii ran off in search of the sisters, and Old Mykhal, gasping, entered the hut. "Vasyl, I am too old for this—much too old." The old man shuffled to the bench, rubbing his forehead.

Vasyl gripped Old Mykhal's arm and helped him to a bench. Over his shoulder Vasyl yelled, "Yurko! Come in here! Pour a cup of *slyvovitsa* for Mykhal! Now, old friend, tell me what this is all about."

Old Mykhal sat heavily on the bench. "I heard about it yesterday, Vasyl, on the way from Bekherov. I met Avhustan Poryanda on the road, and he told me he had seen horsemen in the hills—a small band of them—rough-looking types." Yurko placed a small cup of *slyvovitsa* in front of the old man. "*Dyakuyu*—thank you, Yurko."

"How many men did Avhustan see?" demanded Vasyl.

Old Mykhal tossed the *slyvovitsa* down his throat and wiped his mouth with the back of his hand. "*Chekai*—wait, Vasyl. This morning, not far from here, I saw the men myself. They were off the road and back in the trees. I saw five men, perhaps six at first. But there may have been more in the hills above."

"Were they armed?"

"Yes—I saw rifles across their backs. They saw me but said nothing. Vasyl, there are rumors of fighting to the north, over the mountains, between the Polish army and the Russians and the Ukrainians. They say there are deserters roaming the mountains, stealing and killing men and raping women. I fear these men, Vasyl. I hurried as fast as I could, but Sasha is getting old and he—"

"Mykhal, you did well," smiled Vasyl. "Do you think you can walk down to the river and up to the Senchak place?"

"Yes . . . perhaps . . . if I could have more . . . only . . . only . . . *kus*—a bit."

Vasyl went to the door, motioning to Yurko. "Pour Mykhal one more cup of *slyvovitsa* and then bring him to the Senchak place when he is finished. I'm leaving now." Vasyl grabbed his hat from a peg in the wall and hurried out the door.

ↄ

When Vasyl reached the Senchak hut Paraska was waiting for him. As she spoke her lips trembled and her voice broke.

"Vasyl! Vasyl, what should we do? Andrii told us of these men."

"Go inside, Paraska. Is everyone here?"

"Yes, Vasyl. Yevka and the boys are inside with Andrii."

"Tell them I will come inside when Yurko gets here." Vasyl scanned the hills and watched for movement among the linden trees along the river. When Yurko and Mykhal finally arrived, Vasyl took the old man's arm. "Yurko, I'll take him inside. You stay out here and watch for them." Yurko nodded and began patrolling the grounds around the hut.

Inside, Andrii guided Mykhal to a seat where the women fussed over him and comforted him. On one of the beds, Danko and Myko sat rigidly watching the adults, while Tomashko, lying between the boys, slept with his mouth open.

Yevka left Mykhal's side and stood before Vasyl. "Andrii thinks we should go talk to these men if they enter the village."

Vasyl turned to Andrii. "What would you like to say to these men— '*Vitaite*—Welcome to Stara Polyanka?'"

"Vasyl . . . please. I only—"

"I know—you like to talk, Andrii. But we will not go see these men. If they come here and speak to us, we will speak to them. If they take something, get out of their way. If they ask for something, give it to them. We will stay together as a group. We will tell them that the sisters are our wives. Paraska is your wife, Andrii, and Myko is your son. Do you understand?"

"Yes, Vasyl."

"Mykhal is our father," continued Vasyl. "And Yurko is our brother. Why are you grinning, Andrii?"

"I was thinking that Abraham did something similar, but for less noble reasons."

"Abraham?"

"Yes, Vasyl. It was during the time when Abraham was still called Abram and his wife Sarai—later Sarah—went down to Egypt. Abram called his wife his sister to save himself from being murdered, and—"

Vasyl gripped his brother's arm and squeezed. "Andrii, forget Abraham. There is no time for this now. Do you understand? We are all one family— the sisters are our wives, Mykhal is our father, Yurko is our brother. Do all of you understand what I am saying?"

"Yes, Vasyl," said Old Mykhal. "It is a good idea."

"Yes, Vasyl," said Yevka, now comforting Paraska, whose ashen face twitched.

"Good. Andrii, take Yurko with you to the Kavulya place, tell them what is happening and bring them here if they—what is it, Yurko?"

Yurko had stuck his head inside the room and was nodding to Vasyl. "I see," said Vasyl. "They are here. Andrii, come with me." The two brothers followed Yurko outside and gazed across the valley to the trees Yurko indicated on the hillside above the Rusynko hut.

"Yes, I see them. Maybe they will go around the village," said Andrii. "They are remaining behind the trees near the top of the valley."

Vasyl shook his head. "They want to see who is here in the village. They will come down when they feel it is safe for them." Then Vasyl pointed to the western hills above the village. "*Bozhe!* Look, there are two more horsemen on the other side of the village. These men know what they are doing— they have flanked us. Andrii, take Yurko with you to the Kavulya place, and, if they wish to join us, bring them back with you. Tell them this is very serious. Go quickly."

As the two men ran toward the Kavulya hut, Yevka came outside and stood at Vasyl's side. "Vasyl, Paraska wants to take the boys into the hills."

"No, Yevka. It is too late. Look up there, in the trees. Do you see? And over there—on the other side of the village—there are two more. There is nowhere to go."

"*Moi Bozhe,*" murmured Yevka wretchedly.

"Yevka, tell Paraska to stay inside with the boys."

"Paraska says . . . she . . . she says these men might rape us."

Vasyl grimaced. "Stay close to the boys, both of you," he said, looking at

Yevka. She was biting her lower lip and watching the hills. "Yevka . . . it will be all right."

"Vasyl, during the war . . . they . . . they . . ."

"Who? What happened, Yevka?"

"There were men like these—three of them. They made trouble here. Paraska was sick . . . she sent me up the valley into the forest with the boys until they left. When I returned to our hut . . . Paraska had been . . . Paraska . . ."

"Did they rape her, Yevka?"

Shuddering, Yevka lowered her head and nodded.

Vasyl groaned. *"Bozhe . . . Bozhe . . ."*

Yevka slowly walked back inside the hut. Vasyl ground his jaws and followed the horsemen's progress along the two valley crests. At the southern end of the village the horsemen, descending from each side of the valley, reached the road where they reconstituted themselves in full strength. Then the men rode slowly into Stara Polyanka.

When Andrii and Yurko jogged back from the Kavulya place, Vasyl pointed to the approaching band of men.

"Yes, Vasyl, I see them," said Andrii. "Mariya Kavulya and her sister won't come with us—they are going into the hills with their children and their brother, Hrihorii. Vasyl, do you think . . . do you think the sisters should go to the hills? They seem to think that—"

"It is cold at night, Andrii. If these men stay here in Stara Polyanka for three or four days—what then? The boys will freeze to death in the hills. Go inside—both of you. I will wait out here. Look, they are coming." The horsemen were now approaching the ruins of Yakov's tavern.

"Vasyl, I—"

"Go, Andrii."

"Yes, Vasyl."

The horsemen stopped at the tavern and congregated around Old Mykhal's cart. After a pause, a detachment of two riders turned their horses up the path and made their way cautiously toward Vasyl. The lead rider had a beard and sported a battered Austrian service cap at an angle over black, unkempt hair. On his belt he wore an Austrian officer's revolver. The second man wore a tattered Austrian greatcoat and had an Austrian Steyr rifle slung across his back. Both men had the dark, buffed-leather skin of men who have lived outdoors a very long time. Vasyl inhaled deeply through his mouth and straightened, jutting out his chin slightly.

The lead man wearing the Austrian cap drew his horse up in front of Vasyl. "You are an observant man!" he said to Vasyl. He spoke like the Rusyns north of the mountains. "You have watched us for some time." He jerked his head toward the other rider. "While we were in the hills, I told Pavel we were being watched by a one-armed man. He wondered how I knew you were a one-armed man—and I said that I, too, am an observant man. You see, Pavel? He has one arm. Where did you lose your arm, brother?"

"Near Brody," answered Vasyl quietly.

"Feh! Brody! I've been there. The Jews are everywhere—like crows. They outnumber the peasants."

Vasyl said nothing, and the two men stared at one another before the bearded man continued. "What year, then, did you lose it?"

"Nineteen sixteen—the spring."

The bearded man raised his eyebrows. "You were there? That was a bad business. Brusilov's Russians were on us like locusts. I lost many men to Brusilov's guns. I still carry Russian shrapnel in my shoulder. Whose goat is that?"

The question startled Vasyl, and he followed the man's gaze to the side of the hut, where the sisters' goat nibbled at the ground.

"She's mine," said Vasyl.

The bearded man nodded over his shoulder and snapped his fingers. "Take her down, Pavel, and bring up Hrisha." Pavel, with the Steyr rifle across his back, dismounted and approached the goat with a rope. "We are making a trade," said the bearded man to Vasyl. When the goat bleated in protest at the touch of the rope, Yurko dashed out of the hut and hurried to her aid.

"No, Yurko!" called Vasyl. "They need the goat and they are taking her." Vasyl intercepted Yurko and held him by the arm. "Damn you, Yurko!" he scolded under his breath. "Don't you give me any trouble—not now. Come, stand next to me." Vasyl pulled Yurko to his side, and, for the benefit of the bearded man, said loudly, "Yurko, will you go back inside?" Yurko shook his head.

The bearded man laughed. Then, pointing at Yurko, he said, "You—go help Pavel."

Vasyl released his hold on Yurko's arm and whispered, "Do everything they ask—do you hear me, Yurko? Everything. Do not give me any trouble— do you understand?" Yurko nodded slowly and helped Pavel drag the reluctant goat from the property.

"He is your brother?" asked the bearded man. Vasyl nodded and pointed to his forehead. "Ah," said the bearded man. "I have such a cousin." He turned in his saddle and whistled to his confederates at the old tavern. Then he indicated the hut with a toss of his hand. "Who else is inside?"

Vasyl shrugged. "Only my family."

The bearded man dismounted and tied his horse to a *buk* log protruding from the woodpile. "Let's go meet them," he said, brushing past Vasyl.

☙

Inside the hut, Andrii was shuffling reluctantly toward the door at the insistence of Paraska. "Go on, Andrii," she was saying. "See what is happening." Andrii reached for the latch, but stepped back as the door opened.

"Another brother?" said the bearded man, eyeing Andrii as he entered the hut.

"Yes," said Vasyl, following closely.

"And who are these people?"

"My father, our wives, and our children."

The bearded man studied each member of the family and then pointed to Paraska. "You, move those boys from the bunk. And, you," he pointed to Vasyl. "Go outside and tell them to come in here." Vasyl hesitated, and the man glared at him. "Did you hear me? Go tell them."

Paraska moaned, *"Bozhe moi,"* and closed her eyes. Yevka gathered up the sleeping Tomashko and navigated Paraska and the older boys into a corner, where Myko and Danko cowered, clutching their mothers' skirts.

The bearded man went to the foot of the bunk and then addressed the two sisters. "You women know how to take care of men, yes?" Terrified, Paraska clutched Yevka's arm. Confounded by the sisters' silence, the bearded man snorted in disgust and then opened the door when he heard voices from without. Yurko and the man called Pavel entered the hut carrying a wounded man. The bearded man directed them to the corner bunk. "Put him over there." Yurko and Pavel carefully lowered the groaning man onto the bed.

The bearded man placed his hands on his hips and looked down at his comrade. "He has bled for three days and we cannot stop it. The riding is making it worse. Take care of him—his name is Hrisha. I don't know if we will come this way soon or ever again. You," he pointed to Vasyl. "You, come outside. Pavel, you too—we'll leave now."

Vasyl followed the two men outside, where Pavel mounted his horse. Two other horsemen were already making their way down the path with a rider-less horse between them. The bearded man untied his horse, hoisted him-self into his saddle, and said, "Tell me, brother, what was your rank in the army?"

"Sergeant," said Vasyl.

The man pushed his cap back on his head and nodded solemnly. "So was I. It was an awful mess, wasn't it? Where would an army be without its ser-geants? The men were young and knew nothing—it was up to us sergeants to teach them." He shook his head. "The lieutenants died faster than they could be replaced. But there were always sergeants like us, yes? Good men with the sense to survive and live." He paused and gazed up into the hills, and then leaned over and said something to Pavel, who turned his horse down the path. Then he addressed Vasyl. "Sergeant, call your brother—the quiet one. I want him to follow Pavel and bring something back here."

Vasyl called into the hut, "Yurko, come out here. It's all right, Yurko. Follow that man."

Yurko obeyed and went down the trail behind Pavel. The bearded man pointed to the trees on the hills. "When he dies, bury him up there in the *buk* forest—the beech forest. Will you do it?"

Vasyl gazed up into the hills and nodded. "Yes."

"His name is Hrisha. He is my brother and we are from the highlands east of here—from a village much like this—a village I will probably never see again. Hrisha would want to be buried up there. Your brother looks strong. Have him bury my brother deep in the ground—deep so the wolves can't smell him and drag him away."

"I will see to it," said Vasyl.

"I have no doubt that you will. What is your name, Sergeant?"

"Rusynko."

"What do you call this place?"

"Stara Polyanka."

"Stara Polyanka," repeated the bearded sergeant. "*Prekrasna dolyna*—a beautiful valley. Yes . . . *prekrasna*—beautiful. Look, here is your brother now." Yurko reappeared, leading the goat on a rope. "My men have no need of your goat," said the bearded man as he coaxed his horse down the trail. He called over his shoulder, "*Z Bohom*—go with God, Sergeant Rusynko of Stara Polyanka. Have a good life. You have everything here a man should have—everything I will never have." He rode down to the old tavern, where he rejoined his band of irregulars, and together they crossed the Ondava, riding eastward up into the *buk* forest and toward Poland beyond.

Andrii emerged from the hut and went to Vasyl's side. "Are they gone, Vasyl?"

"Yes. They won't come back. How is he?"

"Bad—very bad. He is shot through here." Andrii patted his right flank just above the hip. "It is a gaping wound. It bleeds from many places and is very dark and ugly." Andrii wrinkled his nose. "There is a horrible smell to it. Also, Paraska is crying and the boys are afraid."

"Very well, let us go to them."

By the bunk in the corner of the hut, Yevka tended to Hrisha. Paraska, her eyes red and her lips quivering, limped about the room fetching the items requested by her sister. "Paraska, bring me another clean cloth," ordered Yevka. "And look on our herb shelf for either *devyatsyl*—elecampane—or *ivanok*—Saint John's wort. Bring both if we have them."

Tomashko was sitting on a bench against the wall, rubbing his eyes and yawning. Andrii picked up the boy, tickled him, and then called to Myko and Danko, "Come outside, my little plums! Let's run in the grass!" Myko and Danko squealed with delight, and the four went outside.

Yevka raised her hand to summon Vasyl to the bunk. "Look," she said, uncovering Hrisha's wound. "What do you think?"

Vasyl examined the wound in the dim light. The opening in the man's side was indeed ugly and very wide—nearly big enough for two fists. Hrisha's eyes were closed tightly and his breathing was shallow and spasmodic. Vasyl felt the man's neck and forehead and then motioned Yevka to another corner of the room.

"What do you think?" repeated Yevka when they were out of earshot of Hrisha.

Vasyl shook his head. "He is very hot. His wound is fatal. No amount of herbs will help. But use whatever will make him comfortable. I think two days, maybe three—I suppose it depends on how strong he was before he was wounded."

❧

Hrisha died three days later. As instructed, Yurko dug a deep grave high in the hills among the tall beech trees. Andrii, Yurko, and Vasyl pulled Hrisha's body to the gravesite on a wooden handcart. Andrii read a selection of psalms over the grave, saying it was the least that should be done, since Father Yaroslav was away from the village and unable to pray at the grave.

On the way back to the village, Andrii told Vasyl that Yevka had finally yielded to Paraska on the decision to leave Stara Polyanka.

"Yevka is worried about her sister," explained Andrii. "Since the riders came through the village, Paraska has hardly spoken—she has a type of hysteria, I suppose. Anyway, Yevka told Paraska yesterday that they will go to Ameryka."

"When?" asked Vasyl softly.

"Possibly later this year."

"I see . . ."

"Yevka feels badly that she didn't agree to go to Ameryka earlier."

"I see . . ."

"Vasyl—"

"Yes?"

"It will be difficult, I think . . . when they leave . . ."

"No, Andrii, it will not be difficult. They will go by cart and then by train and then by ship—and then they will arrive in Ameryka. It will not be difficult at all . . ."

CHAPTER FORTY-THREE

Kvota

WHEN ANDRII HEARD that Paraska was feeling better, he visited the Senchak place.

"*Slava Isusu Khrystu*—Glory to Jesus Christ!" Andrii called from the doorway.

"*Slava na vikŷ*—Glory to Him forever!" responded the sisters. Welcoming Andrii inside, Yevka pointed to a pot of hot water on the hearth. "*Chai*—tea?" she offered.

"Yes, that would be nice. Thank you, Yevka. I'll hold Tomashko while you make it." Yevka handed the boy to Andrii, who then sat as directed at the table in the middle of the room. "I hear you are better now, Paraska. I was glad to see you at Liturgy yesterday."

Paraska held her palms up as in supplication. "Every day a little better," she said.

Andrii gazed around the room. "Where are Myko and Danko?"

"They are with the Barna family," said Yevka. "They are collecting blossoms from the *lipŷ*—the linden trees."

Andrii glanced hopefully at the cup Yevka was preparing. "Have they already brought some blossoms home?"

"Yes," replied Yevka. "I'm making your tea with linden blossoms."

Andrii was pleased. "*Dobre*—good."

"Yevka says another letter came from Ameryka—from Anna," said Paraska. "*To pravda*—this is true?"

"Yes," said Andrii. "Anna wrote from Bayonne, Nu Dzyerzi on the eighth of May."

"Almost two months ago," observed Yevka.

"Yes." Andrii nodded. "Almost. She says that there is still no news of our brother Petro. Anna writes that her Petro has visited Yonkers two more times looking for our brother, but that there is no sign of him anywhere. She says not to worry, however. Anna and her Petro will come to pick you up when you arrive in Ameryka. However . . . she also mentions the problem of kvota."

"What is that?" asked Paraska frowning. "What kind of problem is that?"

"Well, kvota is a limit," explained Andrii. "It is a limit on the number of people who can enter Ameryka. I've been reading about it in the newspapers that I buy in Nŷzhnya Polyanka. Some politicians in Ameryka want to re-strict the entrance of certain people into Ameryka. They think that already there are too many of us Slavs in Ameryka—and too many Italians."

Alarmed, Paraska looked at Yevka and then at Andrii. "So what does that mean? Now we can't go to Ameryka?"

"No, you and Yevka and the boys may still go. However, you must go at the right time. The kvota limits people entering Ameryka to a certain num-ber from each country per year."

Yevka placed the cup of tea in front of Andrii. "Give me Tomashko," she said. "He needs to eat." Andrii handed the boy to Yevka, who sat at the table and began breastfeeding Tomashko.

"Do we need a number, then?" asked Paraska.

"No," continued Andrii. "The number of Slavs, for example, who may enter Ameryka is based on the total number of Slavs already in Ameryka from each country of origin. We now live in the new country of Czechoslovakia. So, everything depends on how many people from Czechoslovakia are al-ready in Ameryka and how many are trying to get to Ameryka. The yearly kvota begins in July."

"That's next week," said Paraska.

"Well, no," said Andrii closing his eyes in concentration. "I think it is sooner than that. In Ameryka they use the newer calendar—the Gregorian calendar, not the Julian calendar that we use. Our calendar runs thirteen days behind the Gregorian."

"So, we should leave for Ameryka now," suggested Paraska hopefully.

Andrii tapped his chin with his index finger. "Hmm . . . I don't think there is enough time . . ."

"Enough time? Enough time for what? How long does it take to get to Ameryka?"

"It's not that, Paraska . . ."

"Well, then, what is it? Mariya Guzii is leaving next week to join her husband in Ameryka. Anna Fedorochko is leaving for Ameryka in two months. How much more time do you think Yevka and I need?"

"Well . . . it's not that . . ." Andrii hesitated. "The people you mentioned . . . well, they are able to do something you are not able to do."

Paraska straightened in her seat and raised one eyebrow at Andrii. "What can they do that I cannot?"

"They can read," he said. "When you get to Ameryka you will have to prove that you are able to read."

Paraska opened her mouth, paused, and then said, "Prove to whom?"

Andrii shrugged. "*Ne znam*—I don't know—the border guards, I suppose."

"Will we also have to show that we can write?" asked Yevka.

"Good question, Yevka," said Andrii. "The new law in Ameryka states that immigrants must demonstrate literacy—which means both reading and writing. However, Anna states that she had to show only that she could read."

Paraska scowled. "We don't have to learn *po-Amerykanský*—the Amerykan way—do we?"

"No, Paraska. Anna read from a prayer book in our language. You can learn, Paraska. It is not difficult. You too, Yevka. I could teach you both to read."

Paraska nodded and frowned. "Of course we could learn. There is nothing to it. Only we never bothered to learn before because there was no need to read. Why learn to do something you will never need to do? Is it not so, Yevka?"

Yevka set Tomashko on the bench and stood next to Paraska. "I started to learn to read many years ago—I might remember a little."

"So, Andrii," said Paraska. "How long will it take to learn to read? We are busy women."

"Well, we could start soon. I have paper and pencil at the hut—"

"*Dobre*—good! Go get your paper and show us."

Andrii looked from Paraska to Yevka and back again. "You want to start today?"

"Yes," said Paraska. "To go to Ameryka we must read. Go get the paper and the pencil and show us the letters. Maybe we can leave for Ameryka with Anna Fedorochko in two months. I'll make room on the table. Today Andrii will show us reading. Go on, Andrii."

Andrii pointed to his cup. "But . . . my tea . . ."

Paraska whisked Andrii out the door, assuring him, "We'll keep it warm for you."

❧

Andrii, armed with paper and pencils, soon returned to the Senchak hut along with Yurko, who had shown interest in the project. Andrii set up his classroom at the table, requesting that Yevka sit on his right and Paraska on his left. Yevka finished feeding Tomashko and put him in his cradle suspended from the main roof beam. Then she set Andrii's cup of tea in front of him before taking her assigned seat. Yurko stood behind the bench, observing everything intently. Andrii placed a notebook on the table and held a pencil aloft for all to see. "I will write the letters first so that you see how they are formed. You will then practice writing them until I am satisfied that both of you are proficient enough to begin writing short words and certain letter combinations frequently encountered in our language. You will notice how I hold the pencil in my hand. A proper grip of the pencil is essential in order to master proper writing technique. Note, in particular, the way in which my fingers—"

Paraska interrupted him. "Show us our names."

"What?"

"I want to see what my name looks like. So does Yevka—don't you, Yevka?"

"Well . . ."

"You see? Yevka wants to see also. Write our names so we can see what they look like."

Andrii set the pencil on the table and folded his hands over the notebook. "Paraska, to learn something new, one must proceed in a series of steps, each step being more advanced than the former. In the case of literacy, there are certain complex yet basic skills which, when mastered in an orderly—"

Paraska interrupted again. "You won't show us our names?"

Andrii drummed his fingers on the table and then glanced at Yevka for help. Yevka closed her eyes and answered with a barely perceptible nod.

Andrii sighed and opened his notebook. "*Dobre*—very well, Paraska. I will start with your name. Perhaps your idea is a very good one, after all. In this way, as you learn the alphabet you will already possess knowledge of certain of the letters. This informal familiarity possibly will be of great benefit. And, by the way, your name contains key letters that will help you—"

"Are you going to write my name or not?" asked Paraska.

"Dobre . . . dobre . . . dobre . . ." Andrii nodded. "Let us begin." He drew a short horizontal line on the paper and then drew two parallel lines, each starting from a point near each end of the horizontal line. "Now, Paraska, that is the first letter of your name. It is called *peh.*"

"Oh?" said Paraska, unimpressed. "My name is PA-raska, not PEH-raska."

"Yes, yes, I know. That is only the *name* of the letter. The sound it represents is always *p.* It is the vowel that follows *peh* that determines how the beginning of your name is pronounced. Now the vowel—"

"The what?" interrupted Paraska.

"The vowel."

Paraska squirmed in her seat. *"Dobre*—very well."

"May I continue?" asked Andrii, forcing a smile.

Paraska waved her hand impatiently.

"Now," said Andrii. "The next letter—a vowel—is *ah.* It is a little circle with a tail on the lower right. Do you see? *Dobre.* The next letter is the *er.* I make this letter by drawing a line straight down below the bottom of the previous letters, and then I add a little half-circle on the right side. Now we follow with another *ah* and then the fifth letter in your name, *es.* The *es* is simply a half-circle to the left. Next comes *kah,* a line straight down and then two lines to the right at angles. Finally, the last letter is another *ah.* You have three *ah*s in your name. Put all the letters together and you have 'Paraska.'"

Параска

Paraska squinted at the writing and said her name slowly. "Pa-ra-ska." She smiled and pointed to the paper. "That is my name." Yurko, his brow wrinkled, looked over Paraska's shoulder at the letters.

"Now," continued Andrii, turning to a fresh page in his notebook. "Some words begin with vowels—Yevka's and Yurko's names, for example. Here is the beginning of Yurko's name. It is *yu*—a vertical line and a circle joined together by a little dash—do you see, Yurko? Next comes the same *er* and *kah* from Paraska's name and then a new letter, *oh,* which is simply a small circle."

Юрко

Andrii tore the page from the book and handed it to Yurko. "That is your name, Yurko. You may keep that." Yurko sat at the end of the table, grasping the paper in both hands and studying it with parted lips.

Paraska looked over Yurko's shoulder and then frowned at Andrii. "Why does my name have so many letters? Yurko's doesn't have as many letters."

"That is because your name is longer—that is, it has more syllables. Your name has three and Yurko's has two, but you really don't need to know—"

"Where are they?"

"Where are what?"

"The things you said."

"The syllables?"

"Yes."

"Well, you don't see them. We hear them as we speak: Pa-ra-ska, one-two-three. The three syllables are like beats in music. Do you see? Or, perhaps I should say, do you hear?"

Paraska frowned and looked at her name again. "Well, if I don't have to see them I won't worry about them. Show us Yevka's name."

Andrii took up his pencil again. "Your name is short, Yevka."

Paraska made a face. "Hmph!"

"Yes," said Yevka. "Two beats."

Andrii beamed proudly at his student. "Yes! Yes, that is exactly right. You see, Paraska, Yevka understands how—"

Paraska stared across the room, grinding her jaw.

Andrii continued. "Yes . . . well . . . anyway, the name *Yevka* has two 'beats' just like Yurko's name. The first two letters are new. Your name begins with *yeh,* which is a half-circle, opening to the right and containing a little dash inside. Next, the *veh,* a straight line down with two half-circles on the right. Now we finish with two letters we have already learned: *kah* and *ah.*"

Євка

"And there, Yevka, is your name," said Andrii.

Yevka studied the writing and sounded out her name: "Yev-ka." Then she turned back a page in the notebook and studied her sister's name. "Paraska's name and my name end the same way."

Excited by this student's quick grasp of learning, Andrii clapped his hands and gave Yevka a little pat on the back, eliciting a blush. Then Andrii turned to his other student. "Do you see, Paraska? Yevka has discovered a very important concept. By recognizing patterns in written words, we can begin to read words we may not have seen before but which are familiar to us in our spoken language. Look, Yevka, here is another letter: *shah*. It looks much like the first letter in your name. However, this letter lies on its back with its legs in the air."

"Hmph!" snorted Paraska. "I'm glad *my* name doesn't contain such a shameless letter!"

Confused, Andrii looked at Paraska. "Well . . . no . . . no . . . of course not." Andrii turned to a new page in the notebook and resumed writing. "Now, Yevka, if we place the ending from your name in front of the *shah,* and add an *ah,* we have a new word."

каша

Andrii pointed to the word, then folded his arms dramatically across his chest, and said, "Yevka, can you read this word that describes something we eat almost daily?"

Yevka studied the word and then smiled and pronounced it quietly but distinctly. "Kasha."

"Yes! Kasha!" cried Andrii, clapping his hands again. "Excellent work, Yevka! There is no end to what you will be able to read once you understand how and why words are written as they are. Now I'll write a word for you, Paraska, so that you can try it!"

Paraska ignored Andrii and picked up the pencil. "How do we make the letters?"

"It is simple," said Andrii, tearing the first two pages from the notebook. "You each have before you a piece of paper with your name on it. I have another pencil for Yevka and somewhere . . . somewhere I have a third for me . . . ah, yes . . . here it is. Now, both of you may simply copy your names below my example. Hold the pencil with the thumb and first two fingers of your right hand like this. Yes, Yevka, very good! Now, starting at the left side of the page, write your name as many times as you can. Try and stay within the lines on the paper. *Dobre*—good, Yevka, *dobre*. It is like making *pysankŷ,* yes?"

"Yes, it is," said Yevka, finishing a row of copies of her name.

Andrii smiled. "You showed me how to 'write' *pysankŷ*—now, I am showing you how to write words. Now, Paraska, do you remember what I said? Hold the pencil like this."

Paraska frowned. "It's not working. Something is wrong with the pencil."

"There is nothing wrong with the pencil," explained Andrii. "You are holding it too tightly, and you are not making contact with the paper. Push down closer to the paper. Closer."

"Feh!" cried Paraska. "Look, the end broke off! I told you there was something wrong with the pencil."

"Here, take mine," said Andrii. "I will sharpen yours with a knife. Try it again. Only don't push down quite so hard. No, hold it like this—remember?"

Paraska, grinding her teeth, tried again. "Feh! Another bad pencil!"

Andrii sharpened the other pencil and handed it to Paraska. "*Chekai*— wait," he said, staying her hand. "You also make *pysankŷ*, Paraska, yes? Well then, how do you make the wax lines? That is, in which hand do you hold the writing tool?"

Paraska frowned at Andrii. "We are not making *pysankŷ* now."

"Yes, I understand. The reason I'm asking is this: the same technique used to make lines on *pysankŷ* is used to write words on paper. Show me how you make *pysankŷ*, Paraska. Yurko, hand me one of those potatoes near the hearth."

Yurko fetched the potato and handed it to Andrii, who set it on the table in front of Paraska. "Thank you, Yurko. Now, Paraska, pretend that this is an egg. Pick it up and hold it as if you were going to make a *pysanka*. Then, pick up the pencil."

Paraska snorted. "What sort of childish game is this?"

"Please, Paraska," said Andrii.

Paraska picked up the potato with her right hand and the pencil with her left.

"*Dobre*," nodded Andrii. "You are left-handed. Put down the potato. Now, try writing with the pencil in your left hand."

Paraska was annoyed. "What are you talking about—pencils—potatoes— *pysankŷ*? What do you want me to do?"

"Just put down the potato, Paraska," said Andrii in a soothing voice. "Forget about the potato. Hold the pencil in your left hand, between the thumb and the first two fingers. Yes, *dobre*. Now copy your name."

Paraska pressed the tip of the pencil to the paper, and, working from Andrii's example, drew two parallel vertical lines topped with a horizontal line that did not quite come into contact with the other two lines. Laboring across half the page, she eventually completed a reasonable rendering of her name.

"*Dobre*," nodded Andrii. "Continue writing your name. Try to print it smaller so that it fits in the lines. Do you see how Yevka has written her name? She has written it six or seven times on each line. Very good, Yevka— you have mastered your name and are ready for something else. Without looking at my paper, try to write 'kasha.' Do you remember the new letter it contains?"

Yevka thought for a moment and then wrote:

каша

"*Dobre!*" cried Andrii. "You remembered the letter *shah*. Practice writing 'kasha,' 'Yurko,' and 'Paraska.' You and Paraska have learned ten letters today."

Paraska finished writing her name a second time and set down the pencil and massaged the fingers of her left hand. "How many more letters do we have to learn?"

Andrii thought for a moment. "You are almost a third of the way through the alphabet—twenty-three letters more."

"*Bozhe,*" moaned Paraska.

❧

The sisters practiced the letters they had learned, including two new ones as Andrii now began teaching the letters in the order of their appearance in the alphabet. "I will show you these two because you can make a very important word with them and one additional letter you already know. The first letter is *beh,* which is made similarly to the *veh,* except that the upper half-circle does not close. The second letter is *heh,* which is simply two lines joined at the top like this. Now, if we combine these two letters with the *oh* that we learned earlier, we can form on paper a very important word—perhaps, the most important word you will ever learn. I have shown you the letters—only three letters. Let's see if one or both of you can make a very important word with just those three letters."

As Yevka wrote the three letters on her paper in various combinations, Paraska rose from the bench and busied herself at the hearth.

Yevka suddenly exclaimed, "Oh! I see!"

Andrii looked over Yevka's shoulder and beamed with pride. "Yes, Yevka! That is it! Don't say it aloud yet. Paraska, come see if you can make the same word."

"No, that is enough for today. We have work to do. Come, Yevka. Yurko, I am sure Vasyl needs you."

Yurko looked up from his scrap of paper and then folded it and slid it down into his boot.

Andrii was disappointed. "But Yevka is doing so well."

Silence.

Yevka bit her lip and urged Andrii toward the door with her eyes. Andrii sighed. "We shall continue tomorrow. Come, Yurko. *Dobrÿi den*—good day— to all."

Yurko was looking over Yevka's shoulder. Yevka pointed to the three-letter word she had just written and whispered to Yurko, "*Boh*—God." Yurko nodded solemnly and then followed Andrii out the door of the hut.

Yevka took the paper from the table and read the words to herself and then placed the sheet next to her *pysankÿ* dyes and other supplies on a little shelf on the wall. Then, joining Paraska at the hearth, Yevka asked tentatively, "Are you . . . making supper?"

"Of course! What a question!"

"Would you like help?"

"No."

Yevka paused and then tried again. "What are you making?"

Paraska banged the wooden spoon on the edge of the pot and turned to her sister. "What would you like?"

"Well . . . I . . ."

"Maybe you want kasha?" growled Paraska through clenched teeth.

❧

The sisters, with disparate aptitude, progressed in both their comprehension and transcription of the written word. In six weeks Yevka was sitting at the table in the Senchak hut reading from a brown notebook as Andrii sat next to her with his head propped on an elbow, listening.

"'When they had . . . finished breakfast . . . Isus said to Shimon Petro— Shimon, son of Ivan, do you . . . love me more than these?'"

Andrii interrupted Yevka. "To whom does He refer when He says, 'these'?"

Yevka looked at the words and, after a long pause, shrugged.

"He means the other disciples. Go on."

Yevka followed the words with her finger. "'He . . . said to him—Yes, Lord, you know . . . that I . . . love you—He said to him—Feed . . . my—feed my—'"

"Lambs."

"'—my lambs.'" Yevka squirmed and stretched her neck.

"Go on."

"'Second . . . time, he . . . said to him—Shimon, son of Ivan, do you . . . love me? He . . . said to him—Yes, Lord, you . . . know I . . . love you.'" Yevka stopped.

"No, Yevka," said Andrii leaning forward, his brow contracted. "Continue. You must not stop there. Read."

"'He . . . said to him—Tend . . . my—sheep—'"

"Excellent, Yevka! Yes, *vivtsý*—sheep. Continue."

"'He . . . said to him—'"

"Who is speaking, Yevka?"

"What?"

"The part you are reading now—who is speaking?"

Yevka looked back at the profusion of object and subject pronouns and then shrugged.

"It is Our Lord, Yevka. Continue."

"'. . . third time—Shimon, son of Ivan do you . . . love me? Petro was—Petro was—'"

"Grieved."

"'Petro was grieved . . . because he . . . said to him . . . third time—Do you love me?'"

"Excellent, Yevka. Why was Petro grieved?"

Yevka took a deep breath and stared at the book. "Because he asked him 'Do you love me?' again."

"Yes and what happened on the night Isus was arrested? Where was Petro?" Yevka shook her head.

"He followed Isus, but every time someone asked him if he was one of the disciples, what did Petro do? He denied it. Do you remember, Yevka? So, you see, Our Lord, risen from the dead, asks Petro to affirm three times what he denied three times on that fateful night. Your reading improves every day. I think you will be able to read anything they show you when you get to Ameryka." Andrii stroked his chin. "If I could only get Paraska to read more . . . she recognizes many words now, but . . . she cannot seem to put everything together."

From outside came the sounds of shouting and crying. "Tomashko!" cried Yevka. She and Andrii ran outside to find Paraska hobbling around the corner with a sobbing Tomashko in her arms.

"*Tota proklyata koza*—that damned goat! Look, Yevka! It is Tomashko's hand! That goat rammed Tomashko against the wall! He was making fun of her again. I told you this would happen. Look at Tomashko's hand!"

Blood dripped from the boy's left hand, and he screamed when Andrii inspected the wound.

"Come inside!" shouted Andrii over Tomashko's wailing. Yevka took her son from Paraska's arms and sat at the table with him. "Heat some water, Paraska," ordered Andrii as he tried to reinspect the wound. "Yevka, please hold up Tomashko's hand so I can see how bad the wound is. Yes that is better . . . yes, Tomashko, I know it hurts . . . yes, yes, I know . . . *Bozhe* . . . it doesn't look good. Yevka, look at me! Can you hear me? *Dobre*—good. There is a bad cut on his fourth finger. It will need stitches. There is a doctor in Nŷzhnya Polyanka this week—he was there yesterday when I purchased the latest newspapers. We must take Tomashko to Nŷzhnya Polyanka as soon as we clean his wound and bandage it. Paraska! Do you have any hot water?"

"Yes, yes . . . *chekai*—wait."

Andrii tapped his chin. "Old Mykhal is not in the village and no one else has a cart . . . so . . . we will have to walk. *Dobre,* I'll carry him and you walk alongside so he can see you, Yevka. We should get there quickly—"

"I'll carry him," said Yevka, her face ashen.

Andrii smiled. "Yes, I'm sure you will . . . Paraska, do you have the water!"

"I'm right here—stop shouting. Use this one to clean and this one to wrap the wound," she said, setting a pot of hot water on the table and handing Andrii several strips of linen. "Now, did you say something about a doctor?"

"Yes, there is a doctor from Pryashev in Nŷzhnya Polyanka this week. Yevka and I are going to take Tomashko to see the doctor as soon as we dress his wound."

Paraska gripped Andrii's arm. "A city doctor? We don't need their help. What do they know?"

Andrii released Paraska's grip on his arm. "We have no means of stitching a wound like this. We are taking him to Nŷzhnya Polyanka."

Paraska bit her lip. "Doctors cost money. We can care for Tomashko here. Doctors do very little for a great deal," she said, rubbing her fingers together as though dispensing coins.

Ignoring Paraska, Andrii and Yevka finished cleaning and wrapping Tomashko's wound, and then left immediately for Nÿzhnya Polyanka. They hurried down the path, crossing the Ondava on the little footbridge, while Paraska stood in the little yard watching them.

Yevka called over her shoulder, "Tell Danko I will be home this evening!"

Paraska went back inside the hut and found Bila, the goat, munching nonchalantly on the strips of linen Andrii used to clean Tomashko's wound. The goat ground its jaws, observing Paraska as she picked up a sharp knife from the hearth. Paraska pointed the knife at the goat and growled, "Don't you look at me like that! *Idy von*—get out! Get out or I'll cut your throat like a pig!" The goat darted away, its hooves slipping on the threshold as it hopped through the doorway.

"Hmph," grunted Paraska. "A waste of money . . . a sorry waste of money spent better elsewhere."

ↄ҂ↄ

By the autumn of 1921, when Tomashko was two and a half years old, his finger had healed. However, during his recovery, he developed the habit of sucking on the two middle fingers of his left hand to allay the pain.

The combination of Tomashko's injury and Paraska's struggles with literacy led Andrii to convince the sisters to postpone any attempt to emigrate until the spring of 1922. Such a schedule would allow them the best opportunity of arriving in their new country in July or August, at the beginning of the quota year. When Paraska protested, Andrii reminded her that failure to be admitted under the quota could result in being sent home to begin the process all over again. Paraska quickly yielded.

Andrii told Danko, Myko, and Tomashko that, in the spring, before they left the village, he would take them on a hike into the forested hills where they would see the land of their birth one last time.

CHAPTER FORTY-FOUR

Pchola

ON A SPRING MORNING IN 1922, Andrii arrived at the Senchak hut to take the boys on the hike he had promised the previous fall. Through the open door he could hear Tomashko crying as Paraska scolded her son, Myko. Yevka emerged from the hut and greeted her brother-in-law.

"*Dobre rano*—good morning, Andrii."

"*Dobre rano*, Yevka." Andrii smiled. "All is not well in this house this morning, I think. Are the boys almost ready?"

Yevka bit her lip. "You may have trouble with Tomashko. I don't know if he wants to go. Danko and Myko told Tomashko they didn't want him to go. So, now he is crying."

"Yes, I can hear him."

Tomashko, his eyes red and his cheeks smeared with tears, rushed out of the hut and buried himself in the folds of his mother's dress. Yevka stroked her son's hair and said, "Look, Tomashko. Your *strŷiko*—your uncle—is here. He wants to take all of you boys walking in the woods." Tomashko shook his head in his mother's dress.

Andrii squatted on the ground and placed his hand on Tomashko's shoulder. "Let me pick you up, Tomashko." The boy rubbed his eyes and then wrapped his arms around his uncle's neck. "*Oiii,* you are a big three-year-old!" grunted Andrii as he stood. "Won't you come with us, Tomashko? We will look for berries and we will collect leaves from trees and—"

Andrii's voice was drowned out by Paraska's booming voice from inside the doorway of the hut: "MYKO-DANKO! COME OUTSIDE! ANDRII IS HERE!"

Andrii nodded to Paraska. "*Dobre rano.*"

"*Dobre rano*, Andrii. How long will you be gone with the boys?"

"All afternoon. I want to take them up the river and then into the hills, where we can look down on Stara Polyanka. I want them to remember their village. When do you and Yevka leave for Varadka?"

"We will leave soon. We won't see you again until tomorrow afternoon. The boys know that you will stay here with them tonight." Paraska frowned at Andrii. "Have you seen your brother?"

Andrii lowered his eyes. "Vasyl has been . . . busy."

Paraska snorted. "Yes, I can see how a man with one arm might be too busy to see his son. Perhaps your brother is felling trees or building barns."

Yevka whispered, "Paraska!"

Andrii looked up at Yevka. "He said he will come to say good-bye before all of you leave for Ameryka."

Yevka turned her head and closed her eyes.

"Well, he has two weeks to see if he can remember where we live," said Paraska peering up the hill at the Rusynko hut. "I think the boy in your arms would like to remember his father. The village he will forget. Myko-Danko-Tomashko, go with Andrii and you mind whatever he tells you. It looks like it may rain later—stay dry. Come, Yevka, we have much to do before we can go to Varadka."

❧

Vasyl was sitting on a tree stump in front of the Rusynko hut, inspecting the cutting edge of a scythe, when he saw Andrii coming up the path with Myko and Danko behind him and Tomashko riding on his shoulders.

"Vasyl!" cried Andrii. "May Tomashko stay with you this afternoon?"

"Stay with me?" Vasyl stood up. "Where are his *mamka* and *teta*? Why should he stay with me?"

"They are on their way to Varadka to see their cousin, Mariya Fedorochko, who is ill. They don't want the boys exposed to her—she has a fever. Danko and Myko are coming with me."

"Where?"

"We are going on a walk." Andrii set Tomashko on the tree stump.

Vasyl frowned at the boy. "What about Yurko? Where is he?"

"Yurko is helping to repair his uncle's roof. He will be busy all day. Listen, Vasyl," said Andrii, pulling his brother aside. "I want to take Myko and Danko up the valley and into the forest. I want them to remember *Ondavska*

Dolyna—the Ondava Valley—when they go to Ameryka. It may be a long time before they ever come back here. Tomashko doesn't want to go on the walk. I would continue carrying him on my shoulders, but he's a big boy now and—"

Danko interrupted, "Let him stay with you, Uncle Vasyl!"

"Y-yes, l-l-let him st-t-tay!" echoed Myko.

"Tsh!" hushed Andrii. "I'm talking with Vasyl. If you two want to go with me, be quiet. Now, Vasyl, Tomashko is tired. He probably will sleep this afternoon and not bother you at all."

Vasyl observed his son, who was sitting on the tree stump alternately rubbing his eyes and frowning at his brother and cousin. Vasyl whispered to Andrii, "Maybe he would sleep on your shoulders—"

But Danko's ears were keen and he implored, "Pleeeease, Uncle Vasyl! Myko and I want to have fun in the hills with Uncle Andrii! Pleeeease let Tomashko stay here with you! Tomashko is slow—he wants to sleep all the time—he can't understand the games Myko and I play—he can't . . . Tomashko can't . . ." Danko paused, overwhelmed by his little brother's staggering incompetence. "Tomashko can't do *anything*!"

Vasyl pointed at Danko, "Enough from you!" Vasyl turned to Andrii. "How long will you be gone?"

"Only until late afternoon. Yevka and Paraska will stay the night in Varadka, but I will come back for Tomashko and then stay with the boys tonight at the Senchak hut."

"*Dobre*—very well," sighed Vasyl.

Andrii put his hand on his brother's shoulder. "*Dyakuyu*—thanks, Vasyl. It will be nice for Tomashko to spend a little time with his father. He and the others leave for Ameryka in only two or three weeks."

Vasyl shrugged. "Maybe he will sleep all afternoon."

Andrii beckoned to Myko and Danko. "Come, boys! We'll follow the banks of *Potok* Ondava first, and then—to the hills!"

The boys made faces at Tomashko, who kicked unsuccessfully at his brother and cousin from atop his perch on the tree stump as they marched past.

Vasyl retrieved his pipe and tobacco from his pocket and regarded Tomashko. "I'm going inside to light my pipe, boy. Do you want to stay out here?"

The boy nodded.

Vasyl propped the scythe against the wall of the hut and went inside to a bench near the hearth. He held the pipe between his knees and, with his left hand, filled the pipe bowl with a layer of tobacco, tamped it with his little finger, added a second layer, and tamped it again. When he reached for the hearth door handle, he noticed Tomashko standing inside the doorway. "I thought you wanted to stay outside, boy."

The boy nodded.

Vasyl opened the hearth door, thrust a stick into the coals, lit his pipe, and then tossed the stick onto the coals and closed the door. He puffed on the pipe until he was satisfied the tobacco was burning evenly. "Are you tired, boy? Do you want to sleep now?"

The boy nodded.

"*Dobre*—very well. You can sleep on that bunk. I'm going outside to work." Vasyl picked up a small stool by the door and took it outside to the tree stump. Then he returned to the hut for the scythe. He sat on the stool in front of the tree stump and held down the scythe blade with the heel of his boot against an iron wedge embedded in the stump. He sharpened the blade, working the scythe gradually across the iron wedge with his boot and tapping the edge with a small hammer. Out of the corner of Vasyl's eye, the boy again appeared. Vasyl set the hammer on his knee, pulled his pipe from his mouth, and shook his head. "What am I going to do with you, boy? Do you want to watch me work?"

The boy nodded.

"*Dobre*—very well. Sit there on the grass and watch me work. If you get tired, sleep on the grass." Vasyl puffed his pipe and continued tapping the edge of the scythe.

☙

Andrii and the boys walked along *Potok* Ondava, tossing stones into the water and passing back and forth over the little stream where partially submerged stones allowed a dry crossing. Andrii, pointing to the trees, flowers, and birds, chatted excitedly to the boys.

"Myko, Danko! Remember all that you see today! This is *Ondavska Dolyna*—the Ondava Valley. They say that everything in Ameryka is bigger and better than anywhere else in God's world. So, perhaps, in Ameryka, a little valley like this would go unnoticed. Remember it anyway, Myko and Danko. It is the valley of your birth."

The boys, ignoring Andrii, ran ahead and then stopped to observe something on the ground. "*S-S-Strýiku*—Uncle Andrii!" called Myko. "*Sk-k-koro*—hurry!"

Andrii caught up with the boys, who pointed to a reptile in the grass. "It's a *had*—a snake!" cried Danko.

"Ugh!" Andrii made a face. "Let it slither away and offer its tempting fruit elsewhere. Come, let's go up in the hills. Do you see that copse of oak trees? You boys run to those trees and I will follow. I brought bread and honey—we will sit under the trees and eat."

The boys raced toward the oak trees, while Andrii laughed and encouraged them. Then he abruptly stopped and looked around him. "What was that?" he called. "Who is there?" Except for the boys dashing up the hill through the grass, there was not a soul in sight on either side of the Ondava. "Is it You, Lord?" he whispered. "I heard a voice—I thought it might be You. There! I hear it again! No, it is not Your voice, Lord. Whose is it? Is it my voice?" Andrii laughed. "It is my voice! Yes, I hear it now! Wait! Let me hear again! Yes, I hear you. Wait—my pencil, my paper. Here, I have pencil in hand—where the devil . . . here! In this pocket I have paper! Now, let me hear the voice again!"

Silence.

Andrii moaned. "Now there is nothing. I know I heard it. It was a poem—yes, a poem." A light breeze came out of the upper valley, and Andrii turned to the north, into the breeze. "Is that it? Is that what you want to tell me? Or, are you telling me the obvious—that there is rain in those clouds? Hmm? Nothing." Andrii held his pencil and fluttering paper aloft. "I am ready when you are!"

Danko and Myko called to Andrii as he made his way up the hill to the shade of the oak trees, where they all enjoyed the bread and honey he provided. When they finished eating, the sky darkened and then the clouds broke, releasing a heavy rainfall. Andrii moved the boys under the heavy oak branches, but the driving storm found them nevertheless. Andrii opened his jacket for the boys, who huddled closely to him and laughed and wiped the rain from their eyes.

The heavy shower passed over the valley and continued on its eastward drenching course. Andrii and the boys stepped out from under the tree and into the sunlight, where they shook themselves dry. Danko shouted, "Look!" and pointed to a great rainbow that arched overhead.

"It is . . . it is . . . beautiful," said Andrii, smiling. "It is the most beautiful rainbow I've ever seen. I wonder . . . is this the poem? Is this what you were telling me about earlier?"

Danko looked at his uncle, then at Myko, and finally at his uncle again. "Who are you talking to, *Strŷiku?*"

"Myself, Danko, myself—pay no attention. Isn't it beautiful, boys? It is God's promise to Noah and to us—His promise never again to flood the earth. Look how it soars over us and over Stara Polyanka, and even into the hills beyond. It seems to come down and touch the earth near Varadka. And to the north it comes down in the *buk* forest—the beech forest. Do you see?"

"Y-y-yes!" cried Myko.

"Yes! Let's see where it touches the earth!" cried Danko. And the two boys charged up the hill toward the forest.

"Wait!" called Andrii. "You can't find the end . . . that is, you will never reach the . . . oh, *chom nit*—why not?" And Andrii chased after the boys into the *buk* forest, singing from the book of Genesis as he ran:

> *As long as the Earth lasts,*
> *seedtime and harvest,*
> *cold and heat,*
> *Summer and winter,*
> *and day and night*
> *shall not cease.*

☙

Curving high above Stara Polyanka, the rainbow cast its glowing spectrum on the face of the rain puddles in front of the Rusynko hut.

Vasyl stood in the doorway of the Rusynko hut, smoking his pipe until he was satisfied that the rain had stopped. Then he went inside to the bench near the hearth, where he fetched the second of two scythes he had planned to sharpen that day. He had finished sharpening the first scythe earlier and had started on the second one when the rains came. Tomashko was still asleep in the corner, where Vasyl had deposited him on a bunk after the boy had fallen asleep on the grass before the storm. Vasyl stepped carefully through the mud and around the rain puddles, on his way to the tree stump where, once again, he went to work on the scythe with the hammer.

Soon Tomashko appeared in the doorway of the hut, yawning and rubbing his eyes. When Vasyl heard the sucking sound of the boy's feet on the mud, he called over his shoulder, "The mud is slick, boy. Be careful." Vasyl finished his sharpening and held up the scythe to inspect its edge. Satisfied, he stood and started back toward the hut. But he stopped when he noticed Tomashko sitting on his haunches, staring into one of the puddles.

"What is it, boy? What do you see?" Vasyl went to the puddle and peered over Tomashko's shoulder. "What is it?"

Tomashko pointed to a bee floating on its back.

"*Pchola*—a bee," said Vasyl. "Pull him out of the water."

Tomashko squinted up at his father and shook his head.

"Are you afraid, boy? Don't be afraid. He's dead—he can't hurt you. Pick him up like this." Vasyl made a scooping motion with his hand. "Put your hand into the water and when your hand is under him, lift your hand straight up out of the water. Now, do it. That's it. *Dobre*—good. Hold him up so I can see him. Yes, he's dead, isn't he? He landed in the rainwater and drowned. Look at me, boy. Are you afraid of the bee?"

Tomashko shook his head.

"Are you sad?"

Tomashko nodded.

"Are you sad because the bee is dead?"

Tomashko nodded.

"Come over to the tree stump, boy. Keep your hand open, but don't let him fall. Hold him carefully. I'm going to sit here on the stump while you go inside and get me something. First, put the *pchola* in my hand—carefully. Don't touch his wings. *Dobre.* Now go inside—go to the shelf next to the hearth and bring me *sol*—salt. Do you understand—*sol*? *Dobre.* Just a little salt—open your hand. Now, with your other hand, place a finger on your open hand. Do you see the nail on your finger? Bring me enough *sol* to fit an area the size of your nail. Go, boy. I'll wait here. And make sure the *sol* stays dry."

As Tomashko made his way to the hut, Vasyl shielded the dead bee from both the sunlight and the light breeze. Overhead, a pair of swallows cavorted in fast, tight turns, twisting in a chasing spiral over the Rusynko hut.

When Tomashko returned from the hut, he held open his hand to display the salt to his father.

"*Dobre.* Now sprinkle a small pinch of *sol* on the *pchola*. Not too much. *Dobre.* Let me turn him over. Now sprinkle him again. *Dobre.* Now brush the salt off your hand and then hold up your palm. You will hold him now.

Be careful—don't hurt his wings. That's good—don't worry. He can't hurt you—he's dead—remember? Now, don't take your eyes off of him."

Tomashko held the salt-encrusted bee in his open hand and watched him. The first movement was barely perceptible—it could have been caused by the breeze. But the second movement was unmistakable. The bee's body twitched and then seemed to pulsate slowly. Tomashko looked up at his father with wide eyes.

"Watch him, boy."

The bee stretched out his little legs and struggled to stand on Tomashko's palm. Then he stood, a little unsteadily, his legs working up and down seeking firm footing in Tomashko's hand. The boy giggled and looked up at Vasyl again.

"Now, help him shake the *sol* off his back and wings. Blow across him gently—not too hard. Do you see how the *sol* falls off? *Dobre.* Look, he is buzzing his wings. They work well for him—they have not been harmed. It is time for him to leave your hand and start his life again. Hold him up in the breeze. He will fly again when he is ready."

Tomashko held up his hand. The bee buzzed his wings, shaking more salt from his back, and then stopped. He buzzed his wings again, released his grip on Tomashko's skin, and flew up into the light breeze. Tomashko rubbed his hands together and laughed and pointed at the bee flying higher and higher into the sky.

Vasyl shielded his eyes from the bright sunlight. "Watch him. You made *pchola* live again. This is something you did, and it is something your brother and your cousin cannot do. Remember that."

The bee buzzed over their heads, and Tomashko clapped his hands and giggled.

"Yes, boy, watch him fly. It was not his day to die."

℘

Having failed to find the end of the rainbow in the *buk* forest, Danko and Myko turned their attention toward the ground and argued about the prospects of finding mushrooms.

"Th-th-there m-might be s-s-some here," said Myko kicking his foot into the leafy mulch covering the forest floor.

Danko shook his head. "It is too early. It's too early, isn't it, *Strŷiku?*"

Andrii, who had stopped running after the boys once he reached the edge of the forest, was only now catching up with them. "Too early for what, Danko?"

"Mushrooms. Myko thinks we can find some today."

Andrii stroked his chin. "Hmm. I don't know. It seems too early, but—"

"Do you see, Myko?" laughed Danko. "I told you!"

"I s-said there m-m-m-m—" Myko's face contorted as he tried to pronounce the word.

Andrii held up a finger to silence Danko, who was about to speak. "Let Myko say the word, Danko. He can do it. Take your time, Myko."

"—m-m-m—" Myko's face was red and his eyes were squinted shut.

"Don't forget to breathe, Myko," said Andrii, growing concerned.

Danko bent forward, laughing and slapping his knees. "'Don't forget to breathe!' Yes, Myko, don't forget to breathe!"

"Stop it, Danko. Myko is trying his best. Stop making fun of—"

"—m-m-MIGHT!" gasped Myko.

"Good!" said Andrii, patting Myko on the back. "Now take deep breaths. You are too big for me to carry all the way to Stara Polyanka."

Danko snorted. "'Don't forget to breathe!'" And then he laughed hysterically, wiping his eyes and nose.

"Yes—'Don't forget to breathe'—very funny, Danko," said Andrii dryly. "I was trying to say before that May is usually too early for mushrooms. But after *teplŷi doshch*—a warm rain—some mushrooms could come out the next day. Only, I think this rain today was too *zymnŷi*—too cold. I'm sure there won't be mushrooms tomorrow. Now, I want you boys each to find a good *buk*—beech—leaf. We'll flatten them in a small book with leaves from the *dub, chereshenka,* and *lypa*—the oak, the cherry tree, and the linden tree. We won't see a *chereshenka* until we return to Stara Polyanka—so, for now, just find the other three. You may take the leaves to Ameryka with you. Go find your leaves—and take your time! Choose only the best ones! Did you hear me? Find good specimens!"

"Yes!" cried Danko over his shoulder as he ran into the forest.

"Y-y-yes!" cried Myko, disappearing among the trees with his cousin.

"*Dobre*—good," said Andrii to himself. He sat in the shade of a tall beech, pulled his cap down over his eyes, and immediately dozed off.

ೕ

After sunset, Vasyl sat outside the Rusynko hut enjoying a freshly prepared pipe. From his perch on the tree stump, he could observe Stara Polyanka as it faded with the light. Near *Potok* Ondava, swallows swooped low over the fields of grass as they fed on flying insects and chatted excitedly among themselves. *"Vit-vit! Vit-vit! Vit-vit-vit!"* the birds sang. Along the single dirt path that ran through the village, young Mariya Burii and young Petro Fedorochko each tended a cow grazing on opposite sides of the path. Mariya had brought her cow, Yahoda—Strawberry, from her family's hut at the south end of the village, and Petro had brought his cow, Malyna—Raspberry, from his hut at the north end of the village. There had been talk for some time in the village of a match between Petro and Mariya. Now, here in the center of the village, they chanced to meet together almost every evening. Petro walked behind his cow and gazed contentedly at Mariya. He suddenly stopped and inspected the bottom of one of his boots. Mariya covered her mouth and turned away giggling. Vasyl removed the pipe from his mouth and laughed.

"Vasyl, I haven't heard you laugh in a long time." It was Andrii coming around the corner of the hut with the exhausted Danko and Myko in tow. "What is so funny?"

Vasyl stood and stretched his arm. *"To nich*—it is nothing," he said. Then Vasyl jabbed his pipe toward the boys. "They look tired." Danko and Myko staggered to the front of the hut and collapsed on their sides in the cool grass.

"Yes, we are all tired," said Andrii. "Where is Tomashko?"

"Inside—asleep."

"He hasn't slept all day, has he, Vasyl?"

"No. He was outside with me for a while."

"Did you two go anywhere today?"

"No."

"Did you talk to Tomashko?"

"No."

Andrii frowned. "I was hoping that . . ."

"You were hoping what?"

"I don't know, Vasyl . . . maybe . . . maybe I hoped that since this was the last time you might spend any time with him . . . that maybe . . ."

"The boy is tired, Andrii. You may have to carry him home."

Andrii went to the door of the hut and then turned around and walked quickly to his brother. "I have an idea, Vasyl. Paraska and Yevka won't be back from Varadka until tomorrow. I told them I would stay at their hut with the

boys. But Tomashko could spend the night here with you, instead of coming
with the boys and me. In this way the two of you—"

"Andrii—"

"—could spend more time—"

"Andrii—"

"What, Vasyl?"

"Take the boy with you."

Andrii stared into his brother's eyes. "Very well, Vasyl . . . very well."
Andrii went into the hut and then emerged holding Tomashko by the hand.
"Tomashko was just waking up, Vasyl. He got into mischief before he went
to sleep. The salt tin is on the floor, and the salt has spilled all over."

Vasyl's mouth drooped into a smile. "He didn't spill the salt—I spilled it,
Andrii."

"You did?"

"Yes. I will clean it up. Go on, Andrii—take the boys home."

Andrii motioned to Danko and Myko. "Come, boys." Danko and Myko
grunted, struggled to their feet, and stumbled down the path toward their
mothers' hut. Andrii followed, holding Tomashko by the hand and calling
over his shoulder, "I will see you tomorrow, Vasyl."

"Yes, Andrii, early tomorrow morning. We will begin sectioning some of
the spruce trees we cut down last year for the new church. If Father Yaroslav
wants the church finished by next year, it will take far more wood than we
have brought down so far."

"Yes, yes, I know," said Andrii waving goodnight. Tomashko stared at his
father over his shoulder as he and his uncle Andrii made their way down the
path. Vasyl sat down on the little stool by the tree stump, puffing on his pipe
and watching Tomashko and Andrii until they entered the old Senchak hut
behind Danko and Myko.

Young Mariya Burii and young Petro Fedorochko, now grazing their cows
just down the little slope from Vasyl, were close enough for Vasyl to hear
their conversation.

"It is getting late, Petro," said Mariya.

"Yes," said Petro, looking up at the sky.

Though they stood on opposite sides of the road, and though Petro's hands
were in his pockets and Mariya's hands were clasped behind her back, the
two might as well have been locked in an embrace—their attraction to each
other was obvious. The cows nodded their heads at one another as if involved

in their own bovine conversation. Swallows darted under the cows' swinging tails and looped in the air over Mariya and Petro.

Vasyl removed the pipe from his mouth and leaned forward on his stool, endeavoring to hear every word between Mariya and Petro.

"I must go home," said Mariya. "*Nyanko*—Papa—will wonder where I am."

"Yes, Mariya, he will wonder."

Mariya tapped her cow with her stick and started homeward, while Petro did the same with his cow. Then Petro stopped and turned around. "Mariya."

"Yes?"

"Mariya . . . will I see you tomorrow?"

Vasyl stared intently at the two lovers, standing blue and nebulous in the failing light.

Mariya tossed her head from side to side. "Perhaps," she said coyly.

"Then, I will say *dobrŷi vechur*—good evening—for now, Mariya."

"*Dobrŷi vechur,* Petro."

"Mariya . . ."

"Yes?"

"*Z Bohom*—go with God."

"*Z Bohom,* Petro."

The two young lovers, their cows lumbering behind them, made their way toward their separate homes.

"*Z Bohom,* Mariya and Petro," whispered Vasyl. "*Z Bohom.*" Then Vasyl stood up, entered his hut, and closed the door.

&

The boys had fallen asleep immediately after dinner. Andrii, though exhausted from the day's activity, was restless all evening. Later, he tossed fitfully in his bed, finally turning on his back and staring up into the darkness.

Then he heard the voice again.

Andrii sat up in bed and listened. It came from outside. Andrii slipped out of bed and rummaged in the dark for his shirt, his trousers, and his pencil and paper. He pulled on his clothes, lit a candle from the coals in the hearth, and stepped outside. It was a still, moonless night, and the stars shimmered overhead like distant fires. Andrii listened. "Yes," he said. "I hear you. I hear you very clearly. Give me time to prepare. *Chekai*—wait! I am not ready." He sat on the little bench outside the front door, held the candle at an angle until hot wax dripped on the surface of the bench, and then he pressed the base of the candle onto the wax, securing his source of light.

Then Andrii gazed up at the heavens. "*Dobre.* Now I am ready," he said. "Tell me everything!" And then he wrote quickly, his pencil racing across the paper. He wrote poetry all night long—until the candle was reduced to a smudge on the bench and the dawn waxed anew.

 co

Do you hear Potok Ondava flowing from the Carpathians?
It flows through the village like the blood in your veins.
It is endless and strong like the beat of your heart.
Do you hear it?
It flows to the river and then to the ocean.
Its waters first washed you—
It is here that you were born.

Do you feel the wind breathing in the valley?
We cannot see it, but it rustles the trees and bends the grass—
An invisible hand that strokes the village.
Do you feel it?
When it stings your cheeks or cools your head, remember,
It is the spirit of God, your creator, who knows
It is here that you were born.

Do you see the swallows circling Stara Polyanka?
They stir the air with their flight and
The village breathes in and out with their wing-beats.
Do you see them?
They bring springtime with them and they take summer away with them
*   when they leave.*
They see you and they know that
It is here that you were born.

Do you taste the work of the bee?
Like man does the bee live and work and die,
But unlike man, the fruit of the bee's labor is always sweet.

Do you taste it?
God made the bee to please us and feed us,
And then God made you.
And it is here that you were born.

Do you smell the earth turned by the gazda?
From the earth comes the grain we eat.
We are of the earth and the earth is of us.
Do you smell it?
In Stara Polyanka the earth is rich because
Your forefathers are buried in it.
It is here that they were born.

Will you remember us after you cross the sea?
In the New World you will become Amerychane—Americans.
We who stay in starŷi krai—the old country—will remember you
　　　until we die.
But will you remember us?
Z Bohom!—Live well in Ameryka!
Only, you were born a Rusyn,
And a Rusyn you shall always be.

CHAPTER FORTY-FIVE

Farewell, Stara Polyanka

THREE DAYS LATER, in the early morning, Old Mykhal struggled up the path to the Rusynko hut. He stopped and called out, "Vasyl! Vasyl Rusynko!"

Andrii emerged from the hut and came down the path to meet the old man. "He's not here, Mykhal. Why are you here? I didn't expect to see you until next week."

"So everyone tells me." Old Mykhal's breathing was labored and he massaged his chest.

"Are you not well, Mykhal? Do you want to come inside and sit down?"

"No—it's too far, Andrii." The old man took a few deep breaths. "I'm tired. It is only old age, young Andrii. I need to speak with Vasyl."

"I think he is at Vasyl Rozum's home. Some of the men are cutting wood for the new church today. Are you not well?"

"I'm as well as a man my age can be. I need your help, Andrii."

"What is it?"

"I am here to take Paraska, Yevka, and the boys to Nẏzhnya Polyanka."

"Today! But, Mykhal, you are early by almost two weeks! Vasyl said their train tickets to Prague are dated two weeks from now. You should come inside—I'm afraid you've made this trip for nothing. Why don't you—"

"Andrii, the tickets are dated tomorrow. Vasyl asked me to take the sisters and their boys to Nẏzhnya Polyanka today. From there, they will travel by wagon to Bardeyov. I thought that already he told Paraska and Yevka all this, but . . ." Old Mykhal stroked his chin and glanced down the hill to the old Senchak home. "Well . . . I guess he didn't. I suppose he has his reasons . . ."

"But, Mykhal, Paraska and Yevka aren't ready to go today. There must be a mistake."

Mykhal shook his head. "There is no mistake. I went to the sisters' house and tried to talk to Paraska, but . . . well, she won't listen. She's angry, Andrii. I'm too old for this. I need your help."

"I see . . ."

"Paraska won't listen to me—maybe she will listen to you. I left poor Yurko alone holding Sasha. I'm afraid he's bearing her anger alone right now."

"Yes . . . I see. Come, Mykhal. We will go speak to her and to Yevka together."

❧

When Andrii and Old Mykhal arrived at the Senchak hut, Yurko was standing at the head of the cart stroking Sasha's nose. Paraska was next to Yurko, shaking her finger in his face. When she spotted Andrii and Mykhal, Paraska stormed across the little Senchak yard and thrust her finger in the old man's face. "You knew! He knew, Andrii! Talk to this old fool! We were to leave in two weeks. Now this fool says that to make it to the train on time we must leave today! Even sooner than today—we must leave NOW!"

The old man confirmed the news with raised palms and a slow, wretched sag of his shoulders.

Paraska brushed past Mykhal. "Andrii, where is Vasyl? I want to talk to him! MYKO-DANKO! Pack your things and help Tomashko with his things—and don't step on him! We are going to Ameryka—TODAY."

Wide-eyed, the boys grinned at each other and rushed inside shouting: "AM-M-M—"

"AMERYKA!"

Paraska snarled at Andrii, "Why are you still here? Go find your brother."

Andrii grimaced. "I . . . I know he is very busy. He is . . . very—" Andrii abruptly turned and headed toward the Rusynko hut.

"Yes, of course, your brother is busy!" called Paraska after Andrii. "Probably he is thinking up more lies!" Paraska glared at Old Mykhal and handed him a cloth sack. "Help us load the cart. We haven't much time. If you must be a part of Vasyl's lies, at least help us."

The old man shuffled into the hut and nodded greetings to Yevka, who was packing a small bag. "*Slava Isusu Khrystu*—Glory to Jesus Christ, Yevka."

"*Slava na vikŷ*—Glory to Him forever," she responded.

"I tried to tell your sister it is not my fault," whispered the old man. "But she—"

"Don't speak, *huntsute*—troublemaker! Fill that sack with the pile of things on the floor next to you and do not speak or complain."

Yevka cleared her throat. "Paraska . . ."

"What!"

"Those are things we are leaving behind."

Paraska waved her hand in disgust at Old Mykhal. "Help Yevka." Myko and Danko stood in the corner whispering, but they stopped when Paraska loomed closer and thrust sacks under their noses. "Fill these—NOW!" she said, her voice shaking.

Yevka indicated two full bags on the floor, and Paraska nodded and tied them up. Yevka tied a small bag and handed it to Tomashko. "Can you carry this?" The boy picked it up and nodded. "Good, Tomashko." Yevka picked up her two bags. "Follow me to the cart."

Paraska tied up the boys' two bags and then tossed one to Myko and one to Danko, nearly knocking them both down. "Take those out, get on the cart, and STAY THERE!" Then she stood next to Old Mykhal and watched him slowly place a few last items in a bag. "Give me," she said, grabbing the bag, tying it up, and thrusting it into the old man's midsection. Paraska steered him to the door. "Follow the boys."

Outside, Yevka was standing alone, shielding her eyes against the morning sun and peering up at the Rusynko hut. Paraska went to her sister's side and said gently, "Yevka, we have to go."

Yevka pointed toward the Rusynko place and Paraska squinted up the hill. "What is it, Yevka? Is it Andrii?" Yevka nodded and the sisters stood together and waited as Andrii approached. "Well?" asked Paraska. "Where is he?"

Andrii stood before the sisters and looked at the ground. "He . . . Vasyl is . . . not there. I tried to find him, but I don't know where he is."

Paraska tossed a sack to Andrii. "So, he has disappeared! Yes, I see. Take this to the cart and make sure the boys are there. And make sure that old fool hasn't wandered off. Yevka, you—" Yevka was walking back into the hut. Paraska followed and paused at the door. Yevka, her eyes moist, stood and stared at the walls.

Paraska spoke softly. "Yevka, maybe he will come to say good-bye."

Yevka shrugged and swept her hand around, indicating the nearly empty room. "We were born here, Paraska—our mother, too."

Paraska nodded. "Yes . . . yes she was. It is time, Yevka."

Yevka sighed and walked out of the hut to the spot where she could best see the Rusynko place. The hut was as quiet and still as before, but . . . perhaps there was movement on the path above the old hut . . . a rustle in the bushes . . . or some unusual movements in the trees . . . but, no . . . there was nothing . . . nothing but trembling oak leaves and the mad chase of two swifts, spiraling above the greenery into the blue sky, matching each other's darting flight turn for turn. Yevka heard her sister's soft voice next to her.

"We could wait a little. Maybe he will come, Yevka."

Yevka pointed toward the hills. "Paraska, do you see those two birds?"

"Birds? Where?"

"There, Paraska! Do you see them in the sky above the trees?"

"Yes, I . . . I think so. I'm not sure . . . your eyes are better than mine. What about them?"

"Nothing. I was only wondering if you could see them. They are very small—perhaps they are too small for you to see."

"Yevka, come sit inside. We will wait. Perhaps he will come. After all—"

"Paraska—"

"—he should come and—"

"Paraska—"

"Yes, Yevka? What is it?"

"He won't come."

Paraska squinted at the hills above the village and murmured, "No . . . no, I . . . I suppose he won't."

Yevka watched the frolicking swifts until they disappeared into the trees. Then she bent down, picked up her bag, and walked to Old Mykhal's cart. Paraska picked up her own bag and quickly followed her sister.

Old Mykhal was seated atop his cart with his pipe in his mouth and Sasha's reins in his lap. Andrii and Yurko had loaded the bundles in the back of the cart and were now lifting the boys onto their seats on top of the bundles. Tomashko stood up in the back of the cart when he saw his mother. Yurko helped Yevka onto her seat next to Old Mykhal, and then, when Yevka nodded, Yurko helped Tomashko crawl onto his mother's lap. Paraska, satisfied after an inspection of the boys and the bags, climbed onto the cart and sat on the other side of Old Mykhal.

Andrii hurried away toward the Parish House. "Wait there, Mykhal," he called over his shoulder. "I will bring Father Yaroslav!"

Yurko patted the old horse's side and neck, then walked around in front of the horse and stroked the soft spot between Sasha's nostrils.

Paraska turned in her seat and looked down at the boys, wrestling on the bundles. "Myko-Danko, stop it! You'll tear the bags. If Mykhal has to stop this cart on account of either one of you"—Paraska held up her open hand—"you will both feel this on your bottoms. Do you understand?" The boys nodded solemnly.

"Yes, *Teto.*"

"Y-y-yes, *M-M-Mamko.*"

When Paraska turned around in her seat, the boys looked at one another, snorted, and, covering their mouths, shook with muffled laughter.

Andrii and Father Yaroslav now left the Parish House and made their way to Old Mykhal's cart. Father Yaroslav greeted everyone, and then gave the little group a final blessing.

"*Hospody Isuse Khryste*—Lord Jesus Christ—look down upon Your faithful servants gathered here before You. Today they embark on a great journey and long voyage. Grant them, *Hospody,* courage and strength of faith in the coming weeks, that they may be calmed during difficult times by the memory of Your steps on the water when *Svyatŷi* Petro and the other disciples were so afraid. We ask You to calm the seas for Your people as You once did for Your friends. Grant them safe passage to Ameryka and bless these, Your faithful, in their new home. *Slava Ottsu y Sŷnu y Svyatomu Dukhu*—Glory be to the Father and to the Son and to the Holy Spirit—*nŷni y prisno, y vo vikŷ vikov*—now and ever, and forever."

"*Amin!*"

Father Yaroslav waved. "*Z Bohom*—go with God—all of you."

Old Mykhal tossed the reins. When nothing happened, he tossed them again and clucked his tongue. "Go, Sasha, go." The old horse lurched forward, his nostrils flaring.

Andrii walked awkwardly next to the cart and looked up at his sister-in-law. "Yevka," he said, glancing back briefly at the Rusynko hut. "Yevka . . . he . . . I think he . . ."

"I know, Andrii. Tell him . . . from me . . . from us . . . tell him, *Z Bohom* . . ."

"Yes, Yevka, I will. *Z Bohom,* Yevka."

"*Z Bohom,* Andrii. *Z Bohom,* Yurko."

Yurko nodded and gave Sasha one last affectionate pat and then stopped and stood next to Andrii. The two men watched the cart rumble southward through the village and then they headed up the east side of the valley to their work in the forest.

"Yevka," said Paraska as the cart creaked past the ruins of Yakov's tavern.

"Hold out your hand." Yevka shifted Tomashko to her shoulder and reached out across Old Mykhal. Paraska reached into one of her pockets and sifted a handful of dirt onto Yevka's open palm. "It is from the floor of the hut where you were born. Take it to Ameryka with you if you like."

Old Mykhal removed his pipe from his mouth and said, "That is good— earth from Stara Polyanka to take to Ameryka. That is good."

Yevka looked at the dark earth and then squeezed her hand shut and gazed about her. Two men were carefully rolling foundation stones a short distance down the hillside from the old site of the Church of the Protection of the Mother of God to the new church site. Up the hill, in the old part of the cemetery where the Rozum family reposed, Yurii Rozum leaned on his shovel and wiped his brow. Yurii's father, Old Shtefan Rozum, would undoubtedly breathe his last any day now. Yurii Rozum raised his hat as the cart passed and Old Mykhal gave two rings on his bell. Yevka turned in her seat. Andrii had disappeared, and there was no sign of life at the Rusynko place.

Yevka turned and faced down the valley, opening her fist over the edge of the cart. The dirt sifted through her fingers onto the turning wheel and scattered to the ground.

∾

Vasyl stood among the wild lilacs near the trail that led to the *buk* forest— the beech forest. He shielded his eyes from the sun with his left hand while his empty right sleeve flapped in a light breeze. In the valley below lay the village, its wartime scars almost completely obliterated by relentless nature and the hand of man. Two men worked on the new church foundation stones, and, across the valley, the green fields of a once prominent peasant undulated in the breeze. In the distance, short sections of the road leading southward from Stara Polyanka were visible through the trees. Vasyl breathed deeply and stared intently at the open stretches of road, waiting.

From the trail below came, first, the sound of a voice, and then Andrii and Yurko appeared in a clearing, the latter with an ax balanced on his shoulder. Vasyl jerked his head toward the upper valley. "Yurko, Andrii—you two go on. I will follow soon. Vasyl Kavulya and Pavlo Fedorochko have already started."

Andrii patted Yurko on the back. "Go on, Yurko. I will follow soon. I will speak with Vasyl first."

Yurko nodded at the brothers and proceeded up the trail alone to the *buk* forest.

Andrii and Vasyl stood together quietly, looking out over the valley. Finally, Andrii said, "They will be gone soon, Vasyl."

"Yes . . . I know."

"Perhaps it's not too late, Vasyl. I could run ahead and stop them so you could say goodbye."

"No, Andrii."

"I'm sure they . . . they would want to see you and—"

"No, Andrii."

"*Dobre*—very well," sighed Andrii. "I won't nag you."

Vasyl nodded. "Thank you."

"Vasyl?"

"Yes, Andrii?"

"I think I know why you did it."

"Oh?"

"Yes. At first I was angry with you. You lied about the train dates. But now . . . now I know that it hurts you to see them go and that—"

"Andrii—"

"—and that you really want—"

"Andrii—"

"Yes, Vasyl?"

"Go with Yurko. Go help him with the wood. I will be along soon."

"Yes, Vasyl, I will go. I . . . I told Yevka good-bye for you. She said to tell you, '*Z Bohom*—go with God.'"

Vasyl closed his eyes tightly.

"I told her, '*Z Bohom*,' from you, Vasyl. I hugged Tomashko for you, but I didn't know what to say. I . . . I wasn't sure."

Vasyl opened his eyes. "It's all right, Andrii. A child . . . a child must . . . he . . . he is with his mother. He will be fine. Now go—we have a church to build and we will need wood. Go."

"Of course." Andrii paused. "Vasyl?"

"Yes?"

"It will be good to have a church once again, yes?"

"Yes, Andrii, it will be good to have a church again. Now go with Yurko. I will be there soon."

"*Dobre*, Vasyl." Andrii headed up the trail, leaving Vasyl alone.

The valley was remarkably quiet, except for the distant barking of a dog somewhere on the other side of the Ondava. In the air in front of Vasyl two swifts spiraled toward the heavens, twisting and frolicking. The birds circled behind Vasyl, drawing his eyes upward. The pair flapped their wings vigorously and then swooped playfully in front of Vasyl, their wing-beats stirring the air in a mellifluous and endless blessing: "*Z Bohom*—go with God . . . *Z Bohom* . . . *Z Bohom* . . ."

"A child must have its mother . . ." whispered Vasyl.

Then, from the corner of his eye, Vasyl detected movement south of the village. He peered at an open stretch of road leading southward out of the village, but saw nothing at first. But, then, there was movement again . . . it was the slow, unmistakable progress of a horse-drawn cart. It emerged silently from the trees . . . moving almost imperceptibly. It disappeared among the trees bordering the road . . . reemerged, slowly winding through thickets . . . disappeared again among the trees . . . reemerged one last time . . . now fully visible in the sunlight . . . but only briefly . . . and now . . . now winding away . . . and away . . . and away . . . and, finally . . . gone.

"*Z Bohom*—go with God . . . *Z Bohom* . . . *Z Bohom* . . ."

Vasyl turned and started walking up the trail, working his way slowly toward the sound of Yurko's ax already at work.

PART FOUR

Apostle Row

My sheep hear my voice; I know them,
and they follow me.
I give them eternal life, and they shall never perish.
No one can take them out of my hand.

JOHN 10

CHAPTER FORTY-SIX

Rotterdam

THE LONG PASSENGER TRAIN FROM PRAGUE rumbled into the Rotterdam station, its engine stacks billowing smoke and its boiler valves hissing steam. Leaning out of the windows of the third-class cars, emigrants bound for the New World babbled excitedly to one another in Czech, Slovak, Rusyn, Polish, Magyar, Yiddish, and German. Porters stood on the steps of each passenger car and, as the train slowed to a stop, jumped to the station platform, centering wooden blocks beneath the steel steps.

The engine emitted a long steam sigh as the passengers alighted on the platform, hoisted their bundles over their shoulders, and, huddling their families into tight groups, began the long walk toward the street entrance of the station. As they passed the great locomotive, there came from deep within its sweating, black exterior, a low, rhythmic thump-thump, pause, thump-thump, pause, thump-thump . . .

A jaunty man in a straw hat strutted along the platform against the flow of emigrants and made his way toward the rear of the train. He listened to everyone's speech, nodding to the men and tipping his hat to the peasant girls, who giggled as he passed. At the end of the train he came upon two women and three children struggling with their bags. One of the women asked the other, "Does your leg hurt?" The other woman, obviously annoyed, shot back, "*Bozhe moi!*—*Hei, furt*—Yes, always!"

The man removed his straw hat and bowed graciously to the women. "Excuse me, *Panie*—ladies. You two must hurry if you wish to take the tram to the steamship hotel."

One woman turned to the other and said, "Yevka, do you hear? He speaks our way . . . almost."

"I am Agent Ziegler," said the man, donning his hat. He reached inside his coat and produced an identity card, which he quickly waved before their eyes and just as quickly returned to his pocket. "I am with the steamship line. I am here to protect our passengers' interests and to guard them against the unfortunate presence here in the city of dishonest operators who prey on the trusting nature of our honorable clients from the highlands, the hinterlands, and the green fields of our ancestors."

The two women stared uncomprehendingly at the man. He leaned toward them, smiling. "*Panie*—ladies, I'm here to make sure no one steals your money or belongings."

"Do you hear, Yevka? Someone honest! Pan Zekler, I wish someone from the boat line had met us in Prague. We didn't dare sleep in that station for fear of all the vultures."

Agent Ziegler chuckled. "Yes, I've heard terrible stories about Prague. I don't know that I would feel safe in such a place. *Panie*—ladies, may I call you by name?"

"Yes, of course, yes. I am Parask—I am Pani Ivanchyn and this is my sister, Pani Rusynko."

Agent Ziegler again removed his hat and bowed. "It is indeed my honor. Now, your tickets please, *Panie*. I think we have chased most of the vultures from Rotterdam."

While Paraska reached under her shawl and fumbled through the purse hanging around her neck, Agent Ziegler reached down and stroked Tomashko's cheek. "What is your name, sailor? Ah, you are shy. Your mother has taught you well. Beware of strangers."

"Here, Pan Tseker. I keep the tickets together with our money."

"Paraska . . ."

"What, Yevka? Don't mind my sister, Pan Zakler. She trusts no one after Prague."

Agent Ziegler nodded solemnly. "And your sister is very wise. Trust no one. That is why I work for the steamship company—to help my Slavic brothers and sisters. Leave the purse about your neck and hand me only the tickets. I will check them before your eyes. Do you see here? Do you see where it is stamped 'Rotterdam' with the numbers underneath? Those are the numbers I need to write down. I have a pencil and a paper on which to record them . . . seven—seven—zero—eight—two, and seven—seven—zero—eight—one. Now, permit me to replace the tickets together with your money. Do you see? I am putting the tickets next to the money in your purse. Boys, look. Do you see?"

Paraska frowned. "Myko-Danko! Pan Zekler is speaking to you!"

"Paraska . . ."

"No, Yevka," said Paraska shaking her finger at Myko and Danko. "The boys need to pay attention when someone speaks to them. Forgive our boys, Pan Zekeler. They have forgotten their manners and are becoming wild on this trip."

"They are good boys," laughed Agent Ziegler. "They are not shy like the little one here, but they observe. Always watch carefully when someone handles your tickets or your money, boys. Now, let's get you to the tram and then to the hotel."

The group hoisted their bags, and Agent Ziegler offered to carry Tomashko, but the boy clutched Yevka's free hand and she grasped it tightly. Agent Ziegler walked alongside Paraska, pointing out interesting details in the train station. Paraska nodded vigorously at the agent's words and marveled at all there was to see.

"Do you see up there, *Pani*? That is—" Agent Ziegler stopped abruptly and Yevka bumped into him from behind.

Standing in the middle of the platform was a tall man wearing a dark coat and a dark hat. "Very good, Ziegler, very good," said this new man, smiling slightly and staring into Agent Ziegler's eyes. "We will all stop here now, hmm? How are you today, Ziegler? Is it 'Ziegler' today, or perhaps a different name, hmm? You are helping the ladies, yes?"

Agent Ziegler turned to Paraska and removed his hat and bowed deeply. When he straightened he flung his hat into the tall man's face and ran past him, eluding the man's grasping hands with a deft spin to the right. The tall man gave chase for the length of a railway car, lost his hat, and then stopped and blew a whistle. Two men appeared near the front of the train, caught Agent Ziegler in their arms, and, after a struggle, subdued him, to the delight of the engineers who leaned out of their locomotive cabs, shaking their fists and shouting encouragement to the combatants.

Paraska and Yevka placed the boys between them and watched the drama with wide eyes. The tall man in the black coat walked back, picked up his hat, and approached the women and boys. He addressed them in a mix of Slovak, Polish, and Rusyn words. "*On zlodii*—He is a thief. I am *zhandar*—police. We watch for him. He steal anything?"

Paraska swallowed. "He . . . he said . . . he said he was an agent from the steamship company. He . . . he took nothing from us."

"No? *Proszę*—please—come with me."

The women herded the boys ahead of them and followed warily. At the head of the train, the other two men had pulled Agent Ziegler's coat down around his elbows and were shouting at him. Agent Ziegler's face was bloody, his shirt was torn, and he ignored his interrogators while acknowledging Paraska with a brief smile. One of the policemen handed an envelope to the tall man in the black coat. He inspected the contents of the envelope and then turned to Paraska. "He took nothing from you, *Pani?*"

Paraska shook her head.

Yevka touched her sister's arm. "Paraska, look in your purse."

Paraska blinked at her sister and then pulled the purse out from under her shawl. She stared into the purse and then looked at Agent Ziegler.

Yevka looked over her sister's shoulder. "*Bozhe moi,* Paraska! It is empty." Then Yevka addressed the tall man. "He stole our tickets and all our money."

The tall man nodded and held out the contents of the envelope taken from Agent Ziegler. "*Panie*—ladies, these are yours."

Yevka took the money and tickets, put them in the purse, and handed it to Paraska. "Put it back under your shawl."

Paraska did as she was told but stood very still and stared at a spot on the far side of the station. The tall man tipped his hat to Yevka and pointed to a set of doors across the station. "Outside, tram take you to ship hotel. Have good voyage to Ameryka, ladies." He patted Myko and Danko on their heads. "Take care of your mothers, boys." He turned and whistled to his fellow officers, and the two men followed with Agent Ziegler, now manacled at the wrists, between them.

Yevka studied her sister out of the corner of her eye but said nothing. Paraska's jaw bulged a few times, and then she took a deep breath, lifted her bag to her shoulder, and began the long walk down the platform. The others followed, and the little group headed for the doors to the street.

℘

A light rain began to fall as the tram pulled up in front of the offices of the steamship line. The passengers filed out of the tram and onto the crowded street, where three men wearing hats bearing the steamship company's name called out instructions in several languages. Yevka and Paraska turned their heads when they heard someone shout in Rusyn, "Enter those doors! Have your papers ready! Dinner after the exam! Have your papers ready!"

Myko and Danko heard accordion music coming from the center of a small crowd congregating on a street corner. As the boys drifted toward the source of the music, a thunderous voice brought them to a halt.

"MYKO-DANKO! COME HERE! NOW!" With a trembling finger, Paraska described a small circle on the surface of the earth and the two boys quickly filled it. Now in a low, firm voice, Paraska gave instructions that the boys acknowledged with quick nods. "You two boys stay in front of us— *always*. Never go to the left or to the right unless we tell you—*never*. Never run ahead—never fall behind—*never*. If we stop, you stop. Listen always for my voice—*always*. If you don't answer me when I call, you will feel my open hand against your heads when I find you. Do you understand?" The two boys nodded.

Yevka placed her hand on her sister's shoulder. "Paraska, let's go inside— we are getting wet."

The sisters and the boys joined the crowd of passengers entering the build- ing, and then followed the loud, multilingual instructions. "Line up here for medical exams! Line up here and here and here!"

Paraska, walking stiffly, pushed Yevka ahead of her and mumbled, "*Bozhe moi,* what will they say about my leg? It's worse today."

One by one, they were led behind a canvas screen for medical exami- nations and inoculations. Paraska, however, was whisked into a room by a laughing, red-faced woman in a white apron, who chattered away in an in- comprehensible language with no apparent expectation of response. Enjoying the woman's friendly manner, Paraska smiled and nodded to her. When this woman left the room, two men appeared and began to examine Paraska. One man, rubber tubes connected to his ears, probed Paraska's chest and back, while the other held a ribbon to her side, stared into her eyes, made notes on a piece of paper, and then left the room. The man with the tubes connected to his ears leaned out the door and called for someone. A short, humorless woman entered and stared at Paraska from head to toe as the man spoke with her. After the man finished speaking, the woman addressed Paraska, using a medley of Slavic terms.

"*Pani, lekar*—doctor—want you should walk." She indicated a little course around the room, and Paraska walked self-consciously, trying to mini- mize her limp. The doctor held out his arm to indicate "enough" and con- ferred with the woman. The woman pointed to Paraska's leg. "Show leg, *Pani*. Pull up dress." Humiliated, Paraska slowly raised her dress and then turned away from the doctor, grimacing as his hands explored her exposed thigh. The doctor spoke, and the woman translated as she tapped Paraska's shrapnel scar. "What is this, *Pani?*"

Paraska grimaced.

"What is this, *Pani?*" the woman repeated.

Through gritted teeth, Paraska replied, "*Voina*—the war."

The doctor squeezed and probed the wound, then lowered the dress. He spoke to the woman, who turned to Paraska and asked, "*Lekar* want to know, does it hurt?"

Paraska smiled and shook her head vigorously. "It never hurts."

The woman translated for the doctor; he looked at Paraska, shrugged and signed a paper. The jolly woman in the white apron reappeared and escorted Paraska back to the rest of her family. The woman's joy was infectious, and Paraska laughed along with her. Before the woman walked away, she touched Paraska's arm, said something, and laughed explosively. Paraska snorted and shook with laughter as she wiped her eyes with her sleeve.

Yevka studied her sister as the chuckling woman walked away. "You understood her?" asked Yevka.

Paraska giggled. "Not a word."

Yevka raised her eyebrows and looked at the boys. When Paraska regained her composure, Yevka leaned closer to her. "Does your leg hurt?"

Paraska giggled again and wiped her eyes. "It always hurts."

❧

After the preliminary medical exam, the emigrants presented their passports to uniformed agents of the steamship line, who transcribed names and other pertinent information onto the ship's steerage manifest, using a typewriter with a massive carriage. While one agent confirmed the passport information orally with the emigrants and asked additional questions, another agent tapped at the keyboard, creating a flurry of little metal arms that popped out of the typewriter and whacked the manifest pages. Children standing in line with their parents were transfixed by this mechanical marvel.

When they reached the head of the line, Paraska and Yevka provided the information requested of them—information not included on their passports: last address, address of relative or friend in America, who paid for the passage, and on and on, the data eventually filling thirty-three columns. Yevka was puzzled by one of the questions until the officer explained the meaning of the word "polygamist." She paled and then quickly shook her head.

Next, the sisters and their boys followed the other passengers into a crowded dining room, where they sat at long tables and were served dark bread, apples, and tea. With the bread came a plate of orange preserves, which Myko and Danko quickly devoured, but not before Yevka spread a spoonful on a piece of bread for Tomashko. The boy, sitting in her lap, happily licked the marmalade off the bread.

Paraska sniffed the air. "Yevka, what is that smell?"

"It is fresh-baked bread."

"No, I mean the other smell."

"*Ne znam*—I don't know, Paraska. I noticed it when we got off the tram." Paraska made a face. "It's not a good smell, is it?"

Across the table a woman with a mouth full of bread declared, "*More*— the sea! The water is under this building."

Paraska smiled at the woman and then whispered to her sister, "Is she mad, Yevka? We are on land, not water."

Yevka shrugged. "*Ne znam*—I don't know, Paraska."

After dinner more women in white aprons escorted the passengers to their sleeping quarters in the steamship line hotel. Men were directed to one wing of the building while women and children were directed to another. Paraska, Yevka, and the boys entered a dark room with a low ceiling, furnished with six iron-frame bunks each with three beds stacked on top of one another. One of the attendants explained. "Like ship. You sleep here. Get used to this so ship not so strange."

Myko and Danko tugged at Yevka's dress. She bent down to listen to their whispers, and when she straightened, she addressed her sister. "Paraska, the boys want to walk around the building. They want—"

"No," said Paraska firmly.

Yevka tried again. "Paraska, we may be here for a few days. We can't keep the boys with us all the time. They promise they won't go far."

Paraska closed her eyes and shrugged. Yevka nodded at the boys, and they ran out of the room.

Paraska sat heavily on the bottom bunk, as Yevka hoisted her things onto the middle bunk. Tomashko climbed up to the middle bunk, where he sat dangling his feet over the edge and munching on a piece of bread.

Paraska collapsed on the bottom bunk and massaged her thigh. "*Bozhe moi,* Yevka! I can't walk another step or answer another question. How much more of this do you think there will be?"

Yevka grunted a noncommittal reply as she arranged her things on the middle bunk. Tomashko finished his bread, yawned, and curled up at the end of the bunk, where he quickly fell asleep.

"Yevka?"

"Yes, Paraska?"

"How long will we stay here before we go on the boat?"

"I don't know—I heard maybe three days."

Paraska groaned. "Three days! What will we do for three days?"

At that moment Myko and Danko raced into the room.

"M-M-Mamko! T-T-Teto!"

"Mamko-Teto!"

"C-c-come and s-s-see!"

"Come see what we found!"

Paraska sat up wearily in her bunk. "What the devil is this all about?"

"C-c-come see, *M-M-Mamko!*"

"No, Myko. My leg hurts. Stop pulling on my arm or I will slap you."

Yevka smiled at her son, Danko. "What did you find?"

"Mamko, they have white bowls here and you—" Danko looked at his cousin, Myko, and they both giggled.

"What about the white bowls?" said Yevka.

"There is a room with white bowls and you sit on them, and when you make something in the water you stand up and pull a rope, and everything goes out the bottom of the bowl—*shoosh!*"

Myko giggled, *"Sh-sh-shoosh!"*

Danko laughed and grabbed his cousin by the arm. "Come, Myko! Let's go make something in the bowls again and pull the rope!" The boys ran out of the room shouting.

"Shoosh!"

"Sh-sh-shoosh!"

"Yevka, what the devil are our boys talking about?"

"Ne znam—I don't know, Paraska."

By the time Yevka climbed up next to Tomashko and looked over the edge of the bunk, Paraska was asleep and breathing deeply through her mouth.

❧

Three days later, after breakfast, the shipping hotel attendants announced that the ship was at the dock, and that the passengers should prepare to board. There was turmoil in the women's quarters as several hundred women packed, admonished their bewildered children, and shouldered their earthly possessions. Danko and Myko had disappeared somewhere between the dining hall and the sleeping quarters. Paraska crammed their things into their bags and mumbled about the terrible fate that awaited the boys. When Danko and Myko reappeared, Paraska lunged toward their necks, but Yevka intervened. "Paraska, hand me Tomashko, and help me with my bundle. Danko, your *teta* has packed your things—pick them up. You too, Myko. Come, Paraska—there is no time—the boat will leave without us if we don't hurry."

Paraska, her lower lip quivering, helped Yevka, and then hoisted her own bags to her shoulder and limped out of the room. Yevka and the boys caught up with her outside, and joined the other passengers walking to the dock. The male passengers came from their quarters, and those men with families joined their wives and children in line while the single men walked alone, staring out at the water. As the passengers rounded the corner of the shipping line hotel, a male voice in the crowd called out, "There it is!"

Paraska frowned and looked around. "What is he yelling about? Yevka, what is it—can you see anything?"

Yevka craned her neck. "I think there is another hotel up ahead. Only . . . it is much bigger than the other one."

Paraska nodded. "Yes, I see it. Is that where we are going? Why must we stay in another hotel? I thought we were getting on the boat today."

A male passenger, only slightly older than the sisters and walking alone along the edge of the dock, moved closer to Paraska and touched his cap. "You speak *po-nashomu*—our way," he said, and then he pointed to the great structure. "That is no hotel. That is the ship for Ameryka. They will pack two thousand of us in it before we head to the open sea."

Paraska said nothing, but edged toward Yevka while the male passenger shrugged, touched his cap, and walked ahead. The line came to a halt and Paraska whispered to Yevka, "Is he a madman? Buildings can't float—nothing that big can float. Where do you think our boat is, Yevka?"

A female voice in the crowd said, "He is right—that is our boat. I saw a picture of it." Other voices chattered anxiously, and everyone gazed up at the great ship's black hull and white upper decks, topped with two yellow smokestacks.

"*Bozhe moi,*" Paraska muttered. "*Bozhe moi.* Yevka, how can such a thing float?"

"*Ne znam*—I don't know, Paraska. *Ne znam.*"

Along the length of the dock, stevedores muscled cargo into great nets, which were lifted into the air by cables, swung over to the ship, and deposited on or below the decks.

Myko and Danko were fascinated by the stevedores, who dangled pipes and cigarettes from their lips, and laughed hoarsely among themselves as they spat nonchalantly into the harbor. "L-l-l-look!" cried Myko, pointing to a long ramp that connected the ship to the dock. The first of two thousand steerage passengers were making their way across the ramp, far above the water's surface and into the side of the ship.

A voice behind Paraska said, "I've gone across once before on her. She's a big ship." Paraska turned and saw the same lone male passenger who had addressed her before. He pointed to the gangplank. "We enter the ship there. The next time you step off that ramp, you will be in Ameryka."

Paraska reddened and squeezed closer to Yevka.

"Yes," the man continued. "There will be nothing but water below us until we arrive in Ameryka."

The long line of emigrants began to move once again.

CHAPTER FORTY-SEVEN

The Ship

PARASKA AND YEVKA HERDED THE BOYS up the ramp that led into the side of the great ship. Halfway up, Danko stopped in front of his aunt Paraska and pointed to the murky harbor water below. "Look! Look how far we are above the water!"

As Paraska looked down she quickly grasped the handrail. *"Bozhe moi!* And still we climb! Danko, move on. Myko, don't stop. Keep moving."

"B-b-but l-l-look at the w-w-water!"

"I saw it—MOVE!"

The stream of passengers passed through the opening and found themselves on the steerage deck, where a number of ship's officials shouted and pushed the bewildered people through doorways and down dark stairwells to dimly lit rooms. Here there were more probing exams and another round of inoculations.

Paraska rubbed her shoulder and leaned closer to Yevka. "If one more person touches me or sticks one more thing into me," she said, "I think I will hit him."

"Paraska!"

"I am very serious, Yevka. I am tired of it all . . . so very tired."

The passengers shuffled still farther below decks. Yevka went first, holding Tomashko's hand, followed by Danko, then Myko, then Paraska. Yevka called over her shoulder, "It is dark—be careful."

Paraska moaned. "Be careful? Be careful of what? It is too dark. I can't see my feet . . . I can't see anything . . . *Bozhe!*"

At the bottom of the stairs, a ship's matron, wearing a little white cap and a long, dark dress overlaid with a white apron, pointed toward a doorway to her right. "Come, please . . . come," she said, beckoning with her other hand. She touched Yevka's arm and pointed to Danko. "How old, please, the boy?"

"*On mat visim rokiv*—he is eight years old."

"And this one?" asked the matron, pointing to Myko.

"*Sim*—seven," grunted Paraska.

The matron nodded, "Very good, they sleep in your compartment." And she guided the sisters and their boys to a room similar to those in the shipping hotel on shore, where two dozen women and children were noisily settling into their quarters. The matron pointed to a stack of three iron cots in the last row. "Your family sleep here, hmm?"

While Paraska and Yevka tossed their bundles on their bunks, the matron returned to the doorway of the room and called for everyone's attention. "Here, please—look here. I am Mary, hmm? You want a thing, you call me, hmm? You need a thing, you call me, hmm? I take care of this room and others, hmm?"

Paraska nudged Yevka. "Is she asking us or telling us?"

The matron raised an eyebrow at Paraska. "You have question?"

Paraska forced a smile. "No . . . no question."

"Good. You take beds and store things, hmm? You see this?" She held up a cushion from the foot of one of the beds. "Everyone look, hmm? This help you float in water, hmm? We never need these, but if I tell you"—She placed the cushion around her neck and indicated the canvas straps—"you put it on and tie these, hmm? There are more on the wall for children. You"— she pointed to Paraska, who had paled at the mention of water—"you have question?"

Paraska's eyes were wide. "Why do we need to float in the water?"

The matron chuckled. "No need. Only if ship sink, hmm? But ship never sink. More question, hmm?"

Since there were no more questions, the matron turned and left the room. Paraska sat heavily on a lower bunk and imitated the matron's higher voice, "'Only if ship sink, hmm!' *Ioi!* I'm so tired—let it sink. I don't care anymore." Paraska sighed. "Yevka?"

"Yes?"

"I'll sleep here like I did in the room on land. Is that all right with you?"

"Yes."

"Why does she make that sound—like she's asking a question? 'Hmm— hmm?' Is she asking a question, Yevka?"

Yevka hoisted her bag onto the middle bunk. "I don't know, Paraska."

A woman comforting a small boy on the lower bunk in the next row looked up at Paraska. "Who knows why she says it. She's a German. Just do as she says. She will take care of you. We stayed a month in Hamburg last year and had to go home because of kvota. A woman there talked like this woman. The Germans took good care of us, though."

Paraska studied the woman. "You couldn't go to Ameryka because of kvota?"

The woman tossed her hands in the air. "They said, 'You go home now—no more of your people this year!' So, kvota was filled for our people even before we got to Hamburg. We had to stay in Hamburg until we could find a way back to our village, Ruska Kaina on *Potok* Olka—the Olka Brook. Do you know it?"

"Do I know what?" asked Paraska.

"Our village, Ruska Kaina on *Potok* Olka."

"I never heard of it."

"You've heard of *Potok* Olka, haven't you?"

Paraska shook her head.

"Well, then, where are you from?" asked the woman, squinting at Paraska.

"Stara Polyanka . . . on *Potok* Ondava."

The woman sniffed and turned away. "I never heard of it."

Danko and Myko had tossed their bundles up on the top bunk and now asked if they could go outside on the deck.

"Of course not," said Paraska. "You'll fall in the water."

"N-n-no w-w-we—"

"No we won't, *Teto*!"

Danko and Myko implored Yevka to intercede on their behalf. Yevka nodded reassuringly at the boys and then turned to Paraska. "I'm sure the boys will be safe. The boat people with the uniforms—the guards—they are everywhere. The boys will be safe, Paraska."

Paraska shrugged but said nothing. The boys raised their eyebrows hopefully at Yevka, who nodded her head toward the door. The boys ran to the door but stopped when Paraska barked, "WALK—DON'T RUN!" The boys walked slowly out the door and into the passageway, where their footsteps suddenly accelerated and their shoes slapped the metal treads of the staircase.

Yevka unrolled her pack on the cot above Paraska's and felt Tomashko tugging at her leg. She picked him up and set him on the edge of the bed, then arranged a blanket for him to lie on.

"Your boy is beautiful."

Yevka turned around. A pale young girl stood behind her, arranging a top bunk. "*Dyakuyu*—thank you," Yevka replied, smiling.

The girl pointed to the woman from Ruska Kaina, who was once again engaged in conversation with Paraska. "That is my mother, Anna Perhach, and that is my little brother, Ivanko. I am Mariya. We are going to Ameryka to be with my father. He went to Ameryka over two years ago and sent us money last year, but we couldn't go . . . like *Mamka* said—kvota. I think your boys are looking forward to seeing their father."

Yevka reddened and busied herself with her bundle. "Yes . . . yes, they are."

☙

Later, Paraska called up to Yevka from her bunk. "Where are Myko and Danko?"

"I think they are back up the stairs."

"They shouldn't go up there—they might fall off the boat."

"They won't fall off the boat, Paraska."

"They could drown."

"There are fences—they won't fall off."

"They could climb the fences, fall off, and drown."

"Paraska, they won't drown."

After a pause, Paraska forgot about Myko and Danko. "Yevka, how long did Vasyl say it would take?"

"Ten days, I think."

"Ten days! *Bozhe moi!*" Paraska pulled a short length of yarn from her bag and tied it to the bed frame above her. "Yevka?"

"Yes?"

"I'm hanging a bit of yarn from your bed. Every day I'll tie a knot so we know how long we have to wait until we get to Ameryka."

"That's a good idea, Paraska."

"Yevka?"

"Hmm?"

"Do you think I should tie a knot now or wait until the boat moves?"

"I don't know, Paraska. Do what you think is best. I'm going to close my eyes now."

Paraska tied a loose knot and then changed her mind. "Maybe I'll wait until the boat moves." Untying the knot, she murmured, "Ten knots to go. *Bozhe!*"

&

Yevka was startled from her afternoon nap by a thundering horn blast that reverberated throughout the depths of the ship. Tomashko grasped her arm, and from the bunk below, Paraska groaned, "*Bozhe moi,* Yevka! What the devil is that? Should we tie on the cushions now?"

Yevka sat up, rubbing her eyes. She lowered herself to the floor, saying, "I don't know. Maybe we are leaving."

Myko and Danko, panting and elbowing one another, rushed into the room and slid to a stop next to their mothers' bunks.

"*M-M-Mamko!*"

"*MAMKO!*"

"C-c-come—"

"Come see!"

"The b-b-boa—"

"—is going away—"

"—f-from the l-l-land and—"

"—we are—"

"—l-l-leaving—"

"—LEAVING FOR AMERYKA!"

The boys ran out again without waiting for a response. They raced back up the stairs, their words registering slowly among all the women and children in the compartment. Several other children ran out the door and up the steps as their mothers futilely admonished them.

Yevka leaned over Paraska's bunk. "Shall we go see what is happening?"

Paraska nodded and rolled to the side of the bunk. But then she stopped. "*Chekai*—wait, Yevka." Paraska looped a loose knot in the strand of yarn. "There, now we have started. *Dobre*—very well, Yevka, let's go upstairs." Grabbing her sister's arm for support, Paraska winced when she stood up. "Yes," she said, anticipating Yevka's question. "It always hurts."

Yevka hoisted Tomashko over her left shoulder, and, together with her sister, followed the other women up the stairs. Out on the deck, Myko and Danko spotted their mothers and led them to the railing. Down below, two little boats blew dark gray smoke into the air as they nudged their bows against the side of the great ship.

Paraska gripped Yevka's shoulder. "All that water . . . it is so far down . . . I can't look."

From behind the sisters came a familiar voice: "Saying good-bye to Europe, hmm?" It was the matron from their compartment, standing at the railing and securing her little white cap with one hand in the light breeze.

"I thought it was called Roterdim," Paraska said, gazing at the distant city that seemed to float slowly away.

The matron smiled broadly, showing her teeth. She walked away stroking her chin with one hand and holding her cap in place with the other.

Paraska squeezed Yevka's shoulder and glared across the water. "I don't like that woman. That city is called Roterdim or Roterdom or some damn thing, isn't it? What was she talking about?"

Yevka shrugged, and the sisters stood at the railing with the crowd of steerage passengers. Together they watched Rotterdam, and all that existed far beyond it, gradually recede in the gray mist.

⁋

Supper was a stressful, chaotic event. For women who had spent a lifetime preparing and serving meals, the idea of sitting and being served was peculiar and uncomfortable. They passed around the pail of soup that was delivered to their table; then came the pan of herring and potatoes; and, finally, the plate of rye bread and butter. The stewards, who rushed about picking up dishes the moment a passenger hesitated, unnerved Paraska and she leaned over to Yevka. "I can't eat like this—my stomach hurts. Why do we have to hurry?"

Behind Paraska, the matron stood smiling, with her hands clasped over her apron. Paraska leaned over her plate and ate quickly.

⁋

After supper, in the fading daylight, the passengers stood on the steerage deck and faced into a cool sea breeze. From an upper deck came the sounds of a lively band and the laughter of men and women.

"Yevka, listen. Do you hear the fiddles? I haven't heard fiddles in a long time. I wish we could hear them better. Yevka, look."

High above on an upper deck, an officer of the ship stood with his back to the railing and spoke to the unseen passengers on that deck. Then, using a small flame, he ignited the bases of three sticks, which, after a pause, shot skyward with a loud hiss, and then suddenly exploded in a succession of colorful bursts. The people on the upper deck laughed and applauded.

Tomashko clung tightly to Yevka as she rubbed his back reassuringly. "Paraska, they are like bombs during the war. What does it mean?" she asked.

Paraska shook her head. "*Ne znam*—I don't know." When she saw Danko and Myko running toward them, Paraska stood in their path with her arms on her hips. "Where have you two been?"

The boys spoke at once.

"D-d-did y-y-you—"

"DID YOU SEE?"

"W-w-we . . . we—"

"We stood right below—"

"—and s-s-saw—"

"—and saw EVERYTHING!"

Paraska held up her hands, and the boys, though excited and anxious, knew well to hold their tongues. "I will not listen to you like this. You will speak one at a time. Danko, you first."

Myko was not pleased. "*M-M-Mamko!*"

"Tsh! Danko will go first—he is the oldest. Myko, you will speak when I point my finger at you. Speak, Danko. And get your chin off your chest, Myko, or you will not see my finger when it is your turn. Speak, Danko."

"We met a man on the deck above who speaks *po-nashomu*—our way. He has his own room on this ship, and he's been to Ameryka and he told us many things."

Paraska frowned. "How did you two get up there?"

The boys grinned at one another and Yevka intervened saying, "Please, Paraska—don't ask. It is better we don't know."

Paraska snorted and pointed to her son. "Hmph! Continue, Myko."

"The m-m-man t-t-told us—A-A-Amerych-ch-chane on the b-b-boat are ha-ha-having a b-birthday."

Paraska pointed to Danko. "Whose birthday?"

Danko stepped forward and threw his hands into the air. "They are having a party for Ameryka. A long, long time ago, maybe even thirty years, Ameryka had a tsar called Kink-a-Enklint and he was a bad man, so they threw all his tea into the ocean and made him leave, and then the Amerychane had their own country and every year on this day they fire powder and guns and they call it fort-a-dzalai in their language!"

Paraska frowned first at Danko and then at her son. "What did they throw away?"

"T-t-tea!"

"Tea?"

"Y-y-yes. They th-th-threw it in the w-w-water."

"Why would they do that?"

The boys shrugged. "That's what they did," said Danko. "Then the tsar left Ameryka. Come, Myko, let's go see the ocean again!" Danko grabbed his cousin by the arm and the two ran off together into the crowd of women and children gathered at the ship's rail.

Paraska smiled and shook her head. "Yevka, do you hear all this? Already our boys are learning stories about Ameryka and even how to speak *po-amerykanský*—the Amerykan way—and still we have nine knots to tie on the yarn before we get there!"

CHAPTER FORTY-EIGHT

The Open Sea

THE NEXT MORNING the great ship called at the French port of Boulogne-sur-Mer. The passengers lined the rails to watch new steerage passengers climbing aboard from a barge tied alongside.

Paraska walked out on the deck followed by Myko and Danko, and finally, Yevka, who carried the sleeping Tomashko. "Yevka, why are we stopped? Myko-Danko, why are we stopped?"

A male passenger standing alone at the railing overheard Paraska and turned to face her. "*Zhydy*—Jews—from Russia," he said. "A whole trainload of them." He touched the brim of his cap. "Hello again."

Paraska paled—it was the man from the dock in Rotterdam—the man who had pointed out the ship at the dock. Flustered, Paraska turned away and glanced down at the activity below before turning away at the sight of all the water. "Yevka, look at all the *Zhydy*. Where can they put so many *Zhydy* on this boat?" Paraska looked askance at the man by the rail.

Yevka set Tomashko on the deck and leaned over the railing to get a better look at the line of heavily burdened people, boarding from the barge. "They are taking them to a different place—a place away from our area."

The man at the railing spoke again. "They don't put the *Zhydy* with us. They keep the races separated. *Zhydy* eat their own food—they won't eat what we eat."

Paraska took Yevka's hand and led her away from the railing. "Come, Yevka, we'll stand over here."

Yevka glanced at the man at the rail and whispered, "What is wrong, Paraska? Why are you ignoring him?"

"Yevka, this man sees two women—two women alone with their children. Why would he want to speak with us? Let him find other women to trouble."

Paraska looked over her shoulder. The man nodded at her and tipped his hat. Paraska quickly turned away, biting her lower lip and breathing quickly through her mouth.

☙

During the night, the ship crossed the English Channel and in the morning called at Portsmouth, England. Here, passengers of a different sort boarded and went to the first- and second-class levels, followed by attendants carrying luggage and pushing enormous steamer trunks on wheeled carts.

Below, in the steerage compartments, Paraska whispered to Yevka in the overhead bunk. "Yevka, are you awake?"

"Hmm?"

"Are you awake?"

"Yes."

"I think we stopped. Why did we stop again?"

"I don't know."

"Yevka?"

"Hmm?"

"I feel sick."

No answer.

"Yevka?"

"Hmm?"

"Do you feel sick?"

"No."

"Last night the boat moved up and down and I felt sick. I feel better when the boat stops, though."

"What do you want to do, Paraska? Do you want to go upstairs and get some fresh air?"

"Yes . . . yes, I think I do."

Yevka roused Tomashko and slid off the bunk, landing hard on her bare feet. She slipped on her shoes, and opened her arms for Tomashko: "Come." The boy rubbed his eyes, and then slid into his mother's arms and thrust his head against her neck.

Paraska rolled to her side and sat up moaning. "I was hot. Now I'm cold. Where are Myko and Danko?"

"Still asleep."

"Wake them and let's wash."

The sisters roused their boys and pushed them out to the hall, where they joined other women and children attempting a modest cleaning at a row of sinks. Mary, the matron, appeared behind the row of sinks and prodded the women. "You hurry, hmm? Breakfast is now in hall." She paused a moment to watch Paraska scrub Myko's face and then moved on.

Paraska leaned closer to Yevka and said, "Why does she always look at me like that? I don't like that woman."

"She watches all of us," said Yevka. "I think she means well, Paraska." Yevka dabbed at her eldest son's face with a small cloth. "Hold still, Danko."

Paraska shook her head. "Maybe she watches all of us . . . but . . . I don't like the way she looks at me."

✑

After breakfast, the passengers went up the stairs and out on the deck, where, in a cold wind, the women tightened their shawls over their heads and the men held down the bills of their caps. Yevka carried Tomashko, spreading her shawl over his head, while Paraska called after Myko and Danko, who ran down the deck ignoring her. Paraska frowned and put her hands on her hips. "It is useless to yell in this wind—they cannot hear me."

"Don't worry—they can't go far," said a familiar voice. Yevka and Paraska turned around to see the same man who was by the rail the day before—the same man from the dock in Rotterdam. "I see your boys everywhere on this ship, at all hours of the day and night. This is an exciting trip for them." The sisters blinked at the man and then at one another. The stranger bowed his head slightly and announced, "I am Andrii Kupka from Krasni Brod on *Rika* Laborets—the Laborets River."

The women stared at the speaker and Paraska moved her lips, pondering his words.

Andrii Kupka continued. "You women are from near there—I guess this because of your way of talking. You are Rusyns—so am I. Are you going to Ameryka to join your family?" He was looking at Paraska as he spoke. With a subtle raise of the eyebrows and a slight cock of the head, Yevka encouraged her to answer the man.

Paraska reddened and then looked down at the deck. "I am Paraska Ivanchyn and she is my sister, Yevka Rusynko. I am from—*we* are from Stara Polyanka on *Potok* Ondava."

Andrii Kupka brightened. "Stara Polyanka! I think I know it. I have been to Stropkov on the Ondava. Do you know it? It is below Stara Polyanka."

Paraska moved her lips in confusion and finally said, "We are from Stara Polyanka on *Potok* Ondava."

"Stropkov isn't far from there—only, you've never been there?" The women shook their heads. "And you are joining family in Ameryka?" asked Andrii.

Paraska bit her lip. "Our husbands will meet us in Nu York."

Yevka sniffed, and, looking over the railing at the view of Portsmouth, shifted Tomashko to her other shoulder.

Andrii grabbed the bill of his cap against a strong gust of wind and put one foot on the railing. "I was in Ameryka during the war—Bayonne, Nu Dzyerzi. I went back to my village last year, only"—he shrugged and held up one palm—"I think maybe I should not have gone back. Things are different there now and . . . I think now maybe I will stay in Ameryka . . . I go back to Nu Dzyerzi for good now. Where do your husbands live?"

Paraska looked to Yevka for help, but her sister was gazing at the docks below. "They are in Yonkers," said Paraska quickly.

"Yonkers!" cried Andrii. "I have been there! I have cousins there. Which church do they attend?"

Paraska bit her lower lip and again glanced at her sister. Yevka, her back turned, had disassociated herself from the conversation. "*Ne znam*—I don't know," said Paraska. "I don't remember."

Andrii was persistent. "Are your husbands *Grekokatolytský* or *Pravoslavný*—Greek Catholic or Orthodox?"

"*Grekokatolytský.*"

"Ah, then your husbands are at St. Nicholas Parish, yes?"

"Y-yes . . ." stammered Paraska. "I . . . I think . . . yes, of course they are."

"What are their names? Perhaps I met them on my last visit to Yonkers."

Paraska twisted the ends of her shawl and ground her teeth. "Vasko Ivanchyn and Petro Rusynko."

Andrii repeated the names and shook his head. "I remember a Rusynko in Bayonne, only that was before the war. No . . . I don't know these men." After a pause, Andrii pointed to Tomashko. "He is a good, quiet boy."

Paraska, relieved at the distraction, placed a hand on Yevka's shoulder and turned her away from the railing. "Yevka, show Tomashko to the *pan*—the gentleman." Yevka displayed the sleeping child and then covered him once again with the shawl.

"He looks like you," said Andrii to Yevka. "When did your husband go to Ameryka?"

"Before the war," said Yevka.

"No, I mean when did he go back to your village again? Has he seen his son yet?"

Reddening, Yevka looked away in confusion. Paraska intervened. "No, Petro will see Tomashko for the first time when we reach Ameryka. He left before Tomashko was born. Do you have children, Pan Kupka?"

"No. I had a wife in Krasni Brod, only she was sickly. I left for Ameryka, and then there was the war. Three years ago I received word that she had died during the war. I went back to Krasni Brod, but . . . maybe . . . I should not have gone back. Maybe I was looking for someone else."

"Do you mean a wife?" suggested Paraska, and then bit her lip and looked away frowning.

Andrii smiled. "Perhaps. Look, we are leaving."

The three looked out across the water toward the land, which seemed to be floating away. Paraska held the rail and turned her back to the water. "What place is this?" she asked Andrii Kupka.

"Angliya. The people here call it Enklint."

"Oh, yes," said Paraska. "I heard of it. This is where the tsar went when he lost his tea in Ameryka. Our boys already learned this."

Andrii shrugged. "I know nothing of such things. In Ameryka there is no time for learning these things. I was a farmer in Krasni Brod. In Ameryka I am always working inside buildings. Ameryka is . . . Ameryka is a big place . . . it is a big land, where there are many people like us who come from *starŷi krai*—the old country. The people come from many places to find work in Ameryka, and some speak our way or very close to it. They come from villages like mine, where we worked in fields and forests. We planted barley and wheat, and we cut trees for our homes and for our hearth fires. Then, after the Feast of the Beheading of St. John, we harvested our crops. In my village I knew everyone, and they knew me. Some of us got along, and some of us didn't, but we worked outdoors all year long unless it rained or snowed." Andrii smiled at Paraska. "Is that how things were in your village?"

Paraska nodded quickly. "Yes, yes, it was. It was very much like that."

"Well," said Andrii, looking out over the harbor. "Be ready for changes.

In Ameryka, it is very different from our villages. In *starŷi krai* our work was guided by the seasons and the length of the day. In Ameryka the work is always the same whether it is day or night, snow or rain or heat. In Ameryka 'big boss' watches everything you do and yells at you, '*Skoro*—hurry!' And always there is a clock on the wall and you work for that clock and 'big boss.' That is Ameryka—bosses and clocks and *skoro*—hurry!" Andrii Kupka sighed and pulled up his collar against the stiffening breeze. "And if you don't hurry fast enough for them, they will replace you with someone else. There is always someone else. Before the war and kvota there were endless people waiting to take your job. Now, with kvota, there will be fewer of our people going to Ameryka."

"We waited since last year," said Paraska. "Didn't we, Yevka?"

"Yes, *to pravda*—this is true, Paraska."

"I think now," said Andrii solemnly, "it will be more and more difficult to go to Ameryka. There are many people in Ameryka—people whose families have been there for generations—who don't want any more of us, or people like us to come to Ameryka."

"Why not?" asked Yevka.

Andrii shook his head and then, after a pause, said, "Maybe I shouldn't tell you, but . . . well, you'll hear it soon enough for yourselves. You might as well hear it from me. They say there are too many of us in Ameryka—they say we are dirty, stupid, and Catholic."

Paraska frowned. "How dare they say such things! Who are they to call us dirty and stupid?"

Andrii shrugged. "We live in the oldest buildings in the worst areas of the cities, and we don't speak *po-Amerykanskŷ*—the Amerykan way. We work long hours doing dirty jobs most Amerychane don't want to do. And most of us are Catholic—they say that someday Catholics will outnumber everyone else in Ameryka. I only tell you all of this to prepare you in case you ever hear such talk. I ignore it myself. If it bothered me I wouldn't return to Ameryka." Andrii sighed and tipped his hat to the sisters. "Good evening to you both. Take a last look at Angliya. We won't see land again until we reach Ameryka next week." Then Andrii walked half the length of the steerage deck to the entrance to the men's quarters.

Yevka placed her hand on Paraska's shoulder. "Why did you tell him we have husbands waiting for us?"

Paraska frowned and shrugged saying, "I don't know why I told him that.

It seemed best somehow . . . at least, I thought it was best at the time . . . now . . . now I don't know . . ."

Spotting Myko and Danko at the end of the deck, Yevka set Tomashko on the deck so he could run after them. "Tomashko and I are going to see the boys," she said. "Will you come?"

Paraska motioned Yevka along. "Yes, yes, I'll follow." She stood at the rail and watched Andrii Kupka, who had stopped to chat with two men before entering the stairwell to the men's quarters. Paraska ran a finger along her cheek and then tapped her lips. "I wish I hadn't told him that," she murmured.

☙

By evening, the ship was beyond sight of land but within range of the shrieking seagulls diving at the stern. Below decks, Paraska lay in her bunk moaning and rubbing her belly while Yevka stood over her.

"Yevka?"

"Yes, Paraska? I am here."

"I think I'm going to be sick again."

"You won't be the only one. Most of the women in this room are getting sick."

Paraska pushed herself up on her elbows, leaned over the edge of the bunk, and vomited on the floor. She coughed and wiped her mouth with her sleeve, before once again collapsing on her back. *"Oi!"* she moaned. *"Ioi,* Yevka! I can't take this any longer. Do you hear me?"

Yevka closed her eyes and wrinkled her nose. "Yes, Paraska—I hear you."

Myko and Danko ran into the compartment and began talking at once. "The *Zh—Zh—Zh—*"

"The *Zhydŷ* tried—"

"—to b-b-burn d-down—"

"—the ship!"

"What the devil has happened?" cried Paraska holding up a hand. "One at a time! ONE AT A TIME! Myko, what happened?"

"The *Zh-Zhydŷ* t-t-tried to b-b-urn down the sh-sh-ship!"

Paraska pointed to Danko. "What happened?"

"We were in the Jewish quarters—the *Zhydŷ* lit candles and—"

Paraska frowned. "What were you two doing in the Jewish quarters? How did you get in there?"

Yevka sat on the edge of Paraska's bunk next to her sister's feet. "Don't ask them, Paraska—it is probably better if we don't know."

"Hmph! Go on—Myko, it is your turn."

"The *Zh- Zhydŷ* lit c-c-candles and the m-m-men from the sh-sh-ship t-took them away f-from the *Zh-Zh- Zhydŷ*!"

Paraska pointed to Danko. "Go on."

"The men from the ship were angry and they grabbed the candles from the Jewish women and shouted, *'Dumpke Yuden! Dumpke Yuden!'* They said the women were trying to burn the ship."

"What did they call them?" asked Yevka.

"*Dumpke Yuden, Mamko.* I don't know what it means."

"I know what *dumpke Yuden* means," offered Anna Perhach from her bunk. "It means 'stupid Jews.' I remember hearing that in Hamburg last year."

Myko and Danko ran out of the compartment, ignoring Paraska's cries. "Where are you going! COME BACK HERE!"

"Let them go, Paraska," said Yevka.

Paraska shook her head. "What the devil were the *Zhydŷ* doing with fire? There are no fires allowed down here."

Anna Perhach snorted. "Feh! *Zhydŷ* are always up to something. They'll burn the ship down with their damn candles. *Dumpke Yuden!*"

Yevka inspected Paraska's length of yarn, suspended from the bunk above. "*Ponedilok*—Monday—was the day we boarded the ship in Rotterdam. Isn't that right, Paraska?"

"I don't know—what difference does it make?"

"*Vitorok*—Tuesday—we went to sea," said Yevka, fingering the knots as she recited the days of the week. "*Ponedilok—vitorok—sereda—chetver—pyatnytsa. Pyatnytsa!* Day five, Paraska! Today is *pyatnytsa*—Friday! That is why the *Zhydŷ* lit candles—they are remembering their Sabbath. For them, it starts on Friday evening. Do you remember the *Zhydŷ* in Stara Polyanka, Paraska? They always lit candles on Friday at dusk—the beginning of their Sabbath."

Paraska yawned and reclined on her cot. "Sabbath or not—they could have burned down the ship."

Yevka climbed into her bunk next to Tomashko. "Think of it, Paraska! Even out here in the middle of the ocean—they remembered their Sabbath."

☙

Later that night, Paraska wheezed and called out weakly from her lower bunk. "Yevka?"

"Yes?"

"Where are you?"

"Above you—in my bunk. Tomashko is asleep. I don't want to speak too loudly and awaken him."

"Oh." Pause. "Yevka?"

"Yes?"

"I think I ate too much dinner."

"You did eat a lot."

"I was feeling better, so I ate a lot of herring. Do you think I'm sick because I ate a lot of herring?"

"I don't know, Paraska. The ship never stops rolling. I don't feel well, either. Maybe we should think about something else."

Pause.

"Yevka?"

"Yes?"

"I need to be sick again." Paraska leaned over the bunk again and vomited on the floor. "Yevka?"

"What is it, Paraska?"

"For most of my life I can't get enough to eat. Now there is food everywhere. These people feed us all the time, only I can't keep it in my stomach . . . *oi* . . ." Pause. "Yevka?"

No answer.

"Yevka?"

"What is it, Paraska?"

"Do you think it is bad that I lied?"

"Lied? Lied about what?"

"You know . . . you remember . . . about having . . . about both of us having husbands waiting for us. Was it bad to lie?"

"I don't know."

Paraska leaned over the side of her bunk and retched and coughed. "*Oi, Bozhe!* I have nothing left in my stomach to bring up. Yevka?"

"Yes?"

"I shouldn't have told him I have a husband." Pause. "Did you hear what I said, Yevka?"

"Yes."

"I think maybe I should tell him I lied. What do you think—should I tell him I lied?"

"I don't know, Paraska. I think I'm too sick to think about it." Yevka closed her eyes and turned on her side. She put an arm across Tomashko's body and grasped the side of the bunk.

In her bunk below, Paraska breathed through her mouth and murmured, "I think tomorrow I'll tell him . . . I shouldn't have lied . . . it was foolish to lie . . . I'll tell him . . . yes . . . tomorrow I'll tell him the truth."

CHAPTER FORTY-NINE

A Storm

IN THE MORNING THE MATRON, Mary, entered the compartment, turned on the lights, and announced that breakfast would be served in thirty minutes.

Groaning, Paraska turned on her side and called to her sister. "Yevka? Yevka . . . are you awake?"

"Yes."

"Who the devil can eat breakfast? Is she mad?"

"She's still in the room, Paraska."

Paraska arched her neck and saw Mary's inverted face smiling down at her.

"You will eat this morning," the matron said to Paraska. "Water is quiet. You will eat." Snapping her fingers, Mary then addressed the other women. "Thirty minutes." She turned and marched out of the room.

Paraska swung her legs over the edge of the cot and struggled into a sitting position. "That woman hates me, Yevka."

"She doesn't hate you."

"What did she mean, 'the water is quiet'?"

"I don't know. The boat isn't swaying like it did last night."

"Have we stopped, Yevka? We can't be there already." Paraska inspected the string above her bunk. "Four knots. It is morning—so, I will tie another knot. There—five knots. How many days did Vasyl say it takes?"

"Ten. Help me wake the boys, Paraska. They won't listen to me."

Paraska stood and slapped the bottom of the upper bunk with her open hand. "MYKO-DANKO! UP, NOW!" The boys bolted upright, blinking their eyes. Paraska slipped on her shoes. "Five more days—five more knots— hmph! Hand me Tomashko."

Yevka handed her son to Paraska and then lowered herself to the floor where she stood up on her toes, stretching her arms toward the ceiling. "The boat is still moving, Paraska—but it doesn't seem as bad as yesterday. Let's get the boys washed for breakfast."

ᏒᎧ

In the dining hall the sisters arranged themselves at a table with the boys between them. As the family was being served, Andrii Kupka approached the table. "*Dobre rano*—good morning. May I sit with all of you?"

Paraska swallowed nervously and then lowered her eyes and stared at her plate. Yevka indicated an open seat directly opposite Paraska's and said, "*Proshu*—please."

Andrii Kupka sat down and, taking the folded napkin from the table, snapped it open with a flick of his wrist and tucked it into his open collar. "Have you all slept well these last two nights?"

Paraska glanced at Yevka and then cleared her throat. "Yes . . . yes we have."

Andrii chuckled. "I haven't. You'd think I'd be used to rough seas after two crossings. I don't know when anyone gets used to the ocean. The crew seems fine. But, then, they do this all the time. *Proshu,* pass the jam."

Paraska passed the jam to Andrii and then picked at her food.

"You are not hungry," said Andrii, his mouth full.

"Yes . . . no," said Paraska, confused.

"I know how you feel," smiled Andrii. "I feel sick—then I can't eat. When I feel better, I don't know if I should eat, because I know the sea will become rough again. I made the crossing during the winter once—it was before the war. It was terrible. Even the crew was sick—maybe they were new—I don't know. Try to eat something, though. Drink the juice—it will help."

Paraska drank the juice and nodded happily as if the liquid were just the thing that she needed.

Myko and Danko gulped the rest of their breakfast, finished off their mothers' half-eaten portions, and then stood, announcing together:

"W-w-w-e—"

"—want to go out—"

"—on d-d-deck!"

Yevka nodded to the boys and then stood. "Yes, and I think Tomashko and I will join you." She gathered up Tomashko, who was still munching on a piece of bread, and set him on his feet. "I think it would be good to breathe fresh air."

Paraska looked up at her sister with wide, dark eyes, but Yevka merely smiled reassuringly at her and then walked away, holding Tomashko by the hand.

Andrii Kupka and Paraska were alone now, while around them the dining hall staff cleared the dirty plates and utensils from the tables. Andrii said, "Your boy . . . I don't remember his name."

"Myko."

"Yes, 'Myko,' that's it. He is enjoying the trip, yes?"

Paraska nodded.

"He is a good boy."

"Yes . . . thank you," murmured Paraska. "He is good."

"He will be glad to see his father again."

Paraska lowered her eyes and clasped her fingers together tightly in her lap.

Andrii Kupka yawned and stretched. "Has he always had trouble talking?"

Paraska was confused. "What?"

"Your boy, Myko—he stammers."

Paraska reddened. "Yes . . . yes, he does. I can't make him stop. I hope, maybe when he is older—maybe he will stop then. I . . . I don't know . . . He is not like his father. His father was quick with his tongue—he was very quick."

"'*Was* quick?'"

Paraska looked away and bit her lip. "I . . . I wasn't . . . I must go to my sister now." Paraska stood and began walking slowly toward the dining hall door.

Andrii Kupka wiped his mouth with his napkin and followed Paraska.

At the door Paraska stopped and, swallowing hard, looked up into Andrii Kupka's eyes. "My husband was killed in the war."

"I see . . ."

"I don't know why I told you . . . I . . . I think . . ."

"Then only your sister is meeting her husband in Yonkers?"

"Well . . . no. I . . . I shouldn't have said that. I . . . I lied about that also. Her husband went to Ameryka nine years ago. She never heard from him again. We are going to the house of Yevka's sister-in-law."

"In Yonkers?"

"No . . . I don't think so. I don't remember where it is."

"Passaic? Jersey City? Bayonne?"

"Maybe the last one."

"Bayonne! That is where I live! Which street?"

Paraska closed her eyes. "I . . . I don't know . . ."

Andrii Kupka opened the door leading to the outer deck. "You are not well. It is too warm in here. Would you like to walk outside with me?"

Paraska nodded quickly. "Ye . . . yes, that would be nice."

❧

Yevka smiled when she saw Paraska walking on the deck with Andrii Kupka. As they approached, Yevka busied herself wrapping her shawl around Tomashko, who had fallen asleep in her arms. "Yevka!" cried Paraska. "We have been looking for you. Where are the boys?"

"I don't know. They ran toward the front of the boat, and I haven't seen them since."

Andrii Kupka laughed. "They are excited to be on the ship. I see them every day in a new place—they go everywhere they can and then they go some places they probably shouldn't. But let them enjoy! It is great fun for them."

Paraska touched her sister's arm and said, "Yevka, Pan Kupka wants to—"

Andrii Kupka interrupted Paraska, leaning close to her and murmuring in her ear, "*Proshu*—please—call me Andrii."

Paraska reddened and then continued. "Andrii wants to know the name of the village in Ameryka where Anna and Petro Kotsur live."

"Bayonne, I think."

Andrii beamed at the sisters. "That is where I live! Do you know the street?"

Yevka thought for a moment. "It is a number—twenty-something. I think it is twenty-one."

Andrii slapped his knee. "I live on East Twenty-third Street! You will be two blocks away! The church—*Svyatŷi Yoan Khrestytel*—Saint John the Baptist—is on East Twenty-sixth Street! What is your family's name—Kotsur, did you say? Kotsur . . . Kotsur . . . I think there are two families by that name. When did they leave *starŷi krai*—the old country?"

The sisters looked at each other. "A year?" suggested Paraska.

"A year and a half ago, I think," said Yevka.

Andrii shook his head. "I wouldn't know them. I was already in Krasni Brod a year and a half ago." Andrii shook his head again and laughed. "We were strangers when we boarded the ship, and when we get off the ship we will live two blocks apart! I will see both of you in church with your boys on the first Sunday after we arrive."

The sisters nodded. "Yes, we will see you there."

Paraska touched Andrii's arm. "Andrii, tell Yevka what you heard."

"Yes, of course. I spoke with a crew member as we came out of the dining hall. He said there is a storm in front of us. It is big and the sea will be very rough—rougher than the last two days. So enjoy today—it will not be so good after this."

೦⁊

That evening the sky darkened and a violent rainstorm pummeled the ship. In the morning the ship rolled and pitched on its westward course, while below decks in their steerage bunks, Yevka and Paraska tossed and moaned.

Paraska leaned over the side of her cot and vomited on the floor. "*Oi!* Yevka! Yevka!"

"What is it?"

"Where are the boys?"

"Tomashko is next to me—asleep. Danko and Myko are upstairs somewhere."

Anna Perhach called out from her bunk. "Your boys are fetching bread for my Mariya. They are good boys. They bring us what we need and they spread sawdust on the floor when we vomit. It is good for all of us that they don't get sick. I would give them hugs if I could stand up. Only, if I could stand I would go to the deck and throw myself into the water! Death would be a relief!"

Paraska shifted on her cot and reached for the dangling length of yarn. "*Bozhe moi!* How much longer? Yevka, did I tie a knot yesterday? I can't remember."

"I don't know, Paraska."

"Yevka, there are only five knots. Did I forget to tie one yesterday? I can't take five more knots of this. Yevka?"

"What is it, Paraska?"

"I think I am dying."

"You aren't dying, Paraska."

"How do you know? You aren't as sick as I am." Paraska vomited over the side of her cot onto the floor. "*Oi!*"

"I think maybe I am as sick as you, Paraska."

"Oh? How do you feel?"

"Like I am dying."

"You see! You agree with me!"

"I didn't say I was dying—it just feels that way."

Paraska leaned over the side of her bunk and whooped—the dry heaves this time. "*Oi!* I ate too much herring for lunch—I can taste it. Why did you let me eat so many herring, Yevka?"

"No one forced you to eat any herring."

"I shouldn't have eaten so many herring. I'll never eat herring again." Pause. "Yevka?"

"Yes?"

"I wish I could sleep. The trip would go faster if we could sleep, wouldn't it?" Pause. "Yevka?"

"Yes?"

"Do you wish you could sleep?"

"I'm trying, Paraska."

"Yevka?"

"Yes?"

"I shouldn't have told him I'm a widow."

"What?"

"*Pan* Ku—Andrii. I told him I'm a widow and now look how God punishes me! Why did you let me tell him, Yevka? Why?"

"*Oi,* Paraska! Go to sleep!"

თ

The winds whipped the sea and rocked the ship for three days. Even after the rains stopped, the seas remained rough. For the invalid steerage passengers, the days dissolved into a miserable and endless journey. Crew members filled the sawdust buckets twice each day and swept the congealed human waste from the compartment floor. Hope faded for many immigrants, and they no longer rose to wash themselves. Those strong enough to make the journey to the near-empty dining hall sat alone or in pairs and tried to eat bread and drink juice. Others sat on the hall benches, simply seeking refuge from the smell of vomit and the endless wailing of the sick in the steerage compartments.

თ

Yevka awoke in the dark and felt for Tomashko next to her. She put her arm around him, removed his fingers from his mouth, and then closed her eyes. Something, however, was different. There was a change in the sounds of the ship—sounds she had become so accustomed to for over a week. She raised her head. The familiar rumbling noise from deep inside the ship was now reduced to a muffled hum. Now, fully awake, Yevka murmured, "We're not rolling . . ."

Other women in the compartment began to stir, and children sat up yawning and rubbing their eyes. Paraska rose on one elbow and blurted, "What the devil! What is it now? Yevka, are you awake?"

"Yes. Stop shouting."

"Who's shouting? What's happening? What happened to the noise?"

"I think we've stopped."

Other women called out to one another, while Myko and Danko along with some of the other children jumped down to the deck and scampered out the door and up the steps to the steerage deck.

Yevka slowly swung her legs over the side of her cot. "How many days since we left, Paraska?"

Paraska was already counting the knots. ". . . *shist, sim, visim, devyat*—six, seven, eight, nine." She frowned. "There is one more day to go. Why do we stop with one day to go? Did I tie *desyat*—number ten? No, I don't think so. Yevka, I think today is the tenth day!"

Men and older boys suddenly entered the room, shouting excitedly to wives, daughters, and mothers.

Paraska was alarmed. "Something is wrong, Yevka! What are these men doing in here? This is the women and children's quarters!"

Myko and Danko raced down the stairs and slid to a stop at their mothers' sides. Tugging on their mothers' arms, they exclaimed:

"M-M-Mamko!"

"MAMKO!"

"C-c-come ups-t-t-tairs . . ."

". . . *SKORO*—HURRY . . ."

". . . it is B-B-BIG!"

". . . YOU MUST SEE IT!"

". . . W-W-WE—"

"WE HAVE ARRIVED! WE ARE IN AMERYKA!"

CHAPTER FIFTY

Prekrasna Pani

DANKO TUGGED AT HIS MOTHER'S ARMS. "*Mamko, skoro*—hurry!"

Yevka gingerly lowered herself to the floor, where she swayed on unsteady feet and withdrew her arm from her son's grasping fingers. "Danko, let me go. I must wake up Tomashko."

"*Skoro, Mamko, skoro*—hurry!"

In the lower bunk Paraska fumbled under the cot for her shoes as Myko tugged at her arm.

"*M-M-Mamko, sk-k-koro!*"

Paraska's knees buckled and she dropped to the edge of the cot, holding her head in her hands. "*Bozhe moi!* I can't hurry. I'm too sick to stand. Yevka, I don't know if I can even stand up."

"You can stand, Paraska. You are tired and sick, but you can stand. I will help you. Danko, stop pulling me."

"Hurry, *Mamko!*"

Paraska pointed to the floor. "Myko, help me with my shoes . . . I found one . . . I can't find the other . . . ah, *dobre*—good. Slip them on my feet. That one goes on the other foot—you have them mixed up."

"*M-M-Mamko, skoro*—hurry!"

"I can't hurry, Myko. I'm too sick. Yevka, let the boys go ahead, and we'll follow."

Yevka beckoned to her oldest. "Danko, take your brother's hand and go upstairs to see Ameryka. Myko, you go with them and hold Tomashko's other hand. Stay together. Your mother and I will be there soon. Do you hear what I say? Stay together. Do you hear me, Myko?"

"Y-y-yes, *T-T-Teto!*"

Yevka pointed to her son. "Did you hear me, Danko?"

"YES, *MAMKO*! COME, TOMASHKO, HURRY!"

Myko and Danko grabbed the wide-eyed Tomashko's hands and whisked him off his feet, out the door, and up the stairs to the steerage deck.

Yevka slipped on her shoes and held out her hand for her sister. Paraska looked up and smiled feebly. "All the trouble to come to Ameryka and now . . . now, I don't care whether I see it or not. Never again, Yevka—now and ever and forever—I don't want to be on something that moves. No more boats. I only want to walk for the rest of my life." She took Yevka's hand and, with a grunt, pulled herself to her feet. "*Oi,* Yevka! I feel so old—ten years older— as if I'm already forty!"

Arm in arm, the sisters shuffled out the door to the stairs, where they joined other weakened women climbing slowly to the deck. Paraska and Yevka stepped over the threshold of the watertight door onto the deck and into the cool, gray morning air.

Paraska breathed deeply. "The air is good, Yevka. It is good and cool. I like it. *Bozhe!* Look at all the people."

Men, women, and children were packed tightly along the starboard railing, craning their necks, raising themselves on their toes, and jumping to see over the heads of those in front. Some laughed and pointed; some prayed; others cried, covering their mouths and shaking. Fathers lifted children to their shoulders for a better view, and women embraced one another and made the sign of the cross. Behind the crowds, kneeling on the open deck, a gray-haired woman, clutching a rosary to her chest, prayed aloud in German:

Heilige Maria, Mutter Gottes, bitte für uns Sünder
jetzt und in der Stunde unseres Todes. Amen.

Holy Mary, Mother of God, pray for us sinners
now and at the hour of our death. Amen.

Paraska squinted in the morning light. "Where are the boys? Where is Ameryka?"

"*MAMKO!*"

"*M-M-MAMKO!*"

The sisters scanned the crowd at the railing. "Do you see them, Yevka?"

"No . . . I don't . . . I hear them, but . . . yes, yes, there they are. I see them. Danko, Myko, come here!"

The two boys, only their heads and waving arms visible in the throng, called out:

"W-w-we—"

"We can't come to you—we're stuck!"

"Is Tomashko with you?" cried Yevka.

Myko reached into the crowd and produced a small hand. "Yes!"

Anna Perhach, with her daughter, Mariya, at her side, called out from the crowd, "Yevka! Paraska! Do you see? It is Ameryka! I thought we would never see it! Come look."

"Yes, it is wonderful!" cried Paraska, smiling and waving. She turned to her sister and whispered, "Yevka, I can't see a thing. Can you?"

"No. There are too many people."

"Mamko!"

"M-M-Mamko!"

"Come see! Hurry!"

"C-c-come!"

The boys broke loose from the crowd and jumped up and down, waving their arms. Tomashko, the middle fingers of his left hand stuffed in his mouth, stomped in a circle around his brother and cousin.

Paraska pointed to one of the great cargo hatch covers. "I need to sit, Yevka. I can't take another step—I'll fall down. You and the boys go see Ameryka. I am certain it will still be there later."

Yevka put an arm over Paraska's shoulders and guided her sister to the hatch cover, where Paraska sat with her head in her hands. "I'll sit with you," said Yevka. "When you are ready, we will see Ameryka together."

The boys shouted at their mothers again, but Yevka held up a hand and said, "Boys! We will come soon. Tell us what you see."

The boys dived into the crowd, squirming and disappearing between legs. Myko's head popped out from under a woman's arm. "It is A-m-m-meryka, and it is B-B-BIG!" The head vanished.

Now Danko's head appeared. "There are houses in the water and they go STRAIGHT UP INTO THE SKY!" The head withdrew.

Paraska raised her head. "Houses in the water? What is your Danko talking about?"

Danko appeared again. "There are houses that come out of the water and disappear into the clouds! And there is a train that goes over the water! Everything is . . . BIG!"

"Danko!" cried Yevka. "Where is your brother?" Danko disappeared and then reappeared between two pairs of legs with Tomashko, who grinned at his mother, giggling and waving good-bye as he was enveloped by the crowd once again.

Paraska sighed heavily. "Help me up, Yevka. I think I want to see Ameryka now." The sisters stood up and made their way haltingly to the back of the crowd. "I can't see anything, Yevka."

Myko and Danko appeared at their mothers' sides with Tomashko, and, with prodding elbows, navigated the two women through the crowd.

"*P-p-proshu—*"

"*Proshu*—please—excuse us!"

"*Ioi!* Watch your elbows, boy!" scolded a woman's voice.

"DON'T YOU YELL AT MY SON!"

"Paraska . . . please . . ."

"*M-M-Mamko, skoro*—hurry!"

"Yes, Myko, I'm trying."

"*Mamko,* do you see it?"

"No, Danko, not yet."

"L-l-look—"

"Look now!"

"Th-th-there it is!"

"LOOK! AMERYKA!"

The crowd parted at the ship's rail, and the stunned sisters stared agape at the city rising out of the harbor before them. Paraska was the first to speak. "*Bozhe!* Yevka, what is . . . what is . . . what is all this?"

Danko tugged at his mother's dress. "*Mamko,* we're going to see what is on the other side of the ship."

Yevka nodded slowly without taking her eyes off the city. "Hold Tomashko's hands—both of you." The boys grabbed Tomashko and raced to the port side of the ship.

Paraska spread her hands in front of her. "This is . . . Ameryka?"

"I don't know . . . I . . . I think it must be Nu York."

"All of it? All of this is Nu York, Ameryka?"

"I don't know, Paraska . . . yes . . . maybe . . . I don't know."

"It is so . . . so . . ."

"Big . . . yes . . . yes, it is."

"Yes, that is Nu York," said a familiar voice behind them. The sisters turned, acknowledging Andrii Kupka with nods. "What do you two think of it?"

Paraska shook her head. "I never thought it could be so big."

Andrii laughed. "Yes, it is an unbelievable place."

Paraska was still shaking her head. "How do people live in such a place as this? The houses are so . . . so tall . . . and . . . and everything comes up out of the water."

"It is on an island," said Andrii. "There are roads between the buildings, and there are trains that run over the roads and under the ground. In the tall buildings, there are small rooms on cables that take you all the way to the top." Andrii pointed across the water to the right. "Over there—that is a place called Brooklyn—I've never been there. The trains run over the water, there—do you see the *mostŷ*—the bridges? We can't see Bayonne from this side of the ship. It is over there," said Andrii, pointing to the other side of the ship. "I'll point it out to you later."

A uniformed officer holding a megaphone worked his way through the crowd, making announcements in German, Czech, and Polish. Andrii, listening with his eyes closed and his head cocked to one side, said, "I think they will be loading the first barges for the immigration station soon. Also, we will be issued identification tags with our names and numbers. I know that I am on an early list. I will see who has the tags and find you later." Yevka looked away smiling as Paraska touched hands briefly with Andrii before he walked away.

The two sisters again turned their attention to the skyline of lower Manhattan. "Yevka, where do Anna and Petro Kotsur live?"

"Bayonne. Andrii said we can see it from the other side of the boat. Do you want to go to the other side and—" Yevka stopped. "Paraska, did you hear that?"

"Hear what?"

Yevka flinched. "I hear crying. I think it is Tomashko." Yevka pushed her way out of the crowd, calling, "Tomashko!"

Danko and Myko rounded a corner with the sobbing little boy between them. When he saw his mother, Tomashko angrily pulled away from the older boys and rushed into Yevka's arms, burying his dirty, tear-streaked face in the folds of her dress.

Yevka frowned at her oldest son. "Danko, what happened to Tomashko?"

"Someone stepped on him. Can he stay with you now? Myko and I want to see *Prekrasna Pani*—the Beautiful Lady."

"I told you to hold his hand," scolded Yevka.

"We did, but he got loose. We want to go see *Prekrasna Pani.*"

Yevka stood up with Tomashko clinging to her neck. The boy rested his head on his mother's shoulder, and sucked on the middle fingers of his left hand.

"You boys stay with us now," said Paraska. "It's too crowded. You'll fall in the water."

"M-M-Mamko!"

"Shush!"

Danko placed his fists on his hips and looked up at his mother and his aunt. "But Myko and I want to see *Prekrasna Pani*! Uncle Vasyl said we should see *Prekrasna Pani*—the Beautiful Lady!"

Paraska scowled at her nephew. "What the devil are you talking about?"

Danko raised his palms skyward. "Didn't Uncle Vasyl tell you about *Prekrasna Pani*?"

Yevka and Paraska looked at one another and then back at Danko, shaking their heads.

Danko held up his right arm. "Uncle Vasyl said *Prekrasna Pani* always holds her arm up like this, but he couldn't show us because he doesn't have that arm anymore, so he made Myko and me hold up our arms instead. See? Show them, Myko." Now Myko thrust his own right arm into the air. "Uncle Vasyl said *Prekrasna Pani* stands on a rock in the water and says '*Slava Isusu Khrystu*—Glory to Jesus Christ!' to people like us who come here from across the ocean and so we want to go see her now."

"Well . . ." hesitated Yevka.

Paraska shrugged. "Yevka, let them go. I'm too tired to listen to any more of this. You two boys go, and we'll follow." The boys grinned at one another and dashed around a corner.

The sisters made their way to the other side of the ship, where they found themselves in a crush of excited immigrants, all of them crying, gesticulating, and chattering in any one of a dozen languages. A man next to Yevka grinned and shouted something to her in a non-Slavic language. Paraska intervened, placing herself protectively in front of Yevka and shooing the man away with her hands. "Ox! She doesn't speak your way! Leave her alone!" The man shrugged and shouted to someone in front of him.

Paraska pulled Yevka's arm. "Yevka, let's go back to the other side of the ship. This is too big a crowd. We can come back later."

Danko, balanced on one of the lifeboat hoists overhead, exclaimed, "There she is! *Mamko! Teto* Paraska! *Prekrasna Pani*—the Beautiful Lady! She looks just like Uncle Vasyl said she would!"

Yevka gasped, "Danko! Come down from there!"

"I can't, *Mamko*. My foot is caught in a rope. *Prekrasna Pani* is green, and she is looking at us just as Uncle Vasyl said she would."

"*Bozhe,*" groaned Yevka. "Paraska, can you get him down? I'm going back to the other side of the boat with Tomashko. I can't breathe here." Yevka pushed through the crowd, clutching Tomashko to her chest. Behind her, all devotion to the Beautiful Lady ceased with Paraska's thunderous command: "DANKO! DOWN, NOW!" Helping hands reached skyward and pulled the boy from the hoist.

Yevka returned to the quieter side of the ship and stood alone at the railing with Tomashko in her arms. "Look, Tomashko. It is Ameryka." The boy raised his head from his mother's shoulder and gazed at the great city. "*Bozhe, it is so big,*" said Yevka, shaking her head slowly. "It is so different from *staryî krai*—the old country. But, it is our new home. This is where we will live—this is where you will grow up. *Bozhe moi*—it is so big!"

✌

As Yevka strolled along the deck holding Tomashko's hand, she spotted Paraska and Andrii Kupka at the ship's rail, the skyline of Manhattan in the background. Andrii, his face intent, was speaking and holding hands with Paraska, who earnestly nodded at his words. Yevka smiled but immediately turned around and walked in the opposite direction.

"Yevka!" shouted Paraska. "We are over here! We were looking for you."

Yevka turned around and joined her sister and Andrii at the rail. They no longer held hands but, nevertheless, stood close to one another.

Paraska's face bore a tinge of rose hue, and she spoke breathlessly. "Yevka, Andrii must board the boat now and show his papers at the—" She glanced at Andrii. "Already I forgot."

"The immigration station," he said.

"Yes, that's it," continued Paraska. "He has offered to wait there for us until we are allowed into Ameryka, in case we have any trouble." The demure Paraska looked up into Andrii's eyes. "And that is very kind of you," she said softly.

Yevka smiled to herself and watched the seagulls diving over the bow of the ship.

Now the practical Paraska spoke. "But I told Andrii that he must not keep his brother waiting. It is your brother who is coming to get you, yes?"

"Yes, my brother, Mykhal."

"Yes," said Paraska firmly. "So, you see, you must tend to your family first. Yevka and I will be fine. Anna and Petro Kotsur will come later today and take us to Ameryka. Our names are on a much later list than yours. We will be fine, won't we, Yevka?"

"Of course."

"There, do you see, Andrii? Yevka agrees with me. You go and we will see you in church on Sunday."

Andrii shrugged. "Well, I suppose it will be all right." He smiled. "You two have gotten this far by yourselves. Sometimes there is trouble with the inspectors, but I'm sure you will do well. I suppose there is no reason for me to wait four or five more hours on the inspection island. As you said, I will see you and your families on Sunday."

Paraska nodded. "Yes, you will." Nervously clearing her throat, Paraska stole a glance at Yevka out of the corner of her eye.

Yevka bowed her head to Andrii. "We will see you on Sunday. Paraska, I will go look for the boys."

Andrii touched the brim of his cap. "Yes, I will see you there."

Yevka left the rail and made her way slowly to a shady bench. Not long after she sat down, she was joined by Paraska, who wordlessly sat and dabbed at her moist eyes with the corners of her shawl.

"Did he go to the boat?" asked Yevka.

"Yes," sniffed Paraska. Then she chuckled. "I don't know why I'm crying. I'll see him soon enough."

"He's a good man, yes?"

"Yes, Yevka . . . yes, he is that. I never knew I could . . . I can't tell you how I feel . . . I feel like . . . I . . ."

Yevka squeezed her sister's arm. "I know how you feel, Paraska. I know just how you feel." Then she patted Paraska's leg lightly. "Does it hurt?"

"Hmm?"

"Your leg, does it hurt?"

Paraska waved aside Yevka's concern. "If it does, I don't feel it right now."

"*Dobre*—good, Paraska. Let's go see *Prekrasna Pani.* There are no more crowds at the railing. I want to see her, don't you?"

"Yes, I do."

The sisters walked through a corridor to the other side of the ship and then across the deck to the ship's rail, where only scattered small groups still stood gazing across the water.

Paraska pointed to the large statue off the ship's port bow. "Is that her? Is that the *Prekrasna Pani* we've heard so much about?"

"Yes . . . yes, it is. Oh, Paraska, look at her! She is beautiful, isn't she?"

"Yes, I suppose. Only . . . she certainly is like everything else here—big. What is she holding up? She seems to be showing us something. Is she holding a cross?"

"I think it is a torch. Yes, she is holding up a big torch."

"Yevka, your eyes are better than mine. Is she smiling?"

"No . . ."

"Is she frowning? I don't want to look at her if she is frowning."

"She's not frowning. She is . . . she is *mitsna*—strong."

"*Mitsna?*"

"Yes, Paraska—*mitsna*. She reminds me of you!"

"Me?"

"Yes. She has . . . maybe it is the chin . . . I don't know . . . she has a strong look. She makes me feel . . . strong, Paraska. She makes me feel that all will be well. What did Vasyl tell the boys? She says '*Slava Isusu Khrystu*— Glory to Jesus Christ' to all of us who come to Ameryka."

Paraska peered at the statue. "You think so, Yevka? Well then, I'll look at her. I'll look at her and answer her: '*Slava na viky*—Glory to Him forever!'"

The sisters stood in silence at the railing and stared across the harbor at *Prekrasna Pani*—the Beautiful Lady.

~

Later that morning officials from the ship walked among the masses on the third-class deck, pinning identification cards on each individual. Later, ship's officers announced that, because of the enormous number of people converging at the immigration station from so many ships in the harbor, processing was moving slowly.

Paraska held her head in her hands. "We will never get off this boat. Never."

Yevka placed her arm across Paraska's shoulders. "It is good that we didn't ask Andrii to wait for us."

"Well, that is something, I suppose," Paraska snorted. "But, Yevka, I'm so tired. I feel that I will never be the same."

Children ran about the deck, and men lounged and smoked or spoke in small groups. Mothers suckled their infants, and older women sat in what little shade they could find, fanning themselves with their hands.

Danko, Myko, and Tomashko, each holding something behind their backs, raced up to their mothers' sides.

"*Mamko!*"

"*M-M-Mamko!* Are y-y-you—"

"Are you both hungry?"

Paraska frowned. "Are we hungry? Where have you boys been? What do you have behind you?"

Danko and Myko grinned at one another and produced two long yellow objects. "There is one for each of you," said Danko. "They are fruit and they are called ba-na-na-na." Danko whispered to Tomashko, who nodded solemnly and kept his hands behind his back.

"T-t-try it," said Myko, offering one of the yellow objects to his mother.

Paraska took the fruit. "I can't eat right now. Where did you get these?"

"There is a little boat in the water next to the ship," explained Danko. "There are two men in the boat and they have bags and bags of ba-na-na-na. Some of the men on the ship lowered money in a basket with a rope and the men in the boat filled the basket with the fruit."

"T-t-take a b-bite, *M-Mamko.*"

"Will you stop nagging me if I do?"

"Of c-c-course, *M-M-Mamko!*"

Paraska bit down on the fruit and made a face. "What is this? I can't cut this with my teeth."

The boys giggled and Myko took the fruit from his mother. "You h-h-have to t-t-take the c-cover off f-first."

Danko handed a fruit to his mother and then said to his brother, "Tomashko, show *Mamka* how they look without the cover." Tomashko displayed his half-eaten peeled banana.

Paraska glared at the boys. "You knew I would not be able to bite this. But you think it is clever to make a fool of me. If I weren't so weak I'd slap both of you."

Yevka peeled her banana and took a bite. "Paraska, it is good. Try it."

"Hmph!"

Yevka ate half the banana and gave the rest to Tomashko. "How did you boys get fruit that other men had to pay for?" Yevka asked.

"Mary gave them to us," answered Danko.

Paraska stopped peeling her banana. "Mary? Which Mary?"

"M-M-Mary from our r-r-room on the b-b-boat, *M-M-Mamko*."

"Yes, that Mary," said Danko. "She said, 'Take these to your mothers and tell them *Z Bohom*—go with God.'"

Paraska was surprised. "She said that?"

"Yes," said Danko. "Now we want to go see if there are more boats alongside the ship."

Yevka nodded. "Take Tomashko with you again. He's having fun with you."

Myko and Danko each grabbed Tomashko by the hand and whisked him away.

Paraska took a bite of the banana and nodded approvingly. "It is good. And Mary bought these for us and for our boys—can you believe that, Yevka? Mary, of all people!"

"It was very nice of her, Paraska."

"She was always nice to us—wasn't she?"

Yevka smiled. "Yes, Paraska. She was always nice to us."

જ

Later that afternoon, a tremendous rainstorm passed slowly over the harbor, driving the immigrants below decks for shelter. When the rain stopped, they reemerged on the wet deck. Members of the ship's crew then made their way among the passengers, announcing that processing on Ellis Island was finished for the day. Over the protests of angry passengers, the crew members announced further that all third-class passengers would have to spend one more night aboard the ship. After nightfall, women bade goodnight tearfully to husbands and older sons and herded their reluctant children below decks for one final night in their fetid compartments.

Standing silently on her rocky prominence, *Prekrasna Pani* held aloft her golden torch in the middle of the dark harbor.

CHAPTER FIFTY-ONE

Inspection

IT WAS ALREADY A HOT AND MUGGY Saturday morning on the lower tip of Manhattan when Inspector O'Keefe stepped aboard the government ferry. The lower decks of the boat were crowded with visitors coming to the Federal Immigration Station on Ellis Island to claim family members they hadn't seen in years. Out in the harbor four ships lay anchored, awaiting the barges that would carry steerage passengers to the island.

O'Keefe went to the forward upper deck, where he found Inspector O'Donnell sitting on a bench reading a newspaper. "Well, O'Donnell, I see you didn't drown on the way home last night."

Inspector O'Donnell peered over the top of his glasses. "Morning, O'Keefe. No, I didn't drown, nor was I struck by lightning. Did you hear about that? Three were struck and killed in the afternoon. I thought Wednesday was bad—it says here yesterday's high hit ninety-one about an hour before the storm hit. Ninety-one! On Wednesday three people died of the heat, and yesterday three people died of the rain. What do you suppose will happen today?"

O'Keefe shrugged. "Wouldn't want to guess. The IRT was flooded uptown yesterday. I'm taking the Second Street El if it rains again today. You got the scores?"

"No Yankee score on account of the rain—they'll have to double up with Saint Louis today, I expect. The Cubs beat the Giants in ten."

"And the Dodgers?"

"Five to four over the Reds in Cincinnati."

"Smith pitched, didn't he?"

"You want the paper?"

"Just tell me."

"I'm reading the first pages now—here take the sports page—I'm done with it." O'Donnell pulled the inside pages from the newspaper and handed them to O'Keefe. "When you're done with the scores, you've got to read about the McMichaels."

"The fighters? Jimmy and Packy?"

"The same."

"What happened?"

"You want that page, too?"

"Just tell me what happened."

O'Donnell took out the third page of the paper and handed it to O'Keefe. "Now you have almost as much of the paper as I do. Look there—see? 'Free-for-all at the Battery.' They were waiting for the ferry to Brooklyn, and someone recognized them and wanted to get tough, I guess. Did you ever see Packy fight?"

"I saw one of them fight in Brooklyn years ago. It might have been Jimmy, though. He was a little fellow, I remember."

"They're both bantams."

"Well," said O'Keefe stretching his arms above his head. "Whichever one I saw, beat up some Polack from the Bronx. It wasn't much of a fight, but then, the Polack wasn't much of a fighter." Yawning loudly, he pointed to the ships in the harbor. "We'll be busy today."

"We're busy every day," said O'Donnell, giving up on the newspaper and folding it under his arm. "It's July—the new quota."

"I worked with Frank yesterday."

"The new translator?"

"Yeah."

"Is that his name? 'Frank'?"

O'Keefe shook his head. "No, no. God only knows what his name is. It's Polish or Czech, or maybe even Hungarian for all I know. He repeated it for me three times. After each time, I told him to say it slower, and each time he said it as fast as the first time. 'Call me Frank,' he said. So I do."

"How good a translator is he?"

"I don't know. He speaks English pretty well. But he seems to have trouble with the immigrants. He interviewed some Poles from a Hamburg Line ship yesterday. I don't know who was more confused, him or the Poles. He seems awfully nervous."

"I heard he got sick a couple of times."

"Yeah, he sure did."

"What was wrong with him?"

"The smell—it was his first day. Plus nerves, I guess."

"Well, the smell is bad—thousands of people who haven't had a bath since who-knows-when; people who have spent a week and a half at sea vomiting all over themselves! It's a wonder you and I are used to it at all by now!"

"Frank'll be OK. The smell is hard to take at first. It was hard for me." O'Keefe held up the newspaper. "Here's an announcement about that Valentino show you were telling me about. Did you take your wife to see it?"

"Yeah—twice."

"Twice!"

"She loves him. She thinks he's handsome. I said he looks more like a woman than a man."

"What did she say?"

"What could she say? It's true!"

"Why would she want to go twice?"

O'Donnell shrugged. "Don't know. She wants me to take her again."

"Again!"

"Yeah—tonight."

"You aren't going, are you?"

"Sure, why not? It makes her happy. I'll slip out to the bar next door after it starts. A couple of beers, a couple of cigarettes—she won't even miss me. How about that!"

❦

The barge eased sideways into the dock on Ellis Island and struck it with a resonant thud, jostling the burdened immigrants and evoking exclamations, nervous laughter, a few foreign expletives, and one particularly forceful *"BOZHE MOI!"* Two men at either end of the barge threw ropes to two other men on the dock, while still other men thrust a gangway out from the dock. Uniformed officials using megaphones addressed the crowd in a variety of languages, urging them off the barge and into lines on the dock: one line for men and one line for women and children. The drone of the officials was momentarily interrupted by a voice that needed no artificial amplification.

"DANKO, MYKO—STOP!" The two boys halted and waited for their mothers. Paraska pointed a finger at the boys, who understood the horrible fate that awaited them if they misbehaved again. "Yevka, Ameryka has made the boys wild, and we are not even in Ameryka . . . yet."

Yevka shifted the bundle on her back and set Tomashko on the concrete walkway. "They are excited, Paraska. They have been on the boat too long."

"Hmph! I've been on the boat too long. Do you see me running around like a wild animal?"

Lining up on the dock as instructed, the immigrants fanned themselves in the hot sun. Eventually, they moved forward toward a great glass canopy in front of a massive brick building and then stopped again.

Paraska set down her bundle. "*Bozhe moi!* It is hot, Yevka. No one told us Ameryka was so hot. Did Vasyl tell you Ameryka was this hot?"

"I don't know—maybe. I don't remember."

"You don't remember? He may have told you it was this hot, and you can't remember!"

"Does it really matter, Paraska? I'm as hot as you are."

"No one is as hot as I am!"

Yevka sighed. "Very well, Paraska . . . very well."

The line moved forward briefly but then stopped. Paraska dropped her bundle and groaned. Almost immediately someone shouted and the line moved forward again. Paraska hoisted her bundle to her shoulder, knocking Tomashko lightly on the head. Tomashko glared up at Paraska and, clutching his mother's dress, rubbed his head with his free hand.

Now the line moved closer to the glass canopy. Yevka pointed to the brick structure. "Look, Tomashko. It looks like a big church." The boy looked up at the enormous building and thrust the middle fingers of his left hand into his mouth.

Paraska limped forward, and when the line halted once again, she set her bundle on the ground and massaged her right leg. Yevka placed a hand on her sister's shoulder.

"Yes, it hurts," said Paraska, anticipating Yevka's question. "It's the heat. I think it makes the leg worse."

Myko and Danko, hot and impatient, edged out of the line, one to the right and one to the left. Paraska leaned forward, and sweeping her arms in a wide arc, gathered the boys back in line, knocking their heads together.

"*Oi, Teto!*"

"*M-M-Mamko!*"

"Shush, both of you! Stay in front of us—we are going inside soon."

As they passed under the canopy, uniformed officials observed the immigrants. At one point an official made a mark on Paraska's back with a piece of chalk. Paraska looked over her shoulder.

"Yevka, what did that policeman do to my back?"

"He made a line—you have a line on your back."

"Why would he do that?"

"I don't know."

Suddenly, two officials armed with metal probes quickly and unceremoniously pulled up the eyelids of each member of the family and inspected their eyes. Terrified, Tomashko cried and rubbed his eyes. Yevka, blinking her eyes to ease the pain, picked up Tomashko. Paraska, holding one hand over her eyes, flailed with her other hand, searching for Myko, who, along with Danko, was rubbing his eyes and whimpering. As officials herded the group down a dark hallway, Paraska, her eyes still stinging, was pulled from the line.

"*Bozhe,* what now?" Paraska groaned. She quickly found herself in a small room with a uniformed official and a woman in a long white dress.

"*Pani,* how is it bad, your *noga?*" asked the woman in Polish.

Paraska blinked and looked about her. "*De moi sŷn*—where is my son?"

"Boy is safe—no worry. How is it bad, your *noga?*"

"*Ne rozumim*—I don't understand."

"*Noga,*" the white-clad woman repeated, slapping her own leg for emphasis. Paraska brightened. "*Moya noha*—my leg?"

"*Tak, tak*—yes, yes—*noha.*"

"*Voina*—the war," explained Paraska. "*Velyka pushka*—a big gun . . . *poof!*"

The woman pointed at Paraska's leg. "We look."

Worried, Paraska glanced at the official. The woman said something to the man, who nodded, left the room, and stood just outside the door, his silhouette visible through the rippled glass window in the door. The woman motioned to Paraska to lift her dress and show the old wound. She probed the wound and lowered Paraska's dress.

"You walk well?"

Paraska nodded, and then demonstrated when the woman indicated she should walk up and down the room. The woman opened the door, admitting the uniformed official along with two other men. "Walk," repeated the woman. Self-consciously, Paraska duplicated her walk around the room. After the woman and the three men conferred, one of the men produced a sheet of paper, which all three men signed. The woman brushed off the chalk mark on Paraska's back and smiled. "Go to your boy, *Pani*."

Passed from official to official, Paraska made her way to a hallway at the bottom of a flight of stairs. She felt a small hand take her own hand and looked down to see Myko, who, still rubbing his eyes, escorted her to Yevka and the other boys.

Yevka put her arm on her sister's shoulder. "Paraska, what happened? You disappeared."

"The people here don't like the way I walk. I had to show them the scar. I think everything is fine. What happens now?"

"These men are making us ready to go upstairs."

An official moved among them, inspecting the tags pinned to each passenger and pulling people into individual lines by ship and manifest number. He called to another official. "Artur! Call out page twenty-seven. Tell them to form a line here! I count only eighteen in line—we're missing twelve people!"

Artur appeared and in rapid order bellowed the number twenty-seven in Slovak, Polish, German, and Rusyn: *"Dvadsat sedem! Dwadzieścia siedem! Siebenundzwanzig! Dvadtsyat sim!"*

At the last rendering, Paraska called to Yevka. "Come! The policemen are calling our number. We are *dvadtsyat sim*—twenty-seven!" Paraska held her bundle in front of her, pushing aside everyone in her path, while Yevka and the boys followed in her wake.

An official inspected their tags and directed them into a column by line number of manifest page twenty-seven. "Nineteen, twenty, twenty-one—" He placed Yevka, Danko, and Tomashko into line. "Twenty-two, twenty-three—" He placed Paraska and Myko in line. "Seven more," he called out. The remaining passengers came forward, and the line was complete. "That makes thirty for page twenty-seven! Take them in, Artur!"

Artur led the group to the foot of the staircase, where he stopped and counted out the numbers on the passenger tags as the immigrants ascended the stairs. Progress was slow up the hot, noisy stairwell as everyone jostled one another with their packages and bundles. Once at the top the immigrants entered an enormous room where hordes of people sat on long rows of benches. Hazy sunlight streaming from windows high above illuminated two large flags suspended from the balcony over the main floor.

Island officials directed the group of thirty to the end of one row of benches and gestured for them to sit and wait.

"More waiting," sighed Paraska. "At least now we sit. Can you see what is happening at the other end of the room, Yevka?"

"Yes, I think so. They seem to be calling us by the numbers pinned to our clothes, and then we go over there to the desks. Do you see the last desk? Anna Perhach and her children, Mariya and Ivanko, are at that desk. They are answering questions now. I think the police will ask us the same questions that they asked in Rotterdam. They haven't started with our group yet."

"*Bozhe moi!* More police—more questions. Where is Tomashko?"

"He is under the bench. The soldiers frightened him when they poked his eyes. Paraska, I am afraid. No one here speaks our language very well. How will we understand anyone?"

Paraska shook her head and rubbed her leg. "*Ne znam*—I don't know . . . I don't know. I wish my leg didn't hurt so much."

಄

Inspector O'Keefe rubbed his eyes and leaned back in his chair, yawning loudly. Inspector O'Donnell at the next desk laughed. "No supper for you, O'Keefe! Not until the last bench is cleared."

Inspector O'Keefe yawned again. "It's not supper I need, but a nap from lunch. It's after five o'clock—why are we still processing, anyway? Do these people have any chance of getting off the island tonight? Sullivan! Where is Sullivan?"

The guard, Sullivan, stepped forward. "Here, sir."

"Sullivan, has the last boat sailed for Manhattan?"

"Yes, sir."

"Well, these people will have to spend the night here. Do they know this? Sullivan, are these people being told that they have to spend the night?"

"We are taking care of it through the interpreters, sir," said Sullivan. "Actually, since this is Saturday, they will have to spend two nights here."

"Oh, they'll love to hear that, won't they?" chuckled Inspector O'Keefe. Then he wheeled around in his chair. "Where is Frank? Is he getting sick again?"

"Here he comes, sir."

The translator, Frank, approached the desk and stood unsteadily next to Inspector O'Keefe. "Well, Frank, do you feel any better?" asked Inspector O'Keefe.

"Not really, sir."

"Well, take a few deep breaths. We're halfway through the last page. Call number ten, Frank."

"*Desat'! Dziesięć! Zehn! Desyat!*"

☙

As Yevka and Paraska sat quietly waiting, the boys slid up and down the empty benches and stared at two very dark-skinned workers who were sweeping the empty aisles.

Paraska tapped her sister's arm. "Yevka, I think it is almost our time. Myko-Danko-Tomashko! Come here. Hurry, it is almost time."

The boys sat next to their mothers and Myko pointed to one of the workers who was sweeping the aisles. "L-l-look, *M-M-Mamko,*" he said to Paraska. "L-l-look at that m-man. Why is he s-so d-d-dark?"

Paraska glanced at the man. "He's a *tsygan*—gypsy—you've seen gypsies before."

"B-b-but he's . . . s-s-so . . . *d-dark.*"

"Some gypsies are darker than others. Yevka, I think we are next."

A family at one of the inspectors' desks picked up their belongings and moved on. Someone called out a number that neither Yevka nor Paraska could understand. When the sisters heard the number again, Paraska stood and hoisted her bundle. "Come, Yevka; come, boys—I think it is our time. Someone is trying to speak our way."

The sisters guided the boys to the elevated desk, set their belongings on the floor, and looked up hopefully at the inspector.

Inspector O'Keefe peered over his glasses. "Frank, please tell these ladies to approach the desk only when their number is called and not in a group."

Frank haltingly translated these instructions, and Yevka and Paraska stared at him.

"Well, Frank, do they understand?"

"Well, I . . . I think . . . yes, sir, I think they do."

"Then why are they all still standing here?"

"Well . . ."

Inspector O'Keefe scanned down the manifest before him. "Never mind, Frank. They are obviously together. Number nineteen is Eva Rusynko. Which of you is Eva Rusynko?"

Yevka straightened at the sound of her name and looked at the inspector.

Inspector O'Keefe leaned over the desk and counted the children. "Frank, she is listed as twenty-eight years of age and the mother of two. Ask her to identify her children by name and age."

Frank translated the instructions to Yevka, who thought for a moment and then answered. While the translator spoke to the inspector, Yevka turned to Paraska. "What is this language he is speaking?"

Paraska frowned. "I don't know, but I think he is trying to speak a little Polish."

Inspector O'Keefe made check marks next to the names, 'Eva,' 'Daniel,' 'Tomas,' and then without looking up, addressed the translator. "Frank, do you speak these people's language? They are listed here on the manifest as Czecho-Slovaks. Do you speak Czech or Slovak?"

"Well, yes, sir, I do. However, the ladies are not Czechs or Slovaks. They are . . . well, they are speaking Ruthenian, sir."

"Ah, yes," said the Inspector. "It says 'Ruthene' under the column 'Race.' And I suppose you don't speak Ruthenian?"

"Ruthenian is very much like Russian, sir."

"All right then, do you speak Russian?"

"Not really, sir. But Russian bears some similarities to Polish."

"Frank, do you speak Polish?"

"I'm trying, sir."

Inspector O'Keefe sighed. "Frank, ask these two ladies carefully—*carefully*, mind you—if they know how to read and write any language the three of you happen to agree upon."

Frank made the inquiry and the sisters nodded, Paraska somewhat less vigorously than Yevka. Frank produced a series of placards and presented three to the sisters.

Yevka pointed to the one printed in Cyrillic text and turned to Paraska. "It is Psalm number one."

Frank handed the card to Yevka, who read haltingly, underlining the text with her finger as Paraska looked on over her shoulder, mumbling along with her sister:

> *Happy those who do not follow*
> *the counsel of the wicked,*
> *Nor go the way of sinners,*
> *nor sit in company with scoffers.*

Rather, the law of the Lord is their joy;
  God's law they study day and night.
They are like a tree
  planted near streams of water,
  that yields its fruit in season;
Its leaves never wither;
  whatever they do prospers.

Frank frowned at Paraska throughout the entire reading, and, when the sisters finished, he shook his head at Inspector O'Keefe and opened his mouth to speak. But the inspector held up his hand.

"Frank, are you aware that five years ago, in 1917, the government of the United States of America introduced the requirement that all aliens seeking admission to this country must be able to read and write their own language?"

"Yes sir. I'm very well aware—"

"Frank, this manifest indicates that both these sisters provided evidence at the port of Rotterdam sufficient to convince a ship's officer that they could both read and write. Are you convinced that these two ladies can read and write?"

Frank shook his head and opened his mouth to speak, but, again, Inspector O'Keefe raised his hand, silencing him.

"Before you answer, Frank, tell me this: are you aware that aliens who seek admission to the United States but who cannot read or write their own language must be returned to their country of origin?"

"Well . . . yes . . . I . . ."

Inspector O'Keefe peered over the rims of his glasses at the translator. "Do you understand, Frank, that if one of these ladies is unable to read or write, she will be returned to her country of origin?"

"Well . . . yes . . . I do . . . however . . . I . . ."

"Frank, do you also understand that returning one of these ladies to her country of origin would result in separation from her son and her sister, possibly for the rest of her life?"

The translator bit his lower lip, glanced first at Yevka and then at Paraska, thought for a moment, and then nodded. "Yes, sir. I understand."

"Very well, Frank. I will ask you one more time: are you, a sworn officer of the government of the United States of America, convinced that each of these sisters is able to read and write her own Ruthenian language and, therefore, clearly and beyond a doubt entitled to land in the United States of America?"

Frank cleared his throat and declared, "Yes, sir! I am convinced."

"Proceed, Frank!" cried Inspector O'Keefe, suppressing a smile. "You will make a fine inspector one day!"

"Y-yes, sir."

"Carry on with the questioning, Frank."

Working from his hand-held list of thirty-three questions, Frank began with Yevka, translating her answers to Inspector O'Keefe, who checked the responses against the information recorded in Rotterdam:

Nationality (Country of which citizen or subject)	Czechoslovakia
Race	Ruthene
Last residence	Stara Polyanka, Czechoslovakia
The name and complete address of nearest relative or friend in country whence alien came	Bro. I. L. Vasyl Rusynko, Stara Polyanka, Zupa Sarysska, Czechoslovakia
Final destination	N.J., Bayonne
Whether having a ticket to such final destination	No
By whom was passage paid?	B. I. L. Vasyl Rusynko
Whether in possession of $50 and if less, how much?	$23
Whether going to join a relative or friend; and if so, what relative or friend, and his name and complete address	B. I. L. Kotsur Petro, 65 E. 21st St. Bayonne, N.J.

Yevka answered the remaining questions as she had in Rotterdam, prior to boarding the great ship: yes, she intended to stay in the United States; no, she had never been in prison. Question number twenty-two flustered her as it had in Rotterdam, after the meaning was explained to her:

"Are you a polygamist?"

Pause. "No."

Then translator Frank asked question number twenty-three, a question no one had asked in Rotterdam: "Are you an anarchist?"

Yevka paled and turned to Paraska, whose eyes had widened. "Yevka, what did he say?"

"Paraska," Yevka gasped out of the corner of her mouth. "I think he wants to know if I am the Antichrist!"

Paraska shook her head in disbelief. "They never asked us *that* in Raterdom! *Bozhe moi,* Yevka, tell him you aren't!"

Suspecting trouble, Inspector O'Keefe looked up from the manifest sheet. "Frank, what is happening?"

"I don't know, sir."

"Well, find out. These two women look like they've seen a ghost."

Yevka, her comportment dignified, addressed the translator. "I . . . *we* are *not* the Antichrist!"

Frank reddened. "Well, no . . . no, of course not . . . no . . . I . . . pardon me."

Inspector O'Keefe tapped his pencil on the desk. "Frank, what is happening? What are they saying?"

"She is . . . that is . . . that is to say . . . *they* are not . . . anarchists."

"Of course they aren't. These are two barely literate mountain women who have just stepped off a ship with three young children. They probably haven't had a decent bath in weeks. Do you really think they look like they might throw bombs on Wall Street?"

"Well . . . no, sir. I . . . I suppose not."

"Very well, Frank. Save that question for those who actually look like anarchists: wild-eyed bearded intellectuals, overeducated women—you know the types. Now, can we please finish this?"

"Yes. Of course, sir."

After a cursory review of Paraska's manifest information, Inspector O'Keefe perused a document that had been delivered to his desk earlier. "Frank, this is a certificate issued by the Medical Division for one Paraska Ivanchyn. Apparently she was examined after the line inspection. The doctors identified some sort of leg wound. Frank, please ask Mrs. Ivanchyn about the wound and ask if it is serious enough to prevent her from engaging in normal daily activities."

Frank translated the questions haltingly.

Paraska spoke quickly, slapped her thigh once, and shook her head vigorously.

Frank held up his hand, silencing Paraska. "She says she was injured by a bomb during the war; however, the wound is nothing. She says it never hurts."

As he signed the manifest sheet, Inspector O'Keefe mused, "Well, I doubt that—I'm sure it hurts like hell. I know my leg would hurt if I were blown up." He waved the women and their children around the desk. "Now tell them the bad news, Frank. They will have to spend two nights here. The Kozars or Kokurs, or whatever their name is, can call for them Monday morning. Tell them not to worry—they will be well fed at no cost. Sullivan! Where's Sullivan?"

"Here, sir."

"Sullivan, take these people to the women and children's quarters," said Inspector O'Keefe. "Frank, have you told them they have to stay?"

Frank translated the news and the sisters stared at him in disbelief. Sullivan appeared in front of the women, beckoning them to follow him; the sisters stoically hoisted their bags to their shoulders and herded their boys before them.

Inspector O'Keefe observed the smallest of the three boys accompanying the sisters and said to Frank, "Go ask the women what happened to their husbands."

"Is there something wrong, sir? Shall I call them back to the desk?"

"No, no, Frank. Just ask them. Tell them not to worry—I'm only curious."

A moment later Frank returned. "The sister with only one boy said her husband was killed in the war. The sister with two boys said her husband came to America before the war—1913. But she doesn't know where he is. Actually, she doesn't know if he is dead or alive. Are you sure there is nothing wrong, sir?"

"No, I was only curious. Many interesting people pass through here, Frank. For instance, the one called Eva has a boy who is three years old."

"Yes, sir." The two men watched as the sisters and their boys disappeared down the hall. Frank nodded slowly. "Oh . . . I see, sir. Yes . . . I see . . . interesting . . ."

"Yes, Frank. So many interesting people—so many interesting families. And they all want to come to America. Well, God bless them all. That's what I say—God bless them all. Come, Frank. You've made it through your second day of work on Ellis Island. You did well. And you only got sick once! Very good. Come—it's time to go home."

CHAPTER FIFTY-TWO

Detention

ONE OF THE ISLAND MATRONS led the family to a large dormitory, where, using hand gestures, she indicated that they should leave their things on the stacked iron bunks. Out of habit, everyone assumed the same bunks they had occupied on the ship: Myko and Danko took the top bunk, Yevka and Tomashko the middle, and Paraska the lower. Next, the matron led the family to the dining hall. When Paraska lagged behind, limping and holding her right thigh, the impatient matron clapped her hands insistently. Paraska glowered at the woman, who quickly hurried down the hall to usher Yevka into the dining hall.

The hall was noisy and crowded with other detainees. An island worker directed the family to empty chairs at the end of one table at which other detained women and children waited to be served. The boys stared at a dark-skinned man delivering plates of sliced white bread to the table. "Look, *Mamko,*" whispered Danko. "Another dark gypsy!" Dozens of eager immigrant hands snatched up the bread as soon as the plates were set down in the middle of the table. In this flurry, Yevka and Paraska, confused and distraught, managed to secure only four slices before the bread disappeared. Giving the boys each a slice, the sisters tore the fourth slice in half to share between them. As they tasted the fresh white bread, the five family members looked at one another in astonishment.

"Is this cake?" cried Paraska.

"M-M-Mamko!"

"Mamko, it is good!"

A Slovak woman on the other side of the table laughed. *"Ne je torta*—it's not cake. *Chlieb*—bread!"

Yevka whispered to her sister, "Paraska, how do they make bread so white and so . . . so . . . good?"

"*Ne znam*—I don't know, Yevka. But good as this bread is, I want to cook again. I hope Anna and Petro have a big hearth in their house in Bayonne. I'm tired of people feeding us. It doesn't seem right. You and I will soon cook for our own family. That will be good."

Tomashko stuffed his mouth full of bread and then kicked his legs with delight as he opened his hands for more bread.

When the same dark gypsy appeared with two more plates of bread, Paraska, the patient predator, poised herself at the edge of her chair, eyeing the man's movements carefully. As the dark gypsy set the plates on the table, Paraska lunged forward and scooped up all the bread from one of the plates, distributing a small stack to Yevka and to each of the boys.

Yevka was shocked. "Paraska!"

Paraska, her mouth full, merely shrugged and said, "Ameryka."

Across the table, the Slovak woman laughed again. "*Áno, áno*—yes, yes— Amerika! Amerika!"

Two more island workers placed glasses in front of each diner and filled them with milk from a pitcher. Danko and Myko tasted the milk and made faces. "It's cold!" complained Danko. But the boys took another sip, and then another, and gulped down the remainder of the milk.

Yevka leaned toward her sister. "Paraska, are you sure this food is free?"

"That is what that man said—the one who tried to speak Polish." Paraska shrugged. "On the other hand," she said, "he thought you were the Antichrist." Paraska nodded at the woman across the table. "*Bisidiyete po-nashomu*—do you speak our way?"

The woman answered in Slovak. "I speak almost your way."

Paraska indicated the food and drink on the table. "*Ushŷtko zadarmo*— everything is free?"

The woman nodded. "*Áno. Všetko zadarmo*—everything is free."

"Who pays?" asked Paraska, arching one eyebrow skeptically.

The Slovak woman lifted her cup. "Amerika pays!" Others at the table lifted their cups of cold milk and cried, "Amerika pays!"

ᘗᕽ

When they finished eating, Myko and Danko wandered toward the end of the dining hall, where a steady stream of workers scurried in and out of the kitchen carrying trays of food or stacks of empty plates and cups. They were a mix of light-skinned and dark-skinned workers, shouting, laughing, sweating, and moving constantly. One of the dark gypsies, spotting Myko and Danko outside the kitchen entrance, stopped and dropped down on one knee. When he spoke, the boys shrugged, indicating that they did not understand. The dark gypsy laughed and then stood, jerking his head toward the open kitchen door. The boys giggled and nodded that they understood, and followed the man into the kitchen.

Their guide led the boys around the kitchen, pointing, laughing, and slapping other workers on the back. Some of the workers stopped what they were doing and leaned down to talk to the boys. The guide led them to an area of the kitchen where a delightful aroma filled the air. He lifted the boys onto a table, found two small plates, sliced two servings from a pan, and presented them to the boys. The guide slowly enunciated the name of the food.

Danko listened intently and then repeated the name: "shoklat kek."

The gypsy guide laughed and nodded. Other workers gathered to watch as the boys sampled the food. Myko and Danko took a bite, and immediately grinned.

"Sho-sho-klat k-k—"

"SHOKLAT KEK!"

The workers laughed. Danko, pointing to his cake, said to the guide, "*Dobre*—good!"

The guide nodded and pronounced a word. Danko listened, and then repeated the word: *"Gut."*

As the guide nodded, a shout came from the kitchen entrance. A light-skinned man with a red face bellowed angrily at the kitchen workers, who quickly returned to work. Danko was particularly intrigued by one phrase which the man vigorously repeated numerous times. The red-faced man shouted at Myko and Danko and pointed to the kitchen exit. The boys stuffed the remaining cake into their mouths and walked out of the kitchen. As they passed through the door, the phrase echoed once again from the kitchen.

Danko elbowed Myko in the ribs and whispered, "Got tam snuf pitch!"

"G-G-Got t-t-tam—" stammered Myko.

"Got tam snuf pitch!" confirmed Danko.

❧

During the afternoon a telegram for Paraska and Yevka was delivered to the women's dormitory:

Paraska and Yevka—

Petro will come for you on Monday. I must stay home because my baby will come soon.

Anna and Petro Kotsur

"What does that mean?" said Paraska, frowning. "Petro will come for us on Monday? Does she mean in the morning, afternoon, or later?"

"*Ne znam*—I don't know," said Yevka. "Perhaps we should be ready in the morning."

Paraska chuckled. "Petro Kotsur—hmph! Without Anna there to speak for him, how will we know when he arrives?"

"I'm certain there will be a way," assured Yevka.

"Hmph! I'm glad you are so certain, Yevka. The only thing I'm certain of is that Monday is going to be a very long day."

ᔕᓬ

Later that evening, as women and children languished in the oppressive heat of the dormitory, a matron appeared in the doorway, calling attention by clapping her hands sharply. Speaking only English, she indicated through gestures that everyone should follow her.

Paraska sat up on the edge of her bunk with a groan. "What the devil now?"

Myko tugged at his mother's arm. "C-c-come, *M-M-Mamko*!"

"Stop, Myko. I won't be hurried. I'm too tired."

"Come, *Mamko*!" Danko urged Yevka. "Something is going to happen in the big room."

"How do you know this?" asked Paraska.

Danko shrugged. "Myko and I can understand a little of what that woman says."

Paraska shook her head. "Do you hear this, Yevka? When people around us speak *po-amerykanskŷ*, all I can hear is '*mua mua mua*.' But our boys can understand *po-amerykanskŷ* already. You boys go to the big room. We will follow with Tomashko."

Myko and Danko grinned and ran from the room.

"G-G-Got t-t-tam—"

"GOT TAM SNUF PITCH!"

Paraska smiled as she slipped her feet into her shoes. "Listen to them, Yevka. Listen to our boys already speaking *po-amerykanskŷ*. And speaking it so well!"

Paraska and Yevka joined the women filing out of the dormitory with their children and assembled, as instructed, in the Great Hall. Island workers supervised a group of the detained men who were rearranging some of the benches. Another group worked upstairs, unfolding a canvas sheet and suspending it from the balcony railing. Two men wheeled a large black box into the middle of the room and positioned it in front of the rows of benches. One of the matrons directed the men to turn the black box just so, and then opened a long, hinged lid on one side of the box, exposing a white and black surface. She tapped her fingers on the black and white surface, instantly creating a delightful tune which drew a small crowd of children and adults.

As island workers directed the detainees to the benches, Paraska pointed behind the rows of benches to a small piece of machinery with two protruding wheels. "What do you suppose that is?"

Yevka shrugged. "*Ne znam*—I don't know, Paraska."

While Myko, Danko, and Tomashko joined other children clustered about the contraption, the sisters sat on one of the benches. Paraska slid apart from her sister and placed a hand on the bench. "The boys will sit here. Put your hand on the bench, Yevka. We will save seats for them—otherwise someone might—*Oi!*" A small boy had stepped on Paraska's hand and now stood on the bench between the sisters. Paraska pulled her hand out from under the boy's foot and glared at the child. "This seat is not for you. You understand?" The boy ignored Paraska, who then turned to a woman in the next row. "*Vash sŷn*—your son? Hmm?" The mother shrugged and smiled innocently. "*Bisidiyete po-nashomu*—do you speak our way?" asked Paraska. The woman shrugged indifferently. Paraska squinted and smiled at the woman. "Yevka," said Paraska without taking her eyes off the woman. "The little devil's mother doesn't understand our language. Let's see how fast she can learn it."

"Paraska . . . please . . ." groaned Yevka.

"You there, mother of the devil," said Paraska as she stood. "Call your boy back to his seat or I will beat him." The child's mother merely sniffed and looked away. Paraska grabbed the boy around the back of his neck and lifted him to his toes like a helpless kitten. The boy arched his back and whimpered as Paraska raised her free hand in the air, poised to strike. The horrified mother leaped up, snatching her child and sputtering angrily at Paraska. The mother clutched her child in her arms and retreated to the back row of benches.

Paraska sat down and straightened her skirt. "*Dumam*—I think," she said calmly, "that both mother and child now understand a little of our way." As the lights in the Great Hall began to dim, Paraska grumbled, "*Bozhe moi!* What now?"

Yevka turned around in her seat. "Tomashko, where are you?" The boy appeared next to her and climbed in her lap, pressing his head under her chin. Danko and Myko pushed their way between their mothers and sat down. The smaller children in the room whimpered in alarm as the room darkened and the machine at the back of the room began to whirr and click. Perplexed detainees stared at the machine's turning wheels. Then Danko stood on the bench and cried, "Look!" The white canvas came to life, with light and shadow and strange writing. The matron sitting near the canvas tapped her fingers on the black and white surface of the large black box, and the Great Hall was filled with joyous music. The written letters on the canvas vanished, giving way to movement—to the images of actual human beings walking on a street bordered by tall buildings.

One of the people on the canvas became very large, his image nearly covering the entire canvas.

Paraska recoiled and almost fell off the bench. "*Bozhe moi!* I never saw such a big person—a giant! What kind of magic is this?"

Some of the detainees who had been on the island for many days, or even weeks, laughed and pointed at the man on the canvas, clapping their hands as if greeting an old friend. Yevka and Paraska glanced nervously around them, confused by the excitement. Danko and Myko, however, watched the canvas intently and joined the others in laughter or gasps of surprise as the enormous man found himself in increasing peril at the hands of sinister-looking men.

"G-G-Got t-t-tam—"

"SNUF PITCH!"

Paraska was horrified. "Yevka, why are these people laughing? Myko-Danko, be quiet!" The boys laughed and pointed at the canvas. From the black box came frantic music that grew in intensity with the action on the canvas. *"Bozhe moi!"* cried Paraska. "Can no one do anything for this poor man besides laugh?" Paraska's comments were drowned by a new wave of laughter as the fleeing man on the screen fell against a ladder, dumping paint on his pursuers and leaving a painter dangling helplessly from a second-story ledge. Paraska gasped and gripped her sister's arm. But Yevka was laughing and bouncing a giggling Tomashko on her lap.

The detainees yelled encouragement to the people on the canvas and Myko and Danko stood on the bench for a better view.

"GOT—"

"T-T-TAM SN-N—"

"—SNUF PITCH!"

Yevka leaned closer to her bewildered sister and pointed to the man scampering across the white screen. "I think he is doing these things on purpose!" shouted Yevka above the music and laughter. "I think it is all right to laugh at him, Paraska. He wants us to laugh. He is like the clown we saw many years ago with the gypsies in Stara Polyanka. Do you remember him, Paraska? It was long ago—before the war, when we were young."

Paraska stared at the screen. Yes, long ago everyone in the village had laughed and cheered each time that clown tripped and fell to the ground. Paraska's jaw dropped and she flinched at each roar of laughter from the crowd. Suddenly, a great weight seemed to fall from her shoulders as the strain of the years of war and hunger, and the weeks of travel and sickness receded. There were no longer any troubles in the world except for the misfortunes tormenting a very silly man swinging by one hand from the back of an out-of-control streetcar.

Ordinarily echoing every idiom on earth, the Great Hall now reverberated with laughter, the one universal language. And no one laughed louder than the trembling Rusyn widow wiping her eyes in the fifth row.

CHAPTER FIFTY-THREE

Monday

EARLY MONDAY MORNING those who were approved for admittance to the United States rose and packed their possessions. Island workers then led the anxious immigrants out of the dormitories and down long corridors toward the dining hall for breakfast.

Paraska, Yevka, and the boys, surrounded by other chattering immigrants, shuffled through the dimly lit halls. Paraska shouted to the boys, "MYKO-DANKO STAY IN FRONT OF US. *Bozhe moi*, Yevka, how much more of this? I'm so tired of these guards pushing us and yelling at us! I tell you, Yevka, if someone pushes me again, I think I will—"

"Paraska . . . please . . ."

"No, Yevka, do not interrupt me. If someone pushes me again, I will hit him. I mean what I am saying, Yevka . . . I mean exactly what I am saying. I can't take this any longer." Paraska ground her jaws together as she walked. "I think you should carry Tomashko. Someone might step on him."

"Yes, you're right," said Yevka, hoisting the boy off the floor and balancing him on her left arm. Tomashko thrust the middle fingers of his left hand into his mouth and surveyed the shuffling crowd.

"Look at the people," said Paraska, shaking her head. "So many! Well, it is our last morning on this island. *Slava Bohu*—glory to God! This afternoon we will be at Anna and Petro Kotsur's house. We will be in a real home with a real hearth and maybe we can make *holubkŷ*—stuffed cabbage. Wouldn't that be nice, Yevka?"

"Yes, that would be nice."

"How many weeks has it been since we had *holubkŷ*?"

"I don't know, Paraska."

502

"And maybe a little *slyvovitsa*—plum brandy. What do you think, Yevka? Do you think Anna and Petro have *slyvovitsa* at their home?"

"I don't know. Probably."

"I hope so. After all this, a little glass of *slyvovitsa* would be nice. Maybe two glasses! Hmm, Yevka?"

"Yes, Paraska, that would be nice. Here's the room where we eat."

The dining hall was crowded and noisy. The sisters guided the boys toward a table for women and children on the far side of the hall. At the same table were Anna Perhach of Ruska Kaina with her son, Ivanko, and her daughter, Mariya.

Anna Perhach spoke excitedly as she ate. "*Dobre rano*—good morning, Paraska, Yevka, boys. How did you sleep last night? I slept poorly. Hardly any sleep at all! My husband, Yurii, will be here this morning, and I am suddenly very nervous. Yurii has never seen Ivanko. I hope he will be pleased with the boy. I've done the best I can. Two years! It has been two years since I saw Yurii—no, more than two years—almost two and a half years. *To pravda*—isn't that true, Mariya?"

"Yes, *Mamko* . . . I think so."

Anna Perhach cupped her chin in her hand. "I hope I recognize Yurii. How silly! Of course I will recognize him! I see him every time I close my eyes." Anna ran her hands down the sides of her face. "I only wonder . . . will he . . . will he recognize me? I hope I haven't changed. I hope he will still know me."

"Of course he will recognize you," said Yevka reassuringly. "A man does not forget his wife—" Yevka suddenly lowered her eyes.

"No, of course not," said Anna Perhach. "But, it has been a long time, and I know I don't look the same. I'm older, of course . . . I just hope I haven't changed too much." Anna finished her food and wiped her mouth with a white cloth napkin. "Paraska, tell me, I forgot, who is coming for you and your boys?"

"The husband of Yevka's sister-in-law. Petro Kotsur will be here today, only, we don't know when."

"Where do they live?" asked Anna.

Paraska shook her head. "I don't remember. Yevka, what is it called?"

"Bayonne," said Yevka without looking up from her food.

"We will live in Dzyerzi Sitii," said Anna. "Maybe we will be neighbors."

Paraska shrugged. "*Mozhe býty*—maybe."

༄

After breakfast, island officials announced that the first boat from Manhattan would be arriving soon. Those detainees expecting to be claimed by relatives, the officials continued, should now retrieve their belongings from the dormitories, and then proceed to the designated waiting area, where they would be claimed by family members from the mainland.

The sisters collected their belongings and herded the children through crowded noisy corridors and down a congested staircase. At the base of the stairs, a large mustachioed man in a straw hat shouldered his way through the crush of people, crying, "Helga! *Mein Gott!* HELGA!" A woman in tears pushed through the crowd with two young children close behind, clutching her dress. The man lifted Helga off her feet, kissing her loudly on the forehead, the cheeks, and mouth. He lowered Helga to her feet and, with another joyful shout, scooped up the two startled children who were huddled in the folds of their mother's dress. Balancing his son on one arm and his daughter on the other, the man guided his family down the corridor and out the doors leading to the ferry slip and the boat to Manhattan.

The sisters were ushered into a large adjacent waiting room. Paraska took a seat on a bench just inside the doorway. "Come, Yevka. There is room for you next to me. You boys stand here in front of us where we can see you." As anxious immigrants continued to pack the waiting room, Paraska shook her head. "*Bozhe,* Yevka, how will we ever see Petro Kotsur in this crowd?"

"*Ne znam*—I don't know, Paraska. They seem to be calling out names."

"So, we wait—hmm, Yevka?"

"Yes, I think so."

"Yes, of course we wait," grumbled Paraska. "Always we wait. Always we hurry and always we wait. And if we don't move quickly enough, someone will push us and hurry us along. *Tsy tak*—isn't that so?"

"*Hei*—yes, Paraska."

Anna Perhach and her children joined the sisters on the same bench. Anna set her little boy, Ivanko, on the bench next to Tomashko and the two boys stared at one another. Caressing Ivanko's head, Anna chatted nervously. "Yurii said he would come for us in the morning. He should be here soon. I wrote to Yurii about Ivanko—Yurii is so anxious to see him. I only hope he recognizes me. I hope he will be pleased with the boy. I've done my best with him. I've tried to explain to Ivanko that he will soon meet his *nyanko*—papa. But, I don't know if he understands. I just hope Yurii will know me when he sees me. I think . . . maybe I look older . . . I know I look older . . . maybe he will be disappointed . . ."

Yevka patted Anna's arm. "He won't be disappointed."

"I hope you are right, Yevka." Anna smiled faintly and squeezed Yevka's hand. "I'll try to stop worrying. And soon you and Paraska will—"

At that moment an official appeared in the doorway and announced, "Perhach!"

Immediately, another voice shouted, "ANNA!" from the same doorway.

Startled, Anna Perhach looked up at the man standing next to the official. "Yurii!" she gasped, rising slowly to her feet.

"Anna, it is you!" Yurii removed his hat and rushed to his wife with open arms.

"Yurii! *Bozhe moi!*"

"Anna! Anna!"

Yurii spotted his daughter, pulled her to his side, and kissed her on the forehead. "Mariya, you are a young lady now!" Mariya nodded shyly and bit her lip.

Anna pulled Ivanko from the folds of her dress and gently pushed the boy toward his father. "Yurii . . . Yurii, I . . . Yurii, *to ye tvoi sŷn*—this is your son, Ivanko. Look, Ivanko—*to ye tvoi nyanko*—this is your papa."

Yurii dropped to one knee and made the sign of the cross over his son. "*Slava Ottsu, i Sŷnu, i Svyatomu Dukhu*—Glory be to the Father and to the Son and to the Holy Spirit." Then he lifted the boy into his arms, and, from his pocket, produced two wrapped candies. "*Shokolada!*" he cried, giving each child a sweet. "Open them and eat!" Then he laughed at the children's delighted gasps and kissed their chocolate-covered lips and fingers. Anna, her lips trembling and her eyes moist, bent down to pick up her bag of belongings. But Yurii grabbed the bundle with one hand, tossed it over his shoulder, and pulled Anna close to his side, guiding her toward the door that led to the Manhattan ferry boat. Young Mariya picked up Ivanko and, looking over her shoulder, waved good-bye.

Paraska waved and murmured, "I think Anna didn't change much after all . . . no, not much . . . not much at all."

છ્ડ

The morning wore on and still the family sat on their bench, waiting. Tomashko clutched his mother's skirt in his right hand and sucked on the middle fingers of his left hand. Myko and Danko were becoming restless and began pushing one another. Paraska glared at them, showing them her open hand as a warning. "Both of you, sit still."

"But it's hot," whined Danko. "We want to go outside."

"*To shkoda*—that's too bad," snapped Paraska. "You can't go outside yet—not until Petro Kotsur comes for us. You can go outside when we get to their house. Stop pushing each other or I'll push you both into the wall." The boys stared sullenly at the passing people and muttered threats to one another.

Paraska yawned loudly. "I wish I had eaten more for breakfast. Now I'm hungry. It is too bad that Anna couldn't come with her husband, Petro. He almost never says anything—how would we know if he's here? It is too crowded. He could be here right now, waiting for us to recognize him. He probably doesn't have the sense to speak up."

Yevka removed Tomashko's fingers from his mouth. "If he's here, they would have called us by now."

"Hmph! He's probably here now, but the police wouldn't know because Petro Kotsur never says a word!"

☙

Finally, in the early afternoon, an official appeared in the doorway and called the sisters' names: "Ivanchyn! Rusynko!"

"*Slava Bohu*—Glory to God!" grunted Paraska. "Come, Yevka. We're finally leaving this place. Myko-Danko, pick up your things."

Yevka held out her hand. "Come, Tomashko. Take my hand."

By the time the family passed through the doorway and into the corridor, the official who had called their names had vanished.

Yevka tried to peer above the crowd. "I don't see where that man went, Paraska."

"Never mind him, Yevka. Do you see Petro?"

"No," said Yevka standing on her tiptoes.

Tomashko's hand slipped from Yevka's grasp briefly and he tugged at her dress. "*Mamko . . . Mamko!*"

"No, Tomashko. I can't pick you up right now." Yevka shook her head at her sister. "I don't see Petro anywhere."

Exasperated, Paraska blurted, "He must be here! Why else would the policeman call our names? Where the devil is Petro? He must have slipped into that room as we were leaving—the fool! Yevka, wait here with the boys. I'll go look for him."

"*Mamko . . . Mamko!*" cried Tomashko, still tugging at his mother's dress.

"Yes, yes," said Yevka, trying to soothe her son. "Hold my hand."

Paraska went back into the waiting room to find Petro Kotsur. Her search unsuccessful, she muttered, "*To proklyatŷi* Petro—that damned Petro!" She returned to the corridor and found Yevka and the boys. "He's not there, Yevka. He must be out here. What's wrong, Yevka? You look like you've seen a ghost."

Yevka hesitated. "There is a man staring at us."

"Where?"

"There, by the wall—in the white hat."

Indeed there was a man standing against the wall with his hat pulled down low on his forehead.

"That's not Petro . . . is it, Paraska?"

"I don't think so . . . no, Petro is thinner. That man's shoulders are too broad. Why is he staring at us?"

"He's not staring at us—he's staring at Tomashko."

At the sound of his name, Tomashko beseeched his mother with open arms. "*Mamko!*"

"Pick up Tomashko, Yevka. Let's move away from here. I don't like this man—he looks angry."

Yevka hoisted Tomashko to her shoulder while Paraska herded Myko and Danko ahead of them. "Stay in front of us, you two," she ordered. "Yevka, let's find a policeman to help us. Follow me to the other side of the hall."

When the sisters emerged from the other side of the crowd, they found the same broad-shouldered man in the white straw hat lurking by the wall. Yevka tapped Paraska's arm. "It's that man again."

"Yes, Yevka, I see him. Where are the police when you need them? Always since we arrived in Ameryka, police are pushing me. Now, where are they? Who is this angry man? Who protects honest women and children in Ameryka?"

Yevka hugged Tomashko to her bosom. "Paraska . . ."

"What, Yevka?"

"Paraska . . ."

"What? What is it?"

"I . . . I . . ."

"You want me to hold Tomashko? What's the matter, Yevka?"

"I'm afraid . . . I'm afraid, Paraska . . ."

"Are you faint? Do you want to sit down?"

"I'm afraid . . . Paraska . . . I'm . . . I think . . . I think it is Petro . . ."

"Who?"

"The white hat . . ."

"Him? No, Yevka. Anna's Petro is thin and—"

Yevka covered her mouth with a trembling hand and whispered, "No, Paraska—not Anna's Petro—*my* Petro!"

"What! No, Yevka; no one knows where he . . ." Paraska scrutinized the man who now approached the sisters. "*Ioi! Ioi,* Yevka! I think . . . *ioi! Mash pravdu*—you are right, Yevka! *Mash pravdu!* It is Petro! It is your husband Petro!"

Standing before the women was Petro Rusynko, his cold eyes fixed on Tomashko. Yevka backed up to the wall, clutching Tomashko tightly while Myko and Danko cowered behind Paraska.

Paraska was the first to speak. "Petro . . . it is you . . . we . . . we didn't . . . Yevka and I didn't expect—"

"*Khto yoho nyanko*—who is his papa?" Petro ground the question with his teeth as he glared at Tomashko.

Paraska looked helplessly at Yevka, who had turned white and was staring mutely at the floor, stroking Tomashko's hair. Paraska stammered, "W-we . . . w-we thought Anna's Petro was coming for us . . . and . . . so . . ."

"*Khto yoho nyanko?*"

"Petro, we . . . Yevka and I never thought—"

"*KHTO YOHO NYANKO!?*"

Yevka flinched and Paraska recoiled, wrapping her arms protectively around Myko's and Danko's shoulders. "It has been many years," said Paraska. "The war was long, Petro . . . we didn't know . . . Yevka didn't know . . . look, Petro, look—it is your boy, Danko. Look how he has grown since you last saw him. He's eight years old now."

But Petro was now glaring at Yevka. "*Suko*—you bitch!" he grunted.

Paraska stepped between Petro and Yevka. "P-Petro, look," she faltered. "This is Myko—he is Vasko's boy . . . he . . ."

Petro ground his jaws together furiously.

Paraska pleaded, "Please, Petro . . . please. You should . . . I think you . . . you don't understand—"

"*Rozumim vshytko*—I understand everything!" snarled Petro. "*Suko!*" He abruptly turned and shoved his way through the congested corridor and out of sight.

"*Bozhe!*" cried Paraska. "Yevka, what should we do!" Myko and Danko huddled next to Paraska, while Tomashko pushed his head under his mother's chin and thrust the middle fingers of his left hand in his mouth. Paraska led the ashen Yevka and the boys to the other side of the corridor, weaving around boisterous family reunions.

Paraska propped the stunned Yevka against the wall. "Yevka, I don't know what to do! What should we do? We thought Anna would come . . . then we thought her Petro would come . . . and then, *Bozhe moi,* your Petro comes . . . I don't know what to do . . ."

There was a commotion in the milling crowd. The immigrants stepped aside and Petro Rusynko reappeared with one of the island officials in tow. Petro pointed angrily to Yevka, Paraska, Myko, and Danko. "I take four," he said in heavily accented English. "Only four! Little boy"—he pointed to Tomashko—"little boy go home—go home to papa!" Petro pointed outside toward the harbor. "Boy go home to Stara Polyanka!"

Yevka slid to the floor, clutching Tomashko and sobbing. "*Nygda*—never! *Nygda . . . nygda . . .*"

The island official pushed his hat to the back of his head and put his hands on his hips. "Well, what the hell!" he said to Petro. "What is all this about?"

"I take four—only four."

"Listen, fella, these women and children have been approved for admittance. You can't just leave them here—you understand? They've been discharged to you."

"I take four. Boy go back."

"Well, what the hell! You can't send a little boy home by himself!"

"Only four! *Lem shtyri*—only four!"

Now, Paraska intervened. "Petro, he can't go back. He's Yevka's boy. If he goes back, Yevka would have to go back with him. Petro, Tomashko is a good boy—he is—"

"*On nich*—he is nothing!" Petro shouted. Then Petro thrust four fingers in Paraska's face. "*Lem shtyri*—only four!" Petro pointed to Tomashko. "He is nothing to me!"

Paraska's lips trembled. "But he is only a little boy! *Bozhe moi,* Petro!"

Tomashko peered over his mother's heaving shoulders at the angry man in the straw hat.

Petro barked at the official, "Only four! Only four!" Then he turned and disappeared into the crowd.

The official followed Petro, shouting, "Hey, fella! Come back here! HEY! COME BACK HERE!"

Paraska stood with outstretched arms, shielding her prostrate sister from the pressing crowd. "Yevka! *Bozhe,* Yevka!"

Tomashko ran his fingers through his mother's hair. *"Mamko . . . Mamko . . ."*

The crush of immigrants shuffled slowly past the wretched little group, murmuring to one another and shaking their heads. Somewhere in the crowd a man's voice cried out, "HELENA!" and a woman's voice answered, "ŠTEFAN!" The flow of immigrants parted around an embracing couple and three wide-eyed little girls.

Outside, the ferry boat rubbed against the dock in the afternoon sun and took on another cargo of reunited families bound for Manhattan, America.

CHAPTER FIFTY-FOUR

The Hospital

EARLY THE NEXT MORNING, Yevka awoke in a women's ward in the Ellis Island hospital. A young charwoman mopping the tiled floor noticed her stirring beneath the sheets. The young woman propped her mop against the wall and came to Yevka's bedside.

"You are awake. *Dobre rano*—good morning, Pani Rusynko. I am Mariya. I mop and clean here. Your family will come to visit you this morning after they finish breakfast. I met them yesterday when you were brought to this ward. Your little boy is very sweet. He will be very happy to see you this morning. Do you feel like talking? No? Your sister, Paraska, said that yesterday was a very sad day for you. She said maybe you don't want to talk much now. That's all right. You will talk when you feel like it. Paraska was surprised when I spoke to her—she was happy to talk with someone who speaks her way. I came from Poland—it was Austria then—twenty years ago, with my parents and my two brothers when I was ten years old—only a year or two older than your oldest boy. We came from a village near Drohobych, south of Lemberg. They called the area Galicia in those days. Maybe they still do—I don't know. So, I speak very closely to your way. Ah, look—do you see? The men are here with the breakfast trays. You will eat something and then you will feel better. Here is your tray. You will have to sit up so you can hold the tray on your lap. Yes, that is good. *Dobre*—very good. Now, you eat. I will come by later—we will talk more then."

ↀ

Four mornings later, Paraska herded the boys down a hallway of Ellis Island Hospital for their daily visit with Yevka.

"Myko-Danko! Stay with me! Stop running ahead! Danko, come back here and hold Tomashko's hand! He's anxious to see his *mamka* and he's pulling on my arm. *Bozhe moi!* You boys are becoming wild—like animals!" The group proceeded along the tiled floor to the women's ward.

At the entrance to the ward, Paraska waited for the charwoman, Mariya, to finish emptying trash cans. "You boys take Tomashko to see his *mamka*," ordered Paraska. Myko and Danko escorted Tomashko to Yevka's bed at the end of the ward. Tomashko buried his head in his mother's open arms and thrust the middle fingers of his left hand into his mouth. Danko submitted his head briefly to his mother's caresses and then withdrew to stand against the wall with Myko.

The trash cans emptied, Mariya greeted Paraska. "*Dobre rano*—good morning, Paraska."

"*Dobre.* How is Yevka today?"

"*Dobre*—well. She still hasn't spoken; but she has been eating well, and she is stronger—stronger than she was the day she came to the ward. Will you tell her today, Paraska? I mean, why her husband showed up on the island."

"Yes . . . I will tell her this morning. I should have told her yesterday. She seemed so weak. But, now, she needs to know." Paraska grasped Mariya's hand. "It was good of you and your brother to help us."

Mariya smiled. "*To nich*—it is nothing. One more thing, Paraska. I overheard a nurse say that the doctors think your sister is better now. So, later today, or maybe tomorrow, they will move her out of this ward and send her back to the detention wards with you and the boys."

Paraska nodded. "*Dobre*—good. That will be better for Tomashko . . . better for all of us. Is there a place where the boys can run and play? Every day we come here the boys get restless."

"Yes, I think it would be all right to let them out in the grassy yard. Send them to me—I'll show them the door."

Paraska limped to the other end of the ward and pulled a chair next to Yevka's bed. She motioned to the boys. "Myko-Danko, go to Mariya. She will let you outside to play. *Chekaite*—wait! Not so fast! Come back here. Take Tomashko with you."

Danko whined, "Got tam snuf pitch! We don't want to take Tomashko! He can't do anything!"

Paraska grabbed Danko's arm and yanked him to her side, her nose almost touching his. "Don't you give me any trouble! You boys take Tomashko outside with you. Be nice to him. And don't let him fall in the ocean." Paraska released her grip on Danko, who retreated to Myko's side, rubbing his arm. Paraska stroked Tomashko's hair. "Let him go, Yevka. He needs fresh air. He will have fun with Myko and Danko." Yevka patted Tomashko on the head, pulled his fingers from his mouth, and gently pushed him toward his brother and cousin. Paraska, glaring at the two older boys, said, "Don't worry, Yevka. They will take good care of him." The boys, with Tomashko between them, hurried to the other end of the ward. Yevka watched the boys as they followed Mariya out the door.

Paraska pulled her chair closer to the bedside. *"Bozhe moi,* Yevka! I'm getting old on this island. The boys are getting wilder every day. Myko and Danko run everywhere—they go places they shouldn't. At least they are learning to speak *po-amerykanský.* I don't know how they learn it so fast. But never mind that. The boys and I still sleep in that big room with all the other people who must stay on this island. This last week has been like being on the ship again." Paraska reached into her bag on the floor. "I brought you something, Yevka. Hold out your hand." Paraska placed an egg in her sister's hand. "I got it from the kitchen. A *chornýi tsygan*—a black gypsy— gave it to me. I will get you more eggs. When you leave this room and come back to us, you can make *pysanký* again. It will give you something to do. Mariya will get everything that you need—beeswax, dyes—everything to make *pysanký.* Her mother makes *pysanký,* so she knows what you need. We are lucky to know Mariya. She has been very good to us, Yevka. She knows our ways, and I can talk to her easily. She has a brother who lives in Bayonne, not far from Anna and Petro Kotsur. Petro Kotsur! Feh!" Paraska turned her head to spit on the floor, paused, and swallowed instead. "I have things to tell you . . . I don't know if you feel like hearing them now. I know you don't feel like talking . . . if you want me to keep talking, just nod your head . . . so I know if I should—good! A nod from you is good, Yevka. I told Mariya what happened on Monday when your Petro, who everyone thought was dead, showed up here. Mariya told the story to her brother who lives in Bayonne. So, her brother and his wife went to see Anna. Petro Kotsur was at work, so Anna let them in. Anna was weak from having her baby—she had another girl—but she told them why her husband didn't come for us. Yevka, it is not Anna's fault. She cried and said she is ashamed of her husband. *To ista pravda,* Yevka—that's the honest truth. It is Petro Kotsur's fault. *Ioi,* Yevka! Everything is his fault! His fault and your Petro's fault!"

Yevka stroked the egg with her thumb.

Paraska lowered her voice and hissed, "Petro Kotsur! *To sukŷi sŷn*—that son of a bitch! He didn't want us in his home! Anna thought we were going to stay at her house, but now her husband says that it's hard enough to feed her and the children, so how can he feed us, too! As if we would expect him to! So, behind Anna's back, Petro Kotsur went to Yonkers to find your Petro. And he found him, indeed! He found him living with a woman who owns a boarding house. Your Petro didn't want anyone to know where he was, so he gave Petro Kotsur some money. 'Keep it to yourself,' he said." Paraska paused. "Yevka, did you say something? No? I thought you were trying to say something."

Yevka closed her eyes and turned the egg over and over in her hand.

"So, Yevka, all I can say about Petro Kotsur is, *on sukŷi sŷn*—he is a son of a bitch! All the time we were trying to make the kvota to come to Ameryka— all that time!—Petro Kotsur knew where your Petro was! But he never told Anna. Then, when Petro Kotsur heard that we were coming to Ameryka with the boys, he went to your Petro and told him to come and claim us on this island when we arrived. Your Petro refused. He refused even though Petro Kotsur hadn't told him about Tomashko."

Yevka held the egg to her chest.

"Yevka, do you remember when Anna wrote to Vasyl and told him that his uncle Pavlo had died? Anna said that your Petro had lived with Uncle Pavlo and that after Uncle Pavlo's funeral no one saw Petro again. No one even knew if he was still alive. Well, Petro found Vasyl's money—all the money Vasyl earned in Ameryka before the war—the money he left with his Uncle Pavlo for safekeeping. Your Petro took the money, Yevka. He knew Vasyl had asked Uncle Pavlo to return it to him someday. But your Petro kept it for himself! So Petro Kotsur threatened to go to the police about the money if your Petro didn't come for us. The police probably wouldn't do anything about it, but the idea of talking to the police frightened your Petro. So, he agreed to come to the island for us. Yevka, your Petro stole Vasyl's money! Over four hundred dolar! Such meanness, Yevka! What has Ameryka done to Petro to make him like this?"

Yevka opened her eyes and cocked her head toward the door leading to the outside. There was a brief commotion from the other side of the door before it opened. Tomashko entered and walked silently down the center of the ward, his face contorted in agony. When the boy reached his mother's side, he inhaled deeply and then wept with choking despair. Handing the egg to Paraska, Yevka drew her quivering son to her bosom.

Paraska noticed two shadows beneath the slowly closing door. "MYKO-DANKO!" she whispered hoarsely, trying unsuccessfully not to disturb the other patients. "COME IN HERE!" The boys opened the door and shuffled into the ward. Paraska glared at the boys. "What happened?"

"N-n-n—" stammered Myko.

"Nothing," muttered Danko.

Paraska pointed to the victim in Yevka's arms. "What did you two do to Tomashko?"

"N-n-n—"

"Nothing."

"Why is he crying? Tell me, or I'll slap both of you."

The boys looked at one another and then spoke at once.

"T-T-Tomashko—"

"—can't do anything! We want to climb a—"

"—t-t-tree b-but he—"

"—he can't. So he cries. We want to—"

"—r-r-race across the g-g-g-grass—"

"—but Tomashko can't run fast. So he cries."

"H-h-he t-t-tried to p-pick—"

"—pick up a *pchola*—a bee—from a rain puddle. We had to stop him!"

"It m-m-might have st-st-stung—"

"The bee might have stung him if it wasn't already drowned! Then you would both be mad at us!"

"H-h-he c-c-can't—"

"He can't do ANYTHING. Let the baby stay here with his *mamka*."

Tomashko released his hold on Yevka, kicked Danko in the shins, and then threw himself once again into his mother's arms.

"*Oiii! Teto—Mamko,* look what he did! Snuf pitch—he kicked me!"

Paraska grabbed Danko by the arm. "Quiet! You probably deserved it. You and Myko stand over here, in the corner. And be quiet."

"W-w-will you—"

"—let us go outside?"

"No."

"B-b-but—"

"But we want to run."

"No."

"But we—"

"I will slap both of you if you say one more word."

The boys retreated to the corner, grumbling to one another.

Paraska glared at the boys. "Do you see, Yevka? They are wild. *Bozhe,* I hope Ameryka doesn't make them mean . . . mean like Petro."

Yevka rested her face against Tomashko's head and stroked his neck.

"Now, Yevka," continued Paraska. "I must tell you the latest news. Mariya says that Anna is so ashamed of her Petro that she has told his family what he has done. They are going to make your Petro come for us and take us off this island whether he wants to or not. I don't know if that will work—they seem to think so. Your Petro is afraid of people finding out about the money he stole from Vasyl. Anna would come for us, but she can't—not without her husband. Women can't leave the island with other women. They're afraid we'll become . . . well . . . dishonest women. The people from the shipping company won't take us back across the ocean because we've already been approved to enter Ameryka. Yevka, we've got to get off this island. The boys are wild and I am losing my mind here. *Oi,* Yevka, Ameryka is so close. I can't bear to look across the water anymore. We can almost touch Ameryka, and yet, we might as well be in Rotyerdom still." Sighing heavily, Paraska shook her head. "I don't know what will become of us, Yevka . . . I don't know what will become of us . . ." Paraska inclined her head toward the ward entrance. "Here comes Mariya. She is smiling—perhaps she has something to tell us."

The charwoman, Mariya, arrived at the foot of the bed. "I think there is good news," she announced. "Yevka, you might return to your family today. I overheard two doctors saying that you are well enough to go back to the main dormitories."

Paraska held her sister's hand. "Do you hear, Yevka? It will be good to have you with us again. Mariya's news is good. *Dyakuyu*—thank you, Mariya."

Mariya smiled and, turning to the sullen Danko, said, "Your mother has missed you. Now your family will be together again."

Danko shrugged. "Tso-kay. Got tam snuf pitch."

Mariya blinked her eyes in disbelief, and then leaning over, whispered into Paraska's ear. The blood drained from Paraska's face; she swung her arm in a broad arc, just missing Myko and Danko, who ducked and then scurried to safety on the other side of the bed.

Paraska's voice shook with anger. "If I ever . . . *ever* hear either one of you say that again, I will beat both of you! I will beat you until you cannot sit. You will not sit for a week! Do you both understand me?"

The boys nodded quickly.

While Paraska glared at the boys, Yevka continued to stroke Tomashko's head.

ᏉᏏ

It was a cool early morning three weeks later when Mariya spoke with Paraska in the hallway adjacent to the entrance to the detention dormitory. The hallway alternately brightened and darkened as small, scattered clouds drifted high above the island.

"I hear," said Mariya, "that Anna Kotsur's idea finally worked."

"Yes."

"So, Yevka's husband will come for all of you?"

Paraska began to smile, but her lips grew taut over her teeth, as though she had tasted something bitter. "If Petro wants to keep the money he stole from his brother," she managed to say, "he will come for us."

"Are you leaving today?" asked Mariya.

"Yes, today . . . all five of us . . . including Tomashko."

"Paraska, how will it be for Yevka? You said her husband was so angry. Will she be all right with Petro?"

Paraska, her jaw firm, nodded. "Yevka will be with me . . . she will be all right."

Mariya nodded. "*Dobre*—good. I have said good-bye to Yevka and the boys. When I held Yevka's hand, she squeezed it. So, I know she understood me, even though she did not speak."

Paraska nodded grimly. "She will speak again someday . . . when she is ready."

Mariya reached into her pocket. "Look, Paraska," she said, unwrapping a handkerchief and revealing a brightly decorated egg. "Look at the *pysanka* your sister made for me. *Prekrasna, tak*—beautiful, yes?"

"*Hei, prekrasna*—yes, beautiful."

"I will show it to my mother," said Mariya, turning the egg in her hand. "She will love to see someone else's work. My mother often remembers *starŷi krai*—the old country—especially at *Velykden*—Easter. She makes many *pysankŷ* at that time, and then she gives them to family and friends." Mariya smiled. "She told me that when she was young, she once gave one to my father at *Velykden*—this was before they married. That was how he knew that she liked him."

"Yes," said Paraska. "At *Velykden*. That was our way also. A girl made a *pysanka* and gave it to a boy in the village. That was how she showed a boy she cared for him."

"Did your sister ever give one to Petro?" asked Mariya.

"No, no, no. She never gave one to him." Paraska paused and then said softly, "I remember that she once gave a *pysanka* to someone else . . ."

Smiling and arching her eyebrows, Mariya asked, "Did she love him?"

"Yes." Paraska paused. "Yes, she did—very much." Her chin cupped in her left hand, Paraska stared down the length of the corridor, squinting her eyes as though searching across all space and time for a distant but vanished place.

Mariya interrupted Paraska's reverie. "I hope I will see you and your family again," said Mariya.

Paraska blinked her eyes. "Hmm? Yes . . . yes . . . that will be nice."

Mariya gripped Paraska's shoulder. "*Z Bohom*—go with God, Paraska."

"Yes, *z Bohom*," said Paraska.

Mariya walked slowly down the corridor, stopped, and turned around. "Paraska!" she called.

"Yes?"

"Did he love her?"

"Who?"

"You said your sister once gave an egg to a boy she loved. Did he love her in return?"

Paraska frowned and moved her lips, as if trying to formulate an answer. Finally, she shrugged. "*Ne znam*—I don't know . . . that was a long time ago."

Mariya smiled, and, waving over her shoulder, continued down the corridor and disappeared around a corner.

"That was a long, long time ago," Paraska whispered. "It was springtime . . . long ago . . . before the war . . . when we were young . . ." Paraska opened the door to the detention dormitory and went inside.

EPILOGUE

1909

The Linden and the Oak

"YEVKA! WHERE ARE YOU, YEVKA?" bellowed Paraska as she opened the door to the old Senchak hut. "YEVKA!"

"Yes, yes—I am here."

"Why have you not answered? What are you doing here in the dark? Vasyl will leave soon for Ameryka and you will miss everything. Father Yaroslav will give him a blessing in front of Yakov's tavern and everyone in the village will be there. What are you doing?"

Yevka held an egg aloft and answered, "I am almost finished."

"Ah, a *pysanka* for a boy! Who do you have an eye for? I will guess it is for Ivanko Korba—or, maybe, Shtefan Fedorochko—or, better yet, Petro Barna! But not now, Yevka. Vasyl is leaving soon. The *pysanka* for Petro Barna, or Mykhal Kavulya, or whoever it is, can wait. You are young, Yevka—only fifteen years! Let the boys wait! Finish the *pysanka* later—otherwise, you will be late. It is not every day that one of our people leaves for Ameryka."

"I am almost finished."

"You will miss the blessing."

"I am almost finished."

"You will be late."

"I am almost finished. Yakov's is not that far away."

Paraska shook her head and stepped forward to rebuke her sister, but, at the sound of singing, she went to the doorway and peeked outside. She sprang to her sister's side and whispered giddily, "It is Vasko! He is coming up the path! Hurry, Yevka! Mariya Kavulya says he has been asking about me! Put down the egg. This is no time for *pysanký*. Vasko may want to walk with me to Yakov's tavern! Yevka, do I look all right?"

"Yes . . ."

"Yevka, you didn't even look at me! Listen! He's coming closer! I mustn't appear too anxious—I must calm down. Hurry! You can make all the *pysankŷ* you want later. Hurry."

"I am almost finished."

Paraska skipped to the door and then stopped, locked her hands over her stomach, and inhaled and exhaled until her breathing was slow and rhythmic. Then she affected a stern countenance and opened the door as Vasko entered the little yard in front of the hut.

Vasko stopped, removed his cap, and proclaimed, "*Khrystos voskrese*—Christ is risen!"

"*Voistinu voskrese*—indeed He is risen," responded Paraska. "What do you want?"

Vasko approached the door, turning his hat in his hands. "Only to wish you *dobre rano*—good morning—my beauty!"

Paraska snorted. "I am not *your* 'beauty.'"

"Then you are someone else's beauty—someone who should be ashamed of himself for leaving you alone on a spring day that is almost as beautiful as a girl standing in a doorway."

Paraska reddened and bit her lower lip. "I'm not alone. Yevka is here," she said, pointing inside.

"Then I will come in."

"Your boots are muddy. You will stay outside."

"I'll remove my boots."

"Hmph! Leave them on. Your feet are probably even dirtier!"

Vasko smirked. "If you wash my feet I could come in."

"If I had that much water in the house I would not waste it on your feet. Go to *Potok* Ondava and wash them yourself and stop bothering honest girls."

Vasko replaced his hat on his head at a precarious angle and put his hands on his hips. "The Ondava is too far. But, someday . . . someday, my beauty, maybe you will wash my feet."

"Are you mad? Or are you the devil himself? Not with all the buckets in the village would I bathe your feet!"

"Maybe with your tears, then. I—"

Paraska squinted at Vasko. "What did you say?"

Vasko shifted nervously and looked at the ground. "I . . . I said only . . .

as Father Yaroslav once said about *Isus*—Jesus, and the . . . the woman with the . . . the long hair . . . maybe . . . maybe you could—"

"That is what I thought you said. Blasphemer! Who are you to talk of Father Yaroslav and *Isus*!?" Paraska leaned closer to Vasko, her nostrils flaring. "If I bathe your feet with my tears, it will be because I am sinful—is that what you are saying?"

Vasko considered carefully. "Well . . . no, my dove . . . no . . . You are no more sinful than . . . than . . . than Yevka." Vasko called into the hut, "Yevka! Yevka, are you coming to Yakov's to see Vasyl leave for Ameryka? Father Yaroslav is going to give the blessing soon."

Paraska snorted, "Don't bother Yevka. Look at her, busy at work. She can think only of love! I am going to the tavern to see him off. I don't know about others, but I am going. In fact, I am leaving now."

Vasko stepped aside to let Paraska pass outdoors. "May I walk you to the tavern, my beauty?"

"You may not."

"May I walk *with* you to the tavern?"

"You may not."

"May I walk near you—three, even four arm lengths away, but not directly alongside you?"

"You may not."

"But, my dove, we are both going to the tavern, yes?"

"No. *You* are going to the tavern, and *I* am going to the tavern—*we* are not going to the tavern. If you wish to go to the tavern, I suggest you leave now."

Vasko sighed and shrugged dramatically. "Someday . . . someday, my beauty, you will walk with me." And he shuffled away slowly.

Paraska hurried back inside the hut and bumped into her sister. "*Bozhe moi!* Be careful, Yevka! Are you finished with the *pysanka*?"

"Yes."

"Good. Now hurry. Vasko is getting away."

"I thought you didn't want to walk with him."

Paraska placed her hands on her hips and patiently explained, "Yevka, you are a young girl of only fifteen years who knows almost nothing about men and women and . . . and . . . well . . . men and women. Now hurry!"

The two sisters left the hut and walked down the path toward the tavern.

Vasko had made little progress and was standing by the path with one boot in his hand, evidently trying to empty it of an irritating pebble.

Paraska threw an elbow into Yevka's side and whispered, "Talk to me!"

"*Umph!* What?"

"Talk to me!" Paraska said, her eyes large and dark. "He is looking at us. Talk to me."

"I have nothing to say."

"Say something," Paraska muttered. "Stop arguing with me." Then Paraska exclaimed loudly, "Yevka! Have you heard? Mariya Rozum and her husband, Petro, will soon have a special little blessing in their family."

"What? I didn't even know she was—"

"Yes, you are right, Yevka, and did you also know—" Paraska leaned over and whispered into Yevka's ear, "After I say this, laugh loudly and cover your mouth as if you were embarrassed."

"But I don't—"

"Just do it!" blurted Paraska, and then she threw her head back, laughing boisterously, her neck trembling in the sunlight.

Yevka raised her eyebrows and forced a chuckle. "Heh, heh!"

Vasko stomped his foot back into his boot and hobbled after the sisters. "What is it? What is so funny? Tell me."

Paraska wheeled around. "Are you following us?"

"Well . . . no . . . no, my dove . . . I—"

"Don't call me your 'dove.' I won't allow it . . . not yet . . ."

"No, never . . . only I . . ." The full implication of Paraska's statement registered slowly on Vasko's face in the form of a hopeful smile, which abruptly degenerated into a smirk. He swaggered ahead of the sisters. "You two may walk with me to the tavern."

Paraska held her sister's arm. "Wait, Yevka. Let this smug stork cross the road. There is not enough room in the road for you and me and this much pride."

Now Vasko threw his head back and howled. He continued on to the tavern, his chest swollen and his head swaying side to side with each spring in his step.

Yevka was confused. "But, Paraska, I thought you wanted to walk with him."

"We did."

"But, look, he's getting away."

"No, he isn't," said Paraska, smiling.

The sisters arrived at the tavern, where a crowd was pressed around Old Mykhal's cart, worrying the old man who brushed villagers aside with his old hat. "Back, back! You will frighten Sasha!" The horse, Sasha, his eyes half-closed, nonchalantly shifted his weight from his left rear leg to his right rear leg, while tall, thin Yurko Kryak stroked the soft spot between the horse's nostrils.

Vasko called out from the crowd, "Yes, leave the poor horse alone. If he becomes any more terrified than he is now, he will fall asleep! Yurko! Stop torturing the poor animal! He might choke on his snores! *Bozhe moi!* The horse's eyes are closed—he's not dead, is he?"

Old Mykhal pointed a finger at Vasko. "Feh!"

Vasko pointed up the hill behind the tavern. "Look! Here he comes—on his way to Ameryka! Don't go, Vasyl! Stay here with friends!"

Down the path from the Rusynko homestead came Vasyl, his hat at a jaunty angle, his mother on one arm, his *baba*—his grandmother—on the other. Behind them came Vasyl's sister Anna and his younger brother, Andriiko.

Paraska peered over the top of the crowd and then shook her head at her sister. "What a shame, Yevka. Vasyl's *dido* and *nyanko*—his grandfather and father—and his brother Petro did not come. You would think they could have stayed away from the fields for one morning! I don't see Vasko. Do you see him?"

Just then Vasko shouted over the buzz of the crowd. "Father Yaroslav! A blessing for Vasyl!"

Annoyed, Father Yaroslav nodded. "Yes, Vasko, that is why I am here."

Paraska shouted, "Forgive Vasko, Father! He often thinks he understands what goes on around him, but usually he is wrong."

Vasko's tenor voice responded from somewhere in the crowd. "I understand more than you think I do, my dove; and I understand almost everything when I am around you! Think of how well I could understand everything if my *arms* were around you!"

The women near Paraska laughed and nodded knowingly at one another. Paraska shook her finger in their faces. "It means nothing! *On didko*—he is the devil! Pay no attention to him! It means nothing."

Vasyl knelt beside Old Mykhal's cart, and Father Yaroslav made the sign of the cross over his head. Yevka backed slowly away from her sister's side and skirted around the crowd to the back of Yakov's tavern, where, now hidden from view, she made her way quickly up the path that wound behind the Church of the Protection of the Mother of God and continued down the valley.

After the blessing, Paraska whispered out of the side of her mouth, "Yevka, you know what the girls in the village say about Vasko, yes? Yevka?" Receiving no answer, Paraska turned her head and found, instead of her sister, Vasko's leering face. "*Bozhe moi!* The devil!" cried Paraska, backing away a step. "Where is Yevka?"

Shrugging, Vasko edged closer to Paraska. "*Ne znam*—I don't know. What do the girls say about me, my dove?"

"They say you are the devil. Get back! Stop it! Don't stand so near me." Paraska shooed Vasko away with her hands.

"What do the girls say about me?"

"They say you ask too many questions." Paraska scanned the crowd. "Yevka couldn't wait to give the *pysanka* to Dmytro Dzyamba, or to Andrii Vantsa, or Petro Kryak, or whoever he may be. She should have waited until Vasyl left. *Ai,* so young—so anxious! So in love!"

Vasko peered into Paraska's dark eyes. "Yes, so in love! My dove, do you have a *pysanka* for me?"

Paraska scanned Vasko contemptuously from head to toe and then sniffed loudly.

Vasko looked away, smiling. "No, I guess you don't . . . but . . . someday . . . someday. Look! Vasyl is leaving!"

Sasha pulled the old cart forward and Old Mykhal rang the bell. Vasyl waved and shouted, "*Khrystos voskrese*—Christ is risen!"

"*VOISTINU VOSKRESE*—INDEED HE IS RISEN!" cried the crowd in response.

Vasko followed the cart, calling out, "Old man! Unhitch that horse—let him sleep! Hitch up Yurko—let him pull the cart! You will get there quicker, only it will cost you more in feed!"

Someone yelled, "Vasko, you are the devil!"

Paraska, standing alone at the edge of waving villagers, smiled and whispered, "Yes . . . yes, he is. He is the devil!"

Now, someone began the great Easter Tropar—the hymn of the resurrection—and the crowd joined in song:

Khrystos voskrese iz mertvykh!
Smertiyu smert poprav,
I sushchim vo hrobikh zhivot darovav.

Christ is risen from the dead!
By death He conquered death,
And to those in the graves He granted life.

❧

In front of the wayside crucifix south of the village, Sasha came to a sudden halt. Old Mykhal, confused by the unscheduled stop, turned from his conversation with Vasyl and uttered a belated "Whoa." Both men bowed their heads toward the wayside crucifix and crossed themselves.

Old Mykhal frowned at the back of Sasha's head. "Why did he stop here? Ah, look." The old man tapped Vasyl's arm and pointed behind the crucifix, where Yevka emerged from a stand of young oak trees. "Go on," said the old man smiling. "Take your time. I want to fill my pipe."

Vasyl jumped down from the cart and laughed as he drew near to Yevka. "What are you doing here, Yevka? Why aren't you back at Yakov's with the others?"

Yevka backed into the trees and away from the grinning scrutiny of Old Mykhal.

Vasyl followed her and the corners of his mouth dropped sharply as he smiled. "Yevka, what is it? What do you have there in your hands?"

Yevka pulled a wrapped scarf from her apron and handed it to Vasyl, who opened it, revealing the *pysanka*.

"Yevka, it is beautiful." He looked at Yevka's down-turned face, and when she looked up, he smiled. Yevka reddened and looked away.

"It is a beautiful *pysanka*, Yevka—but, if I take it with me, it may break." Yevka cleared her throat. "Take it."

"If it breaks, I will feel badly, Yevka."

"Take it. I made it for you."

"You will not be upset if it breaks?"

Yevka shook her head. "There must always be *pysankŷ*."

Vasyl laughed. "Yes, my *mamka* says the world will end when the last *pysanka* breaks."

Yevka nodded solemnly. "*Hei, to pravda*—yes, that is true."

Vasyl wrapped the egg in the scarf and placed it inside his vest. "How old are you, Yevka?"

"*Mam pyatnadtsat rokiv*—I am fifteen years old."

"*Uzhe*—already—you are fifteen!" Vasyl seemed surprised.

The two stood in the shade, while above them sparrows chirped in the branches of the oak trees. Vasyl extended his right hand and touched Yevka's shoulder. She hesitated and then shyly touched Vasyl's shoulder. They clasped each other's shoulder briefly, and Yevka looked up into Vasyl's sharply inverted smile. Vasyl abruptly turned and, hurrying out from under the trees, jogged toward Old Mykhal's cart.

Halfway to the cart Vasyl stopped. "Yevka!" he cried.

Yevka peeked out from under the low oak branches.

"Yevka, if the *pysanka* breaks, I will return to Stara Polyanka—you can make me another!"

Yevka smiled. "Yes . . . yes, I will."

Vasyl laughed and waved. Then he ran to the old man's cart and climbed aboard.

By now, Vasko and Yurko, on foot, had reached the wayside crucifix on their way to work in Pan Kapishinskii's lower fields. "Look, Yurko! Do you see?" exclaimed Vasko, pointing to Vasyl. "Our friend has changed his mind. He knows that he will find nothing in Ameryka worth the voyage. Welcome back, Vasyl! If you run back to Yakov's right away, you may still find the farewell party there ready to greet you home again—two great feasts in one day! The girls will cry to see you after such a long absence."

Vasyl laughed. "They will have to wait longer—maybe even three years!"

The cart started forward and Vasko and Yurko walked alongside. "But, Vasyl," argued Vasko. "Why leave? What good is Ameryka to anyone? Did you see all the girls who came to see you off? I didn't know there were so many girls in Stara Polyanka. What will become of them all after you leave?"

Old Mykhal pulled his pipe from his mouth, spat, and looked over his shoulder at Vasko. "Probably, they will all run to the nearest convent to avoid a match with you."

Vasyl slapped his knee with delight while Vasko cried, "All but one, old man! All but one!"

"Only a fool or a gypsy would marry the devil!" said Old Mykhal, jabbing his pipe at Vasko.

"Feh, old man! Feh!"

"Feh yourself, you . . . *didku*—you devil! Feh to you . . ." Old Mykhal rang the bell as the cart, with Vasko and Yurko following close behind, disappeared around a bend in the path. The bickering voices faded, and even the clang of the old bell eventually dissolved in the bright spring air.

Yevka made her way from the stand of oak trees to a spot in the middle of the path, where, alone now, she stood facing the crucifix. Inscribed on the base of the cross were the words, *"Khrest tvoye spaseniye!*—The Cross is your salvation!" Yevka knelt and closed her eyes.

Nearby, under the young leaves of the linden trees growing along its banks, *Potok* Ondava gurgled, flowing ever southward to the lowlands—*tykho*—quietly . . . *tykho . . . tykho . . . tykho . . .*

Yevka crossed herself from right to left in the eastern fashion: *"Slava Ottsu y Sŷnu y Svyatomu Dukhu*—Glory be to the Father and to the Son and to the Holy Spirit. *Y nŷni y prisno, y vo vikŷ vikov*—now and ever, and forever. *Amin.*"

Yevka gazed into the eyes of the crucified Lord. *"Khrest tvoye spaseniye!"*

Yevka rose to her feet, dusted off her skirt, and began the short journey back up the valley to Stara Polyanka and to her home on the banks of *Potok* Ondava.

Acknowledgments

Buffeted for a century by the gales of war and politics, Carpatho-Rusyns today live as minorities in states that once made up much of the old Austro-Hungarian empire: Slovakia, Ukraine, Hungary, Romania, and Poland. Several million descendents of Carpatho-Rusyn immigrants live in Canada and the United States. Any project involving such a stateless people is by necessity an international effort. I am grateful for the generosity, therefore, of many knowledgeable people in Europe and North America who guided me through the history and culture of the Rusyn people.

Canada

I am deeply grateful to Steven Chepa, Chairman of the World Academy of Rusyn Culture, for publishing *The Linden and the Oak*. I especially appreciate his enthusiasm and great love for this story. Many thanks to Colin Rose, also of the World Academy, for his many hours of kind assistance and his always thoughtful advice. I am indebted to Paul Robert Magocsi, Chair of Ukrainian Studies at the University of Toronto for his lifetime of writings on the Rusyn people and for his many helpful and valuable comments on the manuscript.

Slovakia

I am grateful to the beautiful Rusyn people of the Makovytsya region of Northeastern Slovakia who opened their doors and hearts and welcomed me like a prodigal son. I thank Rev. Robert Jager for kindly helping me reconnect with my family. I thank Rev. Petro Savčak for helping me decipher church records and for sharing his intimate knowledge of bees. Many thanks to Anna

Romanova for sharing old family traditions and for singing a lovely rendi-
tion of 'Bŷstra vodichka'(Chapter 40, *Svyatŷi Vechur*). I am grateful to Elena
Gazdíkova of Košice for her great story-telling and for our emotional meeting
("You are a Senčak!" she cried, squeezing my hands and peering into my face
through moist eyes). I was moved by Petro Senčak's kindness and his inspiring life story. Several mayors in Makovytsya, especially Anna Pasternakova
and Ernest Sivak, were of valuable assistance with village archives. I am grateful to the forester Jan Zamborsky for showing me the remnants of World War
One trenches above the Ondava Valley and for sharing his knowledge of local
flora. Others who shared stories and insights include Anna Barnova, Marija
Buryova, Anna Guzyova, Vladislav Korba, Marija Kruškova, František Sivak,
Vladimir Chudik, Silvia Chudikova, Helena Černa and Daniel Černy.

Ukraine

In a Galician village southeast of Lviv, a friend's *baba* asked me, "Why have
you come to Ukraine?" I answered, "I am here to find old cemeteries and
battlefields." *Baba* cupped her chin in her hand and shook her head. "There
are plenty of those here . . . plenty." I owe a very large debt to Volodymyr
Mysak for his invaluable help in research and translation in Ukraine, Poland,
Slovakia, and Hungary. I will always cherish my memories of our many
shared adventures. I thank our driver Taras Kuzyk for finding obscure, un-
mapped sites in Ukraine and Poland and for his infectious joy of discovery in
places like Brody, Rava Ruska, and Przemyśl. I thank Ksavelii Sydor of Rava
Ruska for sharing the history of his town and his memories of the Jews who
once lived there. Many thanks to Sydor's grandson, Mykhailo, who showed
me the peaceful forest clearing where untold numbers of nameless Russian
soldiers have reposed since those violent months of 1914–1915. (As we left the
mass graves and made our way across the vast fields of an old Soviet collective farm, Mykhailo pointed to a distant group of men and women working
the soil. He reported that each fall local farmers plowing these fields turn
up human bones as well as belt buckles, brass buttons, and rusted rifle parts
from the First World War.) I am grateful to Vasyl Strilchuk, director of the
Brody Museum, for sharing his passion for local history and for his work
preserving the grim history that lies just beneath the lush green mantle that
covers Galicia. Taras Hrynchyshyn of the Religious Information Service of
Ukraine in Lviv was of great help with his maps and encyclopedic knowledge

of the people and history of his country. Professor Yaroslav Hrytsak of Ivano Franko National University provided valuable insight into the strategies for survival employed by refugees and other innocent victims caught up in the chaos of war and revolution.

Hungary

For their help and for granting permission to reproduce Volodymyr Mykyta's 'Tsimborky' ('Friends') I am grateful to Stepan Liavinets, Marianna Liavinets, and their associates of the journal 'Rusynskyi svit.'

The United States

I am deeply indebted to Professor Elaine Rusinko of the University of Maryland for her many years of patient assistance and for her valuable input on multiple drafts. I am very grateful for her fervent support for *The Linden and the Oak* and for promoting it among members of the North American Rusyn community. I am thankful to Mary Byers for her sensitive editing and many improvements to the manuscript. Many thanks to Rev. Zugger and the parishioners of Our Lady of Perpetual Help Byzantine Catholic Church of New Mexico for their insights. I thank Barry Moreno of the Ellis Island Immigration Museum for sharing his vast knowledge of immigrant processing on Ellis Island in the 1920s. Bogdan Horbal of the New York Public Library reviewed the manuscript and made many helpful comments. Anna Prizzi provided valuable insights into shared family history. The Pribula family graciously granted many hours of conversation dedicated to Rusyn daily life, customs, and farming. I am forever grateful to my family: my daughters for their understanding, my mother for her endless proofreading, and my wife Dolores for her steadfast support and keen editing skills. And finally, I thank all those from the past who have made life's final crossing and whose presence I often felt as I wrote. I hope you are pleased.